D0344510

STORIES ⬡

OF ADVENTURE

by JACK LONDON

The Complete Novel of

THE GAME

PLUS 46 SHORT STORIES INCLUDING

AN ODYSSEY of the NORTH

BROWN WOLF

LOVE of LIFE

THE SUN-DOG TRAIL

THE DEATH of LIGOUN

SEVEN TALES of the FISH PATROL

Introduced by Russ Kingman
Compiled by Frank Oppel

CASTLE

TABLE of CONTENTS

Introduction

"Please, Miss, could I have something to read?"

The time was 1886. The speaker was ten-year-old Jack London, shabbily clothed, carrying a bundle of old newspapers under his arm. The woman was Ina Coolbrith, librarian in the Oakland Library. The occasion was Jack London's introduction to the wide world of literature.

Ina Coolbrith favored the young enthusiast and guided him through the world of books, earning his undying adoration. For him, she was his "noble lady." And from that day until he died, Jack London read everything he could find. Reading opened the world to him: a man could accomplish anything he wanted if he dared.

Jack London remains one of the world's literary giants. Year after year his books are published in greater numbers, both here and abroad, and few authors have had as many biographers. He was an excellent portrayer of his times and his knowledge of philosophy and psychology added depth to his works while his rich and unusual adventures make them exciting to read. Also, his writings show a fine sense of drama, a poetic soul, a burning passion for social reform, and a determination to give his readers something new, interesting, and vital each time they pick up a story.

Reading Jack London is a magical return to the turn of the century in the Klondike, at the front in the Russo-Japanese War, in the South Sea Islands, in the London slums, with the rough and tough California Fish Patrol, in the middle of smuggling operations with oyster pirates, or on a hike from Carmel through Northern California in search of a home; but that magic carpet which is the Jack London tale will also take you to the household of Pontius Pilate during the crucifixion of Christ, to the infamous Mountain Meadow massacre, in a strait-jacket in the dungeons of San Quentin prison, in a sailing ship as it struggles to round Cape Horn, or in the boxing ring. Wherever his stories take you, you will be on a trail of adventure.

This volume contains some of Jack London's finest work, including *The Game* and 46 short stories. Here you will find his first story appearing in a magazine, *"A Thousand Deaths,"* which Jack London never knew was printed since it hit the newsstands while he was fighting his way over the Chilcoot Pass enroute to the Klondike gold fields.

By the time Jack London had reached high school, he had stuffed pickles into jars in a cannery, had earned the title, "Prince of the Oyster Pirates," and had spent seven months as a seaman aboard the sealing ship, "Sophia Sutherland" on a trip to the Bering Sea. He had also been a member of the California Fish Patrol, had labored in an Oakland jute mill, had worked as a coal heaver in the power plant of the Oakland, San Leandro and Haywards Railroad, and had spent nearly a year as a hobo tramping his way across the United States and Canada.

On July 14, 1897, the S.S. "Excelsior" entered the Golden Gate and tied up in San Francisco. In a matter of hours, the United States and the rest of the world knew about the Klondike gold discoveries. The Klondike gold rush became a national madness and 21-year-old Jack London was right in the thick of it. On July 25th, he left for the Klondike. In July of the following year, he returned with very little gold in his poke but the experiences he lived and heard about were destined to make him the best paid and most popular author in the world.

At that date, his only writing success was the publication of *"A Thousand Deaths."* But Jack London was determined to be a professional writer. He wrote everything — stories, articles, anecdotes, jokes, sonnets, ballads, villanelles, songs, light plays in iambic pentameter and heavy tragedies in blank verse.

Lecturing at Camp Reverie 1901

JACK LONDON

A famous caricature by James Montgomery Flagg

London at age 10 — about the time he met Ina Coolbrith at the Oakland Public Library

In front of his house on the Jack London Ranch

One year later, Overland Monthly accepted *"To the Man on Trail,"* for its January, 1899 issue. Twenty-three-year-old Jack London had arrived. Few authors ever wrote more steadily than did Jack London during that year. He sent off more than 200 manuscripts and began to earn his reputation as a keen observer of the world in which he lived and an unswerving loyalist to his craft.

To fully apppreciate Jack London's stories, you need to understand that their underlying motif is reform of society. The primordial world with all of its savagery is really the sweatshop where the poor work-beast was suffering excessively long hours for barely enough money to keep his family from starving. Jack London attempts to show the worker that no matter what the odds, there is victory for the one who is steadfast in the face of adversity, who fights for his just rights.

In America's early years, prosperity was closely related to expansion. Westward was the cry for the man willing to pay the exacting price to realize his dream. On the frontier, men were equal. There were no trade unions and no capitalist-owned factories. It was equal opportunity for those who were willing to face hardship to carve a home in the wilderness. It was backbreaking work but a man could hold up his head and be proud.

By 1893, when Jack London was beginning to write, the frontier had all but passed except for the northern frontier that was the Klondike. It was the time when the nation declared itself unmistakably capitalistic. Such a system required vast overseas markets, a huge labor force and, especially, a large surplus army of unemployed workers. The working man had to be content with his low wages while his employer became rich because there was always another man ready to take his job. He had to suffer child labor, no job insurance, no savings, and poor working conditions.

Jack London knew the condition of the working man because he was one of them. A glance at the fiction of the time shows it to be sentimental revery. Life as it was seldom, if ever, appeared in print. It was an opportune time for Jack London's debut as a writer. It was a time of war between classes as the working man battled for a better share of the nation's wealth — a just share. Jack London became his spokesman and he was to speak loud and clear.

Jack London wanted to inspire the working man to settle for no less than that which he deserved. He wanted him to explore the unknown, to break trail, because only man could help himself. The Jack London story gives man the courage to push on by showing how the environment can be overcome and success possible, even against great odds, but only for those willing to fight.

Russ Kingman

Haunts of Jack London

BY NINETTA EAMES

THE TRANSLUCENT, ALDER-HUNG POOL OF THE SONOMA

IN something less than eight years Jack London has achieved international renown. At twenty-nine, his books, twelve in number, flood the English-speaking markets. This is rapid growing, even for a twentieth-century author, but Mr. London learned early the straight course to work. Not the spasm of energy usually characteristic of genius, but a steady enforcement of drill, and the comprehensive adjustment of effort to obstacle which is oftenest the essential of success.

"Genius—there is no such thing," he declares. "What is called such is simply another name for hard work; work along natural law—law with no crack or break in the chain that connects the Alpha and Omega of things."

Jack London of to-day has that "holiday in the eye" that bespeaks a man conscious of having enlarged his destiny; made room in his days for ampler work and pastime. He has recently taken up life in the Coast Range—gained title to a wild tract in the Sonoma hills, whereon to set up the kingdom of home. Out of his own rock and sand he purposes to erect a spacious bungalow, the site within sound of village bells, but woods and mountains away from the church-goers. He points with deep content to the dwelling of his nearest neighbor—the house of an eagle—an "airy cart-load of fagots" aswing high up in a splintered fir.

Notwithstanding its sequestration, the London ranch commands a vast freedom of landscape—fifty miles of gardened valley merging into a silver line of bay, and farther to the south, Mount Diablo arching dimly against the azure; across the valley, notching the full-length horizon on the east, the Mayacmas ridge steeples above the bleached adobes of old Sonoma; while to the north and west, sentineled by Hood's Mountain and cloud-buffeted St. Helena, a world of beautiful wooded hills spread their laps to make room for arcadian homes and vineyards.

Mr. London's steep acres run up to a huddle of sky-fronting knolls, some pinnacled with firs and redwoods, and others, the fewer by count, smoothed into softness by yellowing oat-stubble. Lengthwise the ranch, down a giant trench-way, a clear, cold stream plunges through primeval forests, pausing at rifts in the green to hold a shining mirror to the sun. In the crisp, warm sunlight, and throughout the short, dew-cooled nights, one hears always the chorusing of the cascades—the *vox jubilante* of God's wilderness.

While superintending the building of his bungalow, the author makes home with friends whose summer lodge is within a mile's walk, across hills terraced with vines which offer the lure of shade with promise of fruited purple clusters. In this wildwood haunt he lives brotherly with Nature and human hearts, working aye for larger ends, his thoughts so plainly in tune that men catch them on the quick, and are held and moved imperiously to join in the primal harmony.

Whatever his change of abode, Jack London's writing-hours are the same—from early morning until luncheon at one. His afternoons are mainly given to swimming in a translucent,

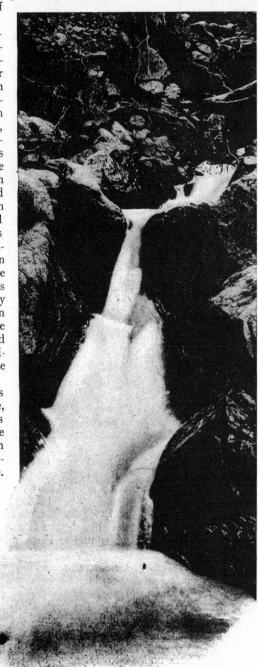

alder-hung pool of the Sonoma, or in horseback rides through this delightfully picturesque region. He is, in fact, an enthusiast over outdoor exercise, accounting a man's muscles of foremost importance, the essential basis of his mental and spiritual vitality.

London's chief attraction lies not so much in his fame as in his personality. He appears to have absorbed the good of the earth and the sun. His naturalness is that of the child, and there is manifest obliviousness of the fact that he has written successfully. In seeing him thus one is forcibly reminded of the "warm human" he portrays as "shot through with flashes and glimmerings of something finer and God-like, with here and there sweetnesses of service and unselfishness, desires for goodness, for renunciation and sacrifice, and with conscience, stern and awful, at times blazingly imperious, demanding the right—nothing more nor less than the right."

When riding through the village, a huge wolf-dog at his horse's heels, Mr. London makes a great stir. The loungers before the one store and the several saloons stare with interest-

A CLEAR, COLD STREAM PLUNGES THROUGH PRIMEVAL FORESTS

ed, friendly faces, while every street urchin shrills after in good-fellowship, "Hello, Jack!" and receives a boyish "Hello!" in response, the rider's eyes smiling, and one hand waving triumphantly a brace of plump chickens, the first product of the new ranch.

He rides bareheaded, his smooth-shaven face and fine column of neck bronzed to matched to corduroy knee-breeches and leggings, the polished dark sorrel of Washoe Ban, and the tawny fur of the wolf-dog.

This trail-worn husky is the hero-to-be of London's forthcoming tale. He is still a fine brute, massive of head and chest, with narrow, inscrutable eyes, and the long sweep of body and tail and swinging

MR. LONDON WRITING "THE SEA WOLF" AT A MAKESHIFT TABLE, DEEP IN THE FERNS AND VINES
ON THE BANK OF THE WILDWATER

delicious warmth of color, his outing shirt thinly veiling the figure of a Greek athlete, and his look that of one who feels it the happiest thing in life to be astride a horse. Not a looker-on but watches from sight the artistically grouped trio—the man, the horse and the dog—a moving study in browns against the rich green of laurels; a crop of sun-burnished hair trot peculiar to his forebear, the wolf. Years of service in harness have broken his spirit, and except when his master rides forth, "Wolf" rests apart, not slinking from proffered attention, but with dignity claiming seclusion as his well-earned right.

A few yards from the lodge, down a steep bank of the Wildwater, a makeshift table,

THE SPOILS OF AN AFTERNOON'S RIDE THROUGH THE PICTURESQUE GLADES OF THE SONOMA VALLEY

backed against a stump, stands deep in the ferns and vines. Here it was that Jack London wrote "The Sea Wolf." Alder, bay and buckeye canopy and curtain this brookside study. The spot embodies the all-tenderness of Nature; the liquid slide of water over stones, nesting twitters in the tree-tops, the soft rustle of breeze-stirred fronds and grasses, and a pervading scent of wine-flowered calycanthus—all strangely out of keeping with the formidable creation of a Wolf Larsen.

And herein London has the advantage: he is largely independent of environment. Whatsoever lies next him, his creative genius absorbs, translates, and fits to the work in hand. His mind runs parallel to Nature's laws, and is made thereby strong with the strength of the immutable, and the sharer of universal force. Thus

writer and book are fundamentally the same—made of the same stuff, since that which befalls his heroes has befallen him or is potential with him. Imagination in him generates the strong, the pictorial and the heroic as inevitably as the sun and soil bring forth oak and sequoia.

Notwithstanding this virility of fancy, Jack London is prone to regard his story-writing as so much needful effort toward a more vital and august end—the social redemption of the race. The soul in him chants the pæan of Brotherhood. The novel that brings him fame and fortune, brings a yet more golden largess—freedom of speech and pen to clarion organized, international, revolutionary social reform. This is the "Game" his soul plays from start to finish, the regnant purpose of his nights and days, the object of his untiring toil.

1
TO THE MAN ON THE TRAIL

TO THE MAN ON THE TRAIL

A KLONDIKE CHRISTMAS

By JACK LONDON

"DUMP it in."

"But I say, Kid, is n't that going it a little too strong? Whisky and alcohol's bad enough; but when it comes to brandy and pepper-sauce and—"

"Dump it in. Who's making this punch, anyway?" And Malemute Kid smiled benignantly through the clouds of steam. "By the time you've been in this country as long as I have, my son, and lived on rabbit-tracks and salmon-belly, you'll learn that Christmas comes only once per annum. And a Christmas without punch is sinking a hole to bedrock with nary a pay-streak."

"Stack up on that fer a high cyard," approved big Jim Belden, who had come down from his claim on Mazy May to spend Christmas, and who, as every one knew, had been living the two months past on straight moose-meat. "Hain't fergot the *hooch* we uns made on the Tanana, hev yeh?"

"Well, I guess yes. Boys, it would have done your hearts good to see that whole tribe fighting drunk—and all because of a glorious ferment of sugar and sour dough. That was before your time," Malemute Kid said as he turned to Stanley Prince, a young mining expert who had been in two years. "No white women in the country then, and Mason wanted to get married. Ruth's father was chief of the Tananas, and objected, like the rest of the tribe. Stiff? Why, I used my last pound of sugar; finest work in that line I ever did in my life. You should have seen the chase down the river and across the portage."

"But the squaw?" asked Louis Savoy, the tall French-Canadian, becoming interested; for he had heard of this wild deed, when at Forty Mile the preceding winter.

Then Malemute Kid, who was a born raconteur, told the unvarnished tale of the Northland Lochinvar. More than one rough adventurer of the North felt his heart-strings draw closer, and experienced vague yearnings for the sunnier pastures of the Southland, where life promised something more than a barren struggle with cold and death.

"We struck the Yukon just behind the first ice-run," he concluded, "and the tribe only a quarter of an hour behind. But that saved us; for the second run broke the jam above and shut them out. When they finally got into Nuklukyeto, the whole post was ready for them. And as to the foregathering, ask Father Roubeau here: he performed the ceremony."

The Jesuit took the pipe from his lips, but could only express his gratification with patriarchal smiles, while Protestant and Catholic vigorously applauded.

"By gar!" ejaculated Louis Savoy, who seemed overcome by the romance of it. "La petite squaw; mon Mason brav; By gar!"

Then, as the first tin cups of punch went round, Bettles the Unquenchable sprang to his feet and struck up his favorite drinking song:—

"There's Henry Ward Beecher
    And Sunday-school teachers,
        All drink of the sassafras root;
But you bet all the same,
If it had its right name,
    It's the juice of the forbidden fruit."

"O the juice of the forbidden fruit,"

roared out the Bacchanalian chorus,—

"O the juice of the forbidden fruit;
    But you bet all the same,
        If it had its right name,
    It's the juice of the forbidden fruit."

Malemute Kid's frightful concoction did its work; the men of the camps and trails unbent in its genial glow, and jest and song and tales of past adventure went round the board. Aliens from a dozen lands, they toasted each and all. It was the Englishman, Prince, who pledged

3

"Uncle Sam, the precocious infant of the New World"; the Yankee, Bettles, who drank to "The Queen, God bless her"; and together, Savoy and Meyers, the German trader, clanged their cups to Alsace and Lorraine.

Then Malemute Kid arose, cup in hand, and glanced at the greased-paper window, where the frost stood full three inches thick. "A health to the man on trail this night; may his grub hold out; may his dogs keep their legs; may his matches never miss fire."

Crack! Crack!—they heard the familiar music of the dog-whip, the whining howl of the Malemutes, and the crunch of a sled at it drew up to the cabin. Conversation languished, while they waited the issue expectantly.

"An old-timer; cares for his dogs and then himself," whispered Malemute Kid to Prince, as they listened to the snapping jaws and the wolfish snarls and yelps of pain which proclaimed to their practiced ears that the stranger was beating back their dogs while he fed his own.

Then came the expected knock, sharp and confident, and the stranger entered. Dazzled by the light, he hesitated a moment at the door, giving to all a chance for scrutiny. He was a striking personage, and a most picturesque one, in his Arctic dress of wool and fur. Standing six foot two or three, with proportionate breadth of shoulders and depth of chest, his smooth-shaven face nipped by the cold to a gleaming pink, his long lashes and eyebrows white with ice, and the ear and neck flaps of his great wolfskin cap loosely raised, he seemed, of a verity, the Frost King, just stepped in out of the night. Clasped outside his Mackinaw jacket, a beaded belt held two large Colt's revolvers and a hunting-knife, while he carried, in addition to the inevitable dog-whip, a smokeless rifle of the largest bore and latest pattern. As he came forward, for all his step was firm and elastic, they could see that fatigue bore heavily upon him.

An awkward silence had fallen, but his hearty "What cheer, my lads?" put them quickly at ease, and the next instant Male-mute Kid and he had gripped hands. Though they had never met, each had heard of the other, and the recognition was mutual. A sweeping introduction and a mug of punch were forced upon him before he could explain his errand.

"How long since that basket-sled, with three men and eight dogs, passed?" he asked.

"An even two days ahead. Are you after them?"

"Yes; my team. Run them off under my very nose, the cusses. I've gained two days on them already,—pick them up on the next run."

"Reckon they'll show spunk?" asked Belden, in order to keep up the conversation, for Malemute Kid already had the coffee-pot on and was busily frying bacon and moose-meat.

The stranger significantly tapped his revolvers.

"When 'd yeh leave Dawson?"

"Twelve o'clock."

"Last night?"—as a matter of course.

"To-day."

A murmur of surprise passed round the circle. And well it might; for it was just midnight and seventy-five miles of rough river trail was not to be sneered at for a twelve hours' run.

The talk soon became impersonal, however, harking back to the trials of childhood. As the young stranger ate of the rude fare, Malemute Kid attentively studied his face. Nor was he long in deciding that it was fair, honest, and open, and that he liked it. Still youthful, the lines had been firmly traced by toil and hardship. Though genial in conversation, and mild when at rest, the blue eyes gave promise of the hard steel-glitter which comes when called into action, especially against odds. The heavy jaw and square-cut chin demonstrated rugged pertinacity and indomitability of purpose. Nor, though the attributes of the lion were there, was there wanting the certain softness, the hint of womanliness, which bespoke an emotional nature—one which could feel, and feel deeply.

"So thet's how me an' the ol' woman got spliced," said Belden, concluding the exciting tale of his courtship. "'Here we be, dad,' sez she. 'An' may yeh be damned,' sez he to her, an' then to me, 'Jim, yeh—yeh git outen them good duds o' yourn; I want a right peart slice o' thet forty acre ploughed 'fore dinner.' An' then he turns on her an' sez, 'An' yeh, Sal; yeh sail inter them dishes.' An' then he sort o' sniffled an' kissed her. An' I was thet happy,—but he seen me an' roars out, 'Yeh, Jim!' An' yeh bet I dusted fer the barn."

"Any kids waiting for you back in the States?" asked the stranger.

"Nope; Sal died 'fore any come. Thet's why I'm here." Belden abstractedly began to light his pipe, which had failed to go out, and then brightened up with, "How 'bout yerself, stranger,—married man?"

For reply, he opened his watch, slipped it from the thong which served for a chain, and passed it over. Belden pricked up the slush-lamp, surveyed the inside of the case critically, and swearing admiringly to himself, handed it over to Louis Savoy. With numerous "By gars!" he finally surrendered it to Prince, and they noticed that his hands trembled and his eyes took on a peculiar softness. And so it passed from horny hand to horny hand—the pasted photograph of a woman, the clinging kind that such men fancy, with a babe at the breast. Those who had not yet seen the wonder were keen with curiosity; those who had, became silent and retrospective. They could face the pinch of famine, the grip of scurvy, or the quick death by field or flood; but the pictured semblance of a stranger woman and child made women and children of them all.

"Never have seen the youngster yet,— he's a boy, she says, and two years old," said the stranger as he received the treasure back. A lingering moment he gazed upon it, then snapped the case and turned away, but not quick enough to hide the restrained rush of tears.

Malemute Kid led him to a bunk and bade him turn in.

"Call me at four, sharp. Don't fail me," were his last words, and a moment later he was breathing in the heaviness of exhausted sleep.

"By Jove, he's a plucky chap," commented Prince. "Three hours' sleep after seventy-five miles with the dogs, and then the trail again. Who is he, Kid?"

"Jack Westondale. Been in going on three years, with nothing but the name of working like a horse, and any amount of bad luck to his credit. I never knew him, but Sitka Charley told me about him."

"It seems hard that a man with a sweet young wife like his should be putting in his years in this God-forsaken land, where every year counts two on the outside."

"The trouble with him is clean grit and stubbornness. He's cleaned up twice with a stake, but lost it both times."

Here the conversation was broken off by an uproar from Bettles, for the effect had begun to wear away. And soon the bleak years of monotonous grub and deadening toil were being forgotten in rough merriment. Malemute Kid alone seemed unable to lose himself, and cast many an anxious look at his watch. Once he put on his mittens and beaver-skin cap, and leaving the cabin, fell to rummaging about in the cache.

Nor could he wait the hour designated; for he was fifteen minutes ahead of time in rousing his guest. The young giant had stiffened badly, and brisk rubbing was necessary to bring him to his feet. He tottered painfully out of the cabin, to find his dogs harnessed and everything ready for the start. The company wished him good luck and a short chase, while Father Roubeau, hurriedly blessing him, led the stampede for the cabin; and small wonder, for it is not good to face seventy-four degrees below zero with naked ears and hands.

Malemute Kid saw him to the main trail, and there, gripping his hand heartily, gave him advice.

"You'll find a hundred pounds of salmon-eggs on the sled," he said. "The dogs will go as far on that as with one hundred and fifty of fish, and you can't get dog-food at Pelly, as you probably expected." The stranger started, and his eyes flashed, but he did not interrupt. "You can't get an ounce of food for dog or man till you reach Five Fingers, and that's a stiff two hundred miles. Watch out for open water on the Thirty Mile

River, and be sure you take the big cut-off above Le Barge."

"How did you know it? Surely the news can't be ahead of me already?"

"I don't know it; and what's more, I don't want to know it. But you never owned that team you're chasing. Sitka Charley sold it to them last spring. But he sized you up to me as square once, and I believe him. I've seen your face; I like it. And I've seen—why, damn you, hit the high places for salt water and that wife of yours, and—" Here the Kid unmittened and jerked out his sack.

"No; I don't need it," and the tears froze on his cheeks as he convulsively gripped Malemute Kid's hand.

"Then don't spare the dogs; cut them out of the traces as fast as they drop; buy them, and think they're cheap at ten dollars a pound. You can get them at Five Fingers, Little Salmon, and the Hootalinqua."

"And watch out for wet feet," was his parting advice. "Keep a-traveling up to twenty-five, but if it gets below that, build a fire and change your socks."

Fifteen minutes had barely elapsed, when the jingle of bells announced new arrivals. The door opened, and a mounted policeman of the Northwest Territory entered, followed by two half-breed dog-drivers. Like Westondale, they were heavily armed and showed signs of fatigue. The half-breeds had been born to the trail, and bore it easily; but the young policeman was badly exhausted. Still the dogged obstinacy of his race held him to the pace he had set, and would hold him till he dropped in his tracks.

"When did Westondale pull out?" he asked. "He stopped here, didn't he?" This was supererogatory, for the tracks told their own tale too well.

Malemute Kid had caught Belden's eye, and he, scenting the wind, replied evasively, "A right peart while back."

"Come, my man; speak up," he admonished.

"Yeh seem to want him right smart. Hez he ben gittin' cantankerous down Dawson way?"

"Held up Harry McFarland's for forty thousand; exchanged it at the A. C. store for a check on Seattle; and who's to stop the cashing of it if we don't overtake him? When did he pull out?"

Every eye suppressed its excitement, for Malemute Kid had given the cue, and the young officer encountered wooden faces on every hand.

Striding over to Prince, he put the question to him. Though it hurt him, gazing into the frank, earnest face of his fellow-countryman, he replied inconsequentially on the state of the trail.

Then he espied Father Roubeau, who could not lie. "A quarter of an hour ago," he answered; "but he had four hours' rest for himself and dogs."

"Fifteen minutes' start, and he's fresh! My God!" The poor fellow staggered back, half-fainting from exhaustion and disappointment, murmuring something about the run from Dawson in ten hours and the dogs being played out.

Malemute Kid forced a mug of punch upon him; then he turned for the door, ordering the dog-drivers to follow. But the warmth and promise of rest was too tempting, and they objected strenuously. The Kid was conversant with their French patois, and followed it anxiously.

They swore that the dogs were gone up; that Siwash and Babette would have to be shot before the first mile was covered; that the rest were almost as bad; and that it would be better for all hands to rest up.

"Lend me five dogs," he asked, turning to Malemute Kid.

But the Kid shook his head.

"I'll sign a check on Captain Constantine for five thousand,—here's my papers,—I'm authorized to draw at my own discretion."

Again the silent refusal.

"Then I'll requisition them in the name of the Queen."

Smiling incredulously, the Kid glanced at his well-stocked arsenal, and the Englishman, realizing his impotency, turned for the door. But the dog-drivers still objecting, he whirled upon them fiercely, calling them women and curs. The swart face of the older half-breed flushed angrily, as he drew himself up and promised in good, round terms that he would travel his leader off his legs, and would then be delighted to plant him in the snow.

The young officer, and it required his whole will, walked steadily to the door, exhibiting a freshness he did not possess. But they all knew and appreciated his proud effort; nor could he veil the twinges of agony that shot across his face. Covered with frost, the dogs were curled up in the snow, and it was almost impossible to get them to their feet. The poor brutes whined under the stinging lash, for the dog-drivers were angry and cruel; nor till Babette, the leader, was cut from the traces, could they break out the sled and get under way.

" A dirty scoundrel and a liar!" " By gar! him no good!" " A thief!" " Worse than an Indian!" It was evident that they were angry—first, at the way they had been deceived; and second, at the outraged ethics of the Northland, where honesty, above all, was man's prime jewel. "An' we gave the cuss a hand; after knowin' what he'd did." All eyes were turned accusingly upon Malemute Kid, who rose from the corner where he had been making Babette comfortable, and silently emptied the bowl for a final round of punch.

" It 's a cold night, boys,—a bitter cold night," was the irrelevant commencement of his defense. " You 've all traveled trail, and know what that stands for. Don't jump a dog when he 's down. You 've only heard one side. A whiter man than Jack Westondale never ate from the same pot nor stretched blanket with you or me. Last fall he gave his whole clean-up, forty thousand, to Joe Castrell, to buy in on Dominion. To-day he 'd be a millionaire. But while he stayed behind at Circle City, taking care of his partner with the scurvy, what does Castrell do? Goes into Mc-Farland's, jumps the limit, and drops the whole sack. Found him dead in the snow the next day. And poor Jack laying his plans to go out this winter to his wife and the boy he 's never seen. Well, he 's gone out; and what are you going to do about it ? "

The Kid glanced round the circle of his judges, noted the softening of their faces, then raised his mug aloft. " So a health to the man on trail this night; may his grub hold out; may his dogs keep their legs; may his matches never miss fire. God prosper him; good luck go with him; and—"

" Confusion to the Mounted Police! " interpolated Bettles, to the crash of the empty cups.

2
AN ODYSSEY OF THE NORTH

AN ODYSSEY OF THE NORTH.

I.

"SIXTY ounces, without even a piece of paper! Ever expect to see it again?"

Malemute Kid shrugged his shoulders.

"Why did he quit?" Prince was interested in the Indian dog-driver whom his partner had just bought out of her Majesty's mail service.

"Don't know. He couldn't desert and then stay here, and he was just wild to remain in the country. Palavered around like a crazy man. Something happened to him when he got to Dawson, — couldn't make out what, — and he made up his mind on the jump; and in the same breath he said he'd been working to this very end for years. He had everything mixed up. Talked of making me rich, putting me onto a mine with more gold than Eldorado and Bonanza together. Never saw a man take on so in my life. It was only sixty ounces, and the look in his face when I agreed was worth the price."

"Who is he, anyway?"

"Don't know. But he's a fellow to whet your curiosity. I never saw him before, but all the Coast was talking about him eight years ago. Sort of mysterious, you know. They called him the 'Strange One,' 'Ulysses,' and the 'Man with the Otter Skins.' He came down out of the north, in the dead of winter, skirting Bering Sea and traveling like mad. No one ever learned where he came from, but he must have come far. He was badly travel-worn when he got food from the Swedish missionary on Golovin Bay, and asked the way south. We heard of this afterward. Then he abandoned the shore line, heading right across Norton Sound. Terrible weather, snowstorms and high winds, but he pulled through where a thousand other men would have died; missing St. Michaels, and making the land at Pastilik. He'd lost all but two dogs, and was nearly gone with starvation.

"He was so anxious to go on that Father Roubeau fitted him out with grub; but he couldn't let him have any dogs, for he was only waiting my arrival to go on trail himself. Mr. Ulysses knew too much to start without animals, and fretted around for several days. He had on his sled a bunch of beautifully cured otter skins, — sea otters, you know, worth their weight in gold. There happened to be at Pastilik an old Shylock of a Russian trader, who had dogs to kill. Well, they didn't dicker very long, but when the Strange One headed south again, it was in the rear of a spanking dog team. Mr. Shylock, by the way, had the otter skins. I saw them. Dogs must have brought him five hundred apiece. And it wasn't as if the Strange One didn't know the value of sea otter: he was Indian; and besides, what little he talked showed he'd been among white men.

"After the ice passed out of the sea, word came up from Nunivak Island that he had gone in there for grub. Then he dropped from sight, and this is the first heard of him in eight years. Now where did he come from? And what was he doing there? And why did he come from there? Another mystery of the north, Prince, for you to solve."

"Thanks, awfully," was the mining engineer's response, muffled and sleepy, from his sleeping-furs; "but you have so many confounded mysteries up here that my hands are full as it is. Anyway, I don't expect I'll ever hear of the chap again, — nor you, either, of your sixty ounces."

The cold weather had come on with the long nights, and the sun had begun to play his ancient game of peekaboo along the southern snow line ere aught was heard of Malemute Kid's grubstake. And then, one bleak morning in early January, a heavily laden dog train pulled into his cabin below Stuart River. He of the Otter Skins was there, and with him walked a man such as the gods have almost forgotten how to fashion. Men never talked of luck and pluck and five-hundred-dollar dirt without bringing in the name of Axel Gunderson; nor could tales of nerve or strength or daring pass up and down the camp fire without the summoning of his presence. And when the conversation flagged, it blazed anew at mention of the woman who shared his fortunes.

As has been noted, in the making of Axel Gunderson the gods had remembered their old-time cunning, and cast him after the manner of men who were born when the world was young. Full seven feet he towered in his picturesque costume which marked a king of Eldorado. His chest, neck, and limbs were those of a giant. To bear his three hundred pounds of bone and muscle, his snowshoes were greater by a generous yard than those of other men. Rough-hewn, with rugged brow and massive jaw and unflinching eyes of palest blue, his face told the tale of one who knew but the law of might. Of the yellow of ripe corn silk, his frost-incrusted hair swept like day across the night, and fell far down his coat of bearskin. A vague tradition of the sea seemed to cling about him, as he swung down the narrow trail in advance of the dogs; and he brought the butt of his dogwhip against Malemute Kid's door as a Norse sea rover, on southern foray, might thunder for admittance at the castle gate.

Prince bared his womanly arms and kneaded sour-dough bread, casting, as he did so, many a glance at the three guests, — three guests the like of which might never come under a man's roof in a lifetime. The Strange One, whom Malemute Kid had surnamed " Ulysses," still

fascinated him; but his interest chiefly gravitated between Axel Gunderson and Axel Gunderson's wife. She felt the day's journey, for she had softened in comfortable cabins during the many days since her husband mastered the wealth of frozen pay streaks, and she was tired. She rested against his great breast like a slender flower against a wall, replying lazily to Malemute Kid's good-natured banter, and stirring Prince's blood strangely with an occasional sweep of her deep, dark eyes. For Prince was a man, and healthy, and had seen few women in many months. And she was older than he, and an Indian besides. But she was different from all native wives he had met: she had traveled, — had been in his country among others, he gathered from the conversation; and she knew most of the things the women of his own race knew, and much more that it was not in the nature of things for them to know. She could make a meal of sun-dried fish or a bed in the snow; yet she teased them with tantalizing details of many-course dinners, and caused strange internal dissensions to arise at the mention of various quondam dishes which they had well-nigh forgotten. She knew the ways of the moose, the bear, and the little blue fox, and of the wild amphibians of the northern seas; she was skilled in the lore of the woods and the streams, and the tale writ by man and bird and beast upon the delicate snow crust was to her an open book; yet Prince caught the appreciative twinkle in her eye as she read the Rules of the Camp. These Rules had been fathered by the Unquenchable Bettles at a time when his blood ran high, and were remarkable for the terse simplicity of their humor. Prince always turned them to the wall before the arrival of ladies; but who could suspect that this native wife — Well, it was too late now.

This, then, was the wife of Axel Gunderson, a woman whose name and fame had traveled with her husband's, hand in hand, through all the northland. At table, Malemute Kid baited her with the assurance of an old friend, and Prince shook off the shyness of first acquaintance and joined in. But she held her own in the unequal contest, while her husband, slower in wit, ventured naught but applause. And he was very proud of her; his every look and action revealed the magnitude of the place she occupied in his life. He of the Otter Skins ate in silence, forgotten in the merry battle; and long ere the others were done he pushed back from the table and went out among the dogs. Yet all too soon his fellow travelers drew on their mittens and *parkas,* and followed him.

There had been no snow for many days, and the sleds slipped along the hard-packed Yukon trail as easily as if it had been glare ice. Ulysses led the first sled; with the second came Prince and Axel Gunderson's wife; while Malemute Kid and the yellow-haired giant brought up the third.

"It's only a 'hunch,' Kid," he said; "but I think it's straight. He's never bēen there, but he tells a good story, and shows a map I heard of when I was in the Kootenay country, years ago. I'd like to have you go along; but he's a strange one, and swore point-blank to throw it up if any one was brought in. But when I come back you'll get first tip, and I'll stake you next to me, and give you a half share in the town site besides.

"No! no!" he cried, as the other strove to interrupt. "I'm running this, and before I'm done it'll need two heads. If it's all right, why it'll be a second Cripple Creek, man; do you hear? — a second Cripple Creek! It's quartz, you know, not placer; and if we work it right we'll corral the whole thing, — millions upon millions. I've heard of the place before, and so have you. We'll build a town — thousands of workmen — good waterways — steam-ship lines — big carrying trade — light-draught steamers for head-reaches — survey a railroad, perhaps — sawmills — electric-light plant — do our own banking — commercial company — syndicate — Say! just you hold your hush till I get back, and then we'll see!"

The sleds came to a halt where the trail crossed the mouth of Stuart River. An unbroken sea of frost, its wide expanse stretched away into the unknown east. The snowshoes were withdrawn from the lashings of the sleds. Axel Gunderson shook hands and stepped to the fore, his great webbed shoes sinking a fair half yard into the feathery surface and packing the snow so the dogs should not wallow. His wife fell in behind the last sled, betraying long practice in the art of handling the awkward footgear. The stillness was broken with cheery farewells; the dogs whined; and He of the Otter Skins talked with his whip to a recalcitrant wheeler.

An hour later, the train had taken on the likeness of a black pencil crawling in a long, straight line across a mighty sheet of foolscap.

II.

One night, many weeks later, Malemute Kid and Prince fell to solving chess problems from the torn page of an ancient magazine. The Kid had just returned from his Bonanza properties, and was resting up preparatory to a long moose hunt. Prince too had been on creek and trail nearly all winter, and had grown hungry for a blissful week of cabin life.

"Interpose the black knight, and force the king. No, that won't do. See, the next move" —

"Why advance the pawn two squares? Bound to take it in transit, and with the bishop out of the way" —

"But hold on! That leaves a hole, and" —

"No; it's protected. Go ahead! You'll see it works."

It was very interesting. Somebody knocked at the door a second time before Malemute Kid said, "Come in." The door swung open. Something staggered in. Prince caught one square look, and sprang to his feet. The horror in his eyes caused Malemute Kid to whirl about; and he too was startled, though he had seen bad things before. The thing tottered blindly toward them. Prince edged away till he reached the nail from which hung his Smith & Wesson.

"My God! what is it?" he whispered to Malemute Kid.

"Don't know. Looks like a case of freezing and no grub," replied the Kid, sliding away in the opposite direction. "Watch out! It may be mad," he warned, coming back from closing the door.

The thing advanced to the table. The bright flame of the slush lamp caught its eye. It was amused, and gave voice to eldritch cackles which betokened mirth. Then, suddenly, he — for it was a man — swayed back, with a hitch to his skin trousers, and began to sing a chanty, such as men lift when they swing around the capstan circle and the sea snorts in their ears : —

"Yan-kee ship come down de ri-ib-er,
　　　Pull! my bully boys! Pull!
D' yeh want — to know de captain ru-uns her?
　　　Pull! my bully boys! Pull!
Jon-a-than Jones ob South Caho-li-in-a,
　　　Pull! my bully " —

He broke off abruptly, tottered with a wolfish snarl to the meat shelf, and before they could intercept was tearing with his teeth at a chunk of raw bacon. The struggle was fierce between him and Malemute Kid; but his mad strength left him as suddenly as it had come, and he weakly surrendered the spoil. Between them they got him upon a stool, where he sprawled with half his body across the table. A small dose of whis-key strengthened him, so that he could dip a spoon into the sugar caddy which Malemute Kid placed before him. After his appetite had been somewhat cloyed, Prince, shuddering as he did so, passed him a mug of weak beef tea.

The creature's eyes were alight with a sombre frenzy, which blazed and waned with every mouthful. There was very little skin to the face. The face, for that matter, sunken and emaciated, bore very little likeness to human countenance. Frost after frost had bitten deeply, each depositing its stratum of scab upon the half-healed scar that went before. This dry, hard surface was of a bloody-black color, serrated by grievous cracks wherein the raw red flesh peeped forth. His skin garments were dirty and in tatters, and the fur of one side was singed and burned away, showing where he had lain upon his fire.

Malemute Kid pointed to where the sun-tanned hide had been cut away, strip by strip, — the grim signature of famine.

"Who — are — you?" slowly and distinctly enunciated the Kid.

The man paid no heed.

"Where do you come from?"

"Yan-kee ship come down de ri-ib-er," was the quavering response.

"Don't doubt the beggar came down the river," the Kid said, shaking him in an endeavor to start a more lucid flow of talk.

But the man shrieked at the contact, clapping a hand to his side in evident pain. He rose slowly to his feet, half leaning on the table.

"She laughed at me — so — with the hate in her eye; and she — would — not — come."

His voice died away, and he was sinking back, when Malemute Kid gripped him by the wrist and shouted, "Who? Who would not come?"

"She, Unga. She laughed, and struck at me, so, and so. And then " —

"Yes?"

"And then" —

"And then what?"

"And then he lay very still, in the snow, a long time. He is — still in — the — snow."

The two men looked at each other helplessly.

"Who is in the snow?"

"She, Unga. She looked at me with the hate in her eye, and then" —

"Yes, yes."

"And then she took the knife, so; and once, twice — she was weak. I traveled very slow. And there is much gold in that place, very much gold."

"Where is Unga?" For all Malemute Kid knew, she might be dying a mile away. He shook the man savagely, repeating again and again, "Where is Unga?"

"She — is — in — the — snow."

"Go on!" The Kid was pressing his wrist cruelly.

"So — I — would — be — in — the snow — but — I — had — a — debt — to — pay. It — was — heavy — I — had — a — debt — to — pay — a — debt — to — pay — I — had" — The faltering monosyllables ceased, as he fumbled in his pouch and drew forth a buckskin sack. "A — debt — to — pay — five — pounds — of — gold — grub — stake — Mal — e — mute — Kid — I" — The exhausted head dropped upon the table; nor could Malemute Kid rouse it again.

"It's Ulysses," he said quietly, tossing the bag of dust on the table. "Guess it's all day with Axel Gunderson and the woman. Come on, let's get him between the blankets. He's Indian: he 'll pull through, and tell a tale besides."

As they cut his garments from him, near his right breast could be seen two unhealed, hard-lipped knife thrusts.

III.

"I will talk of the things which were, in my own way; but you will understand. I will begin at the beginning, and tell of myself and the woman, and, after that, of the man."

He of the Otter Skins drew over to the stove as do men who have been deprived of fire and are afraid the Promethean gift may vanish at any moment. Malemute Kid pricked up the slush lamp, and placed it so its light might fall upon the face of the narrator. Prince slid his body over the edge of the bunk and joined them.

"I am Naass, a chief, and the son of a chief, born between a sunset and a rising, on the dark seas, in my father's *oomiak*. All of a night the men toiled at the paddles, and the women cast out the waves which threw in upon us, and we fought with the storm. The salt spray froze upon my mother's breast till her breath passed with the passing of the tide. But I, — I raised my voice with the wind and the storm, and lived.

"We dwelt in Akatan" —

"Where?" asked Malemute Kid.

"Akatan, which is in the Aleutians; Akatan, beyond Chignik, beyond Kardalak, beyond Unimak. As I say, we dwelt in Akatan, which lies in the midst of the sea on the edge of the world. We farmed the salt seas for the fish, the seal, and the otter; and our homes shouldered about one another on the rocky strip between the rim of the forest and the yellow beach where our *kayaks* lay. We were not many, and the world was very small. There were strange lands to the east, — islands like Akatan; so we thought all the world was islands, and did not mind.

"I was different from my people. In the sands of the beach were the crooked timbers and wave-warped planks of a boat such as my people never built; and I remember on the point of the island which overlooked the ocean three ways there stood a pine tree which never grew there, smooth and straight and tall. It is said the two men came to that spot, turn about, through many days, and watched with the passing of the light. These two men came from out of the sea in the boat which lay in pieces on the beach. And they were white, like you, and weak as the little children when the seal have gone away and the hunters come home empty. I know of these things from the old men and the old women, who got them from their fathers and mothers before them. These strange white men did not take kindly to our ways at first, but they grew strong, what of the fish and the oil, and fierce. And they built them each his own house, and took the pick of our women, and in time children came. Thus he was born who was to become the father of my father's father.

"As I said, I was different from my people, for I carried the strong, strange blood of this white man who came out of the sea. It is said we had other laws in the days before these men; but they were fierce and quarrelsome, and fought with our men till there were no more left who dared to fight. Then they made themselves chiefs, and took away our old laws and gave us new ones, insomuch that the man was the son of his father, and not his mother, as our way had been. They also ruled that the son, firstborn, should have all things which were his father's before him, and that the brothers and sisters should shift for themselves. And they gave us other laws. They showed us new ways in the catching of fish and the killing of bear which were thick in the woods; and they taught us to lay by bigger stores for the time of famine. And these things were good.

"But when they had become chiefs, and there were no more men to face their anger, they fought, these strange white men, each with the other. And the one whose blood I carry drove his seal spear the length of an arm through the other's body. Their children took up the fight, and their children's children; and there was great hatred between them, and

black doings, even to my time, so that in each family but one lived to pass down the blood of them that went before. Of my blood I was alone; of the other man's there was but a girl, Unga, who lived with her mother. Her father and my father did not come back from the fishing one night; but afterward they washed up to the beach on the big tides, and they held very close to each other.

"The people wondered, because of the hatred between the houses, and the old men shook their heads and said the fight would go on when children were born to her and children to me. They told me this as a boy, till I came to believe, and to look upon Unga as a foe, who was to be the mother of children which were to fight with mine. I thought of these things day by day, and when I grew to a stripling I came to ask why this should be so. And they answered, 'We do not know, but that in such way your fathers did.' And I marveled that those which were to come should fight the battles of those that were gone, and in it I could see no right. But the people said it must be, and I was only a stripling.

"And they said I must hurry, that my blood might be the older and grow strong before hers. This was easy, for I was head man, and the people looked up to me because of the deeds and the laws of my fathers, and the wealth which was mine. Any maiden would come to me, but I found none to my liking. And the old men and the mothers of maidens told me to hurry, for even then were the hunters bidding high to the mother of Unga; and should her children grow strong before mine, mine would surely die.

"Nor did I find a maiden till one night coming back from the fishing. The sunlight was lying, so, low and full in the eyes, the wind free, and the kayaks racing with the white seas. Of a sudden the kayak of Unga came driving past me, and she looked upon me, so, with her black hair flying like a cloud of night and the spray wet on her cheek. As I say, the sunlight was full in the eyes, and I was a stripling; but somehow it was all clear, and I knew it to be the call of kind to kind. As she whipped ahead she looked back within the space of two strokes, — looked as only the woman Unga could look, — and again I knew it as the call of kind. The people shouted as we ripped past the lazy oomiaks and left them far behind. But she was quick at the paddle, and my heart was like the belly of a sail, and I did not gain. The wind freshened, the sea whitened, and, leaping like the seals on the windward breech, we roared down the golden pathway of the sun."

Naass was crouched half out of his stool, in the attitude of one driving a paddle, as he ran the race anew. Somewhere across the stove he beheld the tossing kayak and the flying hair of Unga. The voice of the wind was in his ears, and its salt beat fresh upon his nostrils.

"But she made the shore, and ran up the sand, laughing, to the house of her mother. And a great thought came to me that night, — a thought worthy of him that was chief over all the people of Akatan. So, when the moon was up, I went down to the house of her mother, and looked upon the goods of Yash-Noosh, which were piled by the door, — the goods of Yash-Noosh, a strong hunter who had it in mind to be the father of the children of Unga. Other young men had piled their goods there, and taken them away again; and each young man had made a pile greater than the one before.

"And I laughed to the moon and the stars, and went to my own house where my wealth was stored. And many trips I made, till my pile was greater by the fingers of one hand than the pile of Yash-Noosh. There were fish, dried in

the sun and smoked; and forty hides of the hair seal, and half as many of the fur, and each hide was tied at the mouth and big-bellied with oil; and ten skins of bear which I killed in the woods when they came out in the spring. And there were beads and blankets and scarlet cloths, such as I got in trade from the people who lived to the east, and who got them in trade from the people who lived still beyond in the east. And I looked upon the pile of Yash-Noosh and laughed; for I was head man in Akatan, and my wealth was greater than the wealth of all my young men, and my fathers had done deeds, and given laws, and put their names for all time in the mouths of the people.

"So, when the morning came, I went down to the beach, casting out of the corner of my eye at the house of the mother of Unga. My offer yet stood untouched. And the women smiled, and said sly things one to the other. I wondered, for never had such a price been offered; and that night I added more to the pile, and put beside it a kayak of well-tanned skins which never yet had swam in the sea. But in the day it was yet there, open to the laughter of all men. The mother of Unga was crafty, and I grew angry at the shame in which I stood before my people. So that night I added till it became a great pile, and I hauled up my oomiak, which was of the value of twenty kayaks. And in the morning there was no pile.

"Then made I preparation for the wedding, and the people that lived even to the east came for the food of the feast and the *potlach* token. Unga was older than I by the age of four suns in the way we reckoned the years. I was only a stripling; but then I was a chief, and the son of a chief, and it did not matter.

"But a ship shoved her sails above the floor of the ocean, and grew larger with the breath of the wind. From her scuppers she ran clear water, and the men were in haste and worked hard at the pumps. On the bow stood a mighty man, watching the depth of the water and giving commands with a voice of thunder. His eyes were of the pale blue of the deep waters, and his head was maned like that of a sea lion. And his hair was yellow, like the straw of a southern harvest or the manila rope-yarns which sailormen plait.

"Of late years we had seen ships from afar, but this was the first to come to the beach of Akatan. The feast was broken, and the women and children fled to the houses, while we men strung our bows and waited with spears in hand. But when the ship's forefoot smelt the beach the strange men took no notice of us, being busy with their own work. With the falling of the tide they careened the schooner and patched a great hole in her bottom. So the women crept back, and the feast went on.

"When the tide rose, the sea wanderers kedged the schooner to deep water, and then came among us. They bore presents and were friendly; so I made room for them, and out of the largeness of my heart gave them tokens such as I gave all the guests; for it was my wedding day, and I was head man in Akatan. And he with the mane of the sea lion was there, so tall and strong that one looked to see the earth shake with the fall of his feet. He looked much and straight at Unga, with his arms folded, so, and stayed till the sun went away and the stars came out. Then he went down to his ship. After that I took Unga by the hand and led her to my own house. And there was singing and great laughter, and the women said sly things, after the manner of women at such times. But we did not care. Then the people left us alone and went home.

"The last noise had not died away, when the chief of the sea wanderers came in by the door. And he had with

him black bottles, from which we drank and made merry. You see, I was only a stripling, and had lived all my days on the edge of the world. So my blood became as fire, and my heart as light as the froth that flies from the surf to the cliff. Unga sat silent among the skins in the corner, her eyes wide, for she seemed to fear. And he with the mane of the sea lion looked upon her straight and long. Then his men came in with bundles of goods, and he piled before me wealth such as was not in all Akatan. There were guns, both large and small, and powder and shot and shell, and bright axes and knives of steel, and cunning tools, and strange things the like of which I had never seen. When he showed me by sign that it was all mine, I thought him a great man to be so free; but he showed me also that Unga was to go away with him in his ship. Do you understand? — that Unga was to go away with him in his ship. The blood of my fathers flamed hot on the sudden, and I made to drive him through with my spear. But the spirit of the bottles had stolen the life from my arm, and he took me by the neck, so, and knocked my head against the wall of the house. And I was made weak like a newborn child, and my legs would no more stand under me. Unga screamed, and she laid hold of the things of the house with her hands, till they fell all about us as he dragged her to the door. Then he took her in his great arms, and when she tore at his yellow hair laughed with a sound like that of the big bull seal in the rut.

"I crawled to the beach and called upon my people; but they were afraid. Only Yash-Noosh was a man, and they struck him on the head with an oar, till he lay with his face in the sand and did not move. And they raised the sails to the sound of their songs, and the ship went away on the wind.

"The people said it was good, for there would be no more war of the bloods in Akatan; but I said never a word, waiting till the time of the full moon, when I put fish and oil in my kayak, and went away to the east. I saw many islands and many people, and I, who had lived on the edge, saw that the world was very large. I talked by signs; but they had not seen a schooner nor a man with the mane of a sea lion, and they pointed always to the east. And I slept in queer places, and ate odd things, and met strange faces. Many laughed, for they thought me light of head; but sometimes old men turned my face to the light and blessed me, and the eyes of the young women grew soft as they asked me of the strange ship, and Unga, and the men of the sea.

"And in this manner, through rough seas and great storms, I came to Unalaska. There were two schooners there, but neither was the one I sought. So I passed on to the east, with the world growing ever larger, and in the Island of Unamok there was no word of the ship, nor in Kadiak, nor in Atognak. And so I came one day to a rocky land, where men dug great holes in the mountain. And there was a schooner, but not my schooner, and men loaded upon it the rocks which they dug. This I thought childish, for all the world was made of rocks; but they gave me food and set me to work. When the schooner was deep in the water, the captain gave me money and told me to go; but I asked which way he went, and he pointed south. I made signs that I would go with him; and he laughed at first, but then, being short of men, took me to help work the ship. So I came to talk after their manner, and to heave on ropes, and to reef the stiff sails in sudden squalls, and to take my turn at the wheel. But it was not strange, for the blood of my fathers was the blood of the men of the sea.

"I had thought it an easy task to find him I sought, once I got among his own people; and when we raised the land one day, and passed between a gateway of the sea to a port, I looked for perhaps as many schooners as there were fingers to my hands. But the ships lay against the wharves for miles, packed like so many little fish; and when I went among them to ask for a man with the mane of a sea lion, they laughed, and answered me in the tongues of many peoples. And I found that they hailed from the uttermost parts of the earth.

"And I went into the city to look upon the face of every man. But they were like the cod when they run thick on the banks, and I could not count them. And the noise smote upon me till I could not hear, and my head was dizzy with much movement. So I went on and on, through the lands which sang in the warm sunshine; where the harvests lay rich on the plains; and where great cities were, fat with men that lived like women, with false words in their mouths and their hearts black with the lust of gold. And all the while my people of Akatan hunted and fished, and were happy in the thought that the world was small.

"But the look in the eyes of Unga coming home from the fishing was with me always, and I knew I would find her when the time was met. She walked down quiet lanes in the dusk of the evening, or led me chases across the thick fields wet with the morning dew, and there was a promise in her eyes such as only the woman Unga could give.

"So I wandered through a thousand cities. Some were gentle and gave me food, and others laughed, and still others cursed; but I kept my tongue between my teeth, and went strange ways and saw strange sights. Sometimes, I, who was a chief and the son of a chief, toiled for men, — men rough of speech and hard as iron, who wrung gold from the sweat and sorrow of their fellow men. Yet no word did I get of my quest, till I came back to the sea like a homing seal to the rookeries. But this was at another port, in another country which lay to the north. And there I heard dim tales of the yellow-haired sea wanderer, and I learned that he was a hunter of seals, and that even then he was abroad on the ocean.

"So I shipped on a seal schooner with the lazy Siwashes, and followed his trackless trail to the north where the hunt was then warm. And we were away weary months, and spoke many of the fleet, and heard much of the wild doings of him I sought; but never once did we raise him above the sea. We went north, even to the Pribyloffs, and killed the seals in herds on the beach, and brought their warm bodies aboard till our scuppers ran grease and blood and no man could stand upon the deck. Then were we chased by a ship of slow steam, which fired upon us with great guns. But we put on sail till the sea was over our decks and washed them clean, and lost ourselves in a fog.

"It is said, at this time, while we fled with fear at our hearts, that the yellow-haired sea wanderer put into the Pribyloffs, right to the factory, and while the part of his men held the servants of the company, the rest loaded ten thousand green skins from the salt-houses. I say it is said, but I believe; for in the voyages I made on the coast with never a meeting, the northern seas rang with his wildness and daring, till the three nations which have lands there sought him with their ships. And I heard of Unga, for the captains sang loud in her praise, and she was always with him. She had learned the ways of his people, they said, and was happy. But I knew better, — knew that her heart harked back to her own people by the yellow beach of Akatan.

"So, after a long time, I went back to the port which is by a gateway of the sea, and there I learned that he had gone across the girth of the great ocean to hunt for the seal to the east of the warm land which runs south from the Russian Seas. And I, who was become a sailorman, shipped with men of his own race, and went after him in the hunt of the seal. And there were few ships off that new land; but we hung on the flank of the seal pack and harried it north through all the spring of the year. And when the cows were heavy with pup and crossed the Russian line, our men grumbled and were afraid. For there was much fog, and every day men were lost in the boats. They would not work, so the captain turned the ship back toward the way it came. But I knew the yellow-haired sea wanderer was unafraid, and would hang by the pack, even to the Russian Isles, where few men go. So I took a boat, in the black of night, when the lookout dozed on the fok'slehead, and went alone to the warm, long land. And I journeyed south to meet the men by Yeddo Bay, who are wild and unafraid. And the Yoshiwara girls were small, and bright like steel, and good to look upon; but I could not stop, for I knew that Unga rolled on the tossing floor by the rookeries of the north.

"The men by Yeddo Bay had met from the ends of the earth, and had neither gods nor homes, sailing under the flag of the Japanese. And with them I went to the rich beaches of Copper Island, where our salt-piles became high with skins. And in that silent sea we saw no man till we were ready to come away. Then, one day, the fog lifted on the edge of a heavy wind, and there jammed down upon us a schooner, with close in her wake the cloudy funnels of a Russian man-of-war. We fled away on the beam of the wind, with the schooner jamming still closer and plunging ahead three feet to our two. And upon her poop was the man with the mane of the sea lion, pressing the rails under with the canvas and laughing in his strength of life. And Unga was there, — I knew her on the moment, —

but he sent her below when the cannons began to talk across the sea. As I say, with three feet to our two, till we saw the rudder lift green at every jump, — and I swinging on to the wheel and cursing, with my back to the Russian shot. For we knew he had it in mind to run before us, that he might get away while we were caught. And they knocked our masts out of us till we dragged into the wind like a wounded gull ; but he went on over the edge of the sky-line, — he and Unga.

"What could we ? The fresh hides spoke for themselves. So they took us to a Russian port, and after that to a lone country, where they set us to work in the mines to dig salt. And some died, and — and some did not die."

Naass swept the blanket from his shoulders, disclosing the gnarled and twisted flesh, marked with the unmistakable striations of the knout. Prince hastily covered him, for it was not nice to look upon.

"We were there a weary time ; and sometimes men got away to the south, but they always came back. So, when we who hailed from Yeddo Bay rose in the night and took the guns from the guards, we went to the north. And the land was very large, with plains, soggy with water, and great forests. And the cold came, with much snow on the ground, and no man knew the way. Weary months we journeyed through the endless forest, — I do not remember, now, for there was little food and often we lay down to die. But at last we came to the cold sea, and but three were left to look upon it. One had shipped from Yeddo as captain, and he knew in his head the lay of the great lands, and of the place where men may cross from one to the other on the ice. And he led us, — I do not know, it was so long, — till there were but two. When we came to that place we found five of the strange people which live in that country, and they had dogs and skins, and we were

very poor. We fought in the snow till they died, and the captain died, and the dogs and skins were mine. Then I crossed on the ice, which was broken, and once I drifted till a gale from the west put me upon the shore. And after that, Golovin Bay, Pastilik, and the priest. Then south, south, to the warm sunlands where first I wandered.

"But the sea was no longer fruitful, and those who went upon it after the seal went to little profit and great risk. The fleets scattered, and the captains and the men had no word of those I sought. So I turned away from the ocean which never rests, and went among the lands, where the trees, the houses, and the mountains sit always in one place and do not move. I journeyed far, and came to learn many things, even to the way of reading and writing from books. It was well I should do this, for it came upon me that Unga must know these things, and that some day, when the time was met — we — you understand, when the time was met.

"So I drifted, like those little fish which raise a sail to the wind, but cannot steer. But my eyes and my ears were open always, and I went among men who traveled much, for I knew they had but to see those I sought, to remember. At last there came a man, fresh from the mountains, with pieces of rock in which the free gold stood to the size of peas, and he had heard, he had met, he knew them. They were rich, he said, and lived in the place where they drew the gold from the ground.

"It was in a wild country, and very far away ; but in time I came to the camp, hidden between the mountains, where men worked night and day, out of the sight of the sun. Yet the time was not come. I listened to the talk of the people. He had gone away, — they had gone away, — to England, it was said, in the matter of bringing men with much money together to form companies. I saw the house they had lived in ; more like a palace, such as one sees in the old countries. In the nighttime I crept in through a window that I might see in what manner he treated her. I went from room to room, and in such way thought kings and queens must live, it was all so very good. And they all said he treated her like a queen, and many marveled as to what breed of woman she was; for there was other blood in her veins, and she was different from the women of Akatan, and no one knew her for what she was. Ay, she was a queen; but I was a chief, and the son of a chief, and I had paid for her an untold price of skin and boat and bead.

"But why so many words? I was a sailorman, and knew the way of the ships on the seas. I followed to England, and then to other countries. Sometimes I heard of them by word of mouth, sometimes I read of them in the papers; yet never once could I come by them, for they had much money, and traveled fast, while I was a poor man. Then came trouble upon them, and their wealth slipped away, one day, like a curl of smoke. The papers were full of it at the time; but after that nothing was said, and I knew they had gone back where more gold could be got from the ground.

"They had dropped out of the world, being now poor; and so I wandered from camp to camp, even north to the Kootenay Country, where I picked up the cold scent. They had come and gone, some said this way, and some that, and still others that they had gone to the country of the Yukon. And I went this way, and I went that, ever journeying from place to place, till it seemed I must grow weary of the world which was so large. But in the Kootenay I traveled a bad trail, and a long trail, with a 'breed' of the Northwest, who saw fit to die when the famine pinched. He had been to the Yukon by an unknown way over the mountains, and when he knew his time was near gave me the map and the secret of a place where he swore by his gods there was much gold.

"After that all the world began to flock into the north. I was a poor man; I sold myself to be a driver of dogs. The rest you know. I met him and her in Dawson. She did not know me, for I was only a stripling, and her life had been large, so she had no time to remember the one who had paid for her an untold price.

"So? You bought me from my term of service. I went back to bring things about in my own way; for I had waited long, and now that I had my hand upon him was in no hurry. As I say, I had it in mind to do my own way; for I read back in my life, through all I had seen and suffered, and remembered the cold and hunger of the endless forest by the Russian Seas. As you know, I led him into the east,— him and Unga,— into the east where many have gone and few returned. I led them to the spot where the bones and the curses of men lie with the gold which they may not have.

"The way was long and the trail unpacked. Our dogs were many and ate much; nor could our sleds carry till the break of spring. We must come back before the river ran free. So here and there we cached grub, that our sleds might be lightened and there be no chance of famine on the back trip. At the McQuestion there were three men, and near them we built a cache, as also did we at the Mayo, where was a hunting-camp of a dozen Pellys which had crossed the divide from the south. After that, as we went on into the east, we saw no men; only the sleeping river, the moveless forest, and the White Silence of the North. As I say, the way was long and the trail unpacked. Sometimes, in a day's toil, we made no more than eight miles, or ten, and at night we slept like dead men. And never once did they dream that I was Naass, head man of Akatan, the righter of wrongs.

" We now made smaller caches, and in the nighttime it was a small matter to go back on the trail we had broken, and change them in such way that one might deem the wolverines the thieves. Again, there be places where there is a fall to the river, and the water is unruly, and the ice makes above and is eaten away beneath. In such a spot the sled I drove broke through, and the dogs; and to him and Unga it was ill luck, but no more. And there was much grub on that sled, and the dogs the strongest. But he laughed, for he was strong of life, and gave the dogs that were left little grub till we cut them from the harnesses, one by one, and fed them to their mates. We would go home light, he said, traveling and eating from cache to cache, with neither dogs nor sleds; which was true, for our grub was very short, and the last dog died in the traces the night we came to the gold and the bones and the curses of men.

" To reach that place, — and the map spoke true, — in the heart of the great mountains, we cut ice steps against the wall of a divide. One looked for a valley beyond, but there was no valley; the snow spread away, level as the great harvest plains, and here and there about us mighty mountains shoved their white heads among the stars. And midway on that strange plain which should have been a valley, the earth and the snow fell away, straight down toward the heart of the world. Had we not been sailormen our heads would have swung round with the sight; but we stood on the dizzy edge that we might see a way to get down. And on one side, and one side only, the wall had fallen away till it was like the slope of the decks in a topsail breeze. I do not know why this thing should be so, but it was so. ' It is the mouth of hell,' he said; ' let us go down.' And we went down.

" And on the bottom there was a cabin, built by some man, of logs which he had cast down from above. It was a very old cabin; for men had died there alone at different times, and on pieces of birch bark which were there we read their last words and their curses. One had died of scurvy; another's partner had robbed him of his last grub and powder and stolen away; a third had been mauled by a bald-face grizzly; a fourth had hunted for game and starved, — and so it went, and they had been loath to leave the gold, and had died by the side of it in one way or another. And the worthless gold they had gathered yellowed the floor of the cabin like in a dream.

" But his soul was steady, and his head clear, this man I had led thus far. ' We have nothing to eat,' he said, ' and we will only look upon this gold, and see whence it comes and how much there be. Then we will go away quick, before it gets into our eyes and steals away our judgment. And in this way we may return in the end, with more grub, and possess it all.' So we looked upon the great vein, which cut the wall of the pit as a true vein should; and we measured it, and traced it from above and below, and drove the stakes of the claims and blazed the trees in token of our rights. Then, our knees shaking with lack of food, and a sickness in our bellies, and our hearts chugging close to our mouths, we climbed the mighty wall for the last time and turned our faces to the back trip.

" The last stretch we dragged Unga between us, and we fell often, but in the end we made the cache. And lo, there was no grub. It was well done, for he thought it the wolverines, and damned them and his gods in the one breath. But Unga was brave, and smiled, and put her hand in his, till I turned away that I might hold myself. ' We will rest by the fire,' she said, ' till morning, and we will gather strength from our moccasins.' So we cut the tops of our moccasins in strips, and boiled them half of the night, that we might chew them and swallow them. And in the morning we talked of our chance. The next cache was five days' journey; we could not make it. We must find game.

" ' We will go forth and hunt,' he said.

" ' Yes,' said I, ' we will go forth and hunt.'

" And he ruled that Unga stay by the fire and save her strength. And we went forth, he in quest of the moose, and I to the cache I had changed. But I ate little, so they might not see in me much strength. And in the night he fell many times as he drew into camp. And I too made to suffer great weakness, stumbling over my snowshoes as though each step might be my last. And we gathered strength from our moccasins.

" He was a great man. His soul lifted his body to the last; nor did he cry aloud, save for the sake of Unga. On the second day I followed him, that I might not miss the end. And he lay down to rest often. That night he was near gone; but in the morning he swore weakly and went forth again. He was like a drunken man, and I looked many times for him to give up; but his was the strength of the strong, and his soul the soul of a giant, for he lifted his body through all the weary day. And he shot two ptarmigan, but would not eat them. He needed no fire; they meant life; but his thought was for Unga, and he turned toward camp. He no longer walked, but crawled on hand and knee through the snow. I came to him, and read death in his eyes. Even then it was not too late to eat of the ptarmigan. He cast away his rifle, and carried the birds in his mouth like a dog. I walked by his side, upright. And he looked at me during the moments he rested, and wondered that I was so strong. I could see it, though he no longer spoke; and when his lips moved, they moved without sound. As I say, he was a great man, and my heart spoke for softness; but I read back in my life, and remem-

bered the cold and hunger of the endless forest by the Russian Seas. Besides, Unga was mine, and I had paid for her an untold price of skin and boat and bead.

" And in this manner we came through the white forest, with the silence heavy upon us like a damp sea mist. And the ghosts of the past were in the air and all about us; and I saw the yellow beach of Akatan, and the kayaks racing home from the fishing, and the houses on the rim of the forest. And the men who had made themselves chiefs were there, the lawgivers whose blood I bore, and whose blood I had wedded in Unga. Ay, and Yash-Noosh walked with me, the wet sand in his hair, and his war spear, broken as he fell upon it, still in his hand. And I knew the time was met, and saw in the eyes of Unga the promise.

" As I say, we came thus through the forest, till the smell of the camp smoke was in our nostrils. And I bent above him, and tore the ptarmigan from his teeth. He turned on his side and rested, the wonder mounting in his eyes, and the hand which was under slipping slow toward the knife at his hip. But I took it from him, smiling close in his face. Even then he did not understand. So I made to drink from black bottles, and to build high upon the snow a pile of goods, and to live again the things which happened on the night of my marriage. I spoke no word, but he understood. Yet was he unafraid. There was a sneer to his lips, and cold anger, and he gathered new strength with the knowledge. It was not far, but the snow was deep, and he dragged himself very slow. Once, he lay so long, I turned him over and gazed into his eyes. And sometimes he looked forth, and sometimes death. And when I loosed him he struggled on again. In this way we came to the fire. Unga was at his side on the instant. His lips moved, without sound; then he pointed at me, that Unga might understand.

And after that he lay in the snow, very still, for a long while. Even now is he there in the snow.

"I said no word till I had cooked the ptarmigan. Then I spoke to her in her own tongue, which she had not heard in many years. She straightened herself, so, and her eyes were wonder-wide, and she asked who I was, and where I had learned that speech.

"'I am Naass,' I said.

"'You?' she said. 'You?' And she crept close that she might look upon me.

"'Yes,' I answered; 'I am Naass, head man of Akatan, the last of the blood, as you are the last of the blood.'

"And she laughed. By all the things I have seen and the deeds I have done, may I never hear such a laugh again. It put the chill to my soul, sitting there in the White Silence, alone with death and this woman who laughed.

"'Come!' I said, for I thought she wandered. 'Eat of the food and let us be gone. It is a far fetch from here to Akatan.'

"But she shoved her face in his yellow mane, and laughed till it seemed the heavens must fall about our ears. I had thought she would be overjoyed at the sight of me, and eager to go back to the memory of old times; but this seemed a strange form to take.

"'Come!' I cried, taking her strong by the hand. 'The way is long and dark. Let us hurry!'

"'Where?' she asked, sitting up, and ceasing from her strange mirth.

"'To Akatan,' I answered, intent on the light to grow on her face at the thought. But it became like his, with a sneer to the lips, and cold anger.

"'Yes,' she said; 'we will go, hand in hand, to Akatan, you and I. And we will live in the dirty huts, and eat of the fish and oil, and bring forth a spawn, — a spawn to be proud of all the days of our life. We will forget the world and be happy, very happy. It is good, most good. Come! Let us hurry. Let us go back to Akatan.'

"And she ran her hand through his yellow hair, and smiled in a way which was not good. And there was no promise in her eyes.

"I sat silent, and marveled at the strangeness of woman. I went back to the night when he dragged her from me, and she screamed and tore at his hair, — at his hair which now she played with and would not leave. Then I remembered the price and the long years of waiting; and I gripped her close, and dragged her away as he had done. And she held back, even as on that night, and fought like a she-cat for its whelp. And when the fire was between us and the man, I loosed her, and she sat and listened. And I told her of all that lay between, of all that had happened me on strange seas, of all that I had done in strange lands; of my weary quest, and the hungry years, and the promise which had been mine from the first. Ay, I told all, even to what had passed that day between the man and me, and in the days yet young. And as I spoke I saw the promise grow in her eyes, full and large like the break of dawn. And I read pity there, the tenderness of woman, the love, the heart and the soul of Unga. And I was a stripling again, for the look was the look of Unga as she ran up the beach, laughing, to the home of her mother. The stern unrest was gone, and the hunger, and the weary waiting. The time was met. I felt the call of her breast, and it seemed there I must pillow my head and forget. She opened her arms to me, and I came against her. Then, sudden, the hate flamed in her eye, her hand was at my hip. And once, twice, she passed the knife.

"'Dog!' she sneered, as she flung me into the snow. 'Swine!' And then she laughed till the silence cracked, and went back to her dead.

"As I say, once she passed the

knife, and twice; but she was weak with hunger, and it was not meant that I should die. Yet was I minded to stay in that place, and to close my eyes in the last long sleep with those whose lives had crossed with mine and led my feet on unknown trails. But there lay a debt upon me which would not let me rest.

"And the way was long, the cold bitter, and there was little grub. The Pellys had found no moose, and had robbed my cache. And so had the three white men; but they lay thin and dead in their cabin as I passed. After that I do not remember, till I came here, and found food and fire, — much fire."

As he finished, he crouched closely, even jealously, over the stove. For a long while the slush-lamp shadows played tragedies upon the wall.

"But Unga!" cried Prince, the vision still strong upon him.

"Unga? She would not eat of the ptarmigan. She lay with her arms about his neck, her face deep in his yellow hair. I drew the fire close, that she might not feel the frost; but she crept to the other side. And I built a fire there; yet it was little good, for she would not eat. And in this manner they still lie up there in the snow."

"And you?" asked Malemute Kid.

"I do not know; but Akatan is small, and I have little wish to go back and live on the edge of the world. Yet is there small use in life. I can go to Constantine, and he will put irons upon me, and one day they will tie a piece of rope, so, and I will sleep good. Yet — no; I do not know."

"But, Kid," protested Prince, "this is murder!"

"Hush!" commanded Malemute Kid. "There be things greater than our wisdom, beyond our justice. The right and the wrong of this we cannot say, and it is not for us to judge."

Naass drew yet closer to the fire. There was a great silence, and in each man's eyes many pictures came and went.

Jack London.

3
A THOUSAND DEATHS

A Thousand Deaths.

BY JACK LONDON.

HAD been in the water about an hour, and cold, exhausted, with a terrible cramp in my right calf, it seemed as though my hour had come. Fruitlessly struggling against the strong ebb tide, I had beheld the maddening procession of the water-front lights slip by; but now I gave up attempting to breast the stream and contented myself with the bitter thoughts of a wasted career, now drawing to a close.

It had been my luck to come of good, English stock, but of parents whose account with the bankers far exceeded their knowledge of child-nature and the rearing of children. While born with a silver spoon in my mouth, the blessed atmosphere of the home circle was to me unknown. My father, a very learned man and a celebrated antiquarian, gave no thought to his family, being constantly lost in the abstractions of his study; while my mother, noted far more for her good looks than her good sense, sated herself with the adulation of the society in which she was perpetually plunged. I went through the regular school and college routine of a boy of the English bourgeois, and as the years brought me increasing strength and passions, my parents suddenly became aware that I was possessed of an immortal soul, and endeavored to draw the curb. But it was too late; I perpetrated the wildest and most audacious folly, and was disowned by my people, ostracized by the society I had so long outraged, and with the thousand pounds my father gave me, with the declaration that he would neither see me again nor give me more, I took a first-class passage to Australia.

Since then my life had been one long peregrination — from the Orient to the Occident, from the Arctic to the Antarctic — to find myself at last, an able seaman at thirty, in the full vigor of my manhood, drowning in San Francisco bay because of a disastrously successful attempt to desert my ship.

My right leg was drawn up by the cramp, and I was suffering the keenest agony. A slight breeze stirred up a choppy sea, which washed into my mouth and down my throat, nor could I prevent it. Though I still contrived to keep afloat, it was merely mechanical, for I was rapidly becoming unconscious. I have a d m recollection of drifting past the sea-wall, and of catching a glimpse of an up-river steamer's starboard light; then everything became a blank.

.   .   .   .

I heard the low hum of insect life, and felt the balmy air of a spring morning fanning my cheek. Gradually it assumed a rhythmic flow, to whose soft pulsations my body seemed to respond. I floated on the gentle bosom of a summer's sea, rising and falling with dreamy pleasure on each crooning wave. But the pulsations grew stronger; the humming, louder; the waves, larger, fiercer — I was dashed about on a stormy sea. A great agony fastened upon me. Brilliant, intermittent sparks of light flashed athwart my inner consciousness; in my ears there was the sound of many waters; then a sudden snapping of an intangible something, and I awoke.

The scene, of which I was protagonist, was a curious one. A glance sufficed to inform me that I lay on the cabin floor of some gentleman's yacht, in a most uncomfortable posture. On either side, grasping my arms and working them up and down like pump handles, were two peculiarly clad, dark-skinned creatures. Though conversant with most aboriginal types, I could not conjecture their nationality. Some attachment had been fastened about my head, which connected my respiratory organs with the machine I shall next describe. My nostrils, however, had been closed, forcing me to breathe through the mouth. Foreshortened by the obliquity of my line of vision, I beheld two tubes, similar to small hosing but of different composition, which emerged from my mouth and went off at an acute angle from each other. The first came to an abrupt termination and lay on the floor beside me; the second traversed the floor in numerous coils, connecting with the apparatus I have promised to describe.

In the days before my life had become tangential, I had dabbled not a little in science, and, conversant with the appurtenances and general paraphernalia of the laboratory, I appreciated the machine I now beheld. It was composed chiefly of glass, the construction being of that crude sort which is employed for experimentative purposes. A vessel of water was surrounded by an air chamber, to which was fixed a vertical tube, surmounted by a globe. In the center of this was a vacuum gauge. The water in the tube moved upward and downward, creating alternate inhalations and exhalations, which were in turn communicated to me through the hose. With this, and the aid of the men who pumped my arms so vigorously, had the process of breathing been artificially carried on, my chest rising and falling and my lungs expanding and contracting, till nature could be persuaded to again take up her wonted labor.

As I opened my eyes the appliance about my head, nostrils and mouth was removed. Draining a stiff three fingers of brandy, I staggered to my feet to thank my preserver, and confronted — my father. But long years of fellowship with danger had taught me self-control, and I waited to see if he would recognize me. Not so ; he saw in me no more than a runaway sailor and treated me accordingly.

Leaving me to the care of the blackies, he fell to revising the notes he had made on my resuscitation. As I ate of the handsome fare served up to me, confusion began on deck, and from the chanteys of the sailors and the rattling of blocks and tackles I surmised that we were getting under way. What a lark ! Off on a cruise with my recluse father into the wide Pacific ! Little did I realize, as I laughed to myself, which side the joke was to be on. Aye, had I known, I would have plunged overboard and welcomed the dirty fo'k'sle from which I had just escaped.

I was not allowed on deck till we had sunk the Farallones and the last pilot boat. I appreciated this forethought on the part of my father and made it a point to thank him heartily, in my bluff seaman's manner. I could not suspect that he had his own ends in view, in thus keeping my presence secret to all save the crew. He told me briefly of my rescue by his sailors, assuring me that the obligation was on his side, as my appearance had been most

opportune. He had constructed the apparatus for the vindication
of a theory concerning certain biological phenomena, and had been
waiting for an opportunity to use it.

" You have proved it beyond all doubt," he said ; then added
with a sigh, " But only in the small matter of drowning."

But, to take a reef in my yarn — he offered me an advance of
two pounds on my previous wages to sail with him, and this I
considered handsome, for he really did not need me.   Contrary to
my expectations, I did not join the sailors' mess, for'ard, being
assigned to a comfortable stateroom and eating at the captain's
table.   He had perceived that I was no common sailor, and I resolved to take this chance for reinstating myself in his good graces.
I wove a fictitious past to account for my education and present
position, and did my best to come in touch with him.   I was not
long in disclosing a predilection for scientific pursuits, nor he in
appreciating my aptitude.   I became his assistant, with a corre-
sponding increase in wages, and before long, as he grew confidential and expounded his theories, I was as enthusiastic as himself.

The days flew quickly by, for I was deeply interested in my
new studies, passing my waking hours in his well-stocked library,
or listening to his plans and aiding him in his laboratory work.
But we were forced to forego many enticing experiments, a rolling ship not being exactly the proper place for delicate or intri-
cate work.   He promised me, however, many delightful hours in
the magnificent laboratory for which we were bound.   He had
taken possession of an uncharted South Sea island, as he said, and
turned it into a scientific paradise.

We had not been on the island long, before I discovered the
horrible mare's nest I had fallen into.   But before I describe the
strange things which came to pass, I must briefly outline the
causes which culminated in as startling an experience as ever fell
to the lot of man.

Late in life, my father had abandoned the musty charms of
antiquity and succumbed to the more fascinating ones embraced
under the general head of biology.   Having been thoroughly
grounded during his youth in the fundamentals, he rapidly ex-
plored all the higher branches as far as the scientific world had
gone, and found himself on the no man's land of the unknowable.

It was his intention to pre-empt some of this unclaimed territory, and it was at this stage of his investigations that we had been thrown together. Having a good brain, though I say it myself, I had mastered his speculations and methods of reasoning, becoming almost as mad as himself. But I should not say this. The marvelous results we afterward obtained can only go to prove his sanity. I can but say that he was the most abnormal specimen of cold-blooded cruelty I have ever seen.

After having penetrated the dual mysteries of physiology and psychology, his thought had led him to the verge of a great field, for which, the better to explore, he began studies in higher organic chemistry, pathology, toxicology and other sciences and sub-sciences rendered kindred as accessories to his speculative hypotheses. Starting from the proposition that the direct cause of the temporary and permanent arrest of vitality was due to the coagulation of certain elements and compounds in the protoplasm, he had isolated and subjected these various substances to innumerable experiments. Since the temporary arrest of vitality in an organism brought coma, and a permanent arrest death, he held that by artificial means this coagulation of the protoplasm could be retarded, prevented, and even overcome in the extreme states of solidification. Or, to do away with the technical nomenclature, he argued that death, when not violent and in which none of the organs had suffered injury, was merely suspended vitality; and that, in such instances, life could be induced to resume its functions by the use of proper methods. This, then, was his idea: To discover the method — and by practical experimentation prove the possibility — of renewing vitality in a structure from which life had seemingly fled. Of course, he recognized the futility of such endeavor after decomposition had set in; he must have organisms which but the moment, the hour, or the day before, had been quick with life. With me, in a crude way, he had proved this theory. I was really drowned, really dead, when picked from the water of San Francisco bay — but the vital spark had been renewed by means of his aerotherapeutical apparatus, as he called it.

Now to his dark purpose concerning me. He first showed me how completely I was in his power. He had sent the yacht away

for a year, retaining only his two blackies, who were utterly devoted to him.   He then made an exhaustive review of his theory
and outlined the method of proof he had adopted, concluding
with the startling announcement that I was to be his subject.

I had faced death and weighed my chances in many a desperate
venture, but never in one of this nature.   I can swear I am no
coward, yet this proposition of journeying back and forth across
the borderland of death put the yellow fear upon me.   I asked
for time, which he granted, at the same time assuring me that but
the one course was open — I must submit.   Escape from the
island was out of the question; escape by suicide was not to be
entertained, though really preferable to what it seemed I must
undergo; my only hope was to destroy my captors.   But this
latter was frustrated through the precautions taken by my father.
I was subjected to a constant surveillance, even in my sleep being
guarded by one or the other of the blacks.

Having pleaded in vain, I announced and proved that I was his
son.   It was my last card, and I had placed all my hopes upon it.
But he was inexorable; he was not a father but a scientific machine.   I wonder yet how it ever came to pass that he married
my mother or begat me, for there was not the slightest grain of
emotion in his make-up.   Reason was all in all to him, nor could
he understand such things as love or sympathy in others, except
as petty weaknesses which should be overcome.   So he informed
me that in the beginning he had given me life, and who had better
right to take it away than he?   Such, he said, was not his desire,
however; he merely wished to borrow it occasionally, promising
to return it punctually at the appointed time.   Of course, there
was a liability of mishaps, but I could do no more than take the
chances, since the affairs of men were full of such.

The better to insure success, he wished me to be in the best
possible condition, so I was dieted and trained like a great athlete
before, a decisive contest.   What could I do?   If I had to
undergo the peril, it were best to be in good shape.   In my intervals of relaxation he allowed me to assist in the arranging of the
apparatus and in the various subsidiary experiments.   The interest I took in all such operations can be imagined.   I mastered the
work as thoroughly as he, and often had the pleasure of seeing

some of my suggestions or alterations put into effect. After such events I would smile grimly, conscious of officiating at my own funeral.

He began by inaugurating a series of experiments in toxicology. When all was ready, I was killed by a stiff dose of strychnine and allowed to lie dead for some twenty hours. During that period my body was dead, absolutely dead. All respiration and circulation ceased; but the frightful part of it was, that while the protoplasmic coagulation proceeded, I retained consciousness and was enabled to study it in all its ghastly details.

The apparatus to bring me back to life was an air-tight chamber, fitted to receive my body. The mechanism was simple — a few valves, a rotary shaft and crank, and an electric motor. When in operation, the interior atmosphere was alternately condensed and rarefied, thus communicating to my lungs an artificial respiration without the agency of the hosing previously used. Though my body was inert, and, for all I knew, in the first stages of decomposition, I was cognizant of everything that transpired. I knew when they placed me in the chamber, and though all my senses were quiescent, I was aware of hypodermic injections of a compound to react upon the coagulatory process. Then the chamber was closed and the machinery started. My anxiety was terrible; but the circulation became gradually restored, the different organs began to carry on their respective functions, and in an hour's time I was eating a hearty dinner.

It cannot be said that I participated in this series, nor in the subsequent ones, with much verve; but after two ineffectual attempts at escape, I began to take quite an interest. Besides, I was becoming accustomed. My father was beside himself at his success, and as the months rolled by his speculations took wilder and yet wilder flights. We ranged through the three great classes of poisons, the neurotics, the gaseous and the irritants, but carefully avoided some of the mineral irritants and passed the whole group of corrosives. During the poison régime I became quite accustomed to dying, and had but one mishap to shake my growing confidence. Scarifying a number of lesser blood vessels in my arm, he introduced a minute quantity of that most frightful of poisons, the arrow poison, or curare. I lost consciousness at the start, quickly followed by the cessation of respiration and circulation, and so far had the solidification of the protoplasm advanced, that he gave up all hope. But at the last moment he applied a discovery he had been working upon, receiving such encouragement as to redouble his efforts.

In a glass vacuum, similar but not exactly like a Crookes' tube, was placed a magnetic field. When penetrated by polarized light, it gave no phenomena of phosphorescence nor of rectilinear projection of atoms, but emitted non-luminous rays, similar to the X ray. While the X ray could reveal opaque objects hidden in dense mediums, this was possessed of far subtler penetration. By this he photographed my body, and found on the negative an infinite number of blurred shadows, due to the chemical and electric motions still going on. This was an infallible proof that the rigor mortis in which I lay was not genuine; that is, those mysterious forces, those delicate bonds which held my soul to my body, were still in action. The resultants of all other poisons were unapparent, save those of mercurial compounds, which usually left me languid for several days.

Another series of delightful experiments was with electricity. We verified Tesla's assertion that high currents were utterly harmless by passing 100,000 volts through my body. As this did not affect me, the current was reduced to 2,500, and I was quickly electrocuted. This time he ventured so far as to allow me to remain dead, or in a state of suspended vitality, for three days. It took four hours to bring me back.

Once, he superinduced lockjaw; but the agony of dying was so great that I positively refused to undergo similar experiments. The easiest deaths were by asphyxiation, such as drowning, strangling, and suffocation by gas; while those by morphine, opium, cocaine and chloroform, were not at all hard.

Another time, after being suffocated, he kept me in cold storage for three months, not permitting me to freeze or decay. This was without my knowledge, and I was in a great fright on discovering the lapse of time. I became afraid of what he might do with me when I lay dead, my alarm being increased by the predilection he was beginning to betray toward vivisection. The last time I was resurrected, I discovered that he had been tampering with my breast. Though he had carefully dressed and sewed the incisions up, they were so severe that I had to take to my bed for some time. It was during this convalescence that I evolved the plan by which I ultimately escaped.

While feigning unbounded enthusiasm in the work, I asked and received a vacation from my moribund occupation. During this period I devoted myself to laboratory work, while he was too deep in the vivisection of the many animals captured by the blacks to take notice of my work.

It was on these two propositions that I constructed my theory: First, electrolysis, or the decomposition of water into its constituent gases by means of electricity; and, second, by the hypothetical existence of a force, the converse of gravitation, which Astor has named " apergy." Terrestrial attraction, for instance, merely draws objects together but does not combine them; hence, apergy is merely repulsion. Now, atomic or molecular attraction not only draws objects together but integrates them; and it was the converse of this, or a disintegrative force, which I wished to not only discover and produce, but to direct at will. Thus the molecules of hydrogen and oxygen reacting on each other, separate and create new molecules, containing both elements and forming water. Electrolysis causes these molecules to split up and resume their original condition, producing the two gases separately. The force I wished to find must not only do this with two, but with all elements, no matter in what compounds they exist. If I could then entice my father within its radius, he would be instantly disintegrated and sent flying to the four quarters, a mass of isolated elements.

It must not be understood that this force, which I finally came to control, annihilated matter; it merely annihilated form. Nor, as I soon discovered, had it any effect on inorganic structure; but to all organic form it was absolutely fatal. This partiality puzzled me at first, though had I stopped to think deeper I would have seen through it. Since the number of atoms in organic molecules is far greater than in the most complex mineral molecules, organic compounds are characterized by their instability and the ease with which they are split up by physical forces and chemical reagents.

By two powerful batteries, connected with magnets constructed specially for this purpose, two tremendous forces were projected. Considered apart from each other, they were perfectly harmless; but they accomplished their purpose by focusing at an invisible point in mid-air. After practically demonstrating its success, besides narrowly escaping being blown into nothingness, I laid my trap. Concealing the magnets, so that their force made the whole space of my chamber doorway a field of death, and placing by my couch a button by which I could throw on the current from the storage batteries, I climbed into bed.

The blackies still guarded my sleeping quarters, one relieving the other at midnight. I turned on the current as soon as the first man arrived. Hardly had I begun to doze, when I was aroused by a sharp, metallic tinkle. There, on the mid-threshold, lay the collar of Dan, my father's St. Bernard. My keeper ran to pick it up. He disappeared like a gust of wind, his clothes falling to the floor in a heap. There was a slight whiff of ozone in the air, but since the principal gaseous components of his body were hydrogen, oxygen and nitrogen, which are equally colorless and odorless, there was no other manifestation of his departure. Yet when I shut off the current and removed the garments, I found a deposit of carbon in the form of animal charcoal; also other powders, the isolated, solid elements of his organism, such as sulphur, potassium and iron. Resetting the trap, I crawled back to bed. At midnight I got up and removed the remains of the second blacky, and then slept peacefully till morning.

I was awakened by the strident voice of my father, who was calling to me from across the laboratory. I laughed to myself. There had been no one to call him and he had overslept. I could hear him as he approached my room with the intention of rousing me, and so I sat up in bed, the better to observe his translation — perhaps apotheosis -were a better term. He paused a moment at the threshold, then took the fatal step. Puff! It was like the wind sighing among the pines. He was gone. His clothes fell in a fantastic heap on the floor. Besides ozone, I noticed the faint, garlic-like odor of phosphorus. A little pile of elementary solids lay among his garments. That was all. The wide world lay before me. My captors were not.

4
THE PRIESTLY PREROGATIVE

THE PRIESTLY PREROGATIVE

By JACK LONDON

THIS is the story of a man who did not appreciate his wife; also, of a woman who did him too great an honor when she gave herself to him. Incidentally, it concerns a Jesuit priest who had never been known to lie. He was an appurtenance, and a very necessary one, to the Yukon country; but the presence of the other two was merely accidental. They were specimens of the many strange waifs which ride the breast of a gold rush or come tailing along behind.

Edwin Bentham and Grace Bentham were waifs; they were also tailing along behind, for the Klondike rush of '97 had long since swept down the great river and subsided into the famine-stricken city of Dawson. When the Yukon shut up shop and went to sleep under a three-foot ice-sheet, this peripatetic couple found themselves at the Five Finger Rapids, with the City of Gold still a journey of many sleeps to the north.

Many cattle had been butchered at this place in the fall of the year, and the offal made a goodly heap. The three fellow-voyageurs of Edwin Bentham and wife gazed upon this deposit, did a little mental arithmetic, caught a certain glimpse of a bonanza, and decided to remain. And all winter they sold sacks of bones and frozen hides to the famished dog-teams. It was a modest price they asked, a dollar a pound, just as it came. Six months later, when the sun came back and the Yukon awoke, they buckled on their heavy money-belts and journeyed back to the Southland, where they yet live and lie mightily about the Klondike they never saw.

But Edwin Bentham—he was an indolent fellow, and had he not been possessed of a wife, would have gladly joined issues in the dog-meat speculation. As it was, she played upon his vanity, told him how great and strong he was, how a man such as he certainly was could overcome all obstacles and of a surety obtain the Golden Fleece. So he squared his jaw, sold his share in the bones and hides for a sled and one dog, and turned his snow-shoes to the north. Needless to state, Grace Bentham's snow-shoes never allowed his tracks to grow cold. Nay, ere their tribulations had seen three days, it was the man who followed in the rear, and the woman who broke trail in advance. Of course, if anybody hove in sight, the position was instantly reversed. Thus did his manhood remain virgin to the travelers who passed like ghosts on the silent trail. There are such men in this world.

How such a man and such a woman came to take each other for better and for worse is unimportant to this narrative. These things are familiar to us all, and those people who do them, or even question them too closely, are apt to lose a beautiful faith which is known as Eternal Fitness.

Edwin Bentham was a boy, thrust by mischance into a man's body,—a boy who could complacently pluck a butterfly, wing from wing, or cower in abject terror before a lean, nervy fellow, not half his size. He was a selfish cry-baby, hidden behind a man's mustache and stature, and glossed over with a skin-deep veneer of culture and conventionality. Yes; he was a clubman and a society man,—the sort that grace social functions and utter inanities with a charm and unction which is indescribable; the sort that talk big, and cry over a toothache; the sort that put more hell into a woman's life by marrying her than can the most graceless libertine that ever browsed in forbidden pastures. We meet these men every day, but we rarely know them for what they are. Second to marrying them, the best way to get this knowledge is to eat out of the same pot and crawl under the same blanket with them for—well, say a week; no greater margin is necessary.

To see Grace Bentham, was to see a slender, girlish creature; to know her, was to know a soul which dwarfed your own, yet retained all the elements of the eternal feminine. This was the woman

41

who urged and encouraged her husband in his Northland quest, who broke trail for him when no one was looking, and cried in secret over her weakling woman's body.

So journeyed this strangely assorted couple down to old Fort Selkirk, then through fivescore miles of dismal wilderness to Stuart River. And when the short day left them, and the man lay down in the snow and blubbered, it was the woman who lashed him to the sled, bit her lips with the pain of her aching limbs, and helped the dog haul him to Malemute Kid's cabin. Malemute Kid was not at home, but Meyers, the German trader, cooked great moose-steaks and shook up a bed of fresh pine boughs.

Lake, Langham, and Parker, were excited, and not unduly so when the cause was taken into account.

"Oh, Sandy! Say, can you tell a porterhouse from a round? Come out and lend us a hand, anyway!" This appeal emanated from the cache, where Langham was vainly struggling with divers quarters of frozen moose.

"Don't you budge from those dishes!" commanded Parker.

"I say, Sandy; there's a good fellow—just run down to the Missouri Camp and borrow some cinnamon," begged Lake.

"Oh! oh! hurry up! Why don't—" But the crash of meat and boxes, in the cache, abruptly quenched this peremptory summons.

"Come now, Sandy; it won't take a minute to go down to the Missouri—"

"You leave him alone,". interrupted Parker. "How am I to mix the biscuits if the table is n't cleared off?"

Sandy paused in indecision, till suddenly the fact that he was Langham's "man" dawned upon him. Then he apologetically threw down the greasy dishcloth, and went to his master's rescue.

These promising scions of wealthy progenitors had come to the Northland in search of laurels, with much money to burn, and a "man" apiece. Luckily for their souls, the other two men were up the White River in search of a mythical quartz-ledge; so Sandy had to grin under the responsibility of three healthy masters, each of whom was possessed of peculiar

cookery ideas. Twice that morning had a disruption of the whole camp been imminent, only averted by immense concessions from one or the other of these knights of the chafing-dish. But at last their mutual creation, a really dainty dinner, was completed. Then they sat down to a three-cornered game of "cut-throat,"—a proceeding which did away with all *casus belli* for future hostilities, and permitted the victor to depart on a most important mission.

This fortune fell to Parker, who parted his hair in the middle, put on his mittens and bearskin cap, and stepped over to Malemute's Kid's cabin. And when he returned, it was in the company of Grace Bentham and Malemute Kid,—the former very sorry her husband could not share with her their hospitality, for he had gone up to look at the Henderson Creek mines, and the latter still a trifle stiff from breaking trail down the Stuart River. Meyers had been asked, but had declined, being deeply engrossed in an experiment of raising bread from hops.

Well, they could do without the husband; but a woman—why they had not seen one all winter, and the presence of this one promised a new era in their lives. They were college men and gentlemen, these three young fellows, yearning for the flesh-pots they had been so long denied. Probably Grace Bentham suffered from a similar hunger; at least, it meant much to her, the first bright hour in many weeks of darkness.

But that wonderful first course, which claimed the versatile Lake for its parent, had no sooner been served than there came a loud knock at the door.

"Oh! Ah! Won't you come in, Mr. Bentham?" said Parker, who had stepped to see who the newcomer might be.

"Is my wife here?" gruffly responded that worthy.

"Why, yes. We left word with Mr. Meyers." Parker was exerting his most dulcet tones, inwardly wondering what the deuce it all meant. "Won't you come in? Expecting you at any moment, we reserved a place. And just in time for the first course, too."

"Come in, Edwin, dear," chirped Grace Bentham from her seat at the table.

Parker naturally stood aside.

"I want my wife," reiterated Bentham hoarsely, the intonation savoring disagreeably of ownership.

Parker gasped, was within an ace of driving his fist into the face of his boorish visitor, but held himself awkwardly in check. Everybody rose. Lake lost his head and caught himself on the verge of saying, "Must you go?"

Then began the farrago of leave-taking. "So nice of you—" "I am awfully sorry —" "By Jove! how things did brighten—" "Really now, you—" "Thank you ever so much—" "Nice trip to Dawson—" etc., etc.

In this wise the lamb was helped into her jacket and led to the slaughter. Then the door slammed, and they gazed wofuliy upon the deserted table.

"Damn!" Langham had suffered disadvantages in his early training, and his oaths were weak and monotonous. "Damn!" he repeated, vaguely conscious of the incompleteness and vainly struggling for a more virile term.

It is a clever woman who can fill out the many weak places in an inefficient man, by her own indomitability re-enforce his vacillating nature, infuse her ambitious soul into his, and spur him on to great achievements. And it is indeed a very clever and tactful woman who can do all this, and do it so subtly that the man receives all the credit and believes in his inmost heart that everything is due to him and him alone.

This is what Grace Bentham proceeded to do. Arriving in Dawson with a few pounds of flour and several letters of introduction, she at once applied herself to the task of pushing her big baby to the fore. It was she who melted the stony heart and wrung credit from the rude barbarian who presided over the destiny of the P. C. Company; yet it was Edwin Bentham to whom the concession was ostensibly granted. It was she who dragged her baby up and down creeks, over benches and divides, and on a dozen wild stampedes; yet everybody remarked what an energetic fellow that Bentham was. It was she who studied maps, and catechised miners, and hammered geog-raphy and locations into his hollow head, till everybody marveled at his broad grasp of the country and knowledge of its conditions. Of course, they said the wife was a brick, and only a few wise ones appreciated and pitied the brave little woman.

She did the work; he got the credit and reward. In the Northwest Territory a married woman cannot stake or record a creek, bench, or quartz claim; so Edwin Bentham went down to the Gold Commissioner and filed on Bench Claim 23, second tier, of French Hill. And when April came they were washing out a thousand dollars a day, with many, many such days in prospect.

At the base of French Hill lay Eldorado Creek, and on a creek claim stood the cabin of Clyde Wharton. At present he was not washing out a diurnal thousand dollars; but his dumps grew, shift by shift, and there would come a time when those dumps would pass through his sluice-boxes, depositing in the riffles, in the course of half a dozen days, several hundred thousand dollars. He often sat in that cabin, smoked his pipe, and dreamed beautiful little dreams,—dreams in which neither the dumps nor the half-ton of dust in the P. C. Company's big safe, played a part.

And Grace Bentham, as she washed tin dishes in her hillside cabin, often glanced down into Eldorado Creek, and dreamed, —not of dumps nor dust, however. They met frequently, as the trail to the one claim crossed the other, and there is much to talk about in the Northland spring; but never once, by the light of an eye nor the slip of a tongue, did they speak their hearts.

This is as it was at first. But one day Edwin Bentham was brutal. All boys are thus; besides, being a French Hill king now, he began to think a great deal of himself and to forget all he owed to his wife. On this day, Wharton heard of it, and waylaid Grace Bentham, and talked wildly. This made her very happy, though she would not listen, and made him promise to not say such things again. Her hour had not come.

But the sun swept back on its northern journey, the black of midnight changed to the steely color of dawn, the snow slipped away, the water dashed again over the glacial drift, and the wash-up began. Day and night the yellow clay and scraped bedrock hurried through the swift sluices, yielding up its ransom to the strong men from the Southland. And in that time of tumult came Grace Bentham's hour.

To all of us such hours at some time come,—that is, to us who are not too phlegmatic. Some people are good, not from inherent love of virtue, but from sheer laziness. But those of us who know weak moments may understand.

Edwin Bentham was weighing dust over the bar of the saloon at the Forks—altogether too much of his dust went over that pine board—when his wife came down the hill and slipped into Clyde Wharton's cabin. Wharton was not expecting her, but that did not alter the case. And much subsequent misery and idle waiting might have been avoided, had not Father Roubeau seen this and turned aside from the main creek trail.

" My child,—"
" Hold on, Father Roubeau! Though I 'm not of your faith, I respect you; but you can't come in between this woman and me! "
" You know what you are doing? "
" Know! Were you God Almighty, ready to fling me into eternal fire, I'd bank my will against yours in this matter."

Wharton had placed Grace on a stool and stood belligerently before her.
" You sit down on that chair and keep quiet," he continued, addressing the Jesuit. " I 'll take my innings now. You can have yours after."

Father Roubeau bowed courteously and obeyed. He was an easy-going man and had learned to bide his time. Wharton pulled a stool alongside the woman's, smothering her hand in his.
" Then you do care for me, and will take me away? " Her face seemed to reflect the peace of this man, against whom she might draw close for shelter.
" Dear, don't you remember what I said before? Of course I—"
" But how can you?—the wash-up? "
" Do you think that worries? Anyway, I 'll give the job to Father Roubeau, here. I can trust him to safely bank the dust with the company."

" To think of it!—I 'll never see him again."
" A blessing ! "
" And to go—O, Clyde, I can't! I can't ! "
" There, there; of course you can. Just let me plan it. You see, as soon as we get a few traps together, we 'll start, and—"
" Suppose he comes back? "
" I 'll break every—"
" No, no! No fighting, Clyde! Promise me that."
" All right! I 'll just tell the men to throw him off the claim. They 've seen how he 's treated you, and have n't much love for him."
" You must n't do that. You must n't hurt him."
" What then? Let him come right in here and take you away before my eyes? "
" No—o," she half whispered, stroking his hand softly.
" Then let me run it, and don't worry. I 'll see he does n't get hurt. Precious lot he cared whether you got hurt or not! We won't go back to Dawson. I 'll send word down for a couple of the boys to outfit and pole a boat up the Yukon. We 'll cross the divide and raft down the Indian River to meet them. Then—"
" And then? "
Her head was on his shoulder. Their voices sank to softer cadences, each word a caress. The Jesuit fidgeted nervously.
" And then? " she repeated.
" Why we 'll pole up, and up, and up, and portage the White Horse Rapids and the Box Cañon."
" Yes? "
" And the Sixty-Mile River; then the lakes, Chilcoot, Dyea, and Salt Water."
" But, dear, I can't pole a boat."
" You little goose! I 'll get Sitka Charley; he knows all the good water and best camps, and he is the best traveler I ever met, if he is an Indian. All you 'll have to do, is to sit in the middle of the boat, and sing songs, and play Cleopatra, and fight—no, we 're in luck; too early for mosquitoes."
" And then, O my Antony? "
" And then a steamer, San Francisco, and the world! Never to come back to this cursed hole again. Think of it! The world, and ours to choose from! I 'll sell out. Why, we 're rich! The Waldworth

Syndicate will give me half a million for
what's left in the ground, and I've got
twice as much in the dumps and with the
P. C. Company. We'll go to the Fair in
Paris in 1900. We'll go to Jerusalem, if
you say so. We'll buy an Italian palace,
and you can play Cleopatra to your heart's
content. No, you shall be Lucretia, Acte,
or anybody your little heart sees fit to become. But you mustn't, you really
mustn't—"

"The wife of Cæsar shall be above reproach."

"Of course, but—"

"But I won't be your wife, will I,
dear?"

"I didn't mean that."

"But you'll love me just as much, and
never even think—oh! I know you'll be
like other men; you'll grow tired, and
—and—"

"How can you? I—"

"Promise me."

"Yes, yes; I do promise."

"You say it so easily, dear; but how do
you know?—or I know? I have so little
to give, yet it is so much, and all I have.
O, Clyde! promise me you won't?"

"There, there! You mustn't begin to
doubt already. Till death do us part, you
know."

"Think! I once said that to—to him,
and now?"

"And now, little sweetheart, you're not
to bother about such things any more. Of
course, I never, never will, and—"

And for the first time, lips trembled
against lips. Father Roubeau had been
watching the main trail through the
window, but could stand the strain no
longer. He cleared his throat and turned
around.

"Your turn now, Father!" Wharton's
face was flushed with the fire of his first
embrace. There was an exultant ring to
his voice as he abdicated in the other's
favor. He had no doubt as to the result.
Neither had Grace, for a smile played
about her mouth as she faced the priest.

"My child," he began, "my heart
bleeds for you. It is a pretty dream, but
it cannot be."

"And why, Father? I have said yes."

"You knew not what you did. You did
not think of the oath you took, before your

God, to that man who is your husband. It
remains for me to make you realize the
sanctity of such a pledge."

"And if I do realize, and yet refuse?"

"Then God—"

"Which God? My husband has a God
which I care not to worship. There must
be many such."

"Child! unsay those words! Ah! you
do not mean them. I understand. I, too,
have had such moments." For an instant
he was back in his native France, and a
wistful, sad-eyed face came as a mist between him and the woman before him.

"Then, Father, has my God forsaken
me? I am not wicked above women. My
misery with him has been great. Why
should it be greater? Why shall I not
grasp at happiness? I cannot, will not, go
back to him!"

"Rather is your God forsaken. Return.
Throw your burden upon Him, and the
darkness shall be lifted. O my child,—"

"No; it is useless; I have made my
bed and so shall I lie. I will go on. And
if God punishes me, I shall bear it somehow. You do not understand. You are
not a woman."

"My mother was a woman."

"But—"

"And Christ was born of woman."

She did not answer. A silence fell.
Wharton pulled his mustache impatiently
and kept an eye on the trail. Grace leaned
her elbow on the table, her face set with
resolve. The smile had died away. Father
Roubeau shifted his ground.

"You have children?"

"At one time I wished—but now—no.
And I am thankful."

"And a mother?"

"Yes."

"She loves you?"

"Yes." Her replies were whispers.

"And a brother?—no matter, he is a
man. But a sister?"

Her head drooped a quavering "Yes."

"Younger? Very much?"

"Seven years."

"And you have thought well about this
matter? About them? About your
mother? And your sister? She stands
on the threshold of her woman's life, and
this wildness of yours may mean much to
her. Could you go before her, look upon

her fresh young face, hold her hand in yours, or touch your cheek to hers?"

To his words, her brain formed vivid images, till she cried out, "Don't! don't!" and shrank away as do the wolf-dogs from the lash.

"But you must face all this; and better it is to do it now."

In his eyes, which she could not see, there was a great compassion, but his face, tense and quivering, showed no relenting. She raised her head from the table, forced back the tears, struggled for control.

"I shall go away. They will never see me, and come to forget me. I shall be to them as dead. And—and I will go with Clyde—to-day."

It seemed final. Wharton stepped forward, but the priest waved him back.

"You have wished for children?"

A silent "Yes."

"And prayed for them?"

"Often."

"And have you thought, if you should have children?" Father Roubeau's eyes rested for a moment on the man by the window.

A quick light shot across her face. Then the full import dawned upon her. She raised her hand appealingly, but he went on.

"Can you picture an innocent babe in your arms? A boy? The world is not so hard upon a girl. Why, your very breast would turn to gall! And you could be proud and happy of your boy, as you looked on other children?—"

"O, have pity! Hush!"

"A scapegoat—"

"Don't! don't! I will go back!" She was at his feet.

"A child to grow up with no thought of evil, and one day the world to fling a tender name in his face. A child to look back and curse you from whose loins he sprang!"

"O my God! my God!"

She groveled on the floor. The priest sighed and raised her to her feet. Wharton pressed forward, but she motioned him away.

"Don't come near me, Clyde! I am going back!" The tears were coursing pitifully down her face, but she made no effort to wipe them away.

"After all this? You cannot! I will not let you!"

"Don't touch me!" She shivered and drew back.

"I will! You are mine! Do you hear? You are mine!" Then he whirled upon the priest. "O what a fool I was to ever let you wag your silly tongue! Thank your God you are not a common man, for I'd—but the priestly prerogative must be exercised, eh? Well, you have exercised it. Now get out of my house, or I'll forget who and what you are!"

Father Roubeau bowed, took her hand, and started for the door. But Wharton cut them off.

"Grace! You said you loved me?"

"I did."

"And you do now?"

"I do."

"Say it again."

"I do love you, Clyde; I do."

"There, you priest!" he cried. "You have heard it, and with those words on her lips you would send her back to live a lie and a hell with that man?"

But Father Roubeau whisked the woman into the inner room and closed the door. "No words!" he whispered to Wharton, as he struck a casual posture on a stool. "Remember, for her sake," he added.

The room echoed to a rough knock at the door; then the latch raised and Edwin Bentham stepped in.

"Seen anything of my wife?" he asked, as soon as salutations had been exchanged.

Two heads nodded negatively.

"I saw her tracks down from the cabin," he continued tentatively, "and they broke off, just opposite here, on the main trail."

His listeners looked bored.

"And I—I thought—"

"She was here!" thundered Wharton.

The priest silenced him with a look. "Did you see her tracks leading up to this cabin, my son?" Wily Father Roubeau —he had taken good care to obliterate them as he came up the same path an hour before.

"I didn't stop to look, I—" His eyes rested suspiciously on the door to the other room, then interrogated the priest. The latter shook his head; but the doubt seemed to linger.

Father Roubeau breathed a swift, silent prayer, and rose to his feet. " If you doubt me, why—" He made as though to open the door.

A priest could not lie. Edwin Bentham had heard this often, and believed it. " Of course not, Father," he interposed hurriedly. " I was only wondering where my wife had gone, and thought maybe—I guess she 's up at Mrs. Stanton's on French Gulch. Nice weather, is n't it? Heard the news? Flour 's gone down to forty dollars a hundred, and they say the *che-cha-quas* are flocking down the river in droves. But I must be going; so good-by."

The door slammed, and from the window they watched him take his quest up French Gulch.

A few weeks later, just after the June high-water, two men shot a canoe into mid-stream and made fast to a derelict pine. This tightened the painter and jerked the frail craft along as would a tow-boat. Father Roubeau had been directed to leave the Upper Country and return to his swarthy children at Minook. The white men had come among them, and they were devoting too little time to fishing, and too much to a certain deity whose transient habitat was in countless black bottles. Malemute Kid also had business in the Lower Country, so they journeyed together.

But one, in all the Northland, knew the man Paul Roubeau, and that man was Malemute Kid. Before him alone did the priest cast off the sacerdotal garb and stand naked. And why not? These two men knew each other. Had they not shared the last morsel of fish, the last pinch of tobacco, the last and inmost thought, on the barren stretches of Bering Sea, in the heart-breaking mazes of the Great Delta, on the terrible winter journey from Point Barrow to the Porcupine?

Father Roubeau puffed heavily at his trail-worn pipe, and gazed on the red-disked sun, poised somberly on the edge of the northern horizon. Malemute Kid wound up his watch. It was midnight.

" Cheer up, old man ! " The Kid was evidently gathering up a broken thread. " God surely will forgive such a lie. Let me give you the word of a man who strikes a true note :—

If She have spoken a word, remember thy
     lips are sealed,
And the brand of the Dog is upon him by
     whom is the secret revealed.
If there be trouble to Herward, and a lie of
     the blackest can clear,
Lie, while thy lips can move or a man is
     alive to hear."

Father Roubeau removed his pipe and reflected. " The man speaks true, but my soul is not vexed with that. The lie and the penance stand with God ; but—but—"

" What then? Your hands are clean."

" Not so. Kid, I have thought much, and yet the thing remains. I knew, and I made her go back."

The clear note of a robin rang out from the wooded bank, a partridge drummed the call in the distance, a moose lunged noisily in the eddy ; but the twain smoked on in silence.

5
THE MINIONS OF MIDAS

THE MINIONS OF MIDAS.

By Jack London.

WADE ATSHELER is dead—dead by his own hand. To say that this was entirely unexpected by the small coterie which knew him, would be to say an untruth; and yet never once had we, his intimates, ever canvassed the idea. Rather had we been prepared for it in some incomprehensible sub-conscious way. Before the perpetration of the deed, its possibility was remotest from our thoughts; but when we did know he was dead, it seemed, somehow, that we had understood and looked forward to it all the time. This, by retro-spective analysis, we could easily explain by the fact of his great trouble. I use "great trouble" advisedly. Young, handsome, with an assured position as the right-hand man of Eben Hale, the great street-railway magnate, there could be no reason for him to complain of fortune's favors. Yet had we not watched his smooth brow furrow and corrugate as under some carking care or devouring sorrow? Had we not watched his thick, black hair thin and silver as green grain under brazen skies and parching drought? The most cordial of friends and the jolliest of companions, who can forget, in the midst of the hilarious scenes he toward the last sought with greater and greater avidity—who can forget, I say, the deep abstractions and black moods into which he fell? At such times, when the fun rippled and roared from height to height, suddenly, without rhyme or reason, his eyes would turn lack-lustre, his brows knit, as with clenched hands, and face over-shot with spasms of mental pain, he wrestled on the edge of the abyss with some unknown danger.

He never spoke of his trouble, nor were we indiscreet enough to ask. But it was just as well; for had we and had he spoken, our help and strength could have availed nothing. When Eben Hale died, whose confidential secretary he was—nay, well nigh adopted son and full business partner—he no longer came among us. Not, as I now know, that our company was distasteful to him, but because his trouble had so grown that he could not respond to our happiness nor find sur-

cease with us. Why this should be so we could not at the time understand, for when Eben Hale's will was probated, the world learned that he was sole heir to his employer's many millions, and it was expressly stipulated that this great inheritance was given to him without qualification, hitch, or hindrance in the exercise thereof. Not a share of stock, not a penny of cash, were bequeathed to the dead man's relatives. As for his direct family, one astounding clause expressly stated that Wade Atsheler was to dispense to Eben Hale's wife and sons and daughters whatever moneys his judgment dictated, at whatever times he deemed advisable. Had there been any scandal in the dead man's family, or had his sons been wild or undutiful, then there might have been a glimmering of reason in this most unusual action; but Eben Hale's domestic happiness had been proverbial in the community, and one would have to travel far and wide to discover a cleaner, saner, wholesomer progeny of sons and daughters. While his wife—well, by those who knew her best she was endearingly termed "The Mother of the Gracchi." Needless to state, this inexplicable will was a nine days' wonder; but the expectant public was disappointed in that no contest was made.

It was only the other day that Eben Hale was laid away in his stately marble mausoleum. And now Wade Atsheler is dead. The news was printed in this morning's paper. I have just received through the mail a letter from him, posted, evidently, but a short hour before he hurled himself into eternity. This letter, which lies before me, is a narrative in his own handwriting, linking together numerous newspaper clippings and facsimiles of letters. The original correspondence, he has told me, is in the hands of the police. He has begged me, also, as a warning to society against a most frightful and diabolical danger which threatens its very existence, to make public the terrible series of tragedies in which he has been innocently concerned. I herewith append the text in full:

51

"Some ghastly joke, Mr. Hale, and one in very poor taste."

It was in August, 1899, just after my return from my summer vacation, that the blow fell. We did not know it at the time; we had not yet learned to school our minds to such awful possibilities. Mr. Hale opened the letter, read it, and tossed it upon my desk with a laugh. When I had looked it over, I also laughed, saying, "Some ghastly joke, Mr. Hale, and one in very poor taste." Find here, my dear John, an exact duplicate of the letter in question. It may be apparent that it, like the rest of the series, is couched in academical language.

OFFICE OF THE M. of M.,
August 17, 1899.

MR. EBEN HALE, Money Baron.

Dear Sir: We desire you to realize upon whatever portion of your vast holdings necessary to obtain, *in cash*, twenty millions of dollars. This sum we require you to pay over to us or to our agents. You will note we do not specify any given time, for it is not our wish to hurry you in this matter. You may even, if it be easier for you, pay us in ten, fifteen, or twenty instalments; but we will accept no single instalment of less than a million.

Believe us, dear Mr. Hale, when we say that we embark upon this course of action utterly devoid of animus. We are members of that intellectual proletariat, the increasing numbers of which mark in red lettering the last days of the nineteenth century. We have, from a profound study of economics, decided to enter upon this business. It has many merits, chief among which may be noted that we can indulge in large and lucrative operations without capital. So far, we have been fairly successful, and we hope our dealings with you may be pleasant and satisfactory.

Pray attend while we explain our views more fully. At the foundation of the present system of society is to be found the property right. And this right of the individual to hold property is demonstrated, in the last inexorable analysis, to rest solely and wholly upon *might*. The mailed gentlemen of William the Conqueror divided and apportioned England amongst themselves with the naked sword. This, we are sure you will grant, is true of all feudatory possessions. With the invention of steam and the Industrial Revolution there came into existence the Capitalist Class, in the modern sense of the word. These capitalists quickly towered above the ancient nobility. The captains of industry have virtually dispossessed the descendants of the captains of war. Mind, and not muscle, wins in to-day's struggle for existence. But this state of affairs is none the less based upon might. The change has been qualitative. The old-time Feudal Baronage ravaged the world with fire and sword; the modern Money Baronage exploits the world by mastering and applying the world's economic forces. Brain, and not brawn, endures; and those best fitted to survive are the intellectually and commercially powerful.

We, the M. of M., are not content to become wage slaves. The great trusts and business combinations (with which you have your rating) prevent us from rising to the place among you which our intellects qualify us to occupy. Why? Because we are without capital. We are the unwashed, but with this difference: our brains are of the best, and we have no foolish ethical or social scruples. As wage slaves, toiling early and late, and living abstemiously, we could not save in threescore years—nor in twenty times threescore years—a sum of money sufficient to successfully cope with the great aggregations of massed capital which now exist. Nevertheless, we have entered the arena. We now throw down the gauge to the capital of the world. Whether it wishes to fight or not, it shall have to fight.

Mr. Hale, our interests dictate us to demand of you twenty millions of dollars. While we are kind enough to give you reasonable time in which to carry out your share of the transaction, please do not delay too long. When you have agreed to our terms, insert a suitable notice in the agony column of the "Morning Blazer." We shall then acquaint you with our plans for transferring the sum mentioned. You had better do this some time prior to October first. If you do not, and in order to show that we are in earnest, we shall on that date kill a man on East Thirty-ninth Street. He will be a workingman. This man you do not know; nor do we. You represent a force in modern society; we also represent a force—a new force. Without anger or malice, we have grappled in battle. As you will readily discern, we are simply a business proposition. You are the upper, and we the nether, millstone; this man's life shall be ground out between. You may save him if you agree to our conditions and act in time.

There was once a king cursed with a golden touch. His name have we taken to do duty as our official seal. Some day, to protect ourselves against competitors, we shall copyright it.

Until that time, we beg to remain,

THE MINIONS OF MIDAS.

I leave it to you, dear John, why should we not have laughed over such a preposterous communication? The idea, we could not help but grant, was well conceived, but it was too grotesque to be taken seriously. Mr. Hale said he would preserve it as a literary curiosity, and shoved it away in a pigeonhole. Then we promptly forgot its existence. And, as promptly, on the first of October, going over the morning mail, we read the following:

OFFICE OF THE M. of M.,
October 1, 1899.

MR. EBEN HALE, Money Baron.

Dear Sir : Your victim has met his fate. An hour ago, on East Thirty-ninth Street, a working-man was thrust through the heart with a knife. Ere you read this his body will be lying at the Morgue. Go and look upon your handiwork.

On October 14th, in token of our earnestness in this matter, and in case you do not relent, we shall kill a policeman on or near the corner of Polk Street and Clermont Avenue.

Very cordially,

THE MINIONS OF MIDAS.

Again Mr. Hale laughed. His mind was full of a prospective deal with a Chicago syndicate for the sale of all his street railways in that city, and so he went on dictating to the stenographer, never giving it a second thought. But somehow, I know not how, a heavy depression fell upon me. What if it were not a joke? I asked myself, and turned involuntarily to the morning paper. There it was, as befitted an obscure person of the lower classes, a paltry half-dozen lines tucked away in a corner, next a patent medicine advertisement :

Shortly after five o'clock this morning, on East Thirty-ninth Street, a laborer named Pete Lascalle, while on his way to work, was stabbed to the heart by some unknown assailant, who escaped by running. The police have been unable to discover any motive for the murder.

"Impossible!" was Mr. Hale's rejoinder, when I had read the item aloud; but the incident evidently preyed upon his mind, for late in the afternoon, with many epithets denunciatory of his silliness, he asked me to acquaint the police with the affair. I had the pleasure of being laughed at in the Inspector's private office, although I went away with the assurance that they would look into it, and that the vicinity of Polk and Clermont would be doubly patrolled on the night mentioned. There it dropped, till the two weeks had sped by, when the following note came to us through the mail :

OFFICE OF THE M. of M.,
October 15, 1899.

MR. EBEN HALE, Money Baron.

Dear Sir : Your second victim has fallen on schedule time. We are in no hurry; but to increase the pressure we shall henceforth kill weekly.

To protect ourselves against police interference we shall hereafter inform you of the event but a little prior to or simultaneously with the deed. Trusting this finds you in good health,

We are,

THE MINIONS OF MIDAS.

This time Mr. Hale took up the paper, and after a brief search, read to me this account :

A DASTARDLY CRIME.

Joseph Donahue, assigned only last night to special patrol duty in the Eleventh Ward, was shot through the brain and instantly killed at midnight. The tragedy was enacted in the full glare of the street lights on the corner of Polk Street and Clermont Avenue. Our society is indeed unstable when the custodians of its peace are thus openly and wantonly shot down. The police have so far been unable to obtain the slightest clue.

Barely had he finished this than the police arrived—the Inspector himself and two of his keenest sleuths. Alarm sat upon their faces, and it was plain that they were seriously perturbed. Though the facts were so few and simple, we talked long, going over the affair again and again, from Genesis to Revelation. When the Inspector went away, he confidently assured us that everything would soon be straightened out and the assassins run to earth. In the meantime he thought it well to detail guards for the protection of Mr. Hale and myself; also a couple more to be constantly on the vigil about the house and grounds. After the lapse of a week, at one o'clock in the afternoon, this telegram was received :

OFFICE OF THE M. of M.,
October 21, 1899.

MR. EBEN HALE, Money Baron.

Dear Sir : We are sorry to note how completely you have misunderstood us. You have seen fit to surround yourself and household with armed guards, as though, forsooth, we were common criminals, apt to break in upon you and wrest away by force your twenty millions. Believe us, this is farthest from our intentions.

You will readily comprehend, after a little sober thought, that your life is dear to us. Do not be afraid. We would not hurt you for the world. It is our policy to cherish you tenderly and protect you from all harm. Your death means nothing to us. If it did, rest assured that we would not hesitate a moment in destroying you. Think this over, Mr. Hale. When you have paid us our price, there will be need of retrenchment. Dismiss your guards now, and cut down on your expenses.

Within ten minutes of the time you receive this a nurse girl will have been choked to death in Brentwood Park. The body may be found in the shrubbery lining the path which leads off to the left from the band stand.

Cordially yours,

THE MINIONS OF MIDAS.

The next instant Mr. Hale was at the telephone, warning the Inspector of the impending murder. The Inspector excused himself in order to call up Sub-Police Station F and dispatch men to the scene. Fifteen minutes later he rang us up and informed us that the body had been discovered, yet warm, in the place indicated. That evening the papers teemed with glaring Jack-the-Strangler headlines, denouncing the brutality of the deed and complaining at the laxity of the police. We were also closeted with the Inspector, who begged us by all means to keep the affair secret. Success, he said, depended upon silence.

As you know, John, Mr. Hale was a man of iron. He refused to surrender. But, oh, John, it was terrible, nay, horrible—this awful something, this blind force in the dark. We could not fight, could not plan, could do nothing save hold our hands and wait. And week by week, as certain as the rising of the sun, came the notification and death of some person, man or woman, innocent of evil, but just as much killed by us as though we had done it with our own hands. A word from Mr. Hale and the slaughter would have ceased. But he hardened his heart and waited, the lines deepening, the mouth and eyes growing sterner and firmer, and the face aging with the hours. It were needless for me to speak of my own suffering during that frightful period. Find here the letters and telegrams of the M. of M., and the newspaper accounts, etc., of the various murders.

You will notice also the letters warning Mr. Hale of certain machinations of commercial enemies and secret manipulations of stock. The M. of M. seemed to have its hand on the inner pulse of the business and financial world. They possessed themselves of and forwarded to us information which our agents could not obtain. One timely note from them, at a critical moment in a certain deal,

saved all of five millions to Mr. Hale. At another time they sent us a telegram which probably was the means of preventing an anarchist crank from taking my employer's life. Forewarned, forearmed, and we captured the man on his arrival and turned him over to the police, who found upon him enough of a new and powerful explosive to sink a battleship.

However, we hung on. Mr. Hale was clean grit clear through. He disbursed at the rate of one hundred thousand per week for secret service. The aid of the Pinkertons and of countless private detective agencies was called in, and in addition to this virtually thousands were upon our payroll. Our agents swarmed everywhere, in all guises, penetrating all strata of society. They grasped at a myriad clues; hundreds of suspects were jailed, and at various times thousands of suspicious persons were under surveillance, but nothing tangible came to light. With its communications the M. of M. continually changed its method of delivery. And every messenger they sent us was arrested forthwith. But these inevitably proved to be innocent individuals, while their descriptions of the persons who had employed them for the errand never tallied. On the last day of December we received this notification:

OFFICE OF THE M. of M.,
December 31, 1899.

MR. EBEN HALE, Money Baron.

Dear Sir: Pursuant of our policy, with which we flatter ourselves you are already well versed, we beg to state that we shall give a passport from this Vale of Tears to Inspector Bying, with whom, because of our attentions, you have become so well acquainted. It is his custom to be in his private office at this hour. Even as you read this he breathes his last.

Cordially yours,

THE MINIONS OF MIDAS.

I dropped the letter and sprang to the telephone. Great was my relief when I heard the Inspector's hearty voice. But, even as he spoke, his voice died away in the receiver to a gurgling sob, and I heard faintly the crash of a falling body. Then a strange voice hello'd me, sent me the regards of the M. of M., and broke the switch. Like a flash I called up the public office of the Central Police, telling them to go at once to the Inspector's aid in his private office. I then held the line, and a few minutes later received the intelligence that he had been found bathed in his own blood and breathing his last. There were no eye-witnesses, and no trace was discoverable of the murderer.

Upon this Mr. Hale immediately increased his secret service till a quarter of a million flowed weekly from his coffers. He was determined to win out. His graduated rewards aggregated over ten millions. You have a fair idea of his resources and you can see in what manner he drew upon them. It was the principle, he affirmed, he was fighting for, not the gold. And it must be admitted that his course proved the exaltation of his motive. The police departments of all the great cities coöperated, and even the United States Government stepped in, and the affair became one of the highest questions of state. Certain contingent funds of the nation were devoted to the unearthing of the M. of M., and every government agent was on the alert. But all in vain. The Minions of Midas carried on their damnable work unhampered. Imponderable, inexorable, they had their way and struck unerringly.

But while he fought to the last, Mr. Hale could not wash his hands of the blood with which they were dyed. Though not technically a murderer, though no jury of his peers would have ever convicted him, none the less the death of every individual in that carnival of crime was due to him. As I said before, a word from him and the slaughter would have ceased. But he refused to give that word. He insisted that the integrity of society was assailed; that he was not sufficiently a coward to desert his post; and that it was manifestly just that a few should be martyred for the ultimate welfare of the many. Nevertheless this blood was upon his head, and he sank into deep and deeper gloom. I likewise was whelmed with guilt as of an accomplice. Babies were ruthlessly killed, children, aged men; and not only were these murders local, but generously distributed over the country. In the middle of February, one evening, as we sat in the library, there came a sharp knock at the door. On responding to it I found, lying on the carpet of the corridor, the following missive:

OFFICE OF THE M. OF M.,
February 15, 1900.

MR. EBEN HALE, Money Baron.

Dear Sir: O thou hard of heart! Does not your soul cry out upon the red harvest it is reaping? Perhaps we have been too philosophically abstract in conducting our business. Let us now be concrete. Miss Adelaide Laidlaw is a talented young woman, as good and pure, we understand, as she is beautiful. She is the daughter of your old friend, Judge Laidlaw, and we happen to know that you carried her in your arms and petted her when she was an infant. She is your daughter's closest friend, and at present is visiting with you. When your eyes have read thus far her visit shall have terminated. Her doom is signed. Too bad! So young! So beautiful!

Very cordially,
THE MINIONS OF MIDAS.

My God! did we not instantly realize the hideous import! We rushed through the day rooms—she was not there—and on to her own apartments. The door was locked, but we crashed it down by hurling ourselves against it. There she lay, just as she had finished dressing for some reception, smothered with pillows torn from the couch, the flush of life yet on her flesh, the body still flexile and warm. Let me pass over the remainder of this horror. You will surely remember, John, the thrilling newspaper accounts.

Late that night Mr. Hale summoned me to him, and before my God did swear me most solemnly to stand by him and to not compromise, even if all kith and kin were destroyed and the heavens fell.

The next day I was astounded at his cheerfulness. I had thought he would be deeply shocked by this last terrible tragedy—how deep I was soon to learn. All day he was light-hearted and high-spirited, as though at last he had hit upon a way out of the frightful difficulty. The next morning we found him dead in his bed, a peaceful smile upon his careworn face—asphyxiation. Through the connivance of the police and the authorities, it was given out to the world as heart disease. We deemed it politic to withhold the truth; but little good has it done us, little good has anything done us.

Barely had I left that chamber of death, when—but too late—the following extraordinary letter was received:

There she lay . . . smothered with pillows torn from the couch.

MR. EBEN HALE, Money Baron.

Dear Sir : You will pardon our intrusion, we hope, so closely upon the sad event of day before yesterday ; but what we wish to say may be of the utmost importance to you. It is in our mind that you may attempt to escape us. There is but one way, apparently, as you have ere this doubtless discovered. But we wish to inform you that even this one way is debarred. You may die, but you die failing and acknowledging your failure. Note this : *We are part and parcel of your possessions. With your millions we pass down to your heirs and assigns forever.*

We are the inevitable. We are the culmination of industrial and social wrong. We turn upon the society which has created us. We snap the hand which lays the lash upon our backs. We are the successful failures of the age, the regnant giants of debased despair, the degenerate scourges of an unregenerate civilization !

Behold ! we are the creatures of a perverse social selection. We meet force with force. Only the strong shall endure. We believe in the survival of the fittest. You have crushed your wage slaves into the dirt and you have survived. The captains of war, at your behest, have shot down like dogs your employees in a score of bloody strikes. By such means have you endured. We do not grumble at the result, for we acknowledge and have our being in the same natural law. And now the question has arisen : *Under the present social environment, which of us shall survive ?* We believe we are the fittest. You believe you are the fittest. We leave the eventuality to time and law.

In token whereof, we affix, this day, our hand and seal,

THE MINIONS OF MIDAS.

John, do you wonder now that I shunned pleasure and avoided friends ? But why explain ? Surely this narrative will make everything clear. Three weeks ago Adelaide Laidlaw died. Since then I have waited in hope and fear. Yesterday the will was probated and made public. To-day I was notified that a woman of the middle class would be killed in Golden Gate Park, in far-away San Francisco. The dispatches in to-night's papers give the details of the brutal happening— details which correspond with those furnished me.

It is useless. I cannot struggle against that which I know not. I have been faithful to Mr. Hale and have worked hard. Why my faithfulness should have been thus rewarded I cannot understand. Yet I cannot be false to my trust, nor break my word by compromising. Still, I have resolved that no more deaths shall be upon my head. I have willed the many millions I lately received to their rightful owners. Let the stalwart sons of Eben Hale work out their own salvation. Ere you read this I shall have passed over. I may perchance meet Adelaide, and I am tired of life. The Minions of Midas are all-powerful. The police are impotent. I have learned from them that other millionaires have been likewise mulcted or persecuted—how many is not known, for when one yields to the M. of M., his mouth is thenceforth sealed. Those who have not yielded are even now reaping their scarlet harvest. The grim game is being played out. The Federal Government can do nothing. I also understand that similar branch organizations have made their appearance in Europe. Society is shaking to its foundations. Principalities and powers are as brands ripe for the burning. Instead of the masses against the classes, it is a class against the classes. When the pillars of society crash, look out for the superstructure. We, the guardians of human progress, are being singled out and struck down. Law and order have failed to prevail.

The officials have begged me to keep this secret. I have done so, but can do so no longer. It has become a question of public import, fraught with the direst consequences, and I shall do my duty before I leave this world by informing it of its peril. Do you, John, as my last request, make this public. Do not be frightened. The destiny of humanity rests in your hand. Let the press strike off millions of copies ; let the electric currents sweep it round the world ; wherever men meet and speak, let them speak of it in fear and trembling. And then, when thoroughly aroused, let society arise in its might and cast out this abomination !

Yours, in long farewell,

WADE ATSHELER.

6
DIABLE A DOG

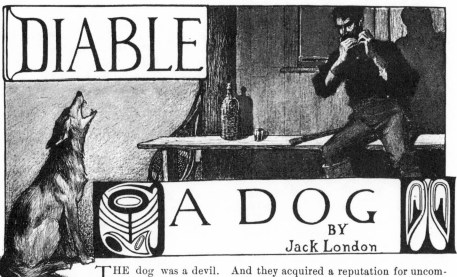

DIABLE

A DOG

BY
Jack London

THE dog was a devil. This was recognized throughout the northland. "Hell's Spawn" he was called by many men, but his master, Black Leclère, chose for him the shameful name, "Diable." Now Black Leclère was also a devil, and the twain were well matched. The first they met, Diable was a puppy, lean and hungry and with bitter eyes; and they met with snap and snarl and wicked looks, for Leclère's upper lip had a wolfish way of lifting and showing the cruel white teeth. And it lifted then and his eyes glinted viciously as he reached for Diable and dragged him out from the squirming litter. It was certain that they divined each other, for on the instant Diable had buried his puppy fangs in Leclère's hand and Leclère, with thumb and finger, was coolly choking his young life out of him.

"Sacrédam!" the Frenchman said softly, flirting the quick blood from his bitten hand and gazing down on the little puppy choking and gasping in the snow.

Leclère turned to John Hamlin, storekeeper of the Sixty Mile Post. "Dat fo' w'at Ah lak heem. 'Ow moch, eh, you, m'sieu'? 'Ow moch? Ah buy heem, now.''

And because he hated him with an exceeding bitter hate, Leclère bought Diable. And for five years the twain adventured across the northland, from St. Michael's and the Yukon Delta to the head-reaches of the Pelly and even so far as the Peace River, Athabasca and the Great Slave.

And they acquired a reputation for uncompromising wickedness the like of which never before had attached itself to man and dog.

Diable's father was a great gray timber-wolf. But the mother of Diable, as he dimly remembered her, was a snarling, bickering husky, full-fronted and heavy-chested, with a malign eye, a cat-like grip on life, and a genius for trickery and evil. There was neither faith nor trust in her. Much of evil and much of strength were there in these, Diable's progenitors, and, bone and flesh of their bone and flesh, he had inherited it all. And then came Black Leclère, to lay his heavy hand on the bit of pulsating puppy-life, to press and prod and mold it till it became a big, bristling beast, acute in knavery, overspilling with hate, sinister, malignant, diabolical. With a proper master the puppy might have made a fairly ordinary, efficient sled-dog. He never got the chance. Leclère but confirmed him in his congenital iniquity.

The history of Leclère and the dog is a history of war—of five cruel, relentless years, of which their first meeting is fit summary. To begin with, it was Leclère's fault, for he hated with understanding and intelligence, while the long-legged, ungainly puppy hated only blindly, instinctively, without reason or method. At first there were no refinements of cruelty (these were to come later), but simple beatings and crude brutalities. In one of these,

Diable had an ear injured. He never regained control of the riven muscles, and ever after the ear drooped limply down to keep keen the memory of his tormentor. And he never forgot.

His puppyhood was a period of foolish rebellion. He was always worsted, but he fought back because it was his nature to fight back. And he was unconquerable. Yelping shrilly from the pain of lash and club, he none the less always contrived to throw in the defiant snarl, the bitter, vindictive menace of his soul, which fetched without fail more blows and beatings. But his was his mother's tenacious grip on life. Nothing could kill him. He flourished under misfortune, grew fat with famine, and out of his terrible struggle for life developed a preternatural intelligence. His was the stealth and cunning of his mother, the fierceness and valor of his wolf sire.

Possibly it was because of his father that he never wailed. His puppy yelps passed with his lanky legs, so that he became grim and taciturn, quick to strike, slow to warn. He answered curse with snarl and blow with snap, grinning the while his implacable hatred; but never again, under the extremest agony, did Leclère bring from him the cry of fear or pain. This unconquerableness only fanned Leclère's wrath and stirred him to greater deviltries. Did Leclère give Diable half a fish and to his mates whole ones, Diable went forth to rob other dogs of their fish. Also he robbed caches and expressed himself in a thousand rogueries till he became a terror to all dogs and the masters of dogs. Did Leclère beat Diable and fondle Babette—Babette, who was not half the worker he was—why, Diable threw her down in the snow and broke her hind leg in his heavy jaws, so that Leclère was forced to shoot her. Likewise, in bloody battles Diable mastered all his team-mates, set them the law of trail and forage, and made them live to the law he set.

In five years he heard but one kind word, received but one soft stroke of a hand, and then he did not know what manner of things they were. He leaped like the untamed thing he was, and his jaws were together in a flash. It was the missionary at Sunrise, a newcomer in the country, who spoke the kind word and gave the soft stroke of the hand. And for six months after, he wrote no letters home to the States, and the surgeon at McQuestion traveled two hundred miles on the ice to save him from blood-poisoning.

Men and dogs looked askance at Diable when he drifted into their camps and posts, and they greeted him with feet threateningly lifted for the kick, or with bristling manes and bared fangs. Once a man did kick Diable, and Diable, with quick wolf-snap, closed his jaws like a steel trap on the man's leg and crunched down to the bone. Whereat the man was determined to have his life, only Black Leclère, with ominous eyes and naked hunting-knife, stepped in between. The killing of Diable —ah, sacrédam! *that* was a pleasure Leclère reserved for himself. Some day it would happen, or else—bah! who was to know? Anyway, the problem would be solved.

For they had become problems to each other, this man and beast, or rather, they had become a problem, the pair of them. The very breath each drew was a challenge and a menace to the other. Their hate bound them together as love could never bind. Leclère was bent on the coming of the day when Diable should wilt in spirit and cringe and whimper at his feet. And Diable—Leclère knew what was in Diable's mind, and more than once had read it in his eyes. And so clearly had he read that when the dog was at his back he made it a point to glance often over his shoulder.

Men marveled when Leclère refused large money for the dog. "Some day you'll kill him and be out his price," said John Hamlin, once, when Diable lay panting in the snow where Leclère had kicked him and no one knew whether his ribs were broken and no one dared look to see.

"Dat," said Leclère dryly, "dat is my biz'ness, m'sieu'."

And the men marveled that Diable did not run away. They did not understand. But Leclère understood. He was a man who had lived much in the open, beyond the sound of human tongue, and he had learned the voices of wind and storm, the sigh of night, the whisper of dawn, the clash of day. In a dim way he could hear the green things growing, the running of the sap, the bursting of the bud. And he knew the subtle speech of the things that moved, of the rabbit in the snare, the moody raven beating the air with hollow wing, the baldface shuffling under the moon, the wolf like a gray shadow gliding betwixt the twilight and the dark. And to him Diable spoke clear and direct. Full well he understood why Diable did not run away, and he looked more often over his shoulder.

When in anger, Diable was not nice to look upon, and more than once had he leaped for Leclère's throat, to be stretched quivering and senseless in the snow by the butt of the ever-ready dog-whip. And so Diable learned to bide his time. When he reached his full strength and prime of youth, he thought the time had come. He was broad-chested, powerfully muscled, of far more than ordinary size, and his neck from head to shoulders was a mass of bristling hair—to all appearances a full-blooded wolf. Leclère was lying asleep in his furs when Diable deemed the time to be ripe. He crept upon him stealthily, head low to earth and lone ear laid back, with a feline softness of tread to which even Leclère's delicate tympanum could not responsively vibrate. The dog breathed gently, very gently, and not till he was close at hand did he raise his head. He paused for a moment and looked at the bronzed bull-throat, naked and knotty and swelling to a deep and steady pulse. The slaver dripped down his fangs and slid off his tongue at the sight, and in that moment he remembered his drooping ear, his uncounted blows and wrongs, and without a sound sprang on the sleeping man.

Leclère awoke to the pang of the fangs in his throat, and, perfect animal that he was, he awoke clear-headed and with full comprehension. He closed on the hound's windpipe with both his hands and rolled out of his furs to get his weight uppermost. But the thousands of Diable's ancestors had clung at the throats of unnumbered moose and caribou and dragged them down, and the wisdom of those ancestors was his. When Leclère's weight came on top of him, he drove his hind legs upward and in and clawed down chest and abdomen, ripping and tearing through skin and muscle. And when he felt the man's body wince above him and lift, he worried and shook at the man's throat. His team-

mates closed around in a snarling, slavering circle, and Diable, with failing breath and fading sense, knew that their jaws were hungry for him. But that did not matter—it was the man, the man above him, and he ripped and clawed and shook and worried to the last ounce of his strength. But Leclère choked him with both his hands till Diable's chest heaved and writhed for the air denied, and his eyes glazed and his jaws slowly loosened and his tongue protruded black and swollen.

"Eh? Bon, you devil!" Leclère gurgled, mouth and throat clogged with his own blood, as he shoved the dizzy dog from him.

And then Leclère cursed the other dogs off as they fell upon Diable. They drew back into a wider circle, squatting alertly on their haunches and licking their chops, each individual hair on every neck bristling and erect.

Diable recovered quickly, and at sound of Leclère's voice, tottered to his feet and swayed weakly back and forth.

"A-h-ah! You beeg devil!" Leclère spluttered. "Ah fix you. Ah fix you plentee, by Gar!"

Diable, the air biting into his exhausted lungs like wine, flashed full into the man's face, his jaws missing and coming together with a metallic clip. They rolled over and over on the snow, Leclère striking madly with his fists. Then they separated, face to face, and circled back and forth before each other for an opening. Leclère could have drawn his knife. His rifle was at his feet. But the beast in him was up and raging. He would do the thing with his hands—and his teeth. The dog sprang in, but Leclère knocked him over with a blow of his fist, fell upon him, and buried his teeth to the bone in the dog's shoulder.

It was a primordial setting and a primordial scene, such as might have been in the savage youth of the world. An open space in a dark forest, a ring of grinning wolf-dogs, and in the center two beasts, locked in combat, snapping and snarling, raging madly about, panting, sobbing, cursing, straining, wild with passion, blind with lust, in a fury of murder, ripping, tearing and clawing in elemental brutishness.

But Leclère caught the dog behind the

ear with a blow from his fist, knocking him over and for an instant stunning him. Then Leclère leaped upon him with his feet, and sprang up and down, striving to grind him into the earth. Both Diable's hind legs were broken ere Leclère ceased that he might catch breath.

"A-a-ah! A-a-ah!" he screamed, incapable of articulate speech, shaking his fist through sheer impotence of throat and larynx.

But Diable was indomitable. He lay there in a hideous, helpless welter, his lip feebly lifting and writhing to the snarl he had not the strength to utter. Leclère kicked him, and the tired jaws closed on the ankle but could not break the skin.

Then Leclère picked up the whip and proceeded almost to cut him to pieces, at each stroke of the lash crying: "Dis taim Ah break you! Eh? By Gar, Ah break you!"

In the end, exhausted, fainting from loss of blood, he crumpled up and fell by his victim, and, when the wolf-dogs closed in to take their vengeance, with his last consciousness dragged his body on top of Diable to shield him from their fangs.

Drawn by E. Hering.

"FLIRTING THE QUICK BLOOD FROM HIS BITTEN HAND."

This occurred not far from Sunrise, and the missionary, opening the door to Leclère a few hours later, was surprised to note the absence of Diable from the team. Nor did his surprise lessen when Leclère threw back the robes from the sled, gathered Diable into his arms, and staggered across the threshold. It happened that the surgeon of McQuestion was up on a gossip, and between them they proceeded to repair Leclère.

"Merci, non," said he. "Do you fix firs' de dog. To die? Non. Eet is not good. Becos' heem Ah mus' yet break. Dat fo' w'at he mus' not die."

The surgeon called it a marvel, the missionary a miracle, that Leclère lived through at all; but so weakened was he that in the spring the fever got him and he went on his back again. The dog had been in even worse plight, but his grip on life prevailed, and the bones of his hind legs knitted and his internal organs righted themselves during the several weeks he lay strapped to the floor. And by the time Leclère, finally convalescent, sallow and shaky, took the sun by the cabin door, Diable had reasserted his supremacy and brought not only his own team-mates but the missionary's dogs into subjection.

He moved never a muscle nor twitched a hair when for the first time Leclère tottered out on the missionary's arm and sank down slowly and with infinite caution on the three-legged stool.

"Bon!" he said. "Bon! De good sun!" And he stretched out his wasted hands and washed them in the warmth.

Then his gaze fell on the dog, and the old light blazed back in his eyes. He touched the missionary lightly on the arm. "Mon père, dat is one beeg devil, dat Diable. You will bring me one pistol, so dat Ah drink the sun in peace."

And thenceforth, for many days, he sat in the sun before the cabin door. He never dozed, and the pistol lay always across his knees. The dog had a way, the first thing each day, of looking for the weapon in its wonted place. At sight of it he would lift his lip faintly in token that he understood, and Leclère would lift his own lip in an answering grin. One day the missionary took note of the trick. "Bless me!" he said. "I really believe the brute comprehends."

Leclère laughed softly. "Look you, mon père. Dat w'at Ah now spik, to dat does he lissen."

As if in confirmation, Diable just perceptibly wriggled his lone ear up to catch the sound.

"Ah say 'keel'———"

Diable growled deep down in his throat, the hair bristled along his neck, and every muscle went tense and expectant.

"Ah lift de gun, so, like dat———" And suiting action to word, he sighted the pistol at the dog.

Diable, with a single leap sidewise, landed around the corner of the cabin out of sight.

"Bless me!" the missionary remarked. "Bless me!" he repeated at intervals, unconscious of his paucity of expression.

Leclère grinned proudly.

"But why does he not run away?"

The Frenchman's shoulders went up in a racial shrug which means all things from total ignorance to infinite understanding.

"Then why do you not kill him?"

Again the shoulders went up.

"Mon père," he said, after a pause, "de taim is not yet. He is one beeg devil.

Some taim Ah break heem, so, an' so, all to leetle bits. Heh? Some taim. Bon!"

A day came when Leclère gathered his dogs together and floated down in a bateau to Forty Mile and on to the Porcupine, where he took a commission from the P. C. Company and went exploring for the better part of a year. After that he poled up the Koyokuk to deserted Arctic City, and later came drifting back, from camp to camp, along the Yukon. And during the long months Diable was well lessoned. He learned many tortures—the torture of hunger, the torture of thirst, the torture of fire, and, worst of all, the torture of music.

Like the rest of his kind, he did not enjoy music. It gave him exquisite anguish, racking him nerve by nerve and ripping apart every fiber of his being. It made him howl, long and wolf-like, as when the wolves bay the stars on frosty nights. He could not help howling. It was his one weakness in the contest with Leclère, and it was his shame. Leclère, on the other hand, passionately loved music—as passionately as he loved strong drink. And when his soul clamored for expression, it usually uttered itself in one or both of the two ways. And when he had drunk, not too much but just enough for the perfect poise of exaltation, his brain alilt with unsung song and the devil in him aroused and rampant, his soul found its supreme utterance in the bearding of Diable.

"Now we will haf a leetle museek," he would say. "Eh? W'at you t'ink, Diable?"

It was only an old and battered harmonica, tenderly treasured and patiently repaired; but it was the best that money could buy, and out of its silver reeds he drew weird, vagrant airs which men had never heard before. Then the dog, dumb of throat, with teeth tight-clenched, would back away, inch by inch, to the farthest cabin corner. And Leclère, playing, playing, a stout club tucked handily under his arm, followed the animal up, inch by inch, step by step, till there was no further retreat.

At first Diable would crowd himself into the smallest possible space, groveling close to the floor; but as the music came nearer and nearer he was forced to uprear, his back jammed into the logs, his fore legs

Drawn by E. Hering.

"A LEETLE FAVOR. . . . FIRS' YOU HANG HEEM, AN' DEN YOU HANG ME."

fanning the air as though to beat off the rippling waves of sound. He still kept his teeth together, but severe muscular contractions attacked his body, strange twitchings and jerkings, till he was all aquiver and writhing in silent torment. As he lost control, his jaws spasmodically wrenched apart and deep, throaty vibrations issued forth, too low in the register of sound for human ear to catch. And then, as he stood reared with nostrils distended, eyes dilated, slaver dripping, hair bristling in helpless rage, arose the long wolf-howl. It came with a slurring rush upward, swelling to a great heartbreaking burst of sound and dying away in sadly cadenced woe—then the next rush upward, octave upon octave; the bursting heart; and the infinite sorrow and misery, fainting, fading, falling, and dying slowly away.

It was fit for hell. And Leclère, with fiendish ken, seemed to divine each particular nerve and heartstring and, with long wails and tremblings and sobbing minors, to make it yield up its last least shred of grief. It was frightful, and for twenty-four hours after, the dog was nervous and unstrung, starting at common sounds, tripping over his own shadow, but withal, vicious and masterful with his team-mates. Nor did he show signs of a breaking spirit. Rather did he grow more grim and taciturn, biding his time with an inscrutable patience which began to puzzle and weigh upon Leclère. The dog would lie in the firelight, motionless, for hours, gazing straight before him at Leclère and hating him with his bitter eyes.

Often the man felt that he had bucked up against the very essence of life—the unconquerable essence that swept the hawk down out of the sky like a feathered thunderbolt, that drove the great gray goose across the zones, that hurled the spawning salmon through two thousand miles of boiling Yukon flood. At such times he felt impelled to express his own unconquerable essence; and with strong drink, wild music and Diable, he indulged in vast orgies, wherein he pitted his puny strength in the face of things and challenged all that was, and had been, and was yet to be. "Dere is somet'ing dere," he affirmed, when the rhythmed vagaries of his mind touched the secret chords of the dog's be-

ing and brought forth the long, lugubrious howl. "Ah pool eet out wid bot' my han's, so, an' so. Ha! Ha! Eet is fonee! Eet is ver' fonee! De mans swear, de leetle bird go peep-peep, Diable heem go yow-yow—an' eet is all de ver' same t'ing."

Father Gautier, a worthy priest, once reproved him with instances of concrete perdition. He never reproved him again.

"Eet may be so, mon père," he made answer. "An' Ah t'ink Ah go troo hell a-snappin', lak de hemlock troo de fire. Eh, mon père?"

But all bad things come to an end as well as good, and so with Black Leclère. On the summer low-water, in a poling-boat, he left McDougall for Sunrise. He left McDougall in company with Timothy Brown, and arrived at Sunrise by himself. Further, it was known that they had quarreled just previous to pulling out; for the "Lizzie," a wheezy ten-ton sternwheeler, twenty-four hours behind, beat Leclère in by three days. And when he did get in, it was with a clean-drilled bullet-hole through his shoulder-muscle and a tale of ambush and murder.

A strike had been made at Sunrise, and things had changed considerably. With the infusion of several hundred gold-seekers, a deal of whisky, and half a dozen equipped gamblers, the missionary had seen the page of his years of labor with the Indians wiped clean. When the squaws became preoccupied with cooking beans and keeping the fire going for the wifeless miners, and the bucks with swapping their warm furs for black bottles and broken timepieces, he took to his bed, said "Bless me!" several times, and departed to his final accounting in a rough-hewn oblong box. Whereupon the gamblers moved their roulette and faro tables into the mission-house, and the click of chips and clink of glasses went up from dawn till dark and to dawn again.

Now Timothy Brown was well beloved among these adventurers of the north. The one thing against him was his quick temper and ready fist—a little thing, for which his kind heart and forgiving hand more than atoned. On the other hand, there was nothing to atone for Black Leclère. He was "black," as more than one remembered deed bore witness, while he was as well hated as the other was beloved. So the men of Sunrise put a dressing on his shoulder and haled him before Judge Lynch.

It was a simple affair. He had quarreled with Timothy Brown at McDougall. With Timothy Brown he had left McDougall. Without Timothy Brown he had arrived at Sunrise. Considered in the light of his evilness, the unanimous conclusion was that he had killed Timothy Brown. On the other hand, Leclère acknowledged their facts, but challenged their conclusion and gave his own explanation. Twenty miles out of Sunrise he and Timothy Brown were poling the boat along the rocky shore. From that shore two rifle-shots rang out. Timothy Brown pitched out of the boat and went down bubbling red, and that was the last of Timothy Brown. He, Leclère, pitched into the bottom of the boat with a stinging shoulder. He lay very quietly, peeping at the shore. After a time two Indians stuck up their heads and came out to the water's edge, carrying between them a birch-bark canoe. As they launched it, Leclère let fly. He potted one, who went over the side after the manner of Timothy Brown. The other dropped into the bottom of the canoe, and then canoe and poling-boat went down the stream in a drifting battle. Only they hung up on a split current, and the canoe passed on one side of an island, the poling-boat on the other. That was the last of the canoe, and he came on into Sunrise. Yes, from the way the Indian in the canoe jumped, he was sure he had potted him. That was all.

This explanation was not deemed adequate. They gave him ten hours' grace while the "Lizzie" steamed down to investigate. Ten hours later she came wheezing back to Sunrise. There had been nothing to investigate. No evidence had been found to back up his statements. They told him to make his will, for he possessed a fifty-thousand-dollar Sunrise claim and they were a law-abiding as well as a law-giving breed.

Leclère shrugged his shoulders. "Bot one t'ing," he said; "a leetle, w'at you call, favor—a leetle favor, dat is eet. I gif my feefty t'ousan' dollair to de church. I gif my husky-dog, Diable, to de devil. De leetle favor? Firs' you hang heem, an' den you hang me. Eet is good, eh?"

Good it was, they agreed, that Hell's Spawn should break trail for his master across the last divide, and the court was adjourned down to the river-bank, where a big spruce-tree stood by itself. Slackwater Charley put a hangman's knot in the end of a hauling-line, and the noose was slipped over Leclère's head and pulled tight around his neck. His hands were tied behind his back, and he was assisted to the top of a cracker-box. Then the running end of the line was passed over an overhanging branch, drawn taut, and made fast. To kick the box out from under would leave him dancing on the air.

"Now for the dog," said Webster Shaw, sometime mining engineer. "You'll have to rope him, Slackwater."

Leclère grinned. Slackwater took a chew of tobacco, rove a running noose, and proceeded leisurely to coil a few turns in his hand. He paused once or twice to brush particularly offensive mosquitoes from off his face. Everybody was brushing mosquitoes, except Leclère, about whose head a small cloud was distinctly visible. Even Diable, lying full-stretched on the ground, with his fore paws rubbed the pests away from eyes and mouth.

But while Slackwater waited for Diable to lift his head, a faint call came down the quiet air and a man was seen waving his arms and running across the flat from Sunrise. It was the storekeeper.

"C—call 'er off, boys," he panted, as he came in among them. "Little Sandy and Bernadotte's jes' got in," he explained with returning breath. "Landed down below an' come up by the short cut. Got the Beaver with 'm. Picked 'm up in his canoe, stuck in a back channel, with a couple of bullet-holes in 'm. Other buck was Klok-Kutz, the one that knocked spots out of his squaw and dusted."

"Eh? W'at Ah say? Eh?" Leclère cried exultantly. "Dat de one fo' sure! Ah know. Ah spik true."

"The thing to do is to teach these damned Siwashes a little manners," spoke Webster Shaw. "They're getting fat and sassy, and we'll have to bring them down a peg. Round in all the bucks and string up the Beaver for an object-lesson. That's the program. Come on and let's see what he's got to say for himself."

"Heh, m'sieu'!" Leclère called, as

the crowd began to melt away through the twilight in the direction of Sunrise, "Ah lak ver' moch to see de fon."

"Oh, we'll turn you loose when we come back," Webster Shaw shouted over his shoulder. "In the mean time, meditate on your sins and the ways of Providence. It will do you good, so be grateful."

As is the way with men who are accustomed to great hazards, whose nerves are healthy and trained to patience, so Leclère settled himself down to the long wait— which is to say that he reconciled his mind to it. There was no settling for the body, for the taut rope forced him to stand rigidly erect. The least relaxation of the leg-muscles pressed the rough-fibered noose into his neck, while the upright position caused him much pain in his wounded shoulder. He projected his under lip and expelled his breath upward along his face to blow the mosquitoes away from his eyes. But the situation had its compensation. To be snatched from the maw of death was well worth a little bodily suffering, only it was unfortunate that he should miss the hanging of the Beaver.

And so he mused, till his eyes chanced to fall upon Diable, head between fore paws and stretched on the ground asleep. And then Leclère ceased to muse. He studied the animal closely, striving to sense if the sleep were real or feigned. The dog's sides were heaving regularly, but Leclère felt that the breath came and went a shade too quickly; also he felt there was a vigilance or an alertness to every hair which belied unshackling sleep. He would have given his Sunrise claim to be assured that the dog was not awake, and once, when one of his joints cracked, he looked quickly and guiltily at Diable to see if he roused.

He did not rouse then, but a few minutes later he got up slowly and lazily, stretched, and looked carefully about him. "Sacrédam!" said Leclère under his breath.

Assured that no one was in sight or hearing, Diable sat down, curled his upper lip almost into a smile, looked up at Leclère, and licked his chops.

"Ah see my feenish," the man said, and laughed sardonically aloud.

Diable came nearer, the useless ear wobbling, the good ear cocked forward with devilish comprehension. He thrust his head on one side, quizzically, and advanced with mincing, playful steps. He rubbed his body gently against the box till it shook and shook again. Leclère teetered carefully to maintain his equilibrium.

"Diable," he said calmly, "look out. Ah keel you."

Diable snarled at the word and shook the box with greater force. Then he upreared and with his fore paws threw his weight against it higher up. Leclère kicked out with one foot, but the rope bit into his neck and checked so abruptly as nearly to overbalance him.

"Hi! Ya! Chook! Mush-on!" he screamed.

Diable retreated for twenty feet or so, with a fiendish levity in his bearing which Leclère could not mistake. He remembered the dog's often breaking the scum of ice on the water-hole by lifting up and throwing his weight upon it; and remembering, he understood what he now had in mind. Diable faced about and paused. He showed his white teeth in a grin, which Leclère answered; and then hurled his body through the air straight for the box.

Fifteen minutes later, Slackwater Charley and Webster Shaw, returning, caught a glimpse of a ghostly pendulum swinging back and forth in the dim light. As they hurriedly drew in closer, they made out the man's inert body, and a live thing that clung to it, and shook and worried, and gave to it the swaying motion.

"Hi! Ya! Chook! you Spawn of Hell!" yelled Webster Shaw.

Diable glared at him, and snarled threateningly, without loosing his jaws.

Slackwater Charley got out his revolver, but his hand was shaking as with a chill and he fumbled.

"Here, you take it," he said, passing the weapon over.

Webster Shaw laughed shortly, drew a sight between the gleaming eyes, and pressed the trigger. Diable's body twitched with the shock, thrashed the ground spasmodically a moment, and went suddenly limp. But his teeth still held fast-locked.

7
IN YEDDO BAY

IN YEDDO BAY.

By Jack London.

Somewhere along Theater Street he had lost it. He remembered being hustled somewhat roughly on the bridge over one of the canals that cross that busy thoroughfare. Possibly some slant-eyed, light-fingered pickpocket was even then enjoying the fifty-odd yen his purse had contained. And then again, he thought, he might have lost it himself, just lost it carelessly.

Hopelessly, and for the twentieth time, he searched in all his pockets for the missing purse. It was not there. His hand lingered in his empty hip-pocket, and he woefully regarded the voluble and vociferous restaurant-keeper, who insanely clamored : " Twenty-five sen ! You pay now ! Twenty-five sen ! "

" But my purse ! " the boy said. " I tell you I 've lost it somewhere."

Whereupon the restaurant-keeper lifted his arms indignantly and shrieked: " Twenty-five ·sen ! Twenty-five sen ! You pay now ! "

Quite a crowd had collected, and it was growing embarrassing for Alf Davis.

It was so ridiculous and petty, Alf thought. Such a disturbance about nothing ! And, decidedly, he must be doing something. Thoughts of diving wildly through that forest of legs, and of striking out at whomsoever opposed him, flashed through his mind ; but, as though divining his purpose, one of the waiters, a short and chunky chap with an evil-looking cast in one eye, seized him by the arm.

" You pay now ! You pay now ! Twenty-five sen ! " yelled the proprietor, hoarse with rage.

Alf was red in the face, too, from mortification ; but he resolutely set out on another exploration. He had given up the purse, pinning his last hope on stray coins. In the little change-pocket of his coat he found a ten-sen piece and five copper sen ; and remembering having recently missed a ten-sen piece, he cut the seam of the pocket and resurrected the coin from the depths of the lining. Twenty-five sen he held in his hand, the sum required to pay for the supper he had eaten. He turned them over to the proprietor, who counted them, grew suddenly calm, and bowed obsequiously — in fact, the whole crowd bowed obsequiously and melted away.

Alf Davis was a young sailor, just turned sixteen, on board the " Annie Mine," an American sealing-schooner which had run into Yokohama to ship its season's catch of skins to London. And in this his second trip ashore he was beginning to catch his first puzzling glimpses of the Oriental mind. He laughed when the bowing and kotowing was over, and turned on his heel to confront another problem. How was he to get aboard ship ? It was eleven o'clock at night, and there would be no ship's boats ashore, while the outlook for hiring a native boatman, with nothing but empty pockets to draw upon, was not particularly inviting.

Keeping a sharp lookout for shipmates, he went down to the pier. At Yokohama there are no long lines of wharves. The shipping lies out at anchor, enabling a few hundred of the short-legged people to make a livelihood by carrying passengers to and from the shore.

A dozen sampan men and boys hailed Alf and offered their services. He selected the most favorable-looking one, an old and beneficent-appearing man with a withered leg. Alf stepped into his sampan and sat down. It was quite dark and he could not see what the old fellow was doing, though he evidently was doing nothing about shoving off and getting under way. At last he limped over and peered into Alf's face.

" Ten sen," he said.

" Yes, I know, ten sen," Alf answered carelessly. " But hurry up. American schooner."

" Ten sen. You pay now," the old fellow insisted.

Alf felt himself grow hot all over at the hateful words "pay now." "You take me to American schooner ; then I pay," he said.

But the man stood up patiently before him, held out his hand, and said, "Ten sen. You pay now."

Alf tried to explain. He had no money. He had lost his purse. But he would pay. As soon as he got aboard the American schooner, then he would pay. No; he would not even go aboard the American schooner. He would call to his shipmates, and they would give the sampan man the ten sen first. After that he would go aboard. So it was all right, of course.

To all of which the beneficent-appearing old man replied: "You pay now. Ten sen." And, to make matters worse, the other sampan men squatted on the pier-steps, listening.

Alf, chagrined and angry, stood up to step ashore. But the old fellow laid a detaining hand on his sleeve. "You give shirt now. I take you 'Merican schooner," he proposed.

Then it was that all of Alf's American independence flamed up in his breast. The Anglo-Saxon has a born dislike of being imposed upon, and to Alf this was sheer robbery! Ten sen was equivalent to six American cents, while his shirt, which was of good quality and was new, had cost him two dollars.

He turned his back on the man without a word, and went out to the end of the pier, the crowd, laughing with great gusto, following at his heels. The majority of them were heavy-set, muscular fellows, and the July night being

one of sweltering heat, they were clad in the least possible raiment. The water-people of any race are rough and turbulent, and it struck Alf that to be out at midnight on a pier-end

"QUITE A CROWD HAD COLLECTED, AND IT WAS GROWING EMBARRASSING FOR ALF DAVIS."

with such a crowd of wharfmen, in a big Japanese city, was not as safe as it might be.

One burly fellow, with a shock of black hair and ferocious eyes, came up. The rest shoved in after him to take part in the discussion.

"Give me shoes," the man said. "Give me shoes now. I take you 'Merican schooner."

Alf shook his head; whereat the crowd clamored that he accept the proposal. Now the Anglo-Saxon is so constituted that to browbeat or bully him is the last way under the sun of getting him to do any certain thing. He will dare willingly, but he will not permit himself to be driven. So this attempt of the boatmen to force Alf only aroused all the dogged stubbornness of his race. The same qualities were in him that are in men who lead forlorn hopes; and there, under the stars, on the lonely pier, encircled by the jostling and shouldering gang, he resolved that he would die rather than submit to the indignity of being robbed of a single stitch of ·clothing. Not value, but principle, was at stake.

Then somebody thrust roughly against him from behind. He whirled about with flashing eyes, and the circle involuntarily gave ground. But the crowd was growing more boisterous. Each and every article of clothing he had on was demanded by one or another, and these demands were shouted simultaneously at the tops of very healthy lungs.

Alf had long since ceased to say anything, but he knew that the situation was getting dangerous, and that the only thing left to him was to get away. His face was set doggedly, his eyes glinted like points of steel, and his body was firmly and confidently poised. This air of determination sufficiently impressed the boatmen to make them give way before him when he started to walk toward the shore-end of the pier. But they trooped along beside him and behind him, shouting and laughing more noisily than ever. One of the youngsters, about Alf's size and build, impudently snatched his cap from his head; but before he could put it on his own head, Alf struck out from the shoulder, and sent the fellow rolling on the stones.

The cap flew out of his hand and disappeared among the many legs. Alf did some quick thinking; his sailor pride would not permit him to leave the cap in their hands. He followed in the direction it had sped, and soon found it under the bare foot of a stalwart fellow, who kept his weight stolidly upon it. Alf tried to get the cap out by a sudden jerk, but failed. He shoved against the man's leg, but the man only grunted. It was challenge direct, and Alf ac-

cepted it. Like a flash one leg was behind the man and Alf had thrust strongly with his shoulder against the fellow's chest. Nothing could save the man from the fierce vigorousness of the trick, and he was hurled over and backward.

Next, the cap was on Alf's head and his fists were up before him. Then Alf whirled about to prevent attack from behind, and all those in that quarter fled precipitately. This was what he wanted. None remained between him and the shore end. The pier was narrow. Facing them and threatening with his fist those who attempted to pass him on either side, he continued his retreat. It was exciting work, walking backward and at the same time checking that surging mass of men. But the dark-skinned peoples, the world over, have learned to respect the white man's fist; and it was the battles fought by many sailors, more than his own warlike front, that gave Alf the victory.

Where the pier adjoins the shore was the station of the harbor police, and Alf backed into the electric-lighted office, very much to the amusement of the dapper lieutenant in charge. The sampan men, grown quiet and orderly, clustered like flies by the open door, through which they could see and hear what passed.

Alf explained his difficulty in few words, and demanded, as the privilege of a stranger in a strange land, that the lieutenant put him aboard in the police-boat. The lieutenant, in turn, who knew all the "rules and regulations" by heart, explained that the harbor police were not ferrymen, and that the police-boats had other functions to perform than that of transporting belated and penniless sailormen to their ships. He also said he knew the sampan men to be natural-born robbers, but that so long as they robbed within the law he was powerless. It was their right to collect fares in advance, and who was he to command them to take a passenger and collect fare at the journey's end? Alf acknowledged the justice of his remarks, but suggested that while he could not command he might persuade. The lieutenant was willing to oblige, and went to the door, from where he delivered a speech to the crowd. But they, too, knew their rights, and, when the officer had finished, shouted in chorus their abominable "Ten sen! You pay now! You pay now!"

"You see, I can do nothing," the lieutenant
said, who, by the way, spoke perfect English.
"But I have warned them not to harm or mo-
lest you, so you will be safe, at least. The
night is warm and half over. Lie down somewhere and go to sleep. I would permit you to
sleep here in the office,
were it not against the
rules and regulations."

Alf thanked him for his
kindness and courtesy;
but the sampan men had
aroused all his pride of
race and doggedness, and
the problem could not be
solved that way. To sleep
out the night on the stones
was an acknowledgment
of defeat.

"The sampan men re-
fuse to take me out?"

The lieutenant nodded.

"And you refuse to take
me out?"

Again the lieutenant
nodded.

"Well, then, it's not in
the rules and regulations
that you can prevent my
taking myself out?"

The lieutenant was per-
plexed. "There is no
boat," he said.

"That's not the ques-
tion," Alf proclaimed
hotly. "If I take myself
out, everybody's satisfied
and no harm done?"

"Yes; what you say is
true," persisted the puz-
zled lieutenant. "But you
cannot take yourself out."

"STRAIGHT TO THE END ALF RAN, AND, WITHOUT PAUSE, DIVED OFF CLEANLY
AND NEATLY INTO THE WATER."

"You just watch me," was the retort.

Down went Alf's cap on the office floor.
Right and left he kicked off his low-cut shoes.
Trousers and shirt followed.

"Remember," he said in ringing tones, "I, as
a citizen of the United States, shall hold you, the
city of Yokohama, and the government of Japan
responsible for those clothes. Good night."

He plunged through the doorway, scattering
the astounded boatmen to either side, and ran
out on the pier. But they quickly recovered
and ran after him, shouting with glee at the new
phase the situation had taken on. It was a
night long remembered among the water-folk
of Yokohama town. Straight to the end Alf
ran, and, without pause, dived off cleanly and
neatly into the water. He struck out with a
lusty, single-overhand stroke till curiosity
prompted him to halt for a moment. Out of
the darkness, from where the pier should be,
voices were calling to him.

He turned on his back, floated, and listened.

"All right! All right!" he could distinguish from the babel. "No pay now; pay bime by! Come back! Come back now; pay bime by!"

"No, thank you," he called back. "No pay at all. Good night."

Then he faced about in order to locate the Annie Mine. She was fully a mile away, and in the darkness it was no easy task to get her bearings. First, he settled upon a blaze of lights which he knew nothing but a man-of-war could make. That must be the United States war-ship "Lancaster." Somewhere to the left and beyond should be the Annie Mine. But to the left he made out three lights close together. That could not be the schooner. For the moment he was confused. He rolled over on his back and shut his eyes, striving to construct a mental picture of the harbor as he had seen it in daytime. With a snort of satisfaction he rolled back again. The three lights evidently belonged to the big English tramp steamer. Therefore the schooner must lie somewhere between the three lights and the Lancaster. He gazed long and steadily, and there, very dim and low, but at the point he expected, burned a single light — the anchor-light of the Annie Mine.

And it was a fine swim under the starshine. The air was warm as the water, and the water as warm as tepid milk. The good salt taste of it was in his mouth, the tingling of it along his limbs; and the steady beat of his heart, heavy and strong, made him glad for living.

But beyond being glorious the swim was uneventful. On the right hand he passed the many-lighted Lancaster, on the left hand the English tramp, and ere long the Annie Mine loomed large above him. He grasped the hanging rope-ladder and drew himself noiselessly on deck. There was no one in sight. He saw a light in the galley, and knew that the captain's son, who kept the lonely anchor-watch, was making coffee. Alf went forward to the forecastle. The men were snoring in their bunks, and in that confined space the heat seemed to him insufferable. So he put on a thin cotton shirt and a pair of dungaree trousers, tucked blanket and pillow under his arm, and went up on deck and out on the forecastle-head.

Hardly had he begun to doze when he was roused by a boat coming alongside and hailing the anchor-watch. It was the police-boat, and to Alf it was given to enjoy the excited conversation that ensued. Yes, the captain's son recognized the clothes. They belonged to Alf Davis, one of the seamen. What had happened? No; Alf Davis had not come aboard. He was ashore. He was not ashore? Then he must be drowned. Here both the lieutenant and the captain's son talked at the same time, and Alf could make out nothing. Then he heard them come forward and rouse out the crew. The crew grumbled sleepily and said that Alf Davis was not in the forecastle; whereupon the captain's son waxed indignant at the Yokohama police and their ways, and the lieutenant quoted rules and regulations in despairing accents.

Alf rose up from the forecastle-head and extended his hand, saying:

"I guess I'll take those clothes. Thank you for bringing them aboard so promptly."

"I don't see why he could n't have brought you aboard inside of them," said the captain's son.

And the police lieutenant said nothing, though he turned the clothes over somewhat sheepishly to their rightful owner.

The next day, when Alf started to go ashore, he found himself surrounded by shouting and gesticulating, though very respectful, sampan men, all extraordinarily anxious to have him for a passenger. Nor did the one he selected say, "You pay now," when he entered his boat. When Alf prepared to step out on to the pier, he offered the man the customary ten sen. But the man drew himself up and shook his head.

"You all right," he said. "You no pay. You never no pay. You bully boy and all right."

And for the rest of the Annie Mine's stay in port, the sampan men refused money at Alf Davis's hand. Out of admiration for his pluck and independence, they had given him the freedom of the harbor.

8
THE LEOPARD MAN'S STORY

THE LEOPARD MAN'S STORY

By JACK LONDON

HE had a dreamy, far-away look in his eyes, and his sad, insistent voice, gentle spoken as a maid's, seemed the placid embodiment of some deep-seated melancholy. He was the Leopard Man, but he did not look it. His business in life, whereby he lived, was to appear in a cage of performing leopards before vast audiences, and to thrill those audiences by certain exhibitions of nerve for which his employers rewarded him on a scale commensurate with the thrills he produced.

As I say, he did not look it. He was narrow-hipped, narrow-shouldered and anæmic, while he seemed not so much oppressed by gloom as by a sweet and gentle sadness, the weight of which was as sweetly and gently borne. For an hour I had been trying to get a story out of him, but he appeared to lack imagination. To him there was no romance in his gorgeous career, no deeds of daring, no thrills—nothing but a gray sameness and infinite boredom.

Lions? Oh, yes! he had fought with them. It was nothing. All you had to do was to stay sober. Anybody could whip a lion to a standstill with an ordinary stick. He had fought one for half an hour once. Just hit him on the nose every time he rushed, and when he got artful and rushed with his head down, why, the thing to do was to stick out your leg. When he grabbed at the leg you drew it back and hit him on the nose again. That was all.

With the far-away look in his eyes and his soft flow of words he showed me his scars. There were many of them, and one recent one where a tigress had reached for his shoulder and gone down to the bone. I could see the neatly-mended rents in the coat he had on. His right arm, from the elbow down, looked as though it had gone through a threshing machine, what of the ravage wrought by claws and fangs. But it was nothing, he said, only the old wounds bothered him somewhat when rainy weather came on.

Suddenly his face brightened with a recollection, for he was really as anxious to give me a story as I was to get it.

"I suppose you've heard of the lion-tamer who was hated by another man?" he asked.

He paused and looked pensively at a sick lion in the cage opposite.

"Got the toothache," he explained. "Well, the lion-tamer's big play to the audience was putting his head in a lion's mouth. The man who hated him attended every performance in the hope sometime of seeing that lion crunch down. He followed the show about all over the country. The years went by and he grew old, and the lion-tamer grew old, and the lion grew old. And at last one day, sitting in a front seat, he saw what he had waited for. The lion crunched down, and there wasn't any need to call a doctor."

The Leopard Man glanced casually over his finger nails in a manner which would have been critical had it not been so sad.

"Now that's what I call patience," he continued, "and it's my style. But it was not the style of a fellow I knew. He was a little, thin, sawed-off, sword-swallowing and juggling Frenchman. De Ville he called himself, and he had a nice wife. She did trapeze work and used to dive from under the roof into a net, turning over once on the way as nice as you please.

"De Ville had a quick temper, as quick as his hand, and his hand was as quick as the paw of a tiger. One day, because the ring-master called him a frogeater, or something like that and maybe a little worse, he shoved him against the soft pine background he used in his knife-throwing act so quick the ringmaster didn't have time to think, and there, before the audience, De Ville kept the air on fire with his knives, sinking them into the wood all around the ringmaster so close that they passed through his clothes and most of them bit into his skin.

"The clowns had to pull the knives out to get him loose, for he was pinned fast. So the word went around to watch out for De Ville, and no one dared be more than barely civil to his wife. And she was a sly bit of baggage, too, only all hands were afraid of De Ville.

"But there was one man, Wallace, who was afraid of nothing. He was the lion-tamer, and he had the self-same trick of putting his head into the lion's mouth. He'd put it into the mouths of any of them, though he preferred Augustus, a big, good-natured beast who could always be depended upon.

"As I was saying, Wallace—'King' Wallace we called him—was afraid of nothing alive or dead. He was a king and no mistake. I've seen him drunk, and on a wager go into the cage of a lion that'd turned nasty and without a stick beat him to a finish. Just did it with his fist on the nose.

"Madame De Ville—"

At an uproar behind us the Leopard Man turned quietly around. It was a divided cage, and a monkey, poking through the bars and around the partition, had had its paw seized by a big gray wolf who was trying to pull it off by main strength. The arm seemed stretching out longer and longer like a thick elastic, and the unfortunate monkey's mates were raising a terrible din. No keeper was at hand, so the Leopard Man stepped over a couple of paces, dealt the wolf a sharp blow on the nose with the light cane he carried, and returned with a sadly apologetic smile to take up his unfinished sentence as though there had been no interruption.

"—looked at King Wallace and King Wallace looked at her, while De Ville looked black. We warned Wallace, but it was no use. He laughed at us, as he laughed at De Ville one day when he shoved De Ville's head into a bucket of paste because he wanted to fight.

"De Ville was in a pretty mess—I helped to scrape him off; but he was cool as a cucumber and made no threats at all. But I saw a glitter in his eyes which I had seen often in the eyes of wild beasts, and I went out of my way to give Wallace a final warning. He laughed, but he did not look so much in Madame De Ville's direction after that.

"Several months passed by. Nothing had happened and I was beginning to think it all a scare over nothing. We were West by that time, showing in 'Frisco. It was during the afternoon performance, and the big tent was filled with women and children, when I went looking for Red Denny, the head canvas-man, who had walked off with my pocket-knife.

"Passing by one of the dressing tents I glanced in through a hole in the canvas to see if I could locate him. He wasn't there, but directly in front of me was King Wallace, in tights, waiting for his turn to go on with his cage of performing lions. He was watching with much amusement a quarrel between a couple of trapeze artists. All the rest of the people in the dressing tent were watching the same thing, with the exception of De Ville, whom I noticed staring at Wallace with undisguised hatred. Wallace and the rest were all too busy following the quarrel to notice this or what followed.

"But I saw it through the hole in the canvas. De Ville drew his handkerchief from his pocket, made as though to mop the sweat from his face with it (it was a hot day), and at the same time walked past Wallace's back. He never stopped, but kept right on to the doorway, where he turned his head, while passing out, and shot a swift look back at the unconscious man. The look troubled me at the time, for not only did I see hatred in it, but I saw triumph as well.

"'De Ville will bear watching,' I said to myself, and I really breathed easier when I saw him go out the entrance to the circus grounds and board an electric car for downtown. A few minutes later I was in the big tent, where I had overhauled Red Denny. King Wallace was doing his turn and holding the audience spellbound. He was in a particularly vicious mood, and he kept the lions stirred up till they were all snarling and growling around him, that is, all of them except old Augustus, and he was just too fat and lazy and old to get stirred up over anything.

"Finally Wallace cracked the old lion's knees with his whip and got him into position. Old Augustus, blinking good-naturedly, opened his mouth and in popped Wallace's head. Then the jaws came together, *crunch*, just like that."

The Leopard Man smiled in a sweetly wistful fashion, and the far-away look came into his eyes.

"And that was the end of King Wallace," he went on in his sad, low voice. "After the excitement cooled down I watched my chance and bent over and smelled Wallace's head. Then I sneezed."

"It . . . it was . . . ?" I queried with halting eagerness.

"Snuff—that De Ville dropped on his hair in the dressing tent. Old Augustus never meant to do it. He only sneezed."

Busy following the quarrel.

- B-CORY-KILVERT
- 1 9 0 3 -

9
LOVE OF LIFE

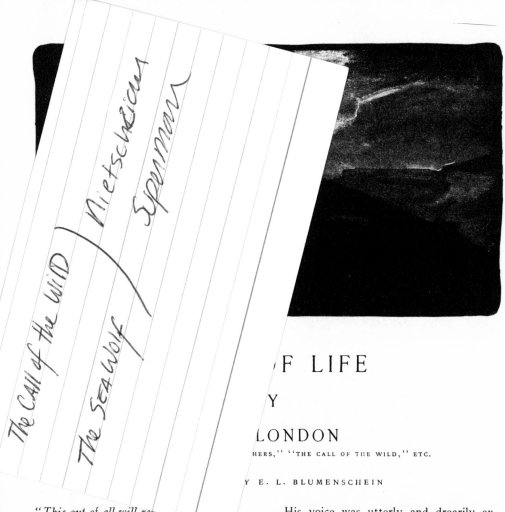

F LIFE

Y

LONDON

HERS," "THE CALL OF THE WILD," ETC.

Y E. L. BLUMENSCHEIN

"This out of all will rem...
They have lived and have tosseu .
So much of the game will be gain,
Though the gold of the dice has been lost."

THEY limped painfully down the bank, and once the foremost of the two men staggered among the rough-strewn rocks. They were tired and weak, and their faces had the drawn expression of patience which comes of hardship long endured. They were heavily burdened with blanket packs which were strapped to their shoulders. Head-straps, passing across the forehead, helped support these packs. Each man carried a rifle. They walked in a stooped posture, the shoulders well forward, the head still farther forward, the eyes bent upon the ground.

"I wish we had just about two of them cartridges that's layin' in that cache of ourn," said the second man.

His voice was utterly and drearily expressionless. He spoke without enthusiasm; but the first man, limping into the milky stream that foamed over the rocks, vouchsafed no reply.

The other man followed at his heels. They did not remove their foot-gear, though the water was icy cold — so cold that their ankles ached and their feet went numb. In places the water dashed against their knees, and both men staggered for footing.

The man who followed slipped on a smooth boulder, nearly fell, but recovered himself with a violent effort, at the same time uttering a sharp exclamation of pain. He seemed faint and dizzy, and put out his free hand while he reeled, as though seeking support against the air. When he had steadied himself he stepped forward, but reeled again and nearly fell. Then he stood still and looked at the other man, who had never turned his head.

"HE CRIED LOUDLY TO THE PITILESS DESOLATION THAT
RINGED HIM AROUND"

The man stood still for fully a minute, as though debating with himself. Then he called out :

"I say, Bill, I've sprained my ankle."

Bill staggered on through the milky water. He did not look around. The man watched him go, and though his face was expressionless as ever, his eyes were like the eyes of a wounded deer.

The other man limped up the farther bank and continued straight on without looking back. The man in the stream watched him. His lips trembled a little, so that the rough thatch of brown hair which covered them was visibly agitated. His tongue even strayed out to moisten them.

"Bill !" he cried out.

It was the pleading cry of a strong man in distress, but Bill's head did not turn. The man watched him go, limping grotesquely and lurching forward with stammering gait up the slow slope toward the soft sky-line of the low-lying hill. He watched him go till he passed over the crest and disappeared. Then he turned his gaze and slowly took in the circle of the world that remained to him now that Bill was gone.

Near the horizon the sun was smoldering dimly, almost obscured by formless mists and vapors, which gave an impression of mass and density without outline or tangibility. The man pulled out his watch, the while resting his weight on one leg. It was four o'clock, and as the season was near the last of July or first of August — he did not know the precise date within a week or two — he knew that the sun roughly marked the northwest. He looked to the south and knew that somewhere beyond those bleak hills lay the Great Bear Lake ; also, he knew that in that direction the Arctic Circle cut its forbidding way across the Canadian Barrens. This stream in which he stood was a feeder to the Coppermine River, which in turn flowed north and emptied into Coronation Gulf and the Arctic Ocean. He had never been there, but he had seen it, once, on a Hudson Bay Company chart.

Again his gaze completed the circle of the world about him. It was not a heartening spectacle. Everywhere was soft sky-line. The hills were all low-lying. There were no trees, no shrubs, no grasses — naught but a tremendous and terrible desolation that sent fear swiftly dawning into his eyes

"Bill !" he whispered, once and twice ; "Bill !"

He cowered in the midst of the milky water, as though the vastness were pressing in upon him with overwhelming force, brutally crushing him with its complacent awfulness. He began to shake as with an ague-fit, till the gun fell from his hand with a splash. This served to rouse him. He fought with his fear and pulled himself together, groping in the water and recovering the weapon. He hitched his pack farther over on his left shoulder, so as to take a portion of its weight from off the injured ankle. Then he proceeded, slowly and carefully, wincing with pain, to the bank.

He did not stop With a desperation that was madness. unmindful of the pain, he hurried up the slope to the crest of the hill over which his comrade had disappeared — more grotesque and comical by far than that limping, jerking comrade. But at the crest he saw a shallow valley, empty of life. He fought with his fear again, overcame it, hitched the pack still farther over on his left shoulder, and lurched on down, the slope.

The bottom of the valley was soggy with water, which the thick moss held, sponge-like, close to the surface. This water squirted out from under his feet at every step, and each time he lifted a foot the action culminated in a sucking sound as the wet moss reluctantly released its grip. He picked his way from muskeg to muskeg, and followed the other man's footsteps along and across the rocky ledges which thrust like islets through the sea of moss.

Though alone he was not lost. Farther on he knew he would come to where dead spruce and fir, very small and weazened, bordered the shore of a little lake, the _tit-chin-nichilie_ — in the tongue of the country, the "land of little sticks." And into that lake flowed a small stream, the water of which was not milky. There was rush-grass on that stream — this he remembered well — but no timber, and he would follow it till its first trickle ceased at a divide. He would cross this divide to the first trickle of another stream, flowing to the west, which he would follow until it emptied into the River Dease, and here he would find a cache under an upturned canoe and piled over with many rocks. And in this cache would be ammunition for his empty gun, fish-hooks and lines, a small net — all the utilities for

"YET THE LIFE THAT WAS IN HIM DROVE HIM ON"

the killing and snaring of food. Also, he would find flour — not much — a piece of bacon and some beans.

Bill would be waiting for him there, and they would paddle away south down the Dease to the Great Bear Lake. And south across the lake they would go, ever south, till they gained the Mackenzie. And south, still south, they would go, while the winter raced vainly after them, and the ice formed in the eddies, and the days grew chill and crisp, south to some warm Hudson Bay Company post, where timber grew tall and generous and there was grub without end.

These were the thoughts of the man as he strove onward. But hard as he strove with his body, he strove equally hard with his mind, trying to think that Bill had not deserted him, that Bill would surely wait for him at the cache. He was compelled to think this thought, or else there would not be any use to strive, and he would have lain down and died. And as the dim ball of the sun sank slowly into the northwest he covered every inch, and many times, of his and Bill's flight south before the downcoming winter. And he conned the grub of the cache and the grub of the Hudson Bay Company post over and over again. He had not eaten for two days; for a far longer time he had not had all he wanted to eat. Often he stooped and picked pale muskeg berries, put them into his mouth and chewed and swallowed them. A muskeg berry is a bit of seed inclosed in a bit of water. In the mouth the water melts away and the seed chews sharp and bitter. The man knew there was no nourishment in the berries, but he chewed them patiently with a hope greater than knowledge and defying experience.

At nine o'clock he stubbed his toe on a rocky ledge, and from sheer weariness and weakness staggered and fell. He lay for some time, without movement, on his side. Then he slipped out of the pack-straps and clumsily dragged himself into a sitting posture. It was not yet dark, and in the lingering twilight he groped about among the rocks for shreds of dry moss. When he had gathered a heap he built a fire — a smoldering, smudgy fire — and put a tin pot of water on to boil.

He unwrapped his pack and the first thing he did was to count his matches. There were sixty-seven. He counted them three times to make sure. He divided them into several portions, wrapping them in oil paper, disposing of one bunch in his empty tobacco pouch, of another bunch in the inside band of his battered hat, of a third bunch under his shirt on the chest. This accomplished, a panic came upon him and he unwrapped them all and counted them again. There were still sixty-seven.

He dried his wet foot-gear by the fire. The moccasins were in soggy shreds. The blanket socks were worn through in places and his feet were raw and bleeding. His ankle was throbbing and he gave it an examination. It had swollen to the size of his knee. He tore a long strip from one of his two blankets and bound the ankle tightly. He tore other strips and bound them about his feet to serve for both moccasins and socks. Then he drank the pot of water, steaming hot, wound his watch, and crawled between his blankets.

He slept like a dead man. The brief darkness around midnight came and went. The sun arose in the northeast — at least the day dawned in that quarter, for the sun was hidden by gray clouds.

At six o'clock he awoke, quietly lying on his back. He gazed straight up into the gray sky and knew that he was hungry. As he rolled over on his elbow he was startled by a loud snort, and saw a bull caribou regarding him with alert curiosity. The animal was not more than fifty feet away, and instantly into the man's mind leaped the vision and the savor of a caribou steak sizzling and frying over a fire. Mechanically he reached for the empty gun, drew a bead, and pulled the trigger. The bull snorted and leaped away, his hoofs rattling and clattering as he fled across the ledges.

The man cursed and flung the empty gun from him. He groaned aloud as he started to drag himself to his feet. It was a slow and arduous task. His joints were like rusty hinges. They worked harshly in their sockets, with much friction, and each bending or unbending was accomplished only through a sheer exertion of will. When he finally gained his feet another minute or so was consumed in straightening up, so that he could stand erect as a man should stand.

He crawled up a small knoll and surveyed the prospect. There were no trees, no bushes, nothing but a gray sea of moss scarcely diversified by gray rocks, gray-colored lakelets, and gray streamlets. The sky was gray. There was no sun or hint of sun. He had no idea of north, and he had forgotten the way he had come to this spot the night before. But he was not lost. He knew that. Soon he would come to the land of the little sticks. He felt that it lay off to the left somewhere, not far — possibly just over the next low hill.

He went back to put his pack into shape for traveling. He assured himself of the existence of his three separate parcels of matches, though he did not stop to count them. But he did linger, debating, over a squat moose-hide sack. It was not large. He could hide it under his two hands. He knew that it weighed fifteen pounds — as much as all the rest of the pack — and it worried him. He finally set it to one side and proceeded to roll the pack. He paused to gaze at the squat moose-hide sack. He picked it up hastily with a defiant glance about him, as though the desolation were trying to rob him of it ; and when he rose to his feet to stagger on into the day, it was included in the pack on his back.

He bore away to the left, stopping now and again to eat muskeg berries. His ankle had stiffened, his limp was more pronounced, but the pain of it was as nothing compared with the pain of his stomach. The hunger pangs were sharp. They gnawed and gnawed until he could not keep his mind steady on the course he must pursue to gain the land of little sticks. The muskeg berries did not allay this gnawing, while they made his tongue and the roof of his mouth sore with their irritating bite.

He came upon a valley where rock ptarmigan rose on whirring wings from the ledges and muskegs. Ker — ker — ker was the cry they made. He threw stones at them but could not hit them. He placed his pack on the ground and stalked them as a cat stalks a sparrow. The sharp rocks cut through his pants' legs till his knees left a trail of blood ; but the hurt was lost in the hurt of his hunger. He squirmed over the wet moss, saturating his clothes and chilling his body ; but he was not aware of it, so great was his fever for food. And always the ptarmigan rose, whirring, before him, till their ker — ker — ker became a mock to him, and he cursed them and cried aloud at them with their own cry.

Once he crawled upon one that must have been asleep. He did not see it till it shot up in his face from its rocky nook. He made a clutch as startled as was the rise of the ptarmigan, and there remained in his hand three tail-feathers. As he watched its flight he hated it, as though it had done him some terrible wrong. Then he returned and shouldered his pack.

As the day wore along he came into valleys or swales where game was more plentiful. A band of caribou passed by, twenty and odd animals, tantalizingly within rifle range. He felt a wild desire to run after them, a certitude that he could run them down. A black fox came toward him, carrying a ptarmigan in his mouth. The man shouted. It was a fearful cry, but the fox leaping away in fright did not drop the ptarmigan.

Late in the afternoon he followed a stream, milky with lime, which ran through sparse patches of rush-grass. Grasping these rushes firmly near the root, he pulled up what resembled a young onion-sprout no larger than a shingle-nail. It was tender and his teeth sank into it with a crunch that promised deliciously of food. But its fibers were tough. It was composed of stringy filaments saturated with water, like the berries, and devoid of nourishment. But he threw off his pack and went into the rush-grass on hands and knees, crunching and munching, like some bovine creature.

He was very weary and often wished to rest — to lie down and sleep ; but he was continually driven on — not so much by his desire to gain the land of little sticks as by his hunger. He searched little ponds for frogs and dug up the earth with his nails for worms, though he knew in spite that neither frogs nor worms existed so far north.

He looked into every pool of water vainly, until, as the long twilight came on, he discovered a solitary fish, the size of a minnow, in such a pool. He plunged his arm in up to the shoulder, but it eluded him. He reached for it with both hands and stirred up the milky mud at the bottom. In his excitement he fell in, wetting himself to the waist. Then the water was too muddy to admit of his seeing the fish and he was compelled to wait until the sediment had settled.

The pursuit was renewed, till the water was again muddied. But he could not wait. He unstrapped the tin bucket and began to bale the pool. He baled wildly at first, splashing himself and flinging the water so short a distance that it ran back into the pool. He worked more carefully, striving

"HIS MIRTH WAS HOARSE AND GHASTLY, LIKE A RAVEN'S CROAK, AND THE
SICK WOLF JOINED HIM, HOWLING LUGUBRIOUSLY"

to be cool, though his heart was pounding against his chest and his hands were trembling. At the end of half an hour the pool was nearly dry. Not a cupful of water remained. And there was no fish. He found a hidden crevice among the stones through which it had escaped to the adjoining and larger pool — a pool which he could not empty in a night and a day. Had he known of the crevice, he could have closed it with a rock at the beginning and the fish would have been his.

Thus he thought, and crumpled up and sank down upon the wet earth. At first he cried softly to himself, then he cried loudly to the pitiless desolation that ringed him around; and for a long time after he was shaken by great dry sobs.

He built a fire and warmed himself by drinking quarts of hot water, and made camp on a rocky ledge in the same fashion he had the night before. The last thing he did was to see that his matches were dry and to wind his watch. The blankets were wet and clammy. His ankle pulsed with pain. But he knew only that he was hungry, and through his restless sleep he dreamed of feasts and banquets and of food served and spread in all imaginable ways.

He awoke chilled and sick. There was no sun. The gray of earth and sky had become deeper, more profound. A raw wind was blowing, and the first flurries of snow were whitening the hilltops. The air about him thickened and grew white while he made a fire and boiled more water. It was wet snow, half rain, and the flakes were large and soggy. At first they melted as soon as they came in contact with the earth, but ever more fell, covering the ground, putting out the fire, spoiling his supply of moss-fuel.

This was the signal for him to strap on his pack and stumble onward he knew not where. He was not concerned with the land of little sticks, nor with Bill and the cache under the upturned canoe by the River Dease. He was mastered by the verb, "to eat." He was hunger-mad. He took no heed of the course he pursued, so long as that course led him through the swale bottoms. He felt his way through the wet snow to the watery muskeg berries, and went by feel as he pulled up the rush-grass by the roots. But it was tasteless stuff and did not satisfy. He found a weed that tasted sour and he ate all he could find of it, which was not much, for it was a creeping growth, easily hidden under the several inches of snow.

He had no fire that night nor hot water, and crawled under his blanket to sleep the broken hunger-sleep. The snow turned into a cold rain. He awakened many times to feel it falling on his upturned face. Day came — a gray day and no sun. It had ceased raining. The keenness of his hunger had departed. Sensibility, so far as concerned the yearning for food, had been exhausted. There was a dull, heavy ache in his stomach, but it did not bother him so much. He was more rational, and once more he was chiefly interested in the land of little sticks and the cache by the River Dease.

He ripped the remnant of one of his blankets into strips and bound his bleeding feet. Also, he recinched the injured ankle and prepared himself for a day of travel. When he came to his pack he paused long over the squat moose-hide sack, but in the end it went with him.

The snow had melted under the rain and only the hilltops showed white. The sun came out and he succeeded in locating the points of the compass, though he knew now that he was lost. Perhaps, in his previous days' wanderings, he had edged away too far to the left. He now bore off to the right to counteract the possible deviation from his true course.

Though the hunger pangs were no longer so exquisite, he realized that he was weak. He was compelled to pause for frequent rests when he attacked the muskeg berries and rush-grass patches. His tongue felt dry and large, as though covered with a fine hairy growth, and it tasted bitter in his mouth. His heart gave him a great deal of trouble. When he had traveled a few minutes it would begin a remorseless thump, thump, thump, and then leap up and away in a painful flutter of beats that choked him and made him go faint and dizzy.

In the middle of the day he found two minnows in a large pool. It was impossible to bale it, but he was calmer now and managed to catch them in his tin bucket. They were no longer than his little finger, but he was not particularly hungry. The dull ache in his stomach had been growing duller and fainter. It seemed almost that his stomach was dozing. He ate the fish raw, masticating with painstaking care, for the eating was

"SLOWLY, WHILE THE WOLF STRUGGLED FEEBLY AND THE HAND CLUTCHED FEEBLY, THE OTHER HAND CREPT ACROSS TO A GRIP"

an act of pure reason. While he had no desire to eat he knew that he must eat to live.

In the evening he caught three more minnows, eating two and saving the third for breakfast. The sun had dried stray shreds of moss, and he was able to warm himself with hot water. He had not covered more than ten miles that day, and the next day, traveling whenever his heart permitted him, he covered no more than five miles. But his stomach did not give him the slightest uneasiness. It had gone to sleep. He was in a strange country, too, and the caribou were growing more plentiful, also the wolves. Often their yelps drifted across the desolation, and once he saw three of them slinking away before his path.

Another night, and in the morning, being more rational, he untied the leather string that fastened the squat moose-hide sack. From its open mouth poured a yellow stream of coarse gold-dust and nuggets. He roughly divided the gold in halves, caching one half on a prominent ledge, wrapped in a piece of blanket, and returning the other half to the sack. He also began to use strips of the one remaining blanket for his feet. He still clung to his gun, for there were cartridges in that cache by the River Dease.

This was a day of fog, and this day hunger awoke in him again. He was very weak and was afflicted with a giddiness which at times blinded him. It was no uncommon thing now for him to stumble and fall; and stumbling once, he fell squarely into a ptarmigan nest. There were four newly hatched chicks a day old — little specks of pulsating life no more than a mouthful; and he ate them ravenously, thrusting them alive into his mouth and crunching them like egg-shells between his teeth. The mother ptarmigan beat about him with great outcry. He used his gun as a club with which to knock her over, but she dodged out of reach. He threw stones at her and with one chance shot broke a wing. Then she fluttered away, running, trailing the broken wing, with him in pursuit.

The little chicks had no more than whetted his appetite. He hopped and bobbed clumsily along on his injured ankle, throwing stones and screaming hoarsely at times; at other times hopping and bobbing silently along, picking himself up grimly and patiently when he fell, or rubbing his eyes with his hand when the giddiness threatened to overpower him.

The chase led him across swampy ground in the bottom of the valley, and he came upon footprints in the soggy moss. They were not his own — he could see that. They must be Bill's. But he could not stop, for the mother ptarmigan was running on. He would catch her first, then he would return and investigate.

He exhausted the mother ptarmigan; but he exhausted himself. She lay panting on her side. He lay panting on his side, a dozen feet away, unable to crawl to her. And as he recovered she recovered, fluttering out of reach as his hungry hand went out to her. The chase was resumed. Night settled down and she escaped. He stumbled from weakness and pitched head-foremost on his face, cutting his cheek, his pack upon his back. He did not move for a long while; then he rolled over on his side, wound his watch, and lay there until morning.

Another day of fog. Half of his last blanket had gone into foot-wrappings. He failed to pick up Bill's trail. It did not matter. His hunger was driving him too compellingly — only — only he wondered if Bill, too, were lost. By midday the irk of his pack became too oppressive. Again he divided the gold, this time merely spilling half of it on the ground. In the afternoon he threw the rest of it away, there remaining to him only the half-blanket, the tin bucket, and the rifle.

An hallucination began to trouble him. He felt confident that one cartridge remained to him. It was in the chamber of the rifle and he had overlooked it. On the other hand, he knew all the time that the chamber was empty. But the hallucination persisted. He fought it off for hours, then threw his rifle open and was confronted with emptiness. The disappointment was as bitter as though he had really expected to find the cartridge.

He plodded on for half an hour, when the hallucination arose again. Again he fought it and still it persisted, till for very relief he opened his rifle to unconvince himself. At times his mind wandered farther afield, and he plodded on, a mere automaton, strange conceits and whimsicalities gnawing at his brain like worms. But these excursions out of the real were of brief duration, for ever the pangs of the hunger-bite called him back. He was jerked back abruptly once from such an excursion by a sight that caused him nearly to faint. He reeled and swayed, doddering like a drunken man to keep from falling. Before him stood a horse. A horse! He could not believe his eyes. A thick mist was in them, intershot with sparkling points of light. He rubbed his eyes savagely to clear his vision, and beheld not a horse but a great brown bear. The animal was studying him with bellicose curiosity.

The man had brought his gun half way to his shoulder before he realized. He lowered it and drew his hunting-knife from its beaded sheath at his hip. Before him was meat and life. He ran his thumb along the edge of his knife. It was sharp. The point was sharp. He would fling himself upon the bear and kill it. But his heart began its warning thump, thump, thump. Then followed the wild upward leap and tattoo of flutters, the pressing as of an iron band about his forehead, the creeping of the dizziness into his brain.

His desperate courage was evicted by a great surge of fear. In his weakness, what if the animal attacked him! He drew himself up to his most imposing stature, gripping the knife and staring hard at the bear. The bear advanced clumsily a couple of steps, reared up and gave vent to a tentative growl. If the man ran he would run after him; but the man did not run. He was animated now with the courage of fear. He, too, growled, savagely, terribly, voicing the fear that is to life germane and that lies twisted about life's deepest roots.

The bear edged away to one side, growling menacingly, himself appalled by this mysterious creature that appeared upright and unafraid. But the man did not move. He stood like a statue till the danger was past, when he yielded to a fit of trembling and sank down into the wet moss.

He pulled himself together and went on, afraid now in a new way. It was not the fear that he should die passively from lack of food, but that he should be destroyed violently before starvation had exhausted the last particle of the endeavor in him that made toward surviving. There were the wolves. Back and forth across the desolation drifted their howls, weaving the very air into a fabric of menace that was so tangible that he found himself, arms in the air, pressing it back from him as it might be the walls of a wind-blown tent.

Now and again the wolves in packs of two and three crossed his path. But they sheered clear of him. They were not in sufficient numbers, and besides they were hunting the caribou which did not battle, while this strange creature that walked erect might scratch and bite.

In the late afternoon he came upon scattered bones where the wolves had made a kill. The débris had been a caribou calf an hour before, squawking and running and very much alive. He contemplated the bones, clean-picked and polished, pink with the cell-life in them which had not yet died. Could it possibly be that he might be that ere the day was done! Such was life, eh? A vain and fleeting thing. It was only life that pained. There was no hurt in death. To die was to sleep. It meant cessation, rest. Then why was he not content to die?

But he did not moralize long. He was squatting in the moss, a bone in his mouth, sucking at the shreds of life that still dyed it faintly pink. The sweet meaty taste, thin and elusive almost as a memory, maddened him. He closed his jaws on the bones and crunched. Sometimes it was the bone that broke, sometimes his teeth. Then he crushed the bones between rocks, pounded them to a pulp and swallowed them. He pounded his fingers, too, in his haste, and yet found a moment in which to feel surprise at the fact that his fingers did not hurt much when caught under the descending rock.

Came frightful days of snow and rain. He did not know when he made camp, when he broke camp. He traveled in the night as much as in the day. He rested wherever he fell, crawled on whenever the dying life in him flickered up and burned less dimly. He as a man no longer strove. It was the life in him, unwilling to die, that drove him on. He did not suffer. His nerves had become blunted, numb, while his mind was filled with weird visions and delicious dreams.

But ever he sucked and chewed on the crushed bones of the caribou calf, the least remnants of which he had gathered up and carried with him. He crossed no more hills or divides, but automatically followed a large stream which flowed through a wide and shallow valley. He did not see this stream or this valley. He saw nothing save visions. Soul and body walked or crawled side by side, yet apart, so slender was the thread that bound them.

He awoke in his right mind, lying on his back on a rocky ledge. The sun was shining bright and warm. Afar off he heard the squawking of caribou calves. He was aware of vague memories of rain and wind and snow, but whether he had been beaten by the storm for two days or two weeks he did not know.

For some time he lay without movement, the genial sunshine pouring upon him and saturating his miserable body with its warmth. A fine day, he thought. Perhaps he could manage to locate himself. By a painful effort he rolled over on his side. Below him flowed a wide and sluggish river. Its unfamiliarity puzzled him. Slowly he followed it with his eyes, winding in wide sweeps among the bleak bare hills, bleaker and barer and lower-lying than any hills he had yet encountered. Slowly, deliberately, without excitement or more than the most casual interest, he followed the course of the strange stream toward the sky-line and saw it emptying into a bright and shining sea. He was still unexcited. Most unusual, he thought, a vision or a mirage — more likely a vision, a trick of his disordered mind. He was confirmed in this by sight of a ship lying at anchor in the midst of the shining sea. He closed his eyes for a while, then opened them. Strange how the vision persisted! Yet not strange. He knew there were no seas or ships in the heart of the barren lands, just as he had known there was no cartridge in the empty rifle.

He heard a snuffle behind him — a half-choking gasp or cough. Very slowly, because of his exceeding weakness and stiffness, he rolled over on his other side. He could see nothing near at hand, but he waited patiently. Again came the snuffle and cough, and outlined between two jagged rocks not a score of feet away he made out the gray head of a wolf. The sharp ears were not pricked so sharply as he had seen them on other wolves; the eyes were bleared and blood-shot, the head seemed to droop limply and forlornly. The animal blinked continually in the sunshine. It seemed sick. As he looked it snuffled and coughed again.

This, at least, was real, he thought, and turned on the other side so that he might see the reality of the world which had been veiled from him before by the vision. But the sea still shone in the distance and the ship's spars were plainly discernible. Was it reality after all? He closed his eyes for a long while and thought, and then it came to him. He had been making north by east, away from the Dease Divide and into the Coppermine Valley. This wide and sluggish river was the Coppermine. That shining sea was the Arctic Ocean. That ship was a whaler, strayed east, far east, from the mouth of the Mackenzie, and it was lying at anchor in Coronation Gulf. He remembered the Hudson Bay Company chart he had seen long ago, and it was all clear and reasonable to him.

He sat up and turned his attention to immediate affairs. He had worn through the blanket-wrappings, and his feet were like shapeless lumps of raw meat. His last blanket was gone. Rifle and knife were both missing. He had lost his hat somewhere, with the bunch of matches in the band, but the matches against his chest were safe and dry inside the tobacco pouch and oil-paper. He looked at his watch. It marked eleven o'clock and was still running. Evidently he had kept it wound.

He was calm and collected. Though extremely weak he had no sensation of pain. He was not hungry. The thought of food was not even pleasant to him, and whatever he did was done by his reason alone. He ripped off his pants' legs to the knees and bound them about his feet. Somehow he had succeeded in retaining the tin bucket. He would have some hot water before he began what he foresaw was to be a terrible journey to the ship.

His movements were slow. He shook as with a palsy. When he started to collect dry moss he found he could not rise to his feet. He tried again and again, then contented himself with crawling about on hands and knees. Once he crawled near to the sick wolf. The animal dragged itself reluctantly out of his way, licking its chops with a tongue which seemed hardly to have the strength to curl. The man noticed that the tongue was not the customary healthful red. It was a yellowish brown and seemed coated with a rough and half-dry mucus.

After he had drunk a quart of hot water the man found he was able to stand, and even to walk as well as a dying man might be supposed to walk. Every minute or so he was compelled to rest. His steps were feeble and uncertain, just as the wolf's that trailed him were feeble and uncertain; and that night, when the shining sea was blotted out by blackness, he knew he was nearer to it by no more than four miles.

Throughout the night he heard the cough of the sick wolf, and now and then the squawking of the caribou calves. There was life all around him, but it was strong life, very much alive and well, and he knew the sick wolf clung to the sick man's trail in the hope that the man would die first. In the morning, on opening his eyes, he beheld it regarding him with a wistful and hungry stare. It stood crouched, with tail between its legs, like a miserable and woebegone dog. It shivered in the chill morning wind, and grinned dispiritedly when the man spoke to it in a voice which achieved no more than a hoarse whisper.

The sun rose brightly, and all morning the man tottered and fell toward the ship on the shining sea. The weather was perfect. It was the brief Indian Summer of the high latitudes. It might last a week. To-morrow or next day it might be gone.

In the afternoon the man came upon a trail. It was of another man, who did not walk, but who dragged himself on all fours. The man thought it might be Bill, but he thought in a dull, uninterested way. He had no curiosity. In fact sensation and emotion had left him. He was no longer susceptible to pain. Stomach and nerves had gone to sleep. Yet the life that was in him drove him on. He was very weary, but it refused to die. It was because it refused to die that he still ate muskeg berries and minnows, drank his hot water, and kept a wary eye on the sick wolf.

He followed the trail of the other man who dragged himself along, and soon came to the end of it — a few fresh-picked bones where the soggy moss was marked by the foot-pads of many wolves. He saw a squat moose-hide sack, mate to his own, which had been torn by sharp teeth. He picked it up, though its weight was almost too much for his feeble fingers. Bill had carried it to the last. Ha! ha! He would have the laugh on Bill. He would survive and carry it to the ship in the shining sea. His mirth was hoarse and ghastly, like a raven's croak, and the sick wolf joined him, howling lugubriously. The man ceased suddenly. How could he have the laugh on Bill if that were Bill; if those bones, so pinky-white and clean, were Bill!

He turned away. Well, Bill had deserted him; but he would not take the gold, nor would he suck Bill's bones. Bill would have, though, had it been the other way around, he mused as he staggered on.

He came to a pool of water. Stooping over in quest of minnows, he jerked his head back as though he had been stung. He had caught sight of his reflected face. So horrible was it that sensibility awoke long enough to be shocked. There were three minnows in the pool, which was too large to drain; and after several ineffectual attempts to catch them in the tin bucket he forbore. He was afraid, because of his great weakness, that he might fall in and drown. It was for this reason that he did not trust himself to the river astride one of the many drift-logs which lined its sand-spits.

That day he decreased the distance between him and the ship by three miles; the next day by two — for he was crawling now as Bill had crawled; and the end of the fifth day found the ship still seven miles away and him unable to make even a mile a day. Still the Indian summer held on, and he continued to crawl and faint, turn and turn about; and ever the sick wolf coughed and wheezed at his heels. His knees had become raw meat like his feet, and though he padded them with the shirt from his back it was a red track he left behind him on the moss and stones. Once glancing back he saw the wolf licking hungrily his bleeding trail, and he saw sharply what his own end might be — unless — unless he could get the wolf. Then began as grim a tragedy of existence as was ever played — a sick man that crawled, a sick wolf that limped, two creatures dragging their dying carcasses across the desolation and hunting each other's lives.

Had it been a well wolf, it would not have mattered so much to the man; but the thought of going to feed the maw of that loathsome and all but dead thing was repugnant to him. He was finicky. His mind had begun to wander again, and to be perplexed by hallucinations, while his lucid intervals grew rarer and shorter.

He was awakened once from a faint by a wheeze close in his ear. The wolf leaped lamely back, losing its footing and falling in its weakness. It was ludicrous, but he was not amused. Nor was he even afraid. He was too far gone for that. But his mind was for the moment clear, and he lay and considered. The ship was no more than four miles away. He could see it quite distinctly when he rubbed the mists out of his eyes, and he could see the white sail of a small boat cutting the water of the shining sea. But he could never crawl those four miles. He knew that, and was very calm in the knowledge. He knew that he could not crawl half a mile. And yet he wanted to live. It was unreasonable that he should die after all he had undergone. Fate asked too much of him. And, dying, he declined to die. It was stark madness, perhaps, but in the very grip of Death he defied Death and refused to die.

He closed his eyes and composed himself with infinite precaution. He steeled himself to keep above the suffocating languor that lapped like a rising tide through all the wells of his being. It was very like a sea, this deadly languor, that rose and rose and drowned his consciousness bit by bit. Sometimes he was all but submerged, swimming through oblivion with a faltering stroke; and again, by some strange alchemy of soul, he would find another shred of will and strike out more strongly.

Without movement he lay on his back, and he could hear slowly drawing near and nearer the wheezing intake and output of the sick wolf's breath. It drew closer, ever closer, through an infinitude of time, and he did not move. It was at his ear. The harsh dry tongue grated like sandpaper against his cheek. His hands shot out — or at least he willed them to shoot out. The fingers were curved like talons, but they closed on empty air. Swiftness and certitude require strength, and the man had not this strength.

The patience of the wolf was terrible. The man's patience was no less terrible. For half a day he lay motionless, fighting off unconsciousness and waiting for the thing that was to feed upon him and upon which he wished to feed. Sometimes the languid sea rose over him and he dreamed long dreams; but ever through it all, waking and dreaming, he waited for the wheezing breath and the harsh caress of the tongue.

He did not hear the breath, and he slipped slowly from some dream to the feel of the tongue along his hand. He waited. The fangs pressed softly; the pressure increased; the wolf was exerting its last strength in an effort to sink teeth in the food for which it had waited so long. But the man had waited long, and the lacerated hand closed on the jaw. Slowly, while the wolf struggled feebly and the hand clutched feebly, the other hand crept across to a grip. Five minutes later the whole weight of the man's body was on top of the wolf. The hands had not sufficient strength to choke the animal, but the face of the man was pressed close to the throat of the wolf and the mouth was full of hair. At the end of half an hour the man was aware of a warm trickle in his throat. It was not pleasant. It was like molten lead being forced into his stomach, but it was forced by his will alone. Later the man rolled over on his back and slept.

There were some members of a scientific expedition on the whaleship *Bedford*. From the deck they remarked a strange object on the shore. It was moving down the beach toward the water. They were unable to classify it, and, being scientific men, they climbed into the whaleboat alongside and went ashore to see. And they saw something that was alive but that could hardly be called a man. It was blind, unconscious. It squirmed along the ground like some monstrous worm. Most of its efforts were ineffectual, but it was persistent, and it writhed and twisted and went ahead perhaps a score of feet an hour.

Three weeks afterward the man lay in a bunk on the whaleship *Bedford*, and with tears streaming down his wasted cheeks told who he was and what he had undergone. He also babbled incoherently of his mother, of sunny Southern California, and a home among the orange groves and flowers.

The days were not many after that when he sat at table with the scientific men and ship's officers. He gloated over the spectacle of so much food, watching it anxiously as it went into the mouths of others. With the disappearance of each mouthful an expression of deep regret came into his eyes. He was quite sane, yet he hated those men at meal-time because they ate so much food. He was haunted by a fear that it would not last. He inquired of the cook, the cabin-boy, the captain, concerning the food stores. They reassured him countless times; but he could not believe them, and pried cunningly about the lazarette to see with his own eyes.

It was noticed that the man was getting fat. He grew stouter with each day. The scientific men shook their heads and theorized. They limited the man at his meals, but still his girth increased and his body swelled prodigiously under his shirt.

The sailors grinned. They knew. And when the scientific men set a watch on the man, they knew too. They saw him slouch for'ard after breakfast, and like a mendicant, with outstretched palm, accost a sailor. The sailor grinned and passed him a fragment of sea biscuit. He clutched it avariciously, looked at it as a miser looks at gold, and thrust it into his shirt bosom. Similar were the donations from other grinning sailors.

The scientific men were discreet. They left him alone. But they privily examined his bunk. It was lined with hardtack; the mattress was stuffed with hardtack; every nook and cranny was filled with hardtack. Yet he was sane. He was taking precautions against another possible famine — that was all. He would recover from it, the scientific men said; and he did, ere the *Bedford's* anchor rumbled down in San Francisco Bay.

10
PLANCHETTE

Planchette

BY JACK LONDON

Illustrated by Charles M. Relyea

I

"I T is my right to know," the girl said.

Her voice was firm. There was no hint of pleading in it, yet it was the determination that is worked up to through a long period of pleading. But in her case it had been pleading, not of speech, but of personality. Her lips had been ever mute, but her face and eyes, and the very attitude of her soul, had been for a long time eloquent with questioning. This the man had known, but he had never answered; and now she was demanding by the spoken word that he answer.

"It is my right," the girl repeated.

"I know it," he answered, desperately.

She waited, in the silence that followed, her eyes fixed upon the light that filtered down through the lofty boughs and bathed the great redwood trunks in mellow warmth. This light, subdued and colored, seemed almost a radiation from the trunks themselves, so strongly did they saturate it with their hue. The girl saw without seeing, as she heard without hearing, the deep gurgling of the stream far below on the canyon bottom.

She looked down at the man. "Well?" she asked, with the firmness that feigns belief that obedience will be forthcoming.

She was sitting upright, her back against a fallen tree, while he lay near her, on his side.

"Dear, dear Lute," he murmured.

She shivered at the sound of his voice, not from repulsion, but from struggle against the fascination of its caressing gentleness. She had come to know well the lure of the man—the wealth of easement and rest that was promised by every caressing intonation of his voice, by the mere touch of hand on hand or the faint impact of his breath on neck or cheek. The man could not express himself by word or look or touch without weaving into the expression, subtly and occultly, the feeling as of a hand that passed and that in passing stroked softly and soothingly, Nor was this all-pervading caress a something that cloyed with too great sweetness; nor was it sickly sentimental; nor was it

Drawn by Charles M. Relyea

HE WOULD NOT SPEAK—SHE KNEW IT; AND SHE KNEW, LIKEWISE, WITH THE SURENESS
OF FAITH, THAT IT WAS BECAUSE HE COULD NOT

maudlin with love's madness. It was vigorous, compelling, masculine. For that matter, it was largely unconscious on the man's part; he was only dimly aware of it. It was a part of him, the breath of his soul as it were.

But now, resolved and desperate, she steeled herself against him. He tried to face her, but her gray eyes looked out at him steadily from under cool, level brows, and he dropped his head upon her knee. Her hand strayed into his hair softly, and her face melted into solicitude and tenderness. But when he looked up again, her eyes were steady, her brows cool and level.

"What more can I tell you?" the man asked. He raised his head and met her gaze. "I cannot marry you. I cannot marry any woman. I love you—you know that—better than my own life. I weigh you in the scales against all the dear things of living, and you outweigh everything. I would give everything to possess you, yet I may not. I can never marry you."

Her lips were compressed with the effort of control. His head was sinking back to her knee, when she checked him.

"You are already married, Chris?"

"No! no!" he cried, vehemently. "I have never been married. I want to marry only you, and I cannot!"

"Then——"

"Don't!" he interrupted; "don't ask me!"

"It is my right to know," she repeated.

"I know it," he again interrupted; "but I cannot tell you."

"You have not considered me, Chris," she went on gently. "You do not know what I have had to bear from my people because of you."

"I did not think they felt so very unkindly toward me," he said bitterly.

"It is true. They can scarcely tolerate you. They do not show it to you, but they almost hate you. It is I who have to bear all this. It was not always so, though. They liked you at first as—as I liked you. But that was four years ago. The time passed by—a year, two years; and then they began to turn against you. They are not to be blamed; you spoke no word. They felt that you were destroying my life. It is four years now, and you have never once mentioned marriage to them. What were they to think? Just what they have thought, that you were destroying my life."

As she talked, she continued to pass her fingers caressingly through his hair, sorrowful for the pain that she was inflicting.

"They did like you at first—who can help liking you? You seem to draw affection from all living things, as the trees draw the moisture from the ground. Aunt Mildred and Uncle Robert thought there was nobody like you. The sun rose and set in you. They thought I was the luckiest girl alive to win the love of a man like you. 'For it looks very much like it,' Uncle Robert used to say, wagging his head wickedly at me. Of course they liked you. Aunt Mildred used to sigh, and look across teasingly at uncle, and say, 'When I think of Chris it almost makes me wish I were younger myself.' And uncle would answer, 'I don't blame you, my dear, not in the least.' And then the pair of them would literally beam upon me their congratulations that I had won the love of a man like you.

"And they knew I loved you as well. How could I hide it—this great, wonderful thing that had entered into my life and swallowed up all my days? For four years, Chris, I have lived only for you. Every moment was yours. Waking I loved you; sleeping I dreamed of you. Every act I have performed was shaped by you, by the thought of you. I had no end, petty or great, that you were not there waiting for me."

"I had no idea of imposing such slavery," he muttered.

"You imposed nothing. You always let me have my own way; it was you who were the obedient slave. You did for me without offending me. You forestalled my wishes without the semblance of forestalling them, so natural and inevitable was everything you did for me. You were no dancing puppet; you made no fuss. Don't you see? You did not seem to do things at all. Somehow they were always there, just done, as a matter of course.

"The slavery was love's slavery. It was just my love for you that made you swallow up all my days. You did not force yourself into my thoughts. You crept in, always, and you were there always—how much you will never know.

"But as time went by, Aunt Mildred and uncle grew afraid. What was to become of me? You were destroying my life. My music — you know how my dream of it has dimmed away. That spring when I first met you, I was twenty, and I was about to start for Germany. I was going to study hard. That was four years ago, and I am still here in California.

"I had other lovers. You drove them away. No! no! I don't mean that. It was I that drove them away. What did I care for lovers, for anything when you were near? But as I said, Aunt Mildred and uncle grew afraid. There has been talk—friends, busybodies, and all the rest. The time went by; you did not speak. I could only wonder, wonder. I knew you loved me. Much was said against you by uncle at first, and then by Aunt Mildred. They were father and mother to me, you know. I could not defend you; yet I was loyal to you. I refused to discuss you. There was half-estrangement in my home —Uncle Robert with a face like an undertaker's, and Aunt Mildred's heart breaking. But what could I do, Chris? What could I do?"

The man, his head resting on her knee again, groaned, but made no other reply.

"Aunt Mildred was mother to me; but I went to her no more with my confidences. My childhood's book was closed. It was a sweet book, Chris. The tears come into my eyes sometimes when I think of it. But never mind that. Great happiness has been mine as well. I am glad I can talk frankly of my love for you. And the attaining of such frankness has been very sweet. I do love you, Chris. I love you— I cannot tell you how. You are everything to me, and more besides. You remember that Christmas tree of the children's, when we played blindman's buff, and you caught me by the arm, so, with such a clutching of fingers that I cried out with the hurt? I never told you, but the arm was badly bruised. And such sweet I got of it you could never guess. There, black and blue, was the imprint of your fingers— your fingers, Chris! It was the touch of you made visible. It was there a week, and I kissed the marks—oh, so often! I was loath to see them go, fain to rebruise the arm and make them linger. I was jealous of the returning white that drove the bruise away. Somehow — oh! I cannot explain, but I loved you so!"

In the silence that fell she continued her caressing of his hair, while she idly watched a great squirrel, boisterous and hilarious, as it scampered back and forth in a distant vista of the redwoods. A crimson-crested woodpecker, energetically drilling a fallen trunk, caught and transferred her gaze. The man did not lift his head. Rather, he crushed his face harder against her knee, while his heaving shoulders marked the hardness with which he breathed.

"You must tell me, Chris," the girl said gently. "This mystery—it is killing me. I must know why we cannot be married. Are we to be ever thus— merely lovers, meeting often, it is true, and yet with the long absences between the meetings? Is it all the world holds for you and me, Chris? Are we never to be more to each other? I want all our days to be together. I want all the companionship, the comradeship, which cannot be ours now, and which will be ours when we are married——" She caught her breath quickly. "But we are never to be married. I forgot. And you must tell me why."

The man raised his head and looked her in the eyes. It was a way he had with whomever he talked.

"I have considered you, Lute," he began, doggedly. "I did consider you at the very first. I should never have gone on with it; I should have gone away. I knew it. And I considered you in the light of that knowledge, and yet—I did not go away. My God! what was I to do? I loved you. I could not go away. I could not help it. I stayed. I resolved, but I broke my resolves. I was like a drunkard. I was drunk of you. I was weak, I know. I failed. I could not go away—I tried. I went away, you will remember, though you did not know why. You know now. I went away, but I could not remain away. Send me away, Lute; I have not the power to go myself."

"But why should you go away?" she asked. "Besides, I must know why before I can send you away."

"Don't ask me."

"Tell me," she said, her voice tenderly imperative.

"Don't, Lute; don't force me," the man pleaded, and there was appeal in his eyes and voice.

"But you must tell me," she insisted. "It is a justice you owe me."

The man wavered. "If I do——" he began. Then he ended with determination, "I should never be able to forgive myself. No, I cannot tell you. Don't try to compel me, Lute. You would be as sorry as I."

"If there is anything—if there are obstacles—if this mystery does really prevent——" She was speaking slowly, with long pauses, seeking the more delicate ways of speech for the framing of her thought. "Chris, I do truly love you. I love you as deeply as it is possible for any woman to love, I am sure. If you were to say to me now, 'Come,' I would arise and go with you. I would follow wherever you led me. I would be your page, as in the days of old when ladies went with their knights to far lands. You are my knight, Chris, and you can do no wrong. Your will is my wish. I was once afraid of the censure of the world; now that you have come into my life I am no longer afraid. I would laugh at the world and its censure for your sake—for my sake, too. I would laugh, for I should have you, and you are more to me than the good will and approval of the world. If you say 'Come,' I will."

"Don't! Don't!" he cried. "It is impossible! Marriage or not, I cannot even say 'Come.' I'll tell you why."

He sat up beside her, the action stamped with resolve. He took her hand in his and held it closely. His lips moved to the verge of speech. The mystery trembled for utterance; the air was palpitant with its presence. As if it were an irrevocable decree of fate, the girl steeled herself to hear. But the man paused, gazing straight out before him. She felt his hand relax in hers, and she pressed it sympathetically, encouragingly. But she felt the rigidity going out of his tense body, and she knew that spirit and flesh were relaxing together. His resolution was ebbing. He would not speak—she knew it; and she knew, likewise, with the sureness of faith, that it was because he could not.

She gazed despairingly before her, a numb feeling at her heart as though hope and happiness had died. She watched the sun flickering down through the warm-trunked redwoods. But she looked at the scene as from a long way off, without interest, herself an alien, no longer an intimate part of the earth and trees she loved so well.

So far removed did she seem that she was aware of a curiosity, strangely impersonal, in what lay around her. Through a near vista she looked at a buckeye tree in full blossom as though her eyes encountered it for the first time. Her eyes paused and dwelt upon a yellow cluster of Diogenes' lanterns that grew on the edge of an open space. It was the way of flowers always to give her quick pleasure - thrills, but no thrill was hers now. She pondered the flowers slowly and thoughtfully, as a hasheesh-eater, heavy with the drug, might ponder some whim-flower that obtruded on his vision. In her ears was the voice of the stream, a hoarse-throated, sleepy old giant muttering and mumbling his somnolent fancies. But her fancy was not in turn aroused, as was its wont; she knew the sound merely for water rushing over the rocks of the deep canyon bottom.

Her gaze wandered beyond the Diogenes' lanterns into the open space. Knee-deep in the wild oats of the hillside grazed two horses, chestnut-sorrels the pair of them, perfectly matched, warm and golden in the sunshine, their spring coats a sheen of high-lights shot through with color-flashes that glowed like fiery jewels. She recognized, almost with a shock, that one of them was hers—Dolly, the companion of her girlhood and womanhood, on whose neck she had sobbed her sorrows and sung her joys. A moisture welled into her eyes at the sight, and she came back from the remoteness of her mood, quick with passion and sorrow, to be part of the world again.

The man sank forward from the hips, relaxing entirely, and with a groan dropped his head on her knee. She leaned over him and pressed her lips softly and lingeringly to his hair.

"Come, let us go," she said softly, almost in a whisper.

She caught her breath in a half sob, then tightened her lips as she arose. His face was white to ghastliness, so shaken was he by the struggle through which he had passed. They did not look at each other, but walked directly to the horses. She leaned against Dolly's neck while he tightened the girths. Then she gathered the reins in her hand and waited. He looked at her as he bent down, an appeal for forgiveness in his eyes; and in that moment her own eyes answered. Her foot rested in his hands, and from there she vaulted into the saddle.

Without speaking, without further looking at each other, they turned the horses' heads and took the narrow trail that wound down through the somber redwood aisles and across the open glades to the pasture lands below. The trail became a cow-path, the cowpath became a wood-road, which later joined with a hay-road; and they ran down through the low-rolling, tawny California hills to where a set of bars let out on the country road that ran along the bottom of the valley. The girl sat her horse while the man dismounted and began taking down the bars.

"No! Wait!" she cried, before he had touched the two lower bars.

She urged the mare forward a couple of strides, and then the animal lifted over the bars in a clean little jump. The man's eyes sparkled, and he clapped his hands.

"You beauty! you beauty!" the girl cried, leaning forward impulsively in the saddle and pressing her cheek to the mare's neck.

"Let's trade horses for the ride in," she suggested, when he had led his horse through and finished putting up the bars. "You've never sufficiently loved Dolly!"

"No, no," he protested.

"You think she is too old, too sedate," Lute insisted. "She's only sixteen, and she can outrun nine colts out of ten. Only she never cuts up. She's too steady and you don't approve of her—no, don't deny it, sir; I know. And I know also that she can outrun your much-vaunted Washoe Ban. There! I challenge you! And furthermore, you may ride her yourself. You know what Ban can do; so you must ride Dolly and see for yourself what she can do."

They proceeded to exchange the saddles, glad of the diversion and making the most of it.

"I'm glad I was born in California," Lute remarked, as she swung astride of Ban. "It's an outrage both to horse and woman to ride in a sidesaddle."

"You look like a young amazon," the man said approvingly.

"Are you ready?" she asked.

"All ready!"

"To the old mill," she called, as the horses sprang forward. "That's less than a mile."

"This is to a finish?" he demanded.

She nodded, and the horses, feeling the urge of the reins, caught the spirit of the race. The dust rose in clouds behind them as they tore along the level road.

They rode side by side, saving the animals for the rush in at the finish, yet putting them at a pace that drew upon vitality and staying power. Curving around a clump of white oaks, the road straightened out before them for several hundred yards, at the end of which they could see the ruined mill.

"Now for it!" the girl cried.

She urged the horse by suddenly leaning forward with her body, at the same time, for an instant, letting the rein slack and touching the neck with her bridle hand. She began to draw away from the man.

"Touch her on the neck!" she cried.

With this, the mare pulled alongside and began gradually to pass the girl. Chris and Lute looked at each other for a moment, the mare still drawing ahead, so that Chris was compelled slowly to turn his head. The mill was a hundred yards away.

"Shall I give him the spurs?" Lute shouted.

The man nodded, and the girl drove the spurs in sharply and quickly, calling upon the horse for its utmost, but saw her own horse forge slowly ahead of her.

"Beaten by three lengths!" Lute beamed triumphantly, as they pulled into a walk. "Confess, sir, confess! You didn't think the old mare had it in her." Lute leaned to the side and rested her hand for a moment on Dolly's wet neck.

"Ban's a sluggard alongside of her," Chris affirmed. "Dolly's all right if she is in her Indian summer."

Lute nodded approval. "That's a sweet way of putting it—Indian summer. It just describes her. But she's not lazy; she has all the fire and none of the folly. She is very wise, what of her years."

"That accounts for it," Chris demurred. "Her folly passed with her youth. Many's the lively time she's given you."

"No," Lute answered; "I never knew her really to cut up. I think the only trouble she ever gave me was when I was training her to open gates. She was afraid when they swung back upon her— the animal's fear of the trap, perhaps. But she bravely got over it. And she never was vicious. She never bolted, nor bucked, nor cut up in all her life—never, not once."

The horses went on at a walk, still breathing heavily from their run. The road wound along the bottom of the valley, now and again crossing the stream. From either side rose the drowsy purr of mowing machines, punctuated by the occasional sharp cries of the men who were gathering the hay crop. On the western side of the valley the hills rose green and dark, but the eastern side was already burned brown and tan by the sun.

"There is summer, here is spring," Lute said. "Oh, beautiful Sonoma Valley!"

Her eyes were glistening and her face was radiant with love of the land. Her gaze wandered on across orchard patches and sweeping vineyard stretches, seeking out the purple which seemed to hang like a dim smoke in the wrinkles of the hills and in the more distant canyon gorges. Far up, among the more rugged crests, where the steep slopes were covered with manzanita and chaparral, she caught a glimpse of a clear space where the wild grass had not yet lost its green.

"Have you ever heard of the secret pasture?" she asked, her eyes still fixed on the remote green.

A snort of fear brought her eyes back to the man beside her. Dolly, upreared, with distended nostrils and wild eyes, was pawing the air madly with her fore legs. Chris threw himself forward against her neck to keep her from falling backward, and at the same time touched her with the spurs to compel her to drop her fore feet to the ground in order to obey the go-ahead impulse of the spurs.

"Why, Dolly, this is most remarkable," Lute began reprovingly.

But to her surprise the mare threw her head down, arched her back as she went up in the air and, returning, struck the ground stiff-legged and bunched.

"A genuine buck!" Chris called out, and the next moment the mare was rising under him in a second buck.

Lute looked on, astounded at the unprecedented conduct of her mare, and admiring her lover's horsemanship. He was quite cool, and was himself evidently enjoying the performance. Again and again, half a dozen times, Dolly arched herself into the air and struck, stiffly bunched. Then she threw her head straight up and rose on her hind legs, pivoting about and striking with her fore feet. Lute whirled the horse she was riding into safety, and as she did so caught a glimpse of Dolly's eyes, with the look in them of blind brute-madness, bulging until it seemed they must burst from her head. The faint pink in the whites of the eyes was gone, replaced by a white that was like dull marble and that yet flashed as from some inner fire.

A faint cry of fear, suppressed in the instant of utterance, slipped past Lute's lips. One hind leg of the mare seemed to collapse under her, and for a moment the whole quivering body, upreared and perpendicular, swayed back and forth, and there was uncertainty as to whether it would fall forward or backward. The man, half slipping sidewise from the saddle, to fall clear if the mare toppled backward, threw his weight to the front and alongside her neck. This overcame the dangerous teetering balance, and the mare struck the ground on her feet again.

But there was no let-up. Dolly straightened out so that the line of the face was almost a continuation of the line of the stretched neck; this position enabled her to master the bit, which she did by bolting straight ahead down the road.

For the first time Lute became really frightened. She spurred Washoe Ban in pursuit, but he could not hold his own with the mad mare, and dropped gradually behind. Lute saw Dolly check and rear in the air again, and caught up just as the mare made a second bolt. As Dolly dashed around a bend, she stopped suddenly, stiff-legged, and Lute saw her lover torn out of the saddle, his thigh-grip broken by the sudden jerk. Though he had lost his seat, he had not been thrown, and as the mare dashed on Lute saw him clinging to the side of the mare, a hand in her mane and a leg across the saddle. With a quick effort he regained his seat and proceeded to fight with the mare for control.

But Dolly swerved from the road and dashed down a grassy slope yellowed with innumerable Mariposa lilies. An old fence at the bottom was no obstacle; she burst through as though it were filmy spider web and disappeared in the underbrush. Lute followed unhesitatingly, putting Ban through the gap in the fence and plunging on into the thicket. She lay along his neck closely, to escape the ripping and

DOLLY, UPREARED, WITH DISTENDED NOSTRILS AND WILD EYES, WAS PAWING THE AIR
MADLY WITH HER FORE LEGS

tearing of the trees and vines. She felt the horse drop down through leafy branches and into the cool gravel of a stream's bottom. From ahead came a splashing of water, and she caught a glimpse of Dolly dashing up the small bank and into a clump of scrub oaks, against the trunks of which she was trying to scrape off her rider.

Lute almost caught up among the trees, but was hopelessly outdistanced on the fallow field adjoining, across which the mare tore with a fine disregard for heavy ground and gopher holes. When she turned at a sharp angle into the thicket land beyond, Lute took the long diagonal, skirted the thicket, and reined in Ban at the other side. She had arrived first. From within the thicket she could hear a tremendous crashing of brush and branches. Then the mare burst through and into the open, falling to her knees, exhausted, on the soft earth. She arose and staggered forward, then came limply to a halt. She was in a lather-sweat of fear, and stood trembling pitiably.

Chris was still on her back. His shirt was in ribbons, the backs of his hands were bruised and lacerated, while his face was streaming with blood from a gash near the temple. Lute had controlled herself well, but now she was aware of a quick nausea and a trembling of weakness.

"Chris!" she said, so softly that it was almost a whisper; then "Thank God!"

"Oh, I'm all right," he cried to her, putting into his voice all the heartiness he could command, which was not much, for he had himself been under no mean nervous strain. He showed the reaction he was undergoing, when he swung down out of the saddle. He began with a brave muscular display as he lifted his leg over, but ended, on his feet, leaning against the limp Dolly for support. Lute flashed out of her saddle, and her arms were about him in an embrace of thankfulness.

"I know where there is a spring," she said, a moment later.

They left the horses standing untethered, and she led her lover to where crystal water bubbled from out the base of the mountain.

"What was that you said about Dolly's never cutting up?" he asked, when the blood had been stanched and his nerves and pulse beats were at normal again.

"I am stunned," Lute answered; "I cannot understand it. She never did anything like it in all her life. Why, she is a child's horse. I was only a little girl when I first rode her, and to this day——"

"Well, this day she was everything but a child's horse," Chris broke in. "She was a devil. She tried to scrape me off against the trees, and to batter my brains out against the limbs. And did you see those bucks?"

Lute nodded.

"Regular bucking-broncho proposition."

"But what should she know about bucking?" Lute demanded. "She was never known to buck—never."

He shrugged his shoulders. "Some forgotten instinct, perhaps, long-lapsed and come to life again."

The girl rose to her feet determinedly. "I'm going to find out," she said.

They went back to the horses, where they subjected Dolly to a rigid examination that disclosed nothing. Hoofs, legs, bit, mouth, body—everything was as it should be. The saddle and saddlecloth were innocent of burr or sticker; the back was smooth and unbroken. They searched for sign of snake bite and sting of fly or insect, but found nothing.

"Whatever it was, it was subjective, that much is certain," Chris said.

"Obsession," Lute suggested.

They laughed together at the idea, for both were twentieth-century products, healthy minded and normal, with souls that delighted in the butterfly-chase of ideals, but that halted before the brink where superstition begins.

"An evil spirit," Chris laughed; "but what evil have I done that I should be so punished?"

"You think too much of yourself, sir," she rejoined. "It is more likely some evil, I don't know what, that Dolly has done. You were a mere accident. I might have been on her back at the time, or Aunt Mildred, or anybody."

As she talked she took hold of the saddle girth and started to loosen it.

"What are you doing?" Chris demanded.

"I'm going to ride Dolly in."

"No, you're not," he announced. "It would be bad discipline. After what has happened I am simply compelled to ride her in myself."

But it was a very weak and very sick mare he rode, stumbling and halting, afflicted with nervous jerks and recurring muscular spasms—the aftermath of a tremendous excitement.

"I feel like a book of verse and a hammock, after all that has happened," Lute said, as they rode into camp.

It was a summer camp of city-tired people, pitched in a grove of towering redwoods through whose lofty boughs the sunshine trickled down, broken and subdued to soft light and cool shadow. Apart from the main camp were the kitchen and the servants' tents; and midway between was the great dining-hall, walled by the living redwood columns, where fresh whispers of air were always to be found, and where no canopy was needed to keep the sun away.

"Poor Dolly, she is really sick," Lute said that evening, when they had returned from a last look at the mare. "But you weren't hurt, Chris, and that's enough for one small woman to be thankful for. I thought I knew, but I really did not know till to-day how much you mean to me."

"My thoughts were of you," Chris answered, and felt the responsive pressure of the hand that rested on his arm.

She turned her face up to his and met his lips.

"Good night," she said.

"Dear Lute, dear Lute," he caressed her with his voice as she moved away among the shadows.

"Who's going for the mail?" called a woman's voice through the trees.

Lute closed the book from which they had been reading, and sighed.

"We weren't going to ride to-day," she said.

"Let me go," Chris proposed; "you stay here. I'll be down and back in no time."

She shook her head.

"Who's going for the mail?" the voice insisted.

"Where's Martin?" Lute called, lifting her voice in answer.

"I don't know," came the voice. "I think Robert took him along somewhere—horse-buying, or fishing, or I don't know what. There's really nobody left but Chris and you. Besides, it will give you an appetite for dinner. You've been lounging in the hammock all day. And Robert *must* have his newspaper."

"All right, aunty, we're starting," Lute called back, getting out of the hammock.

A few minutes later, in riding-clothes, they were saddling the horses. They rode out onto the county road, where blazed the afternoon sun, and turned toward Glen Ellen. The little town slept in the sun, and the somnolent storekeeper and postmaster scarcely kept his eyes open long enough to make up the packet of letters and newspapers.

An hour later Lute and Chris turned aside from the road and dipped along a cowpath down the high bank to water the horses before going into camp.

"Dolly looks as though she'd forgotten all about yesterday," Chris said, as they sat their horses knee-deep in the rushing water. "Look at her."

The mare had raised her head, and cocked her ears at the rustling of a quail in the thicket. Chris leaned over and rubbed around her ears. Her enjoyment was evident, and she drooped her head over against the shoulder of his own horse.

"Like a kitten," was Lute's comment.

"Yet I shall never be able wholly to trust her again," Chris said. "Not after yesterday's mad freak."

"I have a feeling myself that you are safer on Ban," Lute laughed. "It is strange. My trust in Dolly is as implicit as ever. I feel confident so far as I am concerned, but I should never care to see you on her back again. Now with Ban, my faith is still unshaken."

"I feel the same way," Chris laughed back. "Ban could never possibly betray me."

They turned their horses out of the stream. Dolly stopped to brush a fly from her knee with her nose, and Ban urged past into the narrow way of the path. The space was too restricted to make him return, save with much trouble, and Chris allowed him to go on. Lute, riding behind, dwelt with her eyes upon her lover's back, pleasuring in the lines of the bare neck and the sweep out to the muscular shoulders.

Suddenly she reined in her horse. There was nothing else for her to do but look, so brief was the duration of the happening. Beneath and above was the almost perpendicular bank. The path itself was barely wide enough for footing; yet Washoe Ban, whirling and rearing at the same time, toppled for a moment in the air and fell backward off the path.

> Beware Beware Beware Chris Dunbar I intend to destroy you I have already made two attempts upon your life I shall yet succeed So sure am I that I shall succeed that I dare to tell you I do not need to tell you why

Planchette

BY JACK LONDON

Illustrated by Charles M. Relyea

SYNOPSIS: A party of city people is camping in the Sonoma Valley, California. Two of its members, Chris and Lute, ride one afternoon into the redwood forest. They are lovers, but the man tells the girl, as he has often told her before, that he cannot marry her. Lute urges that it is her right to know why; Chris simply repeats that he cannot explain the situation, and says that if he does she will be as sorry as he. It becomes time to return to camp. She mounts her gentle mare, Dolly, and he his horse, Washoe Ban. On the way they trade horses for the ride in. Suddenly, and for no apparent reason, Dolly, with Chris on her back, uprears and paws the air madly. She bolts into a thicket and tries unsuccessfully to scrape her rider off against the trees, stopping finally through exhaustion. Chris is badly shaken but not much hurt. The cause of the mare's performance is a complete mystery. They decide it must be an evil spirit come to punish Chris for something he has done. The next afternoon the young couple go for the mail. On the way back they are riding along a narrow path cut in an almost perpendicular bank. At this point Washoe Ban suddenly rears and topples backward off the path.

II

SO unexpected and so quick was it, that the man was involved in the fall. There had been no time for him to throw himself to the path. He was falling ere he knew it, and he did the only thing possible—slipped the stirrups and threw his body into the air, to the side, and at the same time down. It was twelve feet to the rocks below. He maintained an upright position, his head up and his eyes fixed on the horse above him and falling upon him.

He struck like a cat, on his feet, on the instant making a leap to the side. The next instant Ban crashed down beside him. The animal struggled little, but sounded the terrible cry that horses sometimes make when they have received mortal hurt. He had struck almost squarely on his back, and in that position he remained, his head twisted partly under, his hind legs relaxed and motionless, his fore legs futilely striking the air.

Chris looked up reassuringly.

"I am getting used to it," Lute smiled down to him. "Of course I need not ask if you are hurt. Can I do anything?"

He smiled back and went over to the

113

fallen beast, letting go the girths of the saddle and getting the head straightened out.

"I thought so," he said, after a cursory examination; "I thought so at the time. Did you hear that sort of crunching snap?"

Lute shuddered.

"Well, that was the punctuation of life, the final period dropped at the end of Ban's usefulness." He started around to come up by the path. "I've been astride of Ban for the last time. Let us go home."

At the top of the bank Chris turned and looked down.

"Good-by, Washoe Ban!" he called out; "good-by, old fellow."

The animal was struggling to lift its head. There were tears in Chris's eyes as he turned abruptly away, and tears in Lute's eyes as they met his. She was silent in her sympathy, though the pressure of her hand was firm in his as he walked beside her horse down the dusty road.

"It was done deliberately," Chris burst forth suddenly. "There was no warning. He deliberately flung himself over backward."

"There was no warning," Lute concurred. "I was looking; I saw him. He whirled and threw himself at the same time, just as if you had done it yourself with a tremendous jerk and backward pull on the bit."

"It was not my hand, I swear it. I was not even thinking of him. He was going up with a fairly loose rein, as a matter of course."

"I should have seen it, had you done it," Lute said. "But it was all done before you had a chance to do anything. It was not your hand, not even your unconscious hand."

"Then it was some invisible hand, reaching out from I don't know where."

He looked up whimsically at the sky and smiled at the conceit.

Martin stepped forward to receive Dolly when they came into the stable end of the grove, but his face expressed no surprise at sight of Chris coming in on foot. Chris lingered behind Lute for a moment.

"Can you shoot a horse?" he asked.

The groom nodded, then added, "Yes, sir."

"How do you do it?"

"Draw a line from the eyes to the ears —I mean the opposite ears, sir—and where the lines cross——"

"That will do," Chris interrupted. "You know the watering-place at the second bend. You'll find Ban there with a broken back."

"Oh, here you are, sir. I have been looking for you everywhere since dinner. You are wanted immediately."

Chris tossed his cigar away, then went over and pressed his foot on its glowing fire.

"You haven't told anybody about it?— Ban?" he queried.

Lute shook her head. "They'll learn soon enough. Martin will mention it to Uncle Robert to-morrow. But don't feel too badly about it," she said, after a moment's pause, slipping her hand into his.

"He was my colt," he said; "nobody has ridden him but you. I broke him myself. I knew him from the time he was born. I knew every bit of him, every trick, every caper; and I would have staked my life that it was impossible for him to do a thing like that. There was no warning, no fighting for the bit, no previous unruliness. I have been thinking it over. He didn't fight for the bit, for that matter. He wasn't unruly, nor disobedient, there wasn't time. It was an impulse, and he acted upon it like lightning. I am astounded now at the swiftness with which it took place. Inside the first second we were over the edge and falling.

"It was suicide—deliberate suicide— and attempted murder. It was a trap; I was the victim. He had me, and he threw himself over with me. Yet he did not hate me. He loved me as much as it is possible for a horse to love. I am confounded. I cannot understand it any more than you can understand Dolly's behavior yesterday."

"But horses go insane, Chris," Lute said. "You know that. It's merely a coincidence that two horses in two days should have spells under you."

"That's the only explanation," he answered, starting off with her. "But why am I wanted so urgently?"

"Planchette."

"Oh, I remember. It will be a new experience to me."

"And to all of us," Lute replied, "except Mrs. Grantly. It is her favorite phantom, it seems."

"A weird little thing," he remarked, "a bundle of nerves and black eyes. I'll wager she doesn't weigh ninety pounds, and most of that's magnetism."

"Positively uncanny—at times." Lute shivered involuntarily. "She gives me the creeps."

"Contact of the healthy with the morbid," he explained dryly. "You will notice it is the healthy person that always has the creeps. The morbid one never has the creeps. Morbidness gives the creeps—that's its function. Where did you people pick her up anyway?"

"I don't know—yes, I do, too. Aunt Mildred met her in Boston, I think. Oh, I don't know. At any rate, Mrs. Grantly came to California, and of course had to visit Aunt Mildred. You know the open house we keep."

They halted where a passageway between two great redwood trunks gave entrance to the dining-room. Above, through lacing boughs, could be seen the stars. Candles lighted the tree-columned space. About the table, examining the Planchette contrivance, were four people. Chris's gaze roved over them and he was aware of a guilty sorrow-pang as he paused for a moment on Lute's Aunt Mildred and Uncle Robert, mellow with ripe middle age and genial with the gentle buffets life had dealt them. He passed amusedly over the black-eyed, frail-bodied Mrs. Grantly, and halted on the fourth person, a portly, massive-headed man, whose gray temples belied the youthful solidity of his face.

"Who's that?" Chris whispered.

"A Mr. Barton. The train was late; that's why you didn't see him at dinner. He's only a capitalist—water-power-long-distance-electricity-transmitter, or something like that."

"Doesn't look as though he could give an ox points on imagination."

"He can't. He inherited his money, but he knows enough to hold on to it and hire other men's brains. He is very conservative."

"That is to be expected," was Chris's comment. His gaze went back to the man and woman who had been father and mother to the girl beside him. "Do you know," he said, "it came to me with a shock yesterday when you told me that they had turned against me, that I was scarcely tolerated. I met them afterward, last evening, guiltily, in fear and trembling—

and to-day, too. And yet I could see no difference from of old."

"Dear man," Lute sighed, "hospitality is as natural to them as the act of breathing. But it isn't that, after all. It is all genuine in their dear hearts. No matter how severe the censure they put upon you when you are absent, the moment they are with you they soften and are all kindness and warmth. As soon as their eyes rest on you, affection and love come bubbling up. You are so made. Every animal likes you. All people like you—they can't help it. You can't help it. You are universally lovable, and the best of it is that you don't know it. You don't know it now. Even as I tell it to you, you don't realize it, you won't realize it—and that very incapacity to realize it, is one of the reasons why you are so loved. You are incredulous now, and you shake your head; but I know, who am your slave, as all people know, for they likewise are your slaves.

"Why, in a minute we shall go in and join them. Mark the affection, almost maternal, that will well up in Aunt Mildred's eyes. Listen to the tone of Uncle Robert's voice when he says, 'Well, Chris, my boy?' Watch Mrs. Grantly melt, literally melt, like a dewdrop in the sun.

"Take Mr. Barton, there. You have never seen him before. Why, you will invite him out to smoke a cigar with you when the rest of us have gone to bed— you, a mere nobody, and he a man of many millions, a man of power, a man obtuse and stupid like the ox; and he will follow you about, smoking the cigar, like a little dog, your little dog, trotting at your back. He will not know he is doing it, but he will be doing it just the same. Don't I know, Chris? Oh, I have watched you, watched you, so often, and loved you for it, and loved you again for it, because you were so delightfully and blindly unaware of what you were doing."

"I'm almost bursting with vanity from listening to you," he laughed, passing his arm around her and drawing her against him.

"Yes," she whispered, "and in this very moment when you are laughing at all that I have said, you, the feel of you, your soul —call it what you will, it is you—is calling for all the love that is in me."

She leaned more closely against him, and sighed as with fatigue. He breathed a kiss into her hair and held her with firm tenderness.

Aunt Mildred stirred briskly and looked up from the Planchette board.

"Come, let us begin," she said; "it will soon grow chilly. Robert, where are those children?"

"Here we are," Lute called out, disengaging herself.

"Now for a bundle of creeps," Chris whispered, as they started in.

Lute's prophecy of the manner in which her lover would be received, was realized. Mrs. Grantly, unreal, unhealthy, scintillant with frigid magnetism, warmed and melted as though of truth she were dew and he sun; Mr. Barton beamed broadly upon him, and was colossally gracious; Aunt Mildred greeted him with a glow of fondness and motherly kindness; while Uncle Robert genially and heartily demanded, "Well, Chris, my boy, and what of the riding?"

But Aunt Mildred drew her shawl more closely around her and hastened them to the business in hand. On the table was a sheet of paper. On the paper, riding on three supports, was a small triangular board. Two of the supports were easily moving casters. The third support, placed at the apex of the triangle, was a lead pencil.

"Who's first?" Uncle Robert demanded.

There was a moment's hesitancy, then Aunt Mildred placed her hand on the board, and said,

"Some one always has to be the fool for the delectation of the rest."

"Brave woman," applauded her husband. "Now, Mrs. Grantly, do your worst."

"I?" that lady queried. "I do nothing. The power, or whatever you care to think it, is outside of me, as it is outside of all of you. As to what that power is, I will not dare to say. But there is such a power; I have had evidences of it. And you will undoubtedly have evidences of it. Now please be quiet, everybody. Touch the board very lightly, but firmly, Mrs. Story; but do nothing of your own volition."

Aunt Mildred nodded, and stood with her hand on Planchette, while the rest formed about her in a silent and expectant circle. But nothing happened. The minutes ticked away, and Planchette remained motionless.

"Be patient," Mrs. Grantly counseled.

"Do not struggle against any influences you may feel working on you. But do not do anything yourself, the influences will take care of that. You will feel impelled to do things, and such impulses will be practically irresistible."

"I wish the influences would hurry up," Aunt Mildred protested at the end of five motionless minutes.

"Just a little longer, Mrs. Story, just a little longer," Mrs. Grantly said soothingly.

Suddenly Aunt Mildred's hand began to twitch into movement. A mild concern showed in her face as she observed the movement of her hand and heard the scratching of the pencil-point at the apex of Planchette.

For another five minutes this continued, when Aunt Mildred withdrew her hand with an effort and said, with a nervous laugh:

"I don't know whether I did it myself or not. I do know that I was growing nervous, standing there like a psychic fool with all your solemn faces turned upon me."

"Hen-scratches," was Uncle Robert's judgment, when he looked over the paper upon which she had scrawled.

"Quite illegible," was Mrs. Grantly's dictum. "It does not resemble writing at all. The influences have not got to working yet. Do you try it, Mr. Barton."

That gentleman stepped forward, ponderously willing to please, and placed his hand on the board. And for ten solid, stolid minutes he stood there, motionless as a statue, the frozen personification of the commercial age. Uncle Robert's face began to work. He blinked, stiffened his mouth, uttered suppressed, throaty sounds, deep down, finally snorted, lost his self-control, and broke out in a roar of laughter. All joined in his merriment, including Mrs. Grantly. Mr. Barton laughed with them, but he was vaguely nettled.

"You try it, Story," he said.

Uncle Robert, still laughing and urged on by Lute and his wife, took the board. Suddenly his face sobered. His hand had begun to move, and the pencil could be heard scratching across the paper.

"By George!" he muttered; "that's curious. Look at it. I'm not doing it, I know I'm not doing it. Look at that hand go! Just look at it!"

"Now, Robert, none of your ridiculousness," his wife warned him.

CHRIS LOOKED UP REASSURINGLY. "I AM GETTING USED TO IT," LUTE SMILED DOWN
TO HIM

"I tell you I'm not doing it," he replied indignantly. "The force has got hold of me. Ask Mrs. Grantly. Tell her to make it stop, if you want it to stop. I can't stop it. By George! look at that flourish. I didn't do that; I never wrote a flourish in my life."

"Do try to be serious," Mrs. Grantly warned them. "An atmosphere of levity does not conduce to the best operation of Planchette."

"There, that will do, I guess," Uncle Robert said as he took his hand away. "Now let's see."

He bent over and adjusted his glasses. "It's handwriting at any rate, and that's better than the rest of you did. Here, Lute, your eyes are young."

"Oh, what flourishes!" Lute exclaimed, as she looked at the paper. "And look there, there are two different handwritings."

She began to read: "'*This is the first lecture. Concentrate on this sentence:* "*I am a positive spirit and not negative to any condition.*" *Then follow with concentration on positive love. After that peace and harmony will vibrate through and around your body. Your soul*——' The other writing breaks right in. This is the way it goes: '*Bullfrog* 95, *Dixie* 16, *Golden Anchor* 65, *Gold Mountain* 13, *Jim Butler* 70, *Jumbo* 75, *North Star* 42, *Rescue* 7, *Black Butte* 75, *Brown Hope* 16, *Iron Top* 3.'"

"Iron Top's pretty low," Mr. Barton murmured.

"Robert, you've been dabbling again!" Aunt Mildred cried accusingly.

"No, I've not," he denied; "I only read the quotations. But how the devil—I beg your pardon—they got there on that piece of paper I'd like to know."

"Your subconscious mind," Chris suggested. "You read the quotations in to-day's paper."

"No, I didn't; but last week I glanced over the column."

"A day or a year is all the same in the subconscious mind," said Mrs. Grantly. "The subconscious mind never forgets. But I am not saying that this is due to the subconscious mind. I refuse to state to what I think it is due."

"But how about that other stuff?" Uncle Robert demanded. "Sounds like what I'd think Christian Science ought to sound like."

"Or theosophy," Aunt Mildred volunteered. "Some message to a neophyte."

"Go on, read the rest," her husband commanded.

"'*This puts you in touch with the mightier spirits,*'" Lute read. "'*You shall become one with us, and your name will be* "*Arya,*" *and you will*——*Conqueror* 20, *Empire* 12, *Columbia Mountain* 18, *Midway* 140——' and that is all. Oh, no! here's a last flourish, '*Arya, from Kandor.*' That must surely be the Mahatma."

"I'd like to have you explain that theosophy stuff on the basis of the subconscious mind, Chris," Uncle Robert challenged.

Chris shrugged his shoulders. "No explanation. You must have got a message intended for some one else."

"Lines were crossed, eh?" Uncle Robert chuckled. "Multiplex spiritual wireless telegraphy, I'd call it."

"It *is* nonsense," Mrs. Grantly said. "I never knew Planchette to behave so outrageously. There are disturbing influences at work. I felt them from the first. Perhaps it is because you are all making too much fun of it. You are too hilarious."

"A certain befitting gravity should grace the occasion," Chris agreed, placing his hand on Planchette. "Let me try. And not one of you must laugh or giggle, or even think laugh or giggle. And if you dare to snort, even once, Uncle Robert, there is no telling what occult vengeance may be wreaked upon you."

"I'll be good," Uncle Robert rejoined. "But if I really must snort, may I silently slip away?"

Chris nodded. His hand had already begun to work. There had been no preliminary twitching nor tentative essays at writing. At once his hand had started off, and Planchette was moving swiftly and smoothly across the paper.

"Look at him," Lute whispered to her aunt. "See how white he is."

Chris betrayed disturbance at the sound of her voice, and thereafter silence was maintained. Only the steady scratching of the pencil could be heard. Suddenly, as though it had been stung, he jerked his hand away. With a sigh and a yawn he stepped back from the table, then glanced with the curiosity of a newly awakened man at their faces.

"I think I wrote something," he said.

"I should say you did," Mrs. Grantly

remarked with satisfaction, holding up the sheet of paper and glancing at it.

"Read it aloud," Uncle Robert said.

"Here it is, then. It begins with 'beware' written three times, in a bold hand. '*Beware! Beware! Beware! Chris Dunbar, I intend to destroy you. I have already made two attempts upon your life, and failed. I shall yet succeed. So sure am I that I shall succeed that I dare to tell you. I do not need to tell you why. In your own heart you know. The wrong you are doing——*' and here it abruptly ends."

Mrs. Grantly laid the paper down on the table and looked at Chris, who had already become the center of all eyes, and who was yawning as from an overpowering drowsiness.

"Quite a sanguinary turn, I should say," Uncle Robert remarked.

"'*I have already made two attempts upon your life,*'" Mrs. Grantly read from the paper, which she was going over a second time.

"On my life?" Chris demanded between yawns. "Why, my life hasn't been attempted even once. My! I am sleepy!"

"Ah, my boy, you are thinking of flesh-and-blood men," Uncle Robert laughed. "But this is a spirit. Your life has been attempted by unseen things. Most likely ghostly hands have tried to throttle you in your sleep."

"Oh, Chris!" Lute cried impulsively; "this afternoon! the hand you said must have seized your rein!"

"But I was joking," he objected.

"Nevertheless——" Lute left her thought unspoken.

Mrs. Grantly had become keen on the scent. "What was that about this afternoon? Was your life in danger?"

Chris's drowsiness had disappeared. "I'm becoming interested myself," he acknowledged. "We haven't said anything about it. Ban broke his back this afternoon. He threw himself off the bank, and I ran the risk of being caught underneath."

"I wonder, I wonder," Mrs. Grantly communed aloud. "There is something in this. It is a warning. Ah! You were hurt yesterday riding Miss Story's horse! That makes the two attempts!"

She looked triumphantly at them. Planchette had been vindicated.

"Nonsense," laughed Uncle Robert, but with a slight hint of irritation in his manner.

"Such things do not happen these days. This is the twentieth century, my dear madam. The thing, at the very latest, smacks of mediævalism."

"I have had such wonderful tests with Planchette," Mrs. Grantly began; then broke off suddenly to go to the table and place her hand on the board.

"Who are you?" she asked. "What is your name?"

The board immediately began to write. By this time all heads, with the exception of Mr. Barton's, were bent over the table and following the pencil.

"It's Dick," Aunt Mildred cried, a note of the mildly hysterical in her voice.

Her husband straightened up, his face for the first time grave.

"It's Dick's signature," he said. "I'd know his fist in a thousand."

"'*Dick Curtis,*'" Mrs. Grantly read aloud. "Who is Dick Curtis?"

"By Jove, that's remarkable!" Mr. Barton broke in. "The handwriting in both instances is the same. Clever, I should say, really clever," he added admiringly.

"Let me see," Uncle Robert demanded, taking the paper and examining it. "Yes, it is Dick's handwriting."

"But who is Dick?" Mrs. Grantly insisted. "Who is this Dick Curtis?"

"Dick Curtis, why, he was Captain Richard Curtis," Uncle Robert answered.

"He was Lute's father," Aunt Mildred supplemented. "Lute took our name. She never saw him; he died when she was a few weeks old. He was my brother."

"Remarkable, most remarkable." Mrs. Grantly was revolving the message in her mind. "There were two attempts on Mr. Dunbar's life. The subconscious mind cannot explain that, for none of us knew of the accident to-day."

"I knew," Chris answered, "and it was I that operated Planchette. The explanation is simple."

"But the handwriting," interposed Mr. Barton. "What you wrote and what Mrs. Grantly wrote are identical."

Chris bent over and compared the handwritings.

"Besides," Mrs. Grantly cried, "Mr. Story recognizes the handwriting."

She looked at him for verification.

He nodded his head. "Yes, it is Dick's fist, I'll swear to that."

But to Lute had come a visioning. While the rest argued pro and con, and the air was filled with phrases—"psychic phenomena," "self - hypnotism," "residuum of unexplained truth," and "spiritualism"—she was reviving mentally the girlhood pictures she had conjured of this soldier-father she had never seen. She possessed his sword, there were several old-fashioned daguerreotypes, there was much that had been said of him, stories told of him—and all this had constituted the material out of which she had builded him in her childhood fancy.

"There is the possibility of one mind unconsciously suggesting to another mind," Mrs. Grantly was saying; but through Lute's mind was trooping her father on his great roan war horse. Now he was leading his men. She saw him on lonely scouts, or in the midst of the yelling Indians at Salt Meadows, when of his command he returned with one man in ten. And in the picture she had of him, in the physical semblance she had made of him, was reflected his spiritual nature—reflected by her worshipful artistry in form and feature and expression—his bravery, his quick temper, his impulsive championship, his madness of wrath in a righteous cause, his warm generosity and swift forgiveness, and his chivalry that epitomized codes and ideals primitive as the days of knighthood. And first, last, and always, dominating all, she saw in the face of him the hot passion and quickness of deed that had earned for him the name, "Fighting Dick Curtis."

"Let me put it to the test," she heard Mrs. Grantly saying. "Let Miss Story try Planchette. There may be a further message."

"No, no, I beg of you," Aunt Mildred interposed. "It is too uncanny. It surely is wrong to tamper with the dead. Besides, I am nervous. Or, better, let me go to bed, leaving you to go on with your experiments. That will be the best way, and you can tell me in the morning." Mingled with the "good nights," were half-hearted protests from Mrs. Grantly, as Aunt Mildred withdrew.

"Robert can return," she called back, "as soon as he has seen me to my tent."

"It would be a shame to give it up now," Mrs. Grantly said. "There is no telling what we are on the verge of. Won't you try it, Miss Story?"

Lute obeyed, but when she placed her hand on the board she was conscious of a vague and nameless fear at this toying with the supernatural. She was twentieth century, and the thing in essence, as her uncle had said, was mediæval. Yet she could not shake off the instinctive fear that arose in her—man's inheritance from the wild and howling ages when his hairy, ape-like prototype was afraid of the dark, and personified the elements into things of fear.

Planchette

BY JACK LONDON

Illustrated by Charles M. Relyea

SYNOPSIS: Chris Dunbar and Lute Story are members of a camping party in the Sonoma Valley, California. The man is in love with the girl, but tells her that he cannot marry her. In spite of her questionings, he refuses to say why, simply repeating that he cannot explain. Chris meets with some extraordinary adventures. One day while he is riding Lute's gentle mare she suddenly bolts, and the young man has a narrow escape from injury. The next day his own horse throws itself backward off the path, down an embankment, and breaks its back. Chris is unhurt. Mrs. Grantly, a woman interested in psychic phenomena, comes to the camp as a visitor. She brings a Planchette board, which the company is eager to try. There is little success until Chris places his hand on it. Instantly comes a message warning him that he is to be killed, and telling him that two attempts have already been made upon his life. The latter statement Chris denies. The handwriting is recognized as that of Lute's father, an army officer, long since dead. To get a further message it is proposed that Lute try the board.

III

AS the mysterious influence seized Lute's hand and sent it writing across the paper, all the unusual passed out of the situation and she was unaware of more than a feeble curiosity. For she was intent on another vision—this time of her mother, who was also unremembered in the flesh—not sharp and vivid like that of her father, but dim and nebulous as the picture she shaped of her mother—a saint's head in an aureole of sweetness and good-ness and meekness, and, withal, shot through with a hint of reposeful determination of will, stubborn and unobtrusive, that in life had expressed itself mainly in resignation.

Lute's hand had ceased moving and Mrs. Grantly was already reading the message that had been written.

"It is a different handwriting," she said, "a woman's hand. 'Martha,' it is signed. Who is Martha?"

Lute was not surprised. "It s my mother," she said simply. "What does she say?"

She had not been made sleepy, as Chris had; but the keen edge of her vitality had

121

LUTE WAS OFF HER HORSE, SHE KNEW NOT HOW, AND TO THE EDGE

been blunted, and she was experiencing a sweet and pleasing lassitude. And while the message was being read, in her eyes persisted the vision of her mother.

"'*Dear child*,'" Mrs. Grantly read, "'*do not mind him. He was ever quick of speech and rash. Be no niggard with your love. Love cannot hurt you. To deny love is to sin. Obey your heart and you can do no wrong. Obey worldly considerations, obey pride, obey those that prompt you against your heart's prompting, and you do sin. Do not mind your father. He is angry now, as was his way to be in the earth-life; but he will come to see the wisdom of my counsel, for this, too, was his way in the earth-life. Love, my child, and love well.— Martha.*'"

"Let me see it," Lute cried, seizing the paper and devouring the handwriting with her eyes. She was thrilling with unexpressed love for the mother she had never seen, and this written speech from the grave seemed to give more tangibility to her having ever existed than did the vision of her.

"This *is* remarkable," Mrs. Grantly was reiterating. "There was never anything like it. Think of it, my dear, both your father and mother here with us to-night."

Lute shivered. The lassitude was gone, and she was her natural self again, vibrant with the instinctive fear of the things unseen. And it was offensive to her mind that, real or illusive, the presence or the memoried existence of her father and mother should be touched by these two people who were practically strangers—Mrs. Grantly, unhealthy and morbid, and Mr. Barton, stolid and stupid with a grossness both of the flesh and the spirit. And it further seemed a trespass that these strangers should thus enter into the intimacy between her and Chris.

She could hear the steps of her uncle approaching, and the situation flashed upon her, luminous and clear. She hurriedly folded the sheet of paper and thrust it into her bosom.

"Don't say anything to him about this second message, Mrs. Grantly, please, and Mr. Barton; nor to Aunt Mildred. It will only cause them irritation and needless anxiety."

In her mind there was also the desire to protect her lover, for she knew that the strain of his present standing with her aunt

and uncle would be added to, unconsciously in their minds, by the weird message of Planchette.

"And please don't let us have any more Planchette," Lute continued hastily. "Let us forget all the nonsense that has occurred."

"'Nonsense,' my dear child?" Mrs. Grantly was indignantly protesting when Uncle Robert strode into the circle.

"Hello!" he demanded; "what's being done?"

"Too late," Lute answered lightly. "No more stock quotations for you. Planchette is adjourned, and we're just winding up the discussion of the theory of it. Do you know how late it is?"

"Well, what did you do last night after we left?"

"Oh, took a stroll," Chris answered.

Lute's eyes were quizzical as she asked with a tentativeness that was palpably assumed, "With—a—with Mr. Barton?"

"Why, yes."

"And a smoke?"

"Yes; and now what's it all about?"

Lute broke into merry laughter. "Just as I told you that you would do. Am I not a prophet? But I knew before I saw you that my forecast had come true. I have just left Mr. Barton, and I knew he had walked with you last night, for he is vowing by all his fetiches and idols that you are a perfectly splendid young man. I could see it with my eyes shut. The Chris-Dunbar glamour has fallen upon him. But I have not finished the catechism, by any means. Where have you been all morning?"

"Where I am going to take you this afternoon."

"You plan well without knowing my wishes."

"I knew well what your wishes are. It is to see a horse I have found."

Her voice betrayed her delight as she cried, "Oh, good!"

"He is a beauty," Chris said.

But her face had suddenly gone grave, and apprehension brooded in her eyes.

"He's called 'Comanche,'" Chris went on. "A beauty, a regular beauty, the perfect type of the Californian cow-pony. And his lines—why, what's the matter?"

"Don't let us ride any more," Lute said, "at least for a while. Really, I think I am a tiny bit tired of it, too."

He was looking at her in astonishment, and she was bravely meeting his eyes.

"I see a hearse and flowers for you, and a funeral oration; I see the end of the world, and the stars falling out of the sky, and the heavens rolling up as a scroll; I see the living and the dead gathered together for the final judgment, the sheep and the goats, the lambs and the rams and all the rest of it, the white-robed saints, the sound of golden harps, and the lost souls howling as they fall into the pit—all this I see on the day that you, Lute Story, no longer care to ride a horse—a horse, Lute! a horse!"

"For a while, at least," she pleaded.

"Ridiculous!" he cried. "What's the matter? Aren't you well?—you who are always so abominably and adorably well?"

"No, it's not that," she answered. "I know it is ridiculous, Chris, I know it, but the doubt will arise. I cannot help it. You always say I am so sanely rooted to the earth and reality and all that, but—perhaps it's superstition, I don't know—but the whole occurrence, the messages of Planchette, the possibility of my father's hand, I know not how, reaching out to Ban's rein and hurling him and you to death, the correspondence between my father's statement that he has twice attempted your life and the fact that in the last two days your life has twice been endangered by horses—my father was a great horseman—all this, I say, causes the doubt to arise in my mind. What if there be something in it? I am not so sure. Science may be too dogmatic in its denial of the unseen. The forces of the unseen, of the spirit, may well be too subtle, too sublimated, for science to lay hold of and recognize and formulate. Don't you see, Chris, that there is rationality in the very doubt? It may be a very small doubt— oh, so small—but I love you too much to run even that slight risk. Besides, I am a woman, and that should in itself fully account for my predisposition toward superstition.

"Yes, yes, I know, call it unreality. But I've heard you paradoxing upon the reality of the unreal—the reality of delusion to the mind that is sick. And so with me, if you will, it is delusive and unreal; but to me, constituted as I am, it is very real—is real as a nightmare is real, before one awakes."

"The most logical argument for illogic I have ever heard," Chris smiled. "It is a good gaming proposition, at any rate. You manage to embrace more chances in your philosophy than I do in mine. It reminds me of Sam—the gardener you had a couple of years ago. I overheard him and Martin arguing in the stable. You know what a bigoted atheist Martin is. Well, Martin had deluged Sam with floods of logic. Sam pondered a while, and then he said, 'Foh a fack, Mis' Martin, you jis' tawk like a house afire; but you ain't got de show I has.' 'How's that?' Martin asked. 'Well, you see, Mis' Martin, you has one chance to mah two.' 'I don't see it,' Martin said. 'Mis' Martin, it's dis way. You has jis' de chance, lak you say, to become worms foh de fruitification of de cabbage garden. But I's got de chance to lif' mah voice to de glory of de Lawd as I go paddin' dem golden streets—along 'ith de chance to be jis' worms along 'ith you, Mis' Martin.' "

"You refuse to take me seriously," Lute said, when she had laughed her appreciation.

"How can I take that Planchette rigmarole seriously?" he asked.

"You don't explain it—the handwriting of my father which Uncle Robert recognized—oh, the whole thing, you don't explain it."

"I don't know all the mysteries of mind," Chris answered; "but I believe such phenomena will all yield themselves to scientific explanation in the not distant future."

"Just the same, I have a sneaking desire to find out some more from Planchette," Lute confessed. "The board is still down in the dining-room. We could try it now, you and I, and no one would know."

Chris caught her hand, crying, "Come on! It will be a lark."

Hand in hand they ran down the path to the tree-pillared room.

"The camp is deserted," Lute said, as she placed Planchette on the table. "Mrs. Grantly and Aunt Mildred are lying down, and Mr. Barton has gone off with Uncle Robert. There is nobody to disturb us." She placed her hand on the board. "Now begin."

For a few minutes nothing happened. Chris started to speak, but she hushed him to silence. The preliminary twitchings had appeared in her hand and arm. Then the pencil began to write. They read the message, word by word, as it was written:

"There is wisdom greater than the wisdom of reason. Love proceeds not out of the dry-as-dust way of the mind. Love is of the heart, and is beyond all reason, and logic, and philosophy. Trust your own heart, my daughter. And if your heart bids you have faith in your lover, then laugh at the mind and its cold wisdom, and obey your heart, and have faith in your lover.—Martha."

"But that whole message is the dictate of your own heart," Chris cried. "Don't you see, Lute? The thought is your very own, and your subconscious mind has expressed it there on the paper."

"But there is one thing I don't see," she objected.

"And that?"

"Is the handwriting. Look at it; it does not resemble mine at all. It is mincing, it is old-fashioned, it is the old-fashioned feminine of a generation ago."

"But you don't mean to tell me that you really believe that this is a message from the dead?" he interrupted.

"I don't know, Chris," she wavered; "I am sure I don't know."

"It is absurd!" he cried. "These are cobwebs of fancy. When one dies he is dead; he is dust. He goes to the worms, as Martin says. The dead? I laugh at the dead. They do not exist. They are not. I defy the powers of the grave, the men dead and dust and gone!"

"And what have you to say to that?" he challenged, placing his hand on Planchette.

On the instant his hand began to write. Both were startled by the suddenness of it. The message was brief:

"Beware! Beware! Beware!"

He was distinctly sobered, but he laughed. "It is like a miracle play. Death we have, speaking to us from the grave. But Good Deeds, where art thou? and Kindred? and Joy? and Household Goods? and Friendship? and all the goodly company?"

But Lute did not share his bravado. Her fright showed itself in her face as she laid her trembling hand on his arm.

"Oh, Chris, let us stop. I am sorry we began it. Let us leave the quiet dead to their rest. It is wrong, it must be wrong. I confess I am affected by it. I cannot help it. As my body is trembling, so is my soul. This speech of the grave, this dead man reaching out from the mold of a generation to protect me from you—there *is* reason in

it! There is the living mystery that prevents you from marrying me. Were my father alive he would protect me from you. Dead, he still strives to protect me. His hands, his ghostly hands, are against your life!"

"Do be calm," Chris said soothingly. "Listen to me. It is all a lark. We are playing with the subjective forces of our own being, with phenomena which science has not yet explained, that is all. Psychology is so young a science! The subconscious mind has just been discovered, one might say. It is all mystery as yet; the laws of it are yet to be formulated. This is simply unexplained phenomena. But that is no reason why we should immediately account for it by labeling it spiritualism. As yet we do not know, that is all. As for Planchette——"

He abruptly ceased, for at that moment, to enforce his remark, he had placed his hand on Planchette, and at that moment his hand had been seized, as by a paroxysm, and sent dashing, willy nilly, across the paper, writing as the hand of an angry person would write.

"No, I don't care for any more of it," Lute said, when the message was completed. "It is like witnessing a fight between you and my father in the flesh. There is in it the savor of struggle and blows."

She pointed out a sentence that read, *"You cannot escape me nor the just punishment that is yours."*

"Perhaps I visualize too vividly for my own comfort, for I can see his hands at your throat. I know that he is, as you say, dead and dust. But for all that I see him as a man that is alive and walks the earth; I see the anger in his face, the anger and the vengeance, and I see it all directed against you."

She crumpled up the sheets of paper, and put Planchette away.

"We won't bother with it any more," Chris said. "I didn't think it would affect you so strongly. But it's all subjective, I'm sure, with possibly a bit of suggestion thrown in—that and nothing more. And the whole strain of our situation has made conditions unusually favorable for striking phenomena."

"And about our situation," Lute said, as they went slowly up the path they had run down; "what we are to do, I don't know. Are we to go on, as we have gone on? What is best? Have you thought of anything?"

He debated for a few steps. "I have thought of telling your uncle and aunt."

"What you couldn't tell me?" she asked quickly.

"No," he answered slowly; "but just as much as I have told you. I have no right to tell them more than I have told you."

This time it was she that debated. "No, don't tell them," she said finally; "they wouldn't understand. I don't understand, for that matter, but I have faith in you, and in the nature of things they are not capable of the same implicit faith. You raise up before me a mystery that prevents our marriage, and I believe you; but they could not believe you without doubts arising as to the wrong and ill nature of the mystery. Besides, it would but make their anxieties greater."

"I should go away, I know I should go away," he said, half under his breath. "And I can. I am no weakling. Because I have failed to remain away once is no proof that I shall fail again."

She caught her breath with a quick gasp. "It is like a bereavement to hear you speak of going away and remaining away. I should never see you again. It is too terrible. And do not reproach yourself for weakness. It is I who am to blame. It is I who prevented you from remaining away before, I know. I wanted you so, I want you so.

"There is nothing to be done, Chris, nothing to be done but to go on with it and—and let it work itself out somehow. That is one thing we are sure of: it will work out somehow."

"But it would be easier if I went away," he suggested.

"I am happier when you are here."

"The cruelty of circumstance," he muttered savagely.

"Go or stay—that will be part of the working out. But I do not want you to go, Chris; you know that. And now no more about it. Talk cannot mend it. Let us never mention it again unless—unless some time, some wonderful happy time, you can come to me and say: 'Lute, all is well with me. The mystery no longer binds me. I am free.' Until that time let us bury it, along with Planchette and all the rest, and make the most of the little that is given us.

"And now, to show you how prepared I am to make the most of that little, I am even ready to go with you this afternoon to see the horse—though I wish you wouldn't ride any more, for a few days, anyway, or for a week. What did you say is his name?"

"Comanche," he answered. "I know you will like him."

Chris lay on his back, his head propped by the bare jutting wall of stone, his gaze attentively directed across the canyon to the opposing, tree-covered slope. There was a sound of crashing through underbrush, the ringing of steel-shod hoofs on stone, and an occasional and mossy descent of a dislodged bowlder that bounded from the hill and fetched up with a final splash in the torrent that rushed over a wild chaos of rocks beneath him. Now and again he caught glimpses, framed in green foliage, of the golden-brown of Lute's corduroy riding-habit and of the bay horse which moved beneath her.

She rode out into an open space where a loose earth-slide denied lodgment to trees and grass. She halted the horse at the brink of the slide, and glanced down it with a measuring eye. Forty feet beneath, the slide terminated in a small, firm-surfaced terrace, the banked accumulation of fallen earth and gravel.

"It's a good test," she called across the canyon. "I'm going to put him down it."

The animal gingerly launched himself on the treacherous footing, irregularly losing and gaining his hind feet, keeping his fore legs stiff, and steadily and calmly, without panic or nervousness, extricating the fore feet as fast as they sank too deeply into the sliding earth that surged along in a wave before him. When the firm footing at the bottom was reached, he strode out on the little terrace with a quickness and springiness of gait and with glintings of muscular fires that gave the lie to the calm deliberation of his movements on the slide.

"Bravo!" Chris shouted across the canyon, clapping his hands.

"The wisest-footed, clearest-headed horse I ever saw," Lute called back, as she turned the animal to the side and dropped down a broken slope of rubble into the trees again.

Chris followed her by the sound of her progress, and by occasional glimpses where the foliage was more open, as she zigzagged down the steep and trailless descent. She emerged below him at the rugged rim of the torrent, dropped the horse down a three-foot wall, and halted to study the crossing.

Four feet out in the stream, a narrow ledge thrust above the surface of the water. Beyond the ledge boiled an angry pool. But to the left from the ledge, and several feet lower, was a tiny bed of gravel. A giant bowlder prevented direct access to the gravel bed. The only way to gain it was by first leaping to the ledge of rock. She studied it carefully, and the tightening of her bridle arm advertised that she had made up her mind.

Chris, in his anxiety, had sat up to observe more closely what she meditated.

"Don't tackle it," he called.

"I have faith in Comanche," she replied.

"He can't make that side jump to the gravel," Chris warned. "He'll never keep his legs; he'll topple over into the pool. Only one horse in a thousand could do that stunt."

"And Comanche is that very horse," she called back. "Watch him."

She gave the animal his own head, and he leaped cleanly and accurately to the ledge, striking with feet close together on the narrow space. On the instant he struck, Lute lightly touched his neck with the rein, impelling him to the left; and in that instant, tottering on the insecure footing, with front feet slipping over into the pool beyond, he lifted on his hind legs, with a half turn, sprang to the left, and dropped squarely down to the tiny gravel bed. An easy jump brought him across the stream, and Lute angled him up the bank and halted before her lover.

"Well?" she asked.

"I am all tense," Chris answered. "I was holding my breath."

"Buy him by all means," Lute said, dismounting. "He is a bargain. I could dare anything on him. I never in my life had such confidence in a horse's feet."

"His owner says that he has never been known to lose his feet, that it is impossible to get him down."

"Buy him, buy him at once," she counseled, "before the man changes his mind. If you don't, I shall. Oh, such feet! I feel such confidence in them that when I am on him I don't consider he has feet at all. And he's quick as a cat, and instantly obe-

dient. Bridle-wise is no name for it! You could guide him with silken threads. Oh, I know I'm enthusiastic, but if you don't buy him, Chris, I shall. Remember, I've second refusal."

Chris smiled agreement as he changed the saddles. Meanwhile she compared the two horses.

"Of course he doesn't match Dolly the way Ban did," she concluded regretfully; "but his coat is splendid just the same. And think of the horse that is under the coat."

Chris gave her a hand into the saddle, and followed her up the slope to the county road. She reined in suddenly, saying,

"We won't go straight back to camp."

"You forget dinner," he warned.

"But I remember Comanche," she retorted. "We'll ride directly over to the ranch and buy him. Dinner will keep."

"But the cook won't," Chris laughed. "She's already threatened to leave, what of our late-comings."

"Even so," was the answer. "Aunt Mildred may have to get another cook, but at any rate we shall have got Comanche."

They turned the horses in the other direction, and took the climb of the Nun Canyon road that led over the divide and down into the Napa Valley. But the climb was hard, the going was slow. Sometimes they topped the bed of the torrent by hundreds of feet, and again they dipped down and crossed and recrossed it twenty times in twice as many rods. They rode through the deep shade of clean-trunked maples and towering redwoods, to emerge on open stretches of mountain shoulder where the earth lay dry and cracked under the sun.

On one such shoulder they emerged, where the road stretched level before them for a quarter of a mile. On one side rose the huge bulk of the mountain. On the other side the steep wall of the canyon fell away in impossible slopes and sheer drops to the torrent at the bottom. It was an abyss of green beauty and shady depths, pierced by vagrant shafts of the sun and mottled here and there by the sun's broader blazes. The sound of rushing water ascended on the windless air, and there was a hum of mountain bees.

The horses broke into an easy lope. Chris rode on the outside, looking down into the great depths and pleasuring with his eyes in what he saw. Disassociating itself from the murmur of the bees, a murmur arose of falling water. It grew louder with every stride of the horses.

"Look!" he cried.

Lute leaned well out from her horse to see. Beneath them the water slid foaming down a smooth-faced rock to the lip, whence it leaped clear—a pulsating ribbon of white, a-breath with movement, ever falling and ever remaining, changing its substance but never its form, an aërial waterway as immaterial as gauze and as permanent as the hills, that spanned space and the free air from the lip of the rock to the tops of the trees far below, into whose green screen it disappeared to fall into a secret and unseen pool.

They had flashed past. The descending water became a distant murmur that merged again into the murmur of the bees and ceased. Swayed by a common impulse, they looked at each other.

"Oh, Chris, it is good to be alive—and to have you here by my side!"

He answered her by the warm light in his eyes.

All things tended to key them to an exquisite pitch—the movement of their bodies, at one with the moving bodies of the animals beneath them; the gently stimulated blood, caressing the flesh through and through with the soft vigors of health; the warm air fanning their faces, flowing over the skin with balmy and tonic touch, permeating them and bathing them subtly, with faint, sensuous delight; and the beauty of the world, more subtly still, flowing upon them and bathing them in the delight that is of the spirit and is personal and holy, that is inexpressible, yet communicable by the flash of an eye and the dissolving of the veils of the soul.

So looked they at each other, the horses bounding beneath them, the spring of the world and the spring of their youth astir in their blood, the secret of being trembling in their eyes to the brink of disclosure, as if about to dispel, with one magic word, all the unrealities and riddles of existence.

The road curved before them, so that the upper reaches of the canyon could be seen, the distant bed of it towering high above their heads. They were rounding the curve, leaning toward the inside, gazing before them at the swift-growing picture. There was no sound of warning. Lute heard nothing, but even before the horse went down, she experienced a feeling that

the unison of the two leaping animals was broken. She turned her head, and so quickly that she saw Comanche fall. It was not a stumble nor a trip. He fell as though abruptly, in mid-leap, he had died or been struck a stunning blow.

And in that moment she remembered Planchette; it seared her brain as a lightning flash of all-embracing memory. Her horse was back on its haunches, the weight of her body on the reins; but her head was turned and her eyes were on the falling Comanche. He struck the roadbed squarely, with his legs loose and lifeless beneath him.

It all occurred in one of those age-long seconds that embrace an eternity of happening. There was a slight but perceptible rebound from the impact of Comanche's body with the earth. The violence with which he struck forced the air from his great lungs in an audible groan. His momentum swept him onward and over the edge The weight of the rider on his neck turned him over head first as he pitched to the fall.

Lute was off her horse, she knew not how, and to the edge. Her lover was out of the saddle and clear of Comanche, though held to the animal by his right foot, which was caught in the stirrup. The slope was too steep for them to come to a stop. Earth and small stones, dislodged by their struggles, were rolling down with them and before them in a miniature avalanche. She stood very quietly, holding one hand against her breast and gazing down. But while she saw the real happening, in her eyes was also the vision of her father dealing the spectral blow that had smashed Comanche down in mid-leap and sent horse and rider hurtling over the edge.

Beneath horse and man the steep terminated in an up-and-down wall, from the base of which, in turn, a second slope ran down to a second wall. A third slope terminated in a final wall that based itself on the canyon bed four hundred feet beneath the point where the girl stood and watched. She could see Chris vainly kicking his leg to free the foot from the trap of the stirrup. Comanche fetched up hard against an outjetting point of rock. For a fraction of a second his fall was stopped, and in that slight interval the man managed to grip hold of a young shoot of manzanita. Lute saw him complete the grip with his other hand. Then Comanche's fall began again. She saw the stirrup strap draw taut, then her lover's body and arms. The manzanita shoot yielded its roots, and horse and man plunged over the edge and out of sight.

They came into view on the next slope, together and rolling over and over, with sometimes the man under and sometimes the horse. Chris no longer struggled, and together they dashed over to the third slope. Near the edge of the final wall, Comanche lodged on a hummock of stone. He lay quietly, and near him, still attached to him by the stirrup, face downward, lay his rider.

"If only he will lie quietly," Lute breathed aloud, her mind at work on the means of rescue.

But she saw Comanche begin to struggle again and, clear on her vision, it seemed, was the spectral arm of her father clutching the reins and dragging the animal over. Comanche floundered across the hummock, the inert body following, and together,

horse and man, they plunged from sight. They did not appear again; they had fetched bottom.

Lute looked about her. She stood alone on the world—her lover was gone. There was naught to show of his existence, save the marks of Comanche's hoofs on the road and of his body where it had slid over the brink.

"Chris!" she called once, and twice; but she called hopelessly.

Out of the depths, on the windless air, arose only the murmur of bees and of running water.

"Chris!" she called yet a third time, and sank slowly down in the dust of the road.

She felt the touch of Dolly's muzzle on her arm, and she leaned her head against the mare's neck and waited. She knew not why she waited, nor for what, only there seemed nothing else but waiting left for her to do.

(The End.)

11
THE UNEXPECTED

THE UNEXPECTED*

BY

JACK LONDON

AUTHOR OF ''THE GOD OF HIS FATHERS,'' ''LOVE OF LIFE,'' ETC.

ILLUSTRATED BY E. L. BLUMENSCHEIN

IT is a simple matter to see the obvious, to do the expected. The tendency of the individual life is to be static rather than dynamic, and this tendency is made into a propulsion by civilization, where the obvious only is seen, and the unexpected rarely happens. When the unexpected does happen, however, and when it is of sufficiently grave import, the unfit perish. They do not see what is not obvious, are unable to do the unexpected, are incapable of adjusting their well-grooved lives to other and strange grooves. In short, when they come to the end of their own groove, they die.

On the other hand, there are those who make toward survival, the fit individuals who escape from the rule of the obvious and the expected and adjust their lives to no matter what strange grooves they may stray into or into which they may be forced. Such an individual was Edith Whittlesey. She was born in a rural district of England, where life proceeds by rule of thumb and the unexpected is so very unexpected that when it happens it is looked upon almost as an immorality. She went into service early, and while yet a young woman, by rule-of-thumb progression, she became a lady's maid.

The effect of civilization is to impose human law upon environment until it becomes machine-like in its regularity. The objectionable is eliminated, the inevitable is foreseen. One is not made wet by the rain nor cold by the frost, while death, instead of stalking about gruesome and accidental, becomes a prearranged pageant, moving along a well-oiled groove to the family vault, where the hinges are kept from rusting and the dust from the air is swept continually away.

Such was the environment of Edith Whittlesey. Nothing happened. It could scarcely be called a happening, when, at the age of twenty-five, she accompanied her mistress on a bit of travel to the United States. The groove merely changed its direction. It was

* Mr. London's story is a real human document, based upon actual incidents. Michael Dennin was hanged at Latuya Bay by Mrs. Nelson in 1900.

"SHE CAUGHT HIM BY THE ARM, BUT HER CLINGING TO IT
MERELY IMPEDED HIS EFFORT"

still the same groove and well-oiled. It was a groove that bridged the Atlantic with un-eventfulness, so that the ship was no longer a ship in the midst of the sea, but a capacious many-corridored hotel that moved swiftly and placidly, crushing the waves into submission with its colossal bulk until the sea was as a mill-pond, monotonous with quietude. And at the other side, the groove continued on over the land — a well-disposed, respectable groove that supplied hotels at every stopping-place, and hotels on wheels between the stopping-places.

In Chicago, while her mistress saw one side of social life, Edith Whittlesey saw another side; and when she left her lady's service and became Edith Nelson, she betrayed, perhaps faintly, her ability to grapple with the unexpected and to master it. Hans Nelson, immigrant, Swede by birth and carpenter by occupation, had in him that Teutonic unrest which drives the race ever westward on its great adventure. He was a large-muscled, stolid sort of a man, in whom little imagination was coupled with immense initiative, and who possessed, withal, loyalty and affection as sturdy as his own strength.

"When I have worked hard and saved me some money, I will go to Colorado," he had told Edith on the day after their wedding. A year later they were in Colorado, where Hans Nelson saw his first mining and caught the mining-fever himself. His prospecting led him through the Dakotas, Idaho, and Eastern Oregon, and on into the mountains of British Columbia. In camp and on trail, Edith Nelson was always with him, sharing his luck, his hardship, and his toil. The short step of the house-reared woman she exchanged for the long stride of the mountaineer. She learned to look upon danger clear-eyed and with understanding, losing forever that panic fear which is bred of ignorance and which afflicts the city-reared, making them as silly as silly horses, so that they await fate in frozen horror instead of grappling with it, or stampede in blind self-destroying terror that clutters the way with their crushed carcasses.

Edith Nelson met the unexpected at every turn of the trail, and she trained her vision so that she saw in the landscape, not the obvious, but the concealed. She, who had never cooked in her life, learned to make bread without the mediation of hops, yeast, or baking-powder, and to bake bread, top and bottom, in a frying-pan before an open fire.

And when the last cup of flour was gone and the last rind of bacon, she was able to rise to the occasion, and of moccasins and the softer-tanned bits of leather in the outfit, to make a grub-substitute that somehow held a man's soul in his body and enabled him to stagger on. She learned to pack a horse as well as a man — a task to break the heart and the pride of any city-dweller — and she knew how to throw the hitch best suited for any particular kind of pack. Also, she could build a fire of wet wood in a downpour of rain and not lose her temper. In short, in all its guises, she mastered the unexpected. But the Great Unexpected was yet to come into her life and put its test upon her.

The gold-seeking tide was flooding northward into Alaska, and it was inevitable that Hans Nelson and his wife should be caught up by the stream and swept toward the Klondike. The fall of 1897 found them at Skaguay, but without the money to carry an outfit across Chilcoot Pass and float it down to Dawson. So Hans Nelson worked at his trade that winter and helped rear the mushroom outfitting-town of Skaguay.

He was on the edge of things, and throughout the winter he heard all Alaska calling to him. Latuya Bay called loudest, so that the summer of 1898 found him and his wife threading the mazes of the broken coast-line in seventy-foot Siwash canoes. With them were Indians, also three other men. The Indians landed them and their supplies n a lonely bight of land a hundred miles or so beyond Latuya Bay, and returned to Skaguay; but the three other men remained, for they were members of the organized party. Each had put in an equal share of capital into the outfitting, and the profits were to be divided equally. In that Edith Nelson undertook to cook for the outfit, a man's share was to be her portion.

First, spruce trees were cut down and a three-room cabin constructed. To keep this cabin was Edith Nelson's task. The task of the men was to search for gold, which they did; and to find gold, which they likewise did. It was not a startling find, merely a low-pay placer, where long hours of severe toil earned each man between fifteen and twenty dollars a day. The brief Alaskan summer protracted itself beyond its usual length, and they took advantage of the opportunity, delaying their return to Skaguay to the last moment. And then it was too late. Arrangements had been made to accompany the

"THE SLED SANK DEEP INTO THE DRIFTED SNOW AND PULLED HARD"

several dozen local Indians on their fall trading trip down the coast. The Siwashes had waited on the white people until the eleventh hour, and then departed. There was no course left the party but to wait for chance transportation. In the meantime the claim was cleaned up and firewood stocked in.

The Indian summer had dreamed on and on, and then, suddenly, with the sharpness of bugles, winter came. It came in a single night, and the miners awoke to howling wind, driving snow, and freezing water. Storm followed storm, and between the storms there was the silence, broken only by the boom of the surf on the desolate shore, where the salt spray rimmed the beach with frozen white.

All went well in the cabin. Their gold dust had weighed up something like eight thousand dollars, and they could not but be contented The men made snow-shoes, hunted fresh meat for the larder, and in the long evenings played endless games of whist and pedro. Now that the mining had ceased, Edith Nelson turned over the fire-building and the dish-washing to the men, while she darned their socks and mended their clothes.

There was no grumbling, no bickering nor petty quarreling in the little cabin, and they often congratulated one another on the general happiness of the party. Hans Nelson was stolid and easy-going, while Edith had long before won his unbounded admiration by her capacity for getting on with people. Harkey, a long, lank Texan, was unusually friendly for one with a saturnine disposition, and, so long as his theory that gold grew was not challenged, was quite companionable. The fourth member of the party, Michael Dennin, contributed his Irish wit to the gaiety of the cabin. He was a large, powerful man, prone to sudden rushes of anger over little things, and of unfailing good-humor under the stress and strain of big things. The fifth and last member, Dutchy, was the willing butt of the party. He even went out of his way to raise a laugh at his own expense in order to keep things cheerful. His deliberate aim in life seemed to be that of a maker of laughter. No serious quarrel had ever vexed the serenity of the party ; and, now that each had sixteen hundred dollars to show for a short summer's work, there reigned the well-fed, contented spirit of prosperity.

And then the unexpected happened. They had just sat down to the breakfast-table. Though it was already eight o'clock (late breakfasts had followed naturally upon cessation of the steady work at mining), a candle in the neck of a bottle lighted the meal. Edith and Hans sat at the ends of the table. On one side, with their backs to the door, were Harkey and Dutchy. The place on the other side was vacant. Dennin had not yet come in.

Hans Nelson looked at the empty chair, shook his head slowly, and, with a ponderous attempt at humor, said : "Always is he first at the grub. It is very strange. Maybe he is sick."

"Where is Michael?" Edith asked.

"Got up a little ahead of us and went outside," Harkey answered.

Dutchy's face beamed mischievously. He pretended knowledge of Dennin's absence, and affected a mysterious air, while they clamored for information. Edith, after a peep into the men's bunk-room, returned to the table. Hans looked at her and she shook her head.

"He was never late at meal-time before," she answered.

"I cannot understand," said Hans. "Always has he the great appetite like the horse."

"It is too bad," Dutchy said, with a sad shake of his head.

They were beginning to make merry over their comrade's absence.

"It is a great pity !" Dutchy volunteered.

"What ?" they demanded in chorus.

"Poor Michael," was the mournful reply.

"Well, what's wrong with Michael?" Harkey asked.

"He is not hungry no more," wailed Dutchy. "He has lost der appetite. He do not like der grub."

"Not from the way he pitches into it up to his ears," remarked Harkey.

"He does dot shust to be politeful to Mrs. Nelson," was Dutchy's quick retort. "I know, I know, and it is too pad. Why is he not here ? Pecause he haf gone out. Why haf he gone out ? For der defelopment of der appetite. How does he defelop der appetite? He walks barefoots in der snow. Ach ! don't I know ? It is der way der rich peoples chases after der appetite when it is no more and is running away. Michael haf sixteen hundred dollars. He is rich peoples. He haf no appetite. Derefore, pecause, he is chasing der appetite. Shust you open der door und you will see his barefoots in der snow. No, you will not see der appetite. Dot is

shust his trouble. When he sees der appetite, he will catch it und come to preak-
fast."

They burst into loud laughter at Dutchy's
nonsense. The sound had scarcely died
away when the door opened and Dennin came
in. All turned to look at him. He was
carrying a shot-gun. Even as they looked,
he lifted it to his shoulder and fired twice.
At the first shot Dutchy sank upon the table,
overturning his mug of coffee, his yellow mop
of hair dabbling in his plate of mush. His
forehead, which pressed upon the near edge
of the plate, tilted the plate up against his
hair at an angle of forty-five degrees. Harkey was in the air, in his spring to his feet, at
the second shot, and he pitched face-down
upon the floor, his "My God!" gurgling and
dying in his throat.

It was The Unexpected. Hans and Edith
were stunned. They sat at the table, their
bodies tense, their eyes fixed in a fascinated gaze upon the murderer. Dimly they
saw him through the smoke of the powder,
and in the silence nothing was to be heard
save the drip-drip of Dutchy's spilled coffee
on the floor. Dennin threw open the breech
of the shot-gun, ejecting the empty shells.
Holding the gun with one hand, he reached
with the other into his pocket for fresh shells.

He was thrusting the shells into the gun
when Edith Nelson was aroused to action. It
was patent that he intended to kill Hans and
her. For a space of possibly three seconds
of time she had been dazed and paralyzed
by the horrible and inconceivable form in
which the unexpected had made its appearance. Then she rose to it and grappled with
it. She grappled with it concretely, making
a cat-like leap for the murderer, and gripping
his neck-cloth with both her hands. The
impact of her body sent him stumbling backward several steps. He tried to shake her
loose and at the same time retain his hold on
the gun. This was awkward, for her firm-
fleshed body had become a cat's. She threw
herself to one side, and with her grip at his
throat nearly jerked him to the floor. He
straightened himself and whirled swiftly.
Still faithful to her hold, her body followed
the circle of his whirl so that her feet left
the floor, and she swung through the air
fastened to his throat by her hands. The
whirl culminated in a collision with a chair,
and the man and woman crashed to the floor
in a wild, struggling fall that extended itself
across half the length of the room.

Hans Nelson was half a second behind his
wife in rising to the unexpected. His nerve
processes and mental processes were slower
than hers. His was the grosser organism,
and it had taken him half a second longer
to perceive, and determine, and proceed to
do. She had already flown at Dennin and
gripped his throat, when Hans sprang to his
feet. He was in a blind fury, a Berserker
rage. At the instant he sprang from his
chair his mouth opened, and there issued
forth a sound that was half-roar, half-bellow.
The whirl of the two bodies had already
started, and still roaring, or bellowing, he
pursued this whirl down the room, overtaking it when it fell to the floor.

Hans hurled himself upon the prostrate
man, striking madly with his fists. They
were sledge-like blows, and when Edith felt
Dennin's body relax she loosed her grip and
rolled clear. She lay on the floor, panting
and watching. The fury of the blows continued to rain down. Dennin did not seem
to mind the blows. He did not even move.
Then it dawned upon her that he was unconscious. She cried out to Hans to stop. She
cried out again. But he paid no heed to her
voice. She caught him by the arm, but her
clinging to it merely impeded his effort.

It was no reasoned impulse that stirred her
to do what she then did. Nor was it a sense of
pity, nor obedience to the "Thou shalt not"
of religion. Rather was it some sense of law,
an ethic of her race and early environment,
that compelled her to interpose her body between her husband and the helpless murderer. It was not until Hans knew he was striking his wife that he ceased. He allowed himself to be shoved away by her, in much the
same way that a ferocious but obedient dog
allows itself to be shoved away by its master.
The analogy even went farther. Deep in his
throat, in an animal-like way, Hans's rage
still rumbled, and several times he made as
though to spring back upon his prey and was
only prevented by the woman's swiftly interposed body.

Back and farther back Edith shoved her
husband. She had never seen him in such a
condition, and she was more frightened of
him than she had been of Dennin in the thick
of the struggle. She could not believe that
this raging beast was her Hans, and with a
shock she became suddenly aware of a shrinking instinctive fear that he might snap her
hand in his teeth like any wild animal. For
some seconds, unwilling to hurt her, yet

"RAGING AND STRAINING AT THE RAWHIDE THAT BOUND HIM, AND
THREATENING HER WITH WHAT HE WOULD DO WHEN HE GOT LOOSE"

dogged in his desire to return to the attack, Hans dodged back and forth. But she resolutely dodged with him, until the first glimmerings of reason returned and he gave over.

Both crawled to their feet. Hans staggered back against the wall, where he leaned, his face working, in his throat the deep and continuous rumble that died away with the seconds and at last ceased. The time for the reaction had come. Edith stood in the middle of the floor, wringing her hands, panting and gasping, her whole body trembling violently.

Hans looked at nothing, but Edith's eyes wandered wildly from detail to detail of what had taken place. Dennin lay without movement. The overturned chair, hurled onward in the mad whirl, lay near him. Partly under him lay the shot-gun, still broken open at the breech. Spilling out of his right hand were the two cartridges which he had failed to put into the gun and which he had clutched until consciousness left him. Harkey lay on the floor, face downward, where he had fallen; while Dutchy rested forward on the table, his yellow mop of hair buried in his mush-plate, the plate itself still tilted at an angle of forty-five degrees. This tilted plate fascinated her. Why did it not fall down? It was ridiculous. It was not in the nature of things for a mush-plate to up-end itself on the table even if a man or so had been killed.

She glanced back at Dennin, but her eyes returned to the tilted plate. It was so ridiculous! She felt an hysterical impulse to laugh. Then she noticed the silence, and forgot the plate in a desire for something to happen. The monotonous drip of the coffee from the table to the floor merely emphasized the silence. Why did not Hans do something? say something? She looked at him and was about to speak, when she discovered that her tongue refused its wonted duty. There was a peculiar ache in her throat, and her mouth was dry and furry. She could only look at Hans, who, in turn, looked at her.

Suddenly the silence was broken by a sharp, metallic clang. She screamed, jerking her eyes back to the table. The plate had fallen down. Hans sighed as though awakening from sleep. The clang of the plate had aroused them to life in a new world. The cabin epitomized the new world in which they must thenceforth live and move. The old cabin was gone forever. The horizon of life was totally new and unfamiliar. The unexpected had swept its wizardry over the face of things, changing the perspective, juggling values, and shuffling the real and the unreal into perplexing confusion.

"My God, Hans!" was Edith's first speech.

He did not answer, but stared at her with horror. Slowly his eyes wandered over the room, for the first time taking in its details. Then he put on his cap and started for the door.

"Where are you going?" Edith demanded, in an agony of apprehension.

His hand was on the door-knob, and he half-turned as he answered, "To dig some graves."

"Don't leave me, Hans, with — " her eyes swept the room, "— with this."

"The graves must be dug some time," he said.

"But you do not know how many," she objected desperately. She noted his indecision, and added, "Besides, I'll go with you and help."

Hans stepped back to the table, and mechanically snuffed the candle. Then between them they made the examination. Both Harkey and Dutchy were dead — frightfully dead, because of the close range of the shot-gun. Hans refused to go near Dennin, and Edith was forced to conduct this portion of the investigation by herself.

"He isn't dead," she called to Hans.

He walked over and looked down at the murderer.

"What did you say?" Edith demanded, having caught the rumble of inarticulate speech in her husband's throat.

"I said it was a damn shame that he isn't dead," came the reply.

Edith was bending over the body.

"Leave him alone," Hans commanded harshly, in a strange voice.

She looked at him in sudden alarm. He had picked up the shot-gun dropped by Dennin and was thrusting in the shells.

"What are you going to do?" she cried, rising swiftly from her bending position.

Hans did not answer, but she saw the shot-gun going to his shoulder. She grasped the muzzle with her hand and threw it up.

"Leave me alone!" he cried hoarsely.

He tried to jerk the weapon away from her, but she came in closer and clung to him.

"Hans! Hans! Wake up!" she cried. "Don't be crazy!"

"SHE READ FROM THE NEW TESTAMENT"

"He killed Dutchy and Harkey !" was her husband's reply; "and I am going to kill him."

"But that is wrong," she objected. "There is the law."

He sneered his incredulity of the law's potency in such a region, but he merely iterated, dispassionately, doggedly: "He killed Dutchy and Harkey."

Long she argued with him, but the argument was one-sided, for he contented himself with repeating again and again: "He killed Dutchy and Harkey." But she could not escape from her childhood training, nor from the blood that was in her. The heritage of law was hers, and right conduct, to her, was the fulfilment of the law. She could see no other righteous course to pursue. Hans's taking the law in his own hand was no more justifiable than Dennin's deed. Two wrongs did not make a right, she contended, and there was only one way to punish Dennin, and that was the legal way arranged by society. At last Hans gave in to her.

"All right," he said. "Have it your own way. And to-morrow or next day look to see him kill you and me."

She shook her head, and held out her hand for the shot-gun. He started to hand it to her, then hesitated.

"Better let me shoot him," he pleaded.

Again she shook her head, and again he started to pass her the gun, when the door opened, and an Indian, without knocking, came in. A blast of wind and flurry of snow came in with him. They turned and faced him, Hans still holding the shot-gun. The intruder took in the scene without a quiver. His eyes embraced the dead and wounded in a sweeping glance. No surprise showed in his face, not even curiosity. Harkey lay at his feet, but he took no notice of him. So far as he was concerned, Harkey's body did not exist.

"Much wind," the Indian remarked by way of salutation. "All well? Very well?"

Hans, still grasping the gun, felt sure that the Indian attributed to him the mangled corpses. He glanced appealingly at his wife.

"Good-morning, Negook," she said, her voice betraying her effort. "No, not very well. Much trouble."

"Good-by, I go now, much hurry," the Indian said, and without semblance of haste, with great deliberation stepping clear of a red pool on the floor, he opened the door and went out.

The man and the woman looked at each other.

"He thinks we did it," Hans gasped, "that I did it."

Edith was silent for a space. Then she said, briefly, in a businesslike way:

"Never mind what he thinks. That will come after. At present we have two graves to dig. But, first of all, we've got to tie up Dennin so he can't escape."

Hans refused to touch Dennin, but Edith lashed him securely, hand and foot. Then she and Hans went out into the snow. The ground was frozen. It was impervious to a blow of the pick. They first gathered wood, then scraped the snow away, and on the frozen surface built a fire. When the fire had burned for an hour, several inches of dirt had thawed. This they shoveled out, and then built a fresh fire. Their descent into earth progressed at the rate of two or three inches an hour.

It was hard and bitter work. The flurrying snow did not permit the fire to burn any too well, while the wind cut through their clothes and chilled their bodies. They held but little conversation. The wind interfered with speech. Beyond wondering at what could have been Dennin's motive, they remained silent, oppressed by the horror of the tragedy. At one o'clock, looking toward the cabin, Hans announced that he was hungry.

"No, not now, Hans," Edith answered. "I couldn't go back alone into that cabin the way it is, and cook a meal."

At two o'clock Hans volunteered to go with her; but she held him to his work, and four o'clock found the two graves completed. They were shallow, not more than two feet deep, but they would serve the purpose. Night had fallen. Hans got the sled, and the two dead men were dragged through the darkness and storm to their frozen sepulcher. The funeral procession was anything but a pageant. The sled sank deep into the drifted snow and pulled hard. The man and woman had eaten nothing since the previous day and were weak from hunger and exhaustion. They had not the strength to resist the wind, and at times its buffets hurled them off their feet. On several occasions the sled was overturned, and they were compelled to reload it with its somber freight. The last hundred feet to the graves was up a steep slope, and this they took on all-fours, like sled-dogs, making legs of theirs arms and thrusting their hands into the snow. Even so, they were twice dragged backward by the weight of the sled, and slid and fell down the hill, the living and the dead, the haul-ropes and the sled, in ghastly entanglement.

"To-morrow I will put up head-boards with their names," Hans said, when the graves were filled in.

Edith was sobbing. A few broken sentences had been all she was capable of in the way of a funeral service, and now her husband was compelled to half-carry her back to the cabin.

Dennin was conscious. He had rolled over and over on the floor in vain efforts to free himself. He watched Hans and Edith with glittering eyes, but made no attempt to speak. Hans still refused to touch the murderer, and sullenly watched Edith drag him across the floor to the men's bunk-room. But try as she would, she could not lift him from the floor into his bunk.

"Better let me shoot him, and we'll have no more trouble," Hans said in final appeal.

Edith shook her head and bent again to her task. To her surprise the body rose easily, and she knew Hans had relented and was helping her. Then came the cleansing of the kitchen. But the floor still shrieked the tragedy, until Hans planed the surface of the stained wood away, and with the shavings made a fire in the stove.

The days came and went. There was much of darkness and silence, broken only by the storms and the thunder on the beach of the freezing surf. Hans was obedient to Edith's slightest order. All his splendid initiative had vanished. She had elected to deal with Dennin in her way, and so he left the whole matter in her hands.

The murderer was a constant menace. At all times there was the chance that he might free himself from his bonds, and they were compelled to guard him day and night. The man or the woman sat always beside him, holding the loaded shot-gun. At first, Edith tried eight-hour watches, but the continuous strain was too great, and afterwards she and Hans relieved each other every four hours. As they had to sleep, and as the watches extended through the night, their whole waking time was expended in guarding Dennin. They had barely time left over for the preparation of meals and the getting of fire-wood.

Since Negook's inopportune visit, the Indians had avoided the cabin. Edith sent

Hans to their cabins to get them to take Dennin down the coast in a canoe to the nearest white settlement or trading post, but the errand was fruitless. Then Edith went herself and interviewed Negook. He was head man of the little village, keenly aware of his responsibility, and he elucidated his policy thoroughly, in few words.

"It is white man's trouble," he said, "not Siwash trouble. My people help you, then will it be Siwash trouble, too. When white-man's trouble and Siwash trouble come together and make a trouble, it is a great trouble, beyond understanding and without end. Trouble no good. My people do no wrong. What for they help you and have trouble?"

So Edith Nelson went back to the terrible cabin with its endless alternating four-hour watches. Sometimes, when it was her turn and she sat by the prisoner, the loaded shotgun in her lap, her eyes would close and she would doze. Always she aroused with a start, snatching up the gun and swiftly looking at him. These were distinct nervous shocks, and their effect was not good on her. Such was her fear of the man, that even if she were wide awake, if he moved under the bed-clothes she could not repress the start and the quick reach for the gun.

She was preparing herself for a nervous breakdown, and she knew it. First came a fluttering of the eyeballs, so that she was compelled to close her eyes for relief. A little later the eyelids were afflicted by a nervous twitching that she could not control. To add to the strain, she could not forget the tragedy. She remained as close to the horror as on the first morning when the unexpected stalked into the cabin and took possession. In her daily ministrations upon the prisoner she was forced to grit her teeth and steel herself, body and spirit.

Hans was affected differently. He became obsessed by the idea that it was his duty to kill Dennin; and whenever he waited upon the bound man or watched by him, Edith was troubled by the fear that Hans would add another red entry to the cabin's record. Always he cursed Dennin savagely and handled him roughly. Hans tried to conceal his homicidal mania, and he would say to his wife, "By and by you will want me to kill him, and then I will not kill him. It would make me sick." But more than once, stealing into the room when it was her watch off, she would catch the two men glaring ferociously at each other, wild animals the pair of them, in Hans's face the lust to kill, in Dennin's the fierceness and savagery of the cornered rat. "Hans!" she would cry, "Wake up!" and he would come to a recollection of himself, startled and shamefaced and unrepentant.

So Hans became another factor in the problem the unexpected had given Edith Nelson to solve. At first it had been merely a question of right conduct in dealing with Dennin, and right conduct, as she conceived it, lay in keeping him a prisoner until he could be turned over for trial before a proper tribunal. But now entered Hans, and she saw that his sanity and his salvation were involved. Nor was she long in discovering that her own strength and endurance had become part of the problem. She was breaking down under the strain. Her left arm had developed involuntary jerkings and twitchings. She spilled her food from her spoon, and could place no reliance in her afflicted arm. She judged it to be a form of St. Vitus's dance, and she feared the extent to which its ravages might go. What if she broke down? And the vision she had of the possible future, when the cabin might contain only Dennin and Hans, was an added horror.

After the third day, Dennin had begun to talk. His first question had been, "What are you going to do with me?" And this question he repeated daily and many times a day. And always Edith replied that he would assuredly be dealt with according to law. In turn, she put a daily question to him — "Why did you do it?" To this he never replied. Also, he received the question with outbursts of anger, raging and straining at the rawhide that bound him, and threatening her with what he would do when he got loose, which he said he was sure to do sooner or later. At such times she cocked both triggers of the gun, prepared to meet him with leaden death if he should burst loose, herself trembling and palpitating and dizzy from the tension and shock.

But in time Dennin grew more tractable. It seemed to her that he was growing very weary of his unchanging recumbent position. He began to beg and plead to be released. He made wild promises. He would do them no harm. He would himself go down the coast and give himself up to the officers of the law. He would give them his share of the gold. He would go away into the heart of the wilderness, and never again appear in civilization.

He would take his own life if she would only free him. His pleadings usually culminated in involuntary raving, until it seemed to her that he was passing into a fit; but always she shook her head and denied him the freedom for which he worked himself into a passion.

But the weeks went by, and he continued to grow more tractable. And through it all the weariness was asserting itself more and more. "I am so tired, so tired," he would murmur, rolling his head back and forth on the pillow like a peevish child. At a little later period he began to make impassioned pleas for death, to beg her to kill him, to beg Hans to put him out of his misery so that he might at least rest comfortably.

The situation was fast becoming impossible. Edith's nervousness was continuing, and she knew her breakdown might come any time. She could not even get her proper rest, for she was haunted by the fear that Hans would yield to his mania and kill Dennin while she slept. Though January had already come, months would have to elapse before any trading schooner was even likely to put into the bay. Also, they had not expected to winter in the cabin, and the food was running low; nor could Hans add to the supply by hunting. They were chained to the cabin by the necessity of guarding their prisoner.

Something must be done, and she knew it. She forced herself to go back into a reconsideration of the problem. She could not shake off the legacy of her race, the law that was of her blood and that had been trained into her. She knew that whatever she did she must do according to the law, and in the long hours of watching, the shot-gun on her knees, the murderer restless beside her and the storms thundering without, she made original sociological researches and worked out for herself the evolution of the law. It came to her that the law was nothing more than the judgment and the will of any group of people. It mattered not how large was the group of people. There were little groups, she reasoned, like Switzerland, and there were big groups like the United States. Also, she reasoned, it did not matter how small was the group of people. There might be only ten thousand people in a country, yet their collective judgment and will would be the law of that country. Why, then, could not one thousand people constitute such a group? she asked herself. And if one thousand, why not one hundred? Why not fifty? Why not five? Why not — two?

She was frightened at her own conclusion, and she talked it over with Hans. At first he could not comprehend, and then, when he did, he added convincing evidence. He spoke of miners' meetings, where all the men of a locality came together and made the law and executed the law. There might be only ten or fifteen men altogether, he said, but the will of the majority became the law for the whole ten or fifteen, and whoever violated that will, was punished.

Edith saw her way clear at last. Dennin must hang. Hans agreed with her. Between them they constituted the majority of this particular group. It was the group-will that Dennin should be hanged. In the execution of this will Edith strove earnestly to observe the customary forms, but the group was so small that Hans and she had to serve as witnesses, as jury, and as judges — also, as executioners. She formally charged Michael Dennin with the murder of Dutchy and Harkey, and the prisoner lay in his bunk and listened to the testimony, first of Hans, and then of Edith. He refused to plead guilty or not guilty, and remained silent when she asked him if he had anything to say in his own defense. She and Hans, without leaving their seats, brought in the jury's verdict of guilty. Then, as judge, she imposed the sentence. Her voice shook, her eyelids twitched, her left arm jerked, but she carried it out.

"Michael Dennin, in three days' time you are to be hanged by the neck until you are dead."

Such was the sentence. The man breathed an unconscious sigh of relief, then laughed defiantly, and said, "Thin I'm thinkin' the damn bunk won't be achin' me back anny more, an' that's a consolation."

With the passing of the sentence a feeling of relief seemed to communicate itself to all of them. Especially was it noticeable in Dennin. All sullenness and defiance disappeared, and he talked sociably with his captors, with flashes of his old-time wit. Also, he found great satisfaction in Edith's reading to him from the Bible. She read from the New Testament, and he took keen interest in the prodigal son and the thief on the cross.

On the day preceding that set for the execution, when Edith asked her usual question, "Why did you do it?" Dennin answered, "'Tis very simple. I was thinkin' —— "

But she hushed him abruptly, asked him to wait, and hurried to Hans's bedside. It was his watch off, and he came out of his sleep, rubbing his eyes and grumbling.

"Go," she told him, "and bring up Negook and one other Indian. Michael's going to confess. Make them come. Take the rifle along and bring them up at the point of it if you have to."

Half an hour later Negook and his uncle, Hadikwan, were ushered into the death chamber. They came unwillingly, Hans with his rifle herding them along.

"Negook," Edith said, "there is to be no trouble for you and your people. Only is it for you to sit and do nothing but listen and understand."

Thus did Michael Dennin, under sentence of death, make public confession of his crime. As he talked, Edith wrote his story down, while the Indians listened, and Hans guarded the door for fear the witnesses might bolt.

He had not been home to the old country for fifteen years, Dennin explained, and it had always been his intention to return with plenty of money and make his old mother comfortable for the rest of her days.

"An' how was I to be doin' it on sixteen hundred?" he demanded. "What I was after wantin' was all the goold, the whole eight thousan'. Thin, I cud go back in style. What ud be aisier, thinks I to myself, than to kill all iv yez, report it at Skaguay for an Indian-killin', an' thin pull out for Ireland? An' so I started in to kill all iv yez, but, as Harkey was fond of sayin', I cut out too large a chunk an' fell down on the swallowin' iv it. An' that's me confession. I did me duty to the devil, an' now, God willin', I'll do me duty to God."

"Negook and Hadikwan, you have heard the white man's words," Edith said to the Indians. "His words are here on this paper, and it is for you to make a sign, thus, on the paper, so that white men to come after will know that you have heard."

The two Siwashes put crosses opposite their signatures, received a summons to appear on the morrow with all their tribe for a further witnessing of things, and were allowed to go.

Dennin's hands were released long enough for him to sign the document. Then a silence fell in the room. Hans was restless, and Edith felt uncomfortable. Dennin lay on his back, staring straight up at the moss-chinked roof.

"An' now I'll do me duty to God," he murmured. He turned his head toward Edith. "Read to me," he said, "from the Book," then added, witn a glint of playfulness, "mayhap 'twill help me to forget the bunk."

The day of the execution broke clear and cold. The thermometer was down to twenty-five below zero, and a chill wind was blowing which drove the frost through clothes and flesh to the bones. For the first time in many weeks Dennin stood upon his feet. His muscles had remained inactive so long, and he was so out of practice in maintaining an erect position, that he could scarcely stand. He reeled back and forth, staggered, and clutched hold of Edith with his bound hands for support.

"Sure, an' it's dizzy I am," he laughed weakly.

A moment later he said : "An' it's glad I am that it's over with. That damn bunk would iv been the death iv me, I know."

When Edith put his fur cap on his head and proceeded to pull the flaps down over his ears, he laughed and said :

"What are you doin' that for ?"

"It's freezing cold outside," she answered.

"An' in tin minutes' time what'll matter a frozen ear or so to poor Michael Dennin ?" he asked.

She had nerved herself for the last culminating ordeal, and his remark was like a blow to her self-possession. So far, everything had seemed phantom-like, as in a dream, but the brutal truth of what he had said shocked her eyes wide open to the reality of what was taking place. Nor was her distress unnoticed by the Irishman.

"I'm sorry to be troublin' you with me foolish spache," he said regretfully. "I mint nothin' by it. 'Tis a great day for Michael Dennin, an' he's as gay as a lark."

He broke out into a merry whistle, which quickly became lugubrious and ceased.

"I'm wishin' there was a priest," he said wistfully, then added swiftly ; "But Michael Dennin's too old a campaigner to miss the luxuries when he hits the trail."

He was so very weak and unused to walking that when the door opened and he passed outside, the wind nearly carried him off his feet. Edith and Hans walked on either side of him and supported him, the while he cracked jokes and tried to keep them cheerful, breaking off, once, long enough to arrange the forwarding of his share of the gold to his mother in Ireland.

They climbed a slight hill and came out into an open space among the trees. Here, circled solemnly about a barrel that stood on end in the snow, were Negook and Hadikwan and all the Siwashes down to the babies and the dogs, come to see the way of the white man's law. Nearby was an open grave which Hans had burned into the frozen earth.

Dennin cast a practical eye over the preparations, noting the grave, the barrel, the thickness of the rope, and the diameter of the limb over which the rope was passed.

"Sure, an' I couldn't iv done better meself, Hans, if it'd been for you."

He laughed loudly at his own sally, but Hans's face was frozen into a sullen ghastliness that nothing less than the trump of doom could have broken. Also, Hans was feeling very sick. He had not realized before the enormousness of the task of putting a fellow man out of the world. Edith, on the other hand, had realized ; but the realization did not make the task any easier. She was filled with doubt as to whether she could hold herself together long enough to finish it. She felt incessant impulses to scream, to shriek, to collapse into the snow, to put her hands over her eyes and turn and run blindly away, into the forest, anywhere, away. It was only by a supreme effort of soul that she was able to keep upright and go on and do what she had to do. And in the midst of it all she was grateful to Dennin for the way he helped her.

"Lind me a hand," he said to Hans, with whose assistance he managed to mount the barrel.

He bent over so that Edith could adjust the rope about his neck. Then he stood upright while Hans drew the rope taut across the overhead branch.

"Michael Dennin, have you anything to say ?" Edith asked in a clear voice that shook in spite of her.

Dennin shuffled his feet on the barrel, looked down bashfully like a man making his maiden speech, and cleared his throat.

"I'm glad it's over with," he said. "You've treated me like a Christian, an' I'm thankin' you hearty for your kindness."

"Then may God receive you, a repentant sinner," she said.

"Ay," he answered, his deep voice as a response to her thin one, "may God receive me, a repintant sinner."

"Good-by, Michael," she cried, and her voice sounded desperate.

She threw her weight against the barrel, but it did not overturn.

"Hans! Quick! Help me!" she cried faintly.

She could feel her last strength going, and the barrel resisted her. Hans hurried to her, and the barrel went out from under Michael Dennin.

She turned her back, thrusting her fingers into her ears. Then she began to laugh, harshly, sharply, metallically; and Hans was shocked as he had not been shocked through the whole tragedy. Edith Nelson's breakdown had come. Even in her hysteria she knew it, and she was glad that she had been able to hold up under the strain until everything had been accomplished. She reeled toward Hans.

"Take me to the cabin, Hans," she managed to articulate.

"And let me rest," she added. "Just let me rest, and rest, and rest."

With Hans's arm around her, supporting her weight and directing her helpless steps, she went off across the snow. But the Indians remained solemnly to watch the working of the white man's law that compelled a man to dance upon the air.

12
TWO GOLD BRICKS

TWO GOLD BRICKS.

BY JACK LONDON.

THE heavy portiers were rudely thrust aside and a young man of twenty-two or thereabout, flung himself into the apartment to the evident astonishment of its inmate, who paused long enough in the act of lighting a cigarette to burn his fingers with the paper-lighter.

"Ye gods! preserve us from the faddist!" he cried, dramatically elevating his arms heavenward as though invoking the protection of his divine friends, and then collapsing into the comfortable embrace of the nearest easy-chair.

His audience, having recovered his equanimity at the expense of a muffled curse upon all stage-struck friends, shoved the smoking stand at him. For a space they yielded to the soothing caress of the weed, then proceeded to an elucidation.

"Well, Ollie, old man, out with it. What's the rub?" interrogated he of the burned fingers. Has your tailor taken to dunning on a wheel? Have your auburn love-locks come into demand? or are they trying to enlist your sympathies in that artistic crusade among the unæsthetical denizens of Mott and Mulberry streets.

"No. It's not so bad as that; but what do you think they've been up to?"

"What? which? who? the æsthetes or the non-æsthetes?"

"I mean the crowd—the other crowd, you know, not our crowd."

"Oh, Archie and his friends. What have they been doing? Nothing serious I hope; and yet, they always were a serious crowd."

"It's not serious. Oh, no; and still it concerns a very serious subject. Ha! ha! ha! you'd never guess! He! he! he! you'd— Ho! ho! ho!"

"Confound you and your paradoxes! Not serious—concerns a serious subject; a serious crowd, a fool's laughter—fine material for an epigram. By Jove, if I don't think it up."

"Mercy, Oh, Damon, I pray you. A truce to your epigrams. I plead an arrest of judgment till I explain."

"Proceed, I may be lenient."

"You know I intended going down to Cape Weola for canvas-back and had made all arrangements to start to-day. I packed up, expressed my traps, and said good-by all round, only to find the hunting-party had fallen through. Finding my pleasure nipped in the bud and because I had nothing to do, I became virtuous and made a long-delayed call upon that long-suffering maiden aunt of mine, in Brooklyn. Nice old girl! I tried not to be bored, and made the acquaintance of her two Persian cats, to say nothing of an angular female, who called and spent the afternoon in discussing equal suffrage and all that rot. What with that and the tea, I returned with a very bad headache and a very good intention of going early to bed.

"However, I thought I would drop in and see Archie —nice brother, Archie—and entice him into making a call upon the long-suffering maiden aunt aforesaid. Archie was out, and tired of waiting I made myself comfortable in his boudoir—it's a real boudoir, you know—and fell asleep. I've no idea how long I was there, but suddenly I was awakened by the popping of corks and by conversation in his studio. 'Archie and a lot of his cronies,' I thought. 'Evidently they don't know I'm here.'

"They were as serious as usual. That melancholy rascal Le Blanche, whose 'Bridge of Sighs,' and 'The Requital' you'll remember at the exhibition, was there, as was also Schomberg, his twin brother of personified misery. They were discussing the death of Willis '89— used to chum with Archie and that crowd. The conversation turned to monuments, headstones, and epitaphs, and became quite interesting, I can assure you.

"That idiot, Fessler, opened the ball by deploring the

conventional inconsistency with which our moderns remember the dead by the inscriptions they place on their
headstones; and Schomberg quoted Shakespeare, revised;
'The good that men do lives'—etc., while Le Blanche
favored them with the following from Byron, which I
happened to know:

> " ' When some proud son of man returns to earth,
>   Unknawn to glory but upheld by birth,
>   The Sculptor's art exhausts the pomp of woe,
>   And storied urns record who sests below;
>   When all is done, upon the tomb is seen,
>   Not what he was, but what he should have been.' "

"Finally, that band of morbid-minded pessimists took
up funeral sermons and unmercifully berated our pious
divines for their hypocrisy- in the perpetration of the
same. They decided that the custom was all wrong and
a blot upon our cultured civilization. In the first place,
they decided it was impossible to obtain anything but
flattery when a man was paid to preach the sermon; in
the second place, that it should be delivered by one who
was conversant with the whole life of the deceased; and
in the third place that, if he were an enemy he could not
be induced to officiate, if a friend he would be certain to
flatter. They at last reached the conclusion that all
funeral sermons were snares and deceits, and since the
only one who could properly officiate and tell the brutal,
naked truth, would be the person being buried, it were
better to abolish the wicked and immoral custom.

"Here the subject would have been dropped but for
that brother of mine, who thought it would be 'so
original, you know, for a man to make his own funeral
oration.' Then he was ably supplemented by Moore,
who enthusiastically cried out 'Why not?'

"It dawned upon them all—why not—the phonograph.
Then and there they organized into a 'Voice from the
Beyond,' or 'Every Man His Own Minister,' society.
They gave it some Greek name and this is my free rendi-
tion of it. They elected their officers, swore ironclad
oaths to tell all the mean little things and mean big
things they had done during their lifetime, and promised

to criticize unsparingly each other's faults and vices.
After a voluntary assessment had been levied to procure
a phonograph and the necessary paraphernalia they
adjourned. They expect to have all their sermons in by
this day week, and Archie is to take charge of them.
He is to put them in that little safe you'll remember
stands in a corner of his studio.

"While the crowd was departing I slipped out.by another door, and here I am."

"Like the girl that you are, come to tell me the secret
while yet warm. But, Ollie, it seems to me as though
there is more in it than you have told. I have a scheme."

"A scheme?"

"Yes, we will give an entertainment in your parlors.
You know we have been running too big a margin, and
I, for one, am rather short. This quarter's was all gone
before I received it, and what I shall do till next quarter
is an enigma. You are in just as bad a fix, too, so we'll
give an entertainment."

"An entertainment?"

"Yes, and clear a cool ten hundred apiece."

"Whew! Ten hundred! Why I could square up and
go on swimmingly! But, Damon, how are you going to
do it?"

"Give an entertainment."

"Now don't talk in riddles. Come, explain."

And Damon explained while Ollie went into ecstasies
of delight. Late that night, Ollie departed, and during
the next ten days many were the consultations he held
with Damon regarding the scheme.

.　.　.　.　.　.　.　.　.　.　.

Ten nights later. Ollie's parlors are all ablaze and
perhaps threescore and ten male guests are assembled,
for this is the night of the entertainment. Damon and
Ollie are all bustling and important, and why not? Is
not Professor Armstrong engaged this evening at a hundred dollars? Has not one of Edison's assistants come
all the way from New Jersey with expenses paid and another hundred? And is there not the phonograph specialist? to say nothing of Crooke's tubes, electrical appar-

atus, kinetoscopes, and phonographs? Indeed, is it not
to be a veritable treat to those lovers of popular science
that have received invitations?

By nine, Ollie introduces Professor Armstrong, who
took up Roentgen's discovery and applied it in many
curious and instructive experiments. The kinetoscope
man then engrossed their attention with thrilling scenes
of life, and was followed by Edison's assistant, who presented illustrated demonstrations of several of the
"wizard's" marvelous inventions.

In the meanwhile Damon drew Ollie aside and asked:
"Is Archie's crowd all here?"

"Yes, all except Staunton. He has received the telegram and by this time is speeding across Connecticut."

"Good! But I'm sorry we had to get rid of him.
Won't he be angry when he finds it out?"

"Won't he though."

To conclude the very enjoyable evening in experi-
mental science, the phonograph specialist was introduced.
After a few introductory remarks, in which, incidentally,
the possibility of the voice of the dead coming back, was
mentioned, he proceeded to arrange his apparatus. Taking one from a number of cylinders and inserting it in
the phonograph, he applied the electric current and the
delicate machinery was in motion.

A voice—Staunton's voice—in solemn tones, was heard,
preaching a funeral sermon. The members of the
"Voice from the Beyond," society looked inquiringly
at each other, then in turn, perplexed, indignant, and
amused. Staunton's rich, deep voice ground out of the
machine, sternly moralizing in a manner demoralizing to
the audience. How he criticized his own vices and
trivialities! · He had been weighed by himself in the
balance and found wanting. Then he turned on his
friends and upbraided them unsparingly for their follies.
It was rich! Titters and suppressed giggles turned into
continued roars of laughter, and when the phonograph
ceased, after a bestowal of fatherly advice and solemn
benedictions all round and a *requiescat in pace,* the audience went fairly wild.

The specialist was inserting another cylinder and the members of the "Voice from the Beyond" society were doing some hard thinking. There were hasty reviews of sermons preached recently into phonographic receivers, and many imparted secrets—secrets to be made known only after death—were remembered. They became alarmed. They knew not whose turn was next and they were all convinced that it was a scurvy trick.

Again the phonograph was started; but when Archie's voice was heard, soaring in the eloquent lights of his funeral oration, the members of the "Voice from the Beyond" society sprang to the little platform, stopped the machinery, and took possession of the cylinders. Ollie expostulated; Damon feigned indignation. Finally, amid much confusion and many questions, Damon dismissed the audience, which soon departed, with the exception of the "Voice from the Beyond" society, which remained to talk it over and to take summary vengeance.

Ollie was cool, determined, dramatic—he would have made a model villain. He demanded two hundred and fifty dollars for the return of each of the cylinders. They refused. Why should they pay? Were they not in possession of the cylinders? Then Ollie talked vaguely of duplicate cylinders, which might find their way into the nickle-in-the-slot machines; of funeral orations going abroad from every street and public place in New York; of the possibility of disposing of these same duplicates among friends of the late deceased; and ominiously hinted of many things decidedly worse.

. . . .

"I say, Damon, we've squared up the Doldrums' racket, with interest, haven't we?"

"Didn't we though. By the way, Ollie, how much is ten times two hundred and fifty, minus five hundred, divided by two?"

"Ten hundred! By Jove! You're a brick, Damon, in planning."

"So are you, Ollie, in execution."

"Then we're both bricks, good gold bricks, worth ten hundred apiece."

13
THE HANDSOME CABIN BOY

THE HANDSOME CABIN BOY.

BY JACK LONDON.

"**A**ND the dapper young fellow was——"

"None other than the veiled woman, of course."

"O, pshaw!" I cried. "That's well enough for a Sunday newspaper, but in real life people are not so easily misled."

"Look at the authentic instances—women serving as soldiers, sailors, scouts——"

"Bosh!"

"Why, there's my little brother Bob, as clever an impersonator——"

"Bosh!"

"People are fooled every day and——"

"Stuff and nonsense," I said. "Any one but a ninny should penetrate such a make-up at a glance. I don't think much of a fellow who can't tell a man from a woman. Catch me napping that way."

"I'll catch you," cried Jack.

"I like that," was my reply.

"I'll wager I fool you within six months."

"Done! For how much?"

"The loser to foot a supper; the setting, ordering, and inviting of the same to be at the winner's discretion."

"Done!"

We shook hands, and the fellows crowded round with all sorts of advice and persiflage. Thus was the seed sown, out of which was to spring the never-to-be-forgotten romance of "The Handsome Cabin Boy."

The succeeding fortnight found me in solitary grandeur aboard my schooner yacht Falcon, bound for a short cruise to Honolulu. We had hardly sunk the Farralone

Light, when my suspicions were aroused. From the cook to the sailing master complaints began to pour in about the new cabin boy. They held he was willing enough, but worthless. At the last moment, Billy, the old boy, had left us in the lurch, and my agent, to whom all such matters were entrusted, had hastily procured the present incumbent.

As they said, he was willing enough, but—in short, he was ignorant of his duties and totally unfit for such a position. Yet he tried so hard that everybody was drawn toward him. And he was such a handsome lad. Dark-eyed, rosy-cheeked, with a delicate olive complexion and an exquisite oval—small wonder that he recalled to my mind the bet with Jack Haliday. And then, for the slender lad of fifteen or sixteen that he appeared, there was a vague, insinuating fullness about the figure, which did not fail to corroborate my suspicions.

THE SAILING MASTER GRAPLING THE CABIN BOY

But I held my hush and awaited confirmation. This came sooner than I expected. The sailing master and myself were on the poop, one noon, with our sextants, bent on shooting the sun. The lad came up the companionway with a pan of soot and ashes; he had just cleaned the cabin stove. Instead of going to the lee, he stepped to the weather rail and let fly the refuse. And fly it did—backwards, of course, and all over us.

Digging a handful out of his eyes, the sailing master grabbed the young rascal by the arm. Now, Nelson was a rough son of the sea, and had a mellifluous command of the vernacular which serves for emphasis to those who sail the same. He shook him up and down and cursed him with as virile a combination of English and Scandinavian oaths as was ever my luck to hear.

The boy lost his wits and began to cry. Picking up the pan, he started for the cabin, but just opposite me, reeled and toppled over. I caught him before he could fall, and—well, my arm had strayed in forbidden pastures too often to be mistaken now.

"Why, you're a girl!" I cried.

The man at the wheel began to snicker, so I hurried

her below to save her from confusion before the men. There she cried, and sobbed, and carried on, till I was almost as distracted myself, in my efforts to soothe her. At last she calmed down.

"O, sir," she began, "I hope you won't be angry with me. I—he—Mr.——"

"It's Jack Haliday's doing, isn't it?" I interrupted.

"Yes, sir."

"Then you know all about the bet, and you'll have to testify that I discovered your—er—identity."

"Yes, sir, and he'll be angry because I lost. Boo— hoo—oo——"

"O, you did very well." I thought she needed a little cheering. "The cook would never have discovered— say! how the deuce—you'll have to change your——"

It was indeed embarrassing for both of us. And that blundering cook had never tumbled! I called him into the cabin.

"Tell off that German deck boy to help you," I ordered. "And go to your room and pack up Miss— er——"

"E—E—Eastman," sobbed the disconsolate bundle on the floor.

"And pack up Miss Eastman's belongings. Take them to the spare state room, and make everything comfortable. I'll see you get extra pay for this trip. Go! Don't stand there all day!" I could not help laughing at his round-eyed wonder.

"I don't know what to do in the way of suitable clothes," I said, as she entered her new berth in the wake of a trim little sea-chest.

"That's all right, sir," she replied, between her sobs. "I b—brought some dresses along."

"Strike me blind!" cried the cook, as the door shut. "O, I beg your pardon, sir; but do you mean to tell me, sir, that he's a—a she? Think of it!—and me a married man! What'll my wife say?"

Though I tried to explain that there was no necessity of his wife knowing, he wandered away to the galley,

I BROUGHT DRESSES ALONG, SIR

more woe-begone, if anything, than the poor creature who had caused his distress. Still, I could sympathize with him, realizing as I did, my own false position, and knowing how the sailors must be haw-hawing among themselves.

Dinner was sent in to her, and it was not till next morning that she showed herself. And then it was a demure little maid, in maidenly costume, who came forth—a pretty little maid, for all her short brown locks. It seemed a pity they had been clipped for the sake of a paltry bet.

"What will your people say?" I asked, in the course of explanations. "Do they know?"

"My brother does. I came with his consent."

"Your brother's a scoundrel and ought to be horse-whipped. It's disgraceful, to say the least."

"How?"

This was a poser. How? I began to comprehend the mess Jack Haliday had got me into. How? What innocence!

"You must have been brought up in a convent," I said bluntly.

"Yes, sir; I went to the Sacred Heart until a year ago."

Worse and worse—it was no light responsibility thus thrust upon me. I finally wormed her story from her. She had lost her mother during her childhood, and her father, a small tradesman, had educated her at the Convent of the Sacred Heart. Things had gone from bad to worse with him, and when he died, she and her brother were left penniless. To curtail the story: they had become proteges of Haliday's. She had shown an aptitude for the stage, and Haliday encouraged her, prophesying that some day the metropolitan vaudeville would open its arms to a soubrette of no mean ability.

"And when he asked this favor of me," she concluded, "what could I do? Refuse, after all he had done for me?"

Well, the yacht took on new life. Strange how this

AND THEN IT WAS A
DEMURE LITTLE
WOMAN CAME FORTH

chit of a child, this girl of sixteen, brightened things up! She became the idol of all hands, and even Nelson apologized—first time the stubborn dog ever did such a thing, I'll wager. She could play the piano fairly well, and though her voice was not strong and had no register, her singing was sweet indeed.

When we arrived at Honolulu, I was for making arrangements to send her back by steamer; but the guileless creature would not hear of it, and looked so miserable when I insisted, that I gave in. Besides, nobody knew us. And she—why, she had no conception of evil, and to undeceive her was a task beyond my power. I supplied her with funds, and she soon had a stunning array of gowns and other female fripperies. Then we took in the concerts of the Hawaiian Band, made long drives into the country, and visited many places of interest and recreation. We had a delightful time; but the best of good things must end, and a month later found us off the Golden Gate. To-morrow we should be in San Francisco.

To-morrow—I half sighed as I lighted a cigar, and glanced at her state-room door. What were her dreams, I wondered. Then I thought of my long, lonely cruises. How bright this one had been! Life took on new possibilities, as I began to realize some of its hitherto unknown charms—charms which my benedict friends never ceased to dwell upon. How she had changed things! A neatly turned ankle on the cabin stairs, a twinkling slipper along the deck, a girl's light laughter, a song at twilight, a—in short, the ineffable something of a woman's presence. I was startled at the thought. Let me see: sixteen—twenty-six; nineteen—twenty-nine; no, that would be too long to wait, eighteen—twenty-eight—that's it. And not such a disparity after all. Two years! What would not two years do? Development, the rounding of that mind—aye, and that form, already so rich of promise. Two years, and then——"

I HALF SIGHED AS I LIGHTED A CIGAR—

"Eight bells!"

The clamor of changing watch had destroyed the fairy picture; so I tossed away my cigar and went to bed.

Jack Haliday and the whole crowd were at the club-

THE SUPPER

house pier to meet us. Evidently, the lookout of the Merchants' Exchange had telegraphed our arrival off the Heads the previous night. They trooped aboard in a body, and I trembled for Miss Eastman. However, Clara, as I had come to call her, faced the ordeal bravely. The subdued expectancy and smothered giggles angered me. Jack Haliday opened the ball at once.

"I say, you know, about that supper——"

"What about it?" I asked sharply.

"Well, I've made all the plans, but I thought it better to submit them to you. You might make a few suggestions, you know."

"You've made all the plans!" I shouted. "I have an idea that the ordering of this supper belongs to me."

"Ha! ha! ha!" Everybody began to laugh.

"Hope you had a pleasant trip, Miss Eastman," he said, turning to her.

"O, I did," she assured him, though I could see her lips were trembling.

"How did you discover it?" he asked, addressing me.

"Why, she fainted in my arms, and——"

"Ho! ho! He! he! he!" The crowd fairly roared, and I beamed triumphantly on my discomfited opponent.

"Was he angry?" continued the imperturbable Haliday.

"No," Clara replied, "he was real nice. And when we got to Honolulu he wanted to send me home on the steamer, but I wouldn't let him. Then we had a gorgeous time—bought me candy and gloves, took me buggy-riding, and——"

With this the crowd went mad. They slapped Jack on the shoulder, poked him in the ribs, and hugged each other in ecstasies of glee.

"Why, you ninny!" Jack cried. "That's my brother Bob."

"Impossible," I rejoined. "Why, when she fainted in my arms, I——"

At this juncture speech failed me, for the modest Miss Eastman turned a couple of back-flips, came up smiling, thrust a hand into her maidenly bosom and drew forth—heavens!—a couple of pneumatic cushions, the kind used by football players.

It were needless for me to tell how I led the stampede to the club-house; how the supper came off, with Bob Haliday at the head of the table; or how, to this day, the mere mention of "The Handsome Cabin Boy" arouses a certain choler which I can never hope to overcome.

14
BROWN WOLF

BROWN WOLF

By JACK LONDON
Author of "The Call of the Wild," "The Sea Wolf," etc.

Illustrations by Philip R. Goodwin

SHE had delayed because of the dew-wet grass, in order to put on her rubbers, and when she emerged from the house found her waiting husband absorbed in the wonder of a bursting almond-bud. She sent a questing glance across the tall grass and in and out among the orchard trees.

"Where's Wolf?" she asked.

"He was here a moment ago." Walt Irvine drew himself away with a jerk from the metaphysics and poetry of the organic miracle of blossom, and surveyed the landscape. "He was running a rabbit the last I saw of him."

"Wolf! Wolf! Here, Wolf!" she called, as they left the clearing and took the trail that led down through the waxen-belled manzanita jungle to the country road.

Irvine thrust between his lips the little finger of each hand and lent to her efforts a shrill whistling.

She covered her ears hastily, and made a wry grimace.

"My! for a poet, delicately attuned and all the rest of it, you can make unlovely noises. My ear-drums are pierced. You outwhistle——"

"Orpheus."

"I was about to say a street arab," she concluded severely.

"Poesy does not prevent one from being practical—at least it doesn't prevent *me*. Mine is no futility of genius that can't sell gems to the magazines."

He assumed a mock extravagance, and went on:

"I am no attic singer, no ballroom warbler. And why? Because I am practical. Mine is no squalor of song that cannot transmute itself, with proper exchange value, into a flower-crowned cottage, a sweet mountain meadow, a grove of redwoods, an orchard of thirty-seven trees, one long row of blackberries, and two short rows of strawberries, to say nothing of a quarter of a mile of gurgling brook. I am a beauty merchant, a trader in song, and I pursue beauty utility, dear Madge. I sing a song, and, thanks to the magazine editors, I transmute my song into a waft of the west wind sighing through our redwoods, into a murmur of waters over mossy stones that sings back to me another song than the one I sang and yet the same song wonderfully —er—transmuted."

"Oh, that all your song transmutations were as successful!" she laughed.

"Name one that wasn't."

"Those two beautiful sonnets that you transmuted into the cow that was accounted the worst milker in the township."

"She was beautiful—" he began.

"But she didn't give milk," Madge interrupted.

"But she *was* beautiful, now, wasn't she?" he insisted.

"And here's where beauty and utility fall out," was her reply. "And there's the Wolf!"

From the thicket-covered hillside came a crashing of underbrush, and then, forty feet above them, on the edge of the sheer wall of rock, appeared a wolf's head and shoulders. His braced fore paws dislodged a pebble, and with sharp-pricked ears and peering gaze he watched the fall of the pebble till it struck at their feet. Then he transferred his gaze and with open mouth laughed down at them.

"You Wolf, you!" and "You blessed Wolf!" the man and woman called out to him.

The ears flattened back and down at the sound, and the head seemed to snuggle under the caress of an invisible hand.

They watched him scramble backward into the thicket, then proceeded on their way. Several minutes

WITH OPEN MOUTH LAUGHED DOWN AT THEM.

later, rounding a turn in the trail, where the descent was less precipitous, he joined them in the midst of a miniature avalanche of pebbles and loose soil. He was not demonstrative. A pat and a rub around the ears from the man, and a more prolonged caressing from the woman, and he was away down the trail in front of them, gliding effortlessly over the ground in true wolf fashion.

In build and coat and brush he was a huge timber-wolf; but the lie was given to his wolfhood by his color and marking. There the dog unmistakably advertised itself. No wolf was ever colored like him. He was brown, deep brown, red brown, an orgy of browns. Back and shoulders were a warm brown that paled on the sides and underneath to a yellow that was dingy because of the brown that lingered in it. The white of the throat and paws and the spots over the eyes were dirty because of the persistent and ineradicable brown, while the eyes themselves were twin topazes, golden and brown.

The man and woman loved the dog very much; perhaps this was because it had been such a task to win his love. It had been no easy matter, when he first drifted in mysteriously out of nowhere to their little mountain cottage. Footsore and famished, he had killed a rabbit under their very noses and under their very windows, and then crawled away and slept by the spring at the foot of the blackberry bushes. When Walt Irvine

went down to inspect the intruder, he was snarled at for his pains, and Madge likewise was snarled at when she went down to present, as a peace-offering, a large pan of bread and milk.

A most unsociable dog he proved to be, resenting all their advances, refusing to let them lay hands on him, menacing them with bared fangs and bristling hair. Nevertheless, he remained, sleeping and resting by the spring, and eating the food they gave him after they had set it down at a safe distance and retreated. His wretched physical condition explained why he lingered; and when he had recuperated, after several days' sojourn, he disappeared.

And this would have been the end of him so far as Irvine and his wife were concerned, had not Irvine at that particular time been called away into the northern part of the State. Riding along on the train, near to the line between California and Oregon, he chanced to look out of the window and saw his unsociable guest sliding along the wagon road, brown and wolfish, tired yet tireless, dust-covered and soiled with two hundred miles of travel.

Now, Irvine was a man of impulse, a poet. He got off the train at the next station, bought a piece of meat at a butcher shop, and captured the vagrant on the outskirts of the town. The return trip was made in the baggage-car, and so Wolf came a second time to the mountain cottage. Here he was tied up for a week and made love to by the man and woman. But it was very circumspect love-making. Remote and alien as a traveler from another planet, he snarled down their soft-spoken love-words. He never barked. In all the time they had him he was never known to bark.

To win him became a problem. Irvine liked problems. He had a metal plate made on which was stamped: "RETURN TO WALT IRVINE, GLEN ELLEN, SONOMA COUNTY, CALIFORNIA." This was riveted to a collar and strapped about the dog's neck. Then he was turned loose, and promptly he disappeared. A day later came a telegram from Mendocino County. In twenty hours he had made over a hundred miles to the north, and was still going when captured.

He came back by Wells-Fargo Express, was tied up three days, and was loosed on the fourth and lost. This time he gained southern Oregon before he was caught and returned. Always, as soon as he received his liberty, he fled away, and always he fled north. He was possessed of an obsession that drove him north. The homing instinct, Irvine called it, after he had expended the selling price of a sonnet in getting the animal back from northern Oregon.

Another time the brown wanderer succeeded in traversing half the length of California, all of Oregon, and most of Washington before he was picked up and returned collect. A remarkable thing was the speed with which he traveled. Fed up and rested, as soon as he was loosed he devoted all his energy to getting over the ground. On the first day's run he was known to cover as high as a hundred and fifty miles, and after that he would average a hundred miles a day until caught. He always arrived back lean and hungry and savage, and always departed fresh and vigorous, cleaving his way northward in response to some prompting of his being that no one could understand.

But at last, after a futile year of flight, he accepted the inevitable and elected to remain at the cottage where first he had killed the rabbit and slept by the spring. Even after that, a long time elapsed before the man and woman succeeded in patting him. It was a great victory, for they alone were allowed to put hands on him. He was fastidiously exclusive, and no guest at the cottage ever succeeded in making up to him. A low growl greeted a stranger's approach; if he had the hardihood to come nearer, the lips lifted, the naked fangs appeared, and the growl became a snarl—a snarl so terrible and malignant that it awed the stoutest of them, as it likewise awed the farmers' dogs, that knew ordinary dog-snarling but had never heard wolf-snarling before.

A SNARL SO TERRIBLE AND MALIGNANT THAT IT AWED THE STOUTEST OF THEM.

He was without antecedents. His history began with Walt and Madge. He had come up from the south, but never a clue did they get of the owner from whom he had evidently fled. Mrs. Johnson, their nearest neighbor and the one who supplied them with milk, proclaimed him a Klondike dog. Her brother was burrowing for frozen pay-streaks in that far country, and so she constituted herself an authority on the subject.

But they did not dispute her. There were the tips of Wolf's ears, obviously so severely frozen at some time that they would never quite heal again. Besides, he looked like the photographs of the Alaskan dogs they saw published in magazines and newspapers. They often speculated over his past, and tried to conjure up (from what they had read and heard) what his Northland life had been. That the Northland still drew him they knew; for at night they sometimes heard him crying softly; and when the north wind blew and the bite of frost was in the air, a great restlessness would come upon him and he would lift a mournful lament which they knew to be the long wolf-howl. Yet he never barked. No provocation was great enough to draw from him that canine cry.

Long discussion they had, during the time of winning him, as to whose dog he was. Each claimed him, and each proclaimed loudly any expression of affection made by him. But the man had the best of it at first, chiefly because he was a man. It was patent that Wolf had had no experience with women. He did not understand women. Madge's skirts were something he never quite accepted. The rustle of them was enough to set him a-bristle with suspicion, and on a windy day she could not approach him at all.

On the other hand, it was Madge who fed him; also it was she who ruled the kitchen, and it was by her favor, and her favor alone, that he was permitted to come within that sacred precinct. It was because of these things that she bade fair to overcome the handicap of her garments. Then it was that Walt put forth special effort, making it a practise to have Wolf lie at his feet while he wrote, and, between petting and talking, losing much time from his work. Walt won in the end, and his victory was most probably due to the fact that he was a man, though Madge averred that they would have had another quarter of a mile of gurgling brook, and at least two west winds sighing through their redwoods, had Walt properly devoted his energies to song-transmutation and left Wolf alone to exercise a natural taste and an unbiased judgment.

"It's about time I heard from those triolets," Walt said, after a silence of five minutes, during which they had swung steadily down the trail. "There'll be a check at the post-office, I know, and we'll transmute it into beautiful buckwheat flour, a gallon of maple syrup, and a new pair of rubbers for you."

"And into beautiful milk from Mrs. Johnson's beautiful cow," Madge added. "To-morrow's the first of the month, you know."

Walt scowled unconsciously, then his face brightened and he clapped his hand to his breast pocket.

"Never mind. I have here a nice beautiful new cow, the best milker in California."

"When did you write it?" she demanded eagerly. Then, reproachfully, "And you never showed it to me."

"I saved it to read to you on the way to the post-office, in a spot remarkably like this one," he answered, indicating with a wave of his hand a dry log on which to sit.

A tiny stream flowed out of a dense fern-brake, slipped down a mossy-lipped stone, and ran across the path at their feet. From the valley arose the mellow song of meadow-larks, while about them, in and out, through sunshine and shadow, fluttered great yellow butterflies.

Up from below came another sound that broke in upon Walt reading softly from his manuscript. It was a crunching of heavy feet, punctuated now and again by the clattering of a displaced stone. As Walt finished and looked to his wife for approval, a man came into view around the turn of the trail. He was bareheaded and sweaty. With a handkerchief in one hand he mopped his face, while in the other hand he carried a new hat and a wilted starched collar which he had removed from his neck. He was a well-built man, and his muscles seemed on the point of bursting out of the painfully new and ready-made black clothes he wore.

"Warm day," Walt greeted him. Walt believed in country democracy, and never missed an opportunity to practise it.

The man paused and nodded.

"I guess I ain't used much to the warm," he vouchsafed half-apologetically. "I'm more accustomed to zero weather."

"You don't find any of that in this country," Walt laughed.

"Should say not," the man answered. "An' I ain't here a-lookin' for it, neither. I'm tryin' to find my sister. Mebbe you know where she lives. Her name's Johnson, Mrs. William Johnson."

"You're not her Klondike brother," Madge cried, her eyes bright with interest, "about whom we've heard so much?"

"Yes'm, that's me," he answered modestly. "My name's Miller, Skiff Miller. I just thought I'd s'prise her."

"You are on the right track, then. Only you've come by the foot-path." Madge stood up to direct him, pointing up the canyon a quarter of a mile. "You see that blasted redwood? Take the little trail turning off to the right. It's the short cut to her house. You can't miss it."

"Yes'm, thank you, ma'am," he said.

He made tentative efforts to go, but seemed awkwardly rooted to the spot. He was gazing at her with an open admiration of which he was quite unconscious, and which was drowning, along with him, in the rising sea of embarrassment in which he floundered.

"We'd like to hear you tell about the Klondike," Madge said. "Mayn't we come over some day while you are at your sister's? Or, better yet, won't you come over and have dinner with us?"

"Yes'm; thank you, ma'am," he mumbled mechanically. Then he caught himself up and added, "I ain't stoppin' long. I got to be pullin' north again. I go out on to-night's train. You see, I've got a mail contract with the Government."

When Madge had said that it was too bad, he made another futile effort to go. But he could not take his eyes from her face. He forgot his embarrassment in his admiration, and it was her turn to flush and feel uncomfortable.

It was at this juncture, when Walt had just decided it was time for him to be saying something to relieve the strain, that Wolf, who had been away nosing through the brush, trotted wolf-like into view.

Skiff Miller's abstraction disappeared. The

HE WOULD LIFT A MOURNFUL LAMENT WHICH THEY KNEW
TO BE THE LONG WOLF-HOWL.

pretty woman before him passed out of his field of vision. He had eyes only for the dog, and a great wonder came into his face.

"Well, I'll be durned!" he enunciated slowly and solemnly.

He sat down ponderingly on the log, leaving Madge standing. At the sound of his voice, Wolf's ears had flattened down, and his mouth had opened in a laugh. He trotted slowly up to the stranger and first smelled his hands, then licked them with his tongue.

Skiff Miller patted the dog's head, and

WOLF SPRANG AFTER HIM AND STROVE GENTLY TO MAKE HIM PAUSE.

slowly and solemnly repeated, "Well, I'll be durned!"

"Excuse me, ma'am," he said the next moment; "I was just s'prised some, that was all."

"We're surprised too," she answered

lightly. "We never saw Wolf make up to a stranger before."

"Is that what you call him—Wolf?" the man asked.

Madge nodded. "But I can't understand his friendliness toward you—unless it's because you're from the Klondike. He's a Klondike dog, you know."

"Yes'm," Miller said absently. He lifted one of Wolf's fore legs and examined the footpads, pressing them and denting them with his thumb. "Kind of soft," he remarked. "He ain't been on trail for a long time."

"I say," Walt broke in, "it is remarkable the way he lets you handle him."

Skiff Miller arose, no longer awkward with admiration of Madge, and in a sharp, businesslike manner asked, "How long have you had him?"

But just then the dog, squirming and rubbing against the newcomer's legs, opened his mouth and barked. It was an explosive bark, brief and joyous, but a bark.

"That's a new one on me," Skiff Miller remarked.

Walt and Madge stared at each other. The miracle had happened. Wolf had barked.

"It's the first time he ever barked," Madge said.

"First time I ever heard him, too," Miller volunteered.

Madge smiled at him. The man was evidently a humorist.

"Of course," she said, "since you have only seen him for five minutes."

Skiff Miller looked at her sharply, seeking in her face the guile her words had led him to suspect.

"I thought you understood," he said slowly. "I thought you tumbled to it from his makin' up to me. He's my dog. His name ain't Wolf. It's Brown."

"Oh, Walt!" was Madge's instinctive cry to her husband.

Walt was on the defensive at once.

"How do you know he's your dog?" he demanded.

"Because he is," was the reply.

"Mere assertion," Walt said sharply.

In his slow and pondering way Skiff Miller looked at him, then asked, with a nod of his head toward Madge:

"How d'you know she's your wife? You just say, 'Because she is,' and I'll say it's mere assertion. The dog's mine. I bred 'm an' raised 'm, an' I guess I ought to know. Look here, I'll prove it to you."

Skiff Miller turned to the dog. "Brown!" His voice rang out sharply, and at the sound the dog's ears flattened down as to a caress. "Gee!" The dog made a swinging turn to the right. "Now mush on!" And the dog ceased his swing abruptly and started straight ahead, halting obediently at command.

"I can do it with whistles," Skiff Miller said proudly. "He was my lead dog."

"But you are not going to take him away with you?" Madge asked tremulously.

The man nodded.

"Back into that awful Klondike world of suffering?"

He nodded and added, "Oh, it ain't so bad as all that. Look at me. Pretty healthy specimen, ain't I?"

"But the dog! The terrible hardship, the heart-breaking toil, the starvation, the frost! Oh, I've read about it and I know."

"I nearly ate him once, over on Little Fish River," Miller volunteered grimly. "Gettin' a moose that day was all that saved 'm."

"I'd have died first!" Madge cried.

"Things is different down here," Miller explained. "You don't have to eat dogs. You think differently just about the time you're all in. You've never been all in, so you don't know anything about it."

"That's the very point," she argued warmly. "Dogs are not eaten in California. Why not leave him here? He is happy. He'll never want for food—you know that. He'll never suffer from cold and hardship. Here all is softness and gentleness. Neither the human nor nature is savage. He will never know a whip-lash again. And as for the weather—why, it never snows here."

"But it's all-fired hot in summer, beggin' your pardon," Skiff Miller laughed.

"But you do not answer," Madge continued passionately. "What have you to offer him in that Northland life?"

"Grub, when I've got it, and that's most of the time," came the answer.

"And the rest of the time?"

"No grub."

"And the work?"

"Yes, plenty of work," Miller blurted out impatiently. "Work without end, an' famine, an' frost, an' all the rest of the miseries—that's what he'll get when he comes with me. But he likes it. He is used to it. He knows that life. He was born to it an' brought up to it. An' you don't know anything about it. You don't know what you're talking about. That's where the dog belongs, and that's where he'll be happiest."

"The dog doesn't go," Walt announced in a determined voice. "So there is no need of further discussion."

"What's that?" Skiff Miller demanded, his brows lowering and an obstinate flush of blood reddening his forehead.

"I said the dog doesn't go, and that settles it. I don't believe he's your dog. You may have seen him sometime. You may even sometime have driven him for his owner. But his obeying the ordinary driving-commands of the Alaskan trail is no demonstration that he is yours. Any dog in Alaska would obey you as he obeyed. Besides, he is undoubtedly a valuable dog, as dogs go in Alaska, and that is sufficient explanation of your desire to get possession of him. Anyway, you've got to prove property."

Skiff Miller, cool and collected, the obstinate flush a trifle deeper on his forehead, his huge muscles bulging under the black cloth of his coat, carefully looked the poet up and down as though measuring the strength of his slenderness.

The Klondiker's face took on a contemptuous expression as he said finally, "I reckon there's nothing in sight to prevent me takin' the dog right here an' now."

Walt's face reddened, and the striking-muscles of his arms and shoulders seemed to stiffen and grow tense. His wife fluttered apprehensively into the breach.

"Maybe Mr. Miller is right," she said. "I am afraid that he is. Wolf does seem to know him, and certainly he answers to the name of 'Brown.' He made friends with him instantly, and you know that's something he never did with anybody before. Besides, look at the way he barked. He was just bursting with joy. Joy over what? Without doubt at finding Mr. Miller."

Walt's striking-muscles relaxed, and his

shoulders seemed to droop with hopelessness.

"I guess you're right, Madge," he said. "Wolf isn't Wolf, but Brown, and he must belong to Mr. Miller."

"Perhaps Mr. Miller will sell him," she suggested. "We can buy him."

Skiff Miller shook his head, no longer belligerent, but kindly, quick to be generous in response to generousness.

"I had five dogs," he said, casting about for the easiest way to temper his refusal. "He was the leader. They was the crack team of Alaska. Nothin' could touch 'em. In 1898 I refused five thousand dollars for the bunch. Dogs was high then, anyway; but that wasn't what made the fancy price. It was the team itself. Brown was the best in the team. That winter I refused twelve hundred for 'm. I didn't sell 'm then, an' I ain't a-sellin' 'm now. Besides, I think a mighty lot of that dog. I've been lookin' for 'm for three years. It made me fair sick when I found he'd been stole—not the value of him, but the—well, I liked 'm like hell, that's all, beggin' your pardon. I couldn't believe my eyes when I seen 'm just now. I thought I was dreamin'. It was too good to be true. Why, I was his wet-nurse. I put 'm to bed snug every night. His mother died, an' I brought 'm up on condensed milk at two dollars a can when I couldn't afford it in my own coffee. He never knew any mother but me. He used to suck my finger regular, the darn little cuss—that finger right there!"

And Skiff Miller, too overwrought for speech, held up a forefinger for them to see.

"That very finger," he managed to articulate, as though somehow it clinched the proof of ownership and the bond of affection.

He was still gazing at his extended finger, when Madge began to speak.

"But the dog," she said. "You haven't considered the dog."

Skiff Miller looked puzzled.

"Have you thought about him?" she asked.

"Don't know what you're drivin' at," was the response.

"Maybe the dog has some choice in the matter," Madge went on. "Maybe he has his likes and desires. You have not considered him. You give him no choice. It has never entered your mind that possibly he might prefer California to Alaska. You consider only what you like. You do with him as you would with a sack of potatoes or a bale of hay."

This was a new way of looking at it, and Miller was visibly impressed as he debated it in his mind. Madge took advantage of his indecision.

"If you really love him, what would be happiness to him would be your happiness also," she urged.

Skiff Miller continued to debate with himself, and Madge stole a glance of exultation to her husband, who looked back warm approval.

"What do you think?" the Klondiker suddenly demanded.

It was her turn to be puzzled. "What do you mean?" she asked.

"D'ye think he'd sooner stay in California?"

She nodded her head with positiveness. "I am sure of it."

Skiff Miller again debated with himself, though this time aloud, at the same time running his gaze in a judicial way over the mooted animal.

"He was a good worker. He's done a heap of work for me. He never loafed on me, an' he was a joe-dandy at hammerin' a raw team into shape. He's got a head on him. He can do everything but talk. He knows what you say to him. Look at 'm now. He knows we're talkin' about him."

The dog was lying at Skiff Miller's feet, head close down on paws, ears erect and listening, and eyes that were quick and eager to follow the sound of speech as it fell from the lips of first one and then the other.

"An' there's a lot of work in 'm yet. He's good for years to come. An' I do like him. I do like him!"

Once or twice after that Skiff Miller opened his mouth and closed it again without speaking. Finally he said:

"I'll tell you what I'll do. Your remarks, ma'am, has some weight in them. The dog's worked hard, and maybe he's earned a soft berth an' has got a right to choose. Anyway, we'll leave it up to him. Whatever he says goes. You people stay right here settin' down. I'll say good-by and walk off casual like. If he wants to stay he can stay. If he wants to come with me, let 'm come. I won't call 'm to come and don't you call 'm to come back."

He looked with sudden suspicion at Madge, and added, "Only you must play fair. No persuadin' after my back is turned."

"We'll play fair," Madge began, but Skiff Miller broke in on her assurances.

STRUGGLING WITH ALL HIS BODY TO EXPRESS THE THOUGHT THAT WAS IN HIM.

"I know the ways of women," he announced. "Their hearts is soft. When their hearts is touched they're likely to stack the cards, look at the bottom of the deck, and lie like the devil—beggin' your pardon, ma'am. I'm only discoursin' about women in general."

"I don't know how to thank you," Madge quavered.

"I don't see as you've got any call to thank me," he replied. "Brown ain't decided yet. Now, you won't mind if I go away slow? It's no more'n fair, seein' I'll be out of sight inside a hundred yards."

Madge agreed, and added, "And I promise you faithfully that we won't do anything to influence him."

"Well, then, I might as well be gettin' along," Skiff Miller said in the ordinary tones of one departing.

At this change in his voice Wolf lifted his head quickly, and still more quickly got to his feet when the man and woman shook hands. He sprang up on his hind legs, resting his fore paws on her hip, and at the same time licking Skiff Miller's hand. When the latter shook hands with Walt, Wolf repeated his act, resting his weight on Walt and licking both men's hands.

"It ain't no picnic, I can tell you that," were the Klondiker's last words, as he turned and went slowly up the trail.

For the distance of twenty feet Wolf watched him go, himself all eagerness and expectancy, as though waiting for the man to turn and retrace his steps. Then, with a quick, low whine, Wolf sprang after him, overtook him, caught his hand between his teeth with reluctant tenderness, and strove gently to make him pause.

Failing in this, Wolf raced back to where Walt Irvine sat, catching his coat-sleeve in his teeth and trying vainly to drag him after the retreating man.

Wolf's perturbation began to wax. He desired ubiquity. He wanted to be in two places at the same time, with the old master and the new, and steadily the distance between them was increasing. He sprang about excitedly, making short, nervous leaps and twists, now toward one, now toward the other, in painful indecision, not knowing his own mind, desiring both and unable to choose, uttering quick, sharp whines, and beginning to pant.

He sat down abruptly on his haunches, thrusting his nose upward, the mouth opening and closing with jerking movements, each time opening wider. These jerking movements were in unison with the recurrent spasms that attacked the throat, each spasm severer and more intense than the preceding one. And in accord with jerks and spasms the larynx began to vibrate, at first silently, accompanied by the rush of air expelled from the lungs, then sounding a low, deep note, the lowest in the register of the human ear. All this was the nervous and muscular preliminary to howling.

But just as the howl was on the verge of bursting from the full throat, the wide-opened mouth was closed, the paroxysms ceased, and he looked long and steadily at the retreating man. Suddenly Wolf turned his head and over his shoulder just as steadily regarded Walt. The appeal was unanswered. Not a word nor a sign did the dog receive, no suggestion and no clue as to what his conduct should be.

A glance ahead to where the old master was nearing the curve of the trail excited him again. He sprang to his feet with a whine, and then, struck by a new idea, turned his attention to Madge. Hitherto he had ignored her, but now, both masters failing him, she alone was left. He went over to her and snuggled his head in her lap, nudging her arm with his nose—an old trick of his when begging for favors. He backed away from her and began writhing and twisting playfully, curveting and prancing, half rearing and striking his fore paws to the earth, struggling with all his body, from the wheedling eyes and flattening ears to the wagging tail, to express the thought that was in him and that was denied him utterance.

This, too, he soon abandoned. He was depressed by the coldness of these humans who had never been cold before. No response could he draw from them, no help could he get. They did not consider him. They were as dead.

He turned and silently gazed after the old master. Skiff Miller was rounding the curve. In a moment he would be gone from view. Yet he never turned his head, plodding straight onward, slowly and methodically, as though possessed of no interest in what was occurring behind his back.

And in this fashion he went out of view. Wolf waited for him to reappear. He waited a long moment, silently, quietly, without movement, as though turned to stone—withal stone quick with eagerness and desire. He barked once, and waited. Then he turned and trotted back to Walt Irvine. He sniffed his hand and dropped down heavily at his feet, watching the trail where it curved emptily from view.

The tiny stream slipping down the mossy-lipped stone seemed suddenly to increase the volume of its gurgling noise. Save for the meadow-larks, there was no other sound. The great yellow butterflies drifted silently through the sunshine and lost themselves in the drowsy shadows. Madge gazed triumphantly at her husband.

A few minutes later Wolf got upon his feet. Decision and deliberation marked his movements. He did not glance at the man and woman. His eyes were fixed up the trail. He had made up his mind. They knew it. And they knew, so far as they were concerned, that the ordeal had just begun.

He broke into a trot, and Madge's lips pursed, forming an avenue for the caressing sound that it was the will of her to send forth. But the caressing sound was not made. She was impelled to look at her husband, and she saw the sternness with which he watched her. The pursed lips relaxed, and she sighed inaudibly.

Wolf's trot broke into a run. Wider and wider were the leaps he made. Not once did he turn his head, his wolf's brush standing out straight behind him, his speed not once lessened. He cut sharply across the curve of the trail and was gone.

15
THE SUN-DOG TRAIL

The Sun-dog Trail

BY JACK LONDON

SITKA CHARLEY smoked his pipe and gazed thoughtfully at the newspaper illustration on the wall. For half an hour he had been steadily regarding it, and for half an hour I had been slyly watching him. Something was going on in that mind of his, and, whatever it was, I knew it was well worth knowing. He had lived life, and seen things, and performed that prodigy of prodigies, namely, the turning of his back upon his own people, and, in so far as it was possible for an Indian, becoming a white man even in his mental processes. As he phrased it himself, he had come into the warm, sat among us, by our fires, and become one of us.

We had struck this deserted cabin after a hard day on trail. The dogs had been fed, the supper dishes washed, the beds made, and we were now enjoying that most delicious hour that comes each day, on the Alaskan trail, when nothing intervenes between the tired body and bed save the smoking of the evening pipe.

"Well?" I finally broke the silence.

He took the pipe from his mouth and said, simply, "I do not understand."

He smoked on again, and again removed the pipe, using it to point at the illustration.

"That picture—what does it mean? I do not understand."

I looked at the picture. A man, with a preposterously wicked face, his right hand pressed dramatically to his heart, was falling backward to the floor. Confronting him, with a face that was a composite of destroying angel and Adonis, was a man holding a smoking revolver.

"One man is killing the other man," I said, aware of a distinct bepuzzlement of my own and of failure to explain.

"Why?" asked Sitka Charley.

"I do not know," I confessed.

"That picture is all end," he said. "It has no beginning."

"It is life," I said.

"Life has beginning," he objected.

"Look at that picture," I commanded, pointing to another decoration. "It means something. Tell me what it means to you."

He studied it for several minutes.

"The little girl is sick," he said, finally. "That is the doctor looking at her. They have been up all night—see, the oil is low in the lamp, the first morning light is coming in at the window. It is a great sickness; maybe she will die; that is why the doctor looks so hard. That is the mother. It is a great sickness, because the mother's head is on the table and she is crying."

"And now you understand the picture," I cried.

He shook his head, and asked, "The little girl—does it die?"

It was my turn for silence.

"Does it die?" he reiterated. "You are a painter-man. Maybe you know."

"No, I do not know," I confessed.

"It is not life," he delivered himself, dogmatically. "In life little girl die or get well. Something happen in life. In picture nothing happen. No, I do not understand pictures."

"Pictures are bits of life," I said. "We paint life as we see it. For instance, Charley, you are coming along the trail. It is night. You see a cabin. The window is lighted. You look through the window for one second, or for two seconds; you see something, and you go on your way. You see maybe a man writing a letter. You saw something without beginning or end. Nothing happened. Yet it was a bit of life you saw. You remember it afterward. It is like a picture in your memory. The window is the frame of the picture."

For a long time he smoked in silence. He nodded his head several times, and grunted once or twice. Then he knocked the ashes from his pipe, carefully refilled it, and, after a thoughtful pause, he lighted it again.

"Then have I, too, seen many pictures of life," he began; "pictures not painted but seen with the eyes. I have looked at them like through the window at the man writing the letter. I have seen many pieces of life, without beginning, without end, without understanding."

With a sudden change of position he turned his eyes full upon me and regarded me thoughtfully.

"Look you," he said; "you are a painter-man. How would you paint this which I saw, a picture without beginning, the ending of which I do not understand, a piece of life with the northern lights for a candle and Alaska for a frame?"

"It is a large canvas," I murmured.

"There are many names for this picture," he said. "But in the picture there are many sun-dogs, and it comes into my mind to call it 'The Sun-dog Trail.' It was seven years ago, the fall of '97, when I saw the woman first time. At Lake Linderman I had one canoe. I came over Chilcoot Pass with two thousand letters for Dawson. Everybody rush to Klondike at that time. Many people on trail. Many people chop down trees and make boats. Last water, snow in the air, snow on the ground, ice on the lake, on the river. Every day more snow, more ice, any day maybe freeze-up come; then no more water, all ice, everybody walk; Dawson six hundred miles; long time walk. Boat go very quick. Everybody want to go boat. Everybody say, 'Charley, two hundred dollars you take me in canoe,' 'Charley, three hundred dollars,' 'Charley, four hundred dollars.' I say no; all the time I say no. I am letter-carrier.

"In the morning I get to Lake Linderman; I walk all night and am much tired. I cook breakfast, I eat, then I sleep on the beach three hours. I wake up. It is ten o'clock. Snow is falling. There is wind, much wind that blows fair. Also, there is a woman who sits in the snow alongside. She is white woman, she is young, very pretty; maybe she is twenty years old, maybe twenty-five years old. She look at me. I look at her. She is very tired. She is no dance-woman. I see that right away. She is good woman, and she is very tired.

"'You are Sitka Charley,' she says. 'I go to Dawson,' she says. 'I go in your canoe—how much?'

"I do not want anybody in my canoe. I do not like to say no. So I say, 'One thousand dollars.' She look at me very hard, then she says, 'When you start?' I say right away. Then she says all right, she will give me one thousand dollars.

"What can I say? I do not want the woman, yet have I given my word that for one thousand dollars she can come. And that woman, that young woman, all alone on the trail, there in the snow, she take out one thousand dollars in greenbacks, and she put them in my hand. I look at money, I look at her. What can I say? I say: 'No; my canoe very small. There is no room for outfit.' She laugh. She says: 'I am great traveller. This is my outfit.' She kick one small pack in the snow. It is two fur robes, canvas outside, some woman's clothes inside. I pick it up. Maybe thirty-five pounds. I am surprised. She take it away from me. She says, 'Come, let us start.' She carries pack into canoe. What can I say? I put my blankets into canoe. We start.

"And that is the way I saw the woman first time. The wind was fair. I put up small sail. The canoe went very fast. The woman was much afraid. 'What for you come Klondike much afraid?' I ask. She laugh at me, a hard laugh, but she is still much afraid. Also she is very tired. I run canoe through rapids to Lake Bennett. Water very bad, and woman cry out because she is afraid. We go down Lake Bennett. Snow, ice, wind like a gale, but woman is very tired and go to sleep.

"That night we make camp at Windy Arm. Woman sit by fire and eat supper. I look at her. She is pretty. She fix hair. There is much hair, and it is brown; also sometimes it is like gold in the firelight when she turn her head, so, and flashes come from it like golden fire. The eyes are large and brown. When she smile—how can I say?—when she smile I know white man like to kiss her, just like that, when she smile. She never do hard work. Her hands are soft like a baby's hand. She is not thin, but round like a baby; her arm, her leg, her

Half-tone plate engraved by C. Schwarzburger

"'I GO TO DAWSON IN YOUR CANOE,' SHE SAYS"

muscles, all soft and round like baby. Her waist is small, and when she stand up, when she walk, or move her head or arm, it is—I do not know the word—but it is nice to look at, like—maybe I say she is built on lines like the lines of a good canoe, just like that,—and when she move she is like the movement of the good canoe sliding through still water or leaping through water when it is white and fast and angry. It is very good to see.

"I ask her what is her name. She laugh, then she says, 'Mary Jones; that is my name.' But I know all the time that Mary Jones is not her name.

"It is very cold in canoe, and because of cold sometimes she not feel good. Sometimes she feel good and she sing. Her voice is like a silver bell, and I feel good all over like when I go into church at Holy Cross Mission, and when she sing I feel strong and paddle like hell. Then she laugh and says, 'You think we get to Dawson before freeze-up, Charley?' Sometimes she sit in canoe and is thinking far away, her eyes like that, all empty. She does not see Sitka Charley, nor the ice, nor the snow. She is far away. Sometimes, when she is thinking far away, her face is not good to see. It looks like a face that is angry, like the face of one man when he want to kill another man.

"Last day to Dawson very bad. Shore-ice in all the eddies, mush-ice in the stream. I cannot paddle. The canoe freeze to ice. All the time we go down Yukon in the ice. Then ice stop, canoe stop, everything stop. 'Let us go to shore,' the woman says. I say no; better wait. By and by everything start down-stream again. There is much snow; I cannot see. At eleven o'clock at night everything stop. At one o'clock everything start again. At three o'clock everything stop. Canoe is smashed like egg-shell, but it is on top of ice and cannot sink. I hear dogs howling. We wait; we sleep. By and by morning come. There is no more snow. It is the freeze-up, and there is Dawson. Canoe smash and stop right at Dawson. Sitka Charley has come in with two thousand letters on very last water.

"The woman rent a cabin on the hill, and for one week I see her no more.

Then, one day, she come to me. 'Charley,' she says, 'how do you like to work for me? You drive dogs, make camp, travel with me.' I say that I make too much money carrying letters. She says, 'Charley, I will pay you more money.' I tell her that pick-and-shovel man get fifteen dollars a day in the mines. She says, 'That is four hundred and fifty dollars a month.' And I say, 'Sitka Charley is no pick-and-shovel man.' Then she says: 'I understand, Charley. I will give you seven hundred and fifty dollars each month.' It is a good price, and I go to work for her. I buy for her dogs and sled. We travel up Klondike, up Bonanza and Eldorado, over to Indian River, to Sulphur Creek, to Dominion, back across divide to Gold Bottom and to Too Much Gold, and back to Dawson. All the time she look for something; I do not know what.

"She has a small revolver, which she carries in her belt. Sometimes, on trail, she makes practice with revolver.

"At Dawson comes the man. Which way he come I do not know. Only do I know he is *che-cha-quo*—what you call tenderfoot. His hands are soft. He never do hard work. At first I think maybe he is her husband. But he is too young. He is maybe twenty years old. His eyes blue, his hair yellow; he has a little mustache which is yellow. His name is John Jones. Maybe he is her brother. I do not know.

"One night I am asleep at Dawson. He wake me up. He says, 'Get the dogs ready; we start.' No more do I ask questions, so I get the dogs ready and we start. We go down the Yukon. It is night-time, it is November, and it is very cold—sixty-five below. She is soft. He is soft. The cold bites. They get tired. They cry under their breaths to themselves. By and by I say better we stop and make camp. But they say that they will go on. After that I say nothing. All the time, day after day, it is that way. They are very soft. They get stiff and sore. They do not understand moccasins, and their feet hurt very much. They limp, they stagger like drunken people, they cry under their breaths; and all the time they say: 'On! on! We will go on!'

"We make Circle City. That for

which they look is not there. I think now that we will rest, and rest the dogs. But we do not rest; not for one day do we rest. 'Come,' says the woman to the man, 'let us go on.' And we go on. We leave the Yukon. We cross the divide to the west and swing down into the Tanana Country. There are new diggings there. But that for which they look is not there, and we take the back trail to Circle City.

"It is a hard journey. December is 'most gone. The days are short. It is very cold.

"We limp into Circle City. It is Christmas eve. I dance, drink, make a good time, for to-morrow is Christmas day and we will rest. But no. It is five o'clock in the morning—Christmas morning. I am two hours asleep. The man stand by my bed. 'Come, Charley,' he says; 'harness the dogs. We start.' I harness the dogs, and we start down the Yukon.

"They are very weary. They have travelled many hundreds of miles, and they do not understand the way of the trail. Besides, their cough is very bad—the dry cough that makes strong men swear and weak men cry. Every day they go on. Never do they rest the dogs. Always do they buy new dogs. At every camp, at every post, at every Indian village, do they cut out the tired dogs and put in fresh dogs. They have much money, money without end, and like water they spend it. They are crazy? Sometimes I think so, for there is a devil in them that drives them. They cry aloud in their sleep at night. And in the day, as they stagger along the trail, they cry under their breaths.

"We pass Fort Yukon. We pass Fort Hamilton. We pass Minook. January has come and nearly gone. The days are very short. At nine o'clock comes daylight. At three o'clock comes night. And it is cold. And even I, Sitka Charley, am tired. Will we go on forever this way without end? I do not know. But always do I look along the trail for that which they try to find. There are few people on the trail. Sometimes we travel one hundred miles and never see a sign of life. The northern lights flame in the sky, and the sun-dogs dance, and the air is filled with frost-dust.

"I am Sitka Charley, a strong man. I was born on the trail, and all my days have I lived on the trail. And yet have these two baby wolves made me tired. Their eyes are sunk deep in their heads, bright sometimes as with fever, dim and cloudy sometimes like the eyes of the dead. Their cheeks are black and raw from many freezings. Sometimes it is the woman in the morning who says: 'I cannot get up. I cannot move. Let me die.' And it is the man who stands beside her and says, 'Come, let us go on.'

"Sometimes, at the trading-posts, the man and woman get letters. I do not know what is in the letters. But it is the scent that they follow; these letters themselves are the scent. One time an Indian gives them a letter. I talk with him privately. He says it is a man with one eye who gives him the letter—a man who travels fast down the Yukon. That is all. But I know that the baby wolves are after the man with the one eye.

"It is February, and we have travelled fifteen hundred miles. We are getting near Bering Sea, and there are storms and blizzards. The going is hard. We come to Anvig. I do not know, but I think sure they get a letter at Anvig, for they are much excited, and they say, 'Come, hurry; let us go on.' But I say we must buy grub, and they say we must travel light and fast. Also, they say that we can get grub at Charley McKeon's cabin. Then do I know that they take the big cut-off, for it is there that Charley McKeon lives where the Black Rock stands by the trail.

"Before we start I talk maybe two minutes with the priest at Anvig. Yes, there is a man with one eye who has gone by and who travels fast. And I know that for which they look is the man with the one eye. We leave Anvig with little grub, and travel light and fast. We take the big cut-off, and the trail is fresh. The baby wolves have their noses down to the trail, and they say, 'Hurry!' All the time do they say: 'Hurry! Faster! Faster!' It is hard on the dogs. We have not much food and we cannot give them enough to eat, and they grow weak. Also, they must work hard. The woman has true sorrow for them, and often, because of them, the tears are in her eyes. But the devil in her that drives her on will not let her stop and rest the dogs.

"And then we come upon the man with the one eye. He is in the snow by the trail and his leg is broken. Because of the leg he has made a poor camp, and has been lying on his blankets for three days and keeping a fire going. When we find him he is swearing. Never have I heard a man swear like that man. I am glad. Now that they have found that for which they look, we will have a rest. But the woman says: 'Let us start. Hurry!'

"I am surprised. But the man with the one eye says: 'Never mind me. Give me your grub. You will get more grub at McKeon's cabin to-morrow. Send McKeon back for me. But do you go on.' So we give him our grub, which is not much, and we chop wood for his fire, and we take his strongest dogs and go on. We left the man with one eye there in the snow, and he died there in the snow, for McKeon never went back for him.

"That day and that night we had nothing to eat, and all next day we travelled fast, and we were weak with hunger. Then we came to the Black Rock, which rose five hundred feet above the trail. It was at the end of the day. Darkness was coming, and we could not find the cabin of McKeon. We slept hungry, and in the morning looked for the cabin. It was not there, which was a strange thing, for everybody knew that McKeon lived in a cabin at Black Rock. We were near to the coast, where the wind blows hard and there is much snow. Everywhere were there small hills of snow where the wind had piled it up. I have a thought, and I dig in one and another of the hills of snow. Soon I find the walls of the cabin, and I dig down to the door. I go inside. McKeon is dead. Maybe two or three weeks he is dead. A sickness had come upon him so that he could not leave the cabin. He had eaten his grub and died. I looked for his cache, but there was no grub in it.

"'Let us go on,' said the woman. Her eyes were hungry, and her hand was upon her heart, as with the hurt of something inside. She swayed back and forth like a tree in the wind as she stood there.

"'Yes, let us go on,' said the man. His voice was hollow, like the *klonk* of an old raven, and he was hunger-mad. His eyes were like live coals of fire, and as his body rocked to and fro, so rocked his soul inside. And I, too, said, 'Let us go on.' For that one thought, laid upon me like a lash for every mile of fifteen hundred miles, had burned itself into my soul, and I think that I, too, was mad. Besides, we could only go on, for there was no grub. And we went on, giving no thought to the man with the one eye in the snow.

"The snow had covered the trail, and there was no sign that men had ever come or gone that way. All day the wind blew and the snow fell, and all day we travelled. Then the woman began to fall. Then the man. I did not fall, but my feet were heavy, and I caught my toes and stumbled many times.

"That night is the end of February. I kill three ptarmigan with the woman's revolver, and we are made somewhat strong again. But the dogs have nothing to eat. They try to eat their harness, which is of leather and walrus-hide, and I must fight them off with a club and hang all the harness in a tree. And all night they howl and fight around that tree. But we do not mind. We sleep like dead people, and in the morning get up like dead people out of our graves and go on along the trail.

"That morning is the 1st of March, and on that morning I see the first sign of that after which the baby wolves are in search. It is clear weather, and cold. The sun stay longer in the sky, and there are sun-dogs flashing on either side, and the air is bright with frost-dust. The snow falls no more upon the trail, and I see the fresh sign of dogs and sled. There is one man with that outfit, and I see in the snow that he is not strong. He, too, has not enough to eat. The young wolves see the fresh sign, too, and they are much excited. 'Hurry!' they say. All the time they say: 'Hurry! Faster, Charley, faster!'

"We make hurry very slow. All the time the man and the woman fall down. When they try to ride on sled, the dogs are too weak, and the dogs fall down. Besides, it is so cold that if they ride on the sled they will freeze. It is very easy for a hungry man to freeze. When the woman fall down, the man help her up. Sometimes the woman help the man up. By and by both fall down and cannot get up, and I must help them up all the time, else they will not get up and will die there in the snow. This is very hard work, for I am greatly weary, and as well I must drive the dogs, and the man and woman are very heavy, with no strength in their bodies. So, by and by, I, too, fall down in the snow, and there is no one to help me up. I must get up by myself. And always do I get up by myself, and help them up, and make the dogs go on.

"That night I get one ptarmigan, and we are very hungry. And that night the man says to me, 'What time start to-morrow, Charley?' It is like the voice of a ghost. I say, 'All the time you make start at five o'clock.' 'To-morrow,' he says, 'we will start at three o'clock.'

"And we start at three o'clock. It is clear and cold, and there is no wind. When daylight comes we can see a long way off. And it is very quiet. We can hear no sound but the beat of our hearts, and in the silence that is a very loud sound. We are like sleep-walkers, and we walk in dreams until we fall down; and then we know we must get up, and we see the trail once more and hear the beating of our hearts.

"In the morning we come upon the last-night camp of the man who is before us. It is a poor camp, the kind a man makes who is hungry and without strength. On the snow there are pieces of blanket and of canvas, and I know what has happened. His dogs have eaten their harness, and he has made new harness out of his blankets. The man and woman stare hard at what is to be seen. Their eyes are toil-mad and hunger-mad, and burn like fire deep in their heads. Their faces are like the faces of people who have died of hunger, and their cheeks are black with the dead flesh of many freezings. We come to where we can see a long way over the snow, and that for which they look is before them. A mile away there are black spots upon the snow. The black spots move. My eyes are dim, and I must stiffen my soul to see. And I see one man with dogs and a sled. The baby wolves see, too. They can no longer talk, but they whisper: 'On, on! Let us hurry!'

"And they fall down, but they go on. The man who is before us, his blanket harness breaks often and he must stop and mend it. Our harness is good, for I have hung it in trees each night. At eleven o'clock the man is half a mile away. At one o'clock he is a quarter of a mile away. He is very weak. We see him fall down many times in the snow.

"Now we are three hundred yards away. We go very slow. Maybe in two, three hours we go one mile. We do not walk. All the time we fall down. We stand up and stagger two steps, maybe three steps, then we fall down again. And all the time I must help up the man and woman. Sometimes they rise to their knees and fall forward, maybe four or five times before they can get to their feet again, and stagger two or three steps and fall. But always do they fall forward. Standing or kneeling, always do they fall forward, gaining on the trail each time by the length of their bodies.

"Sometimes they crawl on hands and knees like animals that live in the forest. We go like snails—like snails that are dying we go so slow. And yet we go faster than the man who is before us. For he, too, falls all the time, and there is no Sitka Charley to lift him up. Now he is two hundred yards away. After a long time he is one hundred yards away.

"It is a funny sight. I want to laugh out loud, Ha! ha! just like that, it is so funny. It is a race of dead men and dead dogs. It is like in a dream when you have a nightmare and run away very fast for your life and go very slow. The man who is with me is mad. The woman is mad. I am mad. All the world is mad. And I want to laugh, it is so funny.

"The stranger man who is before us leaves his dogs behind and goes on alone across the snow. After a long time we come to the dogs. They lie helpless in the snow, their harness of blanket and canvas on them, the sled behind them, and as we pass them they whine to us and cry like babies that are hungry.

"Then we, too, leave our dogs and go on alone across the snow. The man and the woman are nearly gone, and they moan and groan and sob, but they go on. I, too, go on. I have but the one thought. It is to come up to the stranger man. Then it is that I shall rest, and not until

Half-tone plate engraved by A. Hayman

"AND THUS I, SITKA CHARLEY, SAW THE BABY WOLVES MAKE THEIR KILL"

then shall I rest, and it seems that I must lie down and sleep for a thousand years, I am so tired.

"The stranger man is fifty yards away, all alone in the white snow. He falls and crawls, staggers, and falls and crawls again. By and by he crawls on hands and knees. He no longer stands up. And the man and woman no longer stand up. They, too, crawl after him on hands and knees. But I stand up. Sometimes I fall, but always do I stand up again.

"On either side the sun are sun-dogs, so that there are three suns in the sky.

"After a long time the stranger man crawls no more. He stands slowly upon his feet and rocks back and forth. Also does he take off one mitten and wait with revolver in his hand, rocking back and forth as he waits. His face is skin and bones, and frozen black. It is a hungry face. The eyes are deep-sunk in his head, and the lips are snarling. The man and woman, too, get upon their feet, and they go toward him very slowly. And all about is the snow and the silence. And in the sky are three suns, and all the air is flashing with the dust of diamonds.

"And thus it was that I, Sitka Charley, saw the baby wolves make their kill. No word is spoken. Only does the stranger man snarl with his hungry face. Also does he rock to and fro, his shoulders drooping, his knees bent, and his legs wide apart so that he does not fall down. The man and the woman stop maybe fifty feet away. Their legs, too, are wide apart so that they do not fall down, and their bodies rock to and fro. The stranger man is very weak. His arm shakes, so that when he shoots at the man his bullet strikes in the snow. The man cannot take off his mitten. The stranger man shoots at him again, and this time the bullet goes by in the air. Then the man takes the mitten in his teeth and pulls it off. But his hand is frozen and he cannot hold the revolver, and it falls in the snow. I look at the woman. Her mitten is off, and the revolver is in her hand. Three times she shoot, quick, just like that. The hungry face of the stranger man is still snarling as he falls forward in the snow.

"They did not look at the dead man.

'Let us go on,' they said. And we went on. But now that they have found that for which they look, they are like dead. The last strength has gone out of them. They can stand no more upon their feet. They will not crawl, but desire only to close their eyes and sleep. I see not far away a place for camp. I kick them. I have my dog-whip, and I give them the lash of it. They cry aloud, but they must crawl. And they do crawl to the place for camp. I build fire so that they will not freeze. Then I go back for sled. Also, I kill the dogs of the stranger man so that we may have food and not die. I put the man and woman in blankets and they sleep. Sometimes I wake them up and give them little bit of food. They are not awake, but they take the food. The woman sleep one day and a half. Then she wake up and go to sleep again. The man sleep two days and wake up and go to sleep again. After that we go down to the coast at St. Michaels. And when the ice goes out of Bering Sea the man and woman go away on a steamship. But first they pay me my seven hundred and fifty dollars a month."

"But why did they kill the man?" I asked.

Sitka Charley delayed reply until he had lighted his pipe. He glanced at the illustration on the wall and nodded his head at it familiarly. Then he said, speaking slowly and ponderingly:

"I have thought much. I do not know. It is something that happened. It is a picture I remember. It is like looking in at the window and seeing the man writing a letter. They came into my life and they went out of my life, and the picture is, as I have said, without beginning, the end without understanding."

"You have painted many pictures in the telling," I said.

"Ay,"—he nodded his head. "But they were without beginning and without end."

"The last picture of all had an end," I said.

"Ay," he answered. "But what end?"

"It was a piece of life," I said.

"Ay," he answered. "It was a piece of life."

16
A RELIC OF THE PLIOCENE

WASH MY HANDS of him at the start. I cannot father his tales, nor will I be responsible for them. I make these preliminary reservations, observe, as a guard upon my own integrity. I possess a certain definite position in a small way, also a wife; and for the good name of the community which honors my existence with its approval, and for the sake of her posterity and mine, I cannot take the chances I once did, nor foster probabilities with the careless improvidence of youth. So, I repeat, I wash my hands of him, this Nimrod, this mighty hunter, this homely, blue-eyed, freckle-faced Thomas Stevens.

Having been honest to myself, and to whatever prospective olive branches my wife may be pleased to tender me, I can now afford to be generous. I shall not criticise the tales told me by Thomas Stevens, and, further, I shall withhold my judgment. If it be asked why, I can only add that judgment I have none. Long have I pondered, weighed and balanced, but never have my conclusions been twice the same—forsooth! because Thomas Stevens is a greater man than I. If he have told truths, well and good; if untruths, still well and good. For who can prove? or who disprove? I eliminate myself from the proposition, while those of little faith may do as I have done—go find the said Thomas Stevens and discuss to his face the various matters, which, if fortune serve, I shall relate. As to where he may be found? The directions are simple: anywhere between 53 north latitude and the Pole, on the one hand; and, on the other, the likeliest hunting grounds which lie between the east coast of Siberia and furthermost Labrador. That he is there, somewhere, within that clearly defined territory, I pledge the word of an honorable man whose expectations entail straight speaking and right living.

Thomas Stevens may have toyed prodigiously with truth, but when we first met (it were well to mark this point), he wandered into my camp when I thought myself a thousand miles beyond the outermost post of civilization. At the sight of his human face, the first in weary months, I could have sprung forward and folded him in my arms (and I am not by any means a demonstrative man); but to him his visit seemed the most casual thing under the sun. He just strolled into the light of my camp, passed the time of day after the custom of men on beaten trails, threw my snowshoes the one way and a couple of dogs the other, and so made room for himself by the fire. Said he'd just dropped in to borrow a pinch of soda and to see if I had any decent tobacco. He plucked forth an ancient pipe, loaded it with painstaking care, and, without as much as by your leave, whacked half the tobacco of my pouch into his. Yes, the stuff was fairly good. He sighed with the contentment of the just, and literally absorbed the smoke from

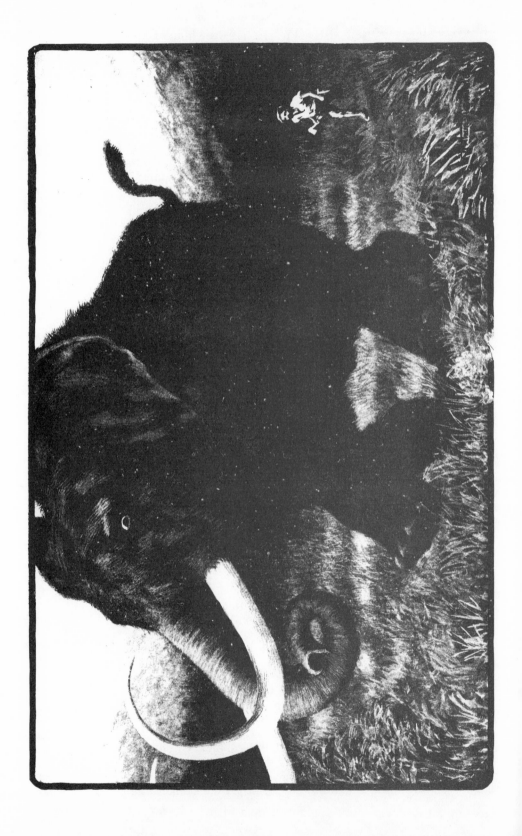

the crisping yellow flakes, and it did my smoker's heart good to behold him.

Hunter? Trapper? Prospector? He shrugged his shoulders No; just sort of knocking round a bit. Had come up from the Great Slave some time since, and was thinking of trapsing over into the Yukon country. The Factor of Koshim had spoken about the discoveries on the Klondike, and he was of a mind to run over for a peep. I noticed that he spoke of the Klondike in the archaic vernacular, calling it the Reindeer River—a conceited custom which the Old Timers employ against the *che-cha-quas* and all tenderfeet in general. But he did it so naïvely and as such a matter of course, that there was no sting, and I forgave him. He also had it in view, he said, before he crossed the divide into the Yukon, to make a little run up Fort o' Good Hope way.

Now Fort o' Good Hope is a far journey to the north, over and beyond the Circle, in a place where the feet of few men have trod; and when a nondescript ragamuffin comes in out of the night, from nowhere in particular, to sit by one's fire and discourse on such in terms of "trapsing" and "a little run," it is fair time to rouse up and shake off the dream. Wherefore I looked about me; saw the fly, and, underneath, the pine boughs spread for the sleeping furs; saw the grub sacks, the camera, the frosty breaths of the dogs circling on the edge of the light; and, above, a great streamer of the aurora bridging the zenith from southeast to northwest I shivered. There is a magic in the Northland night which steals in on one like fevers from malarial marshes. You are clutched and downed before you are aware. Then I looked to the snowshoes, lying prone and crossed where he had flung them. Also I had an eye to my tobacco pouch. Half, at least, of its goodly store had vamosed. That settled it. Fancy had not tricked me after all.

Crazed with suffering, I thought, looking steadfastly at the man. One of those wild stampeders, strayed far from his bearings and wandering like a lost soul through great vastnesses and unknown deeps. Oh, well, let his moods slip on, until, mayhap, he gathers his tangled wits together. Who knows?—the mere sound of a fellow creature's voice may bring all straight again.

So I led him on in talk, and soon I marvelled, for he talked of game and the ways thereof. He had killed the Siberian wolf of westernmost Alaska, and the chamois in the secret Rockies. He averred he knew the haunts where the last buffalo still roamed; that he had hung on the flanks of the caribou when they ran by the hundred thousand, and slept in the Great Barrens on the musk-ox's winter trail.

And I shifted my judgment accordingly (the first revision, but by no account the last), and deemed him a monumental effigy of truth. Why it was I know not, but the spirit moved me to repeat a tale told to me by a man who had dwelt in the land too long to know better. It was of the great bear which hugs the steep slopes of St. Elias, never descending to the levels of the gentler inclines. Now God so constituted this creature for its hillside habitat that the legs of one side are all of a foot longer than those of the other. This is mighty convenient, as will be readily admitted. So I hunted this rare beast in my own name, told it in the first person, present tense, painted the requisite locale, gave it the necessary garnishings and touches of verisimilitude, and looked to see the man stunned by the recital.

Not he. Had he doubted, I could have forgiven him. Had he objected, denying the dangers of such a hunt by virtue of the animal's inability to turn about and go the other way—had he done this, I say, I could have taken him by the hand for the true sportsman that he was. Not he. He sniffed, looked on me, and sniffed again; then gave my tobacco due praise, thrust one foot into my lap, and bade me examine the gear. It was a *mucluc* of the Innuit pattern, sewed together with sinew threads, and devoid of beads or furbelows. But it was the skin itself that was remarkable. In that it was all of half an inch thick it reminded me of walrus-hide; but there the resemblance ceased, for no walrus ever bore so marvellous a growth of hair. On the side and ankles this hair was well-nigh worn away, what of friction with underbrush and snow, but around the top and down the more sheltered back it was coarse, dirty-black, and very thick. I parted it with difficulty and looked beneath for the fine fur which is common with northern animals, but found it in this case to be absent. This, however, was compensated for by the length. Indeed, the tufts which had survived wear and tear measured all of seven or eight inches.

I looked up into the man's face, and he pulled his foot down and asked, "Find hide like that on your St. Elias bear?"

I shook my head. "Nor on any other creature of land or sea," I answered candidly. The thickness of it, and the length of the hair, puzzled me.

"That," he said, and said without the slightest hint of impressiveness, "that came from a mammoth."

"Nonsense!" I exclaimed, for I could not forbear the protest of my unbelief. "The mammoth, my dear sir, long ago vanished from the earth. We know it once existed by the fossil remains which we have unearthed, and by a frozen carcass which the Siberian sun saw fit to melt from out the bosom of a glacier; but we also know that no living specimen exists. Our explorers—"

At this word he broke in impatiently. "Your explorers? Pish! A weakly breed. Let us hear no more of them. But tell me, O man, what you may know of the mammoth and his ways."

Beyond contradiction, this was leading to a yarn; so I baited my hook by ransacking my memory for whatever data I possessed on the subject in hand. To begin with, I emphasized that the animal was prehistoric, and marshalled all my facts in support of this. I mentioned the Siberian sand bars which abounded with ancient mammoth bones; spoke of the large quantities of fossil ivory purchased from the Innuits by the Alaska Commercial Company; and acknowledged having myself mined six and eight-foot tusks from the pay gravel of the Klondike creeks. "All fossils," I concluded, "found in the midst of débris deposited through countless ages."

"I remember when I was a kid," Thomas Stevens sniffed (he had a most confounded way of sniffing), "that I saw a petrified watermelon. Hence, though mistaken people sometimes delude themselves into thinking that they are really raising or eating them, there is no such thing as extant watermelons?"

"But the question of food," I objected, ignoring his point, which was puerile and without bearing. "The soil must bring forth vegetable life in lavish abundance to support such monstrous creations. Nowhere in the North is the soil so prolific. Ergo, the mammoth cannot exist."

"I pardon your ignorance concerning many matters of this Northland, for you are a young man and have travelled little; but, at the same time, I am inclined to agree with you on one thing. The mammoth no longer exists. How do I know? I killed the last one with my own right arm."

Thus spake Nimrod, the Mighty Hunter. I threw a stick of firewood at the dogs and bade them quit their unholy howling, and waited. Undoubtedly this liar of singular felicity would open his mouth and requite me for my St. Elias bear.

"It was this way," he at last began, after the appropriate silence had intervened. "I was in camp one day—"

"Where?" I interrupted.

He waved his hand vaguely in the direction of the northeast, where stretched a terra incognita into which vastness few men have strayed and fewer emerged. "I was in camp one day with Klooch. Klooch was as handsome a little *kamooks* as ever whined betwixt the traces or shoved nose into a camp kettle. Her father was a full-blood Malemute from Russian Pastilik on Bering Sea, and I bred her, and with understanding, out of a clean-legged bitch of the Hudson Bay stock. I tell you, O man, she was a corker combination. And now, on this day I have in mind, she was brought to pup through a pure wild wolf of the woods—gray, and long of limb, with big lungs and no end of staying powers. Say! Was there ever the like? It was a new breed of dog I had started, and I could look forward to big things.

"As I have said, she was brought neatly to pup, and safely delivered. I was squatting on my hams over the litter—seven sturdy, blind little beggars—when from behind came a bray of trumpets and crash of brass. There was a rush, like the wind-squall which kicks the heels of the rain, and I was midway to my feet when knocked flat on my face. At the same instant I heard Klooch sigh, very much as a man does when you've planted your fist in his belly. You can stake your sack I lay quiet, but I twisted my head around and saw a huge bulk swaying above me. Then the blue sky flashed into view and I got to my feet. A hairy mountain of flesh was just disappearing in the underbrush on the edge of the open. I caught a rear-end glimpse, with a stiff tail, as big in girth as my body, standing out straight behind. The next second only a tremendous hole remained in the thicket, though I could still hear the sounds as of a tornado dying quickly away, underbrush ripping and tearing and trees snapping and crashing.

"I cast about for my rifle. It had been lying on the ground with the muzzle against a log; but now the stock was smashed, the barrel out of line and the working-gear in a thousand bits. Then I looked for the slut, and—and what do you suppose?"

I shook my head.

"May my soul burn in a thousand hells if there was anything left of her! Klooch, the seven sturdy, blind little beggars—gone, all gone. Where she had stretched was a slimy, bloody depression in the soft dirt, all of a yard in diameter, and around the edges a few scattered hairs."

I measured three feet on the snow, threw about it a circle, and glanced at Nimrod.

"The beast was thirty long and twenty high," he answered, "and its tusks scaled over six times three feet. I couldn't believe, myself, at the time, for all that it had just happened. But if my senses had played me, there was the broken gun and the hole in the brush. And there was—or, rather, there was not—Klooch and the pups. O man, it makes me hot all over now when I think of it. Klooch! Another Eve! The mother of a new race! And a rampaging, ranting, old bull mammoth, like a second flood wiping them, root and branch, off the face of the earth! Do you wonder that the blood-soaked dirt cried out to high God? Or that I grabbed the hand-axe and took the trail?"

"The hand-axe?" I exclaimed, startled out of myself by the picture. "The hand-axe, and a big bull mammoth, thirty feet long, twenty feet—"

Nimrod joined me in my merriment, chuckling gleefully. "Wouldn't it kill you?" he cried. "Wasn't it a beaver's dream? Many's the time I've laughed about it since, but at the time it was no laughing matter, I was that danged mad, what of the gun and Klooch. Think of it, O man! A brand-new, unclassified, uncopyrighted breed, and wiped out before ever it opened its eyes or took out its intention papers! Well, so be it. Life's full of disappointments, and rightly so. Meat is best after a famine, and a bed soft after a hard trail.

"As I was saying, I took out after the beast with the hand-axe, and hung to its heels down the valley; but when he circled back toward the head I was left winded at the lower end. Speaking of grub, I might as well stop long enough to explain a couple of points. Up thereabouts, in the midst of the mountains, is an almighty curious formation. There are no end of little valleys, each like the other much as peas in a pod, and all neatly tucked away with straight rocky walls rising on all sides. And at the lower ends are always small openings where the drainage or glaciers must have broken out. The only way in is through these mouths, and they are all small, and some smaller than others. As to grub—you've slushed around on the rain-soaked islands of the Alaskan coast down Sitka-way, most likely, seeing as you're a traveller. And you know how stuff grows there—big, and juicy, and jungly. Well, that's the way it was with those valleys. Thick, rich soil, with ferns and grasses and such things in patches higher than your head. Rain three days out of four during the summer months; and food in them for a thousand mammoths, to say nothing of small game tor man.

"But to get back. Down at the lower end of the valley I got winded and gave over. I began to speculate, for when my wind left me my dander got hotter and hotter, and I knew I'd never know peace of mind till I dined on roasted mammoth-foot. And I knew, also, that that stood for *skookum mamook pukapuk*—excuse Chinook, I mean there was a big fight coming. Now the mouth of my valley was very narrow, and the walls steep. High up on one side was one of those big pivot rocks, or balancing rocks as some call them, weighing all of a couple of hundred tons. Just the thing. I hit back for camp, keeping an eye open so the bull couldn't slip past, and got my ammunition. It wasn't worth anything with the rifle smashed; so I opened the shells, planted the powder under the rock, and touched it off with slow fuse. Wasn't much of a charge, but the old bowlder tilted up lazily and dropped down into place, with just space enough to let the creek drain nicely. Now I had him."

"But how did you have him?" I queried. "Who ever heard of a man killing a mammoth with a hand-axe? And, for that matter, with anything else?"

"O man, have I not told you I was mad?" Nimrod replied, with a slight manifestation of sensitiveness. "Mad clean through, what of Klooch and the gun? Also, was I not a hunter? And was this not new and most unusual game? A hand-axe? Pish! I did not need it. Listen, and you shall hear of a hunt, such as might have happened in the youth of the world when caveman rounded up the kill with hand-axe of stone. Such would have served me as well. Now is it not a fact that man can outwalk the dog or horse? That he can wear them out with the intelligence of his endurance?"

I nodded.

"Well?"

The light broke in on me, and I bade him continue.

"My valley was perhaps five miles around. The mouth was closed. There was no way to get out. A timid beast was that bull mammoth, and I had him at my mercy. I got on his heels again, hollered like a fiend, pelted him with cobbles, and raced him around the valley three times before I knocked off for supper. Don't you see? A race-course! A man and a mammoth! A hippodrome, with sun, moon, and stars to referee!

"It took me two months to do it, but I did it. And that's no beaver dream. Round and round I ran him, me travelling on the inner circle, eating jerked meat and salmon berries on the run, and snatching winks of sleep between. Of course, he'd get desperate at times and turn. Then I'd head for soft ground where the creek spread out, and lay anathema upon him and his ancestry, and dare him to come on. But he was too wise to bog in a mud puddle. Once he pinned me in against the walls, and I crawled back into a deep crevice and waited. Whenever he felt for me with his trunk I'd belt him with the hand-axe till he pulled out, shrieking fit to split my ear drums, he was that mad. He knew he had me and didn't have me, and it near drove him wild. But he was no man's fool. He knew he was safe as long as I stayed in the crevice, and he made up his mind to keep me there. And he was dead right, only he hadn't figured on the commissary. There was neither grub nor water around that spot, so on the face of it he couldn't keep up the siege. He'd stand before the opening for hours, keeping an eye on me and flapping mosquitoes away with his big blanket ears. Then the thirst'd come on him, and he'd ramp round and roar till the earth shook, calling me every name he could lay tongue to. This was to frighten me, of course; and when he thought I was sufficiently impressed, he'd back away softly and try to make a sneak for the creek. Sometimes I'd let him get almost there—only a couple of hundred yards away it was—when out I'd pop and back he'd come, lumbering along like the old landslide he was. After I'd done this a few times, and he'd figured it out, he changed his tactics. Grasped the time element, you see. Without a word of warning, away he'd go, tearing for the water like mad, scheming to get there and back before I ran away. Finally, after cursing me most horrible, he raised the siege and deliberately stalked off to the water hole.

"That was the only time he penned me—three days of it—but after that the hippodrome never stopped. Round, and round, and round, like a six days' go-as-I-please, for he never pleased. My clothes went in rags and tatters, but I never stopped to mend, till at last I ran naked as a son of earth, with nothing but the old hand-axe in one hand and a cobble in the other. In fact, I never stopped, save for peeps of sleep in the crannies and ledges of the cliffs. As for the bull, he got perceptibly thinner and thinner—must have lost several tons at least—and as nervous as a schoolmarm on the wrong side of matrimony. When I'd come up with him and yell, or lam him with a rock at long range, he'd jump like a skittish colt and tremble all over. Then he'd pull out on the run, tail and trunk waving stiff, head over one shoulder and wicked eyes blazing, and the way he'd swear at me was something dreadful. A most immoral beast he was, a murderer and a blasphemer.

"But toward the end he quit all this, and fell to whimpering and crying like a baby. His spirit broke and he became a quivering jelly-mountain of misery. He'd get attacks of palpitation of the heart, and stagger around like a drunken man, and fall down and bark his shins. And then he'd cry, but always on the run. O man, the gods themselves would have wept with him, and you yourself or any other man. It was pitiful, and there was so much of it, but I only hardened my heart and hit up the pace. At last I wore him clean out, and he lay down, broken-winded, broken-hearted, hungry and thirsty. When I found he wouldn't budge, I hamstrung him, and spent the better part of the day wading into him with the hand-axe, he a sniffling and sobbing till I worked in far enough to shut him off. Thirty feet long he was, and twenty high, and a man could sling a hammock between his tusks and sleep comfortably. Barring the fact that I had run most of the juices out of him, he was fair eating, and his four feet, alone, roasted whole, would have lasted a man a twelvemonth. I spent the winter there myself."

"And where is this valley?" I asked.

He waved his hand in the direction of the northeast, and said, "Your tobacco is very good. I carry a fair share of it in my pouch, but I shall carry the recollection of it until I die. In token of my appreciation, and in return for the moccasins on your own feet, I will present to you these *muclucs*. They commemorate Klooch and the seven blind little beggars. They are also souvenirs of an unparalleled event in history, namely, the destruction of the oldest breed of animal on earth, and the youngest. And their chief virtue lies in that they will never wear out."

Having effected the exchange, he knocked the ashes from his pipe, gripped my hand good-night, and wandered off through the snow. Concerning this tale, for which I have already disclaimed responsibility, I would recommend those of little faith to make a visit to the Smithsonian Institute. If they bring the requisite credentials and do not come in vacation time, they will undoubtedly gain an audience with Professor Dolvidson. The *muclucs* are in his possession, and he will verify, not the manner in which they were obtained, but the material of which they are composed. When he states that they are made from the skin of the mammoth, the scientific world accepts his verdict. What more would you have?

THE END

17
THE STORY OF JEES UCK

THE STORY OF JEES UCK

There have been renunciations, and renunciations. But, in its essence, renunciation is ever the same. And the paradox of it is that men and women forego the dearest thing in the world for something dearer. It was never otherwise. Thus it was when Abel brought of the firstlings of his flock and of the fat thereof. The firstlings and the fat thereof were to him the dearest things in the world; yet he gave them over that he might be on good terms with God. So it was with Abraham when he prepared to offer up his son Isaac on a stone. Isaac was very dear to him; but God, in incomprehensible ways, was yet dearer. It may be that Abraham feared the Lord. But whether that be true or not, it has since been determined by a few billion people that he loved the Lord and desired to serve Him.

And since it has been determined that love is service, and since to renounce is to serve, then Jees Uck, who was merely a woman of a swart-skinned breed, loved with a great love. She was unversed in history, having learned to read only the signs of weather and of game; so she had never heard of Abel, nor of Abraham; nor, having escaped the good sisters at Holy Cross, had she been told the story of Ruth, the Moabitess, who renounced her very God for the sake of a stranger woman from a strange land. Jees Uck had learned only one way of renouncing, and that was with a club as the dynamic factor, in much the same manner as a dog is made to renounce a stolen marrow-bone. Yet, when the time came, she proved herself capable of rising to the height of the fair-faced royal races and of renouncing in right regal fashion.

So this is the story of Jees Uck, which is also the story of Neil Bonner, and Kitty Bonner, and a couple of Neil Bonner's progeny. Jees Uck was of a swart-skinned breed, it is true, but she was not an Indian; nor was she an Eskimo; nor even an Innuit. Going backward into mouth tradition, there appears the figure of one Skolkz, a Toyaat Indian of the Yukon, who journeyed down in his youth to the Great Delta where dwell the Innuits, and where he forgathered with a woman remembered as Olillie. Now the woman Olillie had been bred from an Eskimo mother by an Innuit man. And from Skolkz and Olillie came Halie, who was one-half Toyaat Indian, one-quarter Innuit, and one-quarter Eskimo. And Halie was the grandmother of Jees Uck.

Now Halie, in whom three stocks had been bastardized, who cherished no prejudice against further admixture, mated with a Russian fur trader called Shpack, also known in his time as the Big Fat. Shpack is herein classed Russian for lack of a more adequate term; for Shpack's father, a Slavonic convict from the Lower Provinces, had escaped from the quicksilver mines into Northern Siberia, where he knew Zimba, who was a woman of the Deer People and who became the mother of Shpack, who became the grandfather of Jees Uck.

Now had not Shpack been captured in his boyhood by the Sea People, who fringe the rim of the Arctic Sea with their misery, he would not have become the grandfather of Jees Uck and there would be no story at all. But he *was* captured by the Sea People, from whom he escaped to Kamchatka, and thence, on a Norwegian whale-ship, to the Baltic. Not long after that he turned up in St. Petersburg, and the years were not many till he went drifting east over the same weary road his father had measured with blood and groans a half-century before. But Shpack was a free man, in the employ of the great Russian Fur Company. And in that employ he fared farther and farther east, until he crossed Bering Sea into Russian America; and at Pastolik, which is hard by the Great Delta of the Yukon, became the husband of Halie, who was the grandmother of Jees Uck. Out of this union came the woman-child, Tukesan.

Shpack, under the orders of the company, made a canoe voyage of a few hundred miles up the Yukon to the post of Nulato. With him he took Halie and the babe Tukesan. This was in 1850, and in 1850 it was that the river Indians fell upon Nulato and wiped it from the face of the earth. And that was the end of Shpack and Halie. On that terrible night Tukesan disappeared. To this day the Toyaats aver they had no hand in the trouble; but, be that as it may, the fact remains that the babe Tukesan grew up among them.

Tukesan was married successively to two Toyaat brothers, to both of whom she was barren. Because of this, other women shook their heads, and no third Toyaat man could be found to dare matrimony with the childless widow. But at this time, many hundred miles above, at Fort Yukon, was a man, Spike O'Brien. Fort Yukon was a Hudson Bay Company post, and Spike O'Brien one of the company's servants. He was a good servant, but he achieved an opinion that the service was bad, and in the course of time vindicated that opinion by deserting. It was a year's journey, by the chain of posts, back to York Factory on Hudson's Bay. Further, being company posts, he knew he could not evade the company's clutches. Nothing remained but to go down the Yukon. It was true no white man had ever gone down the Yukon, and no white man knew whether the Yukon emptied into the Arctic Ocean or Bering Sea; but Spike O'Brien was a Celt, and the promise of danger was a lure he had ever followed.

A few weeks later, somewhat battered, rather famished, and about dead with river-fever, he drove the nose of his canoe into the earth bank by the village of the Toyaats and promptly fainted away. While getting his strength back, in the weeks that followed, he looked upon Tukesan and found her good. Like the father of Shpack, who lived to a ripe old age among the Siberian Deer People, Spike O'Brien might have left his aged bones with the Toyaats. But romance gripped his heart-strings and would not let him stay. As he had journeyed from York Factory to Fort Yukon, so, first among men, might he journey from Fort Yukon to the sea and win the honor of being the first man to make the Northwest

Passage by land. So he departed down the river, won the honor, and was unannaled and unsung. In after years he ran a sailors' boarding-house in San Francisco, where he became esteemed a most remarkable liar by virtue of the gospel truths he told. But a child was born to Tukesan, who had been childless. And this child was Jees Uck. Her lineage has been traced at length to show that she was neither Indian, nor Eskimo, nor Innuit, nor much of anything else; also to show what waifs of the generations we are, all of us, and the strange meanderings of the seed from which we spring.

What with the vagrant blood in her and the heritage compounded of many races, Jees Uck developed a wonderful young beauty. Bizarre, perhaps, it was, and Oriental enough to puzzle any passing ethnologist. A lithe and slender grace characterized her. Beyond a quickened lilt to the imagination, the contribution of the Celt was in no wise apparent. It might possibly have put the warm blood under her skin, which made her face less swart and her body fairer; but that, in turn, might have come from Shpack, the Big Fat, who inherited the color of his Slavonic father. And, finally, she had great, blazing black eyes — the half-caste eye, round, full-orbed, and sensuous, which marks the collision of the dark races with the light. Also, the white blood in her, combined with her knowledge that it was in her, made her, in a way, ambitious. Otherwise, by upbringing and in outlook on life, she was wholly and utterly a Toyaat Indian.

One winter, when she was a young woman, Neil Bonner came into her life. But he came into her life, as he had come into the country, somewhat reluctantly. In fact, it was very much against his will, coming into the country. Between a father who clipped coupons and cultivated roses, and a mother who loved the social round, Neil Bonner had gone rather wild. He was not vicious, but a man with meat in his belly and without work in the world has to expend his energy somehow, and Neil Bonner was such a man. And he expended his energy in such fashion and to such extent that when the inevitable climax came, his father, Neil Bonner, senior, crawled out of his roses in a panic and looked on his son with a wondering eye. Then he hied himself away to a crony of kindred pursuits, with whom he was wont to confer over coupons and roses, and between the two the destiny of young Neil Bonner was made manifest. He must go away, on probation, to live down his harmless follies in order that he might live up to their own excellent standard.

This determined upon, and young Neil a little repentant and a great deal ashamed, the rest was easy. The cronies were heavy stockholders in the P. C. Company. The P. C. Company owned fleets of river-steamers and ocean-going craft, and, in addition to farming the sea, exploited a hundred thousand square miles or so of the land that, on the maps of geographers, usually occupies the white spaces. So the P. C. Company sent young Neil Bonner north, where the white spaces are, to do its work and learn to be good like his father. "Five years of simplicity, close to the soil and far from temptation, will make a man of him," said old Neil Bonner, and forthwith crawled back among his roses. Young Neil set his jaw, pitched his chin at the proper angle, and went to work. As an underling he did his work well and gained the commendation of his superiors. Not that he delighted in the work, but that it was the one thing that prevented him from going mad.

The first year he wished he was dead. The second year he cursed God. The third year he was divided between the two emotions, and in the confusion quarrelled with a man in authority. He had the best of the quarrel, though the man in authority had the last word, — a word that sent Neil Bonner into an exile that made his old billet appear as paradise. But he went without a whimper, for the North had succeeded in making him into a man.

Here and there, on the white spaces on the map, little circlets like the letter "o" are to be found, and, appended to these circlets, on one side or the other, are names such as "Fort Hamilton," "Yanana Station," "Twenty Mile," thus leading one to imagine that the white spaces are plentifully besprinkled with towns and villages. But it is a vain imagining. Twenty Mile, which is very like the rest of the posts, is a log building the size of a corner grocery with rooms to let upstairs. A long-legged caché on stilts may be found in the back yard; also a couple of outhouses. The back yard is unfenced, and extends to the sky-line and an unascertainable bit beyond. There are no other houses in sight, though the Toyaats sometimes pitch a winter camp a mile or two down the Yukon. And this is Twenty Mile, one tentacle of the many-tentacled P. C. Company. Here the agent, with an assistant, barters with the Indians for their furs, and does an erratic trade on a gold-dust basis with the wandering miners. Here, also, the agent and his assistant yearn all winter for the spring, and when the spring comes, camp blasphemously on the roof while the Yukon washes out the establishment. And here, also, in the fourth year of his sojourn in the land, came Neil Bonner to take charge.

He had displaced no agent; for the man that previously ran the post had made away with himself; "because of the rigors of the place," said the assistant, who still remained; though the Toyaats, by their fires, had another version. The assistant was a shrunken-shouldered, hollow-chested man, with a cadaverous face and cavernous cheeks that his sparse black beard could not hide. He coughed much, as though consumption gripped his lungs, while his eyes had that mad, fevered light common to consumptives in the last stage. Pentley was his name, — Amos Pentley, — and Bonner did not like him, though he felt a pity for the forlorn and hopeless devil. They did not get along together, these two men who, of all men, should have been on good terms in the face of the cold and silence and darkness of the long winter.

In the end, Bonner concluded that Amos was partly demented, and left him alone, doing all the work himself except the cooking. Even then, Amos had nothing but bitter looks and an undisguised hatred for him. This was a great loss to Bonner; for the smiling face of one of his own kind, the cheery word, the sympathy of comradeship shared with misfortune — these things meant much; and the winter was yet young when he began to realize the added reasons, with such an assistant, that the previous agent had found to impel his own hand against his life.

It was very lonely at Twenty Mile. The bleak vastness stretched away on every side to the horizon. The snow, which was really frost, flung its mantle over the land and buried everything in the silence of death. For days it was clear and cold, the thermometer steadily recording forty to fifty degrees below zero. Then a change came over the face of things. What little moisture had oozed into the atmosphere gathered into dull gray, formless clouds; it became quite warm, the thermometer rising to twenty below; and the moisture fell out of the sky in hard frost-granules that hissed like dry sugar or driving sand when kicked underfoot. After that it became clear and cold again, until enough moisture had gathered to blanket the earth from the cold of outer space. That was all. Nothing happened. No storms, no churning waters and threshing forests, nothing but the machine-like precipitation of accumulated moisture. Possibly the most notable thing that occurred through the weary weeks was the gliding of the temperature up to the unprecedented height of fifteen below. To atone for this, outer space smote the earth with its cold till the mercury froze and the spirit thermometer remained more than seventy below for a fortnight, when it burst. There was no telling how much colder it was after that. Another occurrence, monotonous in its regularity, was the lengthening of the nights, till day became a mere blink of light between the darknesses.

Neil Bonner was a social animal. The very follies for which he was doing penance had been bred of his excessive sociability. And here, in the fourth year of his exile, he found himself in company — which were to travesty the word — with a morose and speechless creature in whose sombre eyes smouldered a hatred as bitter as it was unwarranted. And Bonner, to whom speech and fellowship were as the breath of life, went about as a ghost might go, tantalized by the gregarious revelries of some former life. In the day his lips were compressed, his face stern; but in the night he clenched his hands, rolled about in his blankets, and cried aloud like a little child. And he would remember a certain man in authority and curse him through the long hours. Also, he cursed God. But God understands. He cannot find it in His heart to blame weak mortals who blaspheme in Alaska.

And here, to the post of Twenty Mile, came Jees Uck, to trade for flour and bacon, and beads, and bright scarlet cloths for her fancy work. And further, and unwittingly, she came to the post of Twenty Mile to make a lonely man more lonely, make him reach out empty arms in his sleep. For Neil Bonner was only a man. When she first came into the store, he looked at her long, as a thirsty man may look at a flowing well. And she, with the heritage bequeathed her by Spike O'Brien, imagined daringly and smiled up into his eyes, not as the swart-skinned peoples should smile at the royal races, but as a woman smiles at a man. The thing was inevitable; only, he did not see it, and fought against her as fiercely and passionately as he was drawn toward her. And she? She was Jees Uck, by upbringing wholly and utterly a Toyaat Indian woman.

She came often to the post to trade. And often she sat by the big wood stove and chatted in broken English with Neil Bonner. And he came to look for her coming; and on the days she did not come he was worried and restless. Sometimes he stopped to think, and then she was met coldly, with a reserve that perplexed and piqued her, and which, she was convinced, was not sincere. But more often he did not dare to think, and then all went well and there were smiles and laughter. And Amos Pentley, gasping like a stranded catfish, his hollow cough a-reek with the grave, looked upon it all and grinned. He, who loved life, could not live, and it rankled his soul that others should be able to live. Wherefore he hated Bonner, who was so very much alive and into whose eyes sprang joy at the sight of Jees Uck. As for Amos, the very thought of the girl was sufficient to send his blood pounding up into a hemorrhage.

Jees Uck, whose mind was simple, who thought elementally and was unused to weighing life in its subtler quantities, read Amos Pentley like a book. She warned Bonner, openly and bluntly, in few words; but the complexities of higher existence confused the situation to him, and he laughed at her evident anxiety. To him, Amos was a poor, miserable devil, tottering desperately into the grave. And Bonner, who had suffered much, found it easy to forgive greatly.

But one morning, during a bitter snap, he got up from the breakfast table and went into the store. Jees Uck was already there, rosy from the trail, to buy a sack of flour. A few minutes later, he was out in the snow lashing the flour on her sled. As he bent over he noticed a stiffness in his neck and felt a premonition of impending physical misfortune. And as he put the last half-hitch into the lashing and attempted to straighten up, a quick spasm seized him and he sank into the snow. Tense and quivering, head jerked back, limbs extended, back arched and mouth twisted and distorted, he appeared as though being racked limb from limb. Without cry or sound, Jees Uck was in the snow beside him; but he clutched both her wrists spasmodically, and as long as the convulsion endured she was helpless. In a few moments the spasm relaxed and he was left weak and fainting, his forehead beaded with sweat, his lips flecked with foam.

"Quick!" he muttered, in a strange, hoarse voice. "Quick! Inside!"

He started to crawl on hands and knees, but she raised him up, and, supported by her young arm, he made faster progress. As he entered the store the spasm seized him again, and his body writhed irresistibly away from her and rolled and curled on the floor. Amos Pentley came and looked on with curious eyes.

"Oh, Amos!" she cried in an agony of apprehension and helplessness, "him die, you think?" But Amos shrugged his shoulders and continued to look on.

Bonner's body went slack, the tense muscles easing down and an expression of relief coming into his face. "Quick!" he gritted between his teeth, his mouth twisting with the on-coming of the next spasm and with his effort to control it. "Quick, Jees Uck! The medicine! Never mind! Drag me!"

She knew where the medicine-chest stood, at the rear of the room, beyond the stove, and thither, by the legs, she dragged the struggling man. As the spasm passed, he began, very faint and very sick, to overhaul the chest. He had seen dogs die exhibiting symptoms similar to his own, and he knew what should be done. He held up a vial of chloral hydrate, but his fingers were too weak and nerveless to draw the cork. This Jees Uck did for him, while he was plunged into another convulsion. As he came out of it he found the open bottle proffered him and looked into the great black eyes of the woman and read what men have always read in the Mate-woman's eyes. Taking a full dose of the stuff, he sank back until another spasm had passed. Then he raised himself limply on his elbow.

"Listen, Jees Uck!" he said very slowly, as though aware of the necessity for haste

and yet afraid to hasten. "Do what I say. Stay by my side, but do not touch me. I must be very quiet, but you must not go away." His jaw began to set and his face to quiver and distort with the forerunning pangs, but he gulped and struggled to master them. "Do not go away. And do not let Amos go away. Understand! Amos must stay right here."

She nodded her head, and he passed off into the first of many convulsions, which gradually diminished in force and frequency. Jees Uck hung over him, remembering his injunction and not daring to touch him. Once Amos grew restless and made as though to go into the kitchen; but a quick blaze from her eyes quelled him, and after that, save for his labored breathing and charnel cough, he was very quiet.

Bonner slept. The blink of light that marked the day disappeared. Amos, followed about by the woman's eyes, lighted the kerosene lamps. Evening came on. Through the north window the heavens were emblazoned with an auroral display, which flamed and flared and died down into blackness. Some time after that, Neil Bonner roused. First he looked to see that Amos was still there, then smiled at Jees Uck and pulled himself up. Every muscle was stiff and sore, and he smiled ruefully, pressing and prodding himself as if to ascertain the extent of the ravage. Then his face went stern and businesslike.

"Jees Uck," he said, "take a candle. Go into the kitchen. There is food on the table — biscuits and beans and bacon; also, coffee in the pot on the stove. Bring it here on the counter. Also, bring tumblers and water and whiskey, which you will find on the top shelf of the locker. Do not forget the whiskey."

Having swallowed a stiff glass of the whiskey, he went carefully through the medicine chest, now and again putting aside, with definite purpose, certain bottles and vials. Then he set to work on the food, attempting a crude analysis. He had not been unused to the laboratory in his college days and was possessed of sufficient imagination to achieve results with his limited materials. The condition of tetanus, which had marked his paroxysms, simplified matters, and he made but one test. The coffee yielded nothing; nor did the beans. To the biscuits he devoted the utmost care. Amos, who knew nothing of chemistry, looked on with steady curiosity. But Jees Uck, who had boundless faith in the white man's wisdom, and especially in Neil Bonner's wisdom, and who not only knew nothing but knew that she knew nothing, watched his face rather than his hands.

Step by step he eliminated possibilities, until he came to the final test. He was using a thin medicine vial for a tube, and this he held between him and the light, watching the slow precipitation of a salt through the solution contained in the tube. He said nothing, but he saw what he had expected to see. And Jees Uck, her eyes riveted on his face, saw something, too, — something that made her spring like a tigress upon Amos and with splendid suppleness and strength bend his body back across her knee. Her knife was out of its sheath and uplifted, glinting in the lamplight. Amos was snarling; but Bonner intervened ere the blade could fall.

"That's a good girl, Jees Uck. But never mind. Let him go!"

She dropped the man obediently, though with protest writ large on her face; and his body thudded to the floor. Bonner nudged him with his moccasined foot.

"Get up, Amos!" he commanded. "You've got to pack an outfit yet to-night and hit the trail."

"You don't mean to say — " Amos blurted savagely.

"I mean to say that you tried to kill me," Neil went on in cold, even tones. "I mean to say that you killed Birdsall, for all the company believes he killed himself. You used strychnine in my case. God knows with what you fixed him. Now I can't hang you. You're too near dead, as it is. But Twenty Mile is too small for the pair of us, and you've got to mush. It's two hundred miles to Holy Cross. You can make it if you're careful not to overexert. I'll give you grub, a sled, and three dogs. You'll be as safe as if you were in jail, for you can't get out of the country. And I'll give you one chance. You're almost dead. Very well. I shall send no word to the company until the spring. In the meantime, the thing for you to do is to die. Now mush!"

"You go to bed!" Jees Uck insisted, when Amos had churned away into the night toward Holy Cross. "You sick man yet, Neil."

"And you're a good girl, Jees Uck," he answered. "And here's my hand on it. But you must go home."

"You don't like me," she said simply.

He smiled, helped her on with her parka, and led her to the door. "Only too well, Jees Uck," he said softly; "only too well."

After that the pall of the Arctic night fell deeper and blacker on the land. Neil Bonner discovered that he had failed to put proper valuation upon even the sullen face of the murderous and death-stricken Amos. It became very lonely at Twenty Mile. "For the love of God, Prentiss, send me a man," he wrote to the agent at Fort Hamilton, three hundred miles up river. Six weeks later the Indian messenger brought back a reply. It was characteristic: "Hell. Both feet frozen. Need him myself — Prentiss."

To make matters worse, most of the Toyaats were in the back country on the flanks of a caribou herd, and Jees Uck was with them. Removing to a distance seemed to bring her closer than ever, and Neil Bonner found himself picturing her, day by day, in camp and on trail. It is not good to be alone. Often he went out of the quiet store, bare-headed and frantic, and shook his fist at the blink of day that came over the southern sky-line. And on still, cold nights he left his bed and stumbled into the frost, where he assaulted the silence at the top of his lungs, as though it were some tangible, sentient thing that he might arouse; or he shouted at the sleeping dogs till they howled and howled again. One shaggy brute he brought into the post, playing that it was the new man sent by Prentiss. He strove to make it sleep decently under blankets at night and to sit at table and eat as a man should; but the beast, mere domesticated wolf that it was, rebelled, and sought out dark corners and snarled and bit him in the leg, and was finally beaten and driven forth.

Then the trick of personification seized upon Neil Bonner and mastered him. All the forces of his environment metamorphosed into living, breathing entities and came to live with him. He re-created the primitive pantheon; reared an altar to the sun and burned candle fat and bacon grease thereon; and in the unfenced yard, by the long-legged caché, made a frost devil which he was wont to make faces at and mock when the mercury oozed down into the bulb. All this in play, of course. He said it to himself that it was in play, and repeated it over and over to make sure, unaware that madness is ever prone to express itself in make-believe and play.

One midwinter day, Father Champreau, a Jesuit missionary, pulled into Twenty Mile. Bonner fell upon him and dragged him into the post, and clung to him and wept, until the priest wept with him from sheer compassion. Then Bonner became madly hilarious and made lavish entertainment, swearing valiantly that his guest should not depart. But Father Champreau was pressing to Salt Water on urgent business for his order, and pulled out next morning, with Bonner's blood threatened on his head.

And the threat was in a fair way toward realization, when the Toyaats returned from their long hunt to the winter camp. They had many furs, and there was much trading and stir at Twenty Mile. Also, Jees Uck came to buy beads and scarlet cloths and things, and Bonner began to find himself again. He fought for a week against her. Then the end came one night when she rose to leave. She had not forgotten her repulse, and the pride that drove Spike O'Brien on to complete the Northwest Passage by land was her pride.

"I go now," she said; "good night, Neil."

But he came up behind her. "Nay, it is not well," he said.

And as she turned her face toward his with a sudden joyful flash, he bent forward, slowly and gravely, as it were a sacred thing, and kissed her on the lips. The Toyaats had never taught her the meaning of a kiss upon the lips, but she understood and was glad.

With the coming of Jees Uck, at once things brightened up. She was regal in her happiness, a source of unending delight. The elemental workings of her mind and her naïve little ways made an immense sum of pleasurable surprise to the over-civilized man that had stooped to catch her up. Not alone was she solace to his loneliness, but her primitiveness rejuvenated his jaded mind. It was as though, after long wandering, he had returned to pillow his head in the lap of Mother Earth. In short, in Jees Uck he found the youth of the world — the youth and the strength and the joy.

And to fill the full round of his need, and that they might not see overmuch of each other, there arrived at Twenty Mile one Sandy MacPherson, as companionable a man as ever whistled along the trail or raised a ballad by a camp-fire. A Jesuit priest had run into his camp, a couple of hundred miles up the Yukon, in the nick of time to say a last word over the body of Sandy's partner. And on departing, the priest had said, "My son, you will be lonely now." And Sandy had bowed his head brokenly. "At Twenty Mile," the priest added, "there is a lonely man. You have need of each other, my son."

So it was that Sandy became a welcome third at the post, brother to the man and woman that resided there. He took Bonner moose-hunting and wolf-trapping; and, in return, Bonner resurrected a battered and wayworn volume and made him friends with Shakespeare, till Sandy declaimed iambic pentameters to his sled-dogs whenever they waxed mutinous. And of the long evenings they played cribbage and talked and disagreed about the universe, the while Jees Uck rocked matronly in an easy-chair and darned their moccasins and socks.

Spring came. The sun shot up out of the south. The land exchanged its austere robes for the garb of a smiling wanton. Everywhere light laughed and life invited. The days stretched out their balmy length and the nights passed from blinks of darkness to no darkness at all. The river bared its bosom, and snorting steamboats challenged the wilderness. There were stir and bustle, new faces, and fresh facts. An assistant arrived at Twenty Mile, and Sandy MacPherson wandered off with a bunch of prospectors to invade the Koyokuk country. And there were newspapers and magazines and letters for Neil Bonner. And Jees Uck looked on in worriment, for she knew his kindred talked with him across the world.

Without much shock, it came to him that his father was dead. There was a sweet letter of forgiveness, dictated in his last hours. There were official letters from the company, graciously ordering him to turn the post over to the assistant and permitting him to depart at his earliest pleasure. A long, legal affair from the lawyers informed him of interminable lists of stocks and bonds, real estate, rents, and chattels that were his by his father's will. And a dainty bit of stationery, sealed and monogrammed, implored dear Neil's return to his heart-broken and loving mother.

Neil Bonner did some swift thinking, and when the *Yukon Belle* coughed in to the bank on her way down to Bering Sea, he departed — departed with the ancient lie of quick return young and blithe on his lips.

"I'll come back, dear Jees Uck, before the first snow flies," he promised her, between the last kisses at the gang-plank.

And not only did he promise, but, like the majority of men under the same circumstances, he really meant it. To John Thompson, the new agent, he gave orders for the extension of unlimited credit to his wife, Jees Uck. Also, with his last look from the deck of the *Yukon Belle*, he saw a dozen men at work rearing the logs that were to make the most comfortable house along a thousand miles of river front — the house of Jees Uck, and likewise the house of Neil Bonner — ere the first flurry of snow. For he fully and fondly meant to come back. Jees Uck was dear to him, and, further, a golden future awaited the North. With his father's money he intended to verify that future. An ambitious dream allured him. With his four years of experience, and aided by the friendly coöperation of the P. C. Company, he would return to become the Rhodes of Alaska. And he would return, fast as steam could drive, as soon as he had put into shape the affairs of his father, whom he had never known, and comforted his mother, whom he had forgotten.

There was much ado when Neil Bonner came back from the Arctic. The fires were lighted and the fleshpots slung, and he took of it all and called it good. Not only was he bronzed and creased, but he was a new man under his skin, with a grip on things and a seriousness and control. His old companions were amazed when he declined to hit up the pace in the good old way, while his father's crony rubbed hands gleefully, and became an authority upon the reclamation of wayward and idle youth.

For four years Neil Bonner's mind had lain fallow. Little that was new had been added to it, but it had undergone a process of selection. It had, so to say, been purged of the trivial and superfluous. He had lived quick years, down in the world; and, up in the wilds, time had been given him to organize the confused mass of his experiences. His superficial standards had been flung to the winds and new standards erected on deeper and broader generalizations. Concerning civilization, he had gone away with one set of values, had returned with another set of values. Aided, also, by the earth smells in his nostrils and the earth sights in his eyes, he laid hold of the inner significance of civilization, beholding with clear vision its futilities and powers. It was a simple little philosophy he evolved. Clean living was the way to grace. Duty performed was sanctification. One must live clean and do his duty in order that he might work. Work was salvation. And to work toward life abundant, and more abundant, was to be in line with the scheme of things and the will of God.

Primarily, he was of the city. And his fresh earth grip and virile conception of humanity gave him a finer sense of civilization and endeared civilization to him. Day by day the people of the city clung closer to him and the world loomed more colossal. And, day by day, Alaska grew more remote and less real. And then he met Kitty Sharon — a woman of his own flesh and blood and kind; a woman who put her hand into his hand and drew him to her, till he forgot the day and hour and the time of the year the first snow flies on the Yukon.

Jees Uck moved into her grand loghouse and dreamed away three golden summer months. Then came the autumn, post-haste before the down rush of winter. The air grew thin and sharp, the days thin and short. The river ran sluggishly, and skin ice formed in the quiet eddies. All migratory life departed south, and silence fell upon the land. The first snow flurries came, and the last homing steamboat bucked desperately into the running mush ice. Then came the hard ice, solid cakes and sheets, till the Yukon ran level with its banks. And when all this ceased the river stood still and the blinking days lost themselves in the darkness.

John Thompson, the new agent, laughed; but Jees Uck had faith in the mischances of sea and river. Neil Bonner might be frozen in anywhere between Chilkoot Pass and St. Michael's, for the last travellers of the year are always caught by the ice, when they exchange boat for sled and dash on through the long hours behind the flying dogs.

But no flying dogs came up the trail, nor down the trail, to Twenty Mile. And John Thompson told Jees Uck, with a certain gladness ill concealed, that Bonner would never come back again. Also, and brutally, he suggested his own eligibility. Jees Uck laughed in his face and went back to her grand log-house. But when midwinter came, when hope dies down and life is at its lowest ebb, Jees Uck found she had no credit at the store. This was Thompson's doing, and he rubbed his hands, and walked up and down, and came to his door and looked up at Jees Uck's house, and waited. And he continued to wait. She sold her dog-team to a party of miners and paid cash for her food. And when Thompson refused to honor even her coin, Toyaat Indians made her purchases, and sledded them up to her house in the dark.

In February the first post came in over the ice, and John Thompson read in the society column of a five months' old paper of the marriage of Neil Bonner and Kitty Sharon. Jees Uck held the door ajar and him outside while he imparted the information; and, when he had done, laughed pridefully and did not believe. In March, and all alone, she gave birth to a man-child, a brave bit of new life at which she marvelled. And at that hour, a year later, Neil Bonner sat by another bed, marvelling at another bit of new life that had fared into the world.

The snow went off the ground and the ice broke out of the Yukon. The sun journeyed north, and journeyed south again; and, the money from the dogs being spent, Jees Uck went back to her own people. Oche Ish, a shrewd hunter, proposed to kill the meat for her and her babe, and catch the salmon, if she would marry him. And Imego and Hah Yo and Wy Nooch, husky young hunters all, made similar proposals. But she elected to live alone and seek her own meat and fish. She sewed moccasins and *parkas* and mittens — warm, serviceable things, and pleasing to the eye, withal, what of the ornamental hairtufts and bead work. These she sold to the miners, who were drifting faster into the land each year. And not only did she win food that was good and plentiful, but she laid money by, and one day took passage on the *Yukon Belle* down the river.

At St. Michael's she washed dishes in the kitchen of the post. The servants of the company wondered at the remarkable woman with the remarkable child, though they asked no questions and she vouch-

safed nothing. But just before Bering Sea closed in for the year, she bought a passage south on a strayed sealing schooner. That winter she cooked for Captain Markheim's household at Unalaska, and in the spring continued south to Sitka on a whiskey sloop. Later, she appeared at Metlakahtla, which is near to St. Mary's on the end of the Pan-Handle, where she worked in the cannery through the salmon season. When autumn came and the Siwash fishermen prepared to return to Puget Sound, she embarked with a couple of families in a big cedar canoe; and with them she threaded the hazardous chaos of the Alaskan and Canadian coasts, till the Straits of Juan de Fuca were passed and she led her boy by the hand up the hard pave of Seattle.

There she met Sandy MacPherson, on a windy corner, very much surprised and, when he had heard her story, very wroth — not so wroth as he might have been, had he known of Kitty Sharon; but of her Jees Uck breathed no word, for she had never believed. Sandy, who read commonplace and sordid desertion into the circumstance, strove to dissuade her from her trip to San Francisco, where Neil Bonner was supposed to live when he was at home. And, having striven, he made her comfortable, bought her tickets and saw her off, the while smiling in her face and muttering "damshame" into his beard.

With roar and rumble, through daylight and dark, swaying and lurching between the dawns, soaring into the winter snows and sinking to summer valleys, skirting depths, leaping chasms, piercing mountains, Jees Uck and her boy were hurled south. But she had no fear of the iron stallion; nor was she stunned by this masterful civilization of Neil Bonner's people. It seemed, rather, that she saw with greater clearness the wonder that a man of such godlike race had held her in his arms. The screaming medley of San Francisco, with its restless shipping, belching factories, and thundering traffic, did not confuse her; instead, she comprehended swiftly the pitiful sordidness of Twenty Mile and the skin-lodged Toyaat village. And she looked down at the boy that clutched her hand and wondered that she had borne him by such a man.

She paid the hack-driver five prices and went up the stone steps to Neil Bonner's front door. A slant-eyed Japanese parleyed with her for a fruitless space, then led her inside and disappeared. She remained in the hall, which to her simple fancy seemed to be the guest room — the show-place wherein were arrayed all the household treasures with the frank purpose of parade and dazzlement. The walls and ceiling were of oiled and panelled redwood. The floor was more glassy than glare ice, and she sought standing place on one of the great skins that gave a sense of security to the polished surface. A huge fireplace — an extravagant fireplace, she deemed it — yawned in the farther wall. A flood of light, mellowed by stained glass, fell across the room, and from the far end came the white gleam of a marble figure.

This much she saw, and more, when the slant-eyed servant led the way past another room — of which she caught a fleeting glance — and into a third, both of which dimmed the brave show of the entrance hall. And to her eyes the great house seemed to hold out a promise of endless similar rooms. There was such length and breadth to them, and the ceilings were so far away! For the first time since her advent into the white man's civilization, a feeling of awe laid hold of her. Neil, her Neil, lived in this house, breathed the air of it, and lay down at night and slept! It was beautiful, all this that she saw, and it pleased her; but she felt, also, the wisdom and mastery behind. It was the concrete expression of power in terms of beauty, and it was the power that she unerringly divined.

And then came a woman, queenly tall, crowned with a glory of hair that was like a golden sun. She seemed to come toward Jees Uck as a ripple of music across still water; her sweeping garment itself a song, her body playing rhythmically beneath. Jees Uck was herself a man compeller. There were Oche Ish and Imego and Hah Yo and Wy Nooch, to say nothing of Neil Bonner and John Thompson and other white men that had looked upon her and felt her power. But she gazed upon the wide blue eyes and rose-white skin of this woman that advanced to meet her, and she measured her with woman's eyes looking through man's eyes; and as a man compeller she felt herself diminish and grow insignificant before this radiant and flashing creature.

"You wish to see my husband?" the woman asked; and Jees Uck gasped at the liquid silver of a voice that had never sounded harsh cries at snarling wolf dogs, nor moulded itself to a guttural speech, nor toughened in storm and frost and camp smoke.

"No," Jees Uck answered slowly and gropingly, in order that she might do justice to her English. "I come to see Neil Bonner."

"He is my husband," the woman laughed.

Then it was true! John Thompson had not lied that bleak February day, when she laughed pridefully and shut the door in his face. As once she had thrown Amos Pentley across her knee and ripped her knife into the air, so now she felt impelled to spring upon this woman and bear her back and down, and tear the life out of her fair body. But Jees Uck was thinking quickly and gave no sign, and Kitty Bonner little dreamed how intimately she had for an instant been related with sudden death.

Jees Uck nodded her head that she understood, and Kitty Bonner explained that Neil was expected at any moment. Then they sat down on ridiculously comfortable chairs, and Kitty sought to entertain her strange visitor, and Jees Uck strove to help her.

"You knew my husband in the North?" Kitty asked, once.

"Sure. I wash um clothes," Jees Uck had answered, her English abruptly beginning to grow atrocious.

"And this is your boy? I have a little girl."

Kitty caused her daughter to be brought, and while the children, after their manner, struck an acquaintance, the mothers indulged in the talk of mothers and drank tea from cups so fragile that Jees Uck feared lest hers should crumble to pieces between her fingers. Never had she seen such cups, so delicate and dainty. In her mind she compared them with the woman who poured the tea, and there uprose in contrast the gourds and pannikins of the Toyaat village and the clumsy mugs of Twenty Mile, to which she likened herself. And in such fashion and such terms the problem presented itself. She was beaten. There was a woman other than herself better fitted to bear and upbring Neil Bonner's children. Just as his people exceeded her people, so did his womenkind exceed her. They were the man compellers, as their men were the world compellers.

She looked at the rose-white tenderness of Kitty Bonner's skin and remembered the sun-beat on her own face. Likewise she looked from brown hand to white — the one, work-worn and hardened by whip handle and paddle, the other as guiltless of toil and soft as a newborn babe's. And, for all the obvious softness and apparent weakness, Jees Uck looked into the blue eyes and saw the mastery she had seen in Neil Bonner's eyes and in the eyes of Neil Bonner's people.

"Why, it's Jees Uck!" Neil Bonner said, when he entered. He said it calmly, with even a ring of joyful cordiality, coming over to her and shaking both her hands, but looking into her eyes with a worry in his own that she understood.

"Hello, Neil!" she said. "You look much good."

"Fine, fine, Jees Uck," he answered heartily, though secretly studying Kitty for some sign of what had passed between the two. Yet he knew his wife too well to expect, even though the worst had passed, such a sign.

"Well, I can't say how glad I am to see you," he went on. "What's happened? Did you strike a mine? And when did you get in?"

"Oo-a, I get in to-day," she replied, her voice instinctively seeking its guttural parts. "I no strike it, Neil. You know Cap'n Markheim, Unalaska? I cook, his house, long time. No spend money. Bime-by, plenty. Pretty good, I think, go down and see White Man's Land. Very fine, White Man's Land, very fine," she added. Her English puzzled him, for Sand and he had sought, constantly, to better her speech, and she had proved an apt pupil. Now it seemed that she had sunk back into her race. Her face was guileless, stolidly guileless, giving no cue. Kitty's untroubled brow likewise baffled him. What had happened? How much had been said? and how much guessed?

While he wrestled with these questions and while Jees Uck wrestled with her problem — never had he looked so wonderful and great — a silence fell.

"To think that you knew my husband in Alaska!" Kitty said softly.

Knew him! Jees Uck could not forbear a glance at the boy she had borne him, and his eyes followed hers mechanically to the window where played the two children. An iron band seemed to tighten across his forehead. His knees went weak and his heart leaped up and pounded like a fist against his breast. His boy! He had never dreamed it!

Little Kitty Bonner, fairylike in gauzy lawn, with pinkest of cheeks and bluest of dancing eyes, arms outstretched and lips puckered in invitation, was striving to kiss the boy. And the boy, lean and lithe, sun-beaten and browned, skin-clad and in hair-fringed and hair-tufted *muclucs* that showed the wear of the sea and rough work, coolly withstood her advances, his body straight and stiff with the peculiar erectness common to children of savage people. A stranger in a strange land, unabashed and unafraid, he appeared more like an untamed animal, silent and watchful, his black eyes flashing from face to face, quiet so long as quiet endured, but prepared to spring and fight and tear and scratch for life, at the first sign of danger.

The contrast between boy and girl was striking, but not pitiful. There was too much strength in the boy for that, waif that he was of the generations of Shpack, Spike O'Brien, and Bonner. In his features, clean cut as a cameo and almost classic in their severity, there were the power and achievement of his father, and his grandfather, and the one known as the Big Fat, who was captured by the Sea People and escaped to Kamchatka.

Neil Bonner fought his emotion down, swallowed it down, and choked over it, though his face smiled with good humor and the joy with which one meets a friend.

"Your boy, eh, Jees Uck?" he said. And then turning to Kitty: "Handsome fellow! He'll do something with those two hands of his in this our world."

Kitty nodded concurrence. "What is your name?" she asked.

The young savage flashed his quick eyes upon her and dwelt over her for a space, seeking out, as it were, the motive beneath the question.

"Neil," he answered deliberately when the scrutiny had satisfied him.

"Injun talk," Jees Uck interposed, glibly manufacturing languages on the spur of the moment. "Him Injun talk, *nee-al*, all the same 'cracker.' Him baby, him like cracker; him cry for cracker. Him say, 'Nee-al, nee-al,' all time him say, 'Nee-al.' Then I say that um name. So um name all time Nee-al."

Never did sound more blessed fall upon Neil Bonner's ear than that lie from Jees Uck's lips. It was the cue, and he knew there was reason for Kitty's untroubled brow.

"And his father?" Kitty asked. "He must be a fine man."

"Oo-a, yes," was the reply. "Um father fine man. Sure!"

"Did you know him, Neil?" queried Kitty.

"Know him? Most intimately," Neil answered, and harked back to dreary Twenty Mile and the man alone in the silence with his thoughts.

And here might well end the story of Jees Uck, but for the crown she put upon her renunciation. When she returned to the North to dwell in her grand log-house, John Thompson found that the P. C. Company could make a shift somehow to carry on its business without his aid. Also, the new agent and the succeeding agents received instructions that the woman Jees Uck should be given whatsoever goods and grub she desired, in whatsoever quantities she ordered, and that no charge should be placed upon the books. Further, the company paid yearly to the woman Jees Uck a pension of five thousand dollars.

When he had attained suitable age, Father Champreau laid hands upon the boy, and the time was not long when Jees Uck received letters regularly from the Jesuit college in Maryland. Later on these letters came from Italy, and still later from France. And in the end there returned to Alaska one Father Neil, a man mighty for good in the land, who loved his mother and who ultimately went into a wider field and rose to high authority in the order.

Jees Uck was a young woman when she went back into the North, and men still looked upon her and yearned. But she lived straight, and no breath was ever raised save in commendation. She stayed for a while with the good sisters at Holy Cross, where she learned to read and write and became versed in practical medicine and surgery. After that she returned to her grand log-house and gathered about her the young girls of the Toyaat village, to show them the way of their feet in the world. It is neither Protestant nor Catholic, this school in the house built by Neil Bonner for Jees Uck, his wife; but the missionaries of all the sects look upon it with equal favor. The latch-string is always out, and tired prospectors and trail-weary men turn aside from the flowing river or frozen trail to rest there for a space and be warm by her fire. And, down in the States, Kitty Bonner is pleased at the interest her husband takes in Alaskan education and the large sums he devotes to that purpose; and, though she often smiles and chaffs, deep down and secretly she is but the prouder of him.

18
THE LEAGUE OF THE OLD MEN

THE LEAGUE OF THE OLD MEN

At the Barracks a man was being tried for his life. He was an old man, a native from the Whitefish River, which empties into the Yukon below Lake Le Barge. All Dawson was wrought up over the affair, and likewise the Yukon-dwellers for a thousand miles up and down. It has been the custom of the land-robbing and sea-robbing Anglo-Saxon to give the law to conquered peoples, and ofttimes this law is harsh. But in the case of Imber the law for once seemed inadequate and weak. In the mathematical nature of things, equity did not reside in the punishment to be accorded him. The punishment was a foregone conclusion, there could be no doubt of that; and though it was capital, Imber had but one life, while the tale against him was one of scores.

In fact, the blood of so many was upon his hands that the killings attributed to him did not permit of precise enumeration. Smoking a pipe by the trailside or lounging around the stove, men made rough estimates of the numbers that had perished at his hand. They had been whites, all of them, these poor murdered people, and they had been slain singly, in pairs, and in parties. And so purposeless and wanton had been these killings, that they had long been a mystery to the mounted police, even in the time of the captains, and later, when the creeks realized, and a governor came from the Dominion to make the land pay for its prosperity.

But more mysterious still was the coming of Imber to Dawson to give himself up. It was in the late spring, when the Yukon was growling and writhing under its ice, that the old Indian climbed painfully up the bank from the river trail and stood blinking on the main street. Men who had witnessed his advent, noted that he was weak and tottery, and that he staggered over to a heap of cabin-logs and sat down. He sat there a full day, staring straight before him at the unceasing tide of white men that flooded past. Many a head jerked curiously to the side to meet his stare, and more than one remark was dropped anent the old Siwash with so strange a look upon his face. No end of men remembered afterward that they had been struck by his extraordinary figure, and forever afterward prided themselves upon their swift discernment of the unusual.

But it remained for Dickensen, Little Dickensen, to be the hero of the occasion. Little Dickensen had come into the land with great dreams and a pocketful of cash; but with the cash the dreams vanished, and to earn his passage back to the States he had accepted a clerical position with the brokerage firm of Holbrook and Mason. Across the street from the office of Holbrook and Mason was the heap of cabin-logs upon which Imber sat. Dickensen looked out of the window at him before he went to lunch; and when he came back from lunch he looked out of the window, and the old Siwash was still there.

Dickensen continued to look out of the window, and he, too, forever afterward prided himself upon his swiftness of discernment. He was a romantic little chap, and he likened the immobile old heathen to the genius of the Siwash race, gazing calm-eyed upon the hosts of the invading Saxon. The hours swept along, but Imber did not vary his posture, did not by a hair's-breadth move a muscle; and Dickensen remembered the man who once sat upright on a sled in the main street where men passed to and fro. They thought the man was resting, but later, when they touched him, they found him stiff and cold, frozen to death in the midst of the busy street. To undouble him, that he might fit into a coffin, they had been forced to lug him to a fire and thaw him out a bit. Dickensen shivered at the recollection.

Later on, Dickensen went out on the sidewalk to smoke a cigar and cool off; and a little later Emily Travis happened along. Emily Travis was dainty and delicate and rare, and whether in London or Klondike she gowned herself as befitted the daughter of a millionnaire mining engineer. Little Dickensen deposited his cigar on an outside window ledge where he could find it again, and lifted his hat.

They chatted for ten minutes or so, when Emily Travis, glancing past Dickensen's shoulder, gave a startled little scream. Dickensen turned about to see, and was startled, too. Imber had crossed the street and was standing there, a gaunt and hungry-looking shadow, his gaze riveted upon the girl.

"What do you want?" Little Dickensen demanded, tremulously plucky.

Imber grunted and stalked up to Emily Travis. He looked her over, keenly and carefully, every square inch of her. Especially did he appear interested in her silky brown hair, and in the color of her cheek, faintly sprayed and soft, like the downy bloom of a butterfly wing. He walked around her, surveying her with the calculating eye of a man who studies the lines upon which a horse or a boat is builded. In the course of his circuit the pink shell of her ear came between his eye and the westering sun, and he stopped to contemplate its rosy transparency. Then he returned to her face and looked long and intently into her blue eyes. He grunted and laid a hand on her arm midway between the shoulder and elbow. With his other hand he lifted her forearm and doubled it back. Disgust and wonder showed in his face, and he dropped her arm with a contemptuous grunt. Then he muttered a few guttural syllables, turned his back upon her, and addressed himself to Dickensen.

Dickensen could not understand his speech, and Emily Travis laughed. Imber turned from one to the other, frowning, but both shook their heads. He was about to go away, when she called out:

"Oh, Jimmy! Come here!"

Jimmy came from the other side of the street. He was a big, hulking Indian clad in approved white-man style, with an Eldorado king's sombrero on his head. He talked with Imber, haltingly, with throaty spasms. Jimmy was a Sitkan, possessed of no more than a passing knowledge of the interior dialects.

"Him Whitefish man," he said to Emily Travis. "Me savve um talk no very much. Him want to look see chief white man."

"The Governor," suggested Dickensen.

Jimmy talked some more with the Whitefish man, and his face went grave and puzzled.

"I t'ink um want Cap'n Alexander," he explained. "Him say um kill white man, white woman, white boy, plenty kill um white people. Him want to die."

"Insane, I guess," said Dickensen.

"What you call dat?" queried Jimmy.

Dickensen thrust a finger figuratively inside his head and imparted a rotary motion thereto.

"Mebbe so, mebbe so," said Jimmy, returning to Imber, who still demanded the chief man of the white men.

A mounted policeman (unmounted for Klondike service) joined the group and heard Imber's wish repeated. He was a stalwart young fellow, broad-shouldered, deep-chested, legs cleanly built and stretched wide apart, and tall though Imber was, he towered above him by half a head. His eyes were cool, and gray, and steady, and he carried himself with the peculiar confidence of power that is bred of blood and tradition. His splendid masculinity was emphasized by his excessive boyishness, — he was a mere lad, — and his smooth cheek promised a blush as willingly as the cheek of a maid.

Imber was drawn to him at once. The fire leaped into his eyes at sight of a sabre slash that scarred his cheek. He ran a withered hand down the young fellow's leg and caressed the swelling thew. He smote the broad chest with his knuckles, and pressed and prodded the thick muscle-pads that covered the shoulders like a cuirass. The group had been added to by curious passers-by — husky miners, mountaineers, and frontiersmen, sons of the long-legged and broad-shouldered generations. Imber glanced from one to another, then he spoke aloud in the Whitefish tongue.

"What did he say?" asked Dickensen.

"Him say um all the same one man, dat p'liceman," Jimmy interpreted.

Little Dickensen was little, and what of Miss Travis, he felt sorry for having asked the question.

The policeman was sorry for him and stepped into the breach. "I fancy there may be something in his story. I'll take him up to the captain for examination. Tell him to come along with me, Jimmy."

Jimmy indulged in more throaty spasms, and Imber grunted and looked satisfied.

"But ask him what he said, Jimmy, and what he meant when he took hold of my arm."

So spoke Emily Travis, and Jimmy put the question and received the answer.

"Him say you no afraid," said Jimmy.

Emily Travis looked pleased.

"Him say you no *skookum*, no strong, all the same very soft like little baby. Him break you, in um two hands, to little pieces. Him t'ink much funny, very strange, how you can be mother of men so big, so strong, like dat p'liceman."

Emily Travers kept her eyes up and unfaltering, but her cheeks were sprayed with scarlet. Little Dickensen blushed and was quite embarrassed. The policeman's face blazed with his boy's blood.

"Come along, you," he said gruffly, setting his shoulder to the crowd and forcing a way.

Thus it was that Imber found his way to the Barracks, where he made full and voluntary confession, and from the precincts of which he never emerged.

Imber looked very tired. The fatigue of hopelessness and age was in his face. His shoulders drooped depressingly, and his eyes were lack-lustre. His mop of hair should have been white, but sun and weatherbeat had burned and bitten it so that it hung limp and lifeless and colorless. He took no interest in what went on around him. The courtroom was jammed with the men of the creeks and trails, and there was an ominous note in the rumble and grumble of their low-pitched voices, which came to his ears like the growl of the sea from deep caverns.

He sat close by a window, and his apathetic eyes rested now and again on the dreary scene without. The sky was overcast, and a gray drizzle was falling. It was flood-time on the Yukon. The ice was gone, and the river was up in the town. Back and forth on the main street, in canoes and poling-boats, passed the people that never rested. Often he saw these boats turn aside from the street and enter the flooded square that marked the Barracks' parade-ground. Sometimes they disappeared beneath him, and he heard them jar against the houselogs and their occupants scramble in through the window. After that came the slush of water against men's legs as they waded across the lower room and mounted the stairs. Then they appeared in the doorway, with doffed hats and dripping seaboots, and added themselves to the waiting crowd.

And while they centred their looks on him, and in grim anticipation enjoyed the penalty he was to pay, Imber looked at them, and mused on their ways, and on their Law that never slept, but went on unceasing, in good times and bad, in flood and famine, through trouble and terror and death, and which would go on unceasing, it seemed to him, to the end of time.

A man rapped sharply on a table, and the conversation droned away into silence. Imber looked at the man. He seemed one in authority, yet Imber divined the square-browed man who sat by a desk farther back to be the one chief over them all and over the man who had rapped. Another man by the same table uprose and began to read aloud from many fine sheets of paper. At the top of each sheet he cleared his throat, at the bottom moistened his fingers. Imber did not understand his speech, but the others did, and he knew that it made them angry. Sometimes it made them very angry, and once a man cursed him, in single syllables, stinging and tense, till a man at the table rapped him to silence.

For an interminable period the man read. His monotonous, sing-song utterance lured Imber to dreaming, and he was dreaming deeply when the man ceased. A voice spoke to him in his own Whitefish tongue, and he roused up, without surprise, to look upon the face of his sister's son, a young man who had wandered away years agone to make his dwelling with the whites.

"Thou dost not remember me," he said by way of greeting.

"Nay," Imber answered. "Thou art Howkan who went away. Thy mother be dead."

"She was an old woman," said Howkan.

But Imber did not hear, and Howkan, with hand upon his shoulder, roused him again.

"I shall speak to thee what the man has spoken, which is the tale of the troubles thou hast done and which thou hast told, O fool, to the Captain Alexander. And thou

"First, there was the man...with cunning traps made of iron, who sought the beaver of the Whitefish. Him I slew"

shalt understand and say if it be true talk or talk not true. It is so commanded."

Howkan had fallen among the mission folk and been taught by them to read and write. In his hands he held the many fine sheets from which the man had read aloud, and which had been taken down by a clerk when Imber first made confession, through the mouth of Jimmy, to Captain Alexander. Howkan began to read. Imber listened for a space, when a wonderment rose up in his face and he broke in abruptly.

"That be my talk, Howkan. Yet from thy lips it comes when thy ears have not heard."

Howkan smirked with self-appreciation. His hair was parted in the middle. "Nay, from the paper it comes, O Imber. Never have my ears heard. From the paper it comes, through my eyes, into my head, and out of my mouth to thee. Thus it comes."

"Thus it comes? It be there in the paper?" Imber's voice sank in whisperful awe as he crackled the sheets 'twixt thumb and finger and stared at the charactery scrawled thereon. "It be a great medicine, Howkan, and thou art a worker of wonders."

"It be nothing, it be nothing," the young man responded carelessly and pridefully. He read at hazard from the document: *In that year, before the break of the ice, came an old man, and a boy who was lame of one foot. These also did I kill, and the old man made much noise —*"

"It be true," Imber interrupted breathlessly. "He made much noise and would not die for a long time. But how dost thou know, Howkan? The chief man of the white men told thee, mayhap? No one beheld me, and him alone have I told."

Howkan shook his head with impatience. "Have I not told thee it be there in the paper, O fool?"

Imber stared hard at the ink-scrawled surface. "As the hunter looks upon the snow and says, Here but yesterday there passed a rabbit; and here by the willow scrub it stood and listened, and heard, and was afraid; and here it turned upon its trail; and here it went with great swiftness, leaping wide; and here, with greater swiftness and wider leapings, came a lynx; and here, where the claws cut deep into the snow, the lynx made a very great leap; and here it struck, with the rabbit under and rolling belly up; and here leads off the trail of the lynx alone, and there is no more rabbit, — as the hunter looks upon the markings of the snow and says thus and so and here, dost thou, too, look upon the paper and say thus and so and here be the things old Imber hath done?"

"Even so," said Howkan. "And now do thou listen, and keep thy woman's tongue between thy teeth till thou art called upon for speech."

Thereafter, and for a long time, Howkan read to him the confession, and Imber remained musing and silent. At the end, he said:

"It be my talk, and true talk, but I am grown old, Howkan, and forgotten things come back to me which were well for the head man there to know. First, there was the man who came over the Ice Mountains, with cunning traps made of iron, who sought the beaver of the Whitefish. Him I slew. And there were three men seeking gold on the Whitefish long ago. Them also I slew, and left them to the wolverines. And at the Five Fingers there was a man with a raft and much meat."

At the moments when Imber paused to remember, Howkan translated and a clerk reduced to writing. The courtroom listened stolidly to each unadorned little tragedy, till Imber told of a red-haired man whose eyes were crossed and whom he had killed with a remarkably long shot.

"Hell," said a man in the forefront of the onlookers. He said it soulfully and sorrowfully. He was red-haired. "Hell," he repeated. "That was my brother Bill." And at regular intervals throughout the session, his solemn "Hell" was heard in the courtroom; nor did his comrades check him, nor did the man at the table rap him to order.

Imber's head drooped once more, and his eyes went dull, as though a film rose up and covered them from the world. And he dreamed as only age can dream upon the colossal futility of youth.

Later, Howkan roused him again, saying: "Stand up, O Imber. It be commanded that thou tellest why you did these troubles, and slew these people, and at the end journeyed here seeking the Law."

Imber rose feebly to his feet and swayed back and forth. He began to speak in a low and faintly rumbling voice, but Howkan interrupted him.

"This old man, he is damn crazy," he said in English to the square-browed man. "His talk is foolish and like that of a child."

"We will hear his talk which is like that of a child," said the square-browed man. "And we will hear it, word for word, as he speaks it. Do you understand?"

Howkan understood, and Imber's eyes flashed, for he had witnessed the play between his sister's son and the man in authority. And then began the story, the epic of a bronze patriot which might well itself be wrought into bronze for the generations unborn. The crowd fell strangely silent, and the square-browed judge leaned head on hand and pondered his soul and the soul of his race. Only was heard the deep tones of Imber, rhythmically alternating with the shrill voice of the interpreter, and now and again, like the bell of the Lord, the wondering and meditative "Hell" of the red-haired man.

"I am Imber of the Whitefish people." So ran the interpretation of Howkan, whose inherent barbarism gripped hold of him, and who lost his mission culture and veneered civilization as he caught the savage ring and rhythm of old Imber's tale. "My father was Otsbaok, a strong man. The land was warm with sunshine and gladness when I was a boy. The people did not hunger after strange things, nor hearken to new voices, and the ways of their fathers were their ways. The women found favor in the eyes of the young men, and the young men looked upon them with content. Babes hung at the breasts of the women, and they were heavy-hipped with increase of the tribe. Men were men in those days. In peace and plenty, and in war and famine, they were men.

"At that time there was more fish in the water than now, and more meat in the. forest. Our dogs were wolves, warm with thick hides and hard to the frost and storm. And as with our dogs so with us, for we were likewise hard to the frost and storm. And when the Pellys came into our land we slew them and were slain. For we were men, we Whitefish, and our fathers and our fathers' fathers had fought against the Pellys and determined the bounds of the land.

"As I say, with our dogs, so with us. And one day came the first white man. He dragged himself, so, on hand and knee, in the snow. And his skin was stretched tight, and his bones were sharp beneath. Never was such a man, we thought, and we wondered of what strange tribe he was, and of its land. And he was weak, most weak, like a little child, so that we gave him a place by the fire, and warm furs to lie upon, and we gave him food as little children are given food.

"And with him was a dog, large as three of our dogs, and very weak. The hair of this dog was short, and not warm, and the tail was frozen so that the end fell off. And this strange dog we fed, and bedded by the fire, and fought from it our dogs, which else would have killed him. And what of the moose meat and the sun-dried salmon, the man and dog took strength to themselves; and what of the strength they became big and unafraid. And the man spoke loud words and laughed at the old men and young men, and looked boldly upon the maidens. And the dog fought with our dogs, and for all of his short hair and softness slew three of them in one day.

"When we asked the man concerning his people, he said, 'I have many brothers,' and laughed in a way that was not good. And when he was in his full strength he went away, and with him went Noda, daughter to the chief. First, after that, was one of our bitches brought to pup. And never was there such a breed of dogs, — big-headed, thick-jawed, and short-haired, and helpless. Well do I remember my father, Otsbaok, a strong man. His face was black with anger at such helplessness, and he took a stone, so, and so, and there was no more helplessness. And two summers after that came Noda back to us with

"And that was the beginning. Came a second white man, with short-haired dogs, which he left behind him when he went. And with him went six of our strongest dogs, for which, in trade, he had given Koo-So-Tee, my mother's brother, a wonderful pistol that fired with great swiftness six times. And Koo-So-Tee was very big, what of the pistol, and laughed at our bows and arrows. 'Woman's things,' he called them, and went forth against the bald-face grizzly, with the pistol in his hand. Now it be known that it is not good to hunt the bald-face with a pistol, but how were we to know? and how was Koo-So-Tee to know? So he went against the bald-face, very brave, and fired the pistol with great swiftness six times; and the bald-face but grunted and broke in his breast like it were an egg, and like honey from a bee's nest dripped the brains of Koo-So-Tee upon the ground. He was a good hunter, and there was no one to bring meat to his squaw and children. And we were bitter, and we said, 'That which for the white men is well, is for us not well.' And this be true. There be many white men and fat, but their ways have made us few and lean.

"Came the third white man, with great wealth of all manner of wonderful foods and things. And twenty of our strongest dogs he took from us in trade. Also, what of presents and great promises, ten of our young hunters did he take with him on a journey which fared no man knew where. It is said they died in the snow of the Ice Mountains where man has never been, or in the Hills of Silence which are beyond the edge of the earth. Be that as it may, dogs and young hunters were seen never again by the Whitefish people.

"And more white men came with the years, and ever, with pay and presents, they led the young men away with them. And sometimes the young men came back with strange tales of dangers and toils in the lands beyond the Pellys, and some times they did not come back. And we said: 'If they be unafraid of life, these white men, it is because they have many lives; but we be few by the Whitefish, and the young men shall go away no more.' But the young men did go away; and the young women went also; and we were very wroth.

"It be true, we ate flour, and salt pork, and drank tea which was a great delight; only, when we could not get tea, it was very bad and we became short of speech and quick of anger. So we grew to hunger for the things the white men brought in trade. Trade! trade! all the time was it trade! One winter we sold our meat for clocks that would not go, and watches with broken guts, and files worn smooth, and pistols without cartridges and worthless. And then came famine, and we were without meat, and two score died ere the break of spring.

"'Now are we grown weak,' we said; 'and the Pellys will fall upon us, and our bounds be overthrown.' But as it fared with us, so had it fared with the Pellys, and they were too weak to come against us.

"My father, Otsbaok, a strong man, was now old and very wise. And he spoke to the chief, saying: 'Behold, our dogs be worthless. No longer are they thick-furred and strong, and they die in the frost and harness. Let us go into the village and kill them, saving only the wolf ones, and these let us tie out in the night that they may mate with the wild wolves of the forest. Thus shall we have dogs warm and strong again.'

"And his word was harkened to, and we Whitefish became known for our dogs, which were the best in the land. But known we were not for ourselves. The best of our young men and women had gone away with the white men to wander on trail and river to far places. And the young women came back old and broken, as Noda had come, or they came not at all. And the young men came back to sit by our fires for a time, full of ill speech and rough ways, drinking evil drinks and gambling through long nights and days, with a great unrest always in their hearts, till the call of the white men came to them and they went away again to the unknown places. And they were without honor and respect, jeering the old-time customs and laughing in the faces of chief and shamans.

"As I say, we were become a weak breed, we Whitefish. We sold our warm skins and furs for tobacco and whiskey and thin cotton things that left us shivering in the cold. And the coughing sickness came upon us, and men and women coughed and sweated through the long nights, and the hunters on trail spat blood upon the snow. And now one, and now another, bled swiftly from the mouth and died. And the women bore few children, and those they bore were weak and given to sickness. And other sicknesses came to us from the white men, the like of which we had never known and could not understand. Smallpox, likewise measles, have I heard these sicknesses named, and we died of them as die the salmon in the still eddies when in the fall their eggs are spawned and there is no longer need for them to live.

"And yet, and here be the strangeness of it, the white men come as the breath of death; all their ways lead to death, their nostrils are filled with it; and yet they do not die. Theirs the whiskey, and tobacco, and short-haired dogs; theirs the many sicknesses, the smallpox and measles, the coughing and mouth-bleeding; theirs the white skin, and softness to the frost and storm; and theirs the pistols that shoot six times very swift and are worthless. And yet they grow fat on their many ills, and prosper, and lay a heavy hand over all the world and tread mightily upon its peoples. And their women, too, are soft as little babes, most breakable and never broken, the mothers of men. And out of all this softness, and sickness, and weakness, come strength, and power, and authority. They be gods, or devils, as the case may be. I do not know. What do I know, I, old Imber of the Whitefish? Only do I know that they are past understanding, these white men, far-wanderers and fighters over the earth that they be.

"As I say, the meat in the forest became less and less. It be true, the white man's gun is most excellent and kills a long way off; but of what worth the gun, when there is no meat to kill? When I was a boy on the Whitefish there was moose on every hill, and each year came the caribou uncountable. But now the hunter may take the trail ten days and not one moose gladden his eyes, while the caribou uncountable come no more at all. Small worth the gun, I say, killing a long way off, when there be nothing to kill.

"And I, Imber, pondered upon these things, watching the while the Whitefish, and the Pellys, and all the tribes of the land, perishing as perished the meat of the forest. Long I pondered. I talked with the shamans and the old men who were wise. I went apart that the sounds of the village might not disturb me, and I ate no meat so that my belly should not press upon me and make me slow of eye and ear. I sat long and sleepless in the forest, wide-eyed for the sign, my ears patient and keen for the word that was to come. And I wandered alone in the blackness of night to the river bank, where was wind-moaning and sobbing of water, and where I sought wisdom from the ghosts of old shamans in the trees and dead and gone.

"And in the end, as in a vision, came to me the short-haired and detestable dogs, and the way seemed plain. By the wisdom of Otsbaok, my father and a strong man, had the blood of our own wolf-dogs been kept clean, wherefore had they remained warm of hide and strong in the harness. So I returned to my village and made oration to the men. 'This be a tribe, these white

men,' I said. 'A very large tribe, and doubtless there is no longer meat in their land, and they are come among us to make a new land for themselves. But they weaken us, and we die. They are a very hungry folk. Already has our meat gone from us, and it were well, if we would live, that we deal by them as we have dealt by their dogs.'

"And further oration I made, counselling fight. And the men of the Whitefish listened, and some said one thing, and some another, and some spoke of other and worthless things, and no man made brave talk of deeds and war. But while the young men were weak as water and afraid, I watched that the old men sat silent, and that in their eyes fires came and went. And later, when the village slept and no one knew, I drew the old men away into the forest and made more talk. And now we were agreed, and we remembered the good young days, and the free land, and the times of plenty, and the gladness and sunshine; and we called ourselves brothers, and swore great secrecy, and a mighty oath to cleanse the land of the evil breed that had come upon it. It be plain we were fools, but how were we to know, we old men of the Whitefish?

"And to hearten the others, I did the first deed. I kept guard upon the Yukon till the first canoe came down. In it were two white men, and when I stood upright upon the bank and raised my hand they changed their course and drove in to me. And as the man in the bow lifted his head, so, that he might know wherefore I wanted him, my arrow sang through the air straight to his throat, and he knew. The second man, who held paddle in the stern, had his rifle half to his shoulder when the first of my three spear-casts smote him.

"'These be the first,' I said, when the old men had gathered to me. 'Later we will bind together all the old men of all the tribes, and after that the young men who remain strong, and the work will become easy.'

"And then the two dead white men we cast into the river. And of the canoe, which was a very good canoe, we made a fire, and a fire, also, of the things within the canoe. But first we looked at the things, and they were pouches of leather which we cut open with our knives. And inside these pouches were many papers, like that from which thou hast read, O Howkan, with markings on them which we marvelled at and could not understand. Now, I am become wise, and I know them for the speech of men as thou hast told me."

A whisper and buzz went around the courtroom when Howkan finished interpreting the affair of the canoe, and one man's voice spoke up: "That was the lost '91 mail, Peter James and Delaney bringing it in and last spoken at Le Barge by Matthews going out." The clerk scratched steadily away, and another paragraph was added to the history of the North.

"There be little more," Imber went on slowly. "It be there on the paper, the things we did. We were old men, and we did not understand. Even I, Imber, do not now understand. Secretly we slew, and continued to slay, for with our years we were crafty and we had learned the swiftness of going without haste. When white men came among us with black looks and rough words, and took away six of the young men with irons binding them helpless, we knew we must slay wider and farther. And one by one we old men departed up river and down to the unknown lands. It was a brave thing. Old we were, and unafraid, but the fear of far places is a terrible fear to men who are old.

"So we slew, without haste and craftily. On the Chilcoot and in the Delta we slew, from the passes to the sea, wherever the white men camped or broke their trails. It be true, they died, but it was without worth. Ever did they come over the mountains, ever did they grow and grow, while we, being old, became less and less. I remember, by the Caribou Crossing, the camp of a white man. He was a very little white man, and three of the old men came upon him in his sleep. And the next day I came upon the four of them. The white man alone still breathed, and there was breath in him to curse me once and well before he died.

"And so it went, now one old man, and now another. Sometimes the word reached us long after of how they died, and sometimes it did not reach us. And the old men of the other tribes were weak and afraid, and would not join us. As I say, one by one, till I alone was left. I am Imber, of the Whitefish people. My father was Otsbaok, a strong man. There are no Whitefish now. Of the old men I am the last. The young men and young women are gone away, some to live with the Pellys, some with the Salmons, and more with the white men. I am very old, and very tired, and it being vain fighting the Law, as thou sayest, Howkan, I am come seeking the Law."

"O Imber, thou art indeed a fool," said Howkan.

But Imber was dreaming. The square-browed judge likewise dreamed, and all his race rose up before him in a mighty phantasmagoria — his steel-shod, mail-clad race, the lawgiver and world-maker among the families of men. He saw it dawn red-flickering across the dark forests and sullen seas; he saw it blaze, bloody and red, to full and triumphant noon; and down the shaded slope he saw the blood-red sands dropping into night. And through it all he observed the Law, pitiless and potent, ever unswerving and ever ordaining, greater than the motes of men who fulfilled it or were crushed by it, even as it was greater than he, his heart speaking for softness.

19
THE ONE THOUSAND DOZEN

THE ONE THOUSAND DOZEN

David Rasmunsen was a hustler, and, like many a greater man, a man of the one idea. Wherefore, when the clarion call of the North rang on his ear, he conceived an adventure in eggs and bent all his energy to its achievement. He figured briefly and to the point, and the adventure became iridescent-hued, splendid. That eggs would sell at Dawson for five dollars a dozen was a safe working premise. Whence it was incontrovertible that one thousand dozen would bring, in the Golden Metropolis, five thousand dollars.

On the other hand, expense was to be considered, and he considered it well, for he was a careful man, keenly practical, with a hard head and a heart that imagination never warmed. At fifteen cents a dozen, the initial cost of his thousand dozen would be one hundred and fifty dollars, a mere bagatelle in face of the enormous profit. And suppose, just suppose, to be wildly extravagant for once, that transportation for himself and eggs should run up eight hundred and fifty more; he would still have four thousand clear cash and clean when the last egg was disposed of and the last dust had rippled into his sack.

"You see, Alma," — he figured it over with his wife, the cosy dining room submerged in a sea of maps, government surveys, guidebooks, and Alaskan itineraries, — "you see, expenses don't really begin till you strike Dyea — fifty dollars'll cover it with a first-class passage thrown in. Now from Dyea to Lake Linderman, Indian packers take your goods over for twelve cents a pound, twelve dollars a hundred, or one hundred and twenty dollars a thousand. Say I have fifteen hundred pounds, it'll cost one hundred and eighty dollars — call it two hundred and be safe. I am creditably informed by a Klondiker just come out that I can buy a boat for three hundred. But the same man says I'm sure to get a couple of passengers for one hundred and fifty each, which will give me

the boat for nothing, and, further, they can help me manage it. And ... that's all; I put my eggs ashore from the boat at Dawson. Now let me see how much is that?"

"Fifty dollars from San Francisco to Dyea, two hundred from Dyea to Linderman, passengers pay for the boat — two hundred and fifty all told," she summed up swiftly.

"And a hundred for my clothes and personal outift," he went on happily; "that leaves a margin of five hundred for emergencies. And what possible emergencies can arise?"

Alma shrugged her shoulders and elevated her brows. If that vast Northland was capable of swallowing up a man and a thousand dozen eggs, surely there was room and to spare for whatever else he might happen to possess. So she thought, but she said nothing. She knew David Rasmunsen too well to say anything.

"Doubling the time because of chance delays, I should make the trip in two months. Think of it, Alma! Four thousand in two months! Beats the paltry hundred a month I'm getting now. Why, we'll build further out where we'll have more space, gas in every room, and a view, and the rent of the cottage'll pay taxes, insurance, and water, and leave something over. And then there's always the chance of my striking it and coming out a millionnaire. Now tell me, Alma, don't you think I'm very moderate?"

And Alma could hardly think otherwise. Besides, had not her own cousin, — though a remote and distant one to be sure, the black sheep, the harum-scarum, the ne'er-do-well, — had not he come down out of that weird North country with a hundred thousand in yellow dust, to say nothing of a half-ownership in the hole from which it came?

David Rasmunsen's grocer was surprised when he found him weighing eggs in the scales at the end of the counter, and

Rasmunsen himself was more surprised when he found that a dozen eggs weighed a pound and a half — fifteen hundred pounds for his thousand dozen! There would be no weight left for his clothes, blankets, and cooking utensils, to say nothing of the grub he must necessarily consume by the way. His calculations were all thrown out, and he was just proceeding to recast them when he hit upon the idea of weighing small eggs. "For whether they be large or small, a dozen eggs is a dozen eggs," he observed sagely to himself; and a dozen small ones he found to weigh but a pound and a quarter. Thereat the city of San Francisco was overrun by anxious-eyed emissaries, and commission houses and dairy associations were startled by a sudden demand for eggs running not more than twenty ounces to the dozen.

Rasmunsen mortgaged the little cottage for a thousand dollars, arranged for his wife to make a prolonged stay among her own people, threw up his job, and started North. To keep within his schedule he compromised on a second-class passage, which, because of the rush, was worse than steerage; and in the late summer, a pale and wabbly man, he disembarked with his eggs on the Dyea beach. But it did not take him long to recover his land legs and appetite. His first interview with the Chilkoot packers straightened him up and stiffened his backbone. Forty cents a pound they demanded for the twenty-eight-mile portage, and while he caught his breath and swallowed, the price went up to forty-three. Fifteen husky Indians put the straps on his packs at forty-five, but took them off at an offer of forty-seven from a Skaguay Croesus in dirty shirt and ragged overalls who had lost his horses on the White Pass Trail and was now making a last desperate drive at the country by way of Chilkoot.

But Rasmunsen was clean grit, and at fifty cents found takers, who, two days later, set his eggs down intact at Linderman. But fifty cents a pound is a thousand dollars a ton, and his fifteen hundred pounds had exhausted his emergency fund and left him stranded at the Tantalus point where each day he saw the fresh-whipsawed boats departing for Dawson. Further, a great anxiety brooded over the camp where the boats were built. Men worked frantically, early and late, at the height of their endur-

ance, calking, nailing, and pitching in a frenzy of haste for which adequate explanation was not far to seek. Each day the snow-line crept farther down the bleak, rock-shouldered peaks, and gale followed gale, with sleet and slush and snow, and in the eddies and quiet places young ice formed and thickened through the fleeting hours. And each morn, toil-stiffened men turned wan faces across the lake to see if the freeze-up had come. For the freeze-up heralded the death of their hope — the hope that they would be floating down the swift river ere navigation closed on the chain of lakes.

To harrow Rasmunsen's soul further, he discovered three competitors in the egg business. It was true that one, a little German, had gone broke and was himself forlornly back-tripping the last pack of the portage; but the other two had boats nearly completed and were daily supplicating the god of merchants and traders to stay the iron hand of winter for just another day. But the iron hand closed down over the land. Men were being frozen in the blizzard, which swept Chilkoot, and Rasmunsen frosted his toes ere he was aware. He found a chance to go passenger with his freight in a boat just shoving off through the rubble, but two hundred, hard cash, was required, and he had no money.

"Ay tank you yust wait one leedle w'ile," said the Swedish boat-builder, who had struck his Klondike right there and was wise enough to know it — "one leedle w'ile und I make you a tam fine skiff boat, sure Pete."

With this unpledged word to go on, Rasmunsen hit the back trail to Crater Lake, where he fell in with two press correspondents whose tangled baggage was strewn from Stone House, over across the Pass, and as far as Happy Camp.

"Yes," he said with consequence. "I've a thousand dozen eggs at Linderman, and my boat's just about got the last seam calked. Consider myself in luck to get it. Boats are at a premium, you know, and none to be had."

Whereupon and almost with bodily violence the correspondents clamored to go with him, fluttered greenbacks before his eyes, and spilled yellow twenties from hand to hand. He could not hear of it, but they overpersuaded him, and he reluctantly consented to take them at three hundred apiece. Also they pressed upon him the passage money in advance. And while they wrote to their respective journals concerning the good Samaritan with the thousand dozen eggs, the good Samaritan was hurrying back to the Swede at Linderman.

"Here, you! Gimme that boat!" was his salutation, his hand jingling the correspondents' gold pieces and his eyes hungrily bent upon the finished craft.

The Swede regarded him stolidly and shook his head.

"How much is the other fellow paying? Three hundred? Well, here's four. Take it."

He tried to press it upon him, but the man backed away.

"Ay tank not. Ay say him get der skiff boat. You yust wait —"

"Here's six hundred. Last call. Take it or leave it. Tell'm it's a mistake."

The Swede wavered. "Ay tank yes," he finally said, and the last Rasmunsen saw of him his vocabulary was going to wreck in a vain effort to explain the mistake to the other fellows.

The German slipped and broke his ankle on the steep hogback above Deep Lake, sold out his stock for a dollar a dozen, and with the proceeds hired Indian packers to carry him back to Dyea. But on the morning Rasmunsen shoved off with his correspondents, his two rivals followed suit.

"How many you got?" one of them, a lean little New Englander, called out.

"One thousand dozen," Rasmunsen answered proudly.

"Huh! I'll go you even stakes I beat you in with my eight hundred."

The correspondents offered to lend him the money; but Rasmunsen declined, and the Yankee closed with the remaining rival, a brawny son of the sea and sailor of ships and things, who promised to show them all a wrinkle or two when it came to cracking on. And crack on he did, with a large tarpaulin squaresail which pressed the bow half under at every jump. He was the first to run out of Linderman, but, disdaining the portage, piled his loaded boat on the rocks in the boiling rapids. Rasmunsen and the Yankee, who likewise had two passengers, portaged across on their backs and then lined their empty boats down through the bad water to Bennett.

Bennett was a twenty-five-mile lake, narrow and deep, a funnel between the mountains through which storms ever romped. Rasmunsen camped on the sand-pit at its head, where were many men and boats bound north in the teeth of the Arctic winter. He awoke in the morning to find a piping gale from the south, which caught the chill from the whited peaks and glacial valleys and blew as cold as north wind ever blew. But it was fair, and he also found the Yankee staggering past the first bold headland with all sail set. Boat after boat was getting under way, and the correspondents fell to with enthusiasm.

"We'll catch him before Cariboo Crossing," they assured Rasmunsen, as they ran up the sail and the *Alma* took the first icy spray over her bow.

Now Rasmunsen all his life had been prone to cowardice on water, but he clung to the kicking steering-oar with set face and determined jaw. His thousand dozen were there in the boat before his eyes, safely secured beneath the correspondents' baggage, and somehow, before his eyes, were the little cottage and the mortgage for a thousand dollars.

It was bitter cold. Now and again he hauled in the steering-sweep and put out a fresh one while his passengers chopped the ice from the blade. Wherever the spray struck, it turned instantly to frost, and the dipping boom of the spritsail was quickly fringed with icicles. The *Alma* strained and hammered through the big seas till the seams and butts began to spread, but in lieu of bailing the correspondents chopped ice and flung it overboard. There was no let-up. The mad race with winter was on, and the boats tore along in a desperate string.

"W-w-we can't stop to save our souls!" one of the correspondents chattered, from cold, not fright.

"That's right! Keep her down the middle, old man!" the other encouraged.

Rasmunsen replied with an idiotic grin. The iron-bound shores were in a lather of foam, and even down the middle the only hope was to keep running away from the big seas. To lower sail was to be overtaken and swamped. Time and again they passed boats pounding among the rocks, and once they saw one on the edge of the breakers about to strike. A little craft behind them, with two men, jibed over and turned bottom up.

"W-w-watch out, old man!" cried he of

the chattering teeth.

Rasmunsen grinned and tightened his aching grip on the sweep. Scores of times had the send of the sea caught the big square stern of the *Alma* and thrown her off from dead before it till the after leach of the spritsail fluttered hollowly, and each time, and only with all his strength, had he forced her back. His grin by then had become fixed, and it disturbed the correspondents to look at him.

They roared down past an isolated rock a hundred yards from shore. From its wave-drenched top a man shrieked wildly, for the instant cutting the storm with his voice. But the next instant the *Alma* was by, and the rock growing a black speck in the troubled froth.

"That settles the Yankee! Where's the sailor?" shouted one of his passengers.

Rasmunsen shot a glance over his shoulder at a black squaresail. He had seen it leap up out of the gray to windward, and for an hour, off and on, had been watching it grow. The sailor had evidently repaired damages and was making up for lost time.

"Look at him come!"

Both passengers stopped chopping ice to watch. Twenty miles of Bennett were behind them — room and to spare for the sea to toss up its mountains toward the sky. Sinking and soaring like a storm god, the sailor drove by them. The huge sail seemed to grip the boat from the crests of the waves, to tear it bodily out of the water, and fling it crashing and smothering down into the yawning troughs.

"The sea'll never catch him!"

"But he'll r-r-run her nose under!"

Even as they spoke, the black tarpaulin swooped from sight behind a big comber. The next wave rolled over the spot, and the next, but the boat did not reappear. The *Alma* rushed by the place. A little riffraff of oars and boxes was seen. An arm thrust up and a shaggy head broke surface a score of yards away.

For a time there was silence. As the end of the lake came in sight, the waves began to leap aboard with such steady recurrence that the correspondents no longer chopped ice but flung the water out with buckets. Even this would not do, and, after a shouted conference with Rasmunsen, they attacked the baggage. Flour, bacon, beans, blankets, cooking stove, ropes, odds and ends, everything they could get hands on,

flew overboard. The boat acknowledged it at once, taking less water and rising more buoyantly.

) "That'll do!" Rasmunsen called sternly, as they applied themselves to the top layer of eggs.

"The h-hell it will!" answered the shivering one, savagely. With the exception of their notes, films, and cameras, they had sacrificed their outfit. He bent over, laid hold of an egg-box, and began to worry it out from under the lashing.

"Drop it! Drop it, I say!"

Rasmunsen had managed to draw his revolver, and with the crook of his arm over the sweep head was taking aim. The correspondent stood up on the thwart, balancing back and forth, his face twisted with menace and speechless anger.

"My God!"

So cried his brother correspondent, hurling himself, face downward, into the bottom of the boat. The *Alma*, under the divided attention of Rasmunsen, had been caught by a great mass of water and whirled around. The after leach hollowed, the sail emptied and jibed, and the boom, sweeping with terrific force across the boat, carried the angry correspondent overboard with a broken back. Mast and sail had gone over the side as well. A drenching sea followed, as the boat lost headway, and Rasmunsen sprang to the bailing bucket.

Several boats hurtled past them in the next half-hour, — small boats, boats of their own size, boats afraid, unable to do aught but run madly on. Then a ten-ton barge, at imminent risk of destruction, lowered sail to windward and lumbered down upon them.

"Keep off! Keep off!" Rasmunsen screamed.

But his low gunwale ground against the heavy craft, and the remaining correspondent clambered aboard. Rasmunsen was over the eggs like a cat and in the bow of the *Alma*, striving with numb fingers to bend the hauling-lines together.

"Come on!" a red-whiskered man yelled at him.

"I've a thousand dozen eggs here," he shouted back. "Gimme a two! I'll pay you!"

"Come on!" they howled in chorus.

A big whitecap broke just beyond, washing over the barge and leaving the *Alma* half swamped. The men cast off, cursing him as they ran up their sail. Rasmunsen cursed back and fell to bailing. The mast and sail, like a sea anchor, still fast by the halyards, held the boat head on to wind and sea and gave him a chance to fight the water out.

Three hours later, numbed, exhausted, blathering like a lunatic, but still bailing, he went ashore on an ice-strewn beach near Cariboo Crossing. Two men, a government courier and a half-breed voyageur, dragged him out of the surf, saved his cargo, and beached the *Alma*. They were paddling out of the country in a Peterborough, and gave him shelter for the night in their storm-bound camp. Next morning they departed, but he elected to stay by his eggs. And thereafter the name and fame of the man with the thousand dozen eggs began to spread through the land. Gold-seekers who made in before the freeze-up carried the news of his coming. Grizzled old-timers of Forty Mile and Circle City, sour doughs with leathern jaws and bean-calloused stomachs, called up dream memories of chickens and green things at mention of his name. Dyea and Skaguay took an interest in his being, and questioned his progress from every man who came over the passes, while Dawson — golden, omeletless Dawson — fretted and worried, and waylaid every chance arrival for word of him.

But of this, Rasmunsen knew nothing. The day after the wreck he patched up the *Alma* and pulled out. A cruel east wind blew in his teeth from Tagish, but he got the oars over the side and bucked manfully into it, though half the time he was drifting backward and chopping ice from the blades. According to the custom of the country, he was driven ashore at Windy Arm; three times on Tagish saw him swamped and beached; and Lake Marsh held him at the freeze-up. The *Alma* was crushed in the jamming of the floes, but the eggs were intact. These he back-tripped two miles across the ice to the shore, where he built a caché, which stood for years after and was pointed out by men who knew.

Half a thousand frozen miles stretched between him and Dawson, and the waterway was closed. But Rasmunsen, with a peculiar tense look in his face, struck back up the lakes on foot. What he suffered on that lone trip, with naught but a single

blanket, an axe, and a handful of beans, is not given to ordinary mortals to know. Only the Arctic adventurer may understand. Suffice that he was caught in a blizzard on Chilkoot and left two of his toes with the surgeon at Sheep Camp. Yet he stood on his feet and washed dishes in the scullery of the *Pawona* to the Puget Sound, and from there passed coal on a P. S. boat to San Francisco.

It was a haggard, unkempt man who limped across the shining office floor to raise a second mortgage from the bank people. His hollow cheeks betrayed themselves through the scraggly beard, and his eyes seemed to have retired into deep caverns where they burned with cold fires. His hands were grained from exposure and hard work, and the nails were rimmed with tight-packed dirt and coal dust. He spoke vaguely of eggs and ice-packs, winds and tides; but when they declined to let him have more than a second thousand, his talk became incoherent, concerning itself chiefly with the price of dogs and dog-food, and such things as snowshoes and moccasins and winter trails. They let him have fifteen hundred, which was more than the cottage warranted, and breathed easier when he scrawled his signature and passed out the door.

Two weeks later he went over Chilkoot with three dog sleds of five dogs each. One team he drove, the two Indians with him driving the others. At Lake Marsh they broke out the caché and loaded up. But there was no trail. He was the first in over the ice, and to him fell the task of packing the snow and hammering away through the rough river jams. Behind him he often observed a camp-fire smoke trickling thinly up through the quiet air, and he wondered why the people did not overtake him. For he was a stranger to the land and did not understand. Nor could he understand his Indians when they tried to explain. This they conceived to be a hardship, but when they balked and refused to break camp of mornings, he drove them to their work at pistol point.

When he slipped through an ice bridge near the White Horse and froze his foot, tender yet and oversensitive from the previous freezing, the Indians looked for him to lie up. But he sacrificed a blanket, and, with his foot incased in an enormous moccasin, big as a water-bucket, continued to take his regular turn with the front sled. Here was the cruelest work, and they respected him, though on the side they rapped their foreheads with their knuckles and significantly shook their heads. One night they tried to run away, but the zip-zip of his bullets in the snow brought them back, snarling but convinced. Whereupon, being only savage Chilkat men, they put their heads together to kill him; but he slept like a cat, and, waking or sleeping, the chance never came. Often they tried to tell him the import of the smoke wreath in the rear, but he could not comprehend and grew suspicious of them. And when they sulked or shirked, he was quick to let drive at them between the eyes, and quick to cool their heated souls with sight of his ready revolver.

And so it went — with mutinous men, wild dogs, and a trail that broke the heart. He fought the men to stay with him, fought the dogs to keep them away from the eggs, fought the ice, the cold, and the pain of his foot, which would not heal. As fast as the young tissue renewed, it was bitten and seared by the frost, so that a running sore developed, into which he could almost shove his fist. In the mornings, when he first put his weight upon it, his head went dizzy, and he was near to fainting from the pain; but later on in the day it usually grew numb, to recommence when he crawled into his blankets and tried to sleep. Yet he, who had been a clerk and sat at a desk all his days, toiled till the Indians were exhausted, and even outworked the dogs. How hard he worked, how much he suffered, he did not know. Being a man of the one idea, now that the idea had come, it mastered him. In the foreground of his consciousness was Dawson, in the background his thousand dozen eggs, and midway between the two his ego fluttered, striving alway to draw them together to a glittering golden point. This golden point was the five thousand dollars, the consummation of the idea and the point of departure for whatever new idea might present itself. For the rest, he was a mere automaton. He was unaware of other things, seeing them as through a glass darkly, and giving them no thought. The work of his hands he did with machine-like wisdom; likewise the work of his head. So the look on his face grew very tense, till even the Indians were afraid of it, and mar-

velled at the strange white man who had made them slaves and forced them to toil with such foolishness.

Then came a snap on Lake Le Barge, when the cold of outer space smote the tip of the planet, and the frost ranged sixty and odd degrees below zero. Here, laboring with open mouth that he might breathe more freely, he chilled his lungs, and for the rest of the trip he was troubled with a dry, hacking cough, especially irritable in smoke of camp or under stress of undue exertion. On the Thirty Mile river he found much open water, spanned by precarious ice bridges and fringed with narrow rim ice, tricky and uncertain. The rim ice was impossible to reckon on, and he dared it without reckoning, falling back on his revolver when his drivers demurred. But on the ice bridges, covered with snow though they were, precautions could be taken. These they crossed on their snowshoes, with long poles, held crosswise in their hands, to which to cling in case of accident. Once over, the dogs were called to follow. And on such a bridge, where the absence of the centre ice was masked by the snow, one of the Indians met his end. He went through as quickly and neatly as a knife through thin cream, and the current swept him from view down under the stream ice.

That night his mate fled away through the pale moonlight, Rasmunsen futilely puncturing the silence with his revolver — a thing that he handled with more celerity than cleverness. Thirty-six hours later the Indian made a police camp on the Big Salmon.

"Um — um — um funny mans — what you call? — top um head all loose," the interpreter explained to the puzzled captain. "Eh? Yep, clazy, much clazy mans. Eggs, eggs, all a time eggs — savvy? Come bimeby."

It was several days before Rasmunsen arrived, the three sleds lashed together, and all the dogs in a single team. It was awkward, and where the going was bad he was compelled to back-trip it sled by sled, though he managed most of the time, through herculean efforts, to bring all along on the one haul. He did not seem moved when the captain of police told him his man was hitting the high places for Dawson, and was by that time, probably, halfway between Selkirk and Stewart. Nor did he appear interested when informed that the police had broken the trail as far as Pelly; for he had attained to a fatalistic acceptance of all natural dispensations, good or ill. But when they told him that Dawson was in the bitter clutch of famine, he smiled, threw the harness on his dogs, and pulled out.

But it was at his next halt that the mystery of the smoke was explained. With the word at Big Salmon that the trail was broken to Pelly, there was no longer any need for the smoke wreath to linger in his wake; and Rasmunsen, crouching over his lonely fire, saw a motley string of sleds go by. First came the courier and the half-breed who had hauled him out from Bennett; then mail-carriers for Circle City, two sleds of them, and a mixed following of ingoing Klondikers. Dogs and men were fresh and fat, while Rasmunsen and his brutes were jaded and worn down to the skin and bone. They of the smoke wreath had travelled one day in three, resting and reserving their strength for the dash to come when broken trail was met with; while each day he had plunged and floundered forward, breaking the spirit of his dogs and robbing them of their mettle.

As for himself, he was unbreakable. They thanked him kindly for his efforts in their behalf, those fat, fresh men, — thanked him kindly, with broad grins and ribald laughter; and now, when he understood, he made no answer. Nor did he cherish silent bitterness. It was immaterial. The idea — the fact behind the idea — was not changed. Here he was and his thousand dozen; there was Dawson; the problem was unaltered.

At the Little Salmon, being short of dog food, the dogs got into his grub, and from there to Selkirk he lived on beans — coarse, brown beans, big beans, grossly nutritive, which griped his stomach and doubled him up at two-hour intervals. But the Factor at Selkirk had a notice on the door of the Post to the effect that no steamer had been up the Yukon for two years, and in consequence grub was beyond price. He offered to swap flour, however, at the rate of a cupful for each egg, but Rasmunsen shook his head and hit the trail. Below the Post he managed to buy frozen horse hide for the dogs, the horses having been slain by the Chilkat cattle men, and the scraps and offal preserved by the Indians. He tackled the hide himself, but the hair worked into the bean sores of his mouth, and was beyond endurance.

Here at Selkirk, he met the forerunners of the hungry exodus of Dawson, and from there on they crept over the trail, a dismal throng. "No grub!" was the song they sang. "No grub, and had to go." "Everybody holding candles for a rise in the spring." "Flour dollar'n a half a pound, and no sellers."

"Eggs?" one of them answered. "Dollar apiece, but they ain't none."

Rasmunsen made a rapid calculation. "Twelve thousand dollars," he said aloud.

"Hey?" the man asked.

"Nothing," he answered, and *mushed* the dogs along.

When he arrived at Stewart River, seventy miles from Dawson, five of his dogs were gone, and the remainder were falling in the traces. He, also, was in the traces, hauling with what little strength was left in him. Even then he was barely crawling along ten miles a day. His cheek-bones and nose, frostbitten again and again, were turned bloody-black and hideous. The thumb, which was separated from the fingers by the gee-pole, had likewise been nipped and gave him great pain. The monstrous moccasin still incased his foot, and strange pains were beginning to rack the leg. At Six Mile, the last beans, which he had been rationing for some time, were finished; yet he steadfastly refused to touch the eggs. He could not reconcile his mind to the legitimacy of it, and staggered and fell along the way to Indian River. Here a fresh-killed moose and an open-handed old-timer gave him and his dogs new strength, and at Ainslie's he felt repaid for it all when a stampede, ripe from Dawson in five hours, was sure he could get a dollar and a quarter for every egg he possessed.

He came up the steep bank by the Dawson barracks with fluttering heart and shaking knees. The dogs were so weak that he was forced to rest them, and, waiting, he leaned limply against the gee-pole. A man, an eminently decorous-looking man, came sauntering by in a great bearskin coat. He glanced at Rasmunsen curiously, then stopped and ran a speculative eye over the dogs and the three lashed sleds.

"What you got?" he asked.

"Eggs," Rasmunsen answered huskily, hardly able to pitch his voice above a whisper.

"Eggs! Whoopee! Whoopee!" He sprang up into the air, gyrated madly, and finished with half a dozen war steps. "You don't say — all of 'em?"

"All of 'em."

"Say, you must be the Egg Man." He walked around and viewed Rasmunsen from the other side. "Come, now, ain't you the Egg Man?"

Rasmunsen didn't know, but supposed he was, and the man sobered down a bit.

"What d'ye expect to get for 'em?" he asked cautiously.

Rasmunsen became audacious. "Dollar'n a half," he said.

"Done!" the man came back promptly. "Gimme a dozen."

"I — I mean a dollar'n a half apiece," Rasmunsen hesitatingly explained.

"Sure. I heard you. Make it two dozen. Here's the dust."

The man pulled out a healthy gold sack the size of a small sausage and knocked it negligently against the gee-pole. Rasmunsen felt a strange trembling in the pit of his stomach, a tickling of the nostrils, and an almost overwhelming desire to sit down and cry. But a curious, wide-eyed crowd was beginning to collect, and man after man was calling out for eggs. He was without scales, but the man with the bearskin coat fetched a pair and obligingly weighed in the dust while Rasmunsen passed out the goods. Soon there was a pushing and shoving and shouldering, and a great clamor. Everybody wanted to buy and be served first. And as the excitement grew, Rasmunsen cooled down. This would never do. There must be something behind the fact of their buying so eagerly. It would be wiser if he rested first and sized up the market. Perhaps eggs were worth two dollars apiece. Anyway, whenever he wished to sell, he was sure of a dollar and a half. "Stop!" he cried, when a couple of hundred had been sold. "No more now. I'm played out. I've got to get a cabin, and then you can come and see me."

A groan went up at this, but the man with the bearskin coat approved. Twenty-four of the frozen eggs went rattling in his capacious pockets and he didn't care whether the rest of the town ate or not. Besides, he could see Rasmunsen was on his last legs.

"There's a cabin right around the second corner from the Monte Carlo," he told him — "the one with the sody-bottle window. It ain't mine, but I've got charge of it. Rents for ten a day and cheap for the money. You move right in, and I'll see you later. Don't forget the sody-bottle window."

"Tra-la-loo!" he called back a moment later. "I'm goin' up the hill to eat eggs and dream of home."

On his way to the cabin, Rasmunsen recollected he was hungry and bought a small supply of provisions at the N. A. T. & T. store — also a beefsteak at the butcher shop and dried salmon for the dogs. He found the cabin without difficulty and left the dogs in the harness while he started the fire and got the coffee under way.

"A dollar'n a half apiece — one thousand dozen — eighteen thousand dollars!" He kept muttering it to himself, over and over, as he went about his work.

As he flopped the steak into the frying-pan the door opened. He turned. It was the man with the bearskin coat. He seemed to come in with determination, as though bound on some explicit errand, but as he looked at Rasmunsen an expression of perplexity came into his face.

"I say — now I say —" he began, then halted.

Rasmunsen wondered if he wanted the rent.

"I say, damn it, you know, them eggs is bad."

Rasmunsen staggered. He felt as though some one had struck him an astounding blow between the eyes. The walls of the cabin reeled and tilted up. He put out his hand to steady himself and rested it on the stove. The sharp pain and the smell of the burning flesh brought him back to himself.

"I see," he said slowly, fumbling in his pocket for the sack. "You want your money back."

"It ain't the money," the man said, "but hain't you got any eggs — good?"

Rasmunsen shook his head. "You'd better take the money."

But the man refused and backed away.

"I'll come back," he said, "when you've taken stock, and get what's comin'."

Rasmunsen rolled the chopping-block into the cabin and carried in the eggs. He went about it quite calmly. He took up the handaxe, and, one by one, chopped the eggs in half. These halves he examined carefully and let fall to the floor. At first he sampled from the different cases, then deliberately emptied one case at a time. The heap on the floor grew larger. The coffee boiled over and the smoke of the burning beefsteak filled the cabin. He chopped steadfastly and monotonously till the last case was finished.

Somebody knocked at the door, knocked again, and let himself in.

"What a mess!" he remarked, as he paused and surveyed the scene.

The severed eggs were beginning to thaw in the heat of the stove, and a miserable odor was growing stronger.

"Must a-happened on the steamer," he suggested.

Rasmunsen looked at him long and blankly.

"I'm Murray, Big Jim Murray, everybody knows me," the man volunteered. "I'm just hearin' your eggs is rotten, and I'm offerin' you two hundred for the batch. They ain't good as salmon, but still they're fair scoffin's for dogs."

Rasmunsen seemed turned to stone. He did not move. "You go to hell," he said passionlessly.

"Now just consider. I pride myself it's a decent price for a mess like that, and it's better'n nothin'. Two hundred. What you say?"

"You go to hell," Rasmunsen repeated softly, "and get out of here."

Murray gaped with a great awe, then went out carefully, backward, with his eyes fixed on the other's face.

Rasmunsen followed him out and turned the dogs loose. He threw them all the salmon he had bought, and coiled a sled-lashing up in his hand. Then he reentered the cabin and drew the latch in after him. The smoke from the cindered steak made his eyes smart. He stood on the bunk, passed the lashing over the ridgepole, and measured the swing-off with his eye. It did not seem to satisfy, for he put the stool on the bunk and climbed upon the stool. He drove a noose in the end of the lashing and slipped his head through. The other end he made fast. Then he kicked the stool out from under.

20
A HYPERBOREAN BREW

A HYPERBOREAN BREW

THOMAS STEVENS'S veracity may have been indeterminate as x, and his imagination the imagination of ordinary men increased to the nth power, but this, at least, must be said: never did he deliver himself of word nor deed that could be branded as a lie outright.... He may have played with probability, and verged on the extremest edge of possibility, but in his tales the machinery never creaked. That he knew the Northland like a book, not a soul can deny. That he was a great traveller, and had set foot on countless unknown trails, many evidences affirm. Outside of my own personal knowledge, I knew men that had met him everywhere, but principally on the confines of Nowhere. There was Johnson, the ex-Hudson Bay Company factor, who had housed him in a Labrador factory until his dogs rested up a bit, and he was able to strike out again. There was McMahon, agent for the Alaska Commercial Company, who had run across him in Dutch Harbor, and later on, among the outlying islands of the Aleutian group. It was indisputable that he had guided one of the earlier United States surveys, and history states positively that in a similar capacity he served the Western Union when it attempted to put through its trans-Alaskan and Siberian telegraph to Europe. Further, there was Joe Lamson, the whaling captain, who, when ice-bound off the mouth of the Mackenzie, had had him come aboard after tobacco.

This last touch proves Thomas Stevens's identity conclusively. His quest for tobacco was perennial and untiring. Ere we became fairly acquainted, I learned to greet him with one hand, and pass the pouch with the other. But the night I met him in John O'Brien's Dawson saloon, his head was wreathed in a nimbus of fifty-cent cigar smoke, and instead of my pouch he demanded my sack. We were standing by a faro table, and forthwith he tossed it upon the "high card." "Fifty," he said, and the gamekeeper nodded. The "high card" turned, and he handed back my sack, called for a "tab," and drew me over to the scales, where the weigher nonchalantly cashed him out fifty dollars in dust.

"And now we'll drink," he said; and later, at the bar, when he lowered his glass: "Reminds me of a little brew I had up Tattarat way. No, you have no knowledge of the place, nor is it down on the charts. But it's up by the rim of the Arctic Sea, not so many hundred miles from the American line, and all of half a thousand God-forsaken souls live there, giving and taking in marriage, and starving and dying inbetween-whiles. Explorers have overlooked them, and you will not find them in the census of 1890. A whale-ship was pinched there once, but the men, who had made shore over the ice, pulled out for the south and were never heard of.

"But it was a great brew we had, Moosu and I," he added a moment later, with just the slightest suspicion of a sigh.

I knew there were big deeds and wild doings behind that sigh, so I haled him into a corner, between a roulette outfit and a poker layout, and waited for his tongue to thaw.

"Had one objection to Moosu," he began, cocking his head meditatively — "one objection, and only one. He was an Indian from over on the edge of the Chippewyan country, but the trouble was, he'd picked up a smattering of the Scriptures. Been campmate a season with a renegade French Canadian who'd studied for the church. Moosu'd never seen applied Christianity, and his head was crammed with miracles, battles, and dispensations, and what not he didn't understand. Otherwise he was a good sort, and a handy man on trail or over a fire.

"We'd had a hard time together and were badly knocked out when we plumped upon Tattarat. Lost outfits and dogs crossing a divide in a fall blizzard, and our bellies clove to our backs and our clothes were in rags when we crawled into the village. They weren't much surprised at seeing us — because of the whalemen — and gave us the meanest shack in the village to live in, and the worst of their leavings to live on. What struck me at the time as strange was that they left us strictly alone. But Moosu explained it.

"'Shaman *sick tumtum*,' he said, meaning the shaman, or medicine man, was jealous, and had advised the people to have nothing to do with us. From the little he'd seen of the whalemen, he'd learned that mine was a stronger race, and a wiser; so he'd only behaved as shamans have always behaved the world over. And before I get done, you'll see how near right he was.

"'These people have a law,' said Moosu: 'Whoso eats of meat must hunt. We be awkward, you and I, O master, in the weapons of this country; nor can we string bows nor fling spears after the manner approved. Wherefore the shaman and Tummasook, who is chief, have put their heads together, and it has been decreed that we work with the women and children in dragging in the meat and tending the wants of the hunters.'

"'And this is very wrong,' I made to answer; 'for we be better men, Moosu, than these people who walk in darkness. Further, we should rest and grow strong, for the way south is long, and on that trail the weak cannot prosper.'

"'But we have nothing,' he objected, looking about him at the rotten timbers of the igloo, the stench of the ancient walrus meat that had been our supper disgusting his nostrils. 'And on this fare we cannot thrive. We have nothing save the bottle of "painkiller," which will not fill emptiness, so we must bend to the yoke of the unbeliever and become hewers of wood and drawers of water. And there be good things in this place, the which we may not have. Ah, master, never has my nose lied to me, and I have followed it to secret cachés and among the fur-bales of the igloos. Good provender did these people extort from the poor whalemen, and this provender has wandered into few hands. The woman Ipsukuk, who dwelleth in the far end of the village next the igloo of the chief, possesseth much flour and sugar, and even have my eyes told me of molasses smeared on her face. And in the igloo of Tummasook, the chief, there be tea — have I not seen the old pig guzzling? And the shaman owneth a caddy of "Star" and two buckets of prime smoking. And what have we? Nothing! Nothing! Nothing!'

"But I was stunned by the word he brought of the tobacco, and made no answer.

"And Moosu, what of his own desire, broke silence: 'And there be Tukeliketa, daughter of a big hunter and wealthy man. A likely girl. Indeed, a very nice girl.'

"I figured hard during the night while Moosu snored, for I could not bear the thought of the tobacco so near which I could not smoke. True, as he had said, we had nothing. But the way became clear to me, and in the morning I said to him: 'Go thou cunningly abroad, after thy fashion, and procure me some sort of bone, crooked like a gooseneck, and hollow. Also, walk humbly, but have eyes awake to the lay of pots and pans and cooking contrivances. And remember, mine is the white man's wisdom, and do what I have bid you, with sureness and despatch.'

"While he was away I placed the whaleoil cooking lamp in the middle of the igloo, and moved the mangy sleeping furs back that I might have room. Then I took apart his gun and put the barrel by handy, and afterward braided many wicks from the cotton that the women gather wild in the summer. When he came back, it was with the bone I had commanded, and with news that in the igloo of Tummasook there was a five-gallon kerosene can and a big copper kettle. So I said he had done well and we would tarry through the day. And when midnight was near I made harangue to him.

"'This chief, this Tummasook, hath a copper kettle, likewise a kerosene can.' I put a rock, smooth and wave-washed, in Moosu's hand. 'The camp is hushed and the stars are winking. Go thou, creep into the chief's igloo softly, and smite him thus upon the belly, and hard. And let the meat and good grub of the days to come put strength into thine arm. There will be uproar and outcry, and the village will come hot afoot. But be thou unafraid. Veil thy movements and lose thy form in the obscurity of the night and the confusion of men. And when the woman Ipsukuk is anigh thee, — she who smeareth her face with molasses, — do thou smite her likewise, and whosoever else that possesseth flour and cometh to thy hand. Then do thou lift thy voice in pain and double up with clasped hands, and make outcry in token that thou, too, hast felt the visitation of the night. And in this way shall we achieve honor and great possessions, and the caddy of "Star" and the prime smoking, and thy Tukeliketa, who is a likely maiden.'

"When he had departed on this errand, I bided patiently in the shack, and the tobacco seemed very near. Then there was a cry of affright in the night, that became an uproar and assailed the sky. I seized the 'painkiller' and ran forth. There was much noise, and a wailing among the women, and fear sat heavily on all. Tummasook and the woman Ipsukuk rolled on the ground in pain, and with them there were divers others, also Moosu. I thrust aside those that cluttered the way of my feet, and put the mouth of the bottle to Moosu's lips. And straightway he became well and ceased his howling. Whereat there was a great clamor for the bottle from the others so stricken. But I made harangue, and ere they tasted and were made well I had mulcted Tummasook of his copper kettle and kerosene can, and the woman Ipsukuk of her sugar and molasses, and the other sick ones of goodly measures of flour. The shaman glowered wickedly at the people around my knees, though he poorly concealed the wonder that lay beneath. But I held my head high, and Moosu groaned beneath the loot as he followed my heels to the shack.

"There I set to work. In Tummasook's copper kettle I mixed three quarts of wheat flour with five of molasses, and to this I added of water twenty quarts. Then I placed the kettle near the lamp, that it might sour in the warmth and grow strong. Moosu understood, and said my wisdom passed understanding and was greater than Solomon's, who he had heard was a wise man of old time. The kerosene can I set over the lamp, and to its nose I affixed a snout, and into the snout the bone that was like a gooseneck. I sent Moosu without to pound ice, while I connected the barrel of his gun with the gooseneck, and midway on the barrel I piled the ice he had pounded. And at the far end of the gun barrel, beyond the pan of ice, I placed a small iron pot. When the brew was strong enough (and it was two days ere it could

stand on its own legs), I filled the kerosene can with it, and lighted the wicks I had braided.

"Now that all was ready, I spoke to Moosu. 'Go forth,' I said, 'to the chief men of the village, and give them greeting, and bid them come into my igloo and sleep the night away with me and the gods.'

"The brew was singing merrily when they began shoving aside the skin flap and crawling in, and I was heaping cracked ice on the gun barrel. Out of the priming hole at the far end, drip, drip, drip into the iron pot fell the liquor — *hooch,* you know. But they'd never seen the like, and giggled nervously when I made harangue about its virtues. As I talked I noted the jealousy in the shaman's eye, so when I had done, I placed him side by side with Tummasook and the woman Ipsukuk. Then I gave them to drink, and their eyes watered and their stomachs warmed, till from being afraid they reached greedily for more; and when I had them well started, I turned to the others. Tummasook made a brag about how he had once killed a polar bear, and in the vigor of his pantomime nearly slew his mother's brother. But nobody heeded. The woman Ipsukuk fell to weeping for a son lost long years agone in the ice, and the shaman made incantation and prophecy. So it went, and before morning they were all on the floor, sleeping soundly with the gods.

"The story tells itself, does it not? The news of the magic potion spread. It was too marvellous for utterance. Tongues could tell but a tithe of the miracles it performed. It eased pain, gave surcease to sorrow, brought back old memories, dead faces, and forgotten dreams. It was a fire that ate through all the blood, and, burning, burned not. It stoutened the heart, stiffened the back, and made men more than men. It revealed the future, and gave visions and prophecy. It brimmed with wisdom and unfolded secrets. There was no end of the things it could do, and soon there was a clamoring on all hands to sleep with the gods. They brought their warmest furs, their strongest dogs, their best meats; but I sold the *hooch* with discretion, and only those were favored that brought flour and molasses and sugar. And such stores poured in that I set Moosu to build a caché to hold them, for there was soon no space in the igloo. Ere three days had passed Tummasook had gone bank-rupt. The shaman, who was never more than half drunk after the first night, watched me closely and hung on for the better part of the week. But before ten days were gone even the woman Ipsukuk exhausted her provisions, and went home weak and tottery.

"But Moosu complained. 'O master,' he said, 'we have laid by great wealth in molasses and sugar and flour, but our shack is yet mean, our clothes thin, and our sleeping furs mangy. There is a call of the belly for meat the stench of which of-fends not the stars, and for tea such as Tummasook guzzles, and there is a great yearning for the tobacco of Neewak, who is shaman and who plans to destroy us. I have flour until I am sick, and sugar and molasses without stint, yet is the heart of Moosu sore and his bed empty.'

"'Peace!' I answered, 'thou art weak of understanding and a fool. Walk softly and wait, and we will grasp it all. But grasp now, and we grasp little, and in the end it will be nothing. Thou art a child in the way of the white man's wisdom. Hold thy tongue and watch, and I will show you the way my brothers do overseas, and, so do-ing, gather to themselves the riches of the earth. It is what is called "business," and what dost thou know about business?'

"But the next day he came in breathless. 'O master, a strange thing happeneth in the igloo of Neewak, the shaman; where-fore we are lost, and we have neither worn the warm furs nor tasted the good tobacco, what of your madness for the molasses and flour. Go thou and witness whilst I watch by the brew.'

"So I went to the igloo of Neewak. And behold, he had made his own still, fash-ioned cunningly after mine. And as he be-held me he could ill conceal his triumph. For he was a man of parts, and his sleep with the gods when in my igloo had not been sound.

"But I was not disturbed, for I knew what I knew, and when I returned to my own igloo, I descanted to Moosu and said: 'Happily the property right obtains amongst this people, who otherwise have been blessed with but few of the institu-tions of men. And because of this respect for property shall you and I wax fat, and, further, we shall introduce amongst them new institutions that other peoples have

worked out through great travail and suf-fering.'

"But Moosu understood dimly, till the shaman came forth, with eyes flashing and a threatening note in his voice, and de-manded to trade with me. 'For look you,' he cried, 'there be of flour and molasses none in all the village. The like have you gathered with a shrewd hand from my people, who have slept with your gods and who now have nothing save large heads, and weak knees, and a thirst for cold water that they cannot quench. This is not good, and my voice has power among them; so it were well that we trade, you and I, even as you have traded with them, for molasses and flour.'

"And I made answer: 'This be good talk, and wisdom abideth in thy mouth. We will trade. For this much of flour and molasses givest thou me the caddy of "Star" and the two buckets of smoking.'

"And Moosu groaned, and when the trade was made and the shaman departed, he upbraided me: 'Now, because of thy madness, are we, indeed, lost! Neewak maketh *hooch* on his own account, and when the time is ripe, he will command the people to drink of no *hooch* but his *hooch*. And in this way are we undone, and our goods worthless, and our igloo mean, and the bed of Moosu cold and empty!'

"And I answered: 'By the body of the wolf, say I, thou art a fool, and thy fathers before thee, and thy children after thee, down to the last generation. Thy wisdom is worse than no wisdom and thine eyes blinded to business, of which I have spoken and whereof thou knowest nothing. Go, thou son of a thousand fools, and drink of the *hooch* that Neewak brews in his igloo, and thank thy gods that thou hast a white man's wisdom to make soft the bed thou liest in. Go! and when thou hast drunken, return with the taste still on thy lips, that I may know.'

"And two days after, Neewak sent greet-ing and invitation to his igloo. Moosu went, but I sat alone, with the song of the still in my ears, and the air thick with the shaman's tobacco; for trade was slack that night, and no one dropped in but Angeit, a young hunter that had faith in me. Later, Moosu came back, his speech thick with chuckling and his eyes wrinkling with laughter.

"'Thou art a great man,' he said. 'Thou

art a great man, O master, and because of thy greatness thou wilt not condemn Moosu, thy servant, who ofttimes doubts and cannot be made to understand.'

"'And wherefore now?' I demanded. 'Hast thou drunk overmuch? And are they sleeping sound in the igloo of Neewak, the shaman?'

"'Nay, they are angered and sore of body, and Chief Tummasook has thrust his thumbs in the throat of Neewak, and sworn by the bones of his ancestors to look upon his face no more. For behold! I went to the igloo, and the brew simmered and bubbled, and the steam journeyed through the gooseneck even as thy steam, and even as thine it became water where it met the ice, and dropped into the pot at the far end. And Neewak gave us to drink, and lo, it was not like thine, for there was no bite to the tongue nor tingling to the eyeballs, and of a truth it was water. So we drank, and we drank overmuch; yet did we sit with cold hearts and solemn. And Neewak was perplexed and a cloud came on his brow. And he took Tummasook and Ipsukuk alone of all the company and sat them apart, and bade them drink and drink and drink. And they drank and drank and drank, and yet sat solemn and cold, till Tummasook arose in wrath and demanded back the furs and the tea he had paid. And Ipsukuk raised her voice, thin and angry. And the company demanded back what they had given, and there was a great commotion.'

"'Does the son of a dog deem me a whale?' demanded Tummasook, shoving back the skin flap and standing erect, his face black and his brows angry.

"'Wherefore I am filled, like a fish-bladder, to bursting, till I can scarce walk, what of the weight within me? Lalah! I have drunken as never before, yet are my eyes clear, my knees strong, my hand steady.'

"'The shaman cannot send us to sleep with the gods,' the people complained, stringing in and joining us, 'and only in thy igloo may the thing be done.'

"So I laughed to myself as I passed the *hooch* around and the guests made merry. For in the flour I had traded to Neewak I had mixed much soda that I had got from the woman Ipsukuk. So how could his brew ferment when the soda kept it sweet? Or his *hooch* be *hooch* when it would not sour?

"After that our wealth flowed in without let or hindrance. Furs we had without number, and the fancy work of the women, all of the chief's tea, and no end of meat. One day Moosu retold for my benefit, and sadly mangled, the story of Joseph in Egypt, but from it I got an idea, and soon I had half the tribe at work building me great meat cachés. And of all they hunted I got the lion's share and stored it away. Nor was Moosu idle. He made himself a pack of cards from birch bark, and taught Neewak the way to play seven-up. He also inveigled the father of Tukeliketa into the game. And one day he married the maiden, and the next day he moved into the shaman's house, which was the finest in the village. The fall of Neewak was complete, for he lost all his possessions, his walrus-hide drums, his incantation tools — everything. And in the end he became a hewer of wood and drawer of water at the beck and call of Moosu. And Moosu — he set himself up as shaman, or high priest, and out of his garbled Scripture created new gods and made incantation before strange altars.

"And I was well pleased, for I thought it good that church and state go hand in hand, and I had certain plans of my own concerning the state. Events were shaping as I had foreseen. Good temper and smiling faces had vanished from the village. The people were morose and sullen. There were quarrels and fighting, and things were in an uproar night and day. Moosu's cards were duplicated and the hunters fell to gambling among themselves. Tummasook beat his wife horribly, and his mother's brother objected and smote him with a tusk of walrus till he cried aloud in the night and was shamed before the people. Also, amid such diversions no hunting was done, and famine fell upon the land. The nights were long and dark, and without meat no *hooch* could be bought; so they murmured against the chief. This I had played for, and when they were well and hungry, I summoned the whole village, made a great harangue, posed as patriarch, and fed the famishing. Moosu made harangue likewise, and because of this and the thing I had done I was made chief. Moosu, who had the ear of God and decreed his judgments, anointed me with whale blubber, and right blubberly he did it, not understanding the ceremony. And between us we interpreted to the people the new theory of the divine right of kings. There was *hooch* galore, and meat and feasting, and they took kindly to the new order.

"So you see, O man, I have sat in the high places, and worn the purple, and ruled populations. And I might yet be a king had the tobacco held out, or had Moosu been more fool and less knave. For he cast eyes upon Esanetuk, eldest daughter to Tummasook, and I objected.

"'O brother,' he explained, 'thou has seen fit to speak of introducing new institutions amongst this people, and I have listened to thy words and gained wisdom thereby. Thou rulest by the God-given right, and by the God-given right I marry.'

"I noted that he 'brothered' me, and was angry and put my foot down. But he fell back upon the people and made incantations for three days, in which all hands joined; and then, speaking with the voice of God, he decreed polygamy by divine fiat. But he was shrewd, for he limited the number of wives by a property qualification, and because of which he, above all men, was favored by his wealth. Nor could I fail to admire, though it was plain that power had turned his head, and he would not be satisfied till all the power and all the wealth rested in his own hands. So he became swollen with pride, forgot it was I that had placed him there, and made preparations to destroy me.

"But it was interesting, for the beggar was working out in his own way an evolution of primitive society. Now I, by virtue of the *hooch* monopoly, drew a revenue in which I no longer permitted him to share. So he meditated for a while and evolved a system of ecclesiastical taxation. He laid tithes upon the people, harangued about fat firstlings and such things, and twisted whatever twisted texts he had ever heard to serve his purpose. Even this I bore in silence, but when he instituted what may be likened to a graduated income tax, I rebelled, and blindly, for this was what he worked for. Thereat, he appealed to the people, and they, envious of my great wealth and well taxed themselves, upheld him. 'Why should we pay,' they asked, 'and not you? Does not the voice of God speak through the lips of Moosu, the shaman?' So I yielded. But at the same time I raised the price of *hooch*, and lo, he was not a whit behind me in raising my taxes.

"Then there was open war. I made a play for Neewak and Tummasook, because of the traditional rights they possessed; but Moosu won out by creating a priesthood and giving them both high office. The problem of authority presented itself to him, and he worked it out as it has often been worked before. There was my mistake. I should have been made shaman, and he chief; but I saw it too late, and in the clash of spiritual and temporal power I was bound to be worsted. A great controversy waged, but it quickly became one-sided. The people remembered that he had anointed me, and it was clear to them that the source of my authority lay, not in me, but in Moosu. Only a few faithful ones clung to me, chief among whom Angeit was; while he headed the popular party and set whispers afloat that I had it in mind to overthrow him and set up my own gods, which were most unrighteous gods. And in this the clever rascal had anticipated me, for it was just what I had intended — forsake my kingship, you see, and fight spiritual with spiritual. So he frightened the people with the iniquities of my peculiar gods — especially the one he named 'Biz-e-Nass' — and nipped the scheme in the bud.

"Now, it happened that Kluktu, youngest daughter to Tummasook, had caught my fancy, and I likewise hers. So I made overtures, but the ex-chief refused bluntly — after I had paid the purchase price — and informed me that she was set aside for Moosu. This was too much, and I was half of a mind to go to his igloo and slay him with my naked hands; but I recollected that the tobacco was near gone, and went home laughing. The next day he made incantation, and distorted the miracle of the loaves and fishes till it became prophecy, and I, reading between the lines, saw that it was aimed at the wealth of meat stored in my cachés. The people also read between the lines, and, as he did not urge them to go on the hunt, they remained at home, and few caribou or bear were brought in.

"But I had plans of my own, seeing that not only the tobacco but the flour and molasses were near gone. And further, I felt it my duty to prove the white man's wisdom and bring sore distress to Moosu, who had waxed high-stomached, what of the power

I had given him. So that night I went to my meat cachés and toiled mightily, and it was noted next day that all the dogs of the village were lazy. No one suspected, and I toiled thus every night, and the dogs grew fat and fatter, and the people lean and leaner. They grumbled and demanded the fulfilment of prophecy, but Moosu restrained them, waiting for their hunger to grow yet greater. Nor did he dream, to the very last, of the trick I had been playing on the empty cachés.

"When all was ready, I sent Angeit, and the faithful ones whom I had fed privily, through the village to call assembly. And the tribe gathered on a great space of beaten snow before my door, with the meat cachés towering stilt-legged in the rear. Moosu came also, standing on the inner edge of the circle opposite me, confident that I had some scheme afoot, and prepared at the first break to down me. But I arose, giving him salutation before all men.

"'O Moosu, thou blessed of God,' I began, 'doubtless thou has wondered in that I have called this convocation together; and doubtless, because of my many foolishnesses, art thou prepared for rash sayings and rash doings. Not so. It has been said, that those the gods would destroy they first make mad. And I have been indeed mad. I have crossed thy will, and scoffed at thy authority, and done divers evil and wanton things. Wherefore, last night a vision was vouchsafed me, and I have seen the wickedness of my ways. And thou stoodst forth like a shining star, with brows aflame, and I knew in mine own heart thy greatness. I saw all things clearly. I knew that thou didst command the ear of God, and that when you spoke he listened. And I remembered that whatever of the good deeds that I had done, I had done through the grace of God, and the grace of Moosu.

"'Yes, my children,' I cried, turning to the people, 'whatever right I have done, and whatever good I have done, have been because of the counsel of Moosu. When I listened to him, affairs prospered; when I closed my ears, and acted according to my folly, things came to folly. By his advice it was that I laid my store of meat, and in time of darkness fed the famishing. By his grace it was that I was made chief. And what have I done with my chiefship? Let me tell you. I have done nothing. My head was turned

with power, and I deemed myself greater than Moosu, and, behold, I have come to grief. My rule has been unwise, and the gods are angered. Lo, ye are pinched with famine, and the mothers are dry-breasted, and the little babies cry through the long nights. Nor do I, who have hardened my heart against Moosu, know what shall be done, nor in what manner of way grub shall be had.'

"At this there was nodding and laughing, and the people put their heads together and I knew they whispered of the loaves and fishes. I went on hastily. 'So I was made aware of my foolishness and of Moosu's wisdom; of my own unfitness and of Moosu's fitness. And because of this, being no longer mad, I make acknowledgment and rectify evil. I did cast unrighteous eyes upon Kluktu, and lo, she was sealed to Moosu. Yet is she mine, for did I not pay to Tummasook the goods of purchase? But I am well unworthy of her, and she shall go from the igloo of her father to the igloo of Moosu. Can the moon shine in the sunshine? And further, Tummasook shall keep the goods of purchase, and she be a free gift to Moosu, whom God hath ordained her rightful lord.

"'And further yet, because I have used my wealth unwisely, and to oppress ye, O my children, do I make gifts of the kerosene can to Moosu, and the gooseneck, and the gun barrel, and the copper kettle. Therefore, I can gather to me no more possessions, and when ye are athirst for *hooch,* he will quench ye and without robbery. For he is a great man, and God speaketh through his lips.

"'And yet further, my heart is softened, and I have repented me of my madness. I, who am a fool and a son of fools; I, who am the slave of the bad god Biz-e-Nass; I, who see thy empty bellies and know not wherewith to fill them — why shall I be chief, and sit above thee, and rule to thine own destruction? Why should I do this, which is not good? But Moosu, who is shaman, and who is wise above men, is so made that he can rule with a soft hand and justly. And because of the things I have related do I make abdication and give my chiefship to Moosu, who alone knoweth how ye may be fed in this day when there be no meat in the land.'

"At this there was a great clapping of hands, and the people cried, '*Kloshe!*

Kloshe!' which means, 'good.' I had seen the wonder-worry in Moosu's eyes; for he could not understand, and was fearful of my white man's wisdom. I had met his wishes all along the line, and even anticipated some; and standing there, selfshorn of all my power, he knew the time did not favor to stir the people against me.

"Before they could disperse I made announcement that while the still went to Moosu, whatever *hooch* I possessed went to the people. Moosu tried to protest at this, for never had we permitted more than a handful to be drunk at a time; but they cried, *'Kloshe! Kloshe!'* and made festival before my door. And while they waxed uproarious without, as the liquor went to their heads, I held council within with Angeit and the faithful ones. I set them the tasks they were to do, and put into their mouths the words they were to say. Then I slipped away to a place back in the woods where I had two sleds, well loaded, with teams of dogs that were not overfed. Spring was at hand, you see, and there was a crust to the snow; so it was the best time to take the way south. Moreover, the tobacco was gone. There I waited, for I had nothing to fear. Did they bestir themselves on my trail, their dogs were too fat, and themselves too lean, to overtake me; also, I deemed their bestirring would be of an order for which I had made due preparation.

"First came a faithful one, running, and after him another. 'O master,' the first cried breathless, 'there be great confusion in the village, and no man knoweth his own mind, and they be of many minds. Everybody hath drunken overmuch, and some be stringing bows, and some be quarrelling one with another. Never was there such a trouble.'

"And the second one: 'And I did as thou biddest, O master, whispering shrewd words in thirsty ears, and raising memories of the things that were of old time. The woman Ipsukuk waileth her poverty and the wealth that no longer is hers. And Tummasook thinketh himself once again chief, and the people are hungry and rage up and down.'

"And a third one: 'And Neewak hath overthrown the altars of Moosu, and maketh incantation before the time-honored and ancient gods. And all the people remember the wealth that ran down their throats, and which they possess no

more. And first, Esanetuk, who be *sick tumtum,* fought with Kluktu, and there was much noise. And next, being daughters of the one mother, did they fight with Tukeliketa. And after that did they three fall upon Moosu, like wind-squalls, from every hand, till he ran forth from the igloo, and the people mocked him. For a man who cannot command his womankind is a fool.'

"Then came Angeit: 'Great trouble hath befallen Moosu, O master, for I have whispered to advantage, till the people came to Moosu, saying they were hungry and demanding the fulfilment of prophecy. And there was a loud shout of "Itlwillie! Itlwillie!" (Meat.) So he cried peace to his womenfolk, who were overwrought with anger and with *hooch,* and led the tribe even to thy meat cachés. And he bade the men open them and be fed. And lo, the cachés were empty. There was no meat. They stood without sound, the people being frightened, and in the silence I lifted my voice. "O Moosu, where is the meat? That there was meat we know. Did we not hunt it and drag it in from the hunt? And it were a lie to say one man hath eaten it; yet have we seen nor hide nor hair. Where is the meat, O Moosu? Thou hast the ear of God. Where is the meat?"

"'And the people cried, "Thou hast the ear of God. Where is the meat?" And they put their heads together and were afraid. Then I went among them, speaking fearsomely of the unknown things, of the dead that come and go like shadows and do evil deeds, till they cried aloud in terror and gathered all together, like little children afraid of the dark. Neewak made harangue, laying this evil that had come upon them at the door of Moosu. When he had done, there was a furious commotion, and they took spears in their hands, and tusks of walrus, and clubs, and stones from the beach. But Moosu ran away home, and because he had not drunken of *hooch* they could not catch him, and fell one over another and made haste slowly. Even now they do howl without his igloo, and his womanfolk within, and what of the noise, he cannot make himself heard.'

"'O Angeit, thou hast done well,' I commended. 'Go now, taking this empty sled and the lean dogs, and ride fast to the igloo of Moosu; and before the people, who are drunken, are aware, throw him quick upon the sled and bring him to me.'

"I waited and gave good advice to the faithful ones till Angeit returned. Moosu was on the sled, and I saw by the finger-marks on his face that his womankind had done well by him. But he tumbled off and fell in the snow at my feet, crying: 'O master, thou wilt forgive Moosu, thy servant, for the wrong things he has done! Thou art a great man! Surely wilt thou forgive!'

"'Call me "brother," Moosu — call me "brother," ' I chided, lifting him to his feet with the toe of my moccasin. 'Wilt thou evermore obey?'

"'Yea, master,' he whimpered, 'evermore.'

"'Then dispose thy body, so, across the sled.' I shifted the dogwhip to my right hand. 'And direct thy face downward, toward the snow. And make haste, for we journey south this day.' And when he was well fixed I laid the lash upon him, reciting, at every stroke, the wrongs he had done me. 'This, for thy disobedience in general

— whack! And this for thy disobedience in particular — whack! whack! And this for Esanetuk! And this for thy soul's welfare! And this for the grace of thy authority! And this for Kluktu! And this for thy rights God-given! And this for thy fat firstlings! And this and this for thy income tax and thy loaves and fishes! And this for all thy disobedience! And this, finally, that thou mayest henceforth walk softly and with understanding! Now cease thy sniffling and get up! Gird on thy snowshoes and go to the fore and break trail for the dogs. *Chook! Mush-on!* Git!'"

Thomas Stevens smiled quietly to himself as he lighted his fifth cigar and sent curling smoke-rings ceilingward.

"But how about the people of Tattarat?" I asked. "Kind of rough, wasn't it, to leave them flat with famine?"

And he answered, laughing, between two smoke-rings, "Were there not the fat dogs?"

21
WHICH MAKE MEN REMEMBER

WHICH MAKE MEN REMEMBER

Fortune La Pearle crushed his way through the snow, sobbing, straining, cursing his luck, Alaska, Nome, the cards, and the man who had felt his knife. The hot blood was freezing on his hands, and the scene yet bright in his eyes, — the man, clutching the table and sinking slowly to the floor; the rolling counters and the scattered deck; the swift shiver throughout the room, and the pause; the game-keepers no longer calling, and the clatter of the chips dying away; the startled faces; the infinite instant of silence; and then the great blood-roar and the tide of vengeance which lapped his heels and turned the town mad behind him.

"All hell's broke loose," he sneered, turning aside in the darkness and heading for the beach. Lights were flashing from open doors, and tent, cabin, and dance-hall let slip their denizens upon the chase. The clamor of men and howling of dogs smote his ears and quickened his feet. He ran on and on. The sounds grew dim, and the pursuit dissipated itself in vain rage and aimless groping. But a flitting shadow clung to him. Head thrust over shoulder, he caught glimpses of it, now taking vague shape on an open expanse of snow, now merging into the deeper shadows of some darkened cabin or beach-listed craft.

Fortune La Pearle swore like a woman, weakly, with the hint of tears that comes of exhaustion, and plunged deeper into the maze of heaped ice, tents, and prospect holes. He stumbled over taut hawsers and piles of dunnage, tripped on crazy guy-ropes and insanely planted pegs, and fell again and again upon frozen dumps and mounds of hoarded driftwood. At times, when he deemed he had drawn clear, his head dizzy with the painful pounding of his heart and the suffocating intake of his breath, he slackened down; and ever the shadow leaped out of the gloom and forced him on in heart-breaking flight. A swift intuition flashed upon him, leaving in its trail the cold chill of superstition. The persistence of the shadow he invested with his gambler's symbolism. Silent, inexorable, not to be shaken off, he took it as the fate which waited at the last turn when chips were cashed in and gains and losses counted up. Fortune La Pearle believed in those rare, illuminating moments, when the intelligence flung from it time and space, to rise naked through eternity and read the facts of life from the open book of chance. That this was such a moment he had no doubt; and when he turned inland and sped across the snow-covered tundra he was not startled because the shadow took upon it greater definiteness and drew in closer. Oppressed with his own impotence, he halted in the midst of the white waste and whirled about. His right hand slipped from its mitten, and a revolver, at level, glistened in the pale light of the stars.

"Don't shoot. I haven't a gun."

The shadow had assumed tangible shape, and at the sound of its human voice a trepidation affected Fortune La Pearle's knees, and his stomach was stricken with the qualms of sudden relief.

Perhaps things fell out differently because Uri Bram had no gun that night when he sat on the hard benches of the El Dorado and saw murder done. To that fact also might be attributed the trip on the Long Trail which he took subsequently with a most unlikely comrade. But be it as it may, he repeated a second time, "Don't shoot. Can't you see I haven't a gun?"

"Then what the flaming hell did you take after me for?" demanded the gambler, lowering his revolver.

Uri Bram shrugged his shoulders. "It don't matter much, anyhow. I want you to come with me."

"Where?"

"To my shack, over on the edge of the camp."

But Fortune La Pearle drove the heel of his moccasin into the snow and attested by his various deities to the madness of Uri Bram.

"Who are you," he perorated, "and what am I, that I should put my neck into the rope at your bidding?"

"I am Uri Bram," the other said simply, "and my shack is over there on the edge of camp. I don't know who you are, but you've thrust the soul from a living man's body, —there's the blood red on your sleeve, — and, like a second Cain, the hand of all mankind is against you, and there is no place you may lay your head. Now, I have a shack —"

"For the love of your mother, hold your say, man," interrupted Fortune La Pearle, "or I'll make you a second Abel for the joy of it. So help me, I will! With a thousand men to lay me by the heels, looking high and low, what do I want with your shack? I want to get out of here — away! away! away! Cursed swine! I've half a mind to go back and run amuck, and settle for a few of them, the pigs! One gorgeous, glorious fight, and end the whole damn business! It's a skin game, that's what life is, and I'm sick of it!"

He stopped, appalled, crushed by his great desolation and Uri Bram seized the moment. He was not given to speech, this man, and that which followed was the longest in his life, save one long afterward in another place.

"That's why I told you about my shack. I can stow you there so they'll never find you, and I've got grub in plenty. Elsewise you can't get away. No dogs, no nothing, the sea closed, St. Michael the nearest post, runners to carry the news before you, the same over the portage to Anvik — not a chance in the world for you! Now wait with me till it blows over. They'll forget all about you in a month or less, what of stampeding to York and what not, and you can hit the trail under their noses and they won't bother. I've got my own ideas of justice. When I ran after you, out of the El Dorado and along the beach, it wasn't to catch you or give you up. My ideas are my own, and that's not one of them."

He ceased as the murderer drew a prayer-book from his pocket. With the aurora borealis glimmering yellow in the northeast, heads bared to the frost and naked hands grasping the sacred book, Fortune La Pearle swore him to the words he had spoken — an oath which Uri Bram never intended breaking, and never broke.

At the door of the shack the gambler hesitated for an instant, marvelling at the strangeness of this man who had befriended him, and doubting. But by the candlelight he found the cabin comfortable and without occupants, and he was quickly rolling a cigarette while the other man made coffee. His muscles relaxed in the warmth and he lay back with half-assumed indolence, intently studying Uri's face through the curling wisps of smoke. It was a powerful face, but its strength was of that peculiar sort which stands girt in and unrelated. The seams were deep-graven, more like scars, while the stern features were in no way softened by hints of sympathy or humor. Under prominent bushy brows the eyes shone cold and gray. The cheekbones, high and forbidding, were undermined by deep hollows. The chin and jaw displayed a steadiness of purpose which the narrow forehead advertised as single, and, if needs be, pitiless. Everything was harsh, the nose, the lips, the voice, the lines about the mouth. It was the face of one who communed much with himself, unused to seeking counsel from the world; the face of one who wrestled oft of nights with angels, and rose to face the day with shut lips that no man might know. He was narrow but deep; and Fortune, his own humanity broad and shallow, could make nothing of him. Did Uri sing when merry and sigh when sad, he could have understood; but as it was, the cryptic features were undecipherable; he could not measure the soul they concealed.

"Lend a hand, Mister Man," Uri ordered when the cups had been emptied. "We've got to fix up for visitors."

Fortune purred his name for the other's benefit, and assisted understandingly. The bunk was built against a side and end of the cabin. It was a rude affair, the bottom being composed of driftwood logs overlaid with moss. At the foot the rough ends of these timbers projected in an uneven row. From the side next the wall Uri ripped back the moss and removed three of the logs. The jagged ends he sawed off and replaced so that the projecting row remained unbroken. Fortune carried in sacks of flour from the cache and piled them on the floor beneath the aperture. On these Uri laid a pair of long sea-bags, and over all spread several thicknesses of moss and blankets. Upon this Fortune could lie, with the sleeping furs stretching over him from one side of the bunk to the other, and all men could look upon it and declare it empty.

In the weeks which followed, several domiciliary visits were paid, not a shack or tent in Nome escaping, but Fortune lay in his cranny undisturbed. In fact, little attention was given to Uri Bram's; for it was the last place under the sun to expect to find the murderer of John Randolph. Except during such interruptions, Fortune lolled about the cabin, playing long games of solitaire and smoking endless cigarettes. Though his volatile nature loved geniality and play of words and laughter, he quickly accommodated himself to Uri's taciturnity. Beyond the actions and plans of his pursuers, the state of the trails, and the price of dogs, they never talked; and these things were only discussed at rare intervals and briefly. But Fortune fell to working out a system, and hour after hour, and day after day, he shuffled and dealt, shuffled and dealt, noted the combinations of the cards in' long columns, and shuffled and dealt again. Toward the end even this absorption failed him, and, head bowed upon the table, he visioned the lively all-night houses of Nome, where the gamekeepers and lookouts worked in shifts and the clattering roulette ball never slept. At such times his loneliness and bankruptcy stunned him till he sat for hours in the same unblinking, unchanging position. At other times, his long-pent bitterness found voice in passionate outbursts; for he had rubbed the world the wrong way and did not like the feel of it.

"Life's a skin-game," he was fond of repeating, and on this one note he rang the changes. "I never had half a chance," he complained. "I was faked in my birth and flim-flammed with my mother's milk. The dice were loaded when she tossed the box, and I was born to prove the loss. But that was no reason she should blame me for it, and look on me as a ctld deck; but she did — ay, she did. Why didn't she give me a show? Why didn't the world? Why did I go broke in Seattle? Why did I take the steerage, and live like a hog to Nome? Why did I go to the El Dorado? I was heading for Big Pete's and only went for matches. Why didn't I have matches? Why did I want to smoke? Don't you see? All worked out, every bit of it, all parts fitting snug. Before I was born, like as not. I'll put the sack I

never hope to get on it, before I was born. That's why! That's why John Randolph passed the word and his checks in at the same time. Damn him! It served him well right! Why didn't he keep his tongue between his teeth and give me a chance? He knew I was next to broke. Why didn't I hold my hand? Oh, why? Why? Why?"

And Fortune La Pearle would roll upon the floor, vainly interrogating the scheme of things. At such outbreaks Uri said no word, gave no sign, save that his gray eyes seemed to turn dull and muddy, as though from lack of interest. There was nothing in common between these two men, and this fact Fortune grasped sufficiently to wonder sometimes why Uri had stood by him.

But the time of waiting came to an end. Even a community's blood lust cannot stand before its gold lust. The murder of John Randolph had already passed into the annals of the camp, and there it rested. Had the murderer appeared, the men of Nome would certainly have stopped stampeding long enough to see justice done, whereas the whereabouts of Fortune La Pearle was no longer an insistent problem. There was gold in the creek beds and ruby beaches, and when the sea opened, the men with healthy sacks would sail away to where the good things of life were sold absurdly cheap.

So, one night, Fortune helped Uri Bram harness the dogs and lash the sled, and the twain took the winter trail south on the ice. But it was not all south; for they left the sea east from St. Michael's, crossed the divide, and struck the Yukon at Anvik, many hundred miles from its mouth. Then on, into the northeast, past Koyokuk, Tanana, and Minook, till they rounded the Great Curve at Fort Yukon, crossed and recrossed the Arctic Circle, and headed south through the Flats. It was a weary journey, and Fortune would have wondered why the man went with him, had not Uri told him that he owned claims and had men working at Eagle. Eagle lay on the edge of the line; a few miles farther on, the British flag waved over the barracks at Fort Cudahy. Then came Dawson, Pelly, the Five Fingers, Windy Arm, Caribou Crossing, Linderman, the Chilcoot and Dyea.

On the morning after passing Eagle, they rose early. This was their last camp, and they were now to part. Fortune's heart was light. There was a promise of spring in the land, and the days were growing longer. The way was passing into Canadian territory. Liberty was at hand, the sun was returning, and each day saw him nearer to the Great Outside. The world was big, and he could once again paint his future in royal red. He whistled about the breakfast and hummed snatches of light song while Uri put the dogs in harness and packed up. But when all was ready, Fortune's feet itching to be off, Uri pulled an unused backlog to the fire and sat down.

"Ever hear of the Dead Horse Trail?"

He glanced up meditatively and Fortune shook his head, inwardly chafing at the delay.

"Sometimes there are meetings under circumstances which make men remember," Uri continued, speaking in a low voice and very slowly, "and I met a man under such circumstances on the Dead Horse Trail. Freighting an outfit over the White Pass in '97 broke many a man's heart, for there was a world of reason when they gave that trail its name. The horses died like mosquitoes in the first frost, and from Skaguay to Bennett they rotted in heaps. They died at the Rocks, they were poisoned at the Summit, and they starved at the Lakes; they fell off the trail, what there was of it, or they went through it; in the river they drowned under their loads, or were smashed to pieces against the boulders; they snapped their legs in the crevices and broke their backs falling backwards with their packs; in the sloughs they sank from sight or smothered in the slime, and they were disembowelled in the bogs where the corduroy logs turned end up in the mud; men shot them, worked them to death, and when they were gone, went back to the beach and bought more. Some did not bother to shoot them, — stripping the saddles off and the shoes and leaving them where they fell. Their hearts turned to stone — those which did not break — and they became beasts, the men on Dead Horse Trail.

"It was there I met a man with the heart of a Christ and the patience. And he was honest. When he rested at midday he took the packs from the horses so that they, too, might rest. He paid $50 a hundred-weight for their fodder, and more. He used his own bed to blanket their backs when they rubbed raw. Other men let the saddles eat holes the size of water-buckets. Other men,

when the shoes gave out, let them wear their hoofs down to the bleeding stumps. He spent his last dollar for horseshoe nails. I know this because we slept in the one bed and ate from the one pot, and became blood brothers where men lost their grip of things and died blaspheming God. He was never too tired to ease a strap or tighten a cinch, and often there were tears in his eyes when he looked on all that waste of misery. At a passage in the rocks, where the brutes upreared hindlegged and stretched their forelegs upward like cats to clear the wall, the way was piled with carcasses where they had toppled back. And here he stood, in the stench of hell, with a cheery word and a hand on the rump at the right time, till the string passed by. And when one bogged he blocked the trail till it was clear again; nor did the man live who crowded him at such time.

"At the end of the trail a man who had killed fifty horses wanted to buy, but we looked at him and at our own, — mountain cayuses from eastern Oregon. Five thousand he offered, and we were broke, but we remembered the poison grass of the Summit and the passage in the Rocks, and the man who was my brother spoke no word, but divided the cayuses into two bunches, — his in the one and mine in the other, — and he looked at me and we understood each other. So he drove mine to the one side and I drove his to the other, and we took with us our rifles and shot them to the last one, while the man who had killed fifty horses cursed us till his throat cracked. But that man, with whom I welded blood-brothership on the Dead Horse Trail —"

"Why, that man was John Randolph," Fortune, sneering the while, completed the climax for him.

Uri nodded, and said, "I am glad you understand."

"I am ready," Fortune answered, the old weary bitterness strong in his face again. "Go ahead, but hurry."

Uri Bram rose to his feet.

"I have had faith in God all the days of my life. I believe He loves justice. I believe He is looking down upon us now, choosing between us. I believe He waits to work His will through my own right arm. And such is my belief, that we will take equal chance and let Him speak His own judgment."

Fortune's heart leaped at the words. He

did not know much concerning Uri's God, but he believed in Chance, and Chance had been coming his way ever since the night he ran down the beach and across the snow. "But there is only one gun," he objected.

"We will fire turn about," Uri replied, at the same time throwing out the cylinder of the other man's Colt and examining it.

"And the cards to decide! One hand of seven up!"

Fortune's blood was warming to the game, and he drew the deck from his pocket as Uri nodded. Surely Chance would not desert him now! He thought of the returning sun as he cut for deal, and he thrilled when he found the deal was his. He shuffled and dealt, and Uri cut him the Jack of Spades. They laid down their hands. Uri's was bare of trumps, while he held ace, deuce. The outside seemed very near to him as they stepped off the fifty paces.

"If God withholds His hand and you drop me, the dogs and outfit are yours. You'll find a bill of sale, already made out, in my pocket," Uri explained, facing the path of the bullet, straight and broad-breasted.

Fortune shook a vision of the sun shining on the ocean from his eyes and took aim. He was very careful. Twice he lowered as the spring breeze shook the pines. But the third time he dropped on one knee, gripped the revolver steadily in both hands, and fired. Uri whirled half about,

threw up his arms, swayed wildly for a moment, and sank into the snow. But Fortune knew he had fired too far to one side, else the man would not have whirled.

When Uri, mastering the flesh and struggling to his feet, beckoned for the weapon, Fortune was minded to fire again. But he thrust the idea from him. Chance had been very good to him already, he felt, and if he tricked now he would have to pay for it afterward. No, he would play fair. Besides Uri was hard hit and could not possibly hold the heavy Colt long enough to draw a bead.

"And where is your God now?" he taunted, as he gave the wounded man the revolver.

And Uri answered: "God has not yet spoken. Prepare that He may speak."

Fortune faced him, but twisted his chest sideways in order to present less surface. Uri tottered about drunkenly, but waited, too, for the moment's calm between the catspaws. The revolver was very heavy, and he doubted, like Fortune, because of its weight. But he held it, arm extended, above his head, and then let it slowly drop forward and down. At the instant Fortune's left breast and the sight flashed into line with his eye, he pulled the trigger. Fortune did not whirl, but gay San Francisco dimmed and faded, and as the sun-bright snow turned black and blacker, he breathed his last malediction on the Chance he had misplayed.

22
THE MASTER OF MYSTERY

THE MASTER OF MYSTERY

There was complaint in the village. The women chattered together with shrill, high-pitched voices. The men were glum and doubtful of aspect, and the very dogs wandered dubiously about, alarmed in vague ways by the unrest of the camp, and ready to take to the woods on the first outbreak of trouble. The air was filled with suspicion. No man was sure of his neighbor, and each was conscious that he stood in like unsureness with his fellows. Even the children were oppressed and solemn, and little Di Ya, the cause of it all, had been soundly thrashed, first by Hooniah, his mother, and then by his father, Bawn, and was now whimpering and looking pessimistically out upon the world from the shelter of the big overturned canoe on the beach.

And to make the matter worse, Scundoo, the shaman, was in disgrace, and his known magic could not be called upon to seek out the evil-doer. Forsooth, a month gone, he had promised a fair south wind so that the tribe might journey to the *potlatch* at Tonkin, where Taku Jim was giving away the savings of twenty years; and when the day came, lo, a grievous north wind blew, and of the first three canoes to venture forth, one was swamped in the big seas, and two were pounded to pieces on the rocks, and a child was drowned. He had pulled the string of the wrong bag, he explained, — a mistake. But the people refused to listen; the offerings of meat and fish and fur ceased to come to his door; and he sulked within — so they thought, fasting in bitter penance; in reality, eating generously from his well-stored cache and meditating upon the fickleness of the mob.

The blankets of Hooniah were missing. They were good blankets, of most marvellous thickness and warmth, and her pride in them was greatened in that they had been come by so cheaply. Ty-Kwan, of the next village but one, was a fool to have so easily parted with them. But then, she did not know they were the blankets of the murdered Englishman, because of whose take-off the United States cutter nosed along the coast for a time, while its launches puffed and snorted among the secret inlets. And not knowing that Ty-Kwan had disposed of them in haste so that his own people might not have to render account to the Government, Hooniah's pride was unshaken. And because the women envied her, her pride was without end and boundless, till it filled the village and spilled over along the Alaskan shore from Dutch Harbor to St. Mary's. Her totem had become justly celebrated, and her name known on the lips of men wherever men fished and feasted, what of the blankets and their marvellous thickness and warmth. It was a most mysterious happening, the manner of their going.

"I but stretched them up in the sun by the sidewall of the house," Hooniah disclaimed for the thousandth time to her Thlinget sisters. "I but stretched them up and turned my back; for Di Ya, dough-thief and eater of raw flour that he is, with head into the big iron pot, overturned and stuck there, his legs waving like the branches of a forest tree in the wind. And I did but drag him out and twice knock his head against the door for riper understanding, and behold, the blankets were not!"

"The blankets were not!" the women repeated in awed whispers.

"A great loss," one added. A second, "Never were there such blankets." And a third, "We be sorry, Hooniah, for thy loss." Yet each woman of them was glad in her heart that the odious, dissension-breeding blankets were gone.

"I but stretched them up in the sun," Hooniah began for the thousand and first time.

"Yea, yea," Bawn spoke up, wearied. "But there were no gossips in the village from other places. Wherefore it be plain that some of our own tribespeople have laid unlawful hand upon the blankets."

"How can that be, O Bawn?" the women chorussed indignantly. "Who should there be?"

"Then has there been witchcraft," Bawn continued stolidly enough, though he stole a sly glance at their faces.

"*Witchcraft!*" And at the dread word their voices hushed and each looked fearfully at each.

"Ay," Hooniah affirmed, the latent malignancy of her nature flashing into a moment's exultation. "And word has been sent to Klok-No-Ton, and strong paddles. Truly shall he be here with the afternoon tide."

The little groups broke up, and fear descended upon the village. Of all misfortune, witchcraft was the most appalling. With the intangible and unseen things only the shamans could cope, and neither man, woman, nor child could know, until the moment of ordeal, whether devils possessed their souls or not. And of all shamans, Klok-No-Ton, who dwelt in the next village, was the most terrible. None found more evil spirits than he, none visited his victims with more frightful tortures. Even had he found, once, a devil residing within the body of a three-months babe — a most obstinate devil which could only be driven out when the babe had lain for a week on thorns and briers. The body was thrown into the sea after that, but the waves tossed it back again and again as a curse upon the village, nor did it finally go away till two strong men were staked out at low tide and drowned.

And Hooniah had sent for this Klok-No-Ton. Better had it been if Scundoo, their own shaman, were undisgraced. For he had ever a gentler way, and he had been known to drive forth two devils from a man who afterward begat seven healthy children. But Klok-No-Ton! They shuddered with dire foreboding at thought of him, and each one felt himself the centre of accusing eyes, and looked accusingly upon his fellows — each one and all, save Sime, and Sime was a scoffer whose evil end was destined with a certitude his successes could not shake.

"Hoh! Hoh!" he laughed. "Devils and Klok-No-Ton! — than whom no greater devil can be found in Thlinket Land."

"Thou fool! Even now he cometh with witcheries and sorceries; so beware thy tongue, lest evil befall thee and thy days be short in the land!"

So spoke La-lah, otherwise the Cheater, and Sime laughed scornfully.

"I am Sime, unused to fear, unafraid of the dark. I am a strong man, as my father before me, and my head is clear. Nor you nor I have seen with our eyes the unseen evil things—"

"But Scundoo hath," La-lah made answer. "And likewise Klok-No-Ton. This we know."

"How dost thou know, son of a fool?" Sime thundered, the choleric blood darkening his thick bull neck.

"By the word of their mouths — even so."

Sime snorted. "A shaman is only a man. May not his words be crooked, even as thine and mine? Bah! Bah! And once more, bah! And this for thy shamans and thy shamans' devils! and this! and this!"

And snapping his fingers to right and left, Sime strode through the on-lookers, who made overzealous and fearsome way for him.

"A good fisher and strong hunter, but an evil man," said one.

"Yet does he flourish," speculated another.

"Wherefore be thou evil and flourish," Sime retorted over his shoulder. "And were all evil, there would be no need for shamans. Bah! You children-afraid-of-the-dark!"

And when Klok-No-Ton arrived on the afternoon tide, Sime's defiant laugh was unabated; nor did he forbear to make a joke when the shaman tripped on the sand in the landing. Klok-No-Ton looked at him sourly, and without greeting stalked straight through their midst to the house of Scundoo.

Of the meeting with Scundoo none of the tribespeople might know, for they clustered reverently in the distance and spoke in whispers while the masters of mystery were together.

"Greeting, O Scundoo!" Klok-No-Ton rumbled, wavering perceptibly from doubt of his reception.

He was a giant in stature, and towered massively above little Scundoo, whose thin voice floated upward like the faint far rasping of a cricket.

"Greeting, Klok-No-Ton," he returned. "The day is fair with thy coming."

"Yet it would seem..." Klok-No-Ton hesitated.

"Yea, yea," the little shaman put in impatiently, "that I have fallen on ill days, else would I not stand in gratitude to you in that you do my work."

"It grieves me, friend Scundoo..."

"Nay, I am made glad, Klok-No-Ton."

"But will I give thee half of that which be given me."

"Not so, good Klok-No-Ton," murmured Scundoo, with a deprecatory wave of the hand. "It is I who am thy slave, and my days shall be filled with desire to befriend thee."

"As I —"

"As thou now befriendest me."

"That being so, it is then a bad business, these blankets of the woman Hooniah?"

The big shaman blundered tentatively in his quest, and Scundoo smiled a wan, gray smile, for he was used to reading men, and all men seemed very small to him.

"Ever hast thou dealt in strong medicine," he said. "Doubtless the evil-doer will be briefly known to thee."

"Ay, briefly known when I set eyes upon him." Again Klok-No-Ton hesitated. "Have there been gossips from other places?" he asked.

Scundoo shook his head. "Behold! Is this not a most excellent mucluc?"

He held up the foot-covering of sealskin and walrus hide, and his visitor examined it with secret interest.

"It did come to me by a close-driven bargain."

Klok-No-Ton nodded attentively.

"I got it from the man La-lah. He is a remarkable man, and often have I thought..."

"So?" Klok-No-Ton ventured impatiently.

"Often have I thought," Scundoo concluded, his voice falling as he came to a full pause. "It is a fair day, and thy medicine be strong, Klok-No-Ton."

Klok-No-Ton's face brightened. "Thou art a great man, Scundoo, a shaman of shamans. I go now. I shall remember thee always. And the man La-lah, as you say, is a remarkable man."

Scundoo smiled yet more wan and gray, closed the door on the heels of his departing visitor, and barred and double-barred it.

Sime was mending his canoe when Klok-No-Ton came down the beach, and he broke off from his work only long enough to ostentatiously load his rifle and place it near him.

The shaman noted the action and called out: "Let all the people come together on this spot! It is the word of Klok-No-Ton, devil-seeker and driver of devils!"

He had been minded to assemble them at Hooniah's house, but it was necessary that all should be present, and he was doubtful of Sime's obedience and did not wish trouble. Sime was a good man to let alone, his judgment ran, and withal, a bad one for the health of any shaman.

"Let the woman Hooniah be brought," Klok-No-Ton commanded, glaring ferociously about the circle and sending chills up and down the spines of those he looked upon.

Hooniah waddled forward, head bent and gaze averted.

"Where be thy blankets?"

"I but stretched them up in the sun, and behold, they were not!" she whined.

"So?"

"It was because of Di Ya."

"So?"

"Him have I beaten sore, and he shall yet be beaten, for that he brought trouble upon us who be poor people."

"The blankets!" Klok-No-Ton bellowed hoarsely, foreseeing her desire to lower the price to be paid. "The blankets, woman! Thy wealth is known."

"I but stretched them up in the sun," she sniffled, "and we be poor people and have nothing."

He stiffened suddenly, with a hideous distortion of the face, and Hooniah shrank back. But so swiftly did he spring forward, with in-turned eyeballs and loosened jaw, that she stumbled and fell down grovelling at his feet. He waved his arms about, wildly flagellating the air, his body writhing and twisting in torment. An epilepsy seemed to come upon him. A white froth flecked his lips, and his body was convulsed with shiverings and tremblings.

The women broke into a wailing chant, swaying backward and forward in abandonment, while one by one the men succumbed to the excitement till only Sime remained. He, perched upon his canoe, looked on in mockery; yet the ancestors whose seed he bore pressed heavily upon him, and he swore his strongest oaths that his courage might be cheered. Klok-No-Ton was horrible to behold. He had cast off his blanket and torn his clothes from him, so that he was quite naked, save for a girdle of eagle-claws about his thighs. Shrieking and yelling, his long black hair flying like a blot of night, he leaped frantically about the circle. A certain rude rhythm characterized his frenzy, and when all were under its sway, swinging their bodies in accord with his and venting their cries in unison, he sat bolt upright, with arm outstretched and long, talon-like finger extended. A low moaning, as of the dead, greeted this, and the people cowered with shaking knees as the dread finger passed them slowly by. For death went with it, and life remained with those who watched it go; and being rejected, they watched with eager intentness.

Finally, with a tremendous cry, the fateful finger rested upon La-lah. He shook like an aspen, seeing himself already dead, his household goods divided, and his widow married to his brother. He strove to speak, to deny, but his tongue clove to his mouth and his throat was sanded with an intolerable thirst. Klok-No-Ton seemed to half swoon away, now that his work was done; but he waited, with closed eyes, listening for the great blood-cry to go up — the great blood-cry, familiar to his ear from a thousand conjurations, when the tribespeople flung themselves like wolves upon the trembling victim. But only was there silence, then a low tittering, from nowhere in particular, which spread and spread until a vast laughter welled up to the sky.

"Wherefore?" he cried.

"Na! Na!" the people laughed. "Thy medicine be ill, O Klok-No-Ton!"

"It be known to all," La-lah stuttered. "For eight weary months have I been gone afar with the Siwash sealers, and but this day am I come back to find the blankets of Hooniah gone ere I came!"

"It be true!" they cried with one accord. "The blankets of Hooniah were gone ere he came!"

"And thou shalt be paid nothing for thy medicine which is of no avail," announced Hooniah, on her feet once more and smarting from a sense of ridiculousness.

But Klok-No-Ton saw only the face of Scundoo and its wan, gray smile, heard only the faint far cricket's rasping. "I got it from the man La-lah, and often have I

thought," and, "It is a fair day and thy medicine be strong."

He brushed by Hooniah, and the circle instinctively gave way for him to pass. Sime flung a jeer from the top of the canoe, the women snickered in his face, cries of derision rose in his wake, but he took no notice, pressing onward to the house of Scundoo. He hammered on the door, beat it with his fists, and howled vile imprecations. Yet there was no response, save that in the lulls Scundoo's voice rose eerily in incantation. Klok-No-Ton raged about like a madman, but when he attempted to break in the door with a huge stone, murmurs arose from the men and women. And he, Klok-No-Ton, knew that he stood shorn of his strength and authority before an alien people. He saw a man stoop for a stone, and a second, and a bodily fear ran through him.

"Harm not Scundoo, who is a master!" a woman cried out.

"Better you return to your own village," a man advised menacingly.

Klok-No-Ton turned on his heel and went down among them to the beach, a bitter rage at his heart, and in his head a just apprehension for his defenceless back. But no stones were cast. The children swarmed mockingly about his feet, and the air was wild with laughter and derision, but that was all. Yet he did not breathe freely until the canoe was well out upon the water, when he rose up and laid a futile curse upon the village and its people, not forgetting to particularly specify Scundoo who had made a mock of him.

Ashore there was a clamor for Scundoo, and the whole population crowded his door, entreating and imploring in confused babel till he came forth and raised his hand.

"In that ye are my children I pardon freely," he said. "But never again. For the last time thy foolishness goes unpunished. That which ye wish shall be granted, and it be already known to me. This night, when the moon has gone behind the world to look upon the mighty dead, let all the people gather in the blackness before the house of Hooniah. Then shall the evil-doer stand forth and take his merited reward. I have spoken."

"It shall be death!" Bawn vociferated, "for that it hath brought worry upon us, and shame."

"So be it," Scundoo replied, and shut his door.

"Now shall all be made clear and plain, and content rest upon us once again," La-lah declaimed oracularly.

"Because of Scundoo, the little man," Sime sneered.

"Because of the medicine of Scundoo, the little man," La-lah corrected.

"Children of foolishness, these Thlinket people!" Sime smote his thigh a resounding blow. "It passeth understanding that grown women and strong men should get down in the dirt to dream-things and wonder tales."

"I am a travelled man," La-lah answered. "I have journeyed on the deep seas and seen signs and wonders, and I know that these things be so. I am La-lah—"

"The Cheater—"

"So called, but the Far-Journeyer right-named."

"I am not so great a traveller—" Sime began.

"Then hold thy tongue," Bawn cut in, and they separated in anger.

When the last silver moonlight had vanished beyond the world, Scundoo came among the people huddled about the house of Hooniah. He walked with a quick, alert step, and those who saw him in the light of Hooniah's slush-lamp noticed that he came empty-handed, without rattles, masks, or shaman's paraphernalia, save for a great sleepy raven carried under one arm.

"Is there wood gathered for a fire, so that all may see when the work be done?" he demanded.

"Yea," Bawn answered. "There be wood in plenty."

"Then let all listen, for my words be few. With me have I brought Jelchs, the Raven, diviner of mystery and seer of things. Him, in his blackness, shall I place under the big black pot of Hooniah, in the blackest corner of her house. The slush-lamp shall cease to burn, and all remain in outer darkness. It is very simple. One by one shall ye go into the house, lay hand upon the pot for the space of one long intake of breath, and withdraw again. Doubtless Jelchs will make outcry when the hand of the evil-doer is nigh him. Or who knows but otherwise he may manifest his wisdom. Are ye ready?"

"We be ready," came the multi-voiced response.

"Then will I call the name aloud, each in his turn and hers, till all are called."

Thereat La-lah was first chosen, and he passed in at once. Every ear strained, and through the silence they could hear his footsteps creaking across the rickety floor. But that was all. Jelchs made no outcry, gave no sign. Bawn was next chosen, for it well might be that a man should steal his own blankets with intent to cast shame upon his neighbors. Hooniah followed, and other women and children, but without result.

"Sime!" Scundoo called out.

"Sime!" he repeated.

But Sime did not stir.

"Art thou afraid of the dark?" La-lah, his own integrity being proved, demanded fiercely.

Sime chuckled. "I laugh at it all, for it is a great foolishness. Yet will I go in, not in belief in wonders, but in token that I am unafraid."

And he passed in boldly, and came out still mocking.

"Some day shalt thou die with great suddenness," La-lah whispered, righteously indignant.

"I doubt not," the scoffer answered airily. "Few men of us die in our beds, what of the shamans and the deep sea."

When half the villagers had safely undergone the ordeal, the excitement, because of its repression, was painfully intense. When two-thirds had gone through, a young woman, close on her first childbed, broke down and in nervous shrieks and laughter gave form to her terror.

Finally the turn came for the last of all to go in, and nothing had happened. And Di Ya was the last of all. It must surely be he. Hooniah let out a lament to the stars, while the rest drew back from the luckless lad. He was half-dead from fright, and his legs gave under him so that he staggered on the threshold and nearly fell. Scundoo shoved him inside and closed the door. A long time went by, during which could be heard only the boy's weeping. Then, very slowly, came the creak of his steps to the far corner, a pause, and the creaking of his return. The door opened and he came forth. Nothing had happened, and he was the last.

"Let the fire be lighted," Scundoo commanded.

The bright flames rushed upward, revealing faces yet marked with vanishing fear, but also clouded with doubt.

"Surely the thing has failed," Hooniah whispered hoarsely.

"Yea," Bawn answered complacently. "Scundoo groweth old, and we stand in need of a new shaman."

"Where now is the wisdom of Jelchs?" Sime snickered in La-lah's ear.

La-lah brushed his brow in a puzzled manner and said nothing.

Sime threw his chest out arrogantly and strutted up to the little shaman. "Hoh! Hoh! As I said, nothing has come of it!"

"So it would seem, so it would seem," Scundoo answered meekly. "And it would seem strange to those unskilled in the affairs of mystery."

"As thou?" Sime queried audaciously.

"Mayhap even as I." Scundoo spoke quite softly, his eyelids drooping, slowly drooping, down, down, till his eyes were all but hidden. "So I am minded of another test. Let every man, woman, and child, now and at once, hold their hands well up above their heads!"

So unexpected was the order, and so imperatively was it given, that it was obeyed without question. Every hand was in the air.

"Let each look on the other's hands, and let all look," Scundoo commanded, "so that—"

But a noise of laughter, which was more of wrath, drowned his voice. All eyes had come to rest upon Sime. Every hand but his was black with soot, and his was guiltless of the smirch of Hooniah's pot.

A stone hurtled through the air and struck him on the cheek.

"It is a lie!" he yelled. "A lie! I know naught of Hooniah's blankets!"

A second stone gashed his brow, a third whistled past his head, the great blood-cry went up, and everywhere were people groping on the ground for missiles. He staggered and half sank down.

"It was a joke! Only a joke!" he shrieked. "I but took them for a joke!"

"Where hast thou hidden them?" Scundoo's shrill, sharp voice cut through the tumult like a knife.

"In the large skin-bale in my house, the one slung by the ridge-pole," came the answer. "But it was a joke, I say, only—"

Scundoo nodded his head, and the air went thick with flying stones. Sime's wife was crying silently, her head upon her knees; but his little boy, with shrieks and laughter, was flinging stones with the rest.

Hooniah came waddling back with the precious blankets. Scundoo stopped her.

"We be poor people and have little," she whimpered. "So be not hard upon us, O Scundoo."

The people ceased from the quivering stonepile they had builded, and looked on.

"Nay, it was never my way, good Hooniah," Scundoo made answer, reaching for the blankets. "In token that I am not hard, these only shall I take."

"Am I not wise, my children?" he demanded.

"Thou art indeed wise, O Scundoo!" they cried in one voice.

And he went away into the darkness, the blankets around him, and Jelchs nodding sleepily under his arm.

23
KEESH, THE SON OF KEESH

KEESH, THE SON OF KEESH

"Thus will I give six blankets, warm and double; six files, large and hard; six Hudson Bay knives, keen-edged and long; two canoes, the work of Mogum, The Maker of Things; ten dogs, heavy-shouldered and strong in the harness; and three guns — the trigger of one be broken, but it is a good gun and can doubtless be mended."

Keesh paused and swept his eyes over the circle of intent faces. It was the time of the Great Fishing, and he was bidding to Gnob for Su-Su his daughter. The place was the St. George Mission by the Yukon, nd the tribes had gathered for many a hundred miles. From north, south, east, and west they had come, even from Tozikakat and far Tana-naw.

"And further, O Gnob, thou art chief of the Tana-naw; and I, Keesh, the son of Keesh, am chief of the Thlunget. Wherefore, when my seed springs from the loins of thy daughter, there shall be a friendship between the tribes, a great friendship, and Tana-naw and Thlunget shall be brothers of the blood in the time to come. What I have said I will do, that will I do. And how is it with you, O Gnob, in this matter?"

Gnob nodded his head gravely, his gnarled and age-twisted face inscrutably masking the soul that dwelt behind. His narrow eyes burned like twin coals through their narrow slits, as he piped in a high-cracked voice, "But that is not all."

"What more?" Keesh demanded. "Have I not offered full measure? Was there ever yet a Tana-naw maiden who fetched so great a price? Then name her!"

An open snicker passed round the circle, and Keesh knew that he stood in shame before these people.

"Nay, nay, good Keesh, thou dost not understand." Gnob made a soft, stroking gesture. "The price is fair. It is a good price. Nor do I question the broken trigger. But that is not all. What of the man?"

"Ay, what of the man?" the circle snarled.

"It is said," Gnob's shrill voice piped, "it is said that Keesh does not walk in the way of his fathers. It is said that he has wandered into the dark, after strange gods, and that he is become afraid."

The face of Keesh went dark. "It is a lie!" he thundered. "Keesh is afraid of no man!"

"It is said," old Gnob piped on, "that he has harkened to the speech of the white man up at the Big House, and that he bends head to the white man's god, and, moreover, that blood is displeasing to the white man's god."

Keesh dropped his eyes, and his hands clenched passionately. The savage circle laughed derisively, and in the ear of Gnob whispered Madwan, the shaman, high-priest of the tribe and maker of medicine.

The shaman poked among the shadows on the rim of the firelight and roused up a slender young boy, whom he brought face to face with Keesh; and in the hand of Keesh he thrust a knife.

Gnob leaned forward. "Keesh! O Keesh! Darest thou to kill a man? Behold! This be Kitz-noo, a slave. Strike, O Keesh, strike with the strength of thy arm!"

The boy trembled and waited the stroke. Keesh looked at him, and thoughts of Mr. Brown's higher morality floated through his mind, and strong upon him was a vision of the leaping flames of Mr. Brown's particular brand of hell-fire. The knife fell to the ground, and the boy sighed and went out beyond the firelight with shaking knees. At the feet of Gnob sprawled a wolf-dog, which bared its gleaming teeth and prepared to spring after the boy. But the shaman ground his foot into the brute's body, and so doing, gave Gnob an idea.

"And then, O Keesh, what wouldst thou do, should a man do this thing to you?" — as he spoke, Gnob held a ribbon of salmon to White Fang, and when the animal attempted to take it, smote him sharply on the nose with a stick. "And afterward, O Keesh, wouldst thou do thus?" — White

Fang was cringing back on his belly and fawning to the hand of Gnob.

"Listen!" — leaning on the arm of Madwan, Gnob had risen to his feet. "I am very old, and because I am very old I will tell thee things. Thy father, Keesh, was a mighty man. And he did love the song of the bowstring in battle, and these eyes have beheld him cast a spear till the head stood out beyond a man's body. But thou art unlike. Since thou left the Raven to worship the Wolf, thou art become afraid of blood, and thou makest thy people afraid. This is not good. For behold, when I was a boy, even as Kitz-noo there, there was no white man in all the land. But they came, one by one, these white men, till now they are many. And they are a restless breed, never content to rest by the fire with a full belly and let the morrow bring its own meat. A curse was laid upon them, it would seem, and they must work it out in toil and hardship."

Keesh was startled. A recollection of a hazy story told by Mr. Brown of one Adam, of old time, came to him, and it seemed that Mr. Brown had spoken true.

"So they lay hands upon all they behold, these white men, and they go everywhere and behold all things. And ever do more follow in their steps, so that if nothing be done they will come to possess all the land and there will be no room for the tribes of the Raven. Wherefore it is meet that we fight with them till none are left. Then will we hold the passes and the land, and perhaps our children and our children's children shall flourish and grow fat. There is a great struggle to come, when Wolf and Raven shall grapple; but Keesh will not fight, nor will he let his people fight. So it is not well that he should take to him my daughter. Thus have I spoken, I, Gnob, chief of the Tana-naw."

"But the white men are good and great," Keesh made answer. "The white men have taught us many things. The white men have given us blankets and knives and guns, such as we have never made and never could make. I remember in what manner we lived before they came. I was unborn then, but I have it from my father. When we went on the hunt we must creep so close to the moose that a spear-cast would cover the distance. To-day we use the white man's rifle, and farther away than can a child's cry be heard. We ate fish and meat and berries — there was nothing else to eat — and we ate without salt. How many be there among you who care to go back to the fish and meat without salt?"

It would have sunk home, had not Madwan leaped to his feet ere silence could come. "And first a question to thee, Keesh. The white man up at the Big House tells you that it is wrong to kill. Yet do we not know that the white men kill? Have we forgotten the great fight on the Koyokuk? or the great fight at Nuklukyeto, where three white men killed twenty of the Tozikakats? Do you think we no longer remember the three men of the Tana-naw that the white man Macklewrath killed? Tell me, O Keesh, why does the Shaman Brown teach you that it is wrong to fight, when all his brothers fight?"

"Nay, nay, there is no need to answer," Gnob piped, while Keesh struggled with the paradox. "It is very simple. The Good Man Brown would hold the Raven tight whilst his brothers pluck the feathers." He raised his voice. "But so long as there is one Tana-naw to strike a blow, or one maiden to bear a man-child, the Raven shall not be plucked!"

Gnob turned to a husky young man across the fire. "And what sayest thou, Makamuk, who art brother to Su-Su?"

Makamuk came to his feet. A long face-scar lifted his upper lip into a perpetual grin which belied the glowing ferocity of his eyes. "This day," he began with cunning irrelevance, "I came by the Trader Macklewrath's cabin. And in the door I saw a child laughing at the sun. And the child looked at me with the Trader Macklewrath's eyes, and it was frightened. The mother ran to it and quieted it. The mother was Ziska, the Thlunget woman."

A snarl of rage rose up and drowned his voice, which he stilled by turning dramatically upon Keesh with outstretched arm and accusing finger.

"So? You give your women away, you Thlunget, and come to the Tana-naw for more? But we have need of our women, Keesh; for we must breed men, many men, against the day when the Raven grapples with the Wolf."

Through the storm of applause, Gnob's voice shrilled clear. "And thou, Nossabok, who art her favorite brother?"

The young fellow was slender and graceful, with the strong aquiline nose and high brows of his type; but from some nervous affliction the lid of one eye drooped at odd times in a suggestive wink. Even as he arose it so drooped and rested a moment against his cheek. But it was not greeted with the accustomed laughter. Every face was grave. "I, too, passed by the Trader Macklewrath's cabin," he rippled in soft, girlish tones, wherein there was much of youth and much of his sister. "And I saw Indians with the sweat running into their eyes and their knees shaking with weariness— I say, I saw Indians groaning under the logs for the store which the Trader Macklewrath is to build. And with my eyes I saw them chopping wood to keep the Shaman Brown's Big House warm through the frost of the long nights. This be squaw work. Never shall the Tana-naw do the like. We shall be blood brothers to men, not squaws; and the Thlunget be squaws."

A deep silence fell, and all eyes centred on Keesh. He looked about him carefully, deliberately, full into the face of each grown man. "So," he said passionlessly. And "So," he repeated. Then turned on his heel without further word and passed out into the darkness.

Wading among sprawling babies and bristling wolf-dogs, he threaded the great camp, and on its outskirts came upon a woman at work by the light of a fire. With strings of bark stripped from the long roots of creeping vines, she was braiding rope for the Fishing. For some time, without speech, he watched her deft hands bringing law and order out of the unruly mass of curling fibres. She was good to look upon, swaying there to her task, strong-limbed, deep-chested, and with hips made for motherhood. And the bronze of her face was golden in the flickering light, her hair blue-black, her eyes jet.

"O Su-Su," he spoke finally, "thou hast looked upon me kindly in the days that have gone and in the days yet young —"

"I looked kindly upon thee for that thou were chief of the Thlunget," she answered quickly, "and because thou wert big and strong."

"Ay—"

"But that was in the old days of the Fishing," she hastened to add, "before the Shaman Brown came and taught thee ill things and led thy feet on strange trails."

"But I would tell thee the—"

She held up one hand in a gesture which reminded him of her father. "Nay, I know already the speech that stirs in thy throat, O Keesh, and I make answer now. It so happeneth that the fish of the water and the beasts of the forest bring forth after their kind. And this is good. Likewise it happeneth to women. It is for them to bring forth their kind, and even the maiden, while she is yet a maiden, feels the pang of the birth, and the pain of the breast, and the small hands at the neck. And when such feeling is strong, then does each maiden look about her with secret eyes for the man — for the man who shall be fit to father her kind. So have I felt. So did I feel when I looked upon thee and found thee big and strong, a hunter and fighter of beasts and men, well able to win meat when I should eat for two, well able to keep danger afar off when my helplessness drew nigh. But that was before the day the Shaman Brown came into the land and taught thee—"

"But it is not right, Su-Su. I have it on good word—"

"It is not right to kill. I know what thou wouldst say. Then breed thou after thy kind, the kind that does not kill; but come not on such quest among the Tana-naw. For it is said in the time to come, that the Raven shall grapple with the Wolf. I do not know, for this be the affair of men; but I do know that it is for me to bring forth men against that time."

"Su-Su," Keesh broke in, "thou must hear me —"

"A *man* would beat me with a stick and make me hear," she sneered. "But thou ...here!" She thrust a bunch of bark into his hand. "I cannot give thee myself, but this, yes. It looks fittest in thy hands. It is squaw work, so braid away."

He flung it from him, the angry blood pounding a muddy path under his bronze.

"One thing more," she went on. "There be an old custom which thy father and mine were not strangers to. When a man falls in battle, his scalp is carried away in token. Very good. But thou, who have forsworn the Raven, must do more. Thou must bring me, not scalps, but heads, two heads, and then will I give thee, not bark, but a brave-beaded belt, and sheath, and long Russian knife. Then will I look kindly upon thee once again, and all will be well."

"So," the man pondered. "So." Then he turned and passed out through the light.

"Nay, O Keesh!" she called after him. "Not two heads, but three at least!"

But Keesh remained true to his conversion, lived uprightly, and made his tribespeople obey the gospel as propounded by the Rev. Jackson Brown. Through all the time of the Fishing he gave no heed to the Tana-naw, nor took notice of the sly things which were said, nor of the laughter of the women of the many tribes. After the Fishing, Gnob and his people, with great store of salmon, sun-dried and smoke-cured, departed for the Hunting on the head reaches of the Tana-naw. Keesh watched them go, but did not fail in his attendance at Mission service, where he prayed regularly and led the singing with his deep bass voice.

The Rev. Jackson Brown delighted in that deep bass voice, and because of his sterling qualities deemed him the most promising convert. Macklewrath doubted this. He did not believe in the efficacy of the conversion of the heathen, and he was not slow in speaking his mind. But Mr. Brown was a large man, in his way, and he argued it out with such convincingness, all of one long fall night, that the trader, driven from position after position, finally announced in desperation, "Knock out my brains with apples, Brown, if I don't become a convert myself, if Keesh holds fast, true blue, for two years!" Mr. Brown never lost an opportunity, so he clinched the matter on the spot with a virile hand-grip, and thenceforth the conduct of Keesh was to determine the ultimate abiding-place of Macklewrath's soul.

But there came news one day, after the winter's rime had settled down over the land sufficiently for travel. A Tana-naw man arrived at the St. George Mission in quest of ammunition and bringing information that Su-Su had set eyes on Nee-Koo, a nervy young hunter who had bid brilliantly for her by old Gnob's fire. It was at about this time that the Rev. Jackson Brown came upon Keesh by the wood-trail which leads down to the river. Keesh had his best dogs in the harness, and shoved under the sled-lashings was his largest and finest pair of snow-shoes.

"Where goest thou, O Keesh? Hunting?" Mr. Brown asked, falling into the Indian manner.

Keesh looked him steadily in the eyes for a full minute, then started up his dogs. Then again, turning his deliberate gaze upon the missionary, he answered, "No; I go to hell."

In an open space, striving to burrow into the snow as though for shelter from the appalling desolateness, huddled three dreary lodges. Ringed all about, a dozen paces away, was the sombre forest. Overhead there was no keen, blue sky of naked space, but a vague, misty curtain, pregnant with snow, which had drawn between. There was no wind, no sound, nothing but the snow and silence. Nor was there even the general stir of life about the camp; for the hunting party had run upon the flank of the caribou herd and the kill had been large. Thus, after the period of fasting had come the plenitude of feasting, and thus, in broad daylight, they slept heavily under their roofs of moosehide.

By a fire, before one of the lodges, five pairs of snow-shoes stood on end in their element, and by the fire sat Su-Su. The hood of her squirrel-skin parka was about her hair, and well drawn up around her throat; but her hands were unmittened and nimbly at work with needle and sinew, completing the last fantastic design on a belt of leather faced with bright scarlet cloth. A dog, somewhere at the rear of one of the lodges, raised a short, sharp bark, then ceased as abruptly as it had begun. Once, her father, in the lodge at her back, gurgled and grunted in his sleep. "Bad dreams," she smiled to herself. "He grows old, and that last joint was too much."

She placed the last bead, knotted the sinew, and replenished the fire. Then, after gazing long into the flames, she lifted her head to the harsh *crunch-crunch* of a moccasined foot against the flinty snow granules. Keesh was at her side, bending slightly forward to a load which he bore upon his back. This was wrapped loosely in a soft-tanned moosehide, and he dropped it carelessly into the snow and sat down. They looked at each other long and without speech.

"It is a far fetch, O Keesh," she said at last, "a far fetch from St. George Mission by the Yukon."

"Ay," he made answer, absently, his eyes fixed keenly upon the belt and taking note of its girth. "But where is the knife?" he demanded.

"Here." She drew it from inside her parka and flashed its naked length in the firelight. "It is a good knife."

"Give it me!" he commanded.

"Nay, O Keesh," she laughed. "It may be that thou wast not born to wear it."

"Give it me!" he reiterated, without change of tone. "I was so born."

But her eyes, glancing coquettishly past him to the moosehide, saw the snow about it slowly reddening. "It is blood, Keesh?" she asked.

"Ay, it is blood. But give me the belt and the long Russian knife."

She felt suddenly afraid, but thrilled when he took the belt roughly from her, thrilled to the roughness. She looked at him softly, and was aware of a pain at the breast and of small hands clutching her throat.

"It was made for a smaller man," he remarked grimly, drawing in his abdomen and clasping the buckle at the first hole.

Su-Su smiled, and her eyes were yet softer. Again she felt the soft hands at her throat. He was good to look upon, and the belt was indeed small, made for a smaller man; but what did it matter? She could make many belts.

"But the blood?" she asked, urged on by a hope new-born and growing. "The blood, Keesh? Is it ... are they ... heads?"

"Ay."

"They must be very fresh, else would the blood be frozen."

"Ay, it is not cold, and they be fresh, quite fresh."

"Oh, Keesh!" Her face was warm and bright. "And for me?"

"Ay; for thee."

He took hold of a corner of the hide, flirted it open, and rolled the heads out before her.

"Three," he whispered savagely; "nay, four at least."

But she sat transfixed. There they lay — the soft-featured Nee-Koo; the gnarled old face of Gnob; Makamuk, grinning at her

with his lifted upper lip; and lastly, Nossabok, his eyelid, up to its old trick, drooped on his girlish cheek in a suggestive wink. There they lay, the firelight flashing upon and playing over them, and from each of them a widening circle dyed the snow to scarlet.

Thawed by the fire, the white crust gave way beneath the head of Gnob, which rolled over like a thing alive, spun around, and came to rest at her feet. But she did not move. Keesh, too, sat motionless, his eyes unblinking, centred steadfastly upon her.

Once, in the forest, an overburdened pine dropped its load of snow, and the echoes reverberated hollowly down the gorge; but neither stirred. The short day had been waning fast, and darkness was wrapping round the camp when White Fang trotted up toward the fire. He paused to reconnoitre, but not being driven back, came closer. His nose shot swiftly to the side, nostrils a-tremble and bristles rising along the spine; and straight and true, he followed the sudden scent to his master's head. He sniffed it gingerly at first and licked the forehead with his red lolling tongue. Then he sat abruptly down, pointed his nose up at the first faint star, and raised the long wolf-howl.

This brought Su-Su to herself. She glanced across at Keesh, who had unsheathed the Russian knife and was watching her intently. His face was firm and set, and in it she read the law. Slipping back the hood of her parka, she bared her neck and rose to her feet. There she paused and took a long look about her, at the rimming forest, at the faint stars in the sky, at the camp, at the snow-shoes in the snow — a last long comprehensive look at life. A light breeze stirred her hair from the side, and for the space of one deep breath she turned her head and followed it around until she met it full-faced.

Then she thought of her children, ever to be unborn, and she walked over to Keesh and said, "I am ready."

Then she walked over to Keesh and said, "I am ready"

24
NAM-BOK THE UNVERACIOUS

NAM-BOK THE UNVERACIOUS

"A bidarka, is it not so? Look! a bidarka, and one man who drives clumsily with a paddle!"

Old Bask-Wah-Wan rose to her knees, trembling with weakness and eagerness, and gazed out over the sea.

"Nam-Bok was ever clumsy at the paddle," she maundered reminiscently, shading the sun from her eyes and staring across the silver-spilled water. "Nam-Bok was ever clumsy. I remember ..."

But the women and children laughed loudly, and there was a gentle mockery in their laughter, and her voice dwindled till her lips moved without sound.

Koogah lifted his grizzled head from his bone-carving and followed the path of her eyes. Except when wide yaws took it off its course, a bidarka was heading in for the beach. Its occupant was paddling with more strength than dexterity, and made his approach along the zigzag line of most resistance. Koogah's head dropped to his work again, and on the ivory tusk between his knees he scratched the dorsal fin of a fish the like of which never swam in the sea.

"It is doubtless the man from the next village," he said finally, "come to consult with me about the marking of things on bone. And the man is a clumsy man. He will never know how."

"It is Nam-Bok," old Bask-Wah-Wan repeated. "Should I not know my son?" she demanded shrilly. "I say, and I say again, it is Nam-Bok."

"And so thou hast said these many summers," one of the women chided softly. "Ever when the ice passed out of the sea hast thou sat and watched through the long day, saying at each chance canoe, 'This is Nam-Bok.' Nam-Bok is dead, O Bask-Wah-Wan, and the dead do not come back. It cannot be that the dead come back."

"Nam-Bok!" the old woman cried, so loud and clear that the whole village was startled and looked at her.

She struggled to her feet and tottered down the sand. She stumbled over a baby lying in the sun, and the mother hushed its crying and hurled harsh words after the old woman, who took no notice. The children ran down the beach in advance of her, and as the man in the bidarka drew closer, nearly capsizing with one of his ill-directed strokes, the women followed. Koogah dropped his walrus tusk and went also, leaning heavily upon his staff, and after him loitered the men in twos and threes.

The bidarka turned broadside and the ripple of surf threatened to swamp it, only a naked boy ran into the water and pulled the bow high up on the sand. The man stood up and sent a questing glance along the line of villagers. A rainbow sweater, dirty and the worse for wear, clung loosely to his broad shoulders, and a red cotton handkerchief was knotted in sailor fashion about his throat. A fisherman's tam-o'-shanter on his close-clipped head, and dungaree trousers and heavy brogans, completed his outfit.

But he was none the less a striking personage to these simple fisherfolk of the great Yukon Delta, who, all their lives, had stared out on Bering Sea and in that time seen but two white men, — the census enumerator and a lost Jesuit priest. They were a poor people, with neither gold in the ground nor valuable furs in hand, so the whites had passed them afar. Also, the Yukon, through the thousands of years, had shoaled that portion of the sea with the detritus of Alaska till vessels grounded out of sight of land. So the sodden coast, with its long inside reaches and huge mud-land archipelagoes, was avoided by the ships of men, and the fisherfolk knew not that such things were.

Koogah, the Bone-Scratcher, retreated backward in sudden haste, tripping over his staff and falling to the ground. "Nam-Bok!" he cried, as he scrambled wildly for footing. "Nam-Bok, who was blown off to sea, come back!"

The men and women shrank away, and the children scuttled off between their legs. Only Opee-Kwan was brave, as befitted the head man of the village. He strode forward and gazed long and earnestly at the newcomer.

"It *is* Nam-Bok," he said at last, and at the conviction in his voice the women wailed apprehensively and drew farther away.

The lips of the stranger moved indecisively, and his brown throat writhed and wrestled with unspoken words.

"La la, it is Nam-Bok," Bask-Wah-Wan croaked, peering up into his face. "Ever did I say Nam-Bok would come back."

"Ay, it is Nam-Bok come back." This time it was Nam-Bok himself who spoke, putting a leg over the side of the bidarka and standing with one foot afloat and one ashore. Again his throat writhed and wrestled as he grappled after forgotten words. And when the words came forth they were strange of sound and a spluttering of the lips accompanied the gutturals. "Greeting, O brothers," he said, "brothers of old time before I went away with the off-shore wind."

He stepped out with both feet on the sand, and Opee-Kwan waved him back.

"Thou art dead, Nam-Bok," he said.

Nam-Bok laughed. "I am fat."

"Dead men are not fat," Opee-Kwan confessed. "Thou hast fared well, but it is strange. No man may mate with the off-shore wind and come back on the heels of the years."

"I have come back," Nam-Bok answered simply.

"Mayhap thou art a shadow, then, a passing shadow of the Nam-Bok that was. Shadows come back."

"I am hungry. Shadows do not eat."

But Opee-Kwan doubted, and brushed his hand across his brow in sore puzzlement. Nam-Bok was likewise puzzled, and as he looked up and down the line found no welcome in the eyes of the fisherfolk. The men and women whispered together. The children stole timidly back among their elders, and bristling dogs fawned up to him and sniffed suspiciously.

"I bore thee, Nam-Bok, and I gave thee suck when thou wast little," Bask-Wah-Wan whimpered, drawing closer; "and

shadow though thou be, or no shadow, I will give thee to eat now."

Nam-Bok made to come to her, but a growl of fear and menace warned him back. He said something in a strange tongue which sounded like "Goddam," and added, "No shadow am I, but a man."

"Who may know concerning the things of mystery?" Opee-Kwan demanded, half of himself and half of his tribespeople. "We are, and in a breath we are not. If the man may become shadow, may not the shadow become man? Nam-Bok was, but is not. This we know, but we do not know if this be Nam-Bok or the shadow of Nam-Bok."

Nam-Bok cleared his throat and made answer. "In the old time long ago, thy father's father, Opee-Kwan, went away and came back on the heels of the years. Nor was a place by the fire denied him. It is said..." He paused significantly, and they hung on his utterance. "It is said," he repeated, driving his point home with deliberation, "that Sipsip, his *klooch,* bore him two sons after he came back."

"But he had no doings with the off-shore wind," Opee-Kwan retorted. "He went away into the heart of the land, and it is in the nature of things that a man may go on and on into the land."

"And likewise the sea. But that is neither here nor there. It is said... that thy father's father told strange tales of the things he saw."

"Ay, strange tales he told."

"I, too, have strange tales to tell," Nam-Bok stated insidiously. And, as they wavered, "And presents likewise."

He pulled from the bidarka a shawl, marvellous of texture and color, and flung it about his mother's shoulders. The women voiced a collective sigh of admiration, and old Bask-Wah-Wan ruffled the gay material and patted it and crooned in childish joy.

"He has tales to tell," Koogah muttered. "And presents," a woman seconded.

And Opee-Kwan knew that his people were eager, and further, he was aware himself of an itching curiosity concerning those untold tales. "The fishing has been good," he said judiciously, "and we have oil in plenty. So come, Nam-Bok, let us feast."

Two of the men hoisted the bidarka on their shoulders and carried it up to the fire. Nam-Bok walked by the side of Opee-Kwan, and the villagers followed after, save those of the women who lingered a moment to lay caressing fingers on the shawl.

There was little talk while the feast went on, though many and curious were the glances stolen at the son of Bask-Wah-Wan. This embarrassed him — not because he was modest of spirit, however, but for the fact that the stench of the seal-oil had robbed him of his appetite, and that he keenly desired to conceal his feelings on the subject.

"Eat; thou art hungry," Opee-Kwan commanded, and Nam-Bok shut both his eyes and shoved his fist into the big pot of putrid fish.

"La la, be not ashamed. The seal were many this year, and strong men are ever hungry." And Bask-Wah-Wan sopped a particularly offensive chunk of salmon into the oil and passed it fondly and dripping to her son.

In despair, when premonitory symptoms warned him that his stomach was not so strong as of old, he filled his pipe and struck up a smoke. The people fed on noisily and watched. Few of them could boast of intimate acquaintance with the precious weed, though now and again small quantities and abominable qualities were obtained in trade from the Eskimos to the northward. Koogah, sitting next to him, indicated that he was not averse to taking a draw, and between two mouthfuls, with the oil thick on his lips, sucked away at the amber stem. And thereupon Nam-Bok held his stomach with a shaky hand and declined the proffered return. Koogah could keep the pipe, he said, for he had intended so to honor him from the first. And the people licked their fingers and approved of his liberality.

Opee-Kwan rose to his feet. "And now, O Nam-Bok, the feast is ended, and we would listen concerning the strange things you have seen."

The fisherfolk applauded with their hands, and gathering about them their work, prepared to listen. The men were busy fashioning spears and carving on ivory, while the women scraped the fat from the hides of the hair seal and made them pliable or sewed muclucs with threads of sinew. Nam-Bok's eyes roved over the scene, but there was not the charm about it that his recollection had warranted him to expect. During the years of his wandering he had looked forward to just this scene, and now that it had come he was disappointed. It was a bare and meagre life, he deemed, and not to be compared to the one to which he had become used. Still, he would open their eyes a bit, and his own eyes sparkled at the thought.

"Brothers," he began, with the smug complacency of a man about to relate the big things he has done, "it was late summer of many summers back, with much such weather as this promises to be, when I went away. You all remember the day, when the gulls flew low, and the wind blew strong from the land, and I could not hold my bidarka against it. I tied the covering of the bidarka about me so that no water could get in, and all of the night I fought with the storm. And in the morning there was no land,—only the sea,—and the off-shore wind held me close in its arms and bore me along. Three such nights whitened into dawn and showed me no land, and the off-shore wind would not let me go.

"And when the fourth day came, I was as a madman. I could not dip my paddle for want of food; and my head went round and round, what of the thirst that was upon me. But the sea was no longer angry, and the soft south wind was blowing, and as I looked about me I saw a sight that made me think I was indeed mad."

Nam-Bok paused to pick away a sliver of salmon lodged between his teeth, and the men and women, with idle hands and heads craned forward, waited.

"It was a canoe, a big canoe. If all the canoes I have ever seen were made into one canoe, it would not be so large."

There were exclamations of doubt, and Koogah, whose years were many, shook his head.

"If each bidarka were as a grain of sand," Nam-Bok defiantly continued, "and if there were as many bidarkas as there be grains of sand in this beach, still would they not make so big a canoe as this I saw on the morning of the fourth day. It was a very big canoe, and it was called a *schooner*. I saw this thing of wonder, this great schooner, coming after me, and on it I saw men—"

"Hold, O Nam-Bok!" Opee-Kwan broke in. "What manner of men were they? — big men?"

"Nay, mere men like you and me."

"Did the big canoe come fast?"

"Ay."

"The sides were tall, the men short." Opee-Kwan stated the premises with conviction. "And did these men dip with long paddles?"

Nam-Bok grinned. "There were no paddles," he said.

Mouths remained open, and a long silence dropped down. Opee-Kwan borrowed Koogah's pipe for a couple of contemplative sucks. One of the younger women giggled nervously and drew upon herself angry eyes.

"There were no paddles?" Opee-Kwan asked softly, returning the pipe.

"The south wind was behind," Nam-Bok explained.

"But the wind-drift is slow."

"The schooner had wings—thus." He sketched a diagram of masts and sails in the sand, and the men crowded around and studied it. The wind was blowing briskly, and for more graphic elucidation he seized the corners of his mother's shawl and spread them out till it bellied like a sail. Bask-Wah-Wan scolded and struggled, but was blown down the beach for a score of feet and left breathless and stranded in a heap of driftwood. The men uttered sage grunts of comprehension, but Koogah suddenly tossed back his hoary head.

"Ho! Ho!" he laughed. "A foolish thing, this big canoe! A most foolish thing! The plaything of the wind! Wheresoever the wind goes, it goes too. No man who journeys therein may name the landing beach, for always he goes with the wind, and the wind goes everywhere, but no man knows where."

"It is so," Opee-Kwan supplemented gravely. "With the wind the going is easy, but against the wind a man striveth hard; and for that they had no paddles these men on the big canoe did not strive at all."

"Small need to strive," Nam-Bok cried angrily. "The schooner went likewise against the wind."

"And what said you made the sch—sch—schooner go?" Koogah asked, tripping craftily over the strange word.

"The wind," was the impatient response.

"Then the wind made the sch—sch—schooner go against the wind." Old Koogah dropped an open leer to Opee-Kwan, and, the laughter growing around him, continued: "The wind blows from the south

and blows the schooner south. The wind blows against the wind. The wind blows one way and the other at the same time. It is very simple. We understand, Nam-Bok. We clearly understand."

"Thou art a fool!"

"Truth falls from thy lips," Koogah answered meekly. "I was over-long in understanding, and the thing was simple."

But Nam-Bok's face was dark, and he said rapid words which they had never heard before. Bone-scratching and skin-scraping were resumed, but he shut his lips tightly on the tongue that could not be believed.

"This sch—sch—schooner," Koogah imperturbably asked; "it was made of a big tree?"

"It was made of many trees," Nam-Bok snapped shortly. "It was very big."

He lapsed into sullen silence again, and Opee-Kwan nudged Koogah, who shook his head with slow amazement and murmured, "It is very strange."

Nam-Bok took the bait. "That is nothing," he said airily; "you should see the *steamer*. As the grain of sand is to the bidarka, as the bidarka is to the schooner, so the schooner is to the steamer. Further, the steamer is made of iron. It is all iron."

"Nay, nay, Nam-Bok," cried the head man; "how can that be? Always iron goes to the bottom. For behold, I received an iron knife in trade from the head man of the next village, and yesterday the iron knife slipped from my fingers and went down, down, into the sea. To all things there be law. Never was there one thing outside the law. This we know. And, moreover, we know that things of a kind have the one law, and that all iron has the one law. So unsay thy words, Nam-Bok, that we may yet honor thee."

"It is so," Nam-Bok persisted. "The steamer is all iron and does not sink."

"Nay, nay; this cannot be."

"With my own eyes I saw it."

"It is not in the nature of things."

"But tell me, Nam-Bok," Koogah interrupted, for fear the tale would go no farther, "tell me the manner of these men in finding their way across the sea when there is no land by which to steer."

"The sun points out the path."

"But how?"

"At midday the head man of the schooner takes a thing through which his eye looks at the sun, and then he makes the sun climb down out of the sky to the edge of the earth."

"Now this be evil medicine!" cried Opee-Kwan, aghast at the sacrilege. The men held up their hands in horror, and the women moaned. "This be evil medicine. It is not good to misdirect the great sun which drives away the night and gives us the seal, the salmon, and warm weather."

"What if it be evil medicine?" Nam-Bok demanded truculently. "I, too, have looked through the thing at the sun and made the sun climb down out of the sky."

Those who were nearest drew away from him hurriedly, and a woman covered the face of a child at her breast so that his eye might not fall upon it.

"But on the morning of the fourth day, O Nam-Bok," Koogah suggested; "on the morning of the fourth day when the sch—sch—schooner came after thee?"

"I had little strength left in me and could not run away. So I was taken on board and water was poured down my throat and good food given me. Twice, my brothers, you have seen a white man. These men were all white and as many as have I fingers and toes. And when I saw they were full of kindness, I took heart, and I resolved to bring away with me report of all that I saw. And they taught me the work they did, and gave me good food and a place to sleep.

"And day after day we went over the sea, and each day the head man drew the sun down out of the sky and made it tell where we were. And when the waves were kind, we hunted the fur seal and I marvelled much, for always did they fling the meat and the fat away and save only the skin."

Opee-Kwan's mouth was twitching violently, and he was about to make denunciation of such waste when Koogah kicked him to be still.

"After a weary time, when the sun was gone and the bite of the frost come into the air, the head man pointed the nose of the schooner south. South and east we travelled for days upon days, with never the land in sight, and we were near to the village from which hailed the men—"

"How did they know they were near?" Opee-Kwan, unable to contain himself longer, demanded. "There was no land to see."

Nam-Bok glowered on him wrathfully. "Did I not say the head man brought the sun down out of the sky?"

Koogah interposed, and Nam-Bok went on.

"As I say, when we were near to that village a great storm blew up, and in the night we were helpless and knew not where we were—"

"Thou hast just said the head man knew—"

"Oh, peace, Opee-Kwan! Thou art a fool and cannot understand. As I say, we were helpless in the night, when I heard, above the roar of the storm, the sound of the sea on the beach. And next we struck with a mighty crash and I was in the water, swimming. It was a rock-bound coast, with one patch of beach in many miles, and the law was that I should dig my hands into the sand and draw myself clear of the surf. The other men must have pounded against the rocks, for none of them came ashore but the head man, and him I knew only by the ring on his finger.

"When day came, there being nothing of the schooner, I turned my face to the land and journeyed into it that I might get food and look upon the faces of the people. And when I came to a house I was taken in and given to eat, for I had learned their speech, and the white men are ever kindly. And it was a house bigger than all the houses built by us and our fathers before us."

"It was a mighty house," Koogah said, masking his unbelief with wonder.

"And many trees went into the making of such a house," Opee-Kwan added, taking the cue.

"That is nothing." Nam-Bok shrugged his shoulders in belittling fashion. "As our houses are to that house, so that house was to the houses I was yet to see."

"And they are not big men?"

"Nay; mere men like you and me," Nam-Bok answered. "I had cut a stick that I might walk in comfort, and remembering that I was to bring report to you, my brothers, I cut a notch in the stick for each person who lived in that house. And I stayed there many days, and worked, for which they gave me money—a thing of which you know nothing, but which is very good.

"And one day I departed from that place to go farther into the land. And as I walked I met many people, and I cut smaller notches in the stick, that there might be room for all. Then I came upon a strange thing. On the ground before me was a bar of iron, as big in thickness as my arm, and a long step away was another bar of iron—"

"Then wert thou a rich man," Opee-Kwan asserted; "for iron be worth more than anything else in the world. It would have made many knives."

"Nay, it was not mine."

"It was a find, and a find be lawful."

"Not so; the white men had placed it there. And further, these bars were so long that no man could carry them away—so long that as far as I could see there was no end to them."

"Nam-Bok, that is very much iron. Opee-Kwan cautioned.

"Ay, it was hard to believe with my own eyes upon it; but I could not gainsay my eyes. And as I looked I heard ..." He turned abruptly upon the head man. "Opee-Kwan, thou hast heard the sea-lion bellow in his anger. Make it plain in thy mind of as many sea-lions as there be waves to the sea, and make it plain that all these sea-lions be made into one sea-lion, and as that one sea-lion would bellow so bellowed the thing I heard."

The fisherfolk cried aloud in astonishment, and Opee-Kwan's jaw lowered and remained lowered.

"And in the distance I saw a monster like unto a thousand whales. It was one-eyed, and vomited smoke, and it snorted with exceeding loudness. I was afraid and ran with shaking legs along the path between the bars. But it came with the speed of the wind, this monster, and I leaped the iron bars with its breath hot on my face..."

Opee-Kwan gained control of his jaw again. "And—and then, O Nam-Bok?"

"Then it came by on the bars, and harmed me not; and when my legs could hold me up again it was gone from sight. And it is a very common thing in that country. Even the women and children are not afraid. Men make them to do work, these monsters."

"As we make our dogs do work?" Koogah asked, with sceptic twinkle in his eye.

"Ay, as we make our dogs do work."

"And how do they breed these—these things?" Opee-Kwan questioned.

"They breed not at all. Men fashion them cunningly of iron, and feed them with stone, and give them water to drink. The stone becomes fire, and the water becomes steam, and the steam of the water

is the breath of their nostrils, and—"

"There, there, O Nam-Bok," Opee-Kwan interrupted. "Tell us of other wonders. We grow tired of this which we may not understand."

"You do not understand?" Nam-Bok asked despairingly.

"Nay, we do not understand," the men and women wailed back. "We cannot understand."

Nam-Bok thought of a combined harvester, and of the machines wherein visions of living men were to be seen, and of the machines from which came the voices of men, and he knew his people could never understand.

"Dare I say I rode this iron monster through the land?" he asked bitterly.

Opee-Kwan threw up his hands, palms outward, in open incredulity. "Say on; say anything. We listen."

"Then did I ride the iron monster, for which I gave money—"

"Thou saidst it was fed with stone."

"And likewise, thou fool, I said money was a thing of which you know nothing. As I say, I rode the monster through the land, and through many villages, until I came to a big village on a salt arm of the sea. And the houses shoved their roofs among the stars in the sky, and the clouds drifted by them, and everywhere was much smoke. And the roar of that village was like the roar of the sea in storm, and the people were so many that I flung away my stick and no longer remembered the notches upon it."

"Hadst thou made small notches," Koogah reproved, "thou mightst have brought report."

Nam-Bok whirled upon him in anger. "Had I made small notches! Listen, Koogah, thou scratcher of bone! If I had made small notches, neither the stick, nor twenty sticks, could have borne them — nay, not all the driftwood of all the beaches between this village and the next. And if all of you, the women and children as well, were twenty times as many, and if you had twenty hands each, and in each hand a stick and a knife, still the notches could not be cut for the people I saw, so many were they and so fast did they come and go."

"There cannot be so many people in all the world," Opee-Kwan objected, for he was stunned and his mind could not grasp such magnitude of numbers.

"What dost thou know of all the world and how large it is?" Nam-Bok demanded.

"But there cannot be so many people in one place."

"Who art thou to say what can be and what can not be?"

"It stands to reason there cannot be so many people in one place. Their canoes would clutter the sea till there was no room. And they could empty the sea each day of its fish, and they would not all be fed."

"So it would seem," Nam-Bok made final answer; "yet it was so. With my own eyes I saw, and flung my stick away." He yawned heavily and rose to his feet. "I have paddled far. The day has been long, and I am tired. Now I will sleep, and to-morrow we will have further talk upon the things I have seen."

Bask-Wah-Wan, hobbling fearfully in advance, proud indeed, yet awed by her wonderful son, led him to her igloo and stowed him away among the greasy, ill-smelling furs. But the men lingered by the fire, and a council was held wherein was there much whispering and low-voiced discussion.

An hour passed, and a second, and Nam-Bok slept, and the talk went on. The evening sun dipped toward the northwest, and at eleven at night was nearly due north. Then it was that the head man and the bone-scratcher separated themselves from the council and aroused Nam-Bok. He blinked up into their faces and turned on his side to sleep again. Opee-Kwan gripped him by the arm and kindly but firmly shook his senses back into him.

"Come, Nam-Bok, arise!" he commanded. "It be time."

"Another feast?" Nam-Bok cried. "Nay, I am not hungry. Go on with the eating and let me sleep."

"Time to be gone!" Koogah thundered.

But Opee-Kwan spoke more softly. "Thou wast bidarka-mate with me when we were boys," he said. "Together we first chased the seal and drew the salmon from the traps. And thou didst drag me back to life, Nam-Bok, when the sea closed over me and I was sucked down to the black rocks. Together we hungered and bore the chill of the frost, and together we crawled beneath the one fur and lay close to each other. And because of these things, and the kindness in which I stood to thee, it grieves me sore that thou shouldst return such a remark-able liar. We cannot understand, and our heads be dizzy with the things thou hast spoken. It is not good, and there has been much talk in the council. Wherefore we send thee away, that our heads may remain clear and strong and be not troubled by the unaccountable things."

"These things thou speakest of be shadows," Koogah took up the strain. "From the shadow-world thou hast brought them, and to the shadow-world thou must return them. Thy bidarka be ready, and the tribespeople wait. They may not sleep until thou art gone."

Nam-Bok was perplexed, but hearkened to the voice of the head man.

"If thou art Nam-Bok," Opee-Kwan was saying, "thou art a fearful and most wonderful liar; if thou art the shadow of Nam-Bok, then thou speakest of shadows, concerning which it is not good that living men have knowledge. This great village thou hast spoken of we deem the village of shadows. Therein flutter the souls of the dead; for the dead be many and the living few. The dead do not come back. Never have the dead come back — save thou with thy wonder-tales. It is not meet that the dead come back, and should we permit it, great trouble may be our portion."

Nam-Bok knew his people well and was aware that the voice of the council was supreme. So he allowed himself to be led down to the water's edge, where he was put aboard his bidarka and a paddle thrust into his hand. A stray wild-fowl honked somewhere to seaward, and the surf broke limply and hollowly on the sand. A dim twilight brooded over land and water, and in the north the sun smouldered, vague and troubled, and draped about with blood-red mists. The gulls were flying low. The off-shore wind blew keen and chill, and the black-massed clouds behind it gave promise of bitter weather.

"Out of the sea thou camest," Opee-Kwan chanted oracularly, "and back into the sea thou goest. Thus is balance achieved and all things brought to law."

Bask-Wah-Wan limped to the froth-mark and cried, "I bless thee, Nam-Bok, for that thou remembered me."

But Koogah, shoving Nam-Bok clear of the beach, tore the shawl from her shoulders and flung it into the bidarka.

"It is cold in the long nights," she wailed; "and the frost is prone to nip old

A shaft of light shot across the dim-lit sea and wrapped
boat and man in a splendor of red and gold

bones."

"The thing is a shadow," the bone-scratcher answered, "and shadows cannot keep thee warm."

Nam-Bok stood up that his voice might carry. "O Bask-Wah-Wan, mother that bore me!" he called. "Listen to the words of Nam-Bok, thy son. There be room in his bidarka for two, and he would that thou camest with him. For his journey is to where there are fish and oil in plenty. There the frost comes not, and life is easy, and the things of iron do the work of men. Wilt thou come, O Bask-Wah-Wan?"

She debated a moment, while the bidarka drifted swiftly from her, then raised her voice to a quavering treble. "I am old, Nam-Bok, and soon I shall pass down among the shadows. But I have no wish to go before my time. I am old, Nam-Bok, and I am afraid."

A shaft of light shot across the dim-lit sea and wrapped boat and man in a splendor of red and gold. Then a hush fell upon the fisherfolk, and only was heard the moan of the off-shore wind and the cries of the gulls flying low in the air.

25
THE DEATH OF LIGOUN

THE DEATH OF LIGOUN

"Hear now the death of Ligoun —"

The speaker ceased, or rather suspended utterance, and gazed upon me with an eye of understanding. I held the bottle between our eyes and the fire, indicated with my thumb the depth of the draught, and shoved it over to him; for was he not Palitlum, the Drinker? Many tales had he told me, and long had I waited for this scriptless scribe to speak of the things concerning Ligoun; for he, of all men living, knew these things best.

He tilted back his head with a grunt that slid swiftly into a gurgle, and the shadow of man's torso, monstrous beneath a huge inverted bottle, wavered and danced on the frown of the cliff at our backs. Palitlum released his lips from the glass with a caressing suck and glanced regretfully up into the ghostly vault of the sky where played the wan white light of the summer borealis.

"It be strange," he said; "cold like water and hot like fire. To the drinker it giveth strength, and from the drinker it taketh away strength. It maketh old men young, and young men old. To the man who is weary it leadeth him to get up and go onward, and to the man unweary it burdeneth him into sleep. My brother was possessed of the heart of a rabbit, yet did he drink of it, and forthwith slay four of his enemies. My father was like a great wolf, showing his teeth to all men, yet did he drink of it and was shot through the back, running swiftly away. It be most strange."

"It is 'Three Star,' and a better than what they poison their bellies with down there," I answered, sweeping my hand, as it were, over the yawning chasm of blackness and down to where the beach fires glinted far below — tiny jets of flame which gave proportion and reality to the night.

Palitlum sighed and shook his head. "Wherefore I am here with thee."

And here he embraced the bottle and me in a look which told more eloquently than speech of his shameless thirst.

"Nay," I said, snuggling the bottle in between my knees. "Speak now of Ligoun. Of the 'Three Star' we will hold speech hereafter."

"There be plenty, and I am not wearied," he pleaded brazenly. "But the feel of it on my lips, and I will speak great words of Ligoun and his last days."

"From the drinker it taketh away strength," I mocked, "and to the man unweary it burdeneth him into sleep."

"Thou art wise," he rejoined, without anger and pridelessly. "Like all of thy brothers, thou art wise. Waking or sleeping, the 'Three Star' be with thee, yet never have I known thee to drink overlong or overmuch. And the while you gather to you the gold that hides in our mountains and the fish that swim in our seas; and Palitlum, and the brothers of Palitlum, dig the gold for thee and net the fish, and are glad to be made glad when out of thy wisdom thou deemest it fit that the 'Three Star' should wet our lips."

"I was minded to hear of Ligoun," I said impatiently. "The night grows short, and we have a sore journey to-morrow."

I yawned and made as though to rise, but Palitlum betrayed a quick anxiety, and with abruptness began:—

"It was Ligoun's desire, in his old age, that peace should be among the tribes. As a young man he had been first of the fighting men and chief over the war-chiefs of the Islands and the Passes. All his days had been full of fighting. More marks he boasted of bone and lead and iron than any other man. Three wives he had, and for each wife two sons; and the sons, eldest born and last all, died by his side in battle. Restless as the bald-face, he ranged wide and far — north to Unalaska and the Shallow Sea; south to the Queen Charlottes, ay, even did he go with the Kakes, it is told, to far Puget Sound, and slay thy brothers in their sheltered houses.

"But, as I say, in his old age he looked for peace among the tribes. Not that he was become afraid, or overfond of the corner by the fire and the well-filled pot. For he slew with the shrewdness and blood-hunger of the fiercest, drew in his belly to famine with the youngest, and with the stoutest faced the bitter seas and stinging trail. But because of his many deeds, and in punishment, a warship carried him away, even to thy country, O Hair-Face and Boston Man; and the years were many ere he came back, and I was grown to something more than a boy and something less than a young man. And Ligoun, being childless in his old age, made much of me, and grown wise, gave me of his wisdom.

"'It be good to fight, O Palitlum,' said he. Nay, O Hair-Face, for I was unknown as Palitlum in those days, being called Olo, the Ever-Hungry. The drink was to come after. 'It be good to fight,' spake Ligoun, 'but it be foolish. In the Boston Man Country, as I saw with mine eyes, they are not given to fighting one with another, and they be strong. Wherefore, of their strength, they come against us of the Islands and Passes, and we are as camp smoke and sea mist before them. Wherefore I say it be good to fight, most good, but it be likewise foolish.'

"And because of this, though first always of the fighting men, Ligoun's voice was loudest, ever, for peace. And when he was very old, being greatest of chiefs and richest of men, he gave a potlatch. Never was there such a potlatch. Five hundred canoes were lined against the river bank, and in each canoe there came not less than ten of men and women. Eight tribes were there; from the first and oldest man to the last and youngest babe were they there. And then there were men from far-distant tribes, great travellers and seekers who had heard of the potlatch of Ligoun. And for the length of seven days they filled their bellies with his meat and drink. Eight thousand blankets did he give to them, as I well know, for who but I kept the tally and apportioned according to degree and rank? And in the end Ligoun was a poor man; but his name was on all men's lips, and other chiefs gritted their teeth in envy that he should be so great.

"And so, because there was weight to his words, he counselled peace; and he journeyed to every potlatch and feast and tribal gathering that he might counsel peace. And so it came that we journeyed together, Ligoun and I, to the great feast given by Niblack, who was chief over the river Indians of the Skoot, which is not far from the Stickeen. This was in the last days, and Ligoun was very old and very close to death. He coughed of cold weather and camp smoke, and often the red blood ran from out his mouth till we looked for him to die.

"'Nay,' he said once at such time; 'it were better that I should die when the blood leaps to the knife, and there is a clash of steel and smell of powder, and men crying aloud what of the cold iron and quick lead.' So, it be plain, O Hair-Face, that his heart was yet strong for battle.

"It is very far from the Chilcat to the Skoot, and we were many days in the canoes. And the while the men bent to the paddles, I sat at the feet of Ligoun and received the Law. Of small need for me to say the Law, O Hair-Face, for it be known to me that in this thou art well skilled. Yet do I speak of the Law of blood for blood, and rank for rank. Also did Ligoun go deeper into the matter, saying:—

"'But know this, O Olo, that there be little honor in the killing of a man less than thee. Kill always the man who is greater, and thy honor shall be according to his greatness. But if, of two men, thou killest the lesser, then is shame thine, for which the very squaws will lift their lips at thee. As I say, peace be good; but remember, O Olo, if kill thou must, that thou killest by the Law.'

"It is a way of the Thlinket-folk," Palitlum vouchsafed half apologetically.

And I remembered the gun-fighters and bad men of my own Western land, and was not perplexed at the way of the Thlinket-folk.

"In time," Palitlum continued, "we came to Chief Niblack and the Skoots. It was a feast great almost as the potlatch of Ligoun. There were we of the Chilcat, and the Sitkas, and the Stickeens who are neighbors to the Skoots, and the Wrangels and the Hoonahs. There were Sundowns and Tahkos from Port Houghton, and their neighbors the Awks from Douglass Channel; the Naass River people, and the Tongas from north of Dixon, and the Kakes who come from the island called Kupreanoff. Then there were Siwashes from Vancouver, Cassiars from the Gold Mountains,

Teslin men, and even Sticks from the Yukon Country.

"It was a mighty gathering. But first of all, there was to be a meeting of the chiefs with Niblack, and a drowning of all enmities in quass. The Russians it was who showed us the way of making quass, for so my father told me, — my father, who got it from his father before him. But to this quass had Niblack added many things, such as sugar, flour, dried apples, and hops, so that it was a man's drink, strong and good. Not so good as 'Three Star,' O Hair-Face, yet good.

"This quass-feast was for the chiefs, and the chiefs only, and there was a score of them. But Ligoun being very old and very great, it was given that I walk with him that he might lean upon my shoulder and that I might ease him down when he took his seat and raise him up when he arose. At the door of Niblack's house, which was of logs and very big, each chief, as was the custom, laid down his spear or rifle and his knife. For as thou knowest, O Hair-Face, strong drink quickens, and old hates flame up, and head and hand are swift to act. But I noted that Ligoun had brought two knives, the one he left outside the door, the other slipped under his blanket, snug to the grip. The other chiefs did likewise, and I was troubled for what was to come.

"The chiefs were ranged, sitting, in a big circle about the room. I stood at Ligoun's elbow. In the middle was the barrel of quass, and by it a slave to serve the drink. First, Niblack made oration, with much show of friendship and many fine words. Then he gave a sign, and the slave dipped a gourd full of quass and passed it to Ligoun, as was fit, for his was the highest rank.

"Ligoun drank it, to the last drop, and I gave him my strength to get on his feet so that he, too, might make oration. He made kind speech for the many tribes, noted the greatness of Niblack to give such a feast, counselled for peace as was his custom, and at the end said that the quass was very good.

"Then Niblack drank, being next of rank to Ligoun, and after him one chief and another in degree and order. And each spoke friendly words and said that the quass was good, till all had drunk. Did I say all? Nay, not all, O Hair-Face. For last of them was one, a lean and cat-like man, young of face, with a quick and daring eye, who drank darkly, and spat forth upon the ground, and spoke no word.

"To not say that the quass was good were insult; to spit forth upon the ground were worse than insult. And this very thing did he do. He was known for a chief over the Sticks of the Yukon, and further naught was known of him.

"As I say, it was an insult. But mark this, O Hair-Face: it was an insult, not to Niblack the feast-giver, but to the man chiefest of rank who sat among those of the circle. And that man was Ligoun. There was no sound. All eyes were upon him to see what he might do. He made no movement. His withered lips trembled not into speech; nor did a nostril quiver, nor an eyelid droop. But I saw that he looked wan and gray, as I have seen old men look of bitter mornings when famine pressed, and the women wailed and the children whimpered, and there was no meat nor sign of meat. And as the old men looked, so looked Ligoun.

"There was no sound. It were as a circle of the dead, but that each chief felt beneath his blanket to make sure, and that each chief glanced to his neighbor, right and left, with a measuring eye. I was a stripling; the things I had seen were few; yet I knew it to be the moment one meets but once in all a lifetime.

"The Stick rose up, with every eye upon him, and crossed the room till he stood before Ligoun.

"'I am Opitsah, the Knife,' he said.

"But Ligoun said naught, nor looked at him, but gazed unblinking at the ground.

"'You are Ligoun,' Opitsah said. 'You have killed many men. I am still alive.'

"And still Ligoun said naught, though he made the sign to me and with my strength arose and stood upright on his two feet. He was as an old pine, naked and gray, but still a-shoulder to the frost and storm. His eyes were unblinking, and as he had not heard Opitsah, so it seemed he did not see him.

"And Opitsah was mad with anger, and danced stiff-legged before him, as men do when they wish to give another shame. And Opitsah sang a song of his own greatness and the greatness of his people, filled with bad words for the Chilcats and for Ligoun. And as he danced and sang, Opitsah threw off his blanket and with his knife drew bright circles before the face of Ligoun. And the song he sang was the Song of the Knife.

"And there was no other sound, only the singing of Opitsah, and the circle of chiefs that were as dead, save that the flash of the knife seemed to draw smouldering fire from their eyes. And Ligoun, also, was very still. Yet did he know his death, and was unafraid. And the knife sang closer and yet closer to his face, but his eyes were unblinking and he swayed not to right or left, or this way or that.

"And Opitsah drove in the knife, so, twice on the forehead of Ligoun, and the red blood leaped after it. And then it was that Ligoun gave me the sign to bear up under him with my youth that he might walk. And he laughed with a great scorn, full in the face of Opitsah, the Knife. And he brushed Opitsah to the side, as one brushes to the side a low-hanging branch on the trail and passes on.

"And I knew and understood, for there was but shame in the killing of Opitsah before the faces of a score of greater chiefs. I remembered the Law, and knew Ligoun had it in mind to kill by the Law. And who, chiefest of rank but himself, was there but Niblack? And toward Niblack, leaning on my arm, he walked. And to his other arm, clinging and striking, was Opitsah, too small to soil with his blood the hands of so great a man. And though the knife of Opitsah bit in again and again, Ligoun noted it not, nor winced. And in this fashion we three went our way across the room, Niblack sitting in his blanket and fearful of our coming.

"And now old hates flamed up and forgotten grudges were remembered. Lamuk, a Kake, had had a brother drowned in the bad water of the Stickeen, and the Stickeens had not paid in blankets for their bad water, as was the custom to pay. So Lamuk drove straight with his long knife to the heart of Klok-Kutz the Stickeen. And Katchahook remembered a quarrel of the Naass River people with the Tongas of north of Dixon, and the chief of the Tongas he slew with a pistol which made much noise. And the blood-hunger gripped all the men who sat in the circle, and chief slew chief, or was slain, as chance might be. Also did they stab and shoot at Ligoun, for whoso killed him won great honor and would be unforgotten for the deed. And they were about him like wolves about a moose, only they were so many they were in their own way, and they slew one another to make room. And there was great confusion.

"But Ligoun went slowly, without haste, as though many years were yet before him. It seemed that he was certain he would make his kill, in his own way, ere they could slay him. And as I say, he went slowly, and knives bit into him, and he was red with blood. And though none sought after me, who was a mere stripling, yet did the knives find me, and the hot bullets burn me. And still Ligoun leaned his weight on my youth, and Opitsah struck at him, and we three went forward. And when we stood by Niblack, he was afraid, and covered his head with his blanket. The Skoots were ever cowards.

"And Goolzug and Kadishan, the one a fish-eater and the other a meat-killer, closed together for the honor of their tribes. And they raged madly about, and in their battling swung against the knees of Opitsah, who was overthrown and trampled upon. And a knife, singing through the air, smote Skulpin, of the Sitkas, in the throat, and he flung his arms out blindly, reeling, and dragged me down in his fall.

"And from the ground I beheld Ligoun bend over Niblack, and uncover the blanket from his head, and turn up his face to the light. And Ligoun was in no haste. Being blinded with his own blood, he swept it out of his eyes with the back of his hand, so he might see and be sure. And when he was sure that the upturned face was the face of Niblack, he drew the knife across his throat as one draws a knife across the throat of a trembling deer. And then Ligoun stood erect, singing his death-song and swaying gently to and fro. And Skulpin, who had dragged me down, shot with a pistol from where he lay, and Ligoun toppled and fell, as an old pine topples and falls in the teeth of the wind."

Palitlum ceased. His eyes, smouldering moodily, were bent upon the fire, and his cheek was dark with blood.

"And thou, Palitlum?" I demanded.

"And thou?"

"I? I did remember the Law, and I slew Opitsah the Knife, which was well. And I drew Ligoun's own knife from the throat of Niblack, and slew Skulpin, who had dragged me down. For I was a stripling, and I could slay any man and it were honor. And further, Ligoun being dead, there was no

...and Ligoun toppled and fell, as an old pine topples and falls in the teeth of the wind

need for my youth, and I laid about me with his knife, choosing the chiefest of rank that yet remained."

Palitlum fumbled under his shirt and drew forth a beaded sheath, and from the sheath, a knife. It was a knife home-wrought and crudely fashioned from a whip-saw file; a knife such as one may find possessed by old men in a hundred Alaskan villages.

"The knife of Ligoun?" I said, and Palitlum nodded.

"And for the knife of Ligoun," I said, "will I give thee ten bottles of 'Three Star.'"

But Palitlum looked at me slowly. "Hair-Face, I am weak as water, and easy as a woman. I have soiled my belly with quass, and hooch, and 'Three Star.' My eyes are blunted, my ears have lost their keenness, and my strength has gone into fat. And I am without honor in these days, and am called Palitlum, the Drinker. Yet honor was mine at the potlatch of Niblack, on the Skoot, and the memory of it, and the memory of Ligoun, be dear to me. Nay, didst thou turn the sea itself into 'Three Star' and say that it were all mine for the knife, yet would I keep the knife. I am Palitlum, the Drinker, but I was once Olo, the Ever-Hungry, who bore up Ligoun with his youth!"

"Thou art a great man, Palitlum," I said, "and I honor thee."

Palitlum reached out his hand.

"The 'Three Star' between thy knees be mine for the tale I have told," he said.

And as I looked on the frown of the cliff at our backs, I saw the shadow of a man's torso, monstrous beneath a huge inverted bottle.

26
LI WAN, THE FAIR

LI WAN, THE FAIR

"The sun sinks, Canim, and the heat of the day is gone!"

So called Li Wan to the man whose head was hidden beneath the squirrel-skin robe, but she called softly, as though divided between the duty of waking him and the fear of him awake. For she was afraid of this big husband of hers, who was like unto none of the men she had known.

The moose-meat sizzled uneasily, and she moved the frying-pan to one side of the red embers. As she did so she glanced warily at the two Hudson Bay dogs dripping eager slaver from their scarlet tongues and following her every movement. They were huge, hairy fellows, crouched to leeward in the thin smoke-wake of the fire to escape the swarming myriads of mosquitoes. As Li Wan gazed down the steep to where the Kondike flung its swollen flood between the hills, one of the dogs bellied its way forward like a worm, and with a deft, catlike stroke of the paw dipped a chunk of hot meat out of the pan to the ground. But Li Wan caught him from out the tail of her eye, and he sprang back with a snap and a snarl as she rapped him over the nose with a stick of firewood.

"Nay, Olo," she laughed, recovering the meat without removing her eye from him. "Thou art ever hungry, and for that thy nose leads thee into endless troubles."

But the mate of Olo joined him, and together they defied the woman. The hair on their backs and shoulders bristled in recurrent waves of anger, and the thin lips writhed and lifted into ugly wrinkles, exposing the flesh-tearing fangs, cruel and menacing. Their very noses serrulated and shook in brute passion, and they snarled as the wolves snarl, with all the hatred and malignity of the breed impelling them to spring upon the woman and drag her down.

"And thou, too, Bash, fierce as thy master and never at peace with the hand that feeds thee! This is not thy quarrel, so that be thine! and that!"

As she cried, she drove at them with the firewood, but they avoided the blows and refused to retreat. They separated and approached her from either side, crouching low and snarling. Li Wan had struggled with the wolf-dog for mastery from the time she toddled among the skin-bales of the teepee, and she knew a crisis was at hand. Bash had halted, his muscles stiff and tense for the spring; Olo was yet creeping into striking distance.

Grasping two blazing sticks by the charred ends, she faced the brutes. The one held back, but Bash sprang, and she met him in mid-air with the flaming weapon. There were sharp yelps of pain and swift odors of burning hair and flesh as he rolled in the dirt and the woman ground the fiery embers into his mouth. Snapping wildly, he flung himself sidewise out of her reach and in a frenzy of fear scrambled for safety. Olo, on the other side, had begun his retreat, when Li Wan reminded him of her primacy by hurling a heavy stick of wood into his ribs. Then the pair retreated under a rain of firewood, and on the edge of the camp fell to licking their wounds and whimpering by turns and snarling.

Li Wan blew the ashes off the meat and sat down again. Her heart had not gone up a beat, and the incident was already old, for this was the routine of life. Canim had not stirred during the disorder, but instead had set up a lusty snoring.

"Come, Canim!" she called. "The heat of the day is gone, and the trail waits for our feet."

The squirrel-skin robe was agitated and cast aside by a brown arm. Then the man's eyelids fluttered and drooped again.

"His pack is heavy," she thought, "and he is tired with the work of the morning."

A mosquito stung her on the neck, and she daubed the unprotected spot with wet clay from a ball she had convenient to hand. All morning, toiling up the divide and enveloped in a cloud of the pests, the man and woman had plastered themselves with the sticky mud, which, drying in the sun, covered their faces with masks of clay. These masks, broken in divers places by the movement of the facial muscles, had constantly to be renewed, so that the deposit was irregular of depth and peculiar of aspect.

Li Wan shook Canim gently but with persistence till he roused and sat up. His first glance was to the sun, and after consulting the celestial timepiece he hunched over to the fire and fell-to ravenously on the meat. He was a large Indian fully six feet in height, deep-chested and heavy-muscled, and his eyes were keener and vested with greater mental vigor than the average of his kind. The lines of will had marked his face deeply, and this, coupled with a sternness and primitiveness, advertised a native indomitability, unswerving of purpose, and prone, when thwarted, to sullen cruelty.

"To-morrow, Li Wan, we shall feast." He sucked a marrow-bone clean and threw it to the dogs. "We shall have *flapjacks* fried in *bacon grease*, and *sugar,* which is more toothsome—"

"*Flapjacks?*" she questioned, mouthing the word curiously.

"Ay," Canim answered with superiority; "and I shall teach you new ways of cookery. Of these things I speak you are ignorant, and of many more things besides. You have lived your days in a little corner of the earth and know nothing. But I," — he straightened himself and looked at her pridefully, — "I am a great traveller, and have been all places, even among the white people, and I am versed in their ways, and in the ways of many peoples. I am not a tree, born to stand in one place always and know not what there be over the next hill; for I am Canim, the Canoe, made to go here and there and to journey and quest up and down the length and breadth of the world."

She bowed her head humbly. "It is true. I have eaten fish and meat and berries all my days and lived in a little corner of the earth. Nor did I dream the world was so large until you stole me from my people and I cooked and carried for you on the endless trails." She looked up at him suddenly. "Tell me, Canim, does this trail ever end?"

"Nay," he answered. "My trail is like the world; it never ends. My trail *is* the world, and I have travelled it since the time my legs could carry me, and I shall travel it until I die. My father and my mother may be dead, but it is long since I looked upon them, and I do not care. My tribe is like your tribe. It stays in the one place — which is far from here, — but I care naught for my tribe, for I am Canim, the Canoe!"

"And must I, Li Wan, who am weary, travel always your trail until I die?"

"You, Li Wan, are my wife, and the wife travels the husband's trail wheresoever it goes. It is the law. And were it not the law, yet would it be the law of Canim, who is lawgiver unto himself and his."

She bowed her head again, for she knew no other law than that man was the master of woman.

"Be not in haste," Canim cautioned her, as she began to strap the meagre camp outfit to her pack. "The sun is yet hot, and the trail leads down and the footing is good."

She dropped her work obediently and resumed her seat.

Canim regarded her with speculative interest. "You do not squat on your hams like other women," he remarked.

"No," she answered. "It never came easy. It tires me, and I cannot take my rest that way."

"And why is it your feet point not straight before you?"

"I do not know, save that they are unlike the feet of other women."

A satisfied light crept into his eyes, but otherwise he gave no sign.

"Like other women, your hair is black; but have you ever noticed that it is soft and fine, softer and finer than the hair of other women?"

"I have noticed," she answered shortly, for she was not pleased at such cold analysis of her sex-deficiencies.

"It is a year, now, since I took you from your people," he went on, "and you are nigh as shy and afraid of me as when first I looked upon you. How does this thing be?"

Li Wan shook her head. "I am afraid of you, Canim, you are so big and strange. And further, before you looked upon me even, I was afraid of all the young men. I do not know ... I cannot say ... only it seemed, somehow, as though I should not be for them, as though ..."

"Ay," he encouraged, impatient at her faltering.

"As though they were not my kind."

"Not your kind?" he demanded slowly. "Then what is your kind?"

"I do not know, I..." She shook her head in a bewildered manner. "I cannot put into words the way I felt. It was strangeness in me. I was unlike other maidens, who sought the young men slyly. I could not care for the young men that way. It would have been a great wrong, it seemed, and an ill deed."

"What is the first thing you remember?" Canim asked with abrupt irrelevance.

"Pow-Wah-Kaan, my mother."

"And naught else before Pow-Wah-Kaan?"

"Naught else."

But Canim, holding her eyes with his, searched her secret soul and saw it waver.

"Think, and think hard, Li Wan!" he threatened.

She stammered, and her eyes were piteous and pleading, but his will dominated her and wrung from her lips the reluctant speech.

"But it was only dreams, Canim, ill dreams of childhood, shadows of things not real, visions such as the dogs, sleeping in the sun-warmth, behold and whine out against."

"Tell me," he commanded, "of the things before Pow-Wah-Kaan, your mother."

"They are forgotten memories," she protested. "As a child I dreamed awake, with my eyes open to the day, and when I spoke of the strange things I saw I was laughed at, and the other children were afraid and drew away from me. And when I spoke of the things I saw to Pow-Wah-Kaan, she chided me and said they were evil; also she beat me. It was a sickness, I believe, like the falling-sickness that comes to old men; and in time I grew better and dreamed no more. And now... I cannot remember" — she brought her hand in a confused manner to her forehead — "they are there, somewhere, but I cannot find them, only ..."

"Only," Canim repeated, holding her.

"Only one thing. But you will laugh at its foolishness, it is so unreal."

"Nay, Li Wan. Dreams are dreams. They may be memories of other lives we have lived. I was once a moose. I firmly believe I was once a moose, what of the things I have seen in dreams, and heard."

Strive as he would to hide it, a growing anxiety was manifest, but Li Wan, groping after the words with which to paint the picture, took no heed.

"I see a snow-tramped space among the trees," she began, "and across the snow the sign of a man where he has dragged himself heavily on hand and knee. And I see, too, the man in the snow, and it seems I am very close to him when I look. He is unlike real men, for he has hair on his face, much hair, and the hair of his face and head is yellow like the summer coat of the weasel. His eyes are closed, but they open and search about. They are blue like the sky, and look into mine and search no more. And his hand moves, slow, as from weakness, and I feel ..."

"Ay," Canim whispered hoarsely. "You feel — ?"

"No! no!" she cried in haste. "I feel nothing. Did I say 'feel'? I did not mean it. It could not be that I should mean it. I see, and I see only, and that is all I see — a man in the snow, with eyes like the sky, and hair like the weasel. I have seen it many times, and always it is the same — a man in the snow —"

"And do you see yourself?" he asked, leaning forward and regarding her intently. "Do you ever see yourself and the man in the snow?"

"Why should I see myself? Am I not real?"

His muscles relaxed and he sank back, an exultant satisfaction in his eyes which he turned from her so that she might not see.

"I will tell you, Li Wan," he spoke decisively; "you were a little bird in some life before, a little moose-bird, when you saw this thing, and the memory of it is with you yet. It is not strange. I was once a moose, and my father's father afterward became a bear — so said the shaman, and the shaman cannot lie. Thus, on the Trail of the Gods we pass from life to life, and the gods know only and understand. Dreams and the shadows of dreams be memories, nothing more, and the dog, whining asleep in the sun-warmth, doubtless sees and remembers things gone before. Bash, there, was a warrior once. I do firmly believe he was once a warrior."

Canim tossed a bone to the brute and got upon his feet. "Come, let us begone. The sun is yet hot, but it will get no cooler."

"And these white people, what are they like?" Li Wan made bold to ask.

"Like you and me," he answered, "only they are less dark of skin. You will be among them ere the day is dead."

Canim lashed the sleeping-robe to his one-hundred-and-fifty-pound pack, smeared his face with wet clay, and sat down to rest till Li Wan had finished loading the dogs. Olo cringed at sight of the club in her hand, and gave no trouble when the bundle of forty pounds and odd was strapped upon him. But Bash was aggrieved and truculent, and could not forbear to whimper and snarl as he was forced to receive the burden. He bristled his back and bared his teeth as she drew the straps tight, the while throwing all the malignancy of his nature into the glances shot at her sideways and backward. And Canim chuckled and said, "Did I not say he was once a very great warrior?"

"These furs will bring a price," he remarked as he adjusted his head-strap and lifted his pack clear of the ground. "A big price. The white men pay well for such goods, for they have no time to hunt and are soft to the cold. Soon shall we feast, Li Wan, as you have feasted never in all the lives you have lived before."

She grunted acknowledgment and gratitude for her lord's condescension, slipped into the harness, and bent forward to the load.

"The next time I am born, I would be born a white man," he added, and swung off down the trail which dived into the gorge at his feet.

The dogs followed close at his heels, and Li Wan brought up the rear. But her thoughts were far away, across the Ice Mountains to the east, to the little corner of the earth where her childhood had been lived. Ever as a child, she remembered, she had been looked upon as strange, as one with an affliction. Truly she had dreamed awake and been scolded and beaten for the remarkable visions she saw, till, after a time, she had outgrown them. But not utterly. Though they troubled her no more waking, they came to her in her sleep, grown woman that she was, and many a night of nightmare was hers, filled with fluttering shapes, vague and meaningless. The talk with Canim had excited her, and down all the twisted slant of the divide she harked back to the mocking fantasies of her dreams.

"Let us take breath," Canim said, when they had tapped midway the bed of the main creek.

He rested his pack on a jutting rock, slipped the head-strap, and sat down. Li Wan joined him, and the dogs sprawled panting on the ground beside them. At their feet rippled the glacial drip of the hills, but it was muddy and discolored, as if soiled by some commotion of the earth.

"Why is this?" Li Wan asked.

"Because of the white men who work in the ground. Listen!" He held up his hand, and they heard the ring of pick and shovel, and the sound of men's voices. "They are made mad by *gold,* and work without ceasing that they may find it. *Gold?* It is yellow and comes from the ground, and is considered of great value. It is also a measure of price."

But Li Wan's roving eyes had called her attention from him. A few yards below and partly screened by a clump of young spruce, the tiered logs of a cabin rose to meet its overhanging roof of dirt. A thrill ran through her, and all her dream-phantoms roused up and stirred about uneasily.

"Canim," she whispered in an agony of apprehension. "Canim, what is that?"

"The white man's teepee, in which he eats and sleeps."

She eyed it wistfully, grasping its virtues at a glance and thrilling again at the unaccountable sensations it aroused. "It must be very warm in time of frost," she said aloud, though she felt that she must make strange sounds with her lips.

She felt impelled to utter them, but did not, and the next instant Canim said, "It is called a *cabin.*"

Her heart gave a great leap. The sounds! the very sounds! She looked about her in sudden awe. How should she know that strange word before ever she heard it? What could be the matter? And then with a shock, half of fear and half of delight, she realized that for the first time in her life there had been sanity and significance in the promptings of her dreams.

"*Cabin,*" she repeated to herself. "*Cabin.*" An incoherent flood of dream-stuff welled up and up till her head was dizzy and her heart seemed bursting. Shadows, and looming bulks of things, and unintelligible associations fluttered and whirled about, and she strove vainly with her consciousness to grasp and hold them. For she felt that there, in that welter of memories, was the key of the mystery; could she but grasp and hold it, all would be clear and plain —

O Canim! O Pow-Wah-Kaan! O shades and shadows, what was that?

She turned to Canim, speechless and trembling, the dream-stuff in mad, overwhelming riot. She was sick and fainting, and could only listen to the ravishing sounds which proceeded from the cabin in a wonderful rhythm.

"Hum, *fiddle,*" Canim vouchsafed.

But she did not hear him, for in the ecstasy she was experiencing, it seemed at last that all things were coming clear. Now! now! she thought. A sudden moisture swept into her eyes, and the tears trickled down her cheeks. The mystery was unlocking, but the faintness was overpowering her. If only she could hold herself long enough! If only — but the landscape bent and crumpled up, and the hills swayed back and forth across the sky as she sprang upright and screamed, "*Daddy! Daddy!*" Then the sun reeled, and darkness smote her, and she pitched forward limp and headlong among the rocks.

Canim looked to see if her neck had been broken by the heavy pack, grunted his satisfaction, and threw water upon her from the creek. She came to slowly, with choking sobs, and sat up.

"It is not good, the hot sun on the head," he ventured.

And she answered, "No, it is not good, and the pack bore upon me hard."

"We shall camp early, so that you may sleep long and win strength," he said gently. "And if we go now, we shall be the quicker to bed."

Li Wan said nothing, but tottered to her feet in obedience and stirred up the dogs. She took the swing of his pace mechanically, and followed him past the cabin, scarce daring to breathe. But no sounds issued forth, though the door was open and smoke curling upward from the sheet-iron stovepipe.

They came upon a man in the bend of the creek, white of skin and blue of eye, and for a moment Li Wan saw the other man in the snow. But she saw dimly, for she was weak and tired from what she had undergone. Still, she looked at him curiously, and stopped with Canim to watch him at his work. He was washing gravel in a large pan, with a circular, tilting movement; and as they looked, giving a deft flirt, he flashed up the yellow gold in a broad streak across the bottom of the pan.

"Very rich, this creek," Canim told her, as they went on. "Sometime I will find such a creek, and then I shall be a big man."

Cabins and men grew more plentiful, till they came to where the main portion of the creek was spread out before them. It was the scene of a vast devastation. Everywhere the earth was torn and rent as though by a Titan's struggles. Where there were no upthrown mounds of gravel, great holes and trenches yawned, and chasms where the thick rime of the earth had been peeled to bed-rock. There was no worn channel for the creek, and its waters, dammed up, diverted, flying through the air on giddy flumes, trickling into sinks and low places, and raised by huge water-wheels, were used and used again a thousand times. The hills had been stripped of their trees, and their raw sides gored and perforated by great timber-slides and prospect holes. And over all, like a monstrous race of ants, was flung an army of men — mud-covered, dirty, dishevelled men, who crawled in and out of the holes of their digging, crept like big bugs along the flumes, and toiled and sweated at the gravel-heaps which they kept in constant unrest — men, as far as the eye could see, even to the rims of the hilltops, digging, tearing, and scouring the face of nature.

Li Wan was appalled at the tremendous upheaval. "Truly, these men are mad," she said to Canim.

"Small wonder. The gold they dig after is a great thing," he replied. "It is the greatest thing in the world."

For hours they threaded the chaos of greed, Canim eagerly intent, Li Wan weak and listless. She knew she had been on the verge of disclosure, and she felt that she was still on the verge of disclosure, but the nervous strain she had undergone had tired her, and she passively waited for the thing, she knew not what, to happen. From every hand her senses snatched up and conveyed to her innumerable impressions, each of which became a dull excitation to her jaded imagination. Somewhere within her, responsive notes were answering to the things without, forgotten and undreamed-of correspondences were being renewed; and she was aware of it in an incurious way, and her soul was troubled, but she was not equal to the mental exultation necessary to transmute and understand. So she plodded wearily on at the heels of her lord, content to wait for that which she knew, somewhere, somehow, must happen.

After undergoing the mad bondage of man, the creek finally returned to its ancient ways, all soiled and smirched from its toil, and coiled lazily among the broad flats and timbered spaces where the valley widened to its mouth. Here the "pay" ran out, and men were loth to loiter with the lure yet beyond. And here, as Li Wan paused to prod Olo with her staff, she heard the mellow silver of a woman's laughter.

Before a cabin sat a woman, fair of skin and rosy as a child, dimpling with glee at the words of another woman in the doorway. But the woman who sat shook about her great masses of dark, wet hair which yielded up its dampness to the warm caresses of the sun.

For an instant Li Wan stood transfixed. Then she was aware of a blinding flash, and a snap, as though something gave way; and the woman before the cabin vanished, and the cabin and the tall spruce timber, and the jagged sky-line, and Li Wan saw another woman, in the shine of another sun, brushing great masses of black hair, and singing as she brushed. And Li Wan heard the words of the song, and understood, and was a child again. She was smitten with a vision, wherein all the troublesome dreams merged and became one, and shapes and shadows took up their accustomed round, and all was clear and plain and real. Many pictures jostled past, strange scenes, and trees, and flowers, and people; and she saw them and knew them all.

"When you were a little bird, a little moose-bird," Canim said, his eyes upon her and burning into her.

"When I was a little moose-bird," she whispered, so faint and low he scarcely heard. And she knew she lied, as she bent her head to the strap and took the swing of the trail.

And such was the strangeness of it, the real now became unreal. The mile tramp and the pitching of camp by the edge of the stream seemed like a passage in a nightmare. She cooked the meat, fed the dogs, and unlashed the packs as in a dream, and it was not until Canim began to sketch his next wandering that she became herself again.

"The Kondike runs into the Yukon," he was saying; "a mighty river, mightier than the Mackenzie, of which you know. So we go, you and I, down to Fort o' Yukon. With dogs, in time of winter, it is twenty sleeps. Then we follow the Yukon away into the west — one hundred sleeps, two hundred — I have never heard. It is very far. And then we come to the sea. You know nothing of the sea, so let me tell you. As the lake is to the island, so the sea is to the land; all the rivers run to it, and it is without end. I have seen it at Hudson Bay; I have yet to see it in Alaska. And then we may take a great canoe upon the sea, you and I, Li Wan, or we may follow the land into the south many a hundred sleeps. And after that I do not know, save that I am Canim, the Canoe, wanderer and far-journeyer over the earth!"

She sat and listened, and fear ate into her heart as she pondered over this plunge into the illimitable wilderness. "It is a weary way," was all she said, head bowed on knee in resignation.

Then it was a splendid thought came to her, and at the wonder of it she was all aglow. She went down to the stream and washed the dried clay from her face. When the ripples died away, she stared long at her mirrored features; but sun and weatherbeat had done their work, and, what of roughness and bronze, her skin was not soft and dimpled as a child's. But the thought was still splendid and the glow unabated as she crept in beside her husband under the sleeping-robe.

She lay awake, staring up at the blue of the sky and waiting for Canim to sink into the first deep sleep. When this came about, she wormed slowly and carefully away, tucked the robe around him, and stood up. At her second step, Bash growled savagely. She whispered persuasively to him and glanced at the man. Canim was snoring profoundly. Then she turned, and with swift, noiseless feet sped up the back trail.

Mrs. Evelyn Van Wyck was just preparing for bed. Bored by the duties put upon her by society, her wealth, and widowed blessedness, she had journeyed into the Northland and gone to housekeeping in a cosey cabin on the edge of the diggings. Here, aided and abetted by her friend and companion, Myrtle Giddings, she played at living close to the soil, and cultivated the primitive with refined abandon.

She strove to get away from the generations of culture and parlor selection, and sought the earth-grip her ancestors had forfeited. Likewise she induced mental states which she fondly believed to approximate those of the stone-folk, and just now, as she put up her hair for the pillow, she was indulging her fancy with a palaeolithic wooing. The details consisted principally of cave-dwellings and cracked marrow-bones, intersprinkled with fierce carnivora, hairy mammoths, and combats with rude flaked knives of flint; but the sensations were delicious. And as Evelyn Van Wyck fled through the sombre forest aisles before the too arduous advances of her slant-browed, skin-clad wooer, the door of the cabin opened, without the courtesy of a knock, and a skin-clad woman, savage and primitive, came in.

"Mercy!"

With a leap that would have done credit to a cave-woman, Miss Giddings landed in safety behind the table. But Mrs. Van Wyck held her ground. She noticed that the intruder was laboring under a strong excitement, and cast a swift glance backward to assure herself that the way was clear to the bunk, where the big Colt's revolver lay beneath a pillow.

"Greeting, O Woman of the Wondrous Hair," said Li Wan.

But she said it in her own tongue, the tongue spoken in but a little corner of the earth, and the women did not understand.

"Shall I go for help?" Miss Giddings quavered.

"The poor creature is harmless, I think," Mrs. Van Wyck replied. "And just look at her skin-clothes, ragged and trail-worn and all that. They are certainly unique. I shall buy them for my collection. Get my sack, Myrtle, please, and set up the scales."

Li Wan followed the shaping of the lips, but the words were unintelligible, and then, and for the first time, she realized, in a moment of suspense and indecision, that there was no medium of communication between them.

And at the passion of her dumbness she cried out, with arms stretched wide apart, "O Woman, thou art sister of mine!"

The tears coursed down her cheeks as she yearned toward them, and the break in her voice carried the sorrow she could not utter. But Miss Giddings was trembling, and even Mrs. Van Wyck was disturbed.

"I would live as you live. Thy ways are my ways, and our ways be one. My husband is Canim, the Canoe, and he is big and strange, and I am afraid. His trail is all the world and never ends, and I am weary. My mother was like you, and her hair was as thine, and her eyes. And life was soft to me then, and the sun warm."

She knelt humbly, and bent her head at Mrs. Van Wyck's feet. But Mrs. Van Wyck drew away, frightened at her vehemence.

Li Wan stood up, panting for speech. Her dumb lips could not articulate her overmastering consciousness of kind.

"Trade? you trade?" Mrs. Van Wyck questioned, slipping, after the fashion of the superior peoples, into pigeon tongue.

She touched Li Wan's ragged skins to indicate her choice, and poured several hundreds of gold into the blower. She stirred the dust about and trickled its yellow lustre temptingly through her fingers. But Li Wan saw only the fingers, milk-white and shapely, tapering daintily to the rosy, jewel-like nails. She placed her own hand alongside, all work-worn and calloused, and wept.

Mrs. Van Wyck misunderstood. "Gold," she encouraged. "Good gold! You trade? You changee for changee?" And she laid her hand again on Li Wan's skin garments.

"How much? You sell? How much?" she persisted, running her hand against the way of the hair so that she might make sure of the sinew-thread seam.

But Li Wan was deaf as well, and the woman's speech was without significance. Dismay at her failure sat upon her. How could she identify herself with these women? For she knew they were of the one breed, blood-sisters among men and the women of men. Her eyes roved wildly about the interior, taking in the soft draperies hanging around, the feminine garments, the oval mirror, and the dainty toilet accessories beneath. And the things haunted her, for she had seen like things before; and as she looked at them her lips involuntarily formed sounds which her throat trembled to utter. Then a thought flashed upon her, and she steadied herself. She must be calm. She must control herself, for there must be no misunderstanding this time, or else, — and she shook with a storm of suppressed tears and steadied herself again.

She put her hand on the table. *"Table,"* she clearly and distinctly enunciated. *"Table,"* she repeated.

She looked at Mrs. Van Wyck, who nodded approbation. Li Wan exulted, but brought her will to bear and held herself steady. *"Stove,"* she went on. *"Stove."*

And at every nod of Mrs. Van Wyck, Li Wan's excitement mounted. Now stumbling and halting, and again in feverish haste, as the recrudescence of forgotten words was fast or slow, she moved about the cabin, naming article after article. And when she paused finally, it was in triumph, with body erect and head thrown back, expectant, waiting.

"Cat," Mrs. Van Wyck, laughing, spelled out in kindergarten fashion. "I—see—the—cat—catch—the—rat."

Li Wan nodded her head seriously. They were beginning to understand her at last, these women. The blood flushed darkly under her bronze at the thought, and she smiled and nodded her head still more vigorously.

Mrs. Van Wyck turned to her companion. "Received a smattering of mission education somewhere, I fancy, and has come to show it off."

"Of course," Miss Giddings tittered. "Little fool! We shall lose our sleep with her vanity."

"All the same I want that jacket. If it *is* old, the workmanship is good — a most excellent specimen." She returned to her visitor. "Changee for changee? You! Changee for changee? How much? Eh? How much, you?"

"Perhaps she'd prefer a dress or something," Miss Giddings suggested.

Mrs. Van Wyck went up to Li Wan and made signs that she would exchange her wrapper for the jacket. And to further the transaction, she took Li Wan's hand and placed it amid the lace and ribbons of the flowing bosom, and rubbed the fingers back and forth so they might feel the texture. But the jewelled butterfly which loosely held the fold in place was insecurely fastened, and the front of the gown slipped to the side, exposing a firm white breast, which had never known the lip-clasp of a child.

Mrs. Van Wyck coolly repaired the mischief; but Li Wan uttered a loud cry, and ripped and tore at her skin-shirt till her own breast showed firm and white as Evelyn Van Wyck's. Murmuring inarticulately and making swift signs, she strove to establish the kinship.

"A half-breed," Mrs. Van Wyck commented. "I thought so from her hair."

Miss Giddings made a fastidious gesture. "Proud of her father's white skin. It's beastly! Do give her something, Evelyn, and make her go."

But the other woman sighed. "Poor creature, I wish I could do something for her."

A heavy foot crunched the gravel without. Then the cabin door swung wide, and Canim stalked in. Miss Giddings saw a vision of sudden death, and screamed; but Mrs. Van Wyck faced him composedly.

"What do you want?" she demanded.

"How do?" Canim answered suavely and directly, pointing at the same time to Li Wan. "Um my wife."

He reached out for her, but she waved him back.

"Speak, Canim! Tell them that I am —"

"Daughter of Pow-Wah-Kaan? Nay, of what is it to them that they should care? Better should I tell them thou art an ill wife, given to creeping from thy husband's bed when sleep is heavy in his eyes."

Again he reached out for her, but she fled away from him to Mrs. Van Wyck, at whose feet she made frenzied appeal, and whose knees she tried to clasp. But the lady stepped back and gave permission with her eyes to Canim. He gripped Li Wan under the shoulders and raised her to her feet. She fought with him, in a madness of despair, till his hest was heaving with the exertion, and they had reeled about over half the room.

"Let me go, Canim," she sobbed.

But he twisted her wrist till she ceased to struggle. "The memories of the little moose-bird are overstrong and make trouble," he began.

"I know! I know!" she broke in. "I see the man in the snow, and as never before I see him crawl on hand and knee. And I, who am a little child, am carried on his back. And this is before Pow-Wah-Kaan and the time I came to live in a little corner of the earth."

"You know," he answered, forcing her toward the door; "but you will go with me down the Yukon and forget."

"Never shall I forget! So long as my skin is white shall I remember!" She clutched frantically at the door-post and looked a last appeal to Mrs. Evelyn Van Wyck.

"Then will I teach thee to forget, I, Canim, the Canoe!"

As he spoke he pulled her fingers clear and passed out with her upon the trail.

27
THE GAME

THE METROPOLITAN MAGAZINE

VOLUME XXII   APRIL, 1905   NUMBER I

THE "GAME"

A TRANSCRIPT FROM REAL LIFE

BY JACK LONDON

ILLUSTRATED BY HENRY HUTT

"He rose from dreams of war's alarms,
To make his daggers keen and bright,
Desiring, in my very arms,
The fiercer rapture of the fight!"

"MANY patterns of carpet lay rolled out before them on the floor—two of Brussels showed the beginning of their quest, and its ending in that direction; while a score of ingrains lured their eyes and prolonged the debate between desire and pocketbook. The head of the department did them the honor of waiting upon them himself—or did Joe the honor, as she well knew, for she had noted the open-mouthed awe of the elevator boy who brought them up. Nor had she been blind to the marked respect shown Joe by the urchins and groups of young fellows on corners, when she walked with him in their own neighborhood down at the west end of the town.

But the head of the department was called away to the telephone, and in her mind the splendid promise of the carpets and the irk of the pocketbook were thrust aside by a greater doubt and anxiety.

"But I don't see what you find to like in it, Joe," she said softly, the note of insistence in her words betraying recent and unsatisfactory discussion.

For a fleeting moment a shadow darkened his boyish face, to be replaced by the glow of tenderness. He was only a boy, as she was only a girl; two young things on the threshold of life, house-renting and buying carpets together.

"What's the good of worrying?" he questioned. "It's the last go, the very last."

He smiled at her, but she saw on his lips the unconscious and all but breathed sigh of renunciation, and with the instinctive monopoly of woman for her mate, she feared this thing she did not understand and which gripped his life so strongly.

"You know the go with O'Neil cleared the last payment on mother's house," he went on. "And that's off my mind. Now this last with Ponta will give me a hundred dollars in bank—an even hundred, that's the purse—for you and me to start on, a nest-egg."

Drawn by Henry Hutt.

HE PRESSED THE ENDS OF HER FINGERS INTO HIS HARD ARM MUSCLES.

She disregarded the money appeal. "But you like it, this—this 'game' you call it. Why?"

He lacked speech-expression. He expressed himself with his hands, at his work, and with his body and the play of his muscles in the squared ring; but to tell with his own lips the charm of the squared ring was beyond him. Yet he essayed, and haltingly at first, to express what he felt and never analyzed when playing the game at the supreme summit of existence.

"All I know, Genevieve, is that you feel good in the ring, when you've got the man where you want him, when he's had a punch up both sleeves waiting for you and you've never given him an opening to land 'em, when you've landed your own little punch, and he's goin' groggy, an' holdin' on, an' the referee's pulling him apart so's you can go in an' finish 'm, an' all the house is shouting an' tearin' itself loose, an' you know you're the best man, an' that you played 'm fair an' won out because you're the best man. I tell you——"

He ceased brokenly, alarmed by his own volubility and by Genevieve's look of alarm. As he talked she had watched his face while fear dawned in her own. As he described the moment of moments to her, on his inward vision were limned the tottering man, the lights, the shouting house, and he swept out and away from her on this tide of life, that was beyond her comprehension, menacing, irresistible, making her love pitiful and weak. The Joe she knew receded, faded, became lost. The fresh boyish face was gone, the tenderness of the eyes, the sweetness of the mouth with its curves and pictured corners. It was a man's face she saw, a face of steel, tense and immobile; a mouth of steel, the lips like the jaws of a trap; eyes of steel, dilated, intent, and the light in them and the glitter were the light and glitter of steel. The face of a man, and she had known only his boy face. This face she did not know at all.

And yet, while it frightened her, she was vaguely stirred with pride in him. His masculinity, the masculinity of the fighting male, made its inevitable appeal to her, a female, moulded by all her heredity to seek out the strong man for mate and to lean against the wall of his strength. She did not understand this force of his being that rose mightier than her love and laid its compulsion upon him; and yet, in her woman's heart she was aware of the sweet pang which told her that for her sake, for Love's own sake, he had surrendered to her, abandoned all that portion of his life, and with this one last fight would never fight again.

"Mrs. Silverstein doesn't like prize fighting," she said. "She's down on it, and she knows something, too."

He smiled indulgently, concealing a hurt, not altogether new, at her persistent inappreciation of this side of his nature and life in which he took the greatest pride. It was to him power and achievement, earned by his own effort and hard work; and in the moment when he had offered himself and all that he was to Genevieve, it was this, and this alone, that he was proudly conscious of laying at her feet. It was the merit of work performed, a guerdon of manhood finer and greater than any other man could offer, and it had been to him his justification and right to possess her. And she had not understood it then, as she did not understand it now, and he might well have wondered what else she found in him to make him worthy.

"Mrs. Silverstein is a dub, and a softy, and a knocker," he said good-humoredly. "What's she know about such things anyway? I tell you it is good, and healthy, too." This last as an afterthought. "Look at me. I tell you I have to live clean to be in condition like this. I live cleaner than she does, or her old man, or anybody you know—baths, rub-downs, exercise, regular hours, good food and no makin' a pig of myself, no drinking, no smoking, nothing that'll hurt me. Why, I live cleaner than you, Genevieve——

"Honest I do," he hastened to add at sight of her shocked face. "I don't mean water an' soap, but look there." His hand closed reverently but firmly on her arm. "Soft, you're all soft, all over. Not like mine. Here, feel this."

He pressed the ends of her fingers into his hard arm-muscles until she winced from the hurt.

"Hard all over, just like that," he went on. "Now, that's what I call clean. Every bit of flesh an' blood an' muscle is clean right down to the bones—an' they're clean, too. No soap an' water only on the skin but clean all the way in. I tell you, it feels clean. It knows it's clean itself. When I wake up in the morning an' go to work, every drop of blood an' bit of meat is

Drawn by Henry Hutt.

HE EXPRESSED HIMSELF WITH HIS HANDS.

shouting right out that it is clean. Oh, I tell you——"

He paused with swift awkwardness, again confounded by his unwonted flow of speech. Never in his life had he been stirred to such utterance, and never in his life had there been cause to be so stirred. For it was the Game that had been questioned, its verity and worth, the Game itself, the biggest thing in the world—or what had been the biggest thing in the world until that chance afternoon and that chance purchase in Silverstein's candy store, when Genevieve loomed suddenly colossal in his life, overshadowing all other things. He was beginning to see, though vaguely, the sharp conflict between woman and career, between a man's work in the world and woman's need of the man. But he was not capable of generalization. He saw only the antagonism between the concrete, flesh-and-blood Genevieve and the great, abstract, living Game. Each resented the other, each claimed him; he was torn with the strife, and yet drifted helpless on the currents of their contention.

His words had drawn Genevieve's gaze to his face, and she had pleasured in the clear skin, the clear eyes, the cheek soft and smooth as a girl's. She saw the force of his argument and disliked it accordingly. She revolted instinctively against this Game which drew him away from her, robbed her of part of him. It was a rival she did not understand. Nor could she understand its seductions. Had it been a woman-rival, another girl, knowledge and light and sight would have been hers. As it was, she grappled in the dark with an intangible adversary about which she knew nothing. What truth she felt in his speech made the Game but the more formidable.

A sudden conception of her weakness came to her. She felt pity for herself, and sorrow. She wanted him, all of him; her woman's need would not be satisfied with less; and he eluded her, slipped away here and there from the all-devouring embrace with which she tried to clasp him. Tears swam into her eyes, and her lips trembled, turning defeat into victory, routing the all-potent Game with the strength of her weakness.

"Don't, Genevieve, don't," the boy pleaded, all contrition, though he was confused and dazed. To his masculine mind there was nothing relevant about her breakdown; yet all else was forgotten at sight of her tears.

She smiled forgiveness through her wet eyes, and though he knew of nothing for which to be forgiven, he melted utterly. His hand went out impulsively to hers, but she avoided the clasp by a sort of bodily stiffening and chill, the while the eyes smiled still more gloriously.

"Here comes Mr. Clausen," she said, at the same time, by some transforming alchemy of woman, presenting to the newcomer eyes that showed no hint of moistness.

"Think I was never coming back, Joe," queried the head of the department, an austere, side-whiskered man, with a pink-and-white face and genial little eyes.

"Now, let me see—hum, yes, we was discussing ingrains," he continued briskly. "That tasty little pattern there catches your eye, don't it now, eh? Yes, yes, I know all about it. I set up housekeeping when I was getting fourteen a week. But nothing's too good for the little nest, eh? Of course I know, and it's only seven cents more, and the dearest is the cheapest, I say. Tell you what I'll do, Joe." This with a burst of philanthropic impulsiveness and a confidential lowering of voice. "Seein's it's you, and I wouldn't do it for anybody else, I'll reduce it five cents. Only "—here his voice became impressively solemn—"only you mustn't ever tell how much you really did pay."

"Sewed, lined, and laid—of course, that's included," he said after Joe and Genevieve had conferred together and announced their decision.

"And the little nest, eh?" he queried. "When do you spread your wings and fly away? To-morrow! So soon? Beautiful! Beautiful!" He rolled his eyes ecstatically for a moment, then beamed upon them with a fatherly air.

Joe had replied sturdily enough, and Genevieve had blushed prettily; but both felt that it was not exactly proper. Not alone because of the privacy and holiness of the subject, but because of what might have been prudery in the middle class but which in them was the modesty and reticence found in individuals of the working class when they strive after clean-living and morality.

Mr. Clausen accompanied them to the elevator, all smiles, patronage, and benefi-

Drawn by Henry Hutt.

GENEVIEVE.

cence, while the clerks turned their heads to follow Joe's retreating figure.

"And to-night, Joe?" Mr. Clausen asked anxiously, as they waited at the shaft. "How do you feel? Think you'll do him?"

"Sure," Joe answered. "Never felt better in my life."

"You feel all right, eh? Good! Good! You see, I was just a-wonderin'—you know, ha! ha!—goin' to get married and the rest—thought you might be unstrung, eh, a trifle?—nerves just a bit off, you know. Know how gettin' married is myself. But you're all right, eh? Of course you are. No use asking *you* that. Ha! ha! Well, good luck, my boy. I know you'll win. Never had the least doubt, of course, of course."

"And good-by, Miss Pritchard," he said to Genevieve, gallantly handing her into the elevator. "Hope you call often. Will be charmed—charmed—I assure you."

"Everybody calls you 'Joe,'" she said reproachfully, as the car dropped downward. "Why don't they call you 'Mr. Fleming?' That's no more than proper."

But he was staring moodily at the elevator boy and did not seem to hear.

"What's the matter, Joe?" she asked, with a tenderness the power of which to thrill him she knew full well.

"Oh, nothing," he said. "I was only thinking—and wishing."

"Wishing—what?" Her voice was seduction itself, and her eyes would have melted stronger than he, though they failed in calling his up to them.

Then, deliberately, his eyes lifted to hers. "I was wishing you could see me fight just once."

She made a gesture of disgust, and his face fell. It came to her sharply that the rival had thrust between and was bearing him away.

"I—I'd like to," she said hastily, with an effort, striving after that sympathy which weakens the strongest men and draws their heads to women's breasts.

"Will you?"

Again his eyes lifted and looked into hers. He meant it—she knew that. It seemed a challenge to the greatness of her love.

"It would be the proudest moment of my life," he said simply.

It may have been the apprehensiveness of love, the wish to meet his need for her sympathy, and the desire to see the Game face to face for wisdom's sake, and it may have been the clarion call of adventure ringing through the narrow confines of uneventful existence; for a great daring thrilled through her, and she said, just as simply, "I will."

"I didn't think you would, or I wouldn't have asked," he confessed, as they walked out to the sidewalk.

"But can't it be done?" she asked anxiously, before her resolution could cool.

"Oh, I can fix that; but I didn't think you would.

"I didn't think you would," he repeated, still amazed, as he helped her upon the electric car and felt in his pocket for the fare.

Genevieve and Joe were working-class aristocrats. In an environment made up largely of sordidness and wretchedness, they had kept themselves unsullied and wholesome. Theirs was a self-respect, a regard for the niceties and clean things of life, which had held them aloof from their kind. Friends did not come to them easily; nor had either ever possessed a really intimate friend, a heart companion with whom to chum and have things in common. The social instinct was strong in them, yet they had remained lonely because they could not satisfy that instinct and at the same time satisfy their desire for cleanness and decency.

If ever a girl of the working class led the sheltered life, Genevieve had. In the midst of roughness and brutality she had shunned all that was rough and brutal. She saw but what she chose to see, and she chose always to see the best, avoiding coarseness and uncouthness without effort, as a matter of instinct. To begin with, she had been peculiarly unexposed. An only child, with an invalid mother upon whom she attended, she had not joined in the street-games and frolics of the children of the neighborhood. Her father, a mild-tempered, narrow-chested, anemic little clerk, domestic because of his inherent disability to mix with men, had done his full share toward giving the home an atmosphere of sweetness and tenderness.

An orphan at twelve, Genevieve had gone straight from her father's funeral to live with the Silversteins in their rooms above the candy store; and here, sheltered by kindly aliens, she earned her keep and clothes by waiting on the shop. Being Gentile, she was especially necessary to the Silversteins, who could not run the business themselves when the day of their Sabbath came around.

And here, in the uneventful little shop, six maturing years had slipped by. Her acquaintances were few. She had elected to have no girl chum for the reason that no satisfactory girl had appeared. Nor did she choose to walk with the young fellows of the neighborhood as was the custom of girls from their fifteenth year. "That stuck-up doll-face," was the way the girls of the neighborhood described her; and though she earned their enmity by her beauty and aloofness, she none the less commanded their respect. "Peaches and cream," she was called by the young men— though softly and amongst themselves, for they were afraid of arousing the ire of the other girls, while they stood in awe of her, in a dimly religious way, as a something mysteriously beautiful and unapproachable.

For she was indeed beautiful. Springing from a long line of American descent, she was one of those wonderful working-class blooms which occasionally appear, defying all precedent of forbears and environment, apparently without cause or explanation. She was a beauty in color, the blood spraying her white skin so deliciously as to earn for her the apt description, "peaches and cream." She was a beauty in the regularity of her features; and, if for no other reason, she was a beauty in the mere delicacy of the lines on which she was moulded. Quiet, low-voiced, stately and dignified, she somehow had the knack of dress, and but befitted her beauty and dignity with anything she put on. Withal, she was sheerly feminine, tender and soft and clinging, with the smouldering passion of the mate and the motherliness of the woman. But this side of her nature had lain dormant through the years, waiting for the mate to appear.

Then Joe came into Silverstein's shop one hot Saturday afternoon to cool himself with ice-cream soda, and all that was woman in her awakened on the instant. And Joe likewise roused, and they drew together with the sharpness and imperativeness of uniting elements. He toyed with his spoon and flushed his embarrassment over his soda, but lingered long; and she spoke softly,

dropped her eyes, and wove her witchery about him till there could be but the one ending. It was the mild nine days' wonder of the neighborhood when she began walking out with Joe.

Both were blessed with an avarice of speech, and because of it their courtship was a long one. As he expressed himself in action, she expressed herself in repose and control, and in the love-light in her eyes— though this latter she would have suppressed in all maiden modesty had she been conscious of the speech her heart printed so plainly there. "Dear" and "darling" were too terribly intimate for them to achieve quickly; and when they did, unlike most mating couples, they did not overwork the love-words. For a long time they were content to walk together in the evenings, or to sit side by side on a bench in the park, neither uttering a word for an hour at a time, merely gazing into each other's eyes, too-faintly luminous in the star-shine to be a cause for self-consciousness and embarrassment.

Came the day, very early in their walking out, when Silverstein chanced upon Joe in his store and stared at him with saucer-eyes. Came likewise the scene, after Joe had departed, when the maternal feelings of Mrs. Silverstein found vent in a diatribe against all prizefighters and against Joe Fleming in particular. Vainly had Silverstein striven to stay his spouse's wrath. There was need for her wrath. All the maternal feelings were hers, but none of the maternal rights.

Genevieve was aware only of the diatribe; she knew a flood of abuse was pouring from the lips of the Jewess, but she was too stunned to hear the details of the abuse. Joe, her Joe, was Joe Fleming the prizefighter. It was abhorrent, impossible, too grotesque to be believable. Her clear-eyed, girl-cheeked Joe might be anything but a prizefighter. She had never seen one, but he in no way resembled her conception of what a prizefighter must be—the human brute with tiger-eyes and a streak for a forehead. Of course she had heard of Joe Fleming—who in West Oakland had not? —but that there should be anything more than a coincidence of names had never crossed her mind.

She came out of her daze to hear Mrs. Silverstein's hysterical sneer, "Keepin' company vit a bruiser." Next, Silverstein and his wife fell to differing on "noted" and "notorious" as applicable to her lover.

"But he iss a good boy," Silverstein was contending. "He make der money, an' he safe der money."

"You tell me dat!" Mrs. Silverstein screamed. "Vat you know? You know too much. You spend good money on der prizefighters. How you know?"

"I know vat I know," Silverstein held on sturdily—a thing Genevieve had never before seen him do when his wife was in the tantrums. "His fader die, he go to work in Hansen's sail-loft. He haf six brudders an' sisters younger as he iss. He iss der liddle fader. He vork hard, all der time. On Saturday night he bring home ten dollar. Den Hansen gif him twelve dollar —vat he do? He iss der liddle fader, he bring it home to der mudder. He vork all der time, he got twenty dollar—vat he do? He bring it home. Der liddle brudders an' sisters go to school, vear good clothes, der mudder lif fat, an' she iss proud for her good boy Joe.

"But he haf der peautiful body—ach, Gott, der peautiful body!—stronger as der ox, k-vicker as der tiger-cat; der head cooler as der ice-box, der eyes vat see eferytings, k-vick, just like dat. He put on der gloves vit der boys at Hansen's loft, he put on der gloves vit der boys at der varehouse. He go before der club; he knock out der Spider, k-vick, one punch, just like dat, der first time. Der purse iss five dollar—vat he do? He bring it home.

"He go many times before der clubs; he get many purses—ten dollar, fifty dollar, one hundred dollar. He buy der good house for der mudder. All der time he vork at Hansen's and fight before der clubs to pay for der house. He buy der piano for der sisters, der carpets, der pictures on der wall. An' he iss all der time straight. He bet on himself—dat iss der good sign. Ven a man bets on himself dat is der time you bet, too, ——"

Here Mrs. Silverstein groaned her horror of gambling, and her husband, aware that his eloquence had betrayed him, collapsed into voluble assurances that he was ahead of the game— "An' all because of Joe Fleming," he concluded. "I back him efery time to vin."

But Genevieve and Joe were pre-eminently mated, and nothing, not even this terrible discovery, could keep them apart. In vain Genevieve tried to steel herself against him; but she fought herself, not him. To her surprise she discovered a thousand excuses for him, found him lovable as ever; and she entered into his life to be his destiny and to control him after the way of women. She saw his future and hers through glowing vistas of reform, and her first great deed was when she wrung from him his promise to cease fighting.

And he, after the way of men, pursuing the dream of love and striving for possession of the precious and deathless object of desire, had yielded. And yet, in the very moment of promising her, he knew vaguely, deep down, that he never could abandon the Game; that somewhere, sometime, in the future, he must go back to it. And he had had a swift vision of his mother and brothers and sisters, their multitudinous wants, the house with its painting and repairing, its street assessments and taxes, and of the coming of children to him and Genevieve, and of his own daily wage in the sail-making loft. But the next moment the vision was dismissed, and he saw before him only Genevieve, and he knew only his hunger for her and the call of his being to her; and he accepted calmly her calm assumption of his life and actions.

He was twenty, she eighteen, boy and girl the pair of them and made for progeny, healthy and normal, with steady blood pounding through their bodies; and wherever they went together, even on Sunday outings across the bay amongst people who did not know him, eyes were continually drawn to them. He matched her girl's beauty with his boy's beauty, her grace with his strength, her delicacy of line and fiber with the harsher vigor and muscle of the male. Frank-faced, fresh-colored, almost ingenious in expression, eyes blue and wide apart, he drew and held the gaze of more than one woman far above him in the social scale. Of such glances and dim maternal promptings, he was quite unconscious, though Genevieve was quick to see and understand; and she knew each time the pang of a fierce joy in that he was hers and that she held him in the hollow of her hand. He did see, however, and rather resented the men's glances drawn by her. These, too, she saw and understood as he did not dream of understanding.

THE "GAME"

A TRANSCRIPT FROM REAL LIFE

BY JACK LONDON

ILLUSTRATED BY HENRY HUTT

Joe Fleming, a youth of twenty, earning his livelihood as a sailmaker and supporting his mother and sisters by his trade, augments his income by prize-fighting before so-called sporting clubs. On the eve of his marriage to Genevieve, an employé in the Silversteins' candy shop, Joe is to fight his last bout before a club, having promised Genevieve to give up " the game," which, while it seems wrong to her, is to him a clean and manly as well as lucrative occupation. It is Joe's desire that Genevieve shall witness the fight, and the girl has reluctantly agreed to do so.

PART II

ENEVIEVE slipped on a pair of Joe's shoes, light-soled and dapper, and laughed with Lottie, who stooped to turn up the trousers for her. Lottie was his sister, and in the secret. To her was due the inveigling of his mother into making a neighborhood call so that they could have the house to themselves. They went down into the kitchen where Joe was waiting. His face brightened as he came to meet her, love shining frankly forth.

"Now get up those skirts, Lottie," he commanded. "Haven't any time to waste. There, that'll do. You see, you only want the bottoms of the pants to show. The coat will cover the rest. Now let's see how it'll fit.

"Borrowed it from Chris; he's a dead sporty sport, little, but oh my!" he went on, helping Genevieve into an overcoat which fell to her heels and which fitted her as a tailor-made overcoat should fit the man for whom it is made.

Joe put a cap on her head and turned up the collar, which was generous to exaggeration, meeting the cap and completely hiding her hair. When he buttoned the collar in front its points served to cover the cheeks, chin and mouth were buried in its depths, and a close scrutiny revealed only shadowy eyes and a little less shadowy nose. She walked across the room, the bottoms of the trousers just showing as the hang of the coat was disturbed by movement.

"A sport with a cold and afraid of catching more, all right, all right," the boy laughed, proudly surveying his handiwork. "How much money you got? I'm layin' ten to six. Will you take the short end?"

"Who's short?" she asked.

"Ponta, of course," Lottie blurted out her hurt, as though there could be any question of it even for an instant.

"Of course," Genevieve said sweetly, "only I don't know about such things."

This time Lottie kept her lips together, but the new hurt showed on her face. Joe looked at his watch and said it was time to go. His sister's arms went about his neck, and she kissed him soundly on the lips. She kissed Genevieve, too, and saw them to the gate, one arm of her brother about her waist.

"What does ten to six mean?" Genevieve asked, the while their footfalls rang out on the frosty air.

"That I'm the long end, the favorite," he answered. "That a man bets ten dollars at the ringside that I win against six dollars another man is betting that I lose."

"But if you're the favorite and everybody thinks you'll win, how does anybody bet against you?"

"That's what makes prize-fighting—difference of opinion," he laughed. "Besides, there's always the chance of a lucky punch, an accident. Lots of chance," he said gravely.

Drawn by Henry Hutt.

PONTA WAS LIKE A MADMAN.

She shrank against him, clingingly and protectingly, and he laughed with surety.

"You wait and you'll see. An' don't get scared at the start. The first few rounds'll be something fierce. That's Ponta's strong point. He's a wild man, with all kinds of punches, a whirlwind, and he gets his man in the first rounds. He's put away a whole lot of cleverer and better men than him. It's up to me to live through it, that's all. Then he'll be all in. When I go after him, just watch. You'll know when I go after him, an' I'll get 'm, too."

They came to the hall, on a dark street-corner, ostensibly the quarters of an athletic club, but in reality an institution designed for pulling off fights and keeping within the police ordinance. Joe drew away from her, and they walked apart to the entrance.

"Keep your hands in your pockets whatever you do," Joe warned her, "and it'll be all right. Only a couple of minutes of it.

"He's with me," Joe said to the door-keeper, who was talking with a policeman.

Both men greeted him familiarly, taking no notice of his companion.

"They never tumbled; nobody'll tumble," Joe assured her, as they climbed the stairs to the second story. "And even if they did, they wouldn't know who it was and they'd keep it mum for me. Here, come in here!"

He whisked her into a little office-like room and left her seated on a dusty, broken-bottomed chair. A few minutes later he was back again, clad in a long bath-robe, canvas shoes on his feet. She began to tremble against him, and his arm passed gently around her.

"It'll be all right, Genevieve," he said encouragingly. "I've got it all fixed. No-body'll tumble."

"It's you, Joe," she said. "I don't care for myself. It's you."

"Don't care for yourself! But that's what I thought you was afraid of!"

He looked at her in amazement, the wonder of woman bursting upon him in a more transcendent glory than ever, and he had seen much of the wonder of woman in Genevieve. He was speechless for a moment, and then stammered:

"You mean me? And you don't care what people think? or anything? or anything?"

A sharp double-knock at the door and a sharper, "Get a move on yerself, you Joe!" brought him back to immediate things.

"Quick, one last kiss, Genevieve," he whispered, almost holily. "It's my last fight, an' I'll fight as never before with you lookin' at me."

The next she knew, the pressure of his lips yet warm on hers, she was in a group of jostling young fellows, none of whom seemed to take the slightest notice of her. Several had their coats off and their shirt sleeves rolled up. They entered the hall from the rear, still keeping the casual formation of the group, and moved slowly up a side aisle.

It was a crowded, ill-lighted hall, barn-like in its proportions, and the smoke-laden air gave a peculiar distortion to everything. She felt as though she would stifle. There were shrill cries of boys selling programs and soda water, and there was a great bass rumble of masculine voices. She heard a voice offering ten to six on Joe Fleming. The utterance was monotonous—hopeless, it seemed to her, and she felt a quick thrill. It was her Joe against whom everybody was afraid to bet.

And she felt other thrills. Her blood was touched, as by fire, with Romance, Adventure—the unknown, the mysterious, the terrible—as she penetrated this haunt of men where women came not. And there were other thrills. It was the only time in her life she had dared the rash thing. For the first time she was overstepping the bounds laid down by that harshest of tyrants, the Mrs. Grundy of the working class. She felt fear, and for herself, though the moment before she had been thinking only of Joe.

Before she knew it, the front of the hall had been reached and she had gone up half a dozen steps into a small dressing-room. This was crowded to suffocation—by men who played the Game, she concluded, in one capacity or another. And here she lost Joe. But before the real personal fright could soundly clutch her, one of the young fellows said gruffly, "Come along with me, you," and as she wedged out at his heels she noticed that another one of the escort was following her. They came upon a sort of stage, which accommodated three rows of men; and she caught her first glimpse of the squared ring. She was on a level with it, and so near that she could have reached out and touched its ropes. She noticed that it was covered with padded canvas. Beyond the ring, and on either side, as in a fog, she could see the crowded house.

The dressing-room she had left abutted upon one corner of the ring. Squeezing her way after her guide through the seated men, she crossed the end of the hall and entered a similar dressing-room at the other corner of the ring.

"Now, don't make no noise, and stay here till I come for you," instructed her guide, pointing out a peep-hole arrangement in the wall of the room.

She hurried to the peep-hole, and found herself against the ring. She could see the whole of it, though part of the audience was shut off. The ring was well-lighted by an overhead cluster of patent gas-burners. The front row of the men she had squeezed past, because of their paper and pencils she decided to be reporters from the local papers up-town. One of them was chewing gum. Behind them, on the other two rows of seats, she could make out firemen from the nearby engine-house and several policemen in uniform. In the middle of the front row, flanked by the reporters, sat the young chief of police. She was startled by catching sight of Mr. Clausen on the opposite side of the ring. There he sat, austere, side-whiskered, pink and white, close up against the front of the ring. Several seats farther on, in the same front row, she discovered Silverstein, his weazened features glowing with anticipation.

A few cheers heralded the advent of several young fellows, in shirt-sleeves, carrying buckets, bottles and towels, who crawled through the ropes and crossed to the diagonal corner from her. One of them sat down on a stool and leaned back against the ropes. She saw that he was bare-legged, with canvas shoes on his feet, and that his body was swathed in a heavy white sweater. In the meantime another group had occupied the corner directly against her. Louder cheers drew her attention to it, and she saw Joe seated on a stool, still clad in the bath-robe, his short chestnut curls within a yard of her eyes.

A young man in a black suit, with a mop of hair and a preposterously tall starched collar, walked to the center of the ring and held up his hand.

"Gentlemen will please stop smoking," he said.

His effort was applauded by groans and cat-calls, and she noticed with indignation that nobody stopped smoking. Mr. Clausen held a burning match in his fingers while the announcement was being made, and then calmly lighted his cigar. She felt that she hated him in that moment. How was her Joe to fight in such an atmosphere? She could scarcely breathe herself, and she was only sitting down.

The announcer came over to Joe. He stood up. His bath-robe fell away from him, and he stepped forth to the center of the ring, naked but for the low canvas shoes and a narrow hip-cloth of white. Genevieve's eyes dropped. She sat alone, with none to see, but her face was burning with shame at sight of the beautiful nakedness of her lover. But she looked again, guiltily, for the joy that was hers in beholding what she knew must be sinful to behold. The leap of something within her and the stir of her being toward him must be sinful. But it was delicious sin, and she did not deny her eyes. In vain Mrs. Grundy admonished her. The Pagan in her, Original Sin, and all Nature urged her on. The mothers of all the past were whispering through her, and there was a clamor of the children unborn. But of this she knew nothing. She knew only that it was sin, and she lifted her head proudly, and recklessly, resolved, in one great surge of revolt, to sin to the uttermost.

She had never dreamed of the form under the clothes. The form, beyond the hands and the face, had no part in her mental processes. A child of garmented civilization, the garment was to her the form. The race of men was to her a race of garmented bipeds, with hands and faces and hair-covered heads. When she thought of Joe, the Joe instantly visualized on her mind was a clothed Joe — girl-cheeked, blue-eyed, curly-headed, but clothed. And there he stood, all but naked, god-like, in a white blaze of light. She had never conceived of the form of God except as nebulously naked, and the thought-association was startling. It seemed to her that her sin partook of sacrilege or blasphemy.

Her chromo-trained æsthetic sense exceeded its education and told her that here was beauty and wonder. She had always liked the physical presentment of Joe, but it was a presentment of clothes, and she had thought the pleasingness of it due to the neatness and taste with which he dressed. She had never dreamed that this lurked beneath. It dazzled her. His skin was fair as a woman's, far more satiny, and no rudimentary hair-growth marred its white luster.

This she perceived, but all the rest, the perfection of line and strength and development, gave pleasure without her knowing why. There was a cleanness and grace about it. His face was like a cameo, and his lips, parted in a smile, made it very boyish.

He smiled as he faced the audience, when the announcer, placing a hand on his shoulder, said: "Joe Fleming, the Pride of West Oakland."

Cheers and hand-clappings stormed up, and she heard affectionate cries of "Oh, you, Joe!" Men shouted it at him again and again.

He walked back to his corner. Never to her did he seem less a fighter than then. His eyes were too mild; there was not a spark of the beast in them, nor in his face, while his body seemed too fragile, what of its fairness and smoothness, and his face too boyish and sweet-tempered and intelligent. She did not have the expert's eye for the depth of chest, the wide nostrils, the recuperative lungs, and the muscles under their satin sheathes—crypts of energy wherein lurked the chemistry of destruction. To her he looked like a something of Dresden china, to be handled gently and with care, liable to be shattered to fragments by the first rough touch.

John Ponta, stripped of his white sweater by the pulling and hauling of two of his seconds, came to the center of the ring. She knew terror as she looked at him. Here was the fighter—the beast with a streak for a forehead, with beady eyes under lowering and bushy brows, flat-nosed, thick-lipped, sullen-mouthed. He was heavy-jawed, bull-necked, and the short straight hair of the head seemed to her frightened eyes the stiff bristles on a hog's back. Here was coarseness and brutishness, a thing savage, primordial, ferocious. He was swarthy to blackness, and his body was covered with a hairy growth that matted like a dog's on his chest and shoulders. He was deep-chested, thick-legged, large-muscled, but unshapely. His muscles were knots, and he was gnarled and knobby, twisted out of beauty by excess of strength.

"John Ponta, West Bay Athletic Club," said the announcer.

A much smaller volume of cheers greeted him. It was evident that the crowd favored Joe with its sympathy.

"Go in an' eat 'm, Ponta! Eat 'm up!" a voice shouted in the lull.

This was received by scornful cries and groans. He did not like it, for his sullen mouth twisted into a half-snarl as he went back to his corner. He was too decided an atavism to draw the crowd's admiration. Instinctively the crowd disliked him. He was an animal, lacking in intelligence and spirit, a menace and a thing of fear as the tiger and the snake are menaces and things of fear, better behind the bars of a cage than running free in the open.

And he felt that the crowd had no relish for him. He was like an animal in the circle of its enemies, and he turned and glared at them with malignant eyes. Little Silverstein, shouting out Joe's name with high glee, shrank away from Ponta's gaze, shriveled as in fierce heat, the sound gurgling and dying in his throat. Genevieve saw the little byplay, and as Ponta's eyes slowly swept round the circle of their hate and met hers, she, too, shriveled and shrank back. The next moment they were past, pausing to center long on Joe. It seemed to her that Ponta was working himself into a rage. Joe returned the gaze with mild boy's eyes, but his face grew serious.

The announcer escorted a third man to the center of the ring, a genial-faced young fellow in shirt-sleeves.

"Eddy Jones, who will referee this contest," said the announcer.

"Oh, you, Eddy!" men shouted in the midst of the applause, and it was apparent to Genevieve that he, too, was well beloved.

Both men were being helped into the gloves by their seconds, and one of Ponta's seconds came over and examined the gloves before they went on Joe's hands. The referee called them to the center of the ring. The seconds followed, and they made quite a group, Joe and Ponta facing each other, the referee in the middle, the seconds leaning with hands on one another's shoulders, their heads craned forward. The referee was talking, and all listened attentively.

The group broke up. Again the announcer came to the front.

"Joe Fleming fights at one hundred and twenty-eight," he said; "John Ponta at one hundred and forty. They will fight as long as one hand is free, and take care of themselves in the break-away. The audience must remember that a decision must be given. There are no draws fought before this club."

He crawled through the ropes and dropped

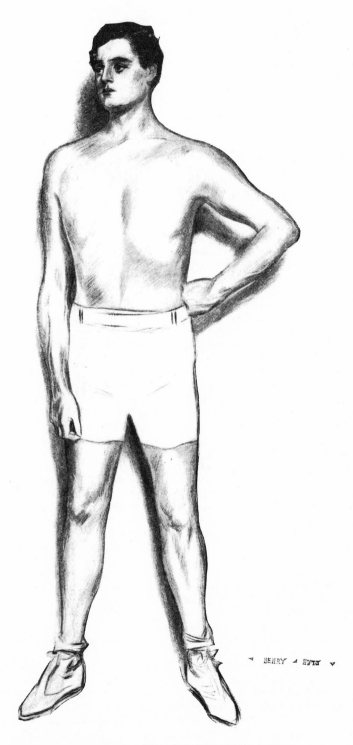

HIS SKIN WAS FAIR AS A WOMAN'S, FAR MORE SATINY.

from the ring to the floor. There was a scuttling in the corners as the seconds cleared out through the ropes, taking with them the stools and buckets. Only remained in the ring the two fighters and the referee. A gong sounded. The two men advanced rapidly to the center. Their right hands extended and for a fraction of an instant met in a perfunctory shake. Then Ponta lashed out savagely, right and left, and Joe escaped by springing back. Like a projectile, Ponta hurled himself after him and upon him.

The fight was on. Genevieve clutched one hand to her breast and watched. She was bewildered by the swiftness and savagery of Ponta's assault, and by the multitude of blows he struck. She felt that Joe was surely being destroyed. At times she could not see his face, so obscured was it by the flying gloves. But she could hear the resounding blows, and with the sound of each blow she felt a sickening sensation in the pit of her stomach. She did not know that what she heard was the impact of glove on glove or shoulder and that no damage was being done.

She was suddenly aware that a change had come over the fight. Both men were clutching each other in a tense embrace; no blows were being struck at all. She recognized it to be what Joe had described to her as the "clinch." Ponta was struggling to free himself, Joe was holding on. The referee shouted, "Break!" Joe made an effort to get away, but Ponta got one hand free and Joe rushed back into a second clinch to escape the blow. But this time she noticed, the heel of his glove was pressed against Ponta's mouth and chin, and at the second "Break!" of the referee, Joe shoved his opponent's head back and sprang clear himself.

For a brief several seconds she had an unobstructed view of her lover. Left foot a trifle advanced, knees slightly bent, he was crouching with his head drawn well down between his shoulders and shielded by them. His hands were in position before him, ready either to attack or defend. The muscles of his body were tense, and as he moved about she could see them bunch up and writhe and crawl like live things under the white skin.

But again Ponta was upon him and he was struggling to live. He crouched a bit more, drew his body more compactly

together, and covered up with his hands, elbows, and fore-arms. Blows rained upon him, and it looked to her as though he were being beaten to death. But he was receiving the blows on his gloves and shoulders, rocking back and forth to the force of them like a tree in a storm, while the house cheered its delight. It was not until she understood this applause, and saw Silverstein half out of his seat and intensely, madly happy, and heard the "Oh, you Joe's!" from many throats, that she realized that instead of being cruelly punished he was acquitting himself well. Then he would emerge, for a moment, to be again enveloped and hidden in the whirlwind of Ponta's ferocity.

The gong sounded. It seemed they had been fighting half an hour, though from what Joe had told her, she knew it had been only three minutes. With the crash of the gong Joe's seconds were through the ropes and running him into his corner for the blessed minute of rest. One man, squatting on the floor between his outstretched feet and elevating them by resting them on his knees, was violently chafing his legs. Joe sat on the stool, leaning far back into the corner, head thrown back and arms outstretched on the ropes to give easy expansion to the chest. With wide-open mouth he was breathing the towel-driven air furnished by one of the seconds, while listening to the counsel of still another second who talked with low voice in his ear and at the same time sponged his face, shoulders and chest.

Hardly had all this been accomplished (it had taken no more than several seconds), than the gong sounded, the seconds scuttled through the ropes with their paraphernalia, and Joe and Ponta were advancing against each other to the center of the ring. Genevieve had no idea that a minute could be so short. For a moment she felt that his rest had been cut and was suspicious of she knew not what.

Ponta lashed out, right and left, savagely as ever, and though Joe blocked the blows, such was the force of them that he was knocked backward several steps. Ponta was after him with the spring of a tiger. In the involuntary effort to maintain equilibrium, Joe had uncovered himself, flinging one arm out and lifting his head from between the sheltering shoulders. So swiftly had Ponta followed him, that a terrible swinging blow was coming at his unguarded jaw. He ducked forward and down, Ponta's fist just missing the back of his head. As he came back to the perpendicular, Ponta's left fist drove at him in a straight punch that would have knocked him backward through the ropes. Again, and with a swiftness an inappreciable fraction of time quicker than Ponta's, he ducked forward. Ponta's fist grazed the backward slope of the shoulder and glanced off into the air. Ponta's right drove straight out, and the graze was repeated as Joe ducked into the safety of a clinch.

Genevieve sighed with relief, her tense body relaxing and a faintness coming over her. The crowd was cheering madly. Silverstein was on his feet, shouting, gesticulating, completely out of himself. And even Mr. Clausen, at the top of his lungs, was yelling his enthusiasm into the ear of his nearest neighbor.

The clinch was broken and the fight went on. Joe blocked, and backed, and slid around the ring, avoiding blows and living somehow through the whirlwind onslaughts. Rarely did he strike blows himself, for Ponta had a quick eye and could defend as well as attack, while Joe had no chance against the other's enormous vitality. His hope lay in that Ponta himself should ultimately consume his own strength.

But Genevieve was beginning to wonder why her lover did not fight. She grew angry. She wanted to see him wreak vengeance on this beast that persecuted him so. Even as she waxed impatient, the chance came and Joe whipped his fist to Ponta's mouth. It was a staggering blow. She saw Ponta's head go back with a jerk and the quick dye of blood on the lips. The blow, and the great shout from the audience, angered him. He rushed like a wild man. The fury of his previous assaults was as nothing compared with the fury of this one. And there was no more opportunity for another blow. Joe was too busy living through the storm he had already caused, blocking, covering up, and ducking into the safety and respite of the clinches.

But the clinch was not all safety and respite. Every instant of it was tense watchfulness, while the break-away was still more dangerous. Genevieve had noticed, with a slight touch of amusement, the curious way in which Joe snuggled his body in against Ponta's in the clinches; but she had not realized why, until, in one such clinch, before the snuggling in could be

effected, Ponta's fist whipped straight up in the air from under, and missed Joe's chin by a hair's breadth. In another and later clinch, when she had already relaxed and sighed her relief at seeing him safely snuggled, Ponta, chin over Joe's shoulder and arms around his waist, lifted his right arm and struck a terrible downward blow on the small of the back. The crowd groaned its apprehension, while Joe quickly locked his opponent's arms to prevent a repetition of the blow.

The gong struck, and after the fleeting minute of rest, they went at it again—in Joe's corner, for Ponta had made a rush to meet him clear across the ring. Where the blow had been struck, over the kidneys, the white skin had become bright red. This splash of color, the size of the glove, fascinated and frightened Genevieve so that she could scarcely take her eyes from it. Promptly, in the next clinch, the blow was repeated; but after that Joe usually managed to give Ponta the heel of the glove on the mouth and so hold his head back. This prevented the striking of the blow, but three times more, before the round ended, Ponta effected the trick, each time striking the same vulnerable part.

Another rest and another round went by, with no further damage to Joe and no diminution of strength on the part of Ponta. But in the beginning of the fifth round, Joe, caught in a corner, made as though to duck into a clinch. Just before it was effected, and at the precise moment that Ponta was ready with his own body to receive the snuggling in of Joe's body, Joe drew back slightly and drove with his fists at his opponent's unprotected stomach. Lightning-like blows they were, four of them, right and left, right and left; and heavy they were, for Ponta winced away from them and staggered back, half dropping his arms, his shoulders drooping forward and in as though he were about to double in at the waist and collapse. Joe's quick eye saw the opening, and he smashed straight out upon Ponta's mouth, following instantly with a half-swing, half-hook for the jaw. It missed, striking the cheek instead, and sending Ponta staggering sideways.

The house was on its feet, shouting, to a man. Genevieve could hear men crying, "He's got 'm, he's got 'm!" and it seemed to her the beginning of the end. She, too, was out of herself; softness and tenderness had vanished; she exulted with each crushing blow her lover delivered.

But Ponta's vitality was yet to be reckoned with. As, like a tiger, he had followed Joe up, Joe now followed him up. He made another half-swing, half-hook for Ponta's jaw, and Ponta, already recovering his wits and strength, ducked cleanly. Joe's fist passed on through empty air, and so great was the momentum of the blow that it carried him around, in a half-twirl, sideways. Then Ponta lashed out with his left. His glove landed on Joe's unguarded neck. Genevieve saw her lover's arms drop to his sides as his body lifted, went backward, and fell limply to the floor. The referee, bending over him, began to count the seconds, emphasizing the passage of each second with a downward sweep of his right arm.

The audience was still as death. Ponta had partly turned to the house to receive the approval that was his due, only to be met by this chill, graveyard silence. Quick wrath surged up in him. It was unfair. His opponent only was applauded—if he struck a blow, if he escaped a blow; he, Ponta, who had forced the fighting from the start, had received no word of cheer.

His eyes blazed as he gathered himself together and sprang to his prostrate foe. He crouched alongside of him, right arm drawn back and ready for a smashing blow the instant Joe should start to rise. The referee, still bending over and counting with his right hand, shoved Ponta back with his left. The latter, crouching, circled around, and the referee circled with him, thrusting him back and keeping between him and the fallen man.

"Four—five—six—" the count went on, and Joe, rolling over on his face, squirmed weakly to draw himself to his knees. This he succeeded in doing, resting on one knee, a hand to the floor on either side and the other leg bent under him to help him rise. "Take the count!   Take the count!" a dozen voices rang out from the audience.

"For God's sake take the full count!" one of Joe's seconds cried warningly from the edge of the ring. Genevieve gave him one swift glance, and saw the young fellow's face, drawn and white, his lips unconsciously moving as he kept the count with the referee.

"Seven—eight—nine—" the seconds went.

The ninth sounded and was gone, when the referee gave Ponta a last backward shove and Joe came to his feet, bunched up, covered up, weak, but cool, very cool. Ponta hurled himself upon him with terrific force, delivering an uppercut and a straight punch. But Joe blocked the two, ducked a third, stepped to the side to avoid a fourth, and was then driven backward into a corner by a hurricane of blows. He was exceedingly weak. He tottered as he kept his footing, and staggered back and forth. His back was against the ropes. There was no further retreat. Ponta paused, as if to make doubly sure, then feinted with his left and struck fiercely with his right with all his strength. But Joe ducked into a clinch and was for the moment saved.

Ponta struggled frantically to free himself. He wanted to give the finish to this foe already so far gone. But Joe was holding on for life, resisting the other's every effort, as fast as one hold or grip was torn loose finding a new one by which to cling. "Break!" the referee commanded. Joe held on tighter. "Make 'm break! Why the hell don't you make 'm break?" Ponta panted at the referee. Again the latter commanded the break. Joe refused, keeping, as he well knew, within his rights. Each moment of the clinch his strength was coming back to him, his brain was clearing, the cobwebs were disappearing from before his eyes. The round was young, and he must live, somehow, through the nearly three minutes of it yet to run.

The referee clutched each by the shoulder and sundered them violently, as they were thrust backward, passing quickly between them in order to make a clean break of it. The moment he was free, Ponta sprang at Joe like a wild animal bearing down its prey. But Joe covered up, blocked, and fell into a clinch. Again Ponta struggled to get free, Joe held on, and the referee thrust them apart. And again Joe avoided damage and clinched.

Genevieve realized that in the clinches he was not being beaten—why then, did not the referee let him hold on? It was cruel. She hated the genial-faced Eddy Jones in those moments, and she partly rose from her chair, her hands clenched with anger, the nails cutting into the palms till they hurt. The rest of the round, the three long minutes of it, was a succession of clinches and breaks. Not once did Ponta succeed in

SHE HURRIED TO THE PEEP-HOLE AND FOUND HERSELF AGAINST THE RING.

striking his opponent the deadly final blow. And Ponta was like a madman, raging because of his impotency in the face of his helpless and all but vanquished foe. One blow, only one blow, and he could not deliver it! Joe's ring-experience and coolness saved him. With shaken consciousness and trembling body, he clutched and held on while the ebbing life turned and flooded up in him again. Once, in his passion, unable to hit him, Ponta made as though to lift him up and hurl him to the floor.

"V'y don't you bite him?" Silverstein taunted shrilly.

In the stillness the sally was heard over the whole house, and the audience, relieved of its anxiety for its favorite, laughed with an uproariousness that had in it the note of hysteria. Even Genevieve felt that there was something irresistibly funny in the remark, and the relief of the audience was communicated to her; yet she felt sick and faint, and was overwrought with horror at what she had seen and was seeing.

"Bite 'm! Bite 'm!" voices from the recovered audience were shouting. "Chew his ear off, Ponta! That's the only way you can get 'm! Eat 'm up! Eat 'm up! Oh, why don't you eat 'm up?"

The effect was bad on Ponta. He became more frenzied than ever, and more impotent. He panted and sobbed, wasting his effort by too much effort, losing sanity and control and futilely trying to compensate for the loss by excess of physical endeavor. He knew only the blind desire to destroy, shook Joe in the clinches as a terrier might a rat, strained and struggled for freedom of body and arms, and all the time Joe calmly clutched and held on. The referee worked manfully and fairly to separate them. Perspiration ran down his face. It took all his strength to split those clinging bodies, and no sooner had he split them than Joe fell unharmed into another embrace and the work had to be done all over again. In vain, when freed, did Ponta try to avoid the clutching arms and twining body. He could not keep away. He had to come close in order to strike, and each time Joe baffled him and caught him in his arms.

And Genevieve, crouched in the little dressing-room and peering through the peep-hole, was baffled, too. She was an interested party in what seemed a death-struggle (was not one of the fighters her Joe?), but the audience understood and she did not. The Game had not unveiled to her. The lure of it was beyond her. It was greater mystery than ever. She could not comprehend its power. What delight could there be for Joe in that brutal, surging and straining of bodies, those fierce clutches, fiercer blows, and terrible hurts? Surely, she, Genevieve, offered more than that— rest, and content, and sweet calm joy. Her bid for the heart of him and the soul of him was finer and more generous than the bid of the Game; yet he dallied with both, held her in his arms but turned his head to listen to that other and siren call she could not understand.

The gong struck. The round ended with a break in Ponta's corner. The white-faced young second was through the ropes with the first clash of sound. He seized Joe in his arms, lifted him clear of the floor, and ran with him across the ring to his own corner. His seconds worked over him furiously, chafing his legs, slapping his abdomen, stretching the hip-cloth out with their fingers so that he might breathe more easily. For the first time Genevieve saw the stomach-breathing of a man, an abdomen that rose and fell far more with every breath than her breast rose and fell after she had run for a car. The pungency of ammonia bit her nostrils, wafted to her from the soaked sponge wherefrom he breathed the fiery fumes that cleared his brain. He gargled his mouth and throat, took a suck at a divided lemon, and all the while the towels worked like mad, driving oxygen into his lungs to purge the pounding blood and send it back revivified for the struggle yet to come. His heated body was sponged with water, doused with it, and bottles were turned mouth downward on his head.

The gong for the sixth round struck, and both men advanced to meet each other, their bodies glistening with water. Ponta rushed two-thirds of the way across the ring, so intent was he on getting at his man before full recovery could be effected. But Joe had lived through. He was strong again, and getting stronger. He blocked several vicious blows and then smashed back, sending Ponta reeling. He attempted to follow up, but wisely forebore and contented himself with blocking and covering up in the whirlwind his blow had raised.

The fight was as it had been at the beginning—Joe protecting, Ponta rushing. But Ponta was never at ease. He did not have it all his own way. At any moment, in his fiercest onslaughts, his opponent was liable to lash out and reach him. Joe saved his strength. He struck one blow to Ponta's ten, but his one blow rarely missed. Ponta overwhelmed him in his attacks, yet could do nothing with him, while Joe's tiger-like strokes, always imminent, compelled respect. They toned Ponta's ferocity. He was no longer able to go in with the complete abandon of destruction which had marked his earlier efforts.

But a change was coming over the fight. The audience was quick to note it, and even Genevieve saw it by the beginning of the ninth round. Joe was taking the offensive.

In the clinches it was he who brought his fist down on the small of the back, striking the terrible kidney blow. He did it once, in each clinch, but with all his strength; and he did it every clinch. Then, in the break-aways, he began to uppercut Ponta on the stomach, or to hook his jaw or strike straight out upon the mouth. But at first sign of a coming whirlwind, Joe would dance nimbly away and cover up.

Two rounds of this went by, and three, but Ponta's strength, though perceptibly less, did not diminish rapidly. Joe's task was to wear down that strength, not with one blow, nor ten, but with blow after blow, without end, until that enormous strength should be beaten sheer out of its body. There was no rest for the man. Joe followed him up, step by step, his advancing left foot making an audible tap, tap, tap on the hard canvas. Then there would come a sudden leap in, tiger-like, a blow struck, or blows, and a swift leap back, whereupon the left foot would take up again its tapping advance. When Ponta made his savage rushes, Joe carefully covered up, only to emerge, his left foot going tap, tap, tap, as he immediately followed up.

Ponta was slowly weakening. To the crowd the end was a foregone conclusion.

"Oh, you Joe!" it yelled its admiration and affection.

"It's a shame to take the money!" it mocked. "Why don't you eat 'm, Ponta? Go on in an' eat 'm!"

In the one-minute intermissions Ponta's seconds worked over him as they had not done before. Their calm trust in his tremendous vitality had been betrayed. Genevieve watched their excited efforts, while she listened to the white-faced second cautioning Joe.

"Take your time," he was saying. "You've got 'm, but you got to take your time. I've seen 'm fight. He's got a punch to the end of the count. I've seen 'm knocked out and clean batty, an' go on punchin' just the same. Mickey Sullivan had 'm goin'. Puts 'm to the mat as fast as he crawls up, six times, an' then leaves an opening. Ponta reaches for his jaw, an' two minutes afterward Mickey's openin' his eyes an' askin' what's doin'. So you've got to watch 'm. No goin' in an' absorbin' one of them lucky punches, now. I got money on this fight, but I don't call it mine till he's counted out."

Ponta was being doused with water. As the gong sounded, one of his seconds inverted a water bottle over his head. He started toward the center of the ring, and the second followed him for several steps, keeping the bottle still inverted. The referee shouted at him, and he fled the ring, dropping the bottle as he fled. It rolled over and over, the water gurgling out upon the canvas till the referee, with a quick flirt of his toe, sent the bottle rolling through the ropes.

In all the previous rounds Genevieve had not seen Joe's fighting face, which had been prefigured to her that morning in the department store. Sometimes his face had been quite boyish; other times, when taking his fiercest punishment, it had been bleak and gray; and still later, when living through and clutching and holding on, it had taken on a wistful expression. But now, out of danger himself and as he forced the fight, his fighting face came upon him. She saw it and shuddered. It removed him so far from her. She had thought she knew him, all of him, and held him in the hollow of her hand; but this she did not know—this face of steel, this mouth of steel, these eyes of steel flashing the light and glitter of steel. It seemed to her the passionless face of an avenging angel, stamped only with the purpose of the Lord.

Ponta attempted one of his old-time rushes, but was stopped on the mouth. Implacable, insistent, ever-menacing, never letting him rest, Joe followed him up. The round, the thirteenth, closed with a rush, in Ponta's corner. He attempted a rally, was brought to his knees, took the nine seconds count, and then tried to clinch into safety, only to receive four of Joe's terrible stomach punches, so that with the gong he fell back, gasping, into the arms of his seconds.

Joe ran across the ring to his own corner.

"Now I'm going to get 'm," he said to his second.

"You sure fixed 'm that time," the latter answered. "Nothin' to stop you now but a lucky punch. Watch out for it."

Joe leaned forward, feet gathered under him for a spring like a foot-racer waiting the start. He was waiting for the gong. When it sounded he shot forward and across the ring, catching Ponta in the midst of his seconds as he rose from his stool. And in the midst of his seconds Ponta went down, knocked down by a right-hand blow. As he arose from the confusion of buckets, stools, and seconds, Joe put him down again. And yet a third time he went down before he could escape from his own corner.

Joe had at last become the whirlwind. Genevieve remembered his, "Just watch, you'll know when I go after him." The house knew it, too. It was on its feet, every voice raised in a fierce yell. It was the blood-cry of the crowd, and it sounded to her like what she imagined must be the howling of wolves. And what of confidence in her lover's victory she found room in her heart to pity Ponta.

In vain he struggled to defend himself, to block, to cover up, to duck, to clinch into a moment's safety. That moment was denied him. Knock-down after knock-down was his portion. He was knocked to the canvas backwards, and sideways, was punched in the clinches and in the break-aways—stiff, jolty blows that dazed his brain and drove the strength from his muscles. He was knocked into the corners and out again, against the ropes, rebounding, and with another blow against the ropes once more. He fanned the air with his arms, showering savage blows upon emptiness. There was nothing human left in him. He was the beast incarnate, roaring and raging and being destroyed. He was smashed down to his knees, but refused to take the count, staggering to his feet only to be met stiff-handed on the mouth and sent hurling back against the ropes.

In sore travail, gasping, reeling, panting, with glazing eyes and sobbing breath, grotesque and heroic, fighting to the last, striving to get at his antagonist, he surged and was driven about the ring. And in that moment Joe's foot slipped on the wet canvas. Ponta's swimming eyes saw and knew the chance. All the fleeing strength of his body gathered itself together for the lightning lucky punch. Even as Joe slipped the other smote him, fairly on the point of the chin. He went over backward. Genevieve saw his muscles relax while he was yet in the air, and she heard the thud of his head on the canvas.

The noise of the yelling house died suddenly. The referee, stooping over the inert body, was counting the seconds. Ponta tottered and fell to his knees. He struggled to his feet, swaying back and forth as he tried to sweep the audience with his hatred. His legs were trembling and bending under

him; he was choking and sobbing, fighting to breathe. He reeled backward and saved himself from falling by a blind clutching for the ropes. He clung there, drooping and bending and giving in all his body, his head upon his chest, until the referee counted the fatal tenth second and pointed to him in token that he had won.

He received no applause, and he squirmed through the ropes, snake-like, into the arms of his seconds, who helped him to the floor and supported him down the aisle into the crowd. Joe remained where he had fallen. His seconds carried him into his corner and placed him on the stool. Men began climbing into the ring, curious to see, but were roughly shoved out by the policemen, who were already there.

Genevieve looked out from her peep-hole. She was not greatly perturbed. Her lover had been knocked out. In so far as disappointment was his, she shared it with him; but that was all. She even felt glad in a way. The Game had played him false, and he was more surely hers. She had heard of knockouts from him. It often took men some time to recover from the effects. It was not till she heard the seconds asking for the doctor that she felt really worried.

They passed his limp body through the ropes to the stage, and it disappeared beyond the limit of her peep-hole. Then the door of her dressing-room was thrust open and a number of men came in. They were carrying Joe. He was laid down on the dusty floor, his head resting on the knee of one of the seconds. No one seemed surprised by her presence. She came over and knelt beside him. His eyes were closed, his lips slightly parted. His wet hair was plastered in straight locks about his face. She lifted one of his hands. It was very heavy, and the lifelessness of it shocked her. She looked suddenly at the faces of the seconds and of the men about her. They seemed frightened, all save one, and he was cursing, in a low voice, horribly. She looked up and saw Silverstein standing beside her. He, too, seemed frightened. He rested a kindly hand on her shoulder, tightening the fingers with a sympathetic pressure.

This sympathy frightened her. She began to feel dazed. There was a bustle as somebody entered the room. The person came forward, proclaiming irritably: "Get out! Get out! You've got to clear the room!"

A number of men silently obeyed.

"Who are you?" he abruptly demanded of Genevieve. "A girl, as I'm alive!"

"That's all right, she's his girl," spoke up a young fellow, she recognized as her guide.

"And you?" the other man blurted explosively at Silverstein.

"I'm vit her," he answered truculently.

"She works for him," explained the young fellow. "It's all right, I tell you."

The newcomer grunted and knelt down. He passed a hand over the damp head, grunted again, and arose to his feet.

"This is no case for me," he said. "Send for the ambulance."

Then the thing became a dream to Genevieve. Maybe she had fainted, she did not know, but for what other reason should Silverstein have his arm around her supporting her? All the faces seemed blurred and unreal. Fragments of a discussion came to her ears.

There was an eruption of new faces, and she saw Joe carried out on a canvas stretcher. Silverstein was buttoning the long overcoat and drawing the collar about her face. She felt the night air on her cheek, and looking up saw the clear, cold stars. She jammed into a seat. Silverstein was beside her. Joe was there, too, still on his stretcher, with blankets over his naked body; and there was a man in a blue uniform, who spoke kindly to her, though she did not know what he said. Horses' hoofs were clattering, and she was lurching somewhere through the night.

Next, lights and voices, and a smell of iodoform. This must be the receiving hospital, she thought; this the operating table, these the doctors. They were examining Joe. One of them, a dark-eyed, dark-bearded, foreign-looking man, rose up from bending over the table.

"Never saw anything like it," he was saying to another man. "The whole back of the skull. Must have been struck by a cannon-ball."

Her lips were hot and dry, and there was an intolerable ache in her throat. But why didn't she cry? She ought to cry; she felt it incumbent upon her. There was Lottie (there had been another change in the dream), across the little narrow cot from her, and she was crying. Somebody was saying something about the coma of death. It was not the foreign-looking doctor, but somebody else. It did not matter who it was. What time was it? As if in answer, she saw the faint white light of dawn on the windows.

"I was going to be married to-day," she said to Lottie.

And from across the cot his sister wailed: "Don't! Don't!" And covering her face sobbed afresh.

This, then, was the end of it all—of the carpets, the furniture, and the little rented house; of the meetings and walking out, the thrilling nights of starshine, the deliciousness of surrender, the loving and the being loved. She was stunned by the awful facts of this Game she did not understand— the grip it laid on men's souls, its irony and faithlessness, its risks, and hazards, and fierce insurgences of the blood, making women pitiful, not the be-all and end-all of man but his toy and his pastime; to women his mothering and care-taking, his moods and his moments, but to the Game his days and nights of striving, the tribute of his head and hand, his most patient toil and wildest effort, all the strain and the stress of his being—to the Game, his heart's desire.

Silverstein was helping her to her feet. She obeyed blindly, the daze of the dream still on her. His hand grasped her arm and he was turning her toward the door.

"Oh, why don't you kiss him?" Lottie cried out, her dark eyes mournful and passionate.

Genevieve stooped obediently over the quiet clay and pressed her lips to the lips yet warm. The door opened and she passed into another room. There stood Mrs. Silverstein, with angry eyes that snapped vindictively at sight of her boy's clothes.

Silverstein looked beseechingly at his spouse, but she burst forth savagely:

"Vot did I tell you, eh? Vot did I tell you? You vood haf a bruiser for your steady! An' now your name vill be in all der papers! You liddle strumpet! You hussy! You——"

But a flood of tears welled into her eyes and voice, and with her fat arms outstretched, ungainly, ludicrous, holy with motherhood, she tottered over to the quiet girl and folded her to her breast. She muttered gasping, inarticulate love-words, rocking slowly to and fro the while and patting Genevieve's shoulder with her ponderous hand.

THE END

28
SIWASH

SIWASH

"If I was a man —" Her words were in themselves indecisive, but the withering contempt which flashed from her black eyes was not lost upon the men-folk in the tent.

Tommy, the English sailor, squirmed, but chivalrous old Dick Humphries, Cornish fisherman and erstwhile American salmon capitalist, beamed upon her benevolently as ever. He bore women too large a portion of his rough heart to mind them, as he said, when they were in the doldrums, or when their limited vision would not permit them to see all around a thing. So they said nothing, these two men who had taken the half-frozen woman into their tent three days back, and who had warmed her, and fed her, and rescued her goods from the Indian packers. This latter had necessitated the payment of numerous dollars, to say nothing of a demonstration in force — Dick Humphries squinting along the sights of a Winchester while Tommy apportioned their wages among them at his own appraisement. It had been a little thing in itself, but it meant much to a woman playing a desperate single-hand in the equally desperate Klondike rush of '97. Men were occupied with their own pressing needs, nor did they approve of women playing, single-handed, the odds of the arctic winter.

"If I was a man, I know what I would do." Thus reiterated Molly, she of the flashing eyes, and therein spoke the cumulative grit of five American-born generations.

In the succeeding silence, Tommy thrust a pan of biscuits into the Yukon stove and piled on fresh fuel. A reddish flood pounded along under his sun-tanned skin, and as he stooped, the skin of his neck was scarlet. Dick palmed a three-cornered sail needle through a set of broken pack straps, his good nature in nowise disturbed by the feminine cataclysm which was threatening to burst in the storm-beaten tent.

"And if you was a man?" he asked, his voice vibrant with kindness. The three-cornered needle jammed in the damp leather, and he suspended work for the moment.

"I'd be a man. I'd put the straps on my back and light out. I wouldn't lay in camp here, with the Yukon like to freeze most any day, and the goods not half over the portage. And you — you are men, and you sit here, holding your hands, afraid of a little wind and wet. I tell you straight, Yankee-men are made of different stuff. They'd be hitting the trail for Dawson if they had to wade through hell-fire. And you, you — I wish I was a man."

"I'm very glad, my dear, that you're not." Dick Humphries threw the bight of the sail twine over the point of the needle and drew it clear with a couple of deft turns and a jerk.

A snort of the gale dealt the tent a broad-handed slap as it hurtled past, and the sleet rat-tat-tatted with snappy spite against the thin canvas. The smoke, smothered in its exit, drove back through the fire-box door, carrying with it the pungent odor of green spruce.

"Good Gawd! Why can't a woman listen to reason?" Tommy lifted his head from the denser depths and turned upon her a pair of smoke-outraged eyes.

"And why can't a man show his manhood?"

Tommy sprang to his feet with an oath which would have shocked a woman of lesser heart, ripped loose the sturdy reef-knots and flung back the flaps of the tent.

The trio peered out. It was not a heartening spectacle. A few water-soaked tents formed the miserable foreground, from which the streaming ground sloped to a foaming gorge. Down this ramped a mountain torrent. Here and there, dwarf spruce, rooting and grovelling in the shallow alluvium, marked the proximity of the timber line. Beyond, on the opposing slope, the vague outlines of a glacier loomed dead-white through the driving rain. Even as they looked, its massive front crumbled into the valley, on the breast of some subterranean vomit, and it lifted its hoarse thunder above the screeching voice of the storm. Involuntarily, Molly shrank back.

"Look, woman! Look with all your eyes! Three miles in the teeth of the gale to Crater Lake, across two glaciers, along the slippery rimrock, knee-deep in a howling river! Look, I say, you Yankee woman! Look! There's your Yankee-men!" Tommy pointed a passionate hand in the direction of the struggling tents. "Yankees, the last mother's son of them. Are they on trail? Is there one of them with the straps to his back? And you would teach us men our work? Look, I say!"

Another tremendous section of the glacier rumbled earthward. The wind whipped in at the open doorway, bulging out the sides of the tent till it swayed like a huge bladder at its guy ropes. The smoke swirled about them, and the sleet drove sharply into their flesh. Tommy pulled the flaps together hastily, and returned to his tearful task at the fire-box. Dick Humphries threw the mended pack straps into a corner and lighted his pipe. Even Molly was for the moment persuaded.

"There's my clothes," she half-whimpered, the feminine for the moment prevailing. "They're right at the top of the cache, and they'll be ruined! I tell you, ruined!"

"There, there," Dick interposed, when the last quavering syllable had wailed itself out. "Don't let that worry you, little woman. I'm old enough to be your father's brother, and I've a daughter older than you, and I'll tog you out in fripperies when we get to Dawson if it takes my last dollar."

"When we get to Dawson!" The scorn had come back to her throat with a sudden surge. "You'll rot on the way, first. You'll drown in a mudhole. You — you — Britishers!"

The last word, explosive, intensive, had strained the limits of her vituperation. If that would not stir these men, what could? Tommy's neck ran red again, but he kept his tongue between his teeth. Dick's eyes mellowed. He had the advantage over Tommy, for he had once had a white woman for a wife.

The blood of five American-born generations is, under certain circumstances, an uncomfortable heritage; and among these circumstances might be enumerated that of being quartered with next of kin. These men were Britons. On sea and land her ancestry and the generations thereof had thrashed them and theirs. On sea and land they would continue to do so. The traditions of her race clamored for vindication. She was but a woman of the present, but in her bubbled the whole mighty past. It was not alone Molly Travis who pulled on gum boots, mackintosh, and straps; for the phantom hands of ten thousand forbears drew tight the buckles, just so as they squared her jaw and set her eyes with determination. She, Molly Travis, intended to shame these Britishers; they, the innumerable shades, were asserting the dominance of the common race.

The men-folk did not interfere. Once Dick suggested that she take his oilskins, as her mackintosh was worth no more than paper in such a storm. But she sniffed her independence so sharply that he communed with his pipe till she tied the flaps on the outside and slushed away on the flooded trail.

"Think she'll make it?" Dick's face belied the indifference of his voice.

"Make it? If she stands the pressure till she gets to the cache, what of the cold and misery, she'll be stark, raving mad. Stand it? She'll be dumb-crazed. You know it yourself, Dick. You've wind-jammed round the Horn. You know what it is to lay out on a topsail yard in the thick of it, bucking sleet and snow and frozen canvas till you're ready to just let go and cry like a baby. Clothes? She won't be able to tell a bundle of skirts from a gold pan or a teakettle."

"Kind of think we were wrong in letting her go, then?"

"Not a bit of it. So help me, Dick, she'd 'a' made this tent a hell for the rest of the trip if we hadn't. Trouble with her she's got too much spirit. This'll tone it down a bit."

"Yes," Dick admitted, "she's too ambitious. But then Molly's all right. A cussed little fool to tackle a trip like this, but a plucky sight better than those pick-me-up-and-carry-me kind of women. She's the stock that carried you and me, Tommy, and you've got to make allowance for the spirit. Takes a woman to breed a man. You can't suck manhood from the dugs of a creature whose only claim to womanhood is her petticoats. Takes a she-cat, not a cow, to mother a tiger."

"And when they're unreasonable we've got to put up with it, eh?"

"The proposition. A sharp sheath-knife cuts deeper on a slip than a dull one; but that's no reason for to hack the edge off over a capstan bar."

"All right, if you say so, but when it comes to woman, I guess I'll take mine with a little less edge."

"What do you know about it?" Dick demanded.

"Some." Tommy reached over for a pair of Molly's wet stockings and stretched them across his knees to dry.

Dick, eying him querulously, went fishing in her hand satchel, then hitched up to the front of the stove with divers articles of damp clothing spread likewise to the heat.

"Thought you said you never were married?" he asked.

"Did I? No more was I — that is — yes, by Gawd! I was. And as good a woman as ever cooked grub for a man."

"Slipped her moorings?" Dick symbolized infinity with a wave of his hand.

"Ay."

"Childbirth," he added, after a moment's pause.

The beans bubbled rowdily on the front lid, and he pushed the pot back to a cooler surface. After that he investigated the biscuits, tested them with a splinter of wood, and placed them aside under cover of a damp cloth. Dick, after the manner of his kind, stifled his interest and waited silently.

"A different woman to Molly. Siwash."

Dick nodded his understanding.

"Not so proud and wilful, but stick by a fellow through thick and thin. Sling a paddle with the next and starve as contentedly as Job. Go for'ard when the sloop's nose was more often under than not, and take in sail like a man. Went prospecting once, up Teslin way, past Surprise Lake and the Little Yellow-Head. Grub gave out, and we ate the dogs. Dogs gave out, and we ate harnesses, moccasins, and furs. Never a whimper; never a pick-me-up-and-carry-me. Before we went she said look out for grub, but when it happened, never a I-told-you-so. 'Never mind, Tommy,' she'd say, day after day, that weak she could bare lift a snow-shoe and her feet raw with the

work. 'Never mind. I'd sooner be flat-bellied of hunger and be your woman, Tommy, than have a potlach every day and be Chief George's klooch.' George was chief of the Chilcoots, you know, and wanted her bad.

"Great days, those. Was a likely chap myself when I struck the coast. Jumped a whaler, the Pole Star, at Unalaska, and worked my way down to Sitka on an otter hunter. Picked up with Happy Jack there — know him?"

"Had charge of my traps for me," Dick answered, "down on the Columbia. Pretty wild, wasn't he, with a warm place in his heart for whiskey and women?"

"The very chap. Went trading with him for a couple of seasons — hooch, and blankets, and such stuff. Then got a sloop of my own, and not to cut him out, came down Juneau way. That's where I met Killisnoo; I called her Tilly for short. Met her at a squaw dance down on the beach. Chief George had finished the year's trade with the Sticks over the Passes, and was down from Dyea with half his tribe. No end of Siwashes at the dance, and I the only white. No one knew me, barring a few of the bucks I'd met over Sitka way, but I'd got most of their histories from Happy Jack.

"Everybody talking Chinook, not guessing that I could spit it better than most; and principally two girls who'd run away from Haine's Mission up the Lynn Canal. They were trim creatures, good to the eye, and I kind of thought of casting that way; but they were fresh as fresh-caught cod. Too much edge, you see. Being a newcomer, they started to twist me, not knowing I gathered in every word of Chinook they uttered.

"I never let on, but set to dancing with Tilly, and the more we danced the more our hearts warmed to each other. 'Looking for a woman,' one of the girls says, and the other tosses her head and answers, 'Small chance he'll get one when the women are looking for men.' And the bucks and squaws standing around began to grin and giggle and repeat what had been said. 'Quite a pretty boy,' says the first one. I'll not deny I was rather smooth-faced and youngish, but I'd been a man amongst men many's the day, and it rankled me. 'Dancing with Chief George's girl,' pipes the second. 'First thing George'll give him the flat of a paddle and send him about his business.' Chief George had been looking pretty black up to now, but at this he laughed and slapped his knees. He was a husky beggar and would have used the paddle too.

"'Who's the girls?' I asked Tilly, as we went ripping down the centre in a reel. And as soon as she told me their names I remembered all about them from Happy Jack. Had their pedigree down fine — several things he'd told me that not even their own tribe knew. But I held my hush, and went on courting Tilly, they a-casting sharp remarks and everybody roaring. 'Bide a wee, Tommy,' I says to myself; 'bide a wee.'

"And bide I did, till the dance was ripe to break up, and Chief George had brought a paddle all ready for me. Everybody was on the lookout for mischief when we stopped; but I marched, easy as you please, slap into the thick of them. The Mission girls cut me up something clever, and for all I was angry I had to set my teeth to keep from laughing. I turned upon them suddenly.

"'Are you done?' I asked.

"You should have seen them when they heard me spitting Chinook. Then I broke loose. I told them all about themselves, and their people before them; their fathers, mothers, sisters, brothers — everybody, everything. Each mean trick they'd played; every scrape they'd got into; every shame that'd fallen them. And I burned them without fear or favor. All hands crowded round. Never had they heard a white man sling their lingo as I did. Everybody was laughing save the Mission girls. Even Chief George forgot the paddle, or at least he was swallowing too much respect to dare to use it.

"But the girls. 'Oh, don't, Tommy,' they cried, the tears running down their cheeks. 'Please don't. We'll be good. Sure, Tommy, sure.' But I knew them well, and I scorched them on every tender spot. Nor did I slack away till they came down on their knees, begging and pleading with me to keep quiet. Then I shot a glance at Chief George; but he did not know whether to have at me or not, and passed it off by laughing hollowly.

"So be. When I passed the parting with Tilly that night I gave her the word that I was going to be around for a week or so, and that I wanted to see more of her. Not thick-skinned, her kind, when it came to showing like and dislike, and she looked

her pleasure for the honest girl she was. Ay, a striking lass, and I didn't wonder that Chief George was taken with her.

"Everything my way. Took the wind from his sails on the first leg. I was for getting her aboard and sailing down Wrangel way till it blew over, leaving him to whistle; but I wasn't to get her that easy. Seems she was living with an uncle of hers — guardian, the way such things go — and seems he was nigh to shuffling off with consumption or some sort of lung trouble. He was good and bad by turns, and she wouldn't leave him till it was over with. Went up to the tepee just before I left, to speculate on how long it'd be; but the old beggar had promised her to Chief George, and when he clapped eyes on me his anger brought on a hemorrhage.

"'Come and take me, Tommy,' she says when we bid good-by on the beach. 'Ay,' I answers; 'when you give the word.' And I kissed her, white-man-fashion and lover-fashion, till she was all of a tremble like a quaking aspen, and I was so beside myself I'd half a mind to go up and give the uncle a lift over the divide.

"So I went down Wrangel way, past St. Mary's and even to the Queen Charlottes, trading, running whiskey, turning the sloop to most anything. Winter was on, stiff and crisp, and I was back to Juneau, when the word came. 'Come,' the beggar says who brought the news. 'Killisnoo say, "Come now."' 'What's the row?' I asks. 'Chief George,' says he. 'Potlach. Killisnoo, makum klooch.'

"Ay, it was bitter — the Taku howling down out of the north, the salt water freezing quick as it struck the deck, and the old sloop and I hammering into the teeth of it for a hundred miles to Dyea. Had a Douglass Islander for crew when I started, but midway up he was washed over from the bows. Jibed all over and crossed the course three times, but never a sign of him."

"Doubled up with the cold most likely," Dick suggested, putting a pause into the narrative while he hung one of Molly's skirts up to dry, "and went down like a pot of lead."

"My idea. So I finished the course alone, half-dead when I made Dyea in the dark of the evening. The tide favored, and I ran the sloop plump to the bank, in the shelter of the river. Couldn't go an inch further, for the fresh water was frozen solid. Halyards and blocks were that iced up I didn't dare lower mainsail or jib. First I broached a pint of the cargo raw, and then, leaving all standing, ready for the start, and with a blanket around me, headed across the flat to the camp. No mistaking, it was a grand layout. The Chilcats had come in a body — dogs, babies, and canoes — to say nothing of the Dog-Ears, the Little Salmons, and the Missions. Full half a thousand of them to celebrate Tilly's wedding, and never a white man in a score of miles.

"Nobody took note of me, the blanket over my head and hiding my face, and I waded knee deep through the dogs and youngsters till I was well up to the front. The show was being pulled off in a big open place among the trees, with great fires burning and the snow moccasin-packed as hard as Portland cement. Next me was Tilly, beaded and scarlet-clothed galore, and against her Chief George and his head men. The shaman was being helped out by the big medicines from the other tribes, and it shivered my spine up and down, the deviltries they cut. I caught myself wondering if the folks in Liverpool could only see me now; and I thought of yellow-haired Gussie, whose brother I licked after my first voyage, just because he was not for having a sailor-man courting his sister. And with Gussie in my eyes I looked at Tilly. A rum old world, thinks I, with man a-stepping in trails the mother little dreamed of when he lay at suck.

"So be. When the noise was loudest, walrus hides booming and priests a-singing, I says, 'Are you ready?' Gawd! Not a start, not a shot of the eyes my way, not the twitch of a muscle. 'I knew,' she answers, slow and steady as a calm spring tide. 'Where?' 'The high bank at the edge of the ice,' I whispers back. 'Jump out when I give the word.'

"Did I say there was no end of huskies? Well, there was no end. Here, there, everywhere, they were scattered about, — tame wolves and nothing less. When the strain runs thin they breed them in the bush with the wild, and they're bitter fighters. Right at the toe of my moccasin lay a big brute, and by the heel another. I doubled the first one's tail, quick, till it snapped in my grip. As his jaws clipped together where my hand should have been, I threw the second one by the scruff straight into his mouth. 'Go!' I cried to Tilly.

"You know how they fight. In the wink of an eye there was a raging hundred of them, top and bottom, ripping and tearing each other, kids and squaws tumbling which way, and the camp gone wild. Tilly'd slipped away, so I followed. But when I looked over my shoulder at the skirt of the crowd, the devil laid me by the heart, and I dropped the blanket and went back.

"By then the dogs'd been knocked apart and the crowd was untangling itself. Nobody was in proper place, so they didn't note that Tilly'd gone. 'Hello,' I says, gripping Chief George by the hand. 'May your potlach-smoke rise often, and the Sticks bring many furs with the spring.'

"Lord love me, Dick, but he was joyed to see me, — him with the upper hand and wedding Tilly. Chance to puff big over me. The tale that I was hot after her had spread through the camps, and my presence did him proud. All hands knew me, without my blanket, and set to grinning and giggling. It was rich, but I made it richer by playing unbeknowing.

"'What's the row?' I asks. 'Who's getting married now?'

"'Chief George,' the shaman says, ducking his reverence to him.

"'Thought he had two *klooches*.'

"'Him takum more, — three,' with another duck.

"'Oh!' And I turned away as though it didn't interest me.

"But this wouldn't do, and everybody begins singing out, 'Killisnoo! Killisnoo!'

"'Killisnoo what?' I asked.

"'Killisnoo, *klooch,* Chief George,' they blathered. 'Killisnoo, *klooch.*'

"I jumped and looked at Chief George. He nodded his head and threw out his chest.

"'She'll be no *klooch* of yours,' I says solemnly. 'No *klooch* of yours,' I repeats, while his face went black and his hand began dropping to his hunting-knife.

"'Look!' I cries, striking an attitude. 'Big medicine. You watch my smoke.'

"I pulled off my mittens, rolled back my sleeves, and made half-a-dozen passes in the air.

"'Killisnoo!' I shouts. 'Killisnoo! Killisnoo!'

"I was making medicine, and they began to scare. Every eye was on me; no time to find out that Tilly wasn't there.

Then I called Killisnoo three times again, and waited; and three times more. All for mystery and to make them nervous. Chief George couldn't guess what I was up to, and wanted to put a stop to the foolery; but the shamans said to wait, and that they'd see me and go me one better, or words to that effect. Besides, he was a superstitious cuss, and I fancy a bit afraid of the white man's magic.

"Then I called Killisnoo, long and soft like the howl of a wolf, till the women were all a-tremble and the bucks looking serious.

"'Look!' I sprang for'ard, pointing my finger into a bunch of squaws — easier to deceive women than men, you know. 'Look!' And I raised it aloft as though following the flight of a bird. Up, up, straight overhead, making to follow it with my eyes till it disappeared in the sky.

"'Killisnoo,' I said, looking at Chief George and pointing upward again. 'Killisnoo.'

"So help me, Dick, the gammon worked. Half of them, at least, saw Tilly disappear in the air. They'd drunk my whiskey at Juneau and seen stranger sights, I'll warrant. Why should I not do this thing, I, who sold bad spirits corked in bottles? Some of the women shrieked. Everybody fell to whispering in bunches. I folded my arms and held my head high, and they drew further away from me. The time was ripe to go. 'Grab him,' Chief George cries. Three or four of them came at me, but I whirled, quick, made a couple of passes like to send them after Tilly, and pointed up. Touch me? Not for the kingdoms of the earth. Chief George harangued them, but he couldn't get them to lift a leg. Then he made to take me himself; but I repeated the mummery and his grit went out through his fingers.

"'Let your shamans work wonders the like of which I have done this night,' I says. 'Let them call Killisnoo down out of the sky whither I have sent her.' But the priests knew their limits. 'May your klooches bear you sons as the spawn of the salmon,' I says, turning to go; 'and may your totem pole stand long in the land, and the smoke of your camp rise always.'

"But if the beggars could have seen me hitting the high places for the sloop as soon as I was clear of them, they'd thought my own medicine had got after me. Tilly'd kept warm by chopping the ice away, and was all ready to cast off. Gawd! how we ran before it, the Taku howling after us and the freezing seas sweeping over at every clip. With everything battened down, me a-steering and Tilly chopping ice, we held on half the night, till I plumped the sloop ashore on Porcupine Island, and we shivered it out on the beach; blankets wet, and Tilly drying the matches on her breast.

"So I think I know something about it. Seven years, Dick, man and wife, in rough sailing and smooth. And then she died, in the heart of the winter, died in childbirth, up there on the Chilcat Station. She held my hand to the last, the ice creeping up inside the door and spreading thick on the gut of the window. Outside, the lone howl of the wolf and the Silence; inside, death and the Silence. You've never heard the Silence yet, Dick, and Gawd grant you don't ever have to hear it when you sit by the side of death. Hear it? Ay, till the breath whistles like a siren, and the heart booms, booms, booms, like the surf on the shore.

"Siwash, Dick, but a woman. White, Dick, white, clear through. Towards the last she says, 'Keep my feather bed, Tommy, keep it always.' And I agreed. Then she opened her eyes, full with the pain. 'I've been a good woman to you, Tommy, and because of that I want you to promise — to promise' — the words seemed to stick in her throat — 'that when you marry, the woman be white. No more Siwash, Tommy. I know. Plenty white women down to Juneau now. I know. Your people call you "squaw-man," your women turn their heads to the one side on the street and you do not go to their cabins like other men. Why? Your wife Siwash. Is it not so? And this is not good. Wherefore I die. Promise me. Kiss me in token of your promise.'

"I kissed her, and she dozed off, whispering, 'It is good.' At the end, that near gone my ear was at her lips, she roused for the last time. 'Remember, Tommy; remember my feather bed.' Then she died, in childbirth, up there on the Chilcat Station."

The tent heeled over and half flattened before the gale. Dick refilled his pipe, while Tommy drew the tea and set it aside against Molly's return.

And she of the flashing eyes and Yankee blood? Blinded, falling, crawling on hand and knee, the wind thrust back in her throat by the wind, she was heading for the tent. On her shoulders a bulky pack caught the full fury of the storm. She plucked feebly at the knotted flaps, but it was Tommy and Dick who cast them loose. Then she set her soul for the last effort, staggered in, and fell exhausted on the floor.

Tommy unbuckled the straps and took the pack from her. As he lifted it there was a clanging of pots and pans. Dick, pouring out a mug of whiskey, paused long enough to pass the wink across her body. Tommy winked back. His lips pursed the monosyllable, "clothes," but Dick shook his head reprovingly.

"Here, little woman," he said, after she had drunk the whiskey and straightened up a bit. "Here's some dry togs. Climb into them. We're going out to extra-peg the tent. After that, give us the call, and we'll come in and have dinner. Sing out when you're ready."

"So help me, Dick, that's knocked the edge off her for the rest of this trip," Tommy spluttered as they crouched to the lee of the tent.

"But it's the edge is her saving grace," Dick replied, ducking his head to a volley of sleet that drove around a corner of the canvas. "The edge that you and I've got, Tommy, and the edge of our mothers before us."

29
PLUCK AND PERTINACITY

PLUCK AND PERTINACITY

To P. T. Barnum is accorded the coinage of the term "stick-to-it-iveness," a strong synonym for "pertinacity." Now he who possesses pertinacity must also possess pluck, another important element in the achievement of success. A man devoid of this cannot be pertinacious; his resolution melts away in the face of obstacles which require pluck to overcome.

The following story of unyielding adherence to purpose, performed under almost unthinkable hardships and dangers, is a true one, for I was personally aware of most of the facts concerned. Some of the incidents, however, were given me by a surgeon travelling into the Yukon country with a detachment of the Northwest mounted police, and still others I obtained from the white trader in charge of the Sixty-Mile Post. The story is of a man who practically achieved the impossible in his hazardous ice-journey in the dead of an Arctic winter. Happily, success crowned the effort.

In the fall of 1897, the cry of famine went up from the hungry town of Dawson. Faint-hearted miners turned their backs on the golden lure. Partners, with food for but one, drew straws to ascertain which should remain and which should go. Canadian citizens and American aliens appealed to their respective governments for aid.

In October, with the last water, which was composed chiefly of running ice, a hungry exodus went down the river to Fort Yukon. Then the price of dogs went up to three hundred dollars, and dog-food to a dollar per pound. Flour was not to be had at one hundred and fifty dollars per hundredweight. In November, with the first ice, another stampeded crowd hurried up the river to civilization and safety.

This scare, which so greatly diminished the number of empty mouths, was all that saved Dawson from a bitter winter. As it was, the gold-seekers managed to pinch through; but those that fled in the height of the panic carried a terrible tale with them to salt water. After that the winter settled down and all communication ceased.

For the many faces turned south on the dismal half-thousand miles of trail, there was one that held unerringly to the north. It belonged to a Dutchman, who knew little English and spoke less. His equipment was more meagre than that of those who passed him, and he was heading into the heart of the famine while they were running away from it. He had barely food enough to last himself and dog to Dawson. He had a dog — a bulldog, the short hair of which made it the worst possible choice of a sledge animal in that frosty land.

The refugees looked at his outfit and laughed. By eloquent signs — for misery speaks a common tongue — they explained the lack of food. When that did not startle him, they painted lurid pictures of starvation and death. But he always remained unperturbed. Then they ceased their grim mirth, and pleaded and entreated him to go back. But he invariably pressed on.

Why not? He had started to go to the Klondike, and he certainly was going there. True, he had already tried the Stikine route and lost his outfit and three comrades in its treacherous waters; true, he had then gone to St. Michaels, only to get there when the Yukon had frozen and to escape on the last vessel before Bering Sea closed; true, his money was gone and he had but a few weeks' food, — all true, — but it was also true that he had left a wife and children down in the States, and he must send yellow dust of the north to them before another year had passed.

And yet again — the real stamp of the man — he had started to go to the Klondike, and he was going there. For the third time he had ventured it, this time over the dreaded Chilkoot Pass in midwinter.

After untold hardship, he arrived at the

345

Big Salmon River, two hundred and fifty miles from the Chilkoot and an equal distance from Dawson. At that point he encountered a squad of the mounted police of the Northwest Territories. They had strict orders to allow no one to pass who did not possess a thousand pounds of provisions. As he had barely fifty pounds, he was turned back. One of the police, who understood his language, explained the terrible condition of affairs.

All others whom they had turned back had retraced their steps cheerfully. But this man was not made of such mettle. Twice nature had conspired to thwart him, and then, when the trip was half completed, came man. However, he ostensibly started back. But that night he broke a trail through the deep snow and crossed the river, regaining the travelled trail far below the encampment.

The next heard of him was at Little Salmon River, when another detachment of police saw an exhausted man and a bulldog limping painfully down the river. They thought the upper camp had passed him on; so, without suspicion, they cordially invited him to their fire to rest and warm up, but he was afraid, and hobbled on.

The thermometer had gone down and then steadily remained at between fifty and sixty degrees below zero — equivalent to between eighty and ninety degrees of frost. The Dutchman had frozen one of his feet, but still pressed on. He passed fleeing men, young men, with frozen limbs or scurvy-rotted flesh — terrible wrecks of the country; but day by day, rigidly adhering to his object, he plodded into the north.

At Fort Selkirk he was forced to lay up, his frozen foot having become so bad that he could no longer travel. But he had been there only two days, when the surgeon from Big Salmon River arrived. He had sledded a hundred miles down the river with a government dog-team, to amputate the limbs of an unfortunate young man who had been trying to get out of the land. After that, the surgeon had gone on to Fort Selkirk, where he expected to wait till the incoming police picked him up.

He recognized the Dutchman and dressed his foot, the flesh of which had begun to slough away, leaving a raw and festered hole in the sole of the foot almost large enough to thrust one's fist into. He happened to explain, by signs, that he was

awaiting the coming of the police.

That was enough for the sufferer. The police were coming. They would send him back. He cut up a blanket and made a gigantic moccasin, folding thickness upon thickness till it was the size of a water-bucket. That night, he and his bulldog

Pluck and Pertinacity

headed down the river to Dawson, one hundred and seventy-five miles away.

The exquisite pain the man must have endured from the cold, the toil, the lack of food, and the injured foot, can only be conjectured. And it was not as if he had comrades, for he suffered alone, and ran the dangers of the ice-journey without hope of help in case of accident.

At Stuart River he was almost gone; but his persistence and indomitability seemed limitless. The fear that the police would capture him and send him back drove him on; and he was the kind of man that did not know the meaning of the word "failure." As it was, the police, with their fine trail equipment of dogs and sleds, never did succeed in overtaking him.

At Sixty-Mile, it seemed that he must at last succumb, for the dog had finally become exhausted, as had also the supply of food. But the white trader at that point bought the dog for two hundred dollars and sufficient food to last the man into Dawson, then only fifty miles away.

Barely had he reached his goal when he was sawing wood at fifteen dollars a day, and slowly but surely curing his foot that he might go prospecting. It is no easy task to work all day in the open in such a frosty clime. But he worked steadily through the winter, while other men idled in their cabins and cursed their ill-luck and the country in general. Not only did he manage to earn subsistence, but he got himself a miner's outfit, and also sent out a snug portion of his earnings to the wife and children down in the States.

In the spring, while the majority of the gold-seekers were preparing to shake the dust of the country from their moccasins, he took part in the stampede to the French Hill benches. A little later, those that passed his claim might have seen a contented-looking man busily engaged in washing out a satisfactory amount of gold a day.

There can be no better way to conclude this narrative of unyielding adherence to purpose, than by stating that one of the first things he did was to hunt up the Sixty-Mile trader and buy back the bulldog that had been the comrade of his hardships and sufferings.

30
THE SICKNESS OF LONE CHIEF

THE SICKNESS OF LONE CHIEF

This is a tale that was told to me by two old men. We sat in the smoke of a mosquito-smudge, in the cool of the day, which was midnight; and ever and anon, throughout the telling, we smote lustily and with purpose at such of the winged pests as braved the smoke for a snack at our hides. To the right, beneath us, twenty feet down the crumbling bank, the Yukon gurgled lazily. To the left, on the rose-leaf rim of the low-lying hills, smouldered the sleepy sun, which saw no sleep that night nor was destined to see sleep for many nights to come.

The old men who sat with me and valorously slew mosquitoes were Lone Chief and Mutsak, erstwhile comrades in arms, and now withered repositories of tradition and ancient happening. They were the last of their generation and without honor among the younger set which had grown up on the farthest fringe of a mining civilization. Who cared for tradition in these days, when spirits could be evoked from black bottles, and black bottles could be evoked from the complaisant white men for a few hours' sweat or a mangy fur? Of what potency the fearful rites and masked mysteries of shamanism, when daily that living wonder, the steamboat, coughed and spluttered up and down the Yukon in defiance of all law, a veritable fire-breathing monster? And of what value was hereditary prestige, when he who now chopped the most wood, or best conned a sternwheeler through the island mazes, attained the chiefest consideration of his fellows?

Of a truth, having lived too long, they had fallen on evil days, these two old men, Lone Chief and Mutsak, and in the new order they were without honor or place. So they waited drearily for death, and the while their hearts warmed to the strange white man who shared with them the torments of the mosquito-smudge and lent ready ear to their tales of old time before the steamboat came.

"So a girl was chosen for me," Lone Chief was saying. His voice, shrill and piping, ever and again dropped plummet-like into a hoarse and rattling bass, and, just as one became accustomed to it, soaring upward into the thin treble — alternate cricket chirpings and bullfrog croakings, as it were.

"So a girl was chosen for me," he was saying. "For my father, who was Kask-ta-ka, the Otter, was angered because I looked not with a needful eye upon women. He was an old man, and chief of his tribe. I was the last of his sons to be alive, and through me, only, could he look to see his blood go down among those to come after and as yet unborn. But know, O White Man, that I was very sick; and when neither the hunting nor the fishing delighted me, and by meat my belly was not made warm, how should I look with favor upon women? or prepare for the feast of marriage? or look forward to the prattle and troubles of little children?"

"Ay," Mutsak interrupted. "For had not Lone Chief fought in the arms of a great bear till his head was cracked and blood ran from out his ears?"

Lone Chief nodded vigorously. "Mutsak speaks true. In the time that followed, my head was well, and it was not well. For though the flesh healed and the sore went away, yet was I sick inside. When I walked, my legs shook under me, and when I looked at the light, my eyes became filled with tears. And when I opened my eyes, the world outside went around and around, and when I closed my eyes, my head inside went around and around, and all the things I had ever seen went around and around inside my head. And above my eyes there was a great pain, as though something heavy rested always upon me, or like a band that is drawn tight and gives much hurt. And speech was slow to me, and I waited long for each right word to come to my tongue. And when I waited not long, all manner of words crowded in, and my tongue spoke foolishness. I was very sick, and when my father, the Otter, brought the girl Kasaan before me—"

"Who was a young girl, and strong, my sister's child," Mutsak broke in. "Strong-hipped for children was Kasaan, and straight-legged and quick of foot. She made better moccasins than any of all the young girls, and the bark-rope she braided was the stoutest. And she had a smile in her eyes, and a laugh on her lips; and her temper was not hasty, nor was she unmindful that men give the law and women ever obey."

"As I say, I was very sick," Lone Chief went on. "And when my father, the Otter, brought the girl Kasaan before me, I said rather should they make me ready for burial than for marriage. Whereat the face of my father went black with anger, and he said that I should be served according to my wish, and that I who was yet alive should be made ready for death as one already dead—"

"Which be not the way of our people, O White Man," spoke up Mutsak. "For know that these things that were done to Lone Chief it was our custom to do only to dead men. But the Otter was very angry."

"Ay," said Lone Chief. "My father, the Otter, was a man short of speech and swift of deed. And he commanded the people to gather before the lodge wherein I lay. And when they were gathered, he commanded them to mourn for his son who was dead —"

"And before the lodge they sang the death-song —O-o-o-o-o-o-a-haa-ha-a-ich-klu-kuk-ich-klu-kuk," wailed Mutsak, in so excellent an imitation that all the tendrils of my spine crawled and curved in sympathy.

"And inside the lodge," continued Lone Chief, "my mother blackened her face with soot, and flung ashes upon her head, and mourned for me as one already dead; for so had my father commanded. So Okiakuta, my mother, mourned with much noise, and beat her breasts and tore her hair; and likewise Hooniak, my sister, and Seenatah, my mother's sister; and the noise they made caused a great ache in my head, and I felt that I would surely and immediately die.

"And the elders of the tribe gathered about me where I lay and discussed the journey my soul must take. One spoke of the thick and endless forests where lost souls wandered crying, and where I, too, might chance to wander and never see the end. And another spoke of the big rivers, rapid with bad water, where evil spirits shrieked and lifted up their formless arms to drag one down by the hair. For these rivers, all said together, a canoe must be provided me. And yet another spoke of the storms, such as no live man ever saw, when the stars rained down out of the sky, and the earth gaped wide in many cracks, and all the rivers in the heart of the earth rushed out and in. Whereupon they that sat by me flung up their arms and wailed loudly; and those outside heard, and wailed more loudly. And as to them I was as dead, so was I to my own mind dead. I did not know when, or how, yet did I know that I had surely died.

"And Okiakuta, my mother, laid beside me my squirrel-skin parka. Also she laid beside me my parka of caribou hide, and my rain coat of seal gut, and my wet-weather muclucs, that my soul should be warm and dry on its long journey. Further, there was mention made of a steep hill, thick with briers and devil's-club, and she fetched heavy moccasins to make the way easy for my feet.

"And when the elders spoke of the great beasts I should have to slay, the young men laid beside me my strongest bow and straightest arrows, my throwing-stick, my spear and knife. And when the elders spoke of the darkness and silence of the great spaces my soul must wander through, my mother wailed yet more loudly and flung yet more ashes upon her head.

"And the girl, Kasaan, crept in, very timid and quiet, and dropped a little bag upon the things for my journey. And in the little bag, I knew, were the flint and steel and the well-dried tinder for the fires my soul must build. And the blankets were chosen which were to be wrapped around me. Also were the slaves selected that were to be killed that my soul might have company. There were seven of these slaves, for my father was rich and powerful, and it was fit that I, his son, should have proper burial. These slaves we had got in war from the Mukumuks, who live down the Yukon. On the morrow, Skolka, the shaman, would kill them, one by one, so that their souls should go questing with mine through the Unknown. Among other things, they would carry my canoe till we came to the big river, rapid with bad water. And there being no room, and their work being done, they would come no farther, but remain and howl forever in the dark and endless forest.

"And as I looked on my fine warm clothes, and my blankets and weapons of war, and as I thought of the seven slaves to be slain, I felt proud of my burial and knew that I must be the envy of many men. And all the while my father, the Otter, sat silent and black. And all that day and night the people sang my death-song and beat the drums, till it seemed that I had surely died a thousand times.

"But in the morning my father arose and made talk. He had been a fighting man all his days, he said, as the people knew. Also the people knew that it were a greater honor to die fighting in battle than on the soft skins by the fire. Ahd since I was to die anyway, it were well that I should go against the Mukumuks and be slain. Thus would I attain honor and chieftainship in the final abode of the dead, and thus would honor remain to my father, who was the Otter. Wherefore he gave command that a war party be made ready to go down the river. And that when we came upon the Mukumuks I was to go forth alone from my party, giving semblance of battle, and so be slain."

"Nay, but hear, O White Man!" cried Mutsak, unable longer to contain himself. "Skolka, the shaman, whispered long that night in the ear of the Otter, and it was his doing that Lone Chief should be sent forth to die. For the Otter being old, and Lone Chief the last of his sons, Skolka had it in mind to become chief himself over the people. And when the people had made great noise for a day and a night and Lone Chief was yet alive, Skolka was become afraid that he would not die. So it was the counsel of Skolka, with fine words of honor and deeds, that spoke through the mouth of the Otter."

"Ay," replied Lone Chief. "Well did I know it was the doing of Skolka, but I was un-mindful, being very sick. I had no heart for anger, nor belly for stout words, and I cared little, one way or the other, only I cared to die and have done with it all. So, O White Man, the war party was made ready. No tried fighters were there, nor elders, crafty and wise — naught but five score of young men who had seen little fighting. And all the village gathered together above the bank of the river to see us depart. And we departed amid great rejoicing and the singing of my praises. Even thou, O White Man, wouldst rejoice at sight of a young man going forth to battle, even though doomed to die.

"So we went forth, the five score young men, and Mutsak came also, for he was likewise young and untried. And by command of my father, the Otter, my canoe was lashed on either side to the canoe of Mutsak and the canoe of Kannakut. Thus was my strength saved me from the work of the paddles, so that, for all of my sickness, I might make a brave show at the end. And thus we went down the river.

"Nor will I weary thee with the tale of the journey, which was not long. And not far above the village of the Mukumuks we came upon two of their fighting men in canoes, that fled at the sight of us. And then, according to the command of my father, my canoe was cast loose and I was left to drift down all alone. Also, according to his command, were the young men to see me die, so that they might return and tell the manner of my death. Upon this, my father, the Otter, and Skolka, the shaman, had been very clear, with stern promises of punishment in case they were not obeyed.

"I dipped my paddle and shouted words of scorn after the fleeing warriors. And the vile things I shouted made them turn their heads in anger, when they beheld that the young men held back, and that I came on alone. Whereupon, when they had made a safe distance, the two warriors drew their canoes somewhat apart and waited side by side for me to come between. And I came between, spear in hand, and singing the war-song of my people. Each flung a spear, but I bent my body, and the spears whistled over me, and I was unhurt. Then, and we were all together, we three, I cast my spear at the one to the right, and it drove into his throat and he pitched backward into the water.

"Great was my surprise thereat, for I had killed a man. I turned to the one on the left and drove strong with my paddle, to meet Death face to face; but the man's second spear, which was his last, but bit into the flesh of my shoulder. Then was I upon him, making no cast, but pressing the point into his breast and working it through him with both my hands. And while I worked, pressing with all my strength, he smote me upon my head, once and twice, with the broad of his paddle.

"Even as the point of the spear sprang out beyond his back, he smote me upon the head. There was a flash, as of bright light, and inside my head I felt something give, with a snap — just like that, with a snap. And the weight that pressed above my eyes so long was lifted, and the band that bound my brows so tight was broken. And a great gladness came upon me, and my heart sang with joy.

"This be death, I thought; wherefore I thought that death was very good. And then I saw the two empty canoes, and I knew that I was not dead, but well again. The blows of the man upon my head had made me well. I knew that I had killed, and the taste of the blood made me fierce, and I drove my paddle into the breast of the Yukon and urged my canoe toward the village of the Mukumuks. The young men behind me gave a great cry. I looked over my shoulder and saw the water foaming white from their paddles—"

"Ay, it foamed white from our paddles," said Mutsak. "For we remembered the command of the Otter, and of Skolka, that we behold with our own eyes the manner of Lone Chief's death. A young man of the Mukumuks, on his way to a salmon trap, beheld the coming of Lone Chief, and of the five score men behind him. And the young man fled in his canoe, straight for the village, that alarm might be given and preparation made. But Lone Chief hurried after him, and we hurried after Lone Chief to behold the manner of his death. Only, in the face of the village, as the young man leaped to the shore, Lone Chief rose up in his canoe and made a mighty cast. And the spear entered the body of the young man above the hips, and the young man fell upon his face.

"Whereupon Lone Chief leaped up the bank war-club in hand and a great war-cry on his lips, and dashed into the village. The first man he met was Itwilie, chief over the Mukumuks, and him Lone Chief smote upon the head with his war-club, so that he fell dead upon the ground. And for fear we might not behold the manner of his death, we too, the five score young men, leaped to the shore and followed Lone Chief

into the village. Only the Mukumuks did not understand, and thought we had come to fight; so their bow-thongs sang and their arrows whistled among us. Whereat we forgot our errand, and fell upon them with our spears and clubs; and they being unprepared, there was great slaughter—"

"With my own hands I slew their shaman," proclaimed Lone Chief, his withered face a-work with memory of that old-time day. "With my own hands I slew him, who was a greater shaman than Skolka, our own shaman. And each time I faced a man, I thought, 'Now cometh Death'; and each time I slew the man, and Death came not. It seemed the breath of life was strong in my nostrils and I could not die—"

"And we followed Lone Chief the length of the village and back again," continued Mutsak. "Like a pack of wolves we followed him, back and forth, and here and there, till there were no more Mukumuks left to fight. Then we gathered together five score men-slaves, and double as many women, and countless children, and we set fire and burned all the houses and lodges, and departed. And that was the last of the Mukumuks."

"And that was the last of the Mukumuks," Lone Chief repeated exultantly. "And when we came to our own village, the people were amazed at our burden of wealth and slaves, and in that I was still alive they were more amazed. And my father, the Otter, came trembling with gladness at the things I had done. For he was an old man, and I the last of his sons. And all the tried fighting men came, and the crafty and wise, till all the people were gathered together. And then I arose, and with a voice like thunder, commanded Skolka, the shaman, to stand forth—"

"Ay, O White Man," exclaimed Mutsak. "With a voice like thunder, that made the people shake at the knees and become afraid."

"And when Skolka had stood forth," Lone Chief went on, "I said that I was not minded to die. Also, I said it were not well that disappointment come to the evil spirits that wait beyond the grave. Wherefore I deemed it fit that the soul of Skolka fare forth into the Unknown, where doubtless it would howl forever in the dark and endless forest. And then I slew him, as he stood there, in the face of all the people. Even I, Lone Chief, with my own hands, slew Skolka, the shaman, in the face of all the people. And when a murmuring arose, I cried aloud—"

"With a voice like thunder," prompted Mutsak.

"Ay, with a voice like thunder I cried aloud: 'Behold, O ye people! I am Lone Chief, slayer of Skolka, the false shaman! Alone among men, have I passed down through the gateway of Death and returned again. Mine eyes have looked upon the unseen things. Mine ears have heard the unspoken words. Greater am I than Skolka, the shaman. Greater than all shamans am I. Likewise am I a greater chief than my father, the Otter. All his days did he fight with the Mukumuks, and lo, in one day have I destroyed them all. As with the breathing of a breath have I destroyed them. Wherefore, my father, the Otter, being old, and Skolka, the shaman, being dead, I shall be both chief and shaman.

Henceforth shall I be both chief and shaman to you, O my people. And if any man dispute my word, let that man stand forth!'

"I waited, but no man stood forth. Then I cried: 'Hoh! I have tasted blood! Now bring meat, for I am hungry. Break open the caches, tear down the fish-racks, and let the feast be big. Let there be merriment, and songs, not of burial, but marriage. And last of all, let the girl Kasaan be brought. The girl Kasaan, who is to be the mother of the children of Lone Chief!'

"And at my words, and because that he was very old, my father, the Otter, wept like a woman, and put his arms about my knees. And from that day I was both chief and shaman. And great honor was mine, and all men yielded me obedience."

"Until the steamboat came," Mutsak prompted.

"Ay," said Lone Chief. "Until the steamboat came."

31
AT THE RAINBOW'S END

AT THE RAINBOW'S END

I

It was for two reasons that Montana Kid discarded his "chaps" and Mexican spurs, and shook the dust of the Idaho ranges from his feet. In the first place, the encroachments of a steady, sober, and sternly moral civilization had destroyed the primeval status of the western cattle ranges, and refined society turned the cold eye of disfavor upon him and his ilk. In the second place, in one of its cyclopean moments the race had arisen and shoved back its frontier several thousand miles. Thus, with unconscious foresight, did mature society make room for its adolescent members. True, the new territory was mostly barren; but its several hundred thousand square miles of frigidity at least gave breathing space to those who else would have suffocated at home.

Montana Kid was such a one. Heading for the sea-coast, with a haste several sheriff's posses might possibly have explained, and with more nerve than coin of the realm, he succeeded in shipping from a Puget Sound port, and managed to survive the contingent miseries of steerage seasickness and steerage grub. He was rather sallow and drawn, but still his own indomitable self, when he landed on the Dyea beach one day in the spring of the year. Between the cost of dogs, grub, and outfits, and the customs exactions of the two clashing governments, it speedily penetrated to his understanding that the Northland was anything save a poor man's Mecca. So he cast about him in search of quick harvests. Between the beach and the passes were scattered many thousands of passionate pilgrims. These pilgrims Montana Kid proceeded to farm. At first he dealt faro in a pine-board gambling shack; but disagreeable necessity forced him to drop a sudden period into a man's life, and to move on up trail. Then he effected a corner in horseshoe nails, and they circulated at par with legal tender, four to the dollar, till an unexpected consignment of a hundred barrels or so broke the market and forced him to disgorge his stock at a loss. After that he located at Sheep Camp, organized the professional packers, and jumped the freight ten cents a pound in a single day. In token of their gratitude, the packers patronized his faro and roulette layouts and were mulcted cheerfully of their earnings. But his commercialism was of too lusty a growth to be long endured; so they rushed him one night, burned his shanty, divided the bank, and headed him up the trail with empty pockets.

Ill-luck was his running mate. He engaged with responsible parties to run whisky across the line by way of precarious and unknown trails, lost his Indian guides, and had the very first outfit confiscated by the Mounted Police. Numerous other misfortunes tended to make him bitter of heart and wanton of action, and he celebrated his arrival at Lake Bennett by terrorizing the camp for twenty straight hours. Then a miners' meeting took him in hand, and commanded him to make himself scarce. He had a wholesome respect for such assemblages, and he obeyed in such haste that he inadvertently removed himself at the tail-end of another man's dog team. This was equivalent to horse-stealing in a more mellow clime, so he hit only the high places across Bennett and down Tagish, and made his first camp a full hundred miles to the north.

Now it happened that the break of spring was at hand, and many of the principal citizens of Dawson were travelling south on the last ice. These he met and talked with, noted their names and possessions, and passed on. He had a good memory, also a fair imagination; nor was veracity one of his virtues.

II

Dawson, always eager for news, beheld Montana Kid's sled heading down the Yukon, and went out on the ice to meet him. No, he hadn't any newspapers; didn't know whether Durrant was hanged yet, nor who had won the Thanksgiving game; hadn't heard whether the United States and Spain had gone to fighting; didn't know who Dreyfus was; but O'Brien? Hadn't they heard? O'Brien, why, he was drowned in the White Horse; Sitka Charley the only one of the party who escaped. Joe Ladue? Both legs frozen and amputated at the Five Fingers. And Jack Dalton? Blown up on the "Sea Lion" with all hands. And Bettles? Wrecked on the "Carthagina," in Seymour Narrows, — twenty survivors out of three hundred. And Swiftwater Bill? Gone through the rotten ice of Lake LeBarge with six female members of the opera troupe he was convoying. Governor Walsh? Lost with all hands and eight sleds on the Thirty Mile. Devereaux? Who was Devereaux? Oh, the courier! Shot by Indians on Lake Marsh.

So it went. The word was passed along. Men shouldered in to ask after friends and partners, and in turn were shouldered out, too stunned for blasphemy. By the time Montana Kid gained the bank he was surrounded by several hundred fur-clad miners. When he passed the Barracks he was the centre of a procession. At the Opera House he was the nucleus of an excited mob, each member struggling for a chance to ask after some absent comrade. On every side he was being invited to drink. Never before had the Klondike thus opened its arms to a che-cha-qua. All Dawson was humming. Such a series of catastrophes had never occurred in its history. Every man of note who had gone south in the spring had been wiped out. The cabins vomited forth their occupants. Wild-eyed men hurried down from the creeks and gulches to seek out this man who had told a tale of such disaster. The Russian half-breed wife of Bettles sought the fireplace, inconsolable, and rocked back and forth, and ever and anon flung white wood-ashes upon her raven hair. The flag at the Barracks flopped dismally at half-mast. Dawson mourned its dead.

Why Montana Kid did this thing no man may know. Nor beyond the fact that the truth was not in him, can explanation be hazarded. But for five whole days he plunged the land in wailing and sorrow, and for five whole days he was the only man in the Klondike. The country gave him its best of bed and board. The saloons granted him the freedom of their bars. Men sought him continuously. The high officials bowed down to him for further information, and he was feasted at the Barracks by Constantine and his brother officers. And then, one day, Devereaux, the government courier, halted his tired dogs before the gold commissioner's office. Dead? Who said so? Give him a moose steak and he'd show them how dead he was. Why, Governor Walsh was in camp on the Little Salmon, and O'Brien coming in on the first water. Dead? Give him a moose steak and he'd show them.

And forthwith Dawson hummed. The Barracks' flag rose to the masthead, and Bettles' wife washed herself and put on clean raiment. The community subtly signified its desire that Montana Kid obliterate himself from the landscape. And Montana Kid obliterated; as usual, at the tail-end of some one else's dog team. Dawson rejoiced when he headed down the Yukon, and wished him godspeed to the ultimate destination of the case-hardened sinner. After that the owner of the dogs bestirred himself, made complaint to Constantine, and from him received the loan of a policeman.

III

With Circle City in prospect and the last ice crumbling under his runners, Montana Kid took advantage of the lengthening days and travelled his dogs late and early. Further, he had but little doubt that the owner of the dogs in question had taken his trail, and he wished to make American territory before the river broke. But by the afternoon of the third day it became evident that he had lost in his race with spring. The Yukon was growling and straining at its fetters. Long detours became necessary, for the trail had begun to fall through into the swift current beneath, while the ice, in constant unrest, was thundering apart in great gaping fissures. Through these and through countless airholes, the water began to sweep across the surface of the ice, and by the time he pulled into a woodchopper's cabin on the point of an island, the dogs were being rushed off their feet and were swimming more often than not. He was greeted sourly by the two residents, but he unharnessed and proceeded to cook up.

Donald and Davy were fair specimens of frontier inefficients. Canadian-born, city-bred Scots, in a foolish moment they had resigned their counting-house desks, drawn upon their savings, and gone Klondiking. And now they were feeling the rough edge of the country. Grubless, spiritless, with a lust for home in their hearts, they had been staked by the P. C. Company to cut wood for its steamers, with the promise at the end of a passage home. Disregarding the possibilities of the ice-run, they had fittingly demonstrated their inefficiency by their choice of the island on which they located. Montana Kid, though possessing little knowledge of the breakup of a great river, looked about him dubiously, and cast yearning glances at the distant bank where the towering bluffs promised immunity from all the ice of the Northland.

After feeding himself and dogs, he lighted his pipe and strolled out to get a better idea of the situation. The island, like all its river brethren, stood higher at the upper end, and it was here that Donald and Davy had built their cabin and piled many cords of wood. The far shore was a full mile away, while between the island and the near shore lay a back-channel perhaps a hundred yards across. At first sight of this, Montana Kid was tempted to take his dogs and escape to the mainland, but on closer inspection he discovered a rapid current flooding on top. Below, the river twisted sharply to the west, and in this turn its breast was studded by a maze of tiny islands.

"That's where she'll jam," he remarked to himself.

Half a dozen sleds, evidently bound upstream to Dawson, were splashing through the chill water to the tail of the island. Travel on the river was passing from the precarious to the impossible, and it was nip and tuck with them till they gained the island and came up the path of the wood-choppers toward the cabin. One of them, snow-blind, towed helplessly at the rear of a sled. Husky young fellows they were, rough-garmented and trail-worn, yet Montana Kid had met the breed before and knew at once that it was not his kind.

"Hello! How's things up Dawson-way?" queried the foremost, passing his eye over Donald and Davy and settling it upon the Kid.

A first meeting in the wilderness is not characterized by formality. The talk quickly became general, and the news of the Upper and Lower Countries was swapped equitably back and forth. But the little the new-comers had was soon over with, for they had wintered at Minook, a thousand miles below, where nothing was doing. Montana Kid, however, was fresh from Salt Water, and they annexed him while they pitched camp, swamping him with questions concerning the outside, from which they had been cut off for a twelvemonth.

A shrieking split, suddenly lifting itself above the general uproar on the river, drew everybody to the bank. The surface water had increased in depth, and the ice, assailed from above and below, was struggling to tear itself from the grip of the shores. Fissures reverberated into life before their eyes, and the air was filled with multitudinous crackling, crisp and sharp, like the sound that goes up on a clear day from the firing line.

From up the river two men were racing a dog team toward them on an uncovered stretch of ice. But even as they looked, the pair struck the water and began to flounder through. Behind, where their feet had sped the moment before, the ice broke up and turned turtle. Through this opening the river rushed out upon them to their waists, burying the sled and swinging the dogs off at right angles in a drowning tangle. But the men stopped their flight to give the animals a fighting chance, and they groped hurriedly in the cold confusion, slashing at the detaining traces with their sheath-knives. Then they fought their way to the bank through swirling water and grinding ice, where, foremost in leaping to the rescue among the jarring fragments, was the Kid.

"Why, blime me, if it ain't Montana Kid!" exclaimed one of the men whom the Kid was just placing upon his feet at the top of the bank. He wore the scarlet tunic of the Mounted Police and jocularly raised his right hand in salute.

"Got a warrant for you, Kid," he continued, drawing a bedraggled paper from his breast pocket, "an' I 'ope as you'll come along peaceable."

Montana Kid looked at the chaotic river and shrugged his shoulders, and the policeman, following his glance, smiled.

"Where are the dogs?" his companion asked.

"Gentlemen," interrupted the policeman, "this 'ere mate o' mine is Jack Sutherland, owner of Twenty-Two Eldorado —"

"Not Sutherland of '92?" broke in the snow-blinded Minook man, groping feebly toward him.

"The same." Sutherland gripped his hand.

"And you?"

"Oh, I'm after your time, but I remember you in my freshman year, — you were doing P.G. work then. Boys," he called, turning half about, "this is Sutherland, Jack Sutherland, erstwhile fullback on the 'Varsity. Come up, you gold-chasers, and fall upon him! Sutherland, this is Greenwich, — played quarter two seasons back."

"Yes, I read of the game," Sutherland said, shaking hands. "And I remember that big run of yours for the first touchdown."

Greenwich flushed darkly under his tanned skin and awkwardly made room for another.

"And here's Matthews, — Berkeley man. And we've got some Eastern cracks knocking about, too. Come up, you Princeton men! Come up! This is Sutherland, Jack Sutherland!"

Then they fell upon him heavily, carried him into camp, and supplied him with dry clothes and numerous mugs of black tea.

Donald and Davy, overlooked, had retired to their nightly game of crib. Montana Kid followed them with the policeman.

"Here, get into some dry togs," he said, pulling them from out his scanty kit. "Guess you'll have to bunk with me, too."

"Well, I say, you're a good 'un," the policeman remarked as he pulled on the other man's socks. "Sorry I've got to take you back to Dawson, but I only 'ope they won't be 'ard on you."

"Not so fast." The Kid smiled curiously. "We ain't under way yet. When I go I'm going down river, and I guess the chances are you'll go along."

"Not if I know myself —"

"Come on outside, and I'll show you, then. These damn fools," thrusting a thumb over his shoulder at the two Scots, "played smash when they located here. Fill your pipe, first — this is pretty good plug — and enjoy yourself while you can. You have n't many smokes before you."

The policeman went with him wonderingly while Donald and Davy dropped their cards and followed. The Minook men noticed Montana Kid pointing now up the river, now down, and came over.

"What's up?" Sutherland demanded.

"Nothing much." Nonchalance sat well upon the Kid. "Just a case of raising hell and putting a chunk under. See that bend down there? That's where she'll jam millions of tons of ice. Then she'll jam in the bends up above, millions of tons. Upper jam breaks first, lower jam holds, pouf!" He dramatically swept the island with his hand. "Millions of tons," he added reflectively.

"And what of the woodpiles?" Davy questioned.

The Kid repeated his sweeping gesture, and Davy wailed, "The labor of months! It canna be! Na, na, lad, it canna be. I doot not it's a jowk. Ay, say that it is," he appealed.

But when the Kid laughed harshly and turned on his heel, Davy flung himself upon the piles and began frantically to toss the cordwood back from the bank.

"Lend a hand, Donald!" he cried. "Can ye no lend a hand? 'Tis the labor of months and the passage home!"

Donald caught him by the arm and shook him, but he tore free. "Did ye no hear, man? Millions of tons, and the island shall be sweepit clean."

"Straighten yersel' up, man," said Donald. "It's a bit fashed ye are."

But Davy fell upon the cordwood. Donald stalked back to the cabin, buckled on his money belt and Davy's, and went out to the point of the island where the ground was highest and where a huge pine towered above its fellows.

The men before the cabin heard the ringing of his axe and smiled. Greenwich returned from across the island with the word that they were penned in. It was impossible to cross the back-channel. The blind Minook man began to sing, and the rest joined in with —

"Wonder if it 's true?
Does it seem so to you?
Seems to me he's lying —
Oh, I wonder if it's true?"

"It's ay sinfu'," Davy moaned, lifting his head and watching them dance in the slanting rays of the sun. "And my guid wood a' going to waste."

"Oh, I wonder if it 's true,"

was flaunted back.

The noise of the river ceased suddenly. A strange calm wrapped about them. The ice had ripped from the shores and was floating higher on the surface of the river, which was rising. Up it came, swift and silent, for twenty feet, till the huge cakes rubbed softly against the crest of the bank. The tail of the island, being lower, was overrun. Then, without effort, the white flood started down-stream. But the sound increased with the momentum, and soon the whole island was shaking and quivering with the shock of the grinding bergs. Under pressure, the mighty cakes, weighing hundreds of tons, were shot into the air like peas. The frigid anarchy increased its riot, and the men had to shout into one another's ears to be heard. Occasionally the racket from the back channel could be heard above the tumult.

The island shuddered with the impact of an enormous cake which drove in squarely upon its point. It ripped a score of pines out by the roots, then swinging around and over, lifted its muddy base from the bottom of the river and bore down upon the cabin, slicing the bank and trees away like a gigantic knife. It seemed barely to graze the corner of the cabin, but the cribbed logs tilted up like matches, and the structure, like a toy house, fell backward in ruin.

"The labor of months! The labor of months, and the passage home!" Davy wailed, while Montana Kid and the policeman dragged him backward from the woodpiles.

"You'll 'ave plenty o' hoppertunity all in good time for yer passage 'ome," the policeman growled, clouting him alongside the head and sending him flying into safety.

Donald, from the top of the pine, saw the devastating berg sweep away the cordwood and disappear down-stream. As though satisfied with this damage, the ice-flood quickly dropped to its old level and began to slacken its pace. The noise likewise eased down, and the others could hear Donald shouting from his eyrie to look down-stream. As forecast, the jam had come among the islands in the bend, and the ice was piling up in a great barrier which stretched from shore to shore. The river came to a standstill, and the water finding no outlet began to rise. It rushed up till the island was awash, the men splashing around up to their knees, and the dogs swimming to the ruins of the cabin. At this stage it abruptly became stationary, with no perceptible rise or fall.

Montana Kid shook his head. "It's jammed above, and no more's coming down."

"And the gamble is, which jam will break first," Sutherland added.

"Exactly," the Kid affirmed. "If the upper jam breaks first, we have n't a chance. Nothing will stand before it."

The Minook men turned away in silence, but soon "Rumsky Ho" floated upon the quiet air, followed by "The Orange and the Black." Room was made in the circle for Montana Kid and the policeman, and they quickly caught the ringing rhythm of the choruses as they drifted on from song to song.

"Oh, Donald, will ye no lend a hand?" Davy sobbed at the foot of the tree into which his comrade had climbed. "Oh, Donald, man, will ye no lend a hand?" he sobbed again, his hands bleeding from vain attempts to scale the slippery trunk.

But Donald had fixed his gaze up river, and now his voice rang out, vibrant with fear: —

"God Almichty, here she comes!"

Standing knee-deep in the icy water, the Minook men, with Montana Kid and the policeman, gripped hands and raised their voices in the terrible "Battle Hymn of the Republic." But the words were drowned in the advancing roar.

And to Donald was vouchsafed a sight such as no man may see and live. A great wall of white flung itself upon the island. Trees, dogs, men, were blotted out, as though the hand of God had wiped the face of nature clean. This much he saw, then swayed an instant longer in his lofty perch and hurtled far out into the frozen hell.

32
THE BANKS OF THE SACRAMENTO

THE BANKS OF THE SACRAMENTO

"And it's blow ye winds, heigh-ho,
For Cal-i-for-ni-o;
For there's plenty of gold, so I've
*   been told,*
On the banks of the Sacramento!"

It was only a little boy, singing in a shrill treble the sea chantey which seamen sing the wide world over when they man the capstan-bars and break the anchors out for "Frisco" port. It was only a little boy who had never seen the sea, but two hundred feet beneath him rolled the Sacramento. "Young" Jerry he was called, after "Old" Jerry, his father, from whom he had learned the song, as well as received his shock of bright-red hair, his blue, dancing eyes, and his fair and inevitably freckled skin.

For Old Jerry had been a sailor, and had followed the sea till middle life, haunted always by the words of the ringing chantey. Then one day he had sung the song in earnest, in an Asiatic port, swinging and thrilling round the capstan-circle with twenty others. And at San Francisco he turned his back upon his ship and upon the sea, and went to behold with his own eyes the banks of the Sacramento.

He beheld the gold, too, for he found employment at the Yellow Dream mine, and proved of utmost usefulness in rigging the great ore-cables across the river and two hundred feet above its surface.

After that he took charge of the cables and kept them in repair, and ran them and loved them, and became himself an indispensable fixture of the Yellow Dream mine. Then he loved pretty Margaret Kelly; but she had left him and Young Jerry, the latter barely toddling, to take up her last long sleep in the little graveyard among the great sober pines.

Old Jerry never went back to the sea. He remained by his cables, and lavished upon them and Young Jerry all the love of his nature. When evil days came to the Yellow Dream, he still remained in the employ of the company as watchman over the all but abandoned property.

But this morning he was not visible. Young Jerry only was to be seen, sitting on the cabin step and singing the ancient chantey. He had cooked and eaten his breakfast all by himself, and had just come out to take a look at the world. Twenty feet before him stood the steel drum round which the endless cable worked. By the drum, snug and fast, was the ore-car. Following with his eyes the dizzy flight of the cables to the farther bank, he could see the other drum and the other car.

The contrivance was worked by gravity, the loaded car crossing the river by virtue of its own weight, and at the same time dragging the empty car back. The loaded car being emptied, and the empty car being loaded with more ore, the performance could be repeated — a performance which had been repeated tens of thousands of times since the day Old Jerry became the keeper of the cables.

Young Jerry broke off his song at the sound of approaching footsteps. A tall, blue-shirted man, a rifle across the hollow of his arm, came out from the gloom of the pine-trees. It was Hall, watchman of the Yellow Dragon mine, the cables of which spanned the Sacramento a mile farther up.

"Hello, younker!" was his greeting. "What you doin' here by your lonesome?"

"Oh, bachin'," Jerry tried to answer unconcernedly, as if it were a very ordinary sort of thing. "Dad's away, you see."

"Where's he gone?" the man asked.

"San Francisco. Went last night. His brother's dead in the old country, and he's gone down to see the lawyers. Won't be back till to-morrow night."

So spoke Jerry, and with pride, because of the responsibility which had fallen to him of keeping an eye on the property of the Yellow Dream, and the glorious adventure of living alone on the cliff above the river and of cooking his own meals.

"Well, take care of yourself," Hall said, "and don't monkey with the cables. I'm goin' to see if I can't pick up a deer in the Cripple Cow Cañon."

"It's goin' to rain, I think," Jerry said, with mature deliberation.

"And it's little I mind a wettin'," Hall laughed, as he strode away among the trees.

Jerry's prediction concerning rain was more than fulfilled. By ten o'clock the pines were swaying and moaning, the cabin windows rattling, and the rain driving by in fierce squalls. At half past eleven he kindled a fire, and promptly at the stroke of twelve sat down to his dinner.

No out-of-doors for him that day, he decided, when he had washed the few dishes and put them neatly away; and he wondered how wet Hall was and whether he had succeeded in picking up a deer.

At one o'clock there came a knock at the door, and when he opened it a man and a woman staggered in on the breast of a great gust of wind. They were Mr. and Mrs. Spillane, ranchers, who lived in a lonely valley a dozen miles back from the river.

"Where's Hall?" was Spillane's opening speech, and he spoke sharply and quickly.

Jerry noted that he was nervous and abrupt in his movements, and that Mrs. Spillane seemed laboring under some strong anxiety. She was a thin, washed-out, worked-out woman, whose life of dreary and unending toil had stamped itself harshly upon her face. It was the same life that had bowed her husband's shoulders and gnarled his hands and turned his hair to a dry and dusty gray.

"He's gone hunting up Cripple Cow," Jerry answered. "Did you want to cross?"

The woman began to weep quietly, while Spillane dropped a troubled exclamation and strode to the window. Jerry joined him in gazing out to where the cables lost themselves in the thick downpour.

It was the custom of the backwoods people in that section of country to cross the Sacramento on the Yellow Dragon cable. For this service a small toll was charged, which tolls the Yellow Dragon Company applied to the payment of Hall's wages.

"We've got to get across, Jerry," Spillane said, at the same time jerking his thumb over his shoulder in the direction of his wife. "Her father's hurt at the Clover Leaf. Powder explosion. Not expected to live. We just got word."

Jerry felt himself fluttering inwardly. He knew that Spillane wanted to cross on the Yellow Dream cable, and in the absence of his father he felt that he dared not assume such a responsibility, for the cable had never been used for passengers; in fact, had not been used at all for a long time.

"Myabe Hall will be back soon," he said.

Spillane shook his head, and demanded, "Where's your father?"

"San Francisco," Jerry answered, briefly.

Spillane groaned, and fiercely drove his clenched fist into the palm of the other hand. His wife was crying more audibly, and Jerry could hear her murmuring, "And daddy's dyin', dyin'!"

The tears welled up in his own eyes, and he stood irresolute, not knowing what he should do. But the man decided for him.

"Look here, kid," he said, with determination, "the wife and me are goin' over on this here cable of yours! Will you run it for us?"

Jerry backed slightly away. He did it unconsciously, as if recoiling instinctively from something unwelcome.

"Better see if Hall's back," he suggested.

"And if he ain't?"

Again Jerry hesitated.

"I'll stand for the risk," Spillane added. "Don't you see, kid, we've simply got to cross!"

Jerry nodded his head reluctantly.

"And there ain't no use waitin' for Hall," Spillane went on. "You know as well as me he ain't back from Cripple Cow this time of day! So come along and let's get started."

No wonder that Mrs. Spillane seemed terrified as they helped her into the ore-car — so Jerry thought, as he gazed into the apparently fathomless gulf beneath her. For it was so filled with rain and cloud, hurtling and curling in the fierce blast, that the other shore, seven hundred feet away, was invisible, while the cliff at their feet dropped sheer down and lost itself in the swirling vapor. By all appearances it might be a mile to bottom instead of two hundred feet.

"All ready?" he asked.

"Let her go!" Spillane shouted, to make himself heard above the roar of the wind.

He had clambered in beside his wife,

He was able to explain the condition of affairs and his errand

and was holding one of her hands in his.

Jerry looked upon this with disapproval. "You'll need all your hands for holdin' on, the way the wind's yowlin'."

The man and the woman shifted their hands accordingly, tightly gripping the sides of the car, and Jerry slowly and carefully released the brake. The drum began to revolve as the endless cable passed round it, and the car slid slowly out into the chasm, its trolley-wheels rolling on the stationary cable overhead, to which it was suspended.

It was not the first time Jerry had worked the cable, but it was the first time he had done so away from the supervising eye of his father. By means of the brake he regulated the speed of the car. It needed regulating, for at times, caught by the stronger gusts of wind, it swayed violently back and forth; and once, just before it was swallowed up in a rain-squall, it seemed about to spill out its human contents.

After that Jerry had no way of knowing where the car was except by means of the cable. This he watched keenly as it glided round the drum. "Three hundred feet," he breathed to himself, as the cable markings went by; "three hundred and fifty, four hundred, four hundred and —"

The cable had stopped. Jerry threw off the brake, but it did not move. He caught the cable with his hands and tried to start it by tugging smartly. Something had gone wrong. What? He could not guess; he could not see. Looking up, he could vaguely make out the empty car, which had been crossing from the opposite cliff at a speed equal to that of the loaded car. It was about two hundred and fifty feet away. That meant, he knew, that somewhere in the gray obscurity, two hundred feet above the river and two hundred and fifty feet from the other bank, Spillane and his wife were suspended and stationary.

Three times Jerry shouted with all the shrill force of his lungs, but no answering cry came out of the storm. It was impossible for him to hear them or to make himself heard. As he stood for a moment, thinking rapidly, the flying clouds seemed to thin and lift. He caught a brief glimpse of the swollen Sacramento beneath, and a briefer glimpse of the car and the man and woman. Then the clouds descended thicker than ever.

The boy examined the drum closely, and found nothing the matter with it. Evidently it was the drum on the other side that had gone wrong. He was appalled at thought of the man and woman out there in the midst of the storm, hanging over the abyss, rocking back and forth in the frail car and ignorant of what was taking place on shore. And he did not like to think of their hanging there while he went round by the Yellow Dragon cable to the other drum.

But he remembered a block and tackle in the tool-house, and ran and brought it. They were double blocks, and he murmured aloud, "A purchase of four," as he made the tackle fast to the endless cable. Then he heaved upon it, heaved until it seemed that his arms were being drawn out from their sockets and that his shoulder muscles would be ripped asunder. Yet the cable did not budge. Nothing remained but to cross over to the other side.

He was already soaking wet, so he did not mind the rain as he ran over the trail to the Yellow Dragon. The storm was with him, and it was easy going, although there was no Hall at the other end of it to man the brake for him and regulate the speed of the car. This he did for himself, however, by means of a stout rope, which he passed, with a turn, round the stationary cable.

As the full force of the wind struck him in mid-air, swaying the cable and whistling and roaring past it, and rocking and careening the car, he appreciated more fully what must be the condition of mind of Spillane and his wife. And this appreciation gave strength to him, as, safely across, he fought his way up the other bank, in the teeth of the gale, to the Yellow Dream cable.

To his consternation, he found the drum in thorough working order. Everything was running smoothly at both ends. Where was the hitch? In the middle, without a doubt.

From this side, the car containing Spillane was only two hundred and fifty feet away. He could make out the man and woman through the whirling vapor, crouching in the bottom of the car and exposed to the pelting rain and the full fury of the wind. In a lull between the squalls he shouted to Spillane to examine the trolley of the car.

Spillane heard, for he saw him rise up cautiously on his knees, and with his hands go over both trolley-wheels. Then he turned his face toward the bank.

"She's all right, kid!"

Jerry heard the words, faint and far, as from a remote distance. Then what was the matter? Nothing remained but the other and empty car, which he could not see, but which he knew to be there, somewhere in that terrible gulf two hundred feet beyond Spillane's car.

His mind was made up on the instant. He was only fourteen years old, slightly and wirily built; but his life had been lived among the mountains, his father had taught him no small measure of "sailoring," and he was not particularly afraid of heights.

In the tool-box by the drum he found an old monkey-wrench and a short bar of iron, also a coil of fairly new Manila rope. He looked in vain for a piece of board with which to rig a "boatswain's chair." There was nothing at hand but large planks, which he had no means of sawing, so he was compelled to do without the more comfortable form of saddle.

The saddle he rigged was very simple. With the rope he made merely a large loop round the stationary cable, to which hung the empty car. When he sat in the loop his hands could just reach the cable conveniently, and where the rope was likely to fray against the cable he lashed his coat, in lieu of the old sack he would have used had he been able to find one.

These preparations swiftly completed, he swung out over the chasm, sitting in the rope saddle and pulling himself along the cable by his hands. With him he carried the monkey-wrench and short iron bar and a few spare feet of rope. It was a slightly uphill pull, but this he did not mind so much as the wind. When the furious gusts hurled him back and forth, sometimes half-twisting him about, and he gazed down into the gray depths, he was aware that he was afraid. It was an old cable. What if it should break under his weight and the pressure of the wind?

It was fear he was experiencing, honest fear, and he knew that there was a "gone" feeling in the pit of his stomach, and a trembling of the knees which he could not quell.

But he held himself bravely to the task. The cable was old and worn, sharp pieces of wire projected from it, and his hands were cut and bleeding by the time he took his first rest, and held a shouted conversation with Spillane. The car was directly beneath him and only a few feet away, so he was able to explain the condition of affairs and his errand.

"Wish I could help you," Spillane shouted at him as he started on, "but the wife's gone all to pieces! Anyway, kid, take care of yourself! I got myself into this fix, but it's up to you to get me out!"

"Oh, I'll do it!" Jerry shouted back. "Tell Mrs. Spillane that she'll be ashore now in a jiffy!"

In the midst of pelting rain, which half-blinded him, swinging from side to side like a rapid and erratic pendulum, his torn hands paining him severely and his lungs panting from his exertions and panting from the very air which the wind sometimes blew into his mouth with strangling force, he finally arrived at the empty car.

A single glance showed him that he had not made the dangerous journey in vain. The front trolley-wheel, loose from long wear, had jumped the cable, and the cable was now jammed tightly between the wheel and the sheave-block.

One thing was clear — the wheel must be removed from the block. A second thing was equally clear — while the wheel was being removed the car would have to be fastened to the cable by the rope he had brought.

At the end of a quarter of an hour, beyond making the car secure, he had accomplished nothing. They key which bound the wheel on its axle was rusted and jammed. He hammered at it with one hand and held on the best he could with the other, but the wind persisted in swinging and twisting his body, and made his blows miss more often than not. Nine-tenths of the strength he expended was in trying to hold himself steady. For fear that he might drop the monkey-wrench he made it fast to his wrist with his handkerchief.

At the end of half an hour Jerry had hammered the key clear, but he could not draw it out. A dozen times it seemed that he must give up in despair, that all the danger and toil he had gone through were for nothing. Then an idea came to him, and he went through his pockets with feverish haste, and found what he sought — a tenpenny nail.

But for that nail, put in his pocket he

knew not when or why, he would have had to make another trip over the cable and back. Thrusting the nail through the looped head of the key, he at last had a grip, and in no time the key was out.

Then came punching and prying with the iron bar to get the wheel itself free from where it was jammed by the cable against the side of the block. After that Jerry replaced the wheel, and by means of the rope, heaved up on the car till the trolley once more rested properly on the cable.

All this took time. More than an hour and a half had elapsed since his arrival at the empty car. And now, for the first time, he dropped out of his rope saddle and down into the car. He removed the detaining ropes, and the trolley-wheels began slowly to revolve. The car was moving, and he knew that somewhere beyond, although he could not see, the car of Spillane was likewise moving, and in the opposite direction.

There was no need for a brake, for his weight sufficiently counterbalanced the weight in the other car; and soon he saw the cliff rising out of the cloud depths and the old familiar drum going round and round.

Jerry climbed out and made the car securely fast. He did it deliberately and carefully, and then, quite unhero-like, he sank down by the drum, regardless of the pelting storm, and burst out sobbing.

There were many reasons why he sobbed — partly from the pain of his hads, which was excruciating; partly from exhaustion; partly from relief and release from the nerve-tension he had been under for so long; and in a large measure from thankfulness that the man and woman were saved.

They were not there to thank him; but somewhere beyond that howling, storm-driven gulf he knew they were hurrying over the trail toward the Clover Leaf.

Jerry staggered to the cabin, and his hand left the white knob red and bloody as he opened the door, but he took no notice of it.

He was too proudly contented with himself, for he was certain that he had done well, and he was honest enough to admit to himself that he had done well. But a small regret arose and persisted in his thoughts — if his father had only been there to see!

33
THE MARRIAGE OF LIT-LIT

THE MARRIAGE OF LIT-LIT

When John Fox came into a country where whiskey freezes solid and may be used as a paper-weight for a large part of the year, he came without the ideals and illusions that usually hamper the progress of more delicately nurtured adventurers. Born and reared on the frontier fringe of the United States, he took with him into Canada a primitive cast of mind, an elemental simplicity and grip on things, as it were, that insured him immediate success in his new career. From a mere servant of the Hudson's Bay Company, driving a paddle with the voyageurs and carrying goods on his back across the portages, he swiftly rose to a Factorship and took charge of a trading post at Fort Angelus.

Here, because of his elemental simplicity, he took himself a native wife, and, by reason of the connubial bliss that followed, he escaped the unrest and vain longings that curse the days of more fastidious men, spoil their work, and conquer them in the end. He lived contentedly, was at single purposes with the business he was set there to do, and achieved a brilliant record in the service of the Company. About this time his wife died, was claimed by her people, and buried with savage circumstance in a tin trunk in the top of a tree.

Two sons she had borne him, and when the Company promoted him, he journeyed with them still deeper into the vastness of the Northwest Territory to a place called Sin Rock, where he took charge of a new post in a more important fur field. Here he spent several lonely and depressing months, eminently disgusted with the unprepossessing appearance of the Indian maidens, and greatly worried by his growing sons who stood in need of a mother's care. Then his eyes chanced upon Lit-lit.

"Lit-lit — well, she is Lit-lit," was the fashion in which he despairingly described her to his chief clerk, Alexander McLean.

McLean was too fresh from his Scottish upbringing — "not dry behind the ears yet," John Fox put it — to take to the marriage customs of the country. Nevertheless he was not averse to the Factor's imperilling his own immortal soul, and, especially, feeling an ominous attraction himself for Lit-lit, he was sombrely content to clinch his own soul's safety by seeing her married to the Factor.

Nor is it to be wondered that McLean's austere Scotch soul stood in danger of being thawed in the sunshine of Lit-lit's eyes. She was pretty, and slender, and willowy, without the massive face and temperamental stolidity of the average squaw. "Lit-lit," so called from her fashion, even as a child, of being fluttery, of darting about from place to place like a butterfly, of being inconsequent and merry, and of laughing as lightly as she darted and danced about.

Lit-lit was the daughter of Snettishane, a prominent chief in the tribe, by a half-breed mother, and to him the Factor fared casually one summer day to open negotiations of marriage. He sat with the chief in the smoke of a mosquito smudge before his lodge, and together they talked about everything under the sun, or, at least, everything that in the Northland is under the sun, with the sole exception of marriage. John Fox had come particularly to talk of marriage; Snettishane knew it, and John Fox knew he knew it, wherefore the subject was religiously avoided. This is alleged to be Indian subtlety. In reality it is transparent simplicity.

The hours slipped by, and Fox and Snettishane smoked interminable pipes, looking each other in the eyes with a guilelessness superbly histrionic. In the mid-afternoon McLean and his brother clerk, McTavish, strolled past, innocently uninterested, on their way to the river. When they strolled back again an hour later, Fox and Snettishane had attained to a ceremonious discussion of the condition and quality of the gunpowder and bacon which the Company was offering in trade.

Meanwhile Lit-lit, divining the Factor's errand, had crept in under the rear wall of the lodge and through the front flap was peeping out at the two logomachists by the mosquito smudge. She was flushed and happy-eyed, proud that no less a man than the Factor (who stood next to God in the Northland hierarchy) had singled her out, femininely curious to see at close range what manner of man he was. Sunglare on the ice, camp smoke, and weather beat had burned his face to a copper-brown, so that her father was as fair as he, while she was fairer. She was remotely glad of this, and more immediately glad that he was large and strong, though his great black beard half frightened her, it was so strange.

Being very young, she was unversed in the ways of men. Seventeen times she had seen the sun travel south and lose itself beyond the sky-line, and seventeen times she had seen it travel back again and ride the sky day and night till there was no night at all. And through these years she had been cherished jealously by Snettishane, who stood between her and all suitors, listening disdainfully to the young hunters as they bid for her hand, and turning them away as though she were beyond price. Snettishane was mercenary. Lit-lit was to him an investment. She represented so much capital, from which he expected to receive, not a certain definite interest, but an incalculable interest.

And having thus been reared in a manner as near to that of the nunnery as tribal conditions would permit, it was with a great and maidenly anxiety that she peeped out at the man who had surely come for her, at the husband who was to teach her all that was yet unlearned of life, at the masterful being whose word was to be her law, and who was to mete and bound her actions and comportment for the rest of her days.

But, peeping through the front flap of the lodge, flushed and thrilling at the strange destiny reaching out for her, she grew disappointed as the day wore along, and the Factor and her father still talked pompously of matters concerning other things and not pertaining to marriage things at all. As the sun sank lower and lower toward the north and midnight approached, the Factor began making unmistakable preparations for departure. As he turned to stride away Lit-lit's heart sank; but it rose again as he halted, half turning on one heel.

"Oh, by the way, Snettishane," he said, "I want a squaw to wash for me and mend my clothes."

Snettishane grunted and suggested Wanidani, who was an old woman and toothless.

"No, no," interposed the Factor. "What I want is a wife. I've been kind of thinking about it, and the thought just struck me that you might know of some one that would suit."

Snettishane looked interested, whereupon the Factor retraced his steps, casually and carelessly to linger and discuss this new and incidental topic.

"Kattou?" suggested Snettishane.

"She has but one eye," objected the Factor.

"Laska?"

"Her knees be wide apart when she stands upright. Kips, your biggest dog, can leap between her knees when she stands upright."

"Senatee?" went on the imperturbable Snettishane.

But John Fox feigned anger, crying: "What foolishness be this? Am I old, that thou shouldst mate me with old women? Am I toothless? lame of leg? blind of eye? Or am I poor that no bright-eyed maiden may look with favor upon me? Behold! I am the Factor, both rich and great, a power in the land, whose speech makes men tremble and is obeyed!"

Snettishane was inwardly pleased, though his sphinxlike visage never relaxed. He was drawing the Factor, and making him break ground. Being a creature so elemental as to have room for but one idea at a time, Snettishane could pursue that one idea a greater distance than could John Fox. For John Fox, elemental as he was, was still complex enough to entertain several glimmering ideas at a time, which debarred him from pursuing the one as single-heartedly or as far as did the chief.

Snettishane calmly continued calling the roster of eligible maidens, which, name by name, as fast as uttered, were stamped ineligible by John Fox, with specified objections appended. Again he gave it up and started to return to the Fort. Snettishane watched him go, making no effort to stop him, but seeing him, in the end, stop himself.

"Come to think of it," the Factor remarked, "we both of us forgot Lit-lit. Now I wonder if she'll suit me?"

Snettishane met the suggestion with a mirthless face, behind the mask of which his soul grinned wide. It was a distinct victory. Had the Factor gone but one step farther, perforce Snettishane would himself have mentioned the name of Lit-lit, but — the Factor had not gone that one step farther.

The chief was non-committal concerning Lit-lit's suitability, till he drove the white man into taking the next step in order of procedure.

"Well," the Factor meditated aloud, "the only way to find out is to make a try of it." He raised his voice. "So I will give for Lit-lit ten blankets and three pounds of tobacco which is good tobacco."

Snettishane replied with a gesture which seemed to say that all the blankets and tobacco in all the world could not compensate him for the loss of Lit-lit and her manifold virtues. When pressed by the Factor to set a price, he coolly placed it at five hundred blankets, ten guns, fifty pounds of tobacco, twenty scarlet cloths, ten bottles of rum, a music-box, and lastly the good-will and best offices of the Factor, with a place by his fire.

The Factor apparently suffered a stroke of apoplexy, which stroke was successful in reducing the blankets to two hundred and in cutting out the place by the fire — an unheard-of condition in the marriages of white men with the daughters of the soil. In the end, after three hours more of chaffering, they came to an agreement. For Lit-lit Snettishane was to receive one hundred blankets, five pounds of tobacco, three guns, and a bottle of rum, good-will and best offices included, which, according to John Fox, was ten blankets and a gun more than she was worth. And as he went home through the wee sma' hours, the three o'clock sun blazing in the due northeast, he was unpleasantly aware that Snettishane had bested him over the bargain.

Snettishane, tired and victorious, sought his bed, and discovered Lit-lit before she could escape from the lodge.

He grunted knowingly: "Thou hast seen. Thou hast heard. Wherefore it be plain to thee thy father's very great wisdom and understanding. I have made for thee a great match. Heed my words and walk in the way of my words, go when I say go, come when I bid thee come, and we shall grow fat with the wealth of this big white man who is a fool according to his bigness."

The next day no trading was done at the store. The Factor opened whiskey before breakfast to the delight of McLean and McTavish, gave his dogs double rations, and wore his best moccasins. Outside the Fort preparations were under way for a *potlatch*. Potlatch means "a giving," and John Fox's intention was to signalize his marriage with Lit-lit by a potlatch as generous as she was good-looking. In the afternoon the whole tribe gathered to the feast. Men, women, children, and dogs gorged to repletion, nor was there one person, even among the chance visitors and stray hunters from other tribes, who failed to receive some token of the bridegroom's largess.

Lit-lit, tearfully shy and frightened, was bedecked by her bearded husband with a new calico dress, splendidly beaded moccasins, a gorgeous silk handkerchief over her raven hair, a purple scarf about her throat, brass earrings and finger-rings, and a whole pint of pinchbeck jewellery, including a Waterbury watch. Snettishane could scarce contain himself at the spectacle, but watching his chance drew her aside from the feast.

"Not this night, nor the next night," he began ponderously, "but in the nights to come, when I shall call live a raven by the river bank, it is for thee to rise up from thy big husband who is a fool and come to me.

"Nay, nay," he went on hastily, at sight of the dismay in her face at turning her back upon her wonderful new life. "For no sooner shall this happen than thy big husband who is a fool will come wailing to my lodge. Then it is for thee to wail likewise, claiming that this thing is not well, and that the other thing thou dost not like, and that to be the wife of the Factor is more than thou didst bargain for, only wilt thou be content with more blankets, and more tobacco, and more wealth of various sorts for thy poor old father Snettishane. Remember well, when I call in the night, like a raven, from the river bank."

Lit-lit nodded; for to disobey her father was a peril she knew well; and, furthermore, it was a little thing he asked, a short separation from the Factor, who would know only greater gladness at having her back. She returned to the feast, and, midnight being well at hand, the Factor sought her out and led her away to the Fort amid joking and outcry in which the squaws were especially conspicuous.

Lit-lit quickly found that married life with the head-man of a fort was even better than she had dreamed. No longer did she have to fetch wood and water and wait hand and foot upon cantankerous menfolk. For the first time in her life she could lie abed till breakfast was on the table. And what a bed! — clean and soft, and comfortable as no bed she had ever known. And such food! Flour, cooked into biscuits, hot-cakes and bread, three times a day and every day, and all one wanted! Such prodigality was hardly believable.

To add to her contentment, the Factor was cunningly kind. He had buried one wife, and he knew how to drive with a slack rein that went firm only on occasion, and then went very firm. "Lit-lit is boss of this place," he announced significantly at the table the morning after the wedding. "What she says goes. Understand?" And McLean and McTavish understood. Also, they knew that the Factor had a heavy hand.

But Lit-lit did not take advantage. Taking a leaf from the book of her husband, she at once assumed charge of his two growing sons, giving them added comforts and a measure of freedom like to that which he gave her. The two sons were loud in the praise of their new mother; McLean and McTavish lifted their voices; and the Factor bragged of the joys of matrimony till the story of her good behavior and her husband's satisfaction became the property of all the dwellers in the Sin Rock district.

Whereupon Snettishane, with visions of his incalculable interest keeping him awake of nights, thought it time to bestir himself. On the tenth night of her wedded life Lit-lit was awakened by the croaking of a raven, and she knew that Snettishane was waiting for her by the river bank. In her great happiness she had forgotten her pact, and now it came back to her with behind it all the childish terror of her father. For a time she lay in fear and trembling, loath to go, afraid to stay. But in the end the Factor won the silent victory, and his kindness, plus his great muscles and

square jaw, nerved her to disregard Snettishane's call.

But in the morning she arose very much afraid, and went about her duties in momentary fear of her father's coming. As the day wore along, however, she began to recover her spirits. John Fox, soundly berating McLean and McTavish for some petty dereliction of duty, helped her to pluck up courage. She tried not to let him go out of her sight, and when she followed him into the huge caché and saw him twirling and tossing great bales around as though they were feather pillows, she felt strengthened in her disobedience to her father. Also (it was her first visit to the warehouse, and Sin Rock was the chief distributing point to several chains of lesser posts), she was astounded at the endlessness of the wealth there stored away.

This sight, and the picture in her mind's eye of the bare lodge of Snettishane, put all doubts at rest. Yet she capped her conviction by a brief word with one of her stepsons. "White daddy good?" was what she asked, and the boy answered that his father was the best man he had ever known. That night the raven croaked again. On the night following the croaking was more persistent. It awoke the Factor, who tossed restlessly for a while. Then he said aloud, "Damn that raven," and Lit-lit laughed quietly under the blankets.

In the morning, bright and early, Snettishane put in an ominous appearance, and was set to breakfast in the kitchen with Wanidani. He refused "squaw food," and a little later bearded his son-in-law in the store where the trading was done. Having learned, he said, that his daughter was such a jewel, he had come for more blankets, more tobacco, and more guns — especially more guns. He had certainly been cheated in her price, he held, and he had come for justice. But the Factor had neither blankets nor justice to spare. Whereupon he was informed that Snettishane had seen the missionary at Three Forks, who had notified him that such marriages were not made in heaven, and that it was his father's duty to demand his daughter back.

"I am good Christian man now," Snettishane concluded. "I want my Lit-lit to go to heaven."

The Factor's reply was short and to the point; for he directed his father-in-law to go to the heavenly antipodes, and by the scruff of the neck and the slack of the blanket propelled him on that trail as far as the door.

But Snettishane sneaked around and in by the kitchen, cornering Lit-lit in the great living-room of the Fort.

"Mayhap thou didst sleep oversound last night when I called by the river bank," he began, glowering darkly.

"Nay, I was awake and heard." Her heart was beating as though it would choke her, but she went on steadily, "And the night before I was awake and heard, and yet again the night before."

And thereat, out of her great happiness and out of the fear that it might be taken from her, she launched into an original and glowing address upon the status and rights of woman — the first new-woman lecture delivered north of Fifty-three.

But it fell on unheeding ears. Snettishane was still in the dark ages. As she paused for breath, he said threateningly, "To-night I shall call again like the raven."

At this moment the Factor entered the room and again helped Snettishane on his way to the heavenly antipodes.

That night the raven croaked more persistently than ever. Lit-lit, who was a light sleeper, heard and smiled. John Fox tossed restlessly. Then he awoke and tossed about with greater restlessness. He grumbled and snorted, swore under his breath and over his breath, and finally flung out of bed. He groped his way to the great living-room and from the rack took down a loaded shot-gun — loaded with bird shot, left therein by the careless McTavis.

The Factor crept carefully out of the Fort and down to the river. The croaking ceased, but he stretched out in the long grass and waited. The air seemed a chilly balm, and the earth, after the heat of the day, now and again breathed soothingly against him. The Factor, gathered into the rhythm of it all, dozed off, with his head upon his arm, and slept.

Fifty yards away, head resting on knees, and with his back to John Fox, Snettishane likewise slept, gently conquered by the quietude of the night. An hour slipped by and then he awoke, and, without lifting his head, set the night vibrating with the hoarse gutturals of the raven call.

The Factor roused, not with the abrupt start of civilized man, but with the swift and comprehensive glide from sleep to waking of the savage. In the night light he made out a dark object in the midst of grass and brought his gun to bear upon it. A second croak began to rise, and he pulled the trigger. The crickets ceased from their sing-song chant, the wild fowl from their squabbling, and the raven croak broke midmost and died away in gasping silence.

John Fox ran to the spot and reached for the thing he had killed, but his fingers closed on a coarse mop of hair and he turned Snettishane's face upward to the starlight. He knew how a shot-gun scattered at fifty yards, and he knew that he had peppered Snettishane across the shoulders and in the small of the back. And Snettishane knew that he knew, but neither referred to it.

"What dost thou here?" the Factor demanded. "It were time old bones should be in bed."

But Snettishane was stately in spite of the bird shot burning under his skin.

"Old bones will not sleep," he said solemnly. "I weep for my daughter, for my daughter Lit-lit, who liveth and who yet is dead, and who goeth without doubt to the white man's hell."

"Weep henceforth on the far bank, beyond earshot of the fort," said John Fox, turning on his heel, "for the noise of thy weeping is exceeding great and will not let one sleep of nights."

"My heart is sore," Snettishane answered, "and my days and nights be black with sorrow."

"As the raven is black," said John Fox.

"As the raven is black," Snettishane said.

Never again was the voice of the raven heard by the river bank. Lit-lit grows matronly day by day and is very happy. Also, there are sisters to the sons of John Fox's first wife who lies buried in a tree. Old Snettishane is no longer a visitor at the Fort, and spends long hours raising a thin, aged voice against the filial ingratitude of children in general and of his daughter Lit-lit in particular. His declining years are embittered by the knowledge that he was cheated, and even John Fox has withdrawn the assertion that the price for Lit-lit was too much by ten blankets and a gun.

SEVEN TALES
OF THE FISH PATROL

WHITE AND YELLOW

The waters of San Francisco Bay contain all manner of fish; therefore its surface is plowed by the keels of all manner of fishing-boats, manned by all manner of fishermen. To protect the fish from this motley floating population many wise laws have been passed, and there is a fish patrol to see that these laws are enforced.

Wildest among the fisherfolk may be accounted the Chinese shrimp-catchers. It is the habit of the shrimp to crawl along the bottom in vast armies till it reaches fresh water, when it turns about and crawls back again to the salt. And where the tide ebbs and flows the Chinese sink great bag nets to the bottom, with gaping mouths, into which the shrimp crawls and from which it is transferred to the boiling-pot.

This in itself would not be bad, were it not for the small mesh of the nets, so small that the tiniest fishes, little new-hatched things not a quarter of an inch long, cannot pass through. The beautiful beaches of Points San Pedro and San Pablo, where are the shrimp-catchers' villages, are made fearful by the stench from myriads of decaying fish; and against this wasteful destruction it has ever been the duty of the fish patrol to act.

When I was a youngster of eighteen, a good sloop sailor and all-round bay-waterman, my sloop, the *Reindeer,* was chartered by the fish commission, and I became a deputy patrolman. After a deal of work among the Greek fishermen of the upper bay and rivers, where knives flashed at the beginning of trouble and men permitted themselves to be made prisoners only after a revolver was thrust in their faces, we hailed with delight an expedition to the lower bay against the Chinese shrimp-catchers.

There were six of us, in two boats, and to avoid suspicion we ran down after dark, and dropped anchor under a projecting bluff of land known as Point Pinole. As the east paled with the first light of dawn, we got under way again, and hauled close on the land-breeze as we slanted across the bay toward Point San Pedro.

The morning mists curled and clung to the water so that we could see nothing; but we busied ourselves driving the chill from our bodies with hot coffee. We had also to devote ourselves to the miserable task of bailing, for in some incomprehensible way the *Reindeer* had sprung a generous leak. Half the night had been spent in overhauling the ballast and exploring the seams, but the labor had been without avail. The water still poured in, and perforce we doubled up in the cockpit and tossed it out again.

After coffee, three of the men withdrew to the other boat, a Columbia River salmon-boat, leaving three of us in the *Reindeer.* Then the two craft proceeded in company till the sun showed over the eastern sky-line. Its fiery rays dispelled the clinging vapors, and there before our eyes, like a picture, lay the shrimping fleet, spread out in a great half-moon, the tips of the crescent fully three miles apart, and each junk moored fast to the buoy of a shrimp-net. But there was no stir, no sign of life.

The situation dawned upon us. While waiting for slack water, in which to lift their heavy nets from the bed of the bay, the Chinese had all gone to sleep below. We were elated, and our plan of battle was swiftly formed.

"Throw each of your two men on to a junk," whispered Le Grant to me from the salmon-boat, "and you make fast to a third yourself. We'll do the same, and there's no reason in the world why we shouldn't capture six junks at the least."

Then we separated. I put the *Reindeer* about on the other tack, ran up under the lee of a junk, shivered the mainsail into the wind and lost headway, and forged past the stern of the junk so slowly and so near that one of the patrolmen stepped lightly aboard. Then I kept off, filled the mainsail, and bore away for a second junk.

Up to this time there had been no noise, but from the first junk captured by the salmon-boat an uproar now broke forth. There was shrill Oriental yelling, a pistol-shot, and more yelling.

"It's all up! They're warning the others," said George, the remaining patrolman, as he stood beside me in the cockpit.

By this time we were in the thick of the fleet, and the alarm was spreading with incredible swiftness. The decks were beginning to swarm with half-awakened and half-naked Chinese. Cries and yells of warning and anger were flying over the quiet water, and somewhere a conch-shell was being blown with great success.

To the right of us I saw the captain of a junk chop away his mooring-line with an ax and spring to help his crew at the hoisting of the huge lug-sail. But to the left, on another junk, the first heads were popping up from below, and I rounded up the *Reindeer* alongside, long enough for George to spring aboard.

The whole fleet was now under way. In addition to the sails they had got out long sweeps, and the bay was being plowed in every direction by the fleeing junks. I was now alone in the *Reindeer,* seeking feverishly to capture a third prize. The first junk I pursued was a clean miss, for it trimmed its sheets and shot away surprisingly into the wind. It outpointed the *Reindeer* by fully half a point, and I began to feel respect for the clumsy craft.

Realizing the hopelessness of the pursuit, I filled away, threw out the main-sheet, and drove down before the wind upon the junks to leeward, where I had them at a disadvantage.

The one I had selected wavered indecisively before me, and as I swung wide to make the boarding gentle, filled suddenly and darted away, the swarthy Mongols shouting a wild rhythm as they bent to the sweeps.

But I had been ready for this. I luffed suddenly. Putting the tiller hard down, and holding it down with my body, I brought the main-sheet in, hand over hand, on the run, so as to retain all possible striking force. The two starboard sweeps of the junk were crumpled up, and then the two boats came together with a crash. The *Reindeer's* bowsprit, like a monstrous hand, reached over and ripped out the junk's chunky mast and towering sail.

This was met by a yell of rage. A big Chinaman, remarkably evil-looking, with his head swathed in a yellow silk handkerchief and his face badly pockmarked, planted a pike-pole on the *Reindeer's* bow and began to shove the entangled boats apart. Pausing long enough to let go the jib halyards, and just as the *Reindeer* cleared and began to drift astern, I leaped aboard the junk with a line and made fast.

He of the yellow handkerchief and pockmarked face came toward me threateningly, but I put my hand into my hip pocket, and he hesitated. I was unarmed, but the Chinese have learned to be fastidiously careful of American hip pockets, and it was upon this that I depended to keep him and his savage crew at a distance.

I ordered him to drop the anchor at the junk's bow, to which he replied, "No sabbe." The crew responded in like fashion, and although I made my meaning plain by signs, they refused to understand. Realizing the inexpediency of discussing the matter, I went forward myself, overran the line, and let the anchor go.

"Now get aboard, four of you!" I said, in a loud voice, indicating with my fingers that four of them were to go with me and the fifth was to remain by the junk. The Yellow Handkerchief hesitated; but I repeated the order fiercely, at the same time sending my hand to my hip. Again the Yellow Handkerchief was overawed, and with surly looks he led three of his men aboard the *Reindeer.*

I cast off at once, and leaving the jib down, steered a course for George's junk. Here it was easier, for there were two of us, and George had a pistol to fall back on if it came to the worst. And here, as with my junk, four Chinese were transferred to the sloop and one left behind to take care of things.

Four more Chinamen were added to our passenger list from the third junk. By this time the salmon-boat had collected its twelve prisoners and come alongside, sadly overloaded. To make matters worse, as it was a small boat, the patrolmen were so jammed in with their prisoners that they would have little chance in case of trouble.

"You'll have to help us out," said Le Grant.

I looked over my prisoners, who had crowded into the cabin and on top of it. "I can take three," I answered.

"Make it four," he suggested, "and I'll take Bill with me." (Bill was the third patrolman.) "We haven't elbow-room here, and in case of a scuffle one white to every two of them will be just about the right proportion."

The exchange was made, and the salmon-boat got up its spritsail and headed down the bay toward the marshes off San Rafael. I ran up the jib and followed with the *Reindeer*. San Rafael, where we were to turn our catch over to the authorities, communicated with the bay by way of a long and tortuous slough, or marsh-land creek, which could be navigated only when the tide was in. Slack water had come, and as the ebb was beginning, there was need for hurry if we cared to escape waiting half a day for the next tide.

But the land-breeze had begun to die away with the rising sun, and now came only in failing puffs. The salmon-boat got out its oars and soon left us far astern. Some of the Chinese stood in the forward part of the cockpit, near the cabin doors, and once, as I leaned over the cockpit-rail to flatten down the jib-sheet a bit, I felt some one brush against my hip pocket. I made no sign, but out of the corner of my eye I saw that the Yellow Handkerchief had discovered the emptiness of the pocket which had hitherto overawed him.

To make matters serious, during all the excitement of boarding the junks the *Reindeer* had not been bailed, and the water was beginning to slush over the cockpit floor. The shrimp-catchers pointed at it and looked to me questioningly.

"Yes," I said. "Bimeby, allee same dlown, velly quick, you no bail now. Sabbe?"

No, they did not "sabbe," or at least they shook their heads to that effect, although they chattered most comprehendingly to one another in their own lingo. I pulled up three or four of the bottom boards, got a couple of buckets from a locker, and by unmistakable sign-language invited them to fall to. But they laughed, and some crowded into the cabin and some climbed up on top.

Their laughter was not good laughter. There was a hint of menace in it, a maliciousness which their black looks verified. The Yellow Handkerchief, since his dis-covery of my empty pocket, had become most insolent in his bearing, and he wormed about among the other prisoners, talking to them with great earnestness.

Swallowing my chagrin, I stepped down into the cockpit and began throwing out the water. But hardly had I begun when the boom swung overhead, the mainsail filled with a jerk, and the *Reindeer* heeled over. The day wind was springing up. George was the veriest of landlubbers, so I was forced to give over bailing and take the tiller. The wind was blowing directly off Point San Pedro and the high mountains behind, and because of this was squally and uncertain, half the time bellying the canvas out, and the other half flapping it idly.

George was about the most all-round helpless man I had ever met. Among his other disabilities, he was a consumptive, and I knew that if he attempted to bail it might bring on a hemorrhage. Yet the rising water warned me that something must be done. Again I ordered the shrimp-catchers to lend a hand with the buckets. They laughed defiantly, and those inside the cabin, the water up to their ankles, shouted back and forth with those on top.

"You'd better get out your gun and make them bail," I said to George.

But he shook his head, and showed all too plainly that he was afraid. The Chinese could see the "funk" he was in as well as I could, and their insolence became insufferable. Those in the cabin broke into the food lockers, and those above scrambled down and joined them in a feast on our crackers and canned goods.

"What do we care?" George said, weakly.

I was fuming with helpless anger. "If they get out of hand it will be too late to care. The best thing you can do, is to get them in check right now."

The water was rising higher and higher, and the gusts, forerunners of a steady breeze, were growing stiffer and stiffer. And between the gusts the prisoners, having got away with a week's provisions, took to crowding first to one side and then to the other till the *Reindeer* rocked like a cockle-shell. Yellow Handkerchief approached me, and pointing out his village on the Point San Pedro beach, gave me to understand that if I turned the *Reindeer* in that direction and put them ashore, they, in turn, would go to bailing. By now the water in the cabin was up to the bunks, and the bedclothes were sopping. It was a foot deep on the cockpit floor. Nevertheless I refused, and I could see by George's face that he was disappointed.

"If you don't show some nerve, they'll throw us overboard!" I said to him. "Better give me your revolver if you want to be safe."

"The safest thing to do," he chattered, "is to put them ashore. I, for one, don't want to be drowned for the sake of a handful of dirty Chinamen."

"And I, for another, don't care to give in to a handful of dirty Chinamen to escape drowning!" I answered, hotly.

"You'll sink the *Reindeer* under us all at this rate," he whined; "and what good that'll do I can't see."

"Every man to his taste!" I retorted.

He made no reply, but I could see he was trembling pitifully. Between the threatening Chinese and the rising water he was beside himself with fright; and more than the Chinese and the water, I feared him and what his fright might impel him to do. I could see him casting longing glances at the small skiff towing astern, so in the next calm I hauled the skiff alongside. As I did so his eyes brightened with hope; but before he could guess my intention, I stove the frail bottom through with a hand-ax, and the skiff filled to its gunwales.

"It's sink or float together," I said, "and if you'll give me your revolver I'll have the *Reindeer* bailed out in a jiffy."

"They're too many for us," he whimpered. "We can't fight them all."

I turned my back on him in disgust. The salmon-boat had long since passed from sight behind a little archipelago known as the Marin Islands, so no help could be looked for from that source. Yellow Handkerchief came up to me in a familiar manner, the water in the cockpit slushing against his legs. I did not like his looks. I felt that beneath the pleasant smile there was an ill purpose. I ordered him back, and so sharply that he obeyed.

"Now keep your distance," I commanded, "and don't you come closer!"

"Wha' fo'?" he demanded, indignantly. "I t'ink-um talkee talkee heap good."

"Talkee talkee!" I answered, bitterly, for I knew now that he had understood all that passed between George and me. "What for talkee talkee? You no sabbe talkee talkee."

He grinned in a sickly fashion. "Yep, I

sabbe velly much. I honest Chinaman."

"All right," I answered. "You sabbe talkee talkee, then you bail water plenty plenty. After that we talkee talkee."

He shook his head, at the same time pointing over his shoulder to his comrades. "No can do. Velly bad Chinamen, heap velly bad. I t'ink-um —"

"Stand back!" I shouted, for I had noticed his hand disappear beneath his blouse and his body prepare for a spring.

Disconcerted, he went back into the cabin, to hold a council, apparently, from the way the jabbering broke forth.

The *Reindeer* was very deep in the water, and its movements had grown quite "logy." In a rough sea it would inevitably have swamped, but the wind, when it did blow, was off the land, and scarcely a ripple disturbed the surface of the bay.

"I think you'd better head for the beach," George said, abruptly, in a manner that told me his fear had forced him to make up his mind to some course of action.

"I think not!" I answered, shortly.

"I command you!" he said, in a bullying tone.

"I was commanded to bring these prisoners into San Rafael," was my reply.

Our voices were gradually raised, and the sound of the altercation brought the Chinese out of the cabin.

"Now will you head for the beach?"

This from George, and I found myself looking into the muzzle of his revolver — of the revolver he dared to use on me, but was too cowardly to use on the prisoners.

My brain seemed smitten with a dazzling brightness. The whole situation, in all its bearings, was focused sharply before me — the shame of losing the prisoners, the worthlessness and cowardice of George, the meeting with Le Grant and the other patrolmen, and the lame explanation; and then there was the fight I had fought so hard, victory wrenched from me just as I thought I had it within my grasp. And out of the tail of my eye I could see the Chinese crowding together by the cabin doors and leering triumphantly. It would never do.

I threw my hand up and my head down. The first act elevated the muzzle; the second removed my head from the path of the bullet which went whistling past. One hand closed on George's wrist, the other on the revolver. Yellow Handkerchief and his gang sprang toward me. It was now or never.

Putting all my strength into a sudden effort, I swung George's body forward to meet them. Then I pulled back with equal suddenness, ripping the revolver out of his fingers and jerking him off his feet. He fell against the knees of Yellow Handkerchief, who stumbled over him, and the pair wallowed in the bailing hole, where the cockpit floor was torn open. The next instant I was covering them with my revolver, and the wild shrimp-catchers were cowering and cringing away.

But I swiftly discovered that there was all the difference in the world between shooting men who are attacking and men who are doing nothing more than simply refusing to obey. For obey they would not when I ordered them into the bailing hole. I threatened them with the revolver, but they sat stolidly in the flooded cabin and on the roof, and would not move.

Fifteen minutes passed, the *Reindeer* sinking deeper and deeper, its mainsail flapping in the calm. But from off the Point San Pedro shore I saw a dark line form on the water and travel toward us. It was the steady breeze I had been expecting so long. I called to the Chinese and pointed it out. They hailed it with exclamations. Then I pointed to the sail and to the water in the *Reindeer*, and indicated by signs that when the wind reached the sail, with the water we had aboard, we should capsize. But they jeered, for they knew it was in my power to luff the helm and let go the mainsheet, so as to spill the wind and escape damage.

But my mind was made up. I hauled in the main-sheet a foot or two, took a turn with it, and bracing my feet, put my back against the tiller. This left me one hand for the sheet and one for the revolver. The dark line drew nearer, and I could see them looking from me to it and back again with an apprehension they could not conceal. My brain and will and endurance were pitted against theirs, and the problem was which

could stand the strain of imminent death the longer and not give in.

Then the wind struck us. The main-sheet tautened with a brisk rattling of the blocks, the boom uplifted, the sail bellied out, and the *Reindeer* heeled over — over and over, till the lee-rail went under, the deck went under, the cabin windows went under, and the bay began to pour in over the cockpit-rail. So violently had it heeled over that the men in the cabin had been thrown on top of one another into the lee bunk, where they squirmed and twisted and were washed about, those underneath being perilously near to drowning.

The wind freshened a bit, and the *Reindeer* went over farther than ever. For the moment I thought it was gone, and I knew that another puff like that and it surely would go.

But while I pressed it under and debated whether I should give up or not, the Chinese cried for mercy. I think it was the sweetest sound I have ever heard. And then, and not until then, did I luff up and ease out the main-sheet. The *Reindeer* righted very slowly, and when it was on an even keel was so much awash that I doubted if it could be saved.

But the Chinese scrambled madly into the cockpit and fell to bailing with buckets, pots, pans, and everything they could lay hands on. It was a beautiful sight to see that water flying over the side! And when the *Reindeer* was high and proud on the water once more, we dashed away with the breeze on our quarter, and at the last possible moment crossed the mud-flats and entered the slough.

The spirit of the Chinese was broken, and so docile did they become that ere we made San Rafael they were out with the tow-rope, Yellow Handkerchief at the head of the line. As for George, it was his last trip with the fish patrol. He did not care for that sort of thing, he explained, and he thought a clerkship ashore was good enough for him.

THE KING OF THE GREEKS

Big Alec had never been captured by the fish patrol. It was his boast that no man could take him alive, and it was certainly true that of the many men who had tried to take him dead none had succeeded. Further, no man violated the fish laws more systematically and deliberately than Big Alec.

He was called "Big Alec" because of his gigantic stature. His height was six feet three inches, and he was correspondingly broad-shouldered and deep-chested. He had splendid muscles and was as hard as steel, and there were innumerable stories in circulation among the fisherfolk concerning his prodigious strength.

He was as bold and domineering as he was strong, and because of this he was widely known by another name, that of "The King of the Greeks." The fishing population was largely Greek, and they looked up to him and obeyed him as their chief. And as their chief, he fought their fights for them, saw that they were protected, saved them from the law when they fell into its clutches, and made them stand by one another and himself in time of trouble.

In the old days the fish patrol had attempted his capture many disastrous times, and had finally given it over, so that when the word was out that he was coming to Benicia, I was most anxious to see him. But I did not have to look for him. In his usual bold way, the first thing he did on arriving was to hunt us up. Charley Le Grant and I were under a patrolman named Carmintel at the time, and the three of us were on the *Reindeer,* preparing for a trip, when Big Alec stepped aboard. Carmintel evidently knew him, for they shook hands in recognition. Big Alec took no notice of Charley or me.

"I've come down to fish sturgeon a couple of months," he said to Carmintel.

His eyes flashed with challenge as he spoke, and we noticed the patrolman's eyes drop.

"That's all right, Alec," Carmintel said, in a low voice. "I'll not bother you. Come on into the cabin and we'll talk things over."

When they had gone inside and shut the doors, Charley winked with slow deliberation at me. But I was only a youngster, new to men and the ways of some men, so I did not understand. Nor did Charley explain, although I felt there was something wrong about the business.

"What are you going to do about his fishing for sturgeon?" I asked. "He's bound to fish with a 'Chinese line.'"

Charley shrugged his shoulders. "We'll see what we shall see," he said, enigmatically.

Now a "Chinese line" is a cunning device invented by the people whose name it bears. By a simple system of floats, weights and anchors, thousands of hooks, each on a separate leader, are suspended at a distance of from six inches to a foot above the bottom. The remarkable thing about such a line is the hook. It is barbless, and in place of the barb the hook is filed long and tapering to a point as sharp as that of a needle. These hooks are only several inches apart, and when a few thousand of them are suspended just above the bottom, like a fringe, for a couple of hundred fathoms, they present a formidable obstacle to the fish that travel along the bottom.

Such a fish is the sturgeon, which goes rooting along like a pig, and indeed is often called "pig-fish." Pricked by the first hook it touches, the sturgeon gives a startled leap and comes in contact with half a dozen more hooks. Then it thrashes about wildly, until it receives hook after hook in its soft flesh; and the hooks, straining from many different angles, hold the luckless fish fast until it is drowned.

Because no sturgeon can pass through a Chinese line, the device is called a trap in the fish laws, and because it bids fair to exterminate the sturgeon, it is branded by the fish laws as illegal. Such a line, we were confident, Big Alec intended setting in open and flagrant violation of the law.

Several days passed after the visit of Big Alec, and Charley and I kept a sharp watch on him. He towed his ark round the Solano wharf and into the big bight at Turner's shipyard. The bight we knew to be good ground for sturgeon, and there we felt sure the King of the Greeks intended to begin operations. The tide circled like a mill-race in and out of this bight, and made it possible to raise, lower or set a Chinese line only at slack water. So, between the tides, Charley and I made it a point for one or the other of us to keep a lookout from the Solano wharf.

On the fourth day I was lying in the sun behind the stringer-piece of the wharf when I saw a skiff leave the distant shore and pull out into the bight. In an instant the glasses were at my eyes and I was following every movement of the skiff. There were two men in it, and although a good two miles away, I yet made out one of them to be Big Alec, and ere the skiff returned to shore I made out enough more to know that the Greek had set his line.

"Big Alec has a Chinese line out in the bight off Turner's shipyard," Charley Le Grant said, that afternoon, to Carmintel.

A fleeting expression of annoyance passed over the patrolman's face, and then he said, "Yes?" in an absent way, and that was all.

Charley bit his lip with suppressed anger, and turned on his heel.

"Are you game, my lad?" he said to me, later on in the evening, just as we had finished washing down the Reindeer's decks and were preparing to turn in.

A lump came up in my throat, and I could only nod my head.

"Well, then," and Charley's eyes glittered in a determined way, "we've got to capture Big Alec between us, you and I, and we've got to do it in spite of Carmintel."

It was no easy task. In order to convict a man of illegal fishing, it was necessary to catch him in the act, with all the evidence of the crime about him — the hooks, the lines, the fish, and the man himself. This meant that we must take Big Alec on the open water, where he could see us coming and prepare for us one of the warm receptions for which he was noted.

"There's no getting around it," said Charley, one morning. "If we can only get alongside it's an even toss, and there's nothing left for us but to try and get alongside. Come on, lad!"

We were in the Columbia River salmonboat, the one we had used against the Chinese shrimp-catchers, as I have related in a previous experience. Slack water had come, and as we dropped round the end of the Solano wharf we saw Big Alec at work running his line and removing the fish.

"Change places," Charley commanded, "and steer just astern of him as if you were going into the shipyard."

I took the tiller, and Charley sat down on a thwart amidships, placing his revolver handily beside him.

"If he begins to shoot," he cautioned, "get down in the bottom and steer from there, so that nothing more than your hand will be exposed."

I nodded, and we kept silent after that, the boat slipping gently through the water and Big Alec growing nearer and nearer. We could see him quite plainly, gaffing the sturgeon and throwing them into the boat, while his companion ran the line and cleared the hooks as he dropped them back into the water. Nevertheless, we were five hundred yards away when the big fisherman hailed us.

"Here! You! What do you want?" he shouted.

"Keep-a-going," Charley whispered, "just as if you didn't hear him."

The next few moments were anxious ones. The fisherman was studying us sharply, while we were gliding up on him every second.

"You keep off if you know what's good for you!" he called out, suddenly, as if he had made up his mind as to who and what we were. "If you don't I'll fix you!"

He brought a rifle to his shoulder and trained it on me.

"Now will you keep off?" he demanded.

I could hear Charley groan with disappointment. "Keep off," he whispered. "It's all up for this time."

I put up the tiller and eased the sheet, and the salmon-boat ran off five or six points. Big Alec watched us till we were out of range, when he returned to his work.

"You'd better leave Big Alec alone," Carmintel said rather sourly to Charley that night.

"So he's been complaining to you, has

The King of the Greeks made his boast

he?" Charley said, significantly.

Carmintel flushed painfully. "You'd better leave him alone, I tell you," he repeated. "He's a dangerous man, and it won't pay to fool with him."

"Yes," Charley answered, softly, "I've heard that it pays better to leave him alone."

This was a direct thrust at Carmintel, and we could see by the expression of his face that it sank home. For it was common knowledge that Big Alec was as willing to bribe as to fight, and that of late years more than one patrolman had handled the fisherman's money.

"Do you mean to say —" Carmintel began, in a bullying tone.

But Charley cut him off shortly. "I mean to say nothing," he said. "You heard what I said, and if the cap fits, why —"

He shrugged his shoulders, and Carmintel glowered at him speechlessly.

"What we want is imagination," Charley said to me one day, when we had attempted to creep up on Big Alec in the gray of dawn, and had been shot at for our trouble.

And thereafter, and for many days, I cudgeled my brains trying to imagine some possible way by which two men, on an open stretch of water, could capture another who knew how to use a rifle, and was never to be found without one. Regularly, every slack water, without slyness, boldly and openly in the broad day, Big Alec was to be seen running his line. And what made it particularly exasperating was the fact that every fisherman from Benicia to Vallejo knew that he was successfully defying us.

Carmintel also bothered us, for he kept us busy among the shad-fishers of San Pablo, so that we had little time to spare on the King of the Greeks. But as Charley's wife and children lived at Benicia, we had made it our headquarters, and always returned to it.

"I'll tell you what we can do," I said, after several fruitless weeks. "We can wait some slack water till Big Alec has run his line and gone ashore with the fish, and then we can go out and capture the line. It will put him to time and expense to make another, and then we'll figure to capture that, too. If we can't capture him, we can discourage him, you see."

Charley saw, and said it was not a bad idea. We watched our chance, and the next low-water slack, after Big Alec had removed the catch and returned ashore, we went out in the salmon-boat. We had the bearings of the line from shore-marks, and we knew we should have no difficulty in locating it. The first of the flood-tide was setting in, when we ran below where we thought the line was stretched and dropped over a fishing-boat anchor. Keeping a short rope to the anchor, so that it barely touched the bottom, we dragged it slowly along until it stuck, and the boat fetched up hard and fast.

"We've got it!" Charley cried. "Come on and lend a hand to get it in!"

Together we hove up the rope till the anchor came in sight with the sturgeon line caught across one of the flukes. Scores of the murderous-looking hooks flashed into sight as we cleared the anchor, and we had just started to run along the line to the end where we could begin to lift it, when a sharp thud in the boat startled us.

We looked about, but saw nothing, and returned to our work. An instant later there was a similar sharp thud, and the gunwale splintered between Charley's body and mine.

"That's remarkably like a bullet, lad," he said, reflectively. "And it's a long shot Big Alec's making."

"He's using smokeless powder," he concluded, after examination of the mile-distant shore. "That's why we can't see where he is."

I looked at the shore, but could see no sign of Big Alec, who was undoubtedly hidden in some rocky nook with us at his mercy. A third bullet struck the water, glanced, passed singing over our heads, and struck the water again beyond.

"I guess we'd better get out of this," Charley remarked, coolly. "What do you think, lad?"

I thought so, too, and said we did not want the line, anyway. Whereupon we cast off and hoisted the spritsail. The bullets ceased at once, and we sailed away, unpleasantly aware that Big Alec was laughing at our discomfiture.

More than that, the next day on the fishing wharf, where we were inspecting nets, he saw fit to laugh and sneer at us, and this before all the fishermen. Charley's face went black with anger; but he controlled himself well, only promising Big Alec that in the end he would surely land him behind the bars.

The King of the Greeks made his boast that no fish patrol had ever taken him or ever could take him, and the fishermen cheered him and said it was true.

They grew excited, and it looked like trouble for a while; but Big Alec asserted his kingship and quelled them.

Carmintel also laughed at Charley, and dropped sarcastic remarks, and made it as hard as he could for him. But Charley refused to be angered, although he told me in confidence that he would capture Big Alec if it took all the rest of his life.

"I don't know how I'll do it," he said, "but do it I will, as sure as I am Charley Le Grant. The idea will come to me at the right and proper time, never fear."

And at the right time it came, and most unexpectedly.

Fully a month had passed, and we were constantly up and down the river, and down and up the bay, with no spare moments to devote to the particular fisherman who ran a Chinese line in the bight of Turner's shipyard. We had called in at Selby's smelter one afternoon while on patrol work, when all unknown to us our opportunity happened along.

It appeared in the guise of a helpless yacht loaded with seasick people, so we could hardly be expected to recognize it as the opportunity. It was a large sloop-yacht, and it was helpless, inasmuch as the trade-wind was blowing half a gale and there were no capable sailors aboard.

From the wharf at Selby's we watched with careless interest the lubberly manoeuver of bringing the yacht to anchor, and the equally lubberly manoeuver of sending the small boat ashore.

A very miserable-looking man in draggled duck, after nearly swamping the boat in the heavy seas, passed us the painter and climbed out. He staggered about as if the wharf were rolling, and told us his troubles, which were the troubles of the yacht.

The only rough-weather sailor aboard, the man on whom they all depended, had been called back to San Francisco by a telegram, and they had attempted to continue the cruise alone. The high wind and big seas of San Pablo Bay had been too much for them, all hands were sick, nobody knew anything or could do anything; and so they had run in to the smelter to desert the yacht or get somebody to bring it to Benicia. In short, did we know of any sailors who would bring the yacht in to Benicia?

Charley looked at me. The *Reindeer* was lying in a snug place. We had nothing on hand in the way of patrol work till midnight. With the wind then blowing we could sail the yacht in to Benicia in a couple of hours, have several more hours ashore, and come back to the smelter on the evening train.

"All right, captain," Charley said to the disconsolate yachtsman, who smiled in sickly fashion at the title.

"I'm only the owner," he explained.

We rowed him aboard in much better style than he had come ashore, and saw for ourselves the helplessness of the passengers.

There were a dozen men and women, and all of them much too sick even to appear grateful at our coming. The yacht was rolling savagely, broadside on, and no sooner had the owner's feet touched the deck than he collapsed and joined the others.

Not one was able to bear a hand, so Charley and I between us cleared the badly tangled running-gear, got up sail and hoisted anchor.

It was a rough trip, although a swift one. The Karquines Straits were a welter of foam and smother, and we came through them wildly before the wind, the big mainsail alternately dipping and flinging its boom skyward as we tore along.

But the people did not mind. They did not mind anything. Two or three, including the owner, sprawled in the cockpit, shuddering when the yacht lifted and raced, or sank dizzily into the trough, and between whiles regarded the shore with yearning eyes. The rest were huddled on the cabin floor among the cushions. Now and again some one groaned, but for the most part they were as limp and uncaring as so many dead persons.

As the bight at Turner's shipyard opened out, Charley edged into it to get the smoother water.

Benicia was in view, and we were bowling along over comparatively easy water, when a speck of a boat danced up ahead of us directly in our course.

It was low-water slack. Charley and I looked at each other. No word was spoken, but at once the yacht began a most astonishing performance, veering and yawing as if the greenest of amateurs were at the wheel.

It was a sight for sailormen to see. To all appearances a runaway yacht was careering madly over the bight, now and again yielding a little bit to control in a desperate effort to make Benicia.

The owner forgot his seasickness long enough to look anxious. The speck of a boat grew larger and larger, till we could see Big Alec and his partner, with a turn of the sturgeon line round a cleat, resting from their labor to laugh at us.

Charley pulled his southwester over his eyes, and I followed his example, although I could not guess the idea he evidently had in mind and intended to carry into execution.

We came foaming down abreast of the skiff, so close that we could hear above the wind the voices of Big Alec and his mate, as they shouted at us with all the scorn that professional watermen feel for amateurs, especially when amateurs are making fools of themselves.

We thundered on past the fishermen, and nothing had happened. Charley grinned at the disappointment he saw in my face, and then shouted:

"Stand by the main-sheet to jibe!"

He put the wheel hard over, and the yacht whirled round obediently. The main-sheet slacked and dipped, then shot over our heads after the boom, and tautened with a crash on the traveller. The yacht heeled over almost on her beamends, and a great wail went up from her seasick passengers as they swept across the cabin floor in a tangled mass and piled into a heap in the starboard bunks.

But there was no time for them. The yacht, completing the manoeuver, headed into the wind with slatting canvas and righted to an even keel. We were still plunging ahead, and directly in our path was the skiff. I saw Big Alec dive swiftly overboard and his mate leap for our bowsprit.

Then came the crash as we struck the boat, and a series of grinding bumps as it passed under our bottom.

"That fixes his rifle!" I heard Charley mutter, as he sprang upon the deck to look for Big Alec somewhere astern.

The wind and sea quickly stopped our forward movement, and we began to drift backward over the spot where the skiff had been. Big Alec's black head and swarthy face popped up within arm's reach; and all unsuspecting and very angry with what he took to be the clumsiness of amateur sailors, he was hauled aboard. Also, he was out of breath, for he had dived deep and stayed down long to escape our keel.

The next instant, to the perplexity and consternation of the owner, Charley was on top of Big Alec in the cockpit, and I was helping bind him with gaskets.

The owner was dancing excitedly about and demanding an explanation, but by that time Big Alec's partner had crawled aft from the bowsprit and was peering apprehensively over the rail into the cockpit. Charley's arm shot round his neck, and the man landed on his back beside Big Alec.

"More gaskets!" Charley shouted, and I made haste to supply them.

The wrecked skiff was rolling sluggishly a short distance to windward, and I trimmed the sheets while Charley took the wheel and steered for it.

"These two men are old offenders," he explained to the angry owner, "and they are most persistent violators of the fish and game laws. You have seen them caught in the act, and you may expect to be subpoenaed as a witness for the state when the trial comes off."

As he spoke he rounded alongside the skiff. It had been torn from the line, a section of which was dragging to it. He hauled in forty or fifty feet, with a young sturgeon still fast in a tangle of barbless hooks, slashed that much of the line free with his knife, and tossed it into the cockpit beside the prisoners.

"And there's the evidence, exhibit A, for the people," Charley continued. "Look it over carefully, so that you may identify it in the court-room with the time and place of capture." Then, in triumph, with no more veering and yawing, we sailed in to Benicia, the King of the Greeks bound hard and fast in the cockpit, and for the first time in his life a prisoner of the fish patrol.

A RAID ON THE OYSTER PIRATES

Of the fish patrolmen we at various times served under, Charley Le Grant and I were agreed, I think, that Neil Partington was the best. He was neither dishonest nor cowardly; and while he demanded strict obedience when we were under his orders, at the same time our relations were those of easy comradeship, and he permitted us a freedom to which we were ordinarily unaccustomed, as the present story will show.

Neil's family lived in Oakland, which is on the Lower Bay, less than six miles across the water from San Francisco. One day, while scouting among the Chinese shrimp-catchers of Point San Pedro, he received word that his wife was very ill, and that day, within the hour, the *Reindeer* was bowling along for Oakland with a stiff northwest breeze astern. We ran up the Oakland estuary and came to anchor, and in the days that followed, while Neil was ashore, we tightened up the *Reindeer's* rigging, overhauled the ballast, scraped down and put the sloop into the best possible condition.

This done, time hung heavy on our hands. Neil's wife was dangerously sick, and the outlook was a week of waiting for the crisis. Charley and I roamed the docks, wondering what we should do, and so came upon the oyster fleet, lying at the Oakland City Wharf. In the main, they were trim boats, made for speed and bad weather, and we sat down on the stringer-piece of the dock to study them.

Pedlers were backing their wagons to the edge of the wharf, and I managed to learn the selling price of the oysters.

"That boat must have at least two hundred dollars' worth aboard," I calculated. "I wonder how long it took to get the load?"

"Three or four days," Charley answered. "Not bad wages for two men."

The boat we were discussing, the *Ghost*, lay directly beneath us. Two men composed its crew, one a squat and broad-shouldered fellow, with remarkably long and gorilla-like arms, the other, tall and well-proportioned, with clear blue eyes and a mat of straight black hair. So unusual and striking was this combination of hair and eyes that Charley and I remained somewhat longer than we had intended, watching this man.

And it was well that we did. A stout, prosperous-looking elderly man came up and stood beside us, looking down upon the deck of the *Ghost*. He appeared angry, and the longer he looked the angrier he grew.

"Those are my oysters," he said, at last. "I know they are my oysters. You raided my beds last night and robbed me of them."

The men on the *Ghost* looked up.

"Hello, Taft!" the short man said, with insolent familiarity. (Among the bay-farers he had gained the nickname of "The Centipede.") "Wot 'r' you growlin' about now?"

"Those are my oysters, that's what I said. You've stolen them from my beds."

"You're mighty wise, ain't ye?" was The Centipede's sneering reply. "S'pose you can tell your oysters wherever you see 'em?"

"I know they're mine!" Mr. Taft cried.

"Prove it!" challenged the tall man, who we afterward learned was known as "The Porpoise" because of his wonderful swimming abilities.

Mr. Taft shrugged his shoulders helplessly. Of course he could not prove the oysters to be his, no matter how certain he might be.

"I'd give a thousand dollars to have you men behind the bars!" he cried. "I'll give fifty dollars a head for your arrest and conviction, all of you!"

A roar of laughter went up from the different boats, for the rest of the crews had been listening to the discussion.

"There's more money in oysters," The Porpoise remarked, dryly.

Mr. Taft turned on his heel and walked away. From out of the corner of his eye

Charley noted the direction in which he went. Several minutes later, when he had disappeared round a corner, Charley rose lazily to his feet. I followed him, and we sauntered off in the opposite direction to that taken by Mr. Taft.

"Come on! Lively!" Charley whispered, as soon as we had passed from the view of the oyster fleet.

Our course was changed at once, and we dodged round corners and raced up side streets till Mr. Taft's form loomed up ahead of us.

"I'm going to interview him about that reward," Charley explained, as we caught up with the oyster-bed owner. "Neil will be delayed here a week, and you and I might as well be doing something in the meanwhile."

"Of course, of course!" Mr. Taft said, when Charley had introduced himself and explained his errand. "Those thieves are robbing me of thousands of dollars every year. As I said, I'll give fifty dollars a head, and call it cheap at that. They've robbed my beds, torn down my signs, terrorized my watchmen, and last year killed one of them. Couldn't prove it. All done in the blackness of night. The detectives could do nothing. We have never succeeded in arresting one of those men. So I say, Mr. — What did you say your name was?"

"Le Grant," Charley answered.

"So I say, Mr. Le Grant, I am deeply obliged to you for the assistance you offer. And I shall be glad to cooperate with you in every way. My watchmen and boats are at your disposal. Come and see me at the San Francisco offices any time, or telephone. And don't be afraid of spending money."

"Now we'll see Neil," Charley said, when Mr. Taft had gone.

Not only did Neil Partington interpose no obstacle to our adventure, but he proved to be of the greatest assistance.

Charley and I knew nothing of the oyster industry, but Neil's head was an encyclopedia of facts concerning it. Also, inside an hour or so, he was able to bring to us a Greek boy of seventeen or eighteen, who knew the ins and outs of oyster piracy.

I may as well explain that we of the fish patrol were free lances, in a way. While Neil Partington, who was a patrolman proper, received a regular salary, Charley and I, being merely deputies, received only what we earned — that is to say, a certain percentage of the fines imposed on convicted violators of the fish laws. Also any rewards that chanced our way were ours.

We offered to share with Partington whatever we should get from Mr. Taft, but the patrolman would not hear of it. He was only too happy, he said, to do a good turn for us, who had done so many for him.

We held a long council of war, and mapped out the following line of action. Our faces were strange ones on the Lower Bay, but as the *Reindeer* was too well known as a fish-patrol sloop, the Greek boy, whose name was Nicholas, and I were to sail some innocent-looking craft down to Asparagus Island and join the oyster pirates' fleet. Here, according to Nicholas's description of the beds and the manner of raiding, it was possible for us to catch the pirates in the act of stealing oysters, and at the same time to get them in our power. Charley was to be on the shore, with Mr. Taft's watchmen and a posse of constables, to help us at the right time.

"I know just the boat," Neil said, at the conclusion of the discussion, "a crazy old sloop that's lying over at Tiburon. You and Nicholas can go over by the ferry, charter it for a song, and sail direct for the beds."

"Good luck be with you, boys," he said at parting, two days later. "Remember, they are dangerous men, so be careful."

Nicholas and I succeeded in chartering the sloop very cheaply, and between laughs, while getting up sail, we agreed that she was even crazier and older than Neil's description had led us to expect. She was a big, flat-bottomed and square-sterned craft, sloop-rigged, with a sprung mast, slack rigging, dilapidated sails and rotten running-gear, clumsy to handle and uncertain in bringing about, and she smelled vilely of coal tar, with which strange stuff she had been smeared from stem to stern and from cabin roof to centerboard. To cap it all, *Coal Tar Maggie* was printed in great white letters the whole length of each side.

It was an uneventful although laughable run from Tiburon to Asparagus Island, where we arrived in the afternoon of the following day. The oyster pirates, a dozen sloops, were lying at anchor on what was known as the "deserted beds." The *Coal Tar Maggie* came sloshing into their midst with a light breeze astern, and they crowded on deck to see us. Nicholas and I

"The Centipede" and "The Porpoise" doubled up on the cabin in paroxysms of laughter

had caught the spirit of the crazy craft, and we handled her in most lubberly fashion.

"Wot is it?" someone called.

"Name it 'n' ye kin have it!" called another.

"I swan, naow, ef it ain't the old ark itself!" mimicked The Centipede, from the *Ghost.*

We took no notice of the joking, but acted, after the manner of greenhorns, as if the *Coal Tar Maggie* required our undivided attention. I rounded her well to windward of the *Ghost,* and Nicholas ran forward to drop the anchor. To all appearances, it was the result of mere awkwardness, the way the chain tangled and kept the anchor from reaching the bottom. And to all appearances, Nicholas and I were excited as we strove to clear it. At any rate, we quite deceived the pirates, who took huge delight in our predicament.

But the chain remained tangled, and amid all kinds of mocking advice we drifted down upon and fouled the *Ghost,* whose bowsprit poked square through our mainsail and ripped a big hole in it. The Centipede and The Porpoise doubled up on the cabin in paroxysms of laughter, and left us to get clear as best we could. This, with much unseamanlike performance, we did, and likewise we cleared the anchor chain, of which we let out about three hundred feet. With only ten feet of water under us, this would permit the *Coal Tar Maggie* to swing in a circle some six hundred feet in diameter, in which circle she would be able to foul at least half the fleet.

The oyster pirates lay snugly together at short hawsers, the weather being fine, and they protested loudly at our ignorance in putting out such an unwarranted length of anchor chain. And not only did they protest, but they made us heave it in again, all but thirty feet.

Having sufficiently impressed them with our general lubberliness, Nicholas and I went below to congratulate ourselves and to cook supper. Hardly had we finished the meal and washed the dishes when a skiff ground against the *Coal Tar Maggie's* side, and heavy feet trampled the deck. Then The Centipede's brutal face appeared in the companionway, and he descended into the cabin, followed by The Porpoise. Before they could seat themselves on a bunk another skiff came alongside, and another and another, till the whole fleet was represented by the gathering in our cabin.

"Where'd you swipe the old tub?" asked a squat and hairy man, with cruel eyes and Mexican features.

"Didn't swipe it!" Nicholas answered, meeting them on their own ground and encouraging the idea that we had stolen the *Coal Tar Maggie.* "And if we did, what of it?"

"I'd rot on the beach first before I'd take a tub that couldn't get out of its own way!" sneered he of the Mexican features.

"How were we to know till we tried her?" Nicholas asked, so innocently as to cause a laugh. "And how do you get the oysters?" he hurried on. "We want a load of them, that's what we came for, a load of oysters."

"What d'ye want 'em for?" demanded The Porpoise.

"Oh, to give away to our friends, of course," Nicholas retorted. "That's what you do with yours, I suppose."

This started another laugh, and as our visitors grew more genial we could see that they had no suspicion of our identity or purpose.

"Didn't I see you on the dock in Oakland the other day?" The Centipede asked me.

"Yes," I answered, boldly. "I was watching you fellows and figuring out whether we'd go oystering or not. It's a pretty good business, I calculate, and so we're in for it. That is," I hastened to add, "if you fellows don't mind."

"I'll tell you one thing," he replied, "and that is, you'll have to look sharp and get a better boat. We won't stand to be disgraced by any such box as this. Understand?"

"Sure!" I said. "Soon as we sell some oysters we'll outfit in style."

"And if you show yourself square and the right sort," he went on, "why, you kin run with us. But if you don't," here his voice became stern and menacing, "why, it'll be the sickest day of your life. Understand?"

"Sure!" I said.

After that, and more warning and advice of similar nature, the conversation became general, and we learned that the beds were to be raided that very night. As they got into their boats, after an hour's stay, we were invited to join them in the raid, with the assurance of "the more the merrier."

"Did you notice that short, Mexican-looking chap?" Nicholas asked, when they had departed to their various sloops. "He's Barchi, of the Sporting Life Gang, and the fellow that came with him is Skilling. They're both out now on five thousand dollars' bail."

I had heard of the Sporting Life Gang before, a crowd of hoodlums and criminals who terrorized the lower quarters of Oakland, and two-thirds of whom were usually to be found in state prisons for crimes that ranged from perjury and ballot-box stuffing to murder.

"They're not regular oyster pirates," Nicholas continued. "They've just come down for the lark and to make a few dollars. But we'll have to watch out for them."

We sat in the cockpit and discussed the details of our plan till eleven o'clock had passed, when we heard the rattle of an oar from the direction of the *Ghost*. We hauled up our own skiff, tossed in a few sacks, and rowed over. There we found all the skiffs assembling, for it was the intention to raid the beds in a body.

To my surprise, I found barely a foot of water where we had dropped anchor in ten feet. It was the big June run-out of the full moon, and as the ebb had yet an hour and a half to run, I knew that our anchorage would be dry ground before slack water.

Mr. Taft's beds were three miles away, and for a long time we rowed silently in the wake of the other boats, once in a while grounding and constantly striking bottom with our oar-blades. At last we came upon mud covered with not more than two inches of water — not enough to float the boats. But the pirates at once jumped over the side, and by pushing and pulling on the flat-bottomed skiffs, we moved steadily along.

After half a mile of the mud, we came upon a deep channel, up which we rowed, with dead oyster shoals looming high and dry on each side. At last we reached the picking-grounds. Two men on one of the shoals warned us off. But The Centipede, The Porpoise, Barchi and Skilling took the lead, and followed by the rest of us, at least thirty men in half as many boats, we rowed right up to the watchmen, who retreated before so overwhelming a force, and rowed their boat along the channel toward where the shore should be. Besides, it was in the plan for them to retreat.

We hauled the noses of the boats up on the shore side of a big shoal, and all hands,

with sacks, spread out and began picking. Every now and again the clouds thinned before the face of the moon, and we could see the big oysters quite distinctly. In almost no time sacks were filled and carried back to the boats, where fresh ones were obtained. Nicholas and I returned often and anxiously to the boats with our little loads, but always found some one of the pirates coming or going.

"Never mind," he said. "No hurry. As they pick farther away it will take too long to carry to the boats. Then they'll stand the full sacks on end, and pick them up when the tide comes in and the skiffs will float to them."

Fully half an hour went by, and the tide had begun to flood when this came to pass. Leaving the pirates at their work, we stole back to the boats. One by one, and noiselessly, we shoved them off and made them fast in an awkward flotilla. Just as we were shoving off the last skiff, our own, one of the men came upon us. It was Barchi. His quick eye took in the situation at a glance, and he sprang for us; but we went clear with a mighty shove, and he was left floundering in water over his head. As soon as he got back to the shoal, he raised his voice and gave the alarm.

We rowed with all our strength, but it was slow going with so many boats in tow. A pistol cracked from the shoal, a second and a third; then a regular fusillade began. The bullets spat and spat all about us; but thick clouds had covered the moon, and in the dim darkness it was no more than random firing. It was only by chance that we could be hit.

"Wish we had a launch!" I panted.

"I'd just as soon the moon stayed hidden!" Nicholas panted back.

It was slow work, but every stroke carried us farther from the shoal and nearer the shore, till at last the shooting died down, and when the moon did come out we were too far away to be in danger. Not long afterward we answered a shoreward hail, and two whitehall boats, each pulled by three pairs of oars, darted up to us. Charley's face bent over to us, and he had us gripped by the hands while he was crying, "O you joys! You joys! Both of you!"

When the flotilla had been landed, Nicholas and I and a watchman rowed out in one of the whitehalls, with Charley in the stern-sheets. Two other whitehalls followed us, and as the moon now shone brightly, we easily made out the oyster pirates on their lonely shoal. As we drew in closer, they fired a volley from their revolvers, and we retreated beyond range.

"Lots of time," Charley said. "The flood is setting in fast, and by the time it's up to their necks there won't be any fight left in them."

So we lay on our oars and waited for the tide to do its work. This was the predicament of the pirates: because of the big run-out, the tide was rushing in like a mill-race, and it was impossible for the strongest swimmer in the world to make against it the three miles to the sloops. Between the pirates and the shore were we, preventing escape in that direction. On the other hand, the water was rising rapidly over the shoals, and it was only a question of a few hours when it would be over their heads.

It was beautifully calm, and in the brilliant white moonlight we watched them through our night-glasses, and told Charley of the voyage of the *Coal Tar Maggie*. One o'clock came, and two o'clock, and the pirates were clustering on the highest shoal, waist-deep in water.

Just then I heard a scarcely audible gurgle of water, and holding up my hand for silence, I turned and pointed to a ripple slowly widening out in a growing circle. It was not more than fifty feet from us.

We kept perfectly quiet and waited. After a minute the water broke six feet away, and a black head and white shoulder showed in the moonlight. With a snort of surprise and of suddenly expelled breath, the head and shoulder went down.

We pulled ahead several strokes and drifted with the current. Four pairs of eyes searched the surface of the water, but never another ripple showed and never another glimpse did we catch of the black head and white shoulder.

"It's The Porpoise," Nicholas said. "It would take broad daylight for us to catch him."

At quarter to three the pirates gave their first sign of weakening. We heard cries for help, in the unmistakable voice of The Centipede, and this time, on rowing closer, we were not fired upon.

The Centipede was in a truly perilous plight. Only the heads and shoulders of his fellow marauders showed above the water as they braced themselves against the current, while his feet were off the bottom, and they were supporting him.

"Now, lads," Charley said, briskly, "we've got you, and you can't get away. If you cut up rough we'll have to leave you alone, and the water will finish you. But if you're good, we'll take you aboard, one man at a time, and you'll all be saved. What do you say?"

"Aye!" they chorused hoarsely.

"Then one man at a time, and the short men first."

The Centipede was the first to be pulled aboard and he came willingly, although he objected when the constable put the handcuffs on him. Barchi was next hauled in, quite meek and resigned from his soaking. When we had ten in our boat we drew back, and the second whitehall was loaded. The third whitehall received nine prisoners only — a catch of twenty-nine in all.

"You didn't get The Porpoise!" The Centipede said, exultantly, as if his escape materially diminished our success.

Charley laughed. "But we saw him just the same," he said, "a-snorting for shore like a puffing pig."

It was a mild and shivering band of pirates that we marched up the beach to the oyster-house. In answer to Charley's knock the door was flung open, and a pleasant wave of warm air rushed out upon us.

"You can dry your clothes here, lads, and get some hot coffee," Charley announced, as they filed in. And there, sitting ruefully by the fire with a steaming mug in his hand, was The Porpoise. With one accord Nicholas and I looked at Charley. He laughed gleefully.

"That comes of imagination," he said. "When you see a thing, you've got to see it all round, or what's the good of seeing it at all? I saw the beach, so I left a couple of constables behind to keep and eye on it. That is all."

THE SIEGE OF THE "LANCASHIRE QUEEN"

Possibly our most exasperating experience on the fish patrol was when Charley Le Grant and I laid siege for two weeks to a big four-masted English ship. Before we had finished with the affair it became a pretty mathematical problem, and it was by the merest chance that we came into possession of the instrument that brought it to a successful solution.

After our raid on the oyster pirates, we had returned to Oakland, where two more weeks passed before Neil Partington's wife was out of danger and on the highroad to recovery. So it was after an absence of a month, all told, that we turned the *Reindeer's* nose toward Benicia.

When the cat's away the mice will play, and in these four weeks the fishermen had become very bold in violating the law. When we passed Point San Pedro we noticed many signs of activity among the shrimp-catchers, and, well into San Pablo Bay, we observed a widely scattered fleet of Upper Bay fishing-boats hastily pulling in their nets and getting up sail.

This was suspicious enough to warrant investigation, and the first and only boat we succeeded in boarding proved to have an illegal net. The two fishermen were forthwith put under arrest. Neil Partington took one of them with him, to help manage the *Reindeer* in pursuit of the fleet, while Charley and I went on ahead with the other in the captured boat.

But the shad fleet had headed over toward the Petaluma shore in wild flight, and for the rest of the run through San Pablo Bay we saw no more fishermen at all.

Our prisoner, a bronzed and bearded Greek, sat sullenly on his net while we sailed his craft. It was a new Columbia River salmon-boat, evidently on its first trip, and it sailed very, very well.

Charley and I ran up the Karquines Strait and edged into the bight at Turner's shipyard for smoother water. Here were lying several English steel sailing-ships, waiting for the wheat harvest; and here, most unexpectedly, in the precise place where we had captured Big Alec, we came upon two Italians, in a skiff that was loaded with a complete "Chinese" sturgeon-line.

The surprise was mutual, and we were on top of them before either they or we were aware. Charley had barely time to luff into the wind and run up to them. I ran forward and tossed them a line, with orders to make it fast. One of the Italians took a turn with it over a cleat, while I hastened to lower our big spritsail. This accomplished, the salmon-boat dropped astern, dragging heavily on the skiff.

Charley came forward to board the prize, but when I tried to haul alongside by means of the line, the Italians cast it off. We at once began drifting to leeward, while they got out two pairs of oars and rowed their light craft directly into the wind. This manoeuver for the moment disconcerted us, for in our large and heavily loaded boat we could not hope to catch them with the oars.

But our prisoner came unexpectedly to our aid. His black eyes were flashing eagerly and his face was flushed with suppressed excitement as he dropped the centerboard, sprang forward with a single leap, and put up the sail.

"I've always heard that Greeks don't like Italians," Charley laughed, as he ran aft to the tiller.

And never in my experience have I seen a man so anxious for the capture of another as was our prisoner in the chase that followed. His eyes fairly snapped, and his nostrils quivered and dilated in a most extraordinary way. Charley steered, while he tended the sheet; and although Charley was as quick and alert as a cat, the Greek could hardly control his impatience.

The Italians were cut off from the shore, which was fully a mile away at its nearest point. Did they attempt to make it, we could haul after them with the wind abeam, and overtake them before they had covered an eighth of the distance.

But they were too wise to attempt it, contenting themselves with rowing lustily to windward along the starboard side of a big ship, the *Lancashire Queen.* Beyond the ship, however, lay an open stretch of fully two miles to the shore in that direction. This, also, they dared not attempt, for we were bound to catch them before they could cover it. So, when they reached the bow of the *Lancashire Queen,* nothing remained but to pass round and row down her port side toward the stern, which meant rowing to leeward and giving us the advantage.

We in the salmon-boat, sailing close on the wind, tacked about and crossed the ship's bow. Then Charley put up the tiller and headed down the port side of the ship, the Greek letting out the sheet and grinning with delight. The Italians were already half-way down the ship, but the stiff breeze at our back drove us after them far faster than they could row. Closer and closer we came, and I, lying down forward, was just reaching out to grasp the skiff when it ducked under the great stern of the *Lancashire Queen.*

The chase was virtually where it had begun. The Italians were rowing up the starboard side of the ship, and we were hauled close on the wind and slowly edging out from the ship as we worked to windward. Then they darted round her bow and began the row down her port side, and we tacked about, crossed her bow, and went plunging down the wind hot after them. And again, just as I was reaching for the skiff, it ducked under the stern of the ship and out of danger. And so it went, round and round, the skiff each time just barely ducking into safety.

By this time the crew of the ship had become aware of what was taking place, and we could see their heads in a long row as they looked at us over the bulwarks. They showered us and the Italians with jokes and advice, and made our Greek so angry that at least once on each circuit he raised his fist and shook it at them in a rage. They came to look for this, and at each display greeted it with uproarious mirth.

"Wot a circus!" cried one.

"Talk about your marine hippodromes, if this ain't one I'd like to know!" declared another.

"Six-days-go-as-yer-please!" announced a third.

On the next tack to windward the Greek offered to change places with Charley.

"Let-a me sail-a de boat," he demanded. "I fix-a them; I catch-a them, sure!"

This was a stroke at Charley's professional pride, but he yielded the tiller to the prisoner and took his place at the sheet. Three times again we made the circuit, and the Greek found that he could get no more speed out of the salmon-boat than Charley had done.

In the meantime my mind had not been idle, and I had finally evolved an idea.

"Keep going, Charley, one time more," I said.

On the next tack to windward I bent a piece of line to a small grappling-hook I had seen lying in the bail-hole. The end of the line I made fast to the ring-bolt in the bow, and with the hook out of sight, I waited for the next opportunity to use it.

Once more the Italians made their leeward pull down the port side of the *Lancashire Queen,* and once more we churned down after them before the wind. Nearer and nearer we drew, and I was making believe to reach for them as before. The stern of the skiff was not six feet away, and they were laughing at me derisively as they ducked under the stern of the ship.

At that instant I suddenly rose and threw the grappling-iron. It caught fairly and squarely on the rail of the skiff, which was jerked backward out of safety as the rope tightened and the salmon-boat plowed on.

A groan went up from the row of sailors above, which quickly changed to a cheer as one of the Italians whipped out a long sheath-knife and cut the rope. But we had drawn them out of safety, and Charley, from his place in the stern-sheets, reached over and clutched the stern of the skiff.

The whole thing happened in a second of time, for the first Italian was cutting the rope and Charley was clutching the skiff when the second Italian dealt him a rap over the head with an oar. Charley released his hold and collapsed, stunned, into the bottom of the salmon-boat, and the Italians bent to their oars and escaped again under the stern of the ship.

The Greek took both tiller and sheet, and continued the chase round the *Lan-*

cashire Queen, while I attended to Charley, on whose head a nasty lump was rising rapidly. Our sailor audience was wild with delight, and to a man encouraged the fleeing Italians. Charley sat up, with one hand on his head, and gazed about him sheepishly.

"It will never do to let them escape now," he said, at the same time drawing his revolver.

On our next circuit he threatened the Italians with the weapon, but they rowed on stolidly. Nor were they to be frightened into surrendering, even when he fired several shots dangerously close to them. It was too much to expect him to shoot unarmed men, and this they knew as well as we did.

"We'll run them down, then!" Charley exclaimed. "We'll wear them out and wind them!"

So the chase continued. But the next time we passed the bow we saw them escaping up the ship's gangway, which had been suddenly lowered. It was an organized move on the part of the sailors, evidently countenanced by the captain; for by the time we arrived where the gangway had been, it was being hoisted up, and the skiff, slung in the davits, was likewise flying aloft out of reach.

The parley that followed with the captain was short and to the point. He absolutely forbade us to board the *Lancashire Queen,* and as absolutely refused to give up the two men.

By this time Charley was as enraged as the Greek. Not only had he been foiled in a long and ridiculous chase, but he had been knocked senseless into the bottom of his boat by the men who had escaped him.

"Knock off my head with little apples," he declared, emphatically, striking the fist of one hand into the palm of the other, "if those two men ever escape me! I'll stay here to get them if it takes the rest of my natural life."

Then began the siege of the *Lancashire Queen,* a siege memorable in the annals of both fishermen and fish patrol.

When the *Reindeer* came along, after a fruitless pursuit of the shad fleet, Charley instructed Neil Partington to send out his own salmon-boat, with blankets, provisions and a fisherman's charcoal stove. By sunset this exchange of boats was made, and we said good-by to our Greek, who, perforce, had to go in to Benicia and be locked up for his own violations of the law.

After supper Charley and I kept alternate four-hour watches till daylight. The fishermen made no attempt to escape that night, although the ship sent out a boat for scouting purposes, to find if the coast was clear.

By the next day we saw that a steady siege was in order, and we perfected our plans with an eye to our own comfort. A dock, known as the Solano wharf, which ran out from the Benicia shore, helped us in this.

It happened that the *Lancashire Queen,* the shore at Turner's shipyard and the Solano wharf were the corners of a big equilateral triangle. From ship to shore — the side of the triangle along which the Italians had to escape — was a distance equal to that from the Solano wharf to the shore, the side of the triangle along which we had to travel to get to the shore before the Italians.

But as we could sail so much faster than they could row, we could permit them to travel just about half their side of the triangle before we darted out along our side. If we allowed them to get more than half-way they were certain to beat us to the shore, while if we started before they were half-way, they were equally certain to beat us back to the ship. The shore in any other direction was too far away to allow them any opportunity of escape.

We found that an imaginary line, drawn from the end of the wharf to a windmill farther along the shore, cut precisely in half the line of the triangle along which the Italians must escape to reach the land. So this line made it easy for us to determine how far to let them run away before we bestirred ourselves in pursuit.

Day after day we would watch them through our glasses, as they rowed leisurely along toward the half-way point, and as they drew close into line with the windmill we would leap into the boat and get up sail. At sight of our preparation they would turn and row slowly back to the *Lancashire Queen,* secure in the knowledge that we could not overtake them.

To guard against calms — when our salmon-boat would be useless — we had in readiness a light rowing-skiff equipped with spoon-oars. But at such times, when the wind failed us, we were forced to row out from the wharf as soon as they rowed from the ship. In the night, on the other hand, we were compelled to patrol the immediate vicinity of the ship, which we did, Charley and I standing four-hour watches turn and turn about.

Friends of the Italians established a code of signals with them from the shore, so that we never dared relax the siege for a moment. And besides this, there were always one or two suspicious-looking fishermen hanging round the Solano wharf and keeping watch on our actions. We could do nothing but "grin and bear it," as Charley said, while it took up all our time and prevented us from doing other work.

The days went by and there was no change in the situation. Not that there were no attempts made to change it. One night friends from the shore came out in a skiff and attempted to confuse us while the two Italians escaped. That they did not succeed was due to the lack of a little oil on the ship's davits; for we were turned back from the pursuit of the strange boat by the creaking of the davits, and arrived at the *Lancashire Queen* just as the Italians were lowering their skiff.

Another night fully half a dozen skiffs rowed round us in the darkness, but we held on like a leech to the side of the ship, and frustrated their plan till they grew angry and showered us with abuse.

Charley laughed to himself in the bottom of the boat.

"It's a good sign, lad," he said to me. "When men begin to abuse, make sure they're losing patience, and shortly after they lose patience they lose their heads. Mark my words, if we only hold out they'll get careless some fine day, and then we'll get them."

But they did not grow careless, and Charley confessed that this was one of the times when all signs failed. Their patience seemed equal to ours, and the second week of the siege dragged monotonously along.

It would have been possible for us to secure the aid of United States marshals and board the English ship backed by government authority. But the instructions of the fish commission were to the effect that the patrolmen should avoid complications, and this one, did we call on the higher powers, might well end in a pretty international tangle.

On the morning of the fourteenth day

the change came, and it was brought about by means as unexpected by us as by the men we were striving to capture.

Charley and I, after our customary night vigil by the side of the *Lancashire Queen*, rowed in to the Solano wharf.

"Hello!" cried Charley, in surprise. "In the name of reason and common sense, what is that? Of all unmannerly craft, did you ever see the like?"

Well he might exclaim, for there, tied up to the dock, lay the strangest-looking launch I had ever seen. Not that it could be called a launch, either, but it seemed to resemble a launch more than any other kind of boat.

It was not more than seventy feet long, but so narrow was it and so bare of superstructure that it appeared much smaller than it really was. It was built wholly of steel and painted black. Three smoke-stacks, a good distance apart and raking well aft, rose in single file amidships, while the bow, long and lean and sharp as a knife, plainly advertised that the boat was made for speed. Passing under the stern, we read *Streak,* painted in small white letters.

In a few minutes we were on board and talking with an engineer, who was watching the sunrise from the deck. He was quite willing to satisfy our curiosity, and in a few minutes we learned that the *Streak* had come in after dark from San Francisco; that this was what might be called the trial trip, and that she was the property of Silas Taft, a young mining millionaire of California, whose fad was high-speed yachts.

There was some talk about turbine engines, direct application of steam and the absence of pistons, rods and cranks. All of this was beyond me, for I was familiar only with sailing craft; but the last words of the engineer I clearly understood.

"Three thousand horse-power and thirty-five knots an hour, though you wouldn't think it," he concluded, proudly.

"Say it again, man! Say it again!" Charley exclaimed in an excited voice.

"Three thousand horse-power and thirty-five knots an hour," the engineer repeated, grinning good-naturedly.

"Where's the owner?" was Charley's next question. "Is there any way I can speak to him?"

The engineer shook his head. "No, I'm

afraid not. He's asleep, you see."

At that moment a young man in blue uniform came on deck farther aft, and stood regarding the sunrise.

"There he is, that's him; that's Mr. Taft," said the engineer.

Charley walked aft and spoke to him, and while he talked earnestly the young man listened with an amused expression on his face. He must have inquired about the depth of water close in to the shore at Turner's shipyard, for I could see Charley making gestures and explaining. A few minutes later he came back in high glee.

"Come on, lad," he said. "We've got them!"

It was our good fortune to leave the *Streak* when we did, for a little later one of the spy fishermen put in his appearance. Charley and I took up our accustomed place on the stringer-piece, a little ahead of the *Streak* and over our own boat, where we could comfortably watch the *Lancashire Queen*.

Nothing occurred till about nine o'clock, when we saw the two Italians leave the ship and pull along their side of the triangle toward the shore. Charley looked as unconcerned as could be, but before they had covered a quarter of the distance he whispered to me:

"Almost forty miles an hour — nothing can save them — they are ours!"

Slowly the two men rowed along till they were nearly in line with the windmill. This was the point where we always jumped into our salmon-boat and got up the sail, and the two men, evidently expecting it, seemed surprised when we gave no sign.

The spy fisherman, sitting beside us on the stringer-piece, was likewise puzzled. He could not make out our inactivity.

The men in the skiff rowed nearer the shore, but stood up again and scanned it, as if they thought we might be in hiding there. But a man came out on the beach and waved a handkerchief to show that the coast was clear. That settled them. They bent to the oars to make a dash for it. Still Charley waited.

Not until they had covered three-quarters of the distance from the *Lancashire Queen*, which left them hardly more than a quarter of a mile to gain the shore, did Charley slap me on the shoulder and cry:

"They're ours! They're ours!"

We ran the few steps to the side of the *Streak* and jumped aboard. Sternline and bowline were cast off in a jiffy. The *Streak*, which had been under steam all the time, shot ahead and away from the wharf. The spy fisherman we had left behind on the stringer-piece pulled out a revolver and fired five shots into the air in rapid succession. The men in the skiff gave instant heed to the warning, for we could see them pulling away like mad.

But if they pulled like mad, I wonder how our progress can be described! We fairly flew. So frightful was the speed with which we displaced the water that a surge rose up on each side of our bow and foamed aft in a series of three stiff, upstanding waves, while astern a great, crested billow pursued us hungrily, as if at each moment it would fall aboard and destroy us.

The *Streak* was pulsing and plunging and roaring like a thing alive. The wind of our progress was like a gale — a forty-mile gale. We could not face it and draw breath without choking and strangling. It blew the smoke straight back from the mouths of the stacks at a direct right angle to the perpendicular. In fact, we were travelling as fast as an express-train.

"We just *streaked* it," was the way Charley told it afterward, and I think his description comes nearer than any I can give.

As for the Italians in the skiff, hardly had we started, it seemed to me, when we were upon them. Naturally we had to slow down long before we got to them; but even then we shot past like a whirlwind, and were compelled to circle back between them and the shore.

They had rowed steadily, rising from the thwarts at every stroke, up to the moment we passed them, when they recognized Charley and me. That took the last bit of fight out of them. They hauled in their oars and sullenly submitted to arrest.

"Well, Charley," Neil Partington said, as we discussed it on the wharf afterward, "I fail to see where your boasted imagination came into play this time."

But Charley was true to his hobby. "Imagination?" he demanded, pointing at the *Streak*. "Look at that! Just look at it! If the invention of that isn't imagination, I should like to know what is?

"Of course," he added, "it's the other fellow's imagination, but it did the work all the same."

CHARLEY'S "COUP"

Charley called it a "coup," having heard Neil Partington use the term; but I think he misunderstood the word, and thought it meant "coop," to catch, to trap.

The fishermen, however, coup or coop, must have called it a Waterloo, for it was the severest stroke ever dealt them by the fish patrol.

During what is called the "open season" the fishermen could catch as many salmon as their luck allowed and their boats could hold. But there was one important restriction. From sundown Saturday night to sunrise Monday morning they were not permitted to set a net.

This was a wise provision on the part of the fish commission, for it was necessary to give the spawning salmon some opportunity to ascend the river and lay their eggs. And this law, with only an occasional violation, had been obediently observed by the Greek fishermen who caught salmon for the canneries and the market.

One Sunday morning Charley received a telephone call from a friend in Collinsville, who told him that the full force of fishermen were out with their nets. Charley and I jumped into our salmon-boat and started for the scene of the trouble. With a light, favoring wind we went through the Karquines Strait, crossed Suisun Bay, passed the Ship Island Light, and came upon the whole fleet at work.

But first let me describe the method by which they worked. The net used is what is known as a gill-net. It has a simple, diamond-shaped mesh, which measures at least seven and one-half inches between the knots. From five to seven and even eight hundred feet in length, these nets are only a few feet wide. They are not stationary, but float with the current, the upper edge supported on the surface by floats, the lower edge sunk by means of leaden weights.

This arrangement keeps the net upright in the current and effectually prevents all but the smaller fish from ascending the river. The salmon, swimming near the surface, as is their custom, run their heads through these meshes, and are prevented from going on through by their larger girth of body, and from going back because of their gills, which catch in the mesh.

It requires two fishermen to set such a net; one to row the boat, while the other, standing in the stern, carefully pays out the net. When it is all out, stretching directly across the stream, the men make their boat fast to one end of the net and drift along with it.

As we drew closer to the fleet, we observed none of the usual flurry and excitement which our appearance invariably produced. Instead, each boat lay quietly to its net, while the fishermen favored us with not the slightest attention.

This did not continue to be the case, however, for as we bore down upon the nearest net, the men to whom it belonged detached their boat and rowed slowly toward the shore. The rest of the boats showed no sign of uneasiness.

"That's funny," was Charley's remark. "But we can confiscate the net, at any rate."

We lowered sail, picked up one end of the net, and began to heave it into the boat. But at the first heave we heard a bullet *zip-zipping* past us on the water, followed by the faint report of a rifle. The men who had rowed ashore were shooting at us.

Charley took a turn round a pin and sat down. There were no more shots. But as soon as he began to heave in, the shooting recommenced.

"That settles it," he said, flinging the end of the net overboard. "You fellows want it worse than we do, and you can have it."

We rowed over toward the next net, for Charley was intent on finding out whether or not we were face to face with an organized defiance.

As we approached, the two fishermen

DRAWN BY GEORGE VARIAN

The consternation we spread among the fishermen was tremendous

proceeded to cast off from their net and row ashore, while the first two rowed back and made fast to the net we had abandoned. And at the second net we were greeted by rifle-shots till we desisted and went on to the third, where the manoeuver was again repeated.

Then we gave it up, completely routed, hoisted sail and started on the long windward beat back to Benicia. A number of Sundays went by, on each of which the law was persistently violated. Yet, unless we had an armed force of soldiers, we could do nothing. The fishermen had hit upon a new idea, and were using it for all it was worth, while there seemed no way by which we could get the better of them.

Then one morning the idea came. We were down on the steamboat wharf, where the river steamers made their landings, and where we found a group of amused longshoremen and loafers listening to the tale of a sleepy-eyed young fellow in long sea-boots. He was a sort of amateur fisherman, he said, fishing for the local market of Berkeley. Now Berkeley was on the Lower Bay, thirty miles away. On the previous night, he said, he had set his net and dozed off to sleep in the bottom of the boat.

That was the last he remembered. The next he knew it was morning, and he opened his eyes to find his boat rubbing softly against the piles of Steamboat Wharf at Benicia. Also, he saw the river steamer, *Apache,* lying ahead of him, and a couple of deck-hands disentangling the shreds of his net from the paddle-wheel.

In short, after he had fallen asleep his fisherman's riding-light had gone out, and the *Apache* had run over his net. After tearing it pretty well to pieces, in some way it still remained foul, and he had been given a thirty-mile tow.

Charley nudged me with his elbow. I grasped his thought on the instant, but objected:

"We can't charter a steamboat."

"Don't intend to," he rejoined. "But let's run over to Turner's shipyard. I've something in my mind there that may be of use to us."

Over we went to the shipyard, where Charley led the way to the *Mary Rebecca,* lying hauled out on the ways, where she had been generally cleaned and overhauled.

She was a scow-schooner we both knew well, carrying a cargo of one hundred and forty tons and a spread of canvas greater than any other schooner on the bay.

"How d'ye do, Ole?" Charley greeted a big blue-shirted Swede who was greasing the jaws of the main-gaff with a piece of pork rind.

Ole Ericsen verified Charley's conjecture that the *Mary Rebecca,* as soon as launched, would run up the San Joaquin River nearly to Stockton for a load of wheat. Then Charley made his proposition, and Ole Ericsen shook his head.

"Just a hook, one good-sized hook," Charley pleaded. "We can put the end of the hook through the bottom from the outside, and fasten it on the inside with a nut. After it's done its work, why, all we have to do is to go down into the hold, unscrew the nut, and out drops the hook. Then drive a wooden peg into the hole, and the *Mary Rebecca* is all right again."

Ole Ericsen was obstinate for a time; but in the end, after we had had dinner with him, he was brought round to consent.

"Ay do it!" he said, striking one huge fist into the palm of the other hand. "But yust hurry you up with der hook. Der *Mary Rebecca* slides into der water to-night."

It was Saturday, and Charley had need to hurry. We went to the shipyard blacksmith shop, where, under Charley's directions, a most generously curved hook of heavy steel was made.

Back we hastened to the *Mary Rebecca.* Aft of the great centerboard case, through what was properly her keel, a hole was bored. The end of the hook was inserted from the outside, and Charley, on the inside, screwed the nut on tightly. As it stood complete, the hook projected more than a foot beneath the bottom of the schooner. Its curve was something like the curve of a sickle, but deeper.

The next morning found the sun shining brightly, but something more than a half-gale shrieking up the Karquines Strait. The *Mary Rebecca* got under way with two reefs in her mainsail and one in her foresail. It was rough in the strait and in Suisun Bay, but as the water grew more landlocked it became quite calm, although there was no let-up in the wind.

Off Ship Island Light the reefs were shaken out, and at Charley's suggestion a big fisherman's staysail was made all ready for hoisting, and the maintopsail, bunched into a cap at the masthead, was overhauled so that it could be set on an instant's notice.

We were tearing along before the wind as we came upon the salmon fleet. There they were, boats and nets, strung out evenly over the river as far as we could see. A narrow space on the right-hand side of the channel was left clear for steamboats, but the rest of the river was covered with the wide-stretching nets. This narrow space was our logical course, but Charley, at the wheel, steered the *Mary Rebecca* straight for the nets.

"Now she takes it!" Charley cried, as we dashed across the middle of a line of floats which marked a net.

At one end of this line was a small barrel buoy, at the other the two fishermen in their boat. Buoy and boat at once began to draw together, and the fishermen cried out as they were jerked after us. A couple of minutes later we hooked a second net, and then a third, and in this fashion we tore straight through the center of the fleet.

The consternation we spread among the fishermen was tremendous. As fast as we hooked a net the two ends of it, buoy and boat, came together as they dragged out astern; and so many buoys and boats, coming together at such breakneck speed, kept the fishermen on the jump to avoid smashing into one another.

The drag of a single net is very heavy, and even in such a wind Charley and Ole Ericsen decided that ten was all the *Mary Rebecca* could take along with her. So, when we had hooked ten nets, with ten boats containing twenty men streaming along behind us, we veered to the left out of the fleet, and headed toward Collinsville.

We were all jubilant. Charley was handling the wheel as if he were steering the winning yacht home in a race. The two sailors, who made up the crew of the *Mary Rebecca*, were grinning and joking. Ole Ericsen was rubbing his huge hands in childlike glee.

"Ay tank you fish patrol fallers never ben so lucky as when you sail with Ole Ericsen," he was saying, when a rifle cracked sharply astern, and a bullet gouged along the newly painted cabin, glanced on a nail, and sang shrilly onward into space.

This was too much for Ole Ericsen. At sight of his beloved paintwork thus defaced, he jumped up and shook his fist at the fishermen; but a second bullet smashed into the cabin not six inches from his head, and he dropped down to the deck under cover of the rail.

All the fishermen had rifles, and they now opened a general fusillade. We were all driven to cover, even Charley, who was compelled to desert the wheel. Had it not been for the heavy drag of the nets, we would inevitably have broached to at the mercy of the enraged fishermen. But the nets, fastened to the bottom of the *Mary Rebecca* well aft, held her stern into the wind, and she continued to plow on, although somewhat erratically.

Then Ole Ericsen bethought himself of a large piece of sheet steel in the empty hold. It was actually a plate from the side of the *New Jersey,* a steamer which had recently been wrecked outside the Golden Gate, and in the salving of which the *Mary Rebecca* had taken part.

Crawling carefully along the deck, the two sailors, Ole and I got the heavy plate on deck and aft, where we reared it as a shield between the wheel and the fishermen. The bullets whanged and banged against it, but Charley grinned in its shelter, and coolly went on steering. So we raced along, behind us a howling, screaming bedlam of wrathful Greeks, Collinsville ahead, and bullets *spat-spatting* all round us.

"Ole," Charley said, in a faint voice, "I don't know what we're going to do!"

Ole Ericsen, lying on his back close to the rail and grinning upward at the sky, turned over on his side and looked at him. "Ay tank we go into Collinsville yust der same," he said.

"But we can't stop!" Charley groaned. "I never thought of it, but we can't stop."

A look of consternation slowly overspread Ole Ericsen's broad face. It was only too true. We had a hornet's nest on our hands, and to stop at Collinsville would be to have it about our ears.

"Every man Jack of them has a gun," one of the sailors remarked, cheerfully.

In a few minutes we were at Collinsville, and went foaming by within biscuit-toss of the wharf.

"I hope the wind holds out," Charley said.

"What of der wind?" Ole demanded, disconsolately. "Der river will not hold out, and then —"

"It's head for the tall timber, and the Greeks take the hindmost," adjudged the cheerful sailor.

We had now reached a dividing of the ways. To the left was the mouth of the Sacramento River, to the right the mouth of the San Joaquin. The cheerful sailor crept forward and jibed over the foresail as Charley put the helm to starboard, and we swerved to the right, into the San Joaquin. The wind, from which we had been running away on an even keel, now caught us on our beam, and the *Mary Rebecca* was pressed down on her port side as if she were about to capsize.

Still we dashed on, and still the fishermen dashed on behind. The value of their nets was greater than the fines they would have to pay for violating the fish laws; so to cast off from their nets and escape, which they could easily do, would profit them nothing. Further, the desire for vengeance was roused, and we could depend upon it that they would follow us to the ends of the earth, if we could tow them that far.

The rifle-firing had ceased, and we looked astern to see what they were doing. The boats were strung along at unequal distances apart, and we saw the four nearest ones bunching together. This was done by the boat ahead trailing a small rope astern to the one behind. When this was caught, they would cast off from their net and heave in on the line till they were brought up to the boat in front.

So great was the speed at which we were travelling, however, that this was very slow work. Sometimes the men would strain to their utmost and fail to get in an inch of the rope; at other times they came ahead more rapidly.

When the four boats were near enough together for a man to pass from one to another, one Greek from each of three got into the nearest boat to us, taking his rifle with him. This made five in the foremost boat, and it was plain that their intention was to board us. This they proceeded to do, by main strength and sweat, running hand over hand the float-line of a net. And although it was slow, and they stopped frequently to rest, they gradually drew nearer.

Charley smiled at their efforts, and said, "Give her the topsail, Ole."

The cap at the mainmasthead was broken out, and sheet and down-haul pulled flat, amid a scattering rifle-fire from the boats; and the *Mary Rebecca* laid over and sprang ahead faster than ever.

But the Greeks were undaunted. Unable, at the increased speed, to draw themselves nearer by means of their hands, they rigged from the blocks of their boat-sail what sailors call a "watch-tackle." One of them, held by the legs by his mates, would lean far over the bow and make the tackle fast to the float-line. Then they would heave in on the tackle till the blocks were together, when the manoeuver would be repeated.

"Have to give her the staysail," Charley said.

Ole Ericsen looked at the straining *Mary Rebecca* and shook his head. "It will take der masts out of her," he said.

"And we'll be taken out of her if you don't," Charley replied.

Ole shot an anxious glance at his masts, another at the boat-load of armed Greeks, and consented.

The five men were in the bow of the boat — a bad place when a craft is towing. I was watching the behavior of their boat as the great fisherman's staysail, far, far larger than the topsail and used only in light breezes, was broken out.

As the *Mary Rebecca* lurched forward with a tremendous jerk, the nose of the boat ducked down into the water, and the men tumbled over one another in a wild rush into the stern to save the boat from being dragged sheer under water.

"That settles them!" Charley remarked, although he was anxiously studying the behavior of the *Mary Rebecca,* which was being driven under far more canvas than it was able to carry safely.

"Next stop is Antioch!" announced the cheerful sailor, after the manner of a railway conductor. "And next comes Merryweather!"

"Come here, quick!" Charley said to me.

I crawled across the deck and stood upright beside him in the shelter of the sheet steel.

"Feel in my inside pocket," he commanded, "and get my note-book. That's right. Tear out a blank page and write what I tell you."

This is what I wrote:

Telephone to Merryweather, to the sheriff, the constable or the judge. Tell them we are coming and to turn out the town. Arm everybody. Have them down on the wharf to meet us or we are gone geese.

"Now make it good and fast to that marlinespike, and stand by to toss it ashore."

I did as he directed. By now we were nearing Antioch. The wind was shouting through our rigging, the *Mary Rebecca* was half-over on her side and rushing ahead like an ocean greyhound. The seafaring folk of Antioch had seen us, and had hurried to the wharf-ends to find out what was the matter.

Straight down the water-front we boomed, Charley edging in till a man could almost leap ashore. When he gave the signal I tossed the marlinespike.

It all happened in a flash, for the next moment Antioch was behind, and we were heeling it up the San Joaquin toward Merryweather, six miles away. The river straightened out here so that our course lay almost due east, and we squared away before the wind.

We strained our eyes for a glimpse of the town, and the first sight we caught of it gave us immense relief. The wharves were black with men. As we came closer, we could see them still arriving, stringing down the main street on the run, nearly every man with a gun in his hand. Charley glanced astern at the fishermen with a look of ownership in his eye which till now had been missing.

The Greeks were plainly overawed by the display of armed strength, and were putting their own rifles away.

We took in topsail and staysail, dropped the main-peak, and as we got abreast of the principal wharf jibed the mainsail. The *Mary Rebecca* shot round into the wind, — the captive fishermen describing a great arc behind her, — and forged ahead till she lost way, when lines were flung ashore and she was made fast.

Ole Ericsen heaved a great sigh. "Ay never tank Ay see my wife never again," he confessed.

"Why, we were never in any danger," said Charley.

Ole looked at him incredulously.

"Sure, I mean it," Charley went on. "All we had to do any time was to let go our end, as I am going to now, so that those Greeks can untangle their nets."

He went below with a monkey-wrench, unscrewed the nut, and let the hook drop off. When the Greeks had hauled their nets into their boats and made everything shipshape, a posse of citizens took them off our hands.

DEMETRIOS CONTOS

It must not be thought from what I have at various times told of the Greek fishermen that they were altogether bad. Far from it. But they were rough men, gathered together in isolated communities, and fighting with the elements for a livelihood. They lived far away from the law and its workings, did not understand it, and thought it tyranny.

Especially did the fish laws seem tyrannical; and because of this the men of the fish patrol were looked upon by them as their natural enemies.

But it is to show that they could act generously as well as hate bitterly that this story of Demetrios Contos is told.

Demetrios Contos lived in Vallejo. Next to "Big Alec," he was the largest, bravest and most influential man among the Greeks. He had given us no trouble, and probably would never have clashed with us had he not invested in a new salmon-boat.

He had had it built upon his own model, in which the lines of the usual salmon-boat were somewhat modified.

To his high elation he found his new boat very fast — in fact, faster than any other boat on the bay or rivers. Forthwith he grew proud and boastful; and our raid with the *Mary Rebecca* on the Sunday salmon-fishers having wrought fear in their hearts, he sent a challenge up to Benicia.

One of the local fishermen told us of it, and it was to the effect that Demetrios Contos would sail up from Vallejo on the following Sunday, and in the plain sight of Benicia set his net and catch salmon, and that Charley Le Grant, patrolman, might come and get him if he could.

Sunday came. The challenge had been bruited abroad, and the fishermen and seafaring folk of Benicia turned out to a man, crowding Steamboat Wharf till it looked like the grand stand at a football-match.

In the afternoon, when the sea-breeze had picked up in strength, the Greek's sail hove into view as he bowled along before the wind. He tacked a score of feet from the wharf, waved his hand theatrically, like a knight about to enter the lists, received a hearty cheer in return, and stood away into the straits for a couple of hundred yards.

Then he lowered sail, and drifting the boat sidewise by means of the wind, proceeded to set his net.

He did not set much of it, possibly fifty feet, yet Charley and I were thunderstruck by the man's effrontery.

We did not know at the time, but we learned afterward that what he used was an old and worthless net. It *could* catch fish, true; but a catch of any size would have torn it into a thousand pieces.

Charley shook his head and said, "I confess it puzzles me. What if he has out only fifty feet? He could never get it in if we once started for him. And why does he come here, anyway, flaunting his lawbreaking in our faces?"

In the meantime the Greek was lolling in the stern of his boat and watching the net-floats. When a large fish is meshed in a gill-net the floats by their agitation advertise the fact. And they evidently advertised it to Demetrios, for he now pulled in about a dozen feet of net, and held aloft for a moment, before he flung it into the bottom of the boat, a big, glistening salmon.

It was greeted by the audience on the wharf with round after round of cheers.

This was more than Charley could stand.

"Come on, lad!" he called to me; and we lost no time jumping into our salmon-boat and getting up sail.

The crowd shouted warning to Demetrios, and as we darted out from the wharf we saw him slash his worthless net clear with a long knife.

His sail was all ready to go up, and a moment later it fluttered in the sunshine. He ran aft, drew in the sheet, and filled on

411

the long tack toward the Contra Costa hills.

By this time we were not more than thirty feet astern. Charley was jubilant. He knew our boat was fast, and he knew, further, that in fine sailing few men were his equals. He was confident that we should surely catch Demetrios, and I shared his confidence. But somehow we did not seem to gain.

It was a pretty sailing breeze. We were gliding sleekly through the water, but Demetrios was sliding away from us. And not only was he going faster, but he was eating into the wind a fraction of a point closer than we. This was sharply impressed upon us when he went about under the Contra Costa hills and passed us on the other track fully one hundred 'feet dead to windward.

"Whew!" Charley exclaimed. "Either that boat is a wonder or there's a five-gallon coal-oil can fast to our keel!"

It certainly looked it, one way or the other; and by the time Demetrios made the Sonoma hills, on the other side of the straits, we were so hopelessly outdistanced that Charley told me to slack off the sheet, and we squared away for Benicia.

The fishermen on Steamboat Wharf showered us with ridicule when we returned and tied up our boat.

Charley and I got out and walked away, feeling rather sheepish, for it is a sore stroke to your pride when you think you have a good boat and know how to sail it and another man comes along and beats you.

Charley mooned over it for a couple of days; then word was brought to us, as before, that on the next Sunday Demetrios Contos would repeat his performance. Charley roused himself. He had our boat out of the water, cleaned and repainted its bottom, made a trifling alteration about the centerboard, overhauled the running-gear, and sat up nearly all of Saturday night, sewing on a new and much larger sail. So large did he make it, in truth, that additional ballast was imperative, and we stowed away nearly five hundred extra pounds of old railroad iron in the bottom of the boat.

Sunday came, and with it came Demetrios Contos. Again we had the afternoon sea-breeze, and again Demetrios cut loose from forty or more feet of his rotten net,

and got up sail and under way under our very noses. But he had anticipated Charley's move, and his own sail peaked higher than ever, while a whole extra cloth had been added to the leech.

By the time we had made the return tack to the Sonoma hills we could not fail to see that, while we footed it at about equal speed, Demetrios had eaten the least bit into the wind more than we.

Of course Charley could have drawn his revolver and fired at Demetrios, but we had long since found it contrary to our natures to shoot at a fleeing man guilty of a petty offense.

Also, a sort of tacit agreement seemed to have been reached between the patrolmen and the fishermen. If we did not shoot while they ran away, they, in turn, did not fight if we once laid hands on them.

Thus Demetrios Contos ran way from us, and we did no more than try very hard to overtake him; and in turn, if our boat proved faster than his, or was sailed better, he would, we knew, make no resistance when we caught up with him.

But it was a vain undertaking for us to attempt to catch him.

"Slack away the sheet!" Charley commanded; and as we fell off before the wind, Demetrios's mocking laugh floated down to us.

Charley shook his head, saying, "It's no use. Demetrios has the better boat. If he tries his performance again we must meet it with some new scheme."

This time it was my imagination which came to the rescue.

"What's the matter," I suggested, on the Wednesday following, "with my chasing Demetrios in the boat next Sunday, and with your waiting for him on the wharf at Vallejo?"

Charley considered it a moment and slapped his knee.

"A good idea! You're beginning to use that head of yours. But everybody'll know I've gone to Vallejo, and you can depend upon it that Demetrios will know, too."

"No," I replied. "On Sunday you and I will be round Benicia up to the very moment Demetrios's sail heaves into sight. This will lull everybody's suspicions. Then, when Demetrios's sail does heave in sight, you stroll leisurely away and up-town. All the fishermen will think you're beaten, and that you know you're beaten."

DRAWN BY GEORGE VARIAN.

And there,...grinning and nodding good-naturedly, sat Demetrios Contos

"So far, so good," Charley commented, while I paused to catch breath.

"When you're once out of sight," I continued, "you leg it for all you're worth for Dan Maloney's. Take that little mare of his, and strike out on the county road for Vallejo. The road's in fine condition, and you can make it in quicker time than Demetrios can beat all the way down against the wind."

"And I'll arrange right away for the mare, first thing in the morning," Charley said.

As usual, Sunday and Demetrios Contos arrived together. It had become the regular thing for the fishermen to assemble on Steamboat Wharf to greet his arrival and laugh at our discomfiture. He lowered sail two hundred yards out, and set his customary fifty feet of rotten net.

"I suppose this nonsense will keep up as long as his old net holds out!" Charley grumbled, with intention, in the hearing of several of the Greeks. "Well, so long, lad!" Charley called to me, a moment later. "I think I'll go up-town to Maloney's."

"Let me take the boat out?" I asked.

"If you want to," was his answer, as he turned on his heel and walked slowly away.

Demetrios pulled two large salmon out of his net, and I jumped into the boat. The fishermen crowded round in a spirit of fun, and when I started to get up sail, overwhelmed me with all sorts of jocular advice.

But I was in no hurry. I waited to give Charley all the time I could, and I pretended dissatisfaction with the stretch of the sail, and slightly shifted the small tackle by which the sprit forces up the peak. It was not until I was sure that Charley had reached Dan Maloney's that I cast off from the wharf and gave the big sail to the wind. A stout puff filled it and suddenly pressed the lee gunwale down till a couple of buckets of water came inboard.

A little thing like this will happen to the best small-boat sailors, and yet, although I instantly let go the sheet and righted, I was cheered sarcastically, as if I had been guilty of a very awkward blunder.

When Demetrios saw only one person in the fish-patrol boat, and that one a boy, he proceeded to play with me. Making a short tack out, he returned, with his sheet a little free, to the Steamboat Wharf. And there he made short tacks, and turned and twisted and ducked round, to the great delight of his sympathetic audience.

I was right behind him all the time, and I dared to do whatever he did, even when he squared away before the wind and jibed his big sail over — a most dangerous trick with such a sail in such a wind.

He depended upon the brisk sea-breeze and strong ebb-tide, which together kicked up a nasty sea, to bring me to grief. But I was on my mettle, and if I do say it, never in all my life did I sail a boat better than on that day.

It was Demetrios who came to grief instead. Something went wrong with his centerboard, so that it jammed in the case and would not go all the way down.

In a short breathing-space, which he had gained from me by a clever trick, I saw him working impatiently with the centerboard, trying to force it down. I gave him little time, and he was compelled quickly to return to the tiller and sheet.

The centerboard made him anxious. He gave over playing with me and started on the long beat to Vallejo.

To my joy, on the first long tack across, I found that I could eat into the wind just a little closer than he. Here was where another man in the boat would have been of value, for with me but a few feet astern, he did not dare let go the tiller and run amidships to try to force down the centerboard.

Unable to hang on as close in the eye of the wind as formerly, he proceeded to slack his sheet a trifle and to ease off a bit, in order to outfoot me. This I permitted him to do till I had worked to windward, when I bore down upon him.

As I drew close, he feinted at coming about. This led me to shoot into the wind to forestall him. But it was only a feint, cleverly executed, and he held back to his course while I hurried to make up lost ground.

He was undeniably abler than I when it came to manoeuvering. Time after time I all but had him, and each time he tricked me and escaped. Besides, the wind was freshening constantly, and each of us had our hands full to avoid a capsize.

The strong ebb-tide, racing down the straits in the teeth of the wind, caused an unusually heavy and spiteful sea, which dashed aboard continually. I was dripping wet, and even the sail was wet half-way up the leech. Once I did succeed in outmanoeuvering Demetrios, so that my bow bumped into him amidships.

Here was where I should have had another man. Before I could run forward and leap aboard he shoved the boats apart with an oar, laughing mockingly in my face as he did so.

We were now at the mouth of the straits, in a bad stretch of water. Here the Vallejo Strait and the Karquines Strait drove directly at each other.

Through the first flowed all the water of Napa River and the great tide-lands; through the second flowed all the water of Suisun Bay and the Sacramento and San Joaquin rivers. And where such immense bodies of water, flowing swiftly, rushed together, a terrible tide-rip was produced.

To make it worse, the wind howled up San Pablo Bay for fifteen miles, and drove in a tremendous sea upon the tide-rip.

Conflicting currents tore about in all directions, colliding, forming whirlpools, sucks and boils, and shooting up spitefully into hollow waves, which fell aboard as often from leeward as from windward. And through it all, confused, driven into a madness of motion, thundered the great, smoking seas from San Pablo Bay.

I was as wildly excited as the water. The boat was behaving splendidly, leaping and lurching through the welter like a race-horse. I could hardly contain myself with the joy of it.

And just then, as I roared along like a conquering hero, the boat received a frightful smash, and came instantly to a dead stop. I was flung forward and into the bottom.

As I sprang up I caught a fleeting glimpse of a greenish, barnacle-covered object, and knew it at once for what it was — that terror of navigation, a sunken pile.

No man may guard against such a thing. Water-logged and floating just beneath the surface, it was impossible to sight it in the troubled water in time to escape.

The whole bow of the boat must have been crushed in, for in a very few seconds the boat was half-full. Then a couple of seas filled it and it sank straight down, dragged to the bottom by the heavy ballast. So quickly did it all happen that I was entangled in the sail and drawn under. When I fought my way to the surface, suffocating, lungs almost bursting, I could see nothing of the oars. They must have been swept away by the chaotic currents. I saw Demetrios Contos looking back from his boat, and heard the vindictive and mocking tones of his voice, as he shouted exultantly. He held steadily on his course, leaving me to perish.

There was nothing to do but swim for it, which, in that wild confusion, was at the best a matter of but a few moments.

Holding my breath and working with my hands, I managed to get off my heavy sea-boots and my jacket. Yet there was very little breath I could catch to hold, and I swiftly discovered that it was not so much a matter of swimming as of breathing.

I was beaten and buffeted, smashed under by the great San Pablo whitecaps, and strangled by the hollow tide-rip waves which flung themselves into my eyes, nose and mouth. Then the strange sucks would grip my legs and drag me under, to spout me up in some fierce boiling, where, even as I tried to catch my breath, a great whitecap would crash down upon me.

It was impossible to survive any length of time. I was breathing more water than air, and drowning all the time. My senses began to leave me, my head to whirl. I struggled on, spasmodically, instinctively, and was barely half-conscious, when I felt myself caught by the shoulders and hauled over the gunwale of a boat.

For some time I lay across a seat, where I had been flung, face downward, and with the water running out of my mouth. After a while, still weak and faint, I turned round to see who was my rescuer. And there, in the stern, sheet in one hand and tiller in the other, grinning and nodding good-naturedly, sat Demetrios Contos.

He had intended to let me drown, — he said so afterward, — but his better self had fought the battle, conquered, and sent him back to me.

"You alla right?" he asked.

I managed to shape a "Yes" with my lips, although I could not yet speak.

"You saila de boat verra gooda," he said. "So gooda as a man."

A compliment from Demetrios Contos was a compliment indeed, and I keenly appreciated it, although I could only nod my head in acknowledgment.

We held no more conversation, for I was busy recovering and he was busy with the boat. He ran in to the wharf at Vallejo, made the boat fast and helped me out. Then it was, as we both stood on the wharf, that Charley stepped out from behind a net-rack and put his hand on Demetrios Contos's arm.

"He saved my life, Charley," I protested, "and I don't think he ought to be arrested."

A puzzled expression came into Charley's face, which cleared immediately in a way it had when he made up his mind.

"I can't help it, lad," he said, kindly. "I can't go back on my duty, and it's my plain duty to arrest him. To-day is Sunday; there are two salmon in his boat which he caught to-day. What else can I do?"

"But he saved my life," I persisted, unable to make any other argument.

Demetrios Contos's face was black with rage when he learned Charley's decision. He had a sense of being unfairly treated. He had performed a generous act and saved a helpless enemy, and in return the enemy was taking him to jail.

Charley and I were out of sorts with each other when we went back to Benicia. I stood for the spirit of the law and not the letter; but by the letter Charley made his stand.

So far as he could see, there was nothing else for him to do.

The law said distinctly that no salmon should be caught on Sunday. He was a patrolman, and it was his duty to enforce that law. That was all there was to it.

Two days later we went down to Vallejo to the trial. I had to go along as a witness, and it was the most hateful task that I ever performed in my life when I testified on the witness-stand to seeing Demetrios catch the two salmon.

Demetrios had engaged a lawyer, but his case was hopeless. The jury was out only fifteen minutes, and returned a verdict of guilty. The judge sentenced Demetrios to pay a fine of one hundred dollars or be sent to jail for fifty days.

Charley stepped quickly up to the clerk of the court.

"I want to pay that fine," he said, at the same time placing five twenty-dollar gold pieces on the desk. "It — it was the only way out of it, lad," he said, turning to me.

The moisture rushed into my eyes as I seized his hand.

"I want to pay —" I began.

"To pay your half?" he interrupted. "I certainly shall expect you to pay it."

In the meantime Demetrios had been informed by his lawyer that his fee had likewise been paid by Charley.

Demetrios came over to shake Charley's hand, and all his warm southern blood flamed in his face.

Then, not to be outdone in generosity, he insisted on paying his fine and his lawyer's fee himself, and flew half-way into a passion because Charley refused to let him.

More than anything else we ever did, I think, did this action of Charley's impress upon the fishermen the deeper significance of the law. Also Charley was raised high in their estimation, while I came in for a little share of praise as a boy who knew how to sail a boat. Demetrios Contos not only never broke the law again, but became a very good friend of ours, and on more than one occasion he ran up to Benicia to have a gossip with us.

"YELLOW HANDKERCHIEF"

"I'm not wanting to dictate to you, lad," Charley said, "but I'm very much against your making a last raid. You've gone safely through rough times with rough men, and it would be a shame to have something happen to you at the very end."

"But how can I get out of making a last raid?" I demanded. "There always has to be a last, you know, to anything."

"Very true. But why not call the capture of Demetrios Contos the last? You're back from it safe and sound and hearty, for all of a good wetting, and — and" — his voice broke and he could not speak for a moment — "and I could never forgive myself if anything happened to you now."

I laughed at Charley's fears while I gave in to the claims of his affection, and agreed to consider the last raid already performed. We had been together for two years, and now I was leaving the fish patrol in order to go back and finish my education. I had earned and saved enough money to take me through four years of high school, and although the beginning of the term was several months away, I intended doing a great deal of studying for the entrance examinations.

My belongings were packed snugly in a sea-chest, and I was all ready to buy my ticket and ride down on the train to Oakland, when Neil Partington arrived in Benicia. The *Reindeer* was needed immediately for work far down on the Lower Bay, and Neil said he intended to run straight for Oakland. As that was his home, and as I was to live with his family while going to school, he saw no reason, he said, why I should not put my trunk aboard and come along.

In the middle of the afternoon we hoisted the *Reindeer's* big mainsail and cast off. It was tantalizing fall weather. The sea-breeze, which had blown steadily all summer, was gone, and in its place were capricious winds and murky skies, which made the time of arriving anywhere extremely problematical.

A great wall of fog advanced across San Pablo Bay to meet us, and in a few minutes the *Reindeer* was running blindly through the damp obscurity.

"It looks as though it were lifting," Neil Partington said, a couple of hours after we had entered the fog. "Where do you say we are, Charley?"

Charley pondered a moment, then answered, "The tide has edged us over a bit out of our course, but if the fog lifts right now, as it is going to lift, you'll find we're not more than half a mile off McNear's Landing."

The three of us were peering intently into the fog when the *Reindeer* struck with a dull crash and came to a standstill. We ran forward and found her bowsprit entangled in the tanned rigging of a short, chunky mast. She had collided, head on, with a Chinese junk lying at anchor.

At the moment we arrived forward, five Chinese came swarming out of the little between-decks cabin, the sleep still in their eyes.

Leading them came a big, muscular man, conspicuous for his pockmarked face and the yellow silk handkerchief swathed about his head. It was "Yellow Handkerchief," the Chinaman whom we had arrested for illegal shrimp-fishing the year before, and who, at that time, had nearly sunk the *Reindeer*, as he had nearly sunk it now by violating the rules of navigation.

"What d'ye mean, lying here in a fairway without a horn going?" Charley cried, hotly.

"Mean?" Neil calmly answered. "Just take a look — that's what he means."

Our eyes followed the direction indicated by Neil's finger, and we saw the open amidships of the junk half-filled with fresh-caught shrimps. Mingled with the shrimps we found, on closer examination, myriads of small fish, from a quarter of an inch upward in size. Yellow Handkerchief

DRAWN BY GEORGE VARIAN.

I went aft and took charge of the prize

had lifted the trap-net at high-water slack, and taking advantage of the concealment offered by the fog, had boldly been lying by, waiting to lift the net again at low-water slack.

"Well," Neil hummed and hawed, "in all my varied and extensive experience as a fish patrolman, I must say this is the easiest capture I ever made. What'll we do with them, Charley?"

"Tow the junk into San Rafael, of course," came the answer. He turned to me. "You stand by the junk, lad, and I'll pass you a towing-line. If the wind doesn't fail us, we'll make the creek before the tide gets too low, sleep at San Rafael, and arrive in Oakland to-morrow by midday."

So saying, Charley and Neil returned to the *Reindeer* and got under way, the junk towing astern. I went aft and took charge of the prize, steering by means of an antiquated tiller and a rudder with large, diamond-shaped holes, through which the water rushed back and forth.

The last of the fog had now vanished, and Charley's estimate of our position was confirmed by the sight of McNear's Landing a short half-mile away. Following along the west shore, we rounded Point San Pedro in plain view of the Chinese shrimp villages, and a great "to-do" was raised when they saw one of their junks towing behind the familiar fish-patrol sloop.

The wind, coming off the land, was rather puffy and uncertain, and it would have been more to our advantage had it been stronger. San Rafael Creek, up which we had to go to reach the town and turn over our prisoners to the authorities, ran through wide-stretching marshes, and was difficult to navigate on a falling tide, while at low tide it was impossible to navigate at all.

So, with the tide already half-ebbed, it was necessary for us to hurry. This the heavy junk prevented, lumbering along behind and holding the *Reindeer* back by just so much dead weight.

"Tell those coolies to get up that sail!" Charley finally called to me. "We don't want to hang up on the mud-flats for the rest of the night."

I repeated the order to Yellow Handkerchief, who mumbled it huskily to his men. He was suffering from a bad cold, which doubled him up in convulsive coughing spells and made his eyes heavy and blood-shot. This caused him to appear more evil-looking than ever, and when he glared viciously at me I remembered with a shiver the time of his previous arrest.

His crew sullenly tailed on to the halyards, and the strange, outlandish sail, lateen in rig and dyed a warm brown, rose in the air. We were sailing on the wind, and when Yellow Handkerchief flattened down the sheet, the junk forged ahead and the tow-line went slack.

Fast as the *Reindeer* was, the junk out-sailed her, and to avoid running her down, I hauled a little closer on the wind. But the junk likewise outpointed, and in a couple of minutes I was abreast of the *Reindeer* and to windward. The tow-line had now tautened at right angles to the two boats, and the predicament was laughable.

"Cast off!" I shouted.

Charley hesitated.

"It's all right," I added. "Nothing can happen. We'll make the creek on this tack, and you'll be right behind me all the way up to San Rafael."

At this Charley cast off, and Yellow Handkerchief sent one of his men forward to haul in the line. In the gathering darkness I could just make out the mouth of San Rafael Creek, and by the time we entered it I could barely see its banks.

The *Reindeer* was fully five minutes astern, and we continued to leave her behind as we beat up the narrow, winding channel. With Charley behind us, it seemed I had little to fear from my five prisoners; but the darkness prevented my keeping a sharp eye on them, so I transferred my revolver from my trousers pocket to the side pocket of my coat, where I could put my hand more easily upon it.

Yellow Handkerchief was the one I feared, and that he knew it and made use of it subsequent events will show. He was sitting a few feet away from me, on what then happened to be the weather side of the junk. I could hardly see the outlines of his form, and I soon became convinced that he was slowly, very slowly, edging closer to me. I watched him carefully. Steering with my left hand, I slipped my right into my pocket and got hold of the revolver.

I saw him shift along for a couple of inches, and I was just about to order him back when I was struck with force by a heavy figure, which had leaped through the air upon me from the lee side.

It was one of the crew. He had pinioned my right arm so that I could not withdraw my hand from my pocket, and at the same time had clapped his other hand over my mouth. Of course I could have struggled away from him and either got my hand clear or my mouth so that I might cry an alarm, but in a trice Yellow Handkerchief was on top of me.

I struggled round to no purpose in the bottom of the junk, while my legs and arms were tied and my mouth securely bound in what I afterward found to be a cotton shirt. Then I was left lying in the bottom.

Yellow Handkerchief took the tiller, issuing his orders in whispers; and from where we were at the time, and from the alteration of the sail, which I could dimly make out above me as a blot against the stars, I knew the junk was being headed into the mouth of a small slough which emptied at that point into San Rafael Creek.

In a couple of minutes we ran softly alongside the bank, and the sail was silently lowered. The Chinese kept very quiet. Yellow Handkerchief sat down in the bottom beside me, and I could feel him straining to repress his raspy, hacking cough. Possibly seven or eight minutes later I heard Charley's voice as the *Reindeer* went past the mouth of the slough.

"I can't tell you how relieved I am," I could plainly hear him saying to Neil, "that the lad has finished with the fish patrol without accident."

Here Neil said something which I could not catch, and then Charley's voice went on:

"The youngster takes naturally to the water, and if, when he finishes high school, he takes a course in navigation and goes deep sea, I see no reason why he shouldn't rise to be master of the finest and biggest ship afloat."

It was all very flattering to me, but lying there, bound and gagged by my own prisoners, I must say I was not quite in the proper situation to enjoy my smiling future.

With the *Reindeer* went my last hope. What was to happen next I could not imagine, for the Chinese were of a different race from mine, and from what I knew I was confident that fair play was no part of their make-up.

After waiting a few minutes longer the crew hoisted the lateen sail, and Yellow Handkerchief steered down toward the mouth of San Rafael Creek. As we passed out of the creek a noisy discussion arose, which I knew related to me. Yellow Handkerchief was vehement, but the other four as vehemently opposed him. It was very evident that he advocated doing away with me, and that they were afraid of the consequences.

My feelings, as my fate hung in the balance, may be guessed. The discussion developed into a quarrel, and in the midst of it Yellow Handkerchief unshipped the heavy tiller and sprang toward me. But his four companions threw themselves between, and a clumsy struggle took place. In the end Yellow Handkerchief was overcome, and he sullenly returned to the steering, while they soundly berated him for his rashness.

Not long after, the sail was run down and the junk slowly urged forward by means of the sweeps. I felt it ground gently on the soft mud. Three of them — they all wore long sea-boots — got over the side, while the remaining two passed me across the rail. With Yellow Handkerchief at my legs and his two companions at my shoulders, they began to flounder along through the mud.

After some minutes of this their feet struck firmer footing, and I knew they were carrying me up some beach. The location of this beach was not doubtful in my mind. It could be none other than one of the Marin Islands, a group of rocky islets which lay off the Marin County shore.

When they reached the firm sand which marked the high-tide limit, I was dropped, and none too gently. Yellow Handkerchief kicked me spitefully in the ribs, and then the trio floundered back through the mud to the junk. A moment later I heard the sail go up and slat in the wind as they drew in the sheet. Then silence fell, and I was left to my own devices.

Although I writhed and squirmed like a good fellow, the knots remained as hard as ever. But in the course of my squirming I rolled over upon a heap of clam-shells — the remains, evidently, of the clambake of some yachting party. This gave me an idea. My hands were tied behind my back, and clutching a shell in them, I rolled over and over, up the beach, till I came to the rocks I knew to be there.

Rolling round and searching, I finally

discovered a narrow crevice, in which I shoved the shell. The edge of it was sharp, and across the sharp edge I proceeded to saw the rope which bound my wrists.

The edge of the shell was brittle, and I broke it by bearing too heavily upon it. Then I rolled back to the heap and returned with as many shells as I could carry in both hands. I broke several shells, cut my hands a number of times, and got cramps in my legs from my strained position and my exertions.

While I was suffering from the cramps and resting, I heard a familiar halloo drift across the water. It was Charley, searching for me. The gag in my mouth prevented me from replying, and I could only lie there, helplessly fuming, while he rowed past the island.

I returned to the sawing process, and at the end of half an hour succeeded in severing the rope. The rest was easy. My hands once free, it was a matter of minutes to loosen my legs and take the gag out of my mouth. I ran round the island to make sure it *was* an island, and not by any chance a portion of the mainland.

An island it certainly was, one of the Marin group, fringed with a sandy beach and surrounded by a sea of mud. Nothing remained but to wait till daylight and to keep warm; for it was a cold, raw night for California, with just enough wind to pierce the skin and cause one to shiver.

To keep up the circulation, I ran round the island a dozen or so times and clambered across its rocky backbone as many times more — all of which was of greater service to me, as I afterward discovered, than merely to warm me up.

In the midst of this exercise I wondered if I had lost anything out of my pockets while rolling over and over in the sand. A search showed the absence of my revolver and pocket-knife. Yellow Handkerchief had taken the first, but the knife had been lost in the sand.

I was hunting for it when the sound of rowlocks came to my ears. At first, of course, I thought of Charley; but on second thought I knew Charley would be calling out as he rowed along. A sudden premonition of danger seized me. The Marin Islands are lonely places, where chance visitors in the dead of night are hardly to be expected.

The sound made by the rowlocks grew more distinct. I crouched in the sand and listened intently. The boat, which I judged a small skiff from the quick stroke of the oars, was landing in the mud about fifty yards up the beach. I heard a raspy, hacking cough, and my heart stood still. It was Yellow Handkerchief! Not to be robbed of his revenge by his more cautious companions, he had stolen away from the village and come back alone!

I did some swift thinking. I was unarmed and helpless on a tiny islet, and a yellow barbarian, whom I had reason to fear, was coming after me. Any place was safer than the island. As he began to flounder ashore through the mud, I started to flounder out into it, going over the same course which the Chinese had taken in landing me and in returning to the junk.

Yellow Handkerchief, believing me to be lying tightly bound, exercised no care, but came ashore noisily. This helped me, for, under the cover of his noise, I managed to make fifty feet by the time he had reached the beach.

Here I lay down in the mud. It was cold and clammy and made me shiver, but I did not care to stand up and run the risk of being discovered by his sharp eyes.

He walked down the beach straight to where he had left me lying, and I had a fleeting feeling of regret at not being able to see his surprise when he did not find me.

What his movements were after that I had largely to deduce from the facts of the situation, for I could hardly see him in the dim starlight. But I was sure that the first thing he did was to make the circuit of the beach to learn if landings had been made by other boats. This he would have known at once by the tracks through the mud.

Convinced that no boat had removed me from the island, he next started to find out what had become of me. Beginning at the pile of clam-shells, he lighted matches to trace my tracks in the sand.

The multiplicity of my footprints puzzled him. Then the idea that I might be out in the mud must have struck him, for he waded out a few yards in my direction, and stooping, with his eyes searched the dim surface long and carefully. He could not have been more than fifteen feet from me, and had he lighted a match he would surely have discovered me.

The thought came to me of going toward Yellow Handkerchief's skiff and escaping in it, but at that very moment he returned to the beach, and as if fearing the very thing I had in mind, he slushed out through the mud to assure himself that the skiff was safe.

I knew he was convinced that I was hiding somewhere in the mud. But to hunt on a dark night for a boy in a sea of mud was like hunting for a needle in a haystack, and he did not attempt it.

At last he waded out to his skiff and rowed away. My relief was great, and I started at once to crawl for the beach. But a thought struck me. What if this departure of Yellow Handkerchief's were a sham? What if he had done it merely to entice me ashore?

The more I thought of it, the more certain I became that he had made a little too much noise with his oars as he rowed away. So I remained, lying in the mud and shivering. I shivered till the muscles of the small of my back ached and pained me as badly as the cold, and I had need of all my self-control to force myself to remain in my miserable situation.

It was well that I did, however, for, possibly an hour later, I thought I could make out something moving on the beach. I watched intently, but my ears were rewarded first, by a raspy cough I knew too well. Yellow Handkerchief had sneaked back, landed on the other side of the island, and crept round to surprise me if I had returned.

After that, although hours passed by without sign of him, I was afraid to return to the island at all. On the other hand, I was almost equally afraid that I should die of the exposure I was undergoing. I had never dreamed one could suffer so. The tide had long since begun to rise, and foot by foot it drove me in toward the beach. High water came at three o'clock, and at three o'clock I drew myself up on the beach, more dead than alive, and too helpless to have offered any resistance had Yellow Handkerchief swooped down upon me.

But no Yellow Handkerchief appeared. He had given me up and gone back to Point San Pedro. Nevertheless, I was in a deplorable, not to say dangerous, condition. I could not stand upon my feet, much less walk. My clammy, muddy garments clung to me like sheets of ice.

Nothing remained but to crawl weakly, like a snail, and at the cost of constant pain, up and down the sand. I kept this up as long as possible, but as the east paled with the coming of dawn I began to succumb. The sky grew rosy-red, and the golden rim of the sun, showing above the horizon, found me lying helpless and motionless among the clam-shells.

As in a dream I saw the familiar mainsail of the *Reindeer* as she slipped out of San Rafael Creek on a light puff of morning air. This dream was very much broken. There are intervals I can never recollect on looking back over it.

Three things, however, I distinctly remember: the first sight of the *Reindeer's* mainsail; her lying to anchor a few hundred feet away, and a small boat leaving her side; and the cabin stove roaring red-hot, myself swathed all over with blankets, except on the chest and shoulders, which Charley was pounding and mauling unmercifully, and my mouth and throat burning with the coffee which Neil Partington was pouring down.

By the time we arrived in Oakland I was as limber and strong as ever, although Charley and Neil Partington were afraid I was going to have pneumonia; and Mrs. Partington, for my first six months of school, kept an anxious eye upon me to discover the first symptoms of consumption.

Time flies. It seems but yesterday that I was a lad of sixteen on the fish patrol. Yet this very morning I know that I arrived from China, with a quick passage to my credit and master of the barkentine *Harvester*. And I know that to-morrow morning I shall run over to Oakland to see Neil Partington and his wife and family, and later on go up to Benicia to see Charley Le Grant and talk over old times with him.

No, I shall not go to Benicia, now that I think about it. I expect to be a highly interested party to a wedding, shortly to take place. Her name is Alice Partington, and since Charley has promised to be best man, he will have to come down to Oakland instead.

41
A DAUGHTER OF THE AURORA

A DAUGHTER OF THE AURORA

"You — what you call — lazy mans, you lazy mans would desire me to haf for wife. It is not good. Nevaire, no, nevaire, will lazy mans my hoosband be."

Thus Joy Molineau spoke her mind to Jack Harrington, even as she had spoken it, but more tritely and in his own tongue, to Louis Savoy the previous night.

"Listen, Joy —"

"No, no; why moos' I listen to lazy mans? It is vaire bad, you hang rount, make visitation to my cabin, and do nothing. How you get grub for the famille? Why haf not you the dust? Odder mans haf plentee."

"But I work hard, Joy. Never a day am I not on trail or up creek. Even now have I just come off. My dogs are yet tired. Other men have luck and find plenty of gold; but I — I have no luck."

"Ah! But when this mans with the wife which is Indian, this mans McCormack, when him discovaire the Klondike, you go not. Odder mans go; odder mans now rich."

"You know I was prospecting over on the head-reaches of the Tanana," Harrington protested, "and knew nothing of the Eldorado or Bonanza until it was too late."

"That is deeferent; only you are — what you call way off."

"What?"

"Way off. In the — yes — in the dark. It is nevaire too late. One vaire rich mine is there, on the creek which is Eldorado. The mans drive the stake and him go 'way. No odder mans know what of him become. The mans, him which drive the stake, is nevaire no more. Sixty days no mans on that claim file the papaire. Then odder mans, plentee odder mans — what you call — jump that claim. Then they race, O so queek, like the wind, to file the papaire. Him be vaire rich. Him get grub for famille."

Harrington hid the major portion of his interest.

"When's the time up?" he asked. "What claim is it?"

"So I speak Louis Savoy last night," she continued, ignoring him. "Him I think the winnaire."

"Hang Louis Savoy!"

"So Louis Savoy speak in my cabin last night. Him say, 'Joy, I am strong mans. I haf good dogs. I haf long wind. I will be winnaire. Then you will haf me for hoosband?' And I say to him, I say —"

"What'd you say?"

"I say, 'If Louis Savoy is winnaire, then will he haf me for wife.'"

"And if he don't win?"

"Then Louis Savoy, him will not be — what you call — the father of my children."

"And If I win?"

"You winnaire? Ha! ha! Nevaire!"

Exasperating as it was, Joy Molineau's laughter was pretty to hear. Harrington did not mind it. He had long since been broken in. Besides, he was no exception. She had forced all her lovers to suffer in kind. And very enticing she was just then, her lips parted, her color heightened by the sharp kiss of the frost, her eyes vibrant with the lure which is the greatest of all lures and which may be seen nowhere save in woman's eyes. Her sled-dogs clustered about her in hirsute masses, and the leader, Wolf Fang, laid his long snout softly in her lap.

"If I do win?" Harrington pressed.

She looked from dog to lover and back again.

"What you say, Wolf Fang? If him strong mans and file the papaire, shall we his wife become? Eh? What you say?"

Wolf Fang picked up his ears and growled at Harrington.

"It is vaire cold," she suddenly added with feminine irrelevance, rising to her feet and straightening out the team.

Her lover looked on stolidly. She had kept him guessing from the first time they met, and patience had been joined unto his virtues.

"Hi! Wolf Fang!" she cried, springing

425

upon the sled as it leaped into sudden motion. "Ai! Ya! Mush-on!"

From the corner of his eye Harrington watched her swinging down the trail to Forty Mile. Where the road forked and crossed the river to Fort Cudahy, she halted the dogs and turned about.

"O Mistaire Lazy Mans!" she called back.

"Wolf Fang, him say yes — if you win-naire!"

But somehow, as such things will, it leaked out, and all Forty Mile, which had hitherto speculated on Joy Molineau's choice between her two latest lovers, now hazarded bets and guesses as to which would win in the forthcoming race. The camp divided itself into two factions, and every effort was put forth in order that their respective favorites might be the first in at the finish. There was a scramble for the best dogs the country could afford, for dogs, and good ones, were essential, above all, to success. And it meant much to the victor. Besides the possession of a wife, the like of which had yet to be created, it stood for a mine worth a million at least.

That fall, when news came down of McCormack's discovery on Bonanza, all the Lower Country, Circle City and Forty Mile included, had stampeded up the Yukon, — at least all save those who, like Jack Harrington and Louis Savoy, were away prospecting in the west. Moose pastures and creeks were staked indiscriminately and promiscuously; and incidentally, one of the unlikeliest of creeks, Eldorado. Olaf Nelson laid claim to five hundred of its linear feet, duly posted his notice, and as duly disappeared. At that time the nearest recording office was in the police barracks at Fort Cudahy, just across the river from Forty Mile; but when it became bruited abroad that Eldorado Creek was a treasure-house, it was quickly discovered that Olaf Nelson had failed to make the down-Yukon trip to file upon his property. Men cast hungry eyes upon the owner-less claim, where they knew a thousand-thousand dollars waited but shovel and sluice-box. Yet they dared not touch it; for there was a law which permitted sixty days to lapse between the staking and the filing, during which time a claim was immune. The whole country knew of Olaf Nelson's disappearance, and scores of men made preparation for the jumping and for the consequent race to Fort Cudahy.

But competition at Forty Mile was limited. With the camp devoting its energies to the equipping either of Jack Harrington or Louis Savoy, no man was unwise enough to enter the contest singlehanded. It was a stretch of a hundred miles to the Recorder's office, and it was planned that the two favorites should have four relays of dogs stationed along the trail. Naturally, the last relay was to be the crucial one, and for these twenty-five miles their respective partisans strove to obtain the strongest possible animals. So bitter did the factions wax, and so high did they bid, that dogs brought stiffer prices than ever before in the annals of the country. And, as it chanced, this scramble for dogs turned the public eye still more searchingly upon Joy Molineau. Not only was she the cause of it all, but she possessed the finest sled-dog from Chilkoot to Bering Sea. As wheel or leader, Wolf Fang had no equal. The man whose sled he led down the last stretch was bound to win. There could be no doubt of it. But the community had an innate sense of the fitness of things, and not once was Joy vexed by overtures for his use. And the factions drew consolation from the fact that if one man did not profit by him, neither should the other.

However, since man, in the individual or in the aggregate, has been so fashioned that he goes through life blissfully obtuse to the deeper subtleties of his womenkind, so the men of Forty Mile failed to divine the inner deviltry of Joy Molineau. They confessed, afterward, that they had failed to appreciate this dark-eyed daughter of the aurora, whose father had traded furs in the country before ever they dreamed of invading it, and who had herself first opened eyes on the scintillant northern lights. Nay, accident of birth had not rendered her less the woman, nor had it limited her woman's understanding of men. They knew she played with them, but they did not know the wisdom of her play, its deepness and its deftness. They failed to see more than the exposed card, so that to the very last Forty Mile was in a state of pleasant obfuscation, and it was not until she cast her final trump that it came to reckon up the score.

Early in the week the camp turned out to start Jack Harrington and Louis Savoy on their way. They had taken a shrewd margin of time, for it was their wish to arrive at Olaf Nelson's claim some days previous to the expiration of its immunity, that they might rest themselves, and their dogs be fresh for the first relay. On the way up they found the men of Dawson already stationing spare dog teams along the trail, and it was manifest that little expense had been spared in view of the millions at stake.

A couple of days after the departure of their champions, Forty Mile began sending up their relays, — first to the seventy-five station, then to the fifty, and last to the twenty-five. The teams for the last stretch were magnificent, and so equally matched that the camp discussed their relative merits for a full hour at fifty below, before they were permitted to pull out. At the last moment Joy Molineau dashed in among them on her sled. She drew Lon McFane, who had charge of Harrington's team, to one side, and hardly had the first words left her lips when it was noticed that his lower jaw dropped with a celerity and emphasis suggestive of great things. He unhitched Wolf Fang from her sled, put him at the head of Harrington's team, and mushed the string of animals into the Yukon trail.

"Poor Louis Savoy!" men said; but Joy Molineau flashed her black eyes defiantly and drove back to her father's cabin.

Midnight drew near on Olaf Nelson's claim. A few hundred fur-clad men had preferred sixty below and the jumping, to the inducements of warm cabins and comfortable bunks. Several score of them had their notices prepared for posting and their dogs at hand. A bunch of Captain Constantine's mounted police had been ordered on duty that fair play might rule. The command had gone forth that no man should place a stake till the last second of the day had ticked itself into the past. In the northland such commands are equal to Jehovah's in the matter of potency; the dum-dum as rapid and effective as the thunderbolt. It was clear and cold. The aurora borealis painted palpitating color revels on the sky. Rosy waves of cold brilliancy swept across the zenith, while great coruscating bars of greenish white blotted out the stars, or a Titan's hand reared mighty arches above the Pole. And at this mighty display the wolf-dogs howled as had their ancestors of old time. A bearskin-coated policeman stepped prominently to the fore, watch in hand.

Men hurried among the dogs, rousing them to their feet, untangling their traces, straightening them out. The entries came to the mark, firmly gripping stakes and notices. They had gone over the boundaries of the claim so often that they could now have done it blindfolded. The policeman raised his hand. Casting off their superfluous furs and blankets, and with a final cinching of belts, they came to attention.

"Time!"

Sixty pairs of hands unmitted; as many pairs of moccasins gripped hard upon the snow.

"Go!"

They shot across the wide expanse, round the four sides, sticking notices at every corner, and down the middle where the two centre stakes were to be planted. Then they sprang for the sleds on the frozen bed of the creek. An anarchy of sound and motion broke out. Sled collided with sled, and dog-team fastened upon dog-team with bristling manes and screaming fangs. The narrow creek was glutted with the struggling mass. Lashes and butts of dog-whips were distributed impartially among men and brutes. And to make it of greater moment, each participant had a bunch of comrades intent on breaking him out of jam.

But one by one, and by sheer strength, the sleds crept out and shot from sight in the darkness of the overhanging banks.

Jack Harrington had anticipated this crush and waited by his sled until it untangled. Louis Savoy, aware of his rival's greater wisdom in the matter of dog-driving, had followed his lead and also waited. The rout had passed beyond earshot when they took the trail, and it was not till they had travelled the ten miles or so down to Bonanza that they came upon it, speeding along in single file, but well bunched. There was little noise, and less chance of one passing another at that stage. The sleds, from runner to runner, measured sixteen inches, the trail eighteen; but the trail, packed down fully a foot by the traffic, was like a gutter. On either side spread the blanket of soft snow crystals. If a man turned into this in an endeavor to pass, his dogs would wallow perforce to their bellies and slow down to a snail's pace. So the men lay close to their leaping sleds and waited. No alteration in position occurred down the fifteen miles of Bonanza and Klondike to Dawson, where the Yukon was encountered. Here the first relays waited. But here, intent to kill their first teams, if necessary, Harrington and Savoy had had their fresh teams placed a couple of miles beyond those of the others. In the confusion of changing sleds they passed full half the bunch. Perhaps thirty men were still leading them when they shot on to the broad breast of the Yukon. Here was the tug. When the river froze in the fall, a mile of open water had been left between two mighty jams. This had but recently crusted, the current being swift, and now it was as level, hard, and slippery as a dance floor. The instant they struck this glare ice Harrington came to his knees, holding precariously on with one hand, his whip singing fiercely among his dogs and fearsome abjurations hurtling about their ears. The teams spread out on the smooth surface, each straining to the uttermost. But few men in the North could lift their dogs as did Jack Harrington. At once he began to pull ahead, and Louis Savoy, taking the pace, hung on desperately, his leaders running even with the tail of his rival's sled.

Midway on the glassy stretch their relays shot out from the bank. But Harrington did not slacken. Watching his chance when the new sled swung in close, he leaped across, shouting as he did so and jumping up the pace of his fresh dogs. The other driver fell off somehow. Savoy did likewise with his relay, and the abandoned teams, swerving to right and left, collided with the others and piled the ice with confusion. Harrington cut out the pace; Savoy hung on. As they neared the end of the glare ice, they swept abreast of the leading sled. When they shot into the narrow trail between the soft snowbanks, they led the race; and Dawson, watching by the light of the aurora, swore that it was neatly done.

When the frost grows lusty at sixty below, men cannot long remain without fire or excessive exercise, and live. So Harrington and Savoy now fell to the ancient custom of "ride and run." Leaping from their sleds, tow-thongs in hand, they ran behind till the blood resumed its wonted channels and expelled the frost, then back to the sleds till the heat again ebbed away. Thus, riding and running, they covered the second and third relays. Several times,

on smooth ice, Savoy spurted his dogs, and as often failed to gain past. Strung along for five miles in the rear, the remainder of the race strove to overtake them, but vainly, for to Louis Savoy alone was the glory given of keeping Jack Harrington's killing pace.

As they swung into the seventy-five-mile station, Lon McFane dashed alongside; Wolf Fang in the lead caught Harrington's eye, and he knew that the race was his. No team in the North could pass him on those last twenty-five miles. And when Savoy saw Wolf Fang heading his rival's team, he knew that he was out of the running, and he cursed softly to himself, in the way woman is most frequently cursed. But he still clung to the other's smoking trail, gambling on chance to the last. And as they churned along, the day breaking in the southeast, they marvelled in joy and sorrow at that which Joy Molineau had done.

Forty Mile had early crawled out of its sleeping furs and congregated near the edge of the trail. From this point it could view the up-Yukon course to its first bend several miles away. Here it could also see across the river to the finish at Fort Cudahy, where the Gold Recorder nervously awaited. Joy Molineau had taken her position several rods back from the trail, and under the circumstances, the rest of Forty Mile forbore interposing itself. So the space was clear between her and the slender line of the course. Fires had been built, and around these men wagered dust and dogs, the long odds on Wolf Fang.

"Here they come!" shrilled an Indian boy from the top of a pine.

Up the Yukon a black speck appeared against the snow, closely followed by a second. As these grew larger, more black specks manifested themselves, but at a goodly distance to the rear. Gradually they resolved themselves into dogs and sleds, and men lying flat upon them.

"Wolf Fang leads," a lieutenant of the police whispered to Joy. She smiled her interest back.

"Ten to one on Harrington!" cried a Birch Creek King, dragging out his sack.

"The Queen, her pay you not mooch?" queried Joy.

The lieutenant shook his head.

"You have some dust, ah, how mooch?" she continued.

He exposed his sack. She gauged it with

a rapid eye.

"Mebbe — say — two hundred, eh? Good. Now I give — what you call — the tip. Covaire the bet." Joy smiled inscrutably. The lieutenant pondered. He glanced up the trail. The two men had risen to their knees and were lashing their dogs furiously, Harrington in the lead.

"Ten to one on Harrington!" bawled the Birch Creek King, flourishing his sack in the lieutenant's face.

"Covaire the bet," Joy prompted.

He obeyed, shrugging his shoulders in token that he yielded, not to the dictate of his reason, but to her charm. Joy nodded to reassure him.

All noise ceased. Men paused in the placing of bets.

Yawing and reeling and plunging, like luggers before the wind, the sleds swept wildly upon them. Though he still kept his leader up to the tail of Harrington's sled, Louis Savoy's face was without hope. Harrington's mouth was set. He looked neither to the right nor to the left. His dogs were leaping in perfect rhythm, firm-footed, close to the trail, and Wolf Fang, head low and unseeing, whining softly, was leading his comrades magnificently.

Forty Mile stood breathless. Not a sound, save the roar of the runners and the voice of the whips.

Then the clear voice of Joy Molineau rose on the air. "Ai! Ya! Wolf Fang! Wolf Fang!"

Wolf Fang heard. He left the trail sharply, heading directly for his mistress. The team dashed after him, and the sled poised an instant on a single runner, then shot Harrington into the snow.

Savoy was by like a flash. Harrington pulled to his feet and watched him skimming across the river to the Gold Recorder's. He could not help hearing what was said.

"Ah, him do vaire well," Joy Molineau was explaining to the lieutenant. "Him — what you call — set the pace. Yes, him set the pace vaire well."

42
THE LOST POACHER

THE LOST POACHER

"But they won't take excuses. You're across the line, and that's enough. They'll take you. In you go, Siberia and the salt-mines. And as for Uncle Sam, why, what's he to know about it? Never a word will get back to the States. 'The *Mary Thomas*,' the papers will say, 'the *Mary Thomas* lost with all hands. Probably in a typhoon in the Japanese seas.' That's what the papers will say, and people too. In you go, Siberia and the salt-mines. Dead to the world and kith and kin, though you live fifty years."

In such manner John Lewis, commonly known as the "sea-lawyer," settled the matter out of hand.

It was a serious moment in the forecastle of the *Mary Thomas*. No sooner had the watch below begun to talk the trouble over, than the watch on deck came down and joined them. As there was no wind, every hand could be spared with the exception of the man at the wheel, and he remained only for the sake of discipline. Even "Bub" Russell, the cabin-boy, had crept forward to hear what was going on.

However, it was a serious moment, as the grave faces of the sailors bore witness. For the three preceding months the *Mary Thomas*, sealing schooner, had hunted the seal pack along the coast of Japan and north to Bering Sea. Here, on the Asiatic side of the sea, they were forced to give over the chase, or rather, to go no farther; for beyond, the Russian cruisers patrolled forbidden ground, where the seals might breed in peace. And here, on the very edge of the line, the *Mary Thomas* had hunted back and forth, picking up the laggards which had not gone on with the pack.

A week before she had fallen into a heavy fog accompanied by calm. Since then the fog-bank had not lifted, and the only wind had been light airs and catspaws. This in itself was not so bad, for the sealing schooners are never in a hurry so long as they are in the midst of the seals; but the trouble lay in the fact that the current at this point bore heavily to the north. Thus the *Mary Thomas* had unwittingly drifted across the line, and every hour she was penetrating, unwillingly, farther and farther into the dangerous waters where the Russian bear kept guard.

How far she had drifted no man knew. The sun had not been visible for a week, nor the stars, and the captain had been unable to take observations in order to determine his position. At any moment a cruiser might swoop down and hale the crew away to Siberia. The fate of other poaching seal-hunters was too well known to the men of the *Mary Thomas*, and there was cause for grave faces.

"Mine friends," spoke up a German boat-steerer, "it vas a pad piziness. Shust as ve make a big catch, und all honest, somedings go wrong, und der Russians nab us, dake our skins und our schooner, und send us mit der anarchists to Siberia. Ach! a pretty pad piziness!"

"Yes, that's where it hurts," the sea-lawyer went on. "Fifteen hundred skins in the salt piles, and all honest, a big pay-day coming to every man Jack of us, and then to be captured and lose it all! It'd be different if we'd been poaching, but it's all honest work in open water."

"But if we haven't done anything wrong, they can't do anything to us, can they?" Bub queried.

"It strikes me as 'ow it ain't the proper thing for a boy o' your age shovin' in when 'is elders is talkin'," protested an English sailor, from over the edge of his bunk.

"Oh, that's all right, Jack," answered the sea-lawyer. "He's a perfect right to. Ain't he just as liable to lose his wages as the rest of us?"

"Wouldn't give thruppence for them!" Jack sniffed back. He had been planning to go home and see his family in Chelsea when he was paid off, and he was now feeling rather blue over the highly possible loss, not only of his pay, but of his liberty.

"How are they to know?" the sea-lawyer asked, in answer to Bub's previous question. "Here we are in forbidden water. How do they know but what we came here of our own accord? Here we are, fifteen hundred skins in the hold. How do they know whether we got them in open water or in the closed sea? Don't you see, Bub, the evidence is all against us. If you caught a man with his pockets full of apples like those which grow on your tree, and if you caught him in your tree besides, what'd you think if he told you he couldn't help it, and had just been sort of blown there, and that anyway those apples came from some other tree — what'd you think, eh?"

Bub saw it clearly when put in that light, and shook his head despondently.

"You'd rather be dead than go to Siberia," one of the boat-pullers said. "They put you into the salt-mines and work you till you die. Never see daylight again. Why, I've heard tell of one fellow that was chained to his mate, and that mate died. And they were both chained together! And if they send you to the quicksilver-mines you get salivated. I'd rather be hung than salivated."

"Wot's salivated?" Jack asked, suddenly sitting up in his bunk at the hint of fresh misfortunes.

"Why, the quicksilver gets into your blood; I think that's the way. And your gums all swell like you had the scurvy, only worse, and your teeth get loose in your jaws. And big ulcers form, and then you die horrible. The strongest man can't last long a-mining quicksilver."

"A pad piziness," the boat-steerer reiterated, dolorously, in the silence which followed. "A pad piziness. I vish I vas In Yokohama. Eh? Vot vas dot?"

Every face lighted up. The Mary Thomas heeled over. The decks were aslant. A tin pannikin rolled down the inclined plane, rattling and banging. From above came the slapping of canvas and the quivering rat-tat-tat of the after-leech of the loosely stretched foresail. Then the mate's voice sang down the hatch, "All hands on deck and make sail!"

Never had such summons been answered with more enthusiasm. The calm had broken. The wind had come which was to carry them south into safety. With a wild cheer all sprang on deck. Working with mad haste, they flung out topsails, flying jibs and staysails. As they worked, the fog-bank lifted and the black vault of heaven, bespangled with the old familiar stars, rushed into view. When all was ship-shape, the Mary Thomas was lying gallantly over on her side to a beam wind and plunging ahead due south.

"Steamer's lights ahead on the port bow, sir!" cried the lookout from his station on the forecastle-head. There was excitement in the man's voice.

The captain sent Bub below for his night-glasses. Everybody crowded to the lee-rail to gaze at the suspicious stranger, which already began to loom up vague and indistinct. In those unfrequented waters the chance was one in a thousand that it could be anything else than a Russian patrol. The captain was still anxiously gazing through the glasses, when a flash of flame left the stranger's side, followed by the loud report of a cannon. The worst fears were confirmed. It was a patrol, evidently firing across the bows of the Mary Thomas in order to make her heave to.

"Hard down with your helm!" the captain commanded the steersman, all the life gone out of his voice. Then to the crew, "Back over the jib and foresail! Run down the flying jib! Clew up the foretopsail! And aft here and swing on to the main-sheet!"

The Mary Thomas ran into the eye of the wind, lost headway, and fell to courtesying gravely to the long seas rolling up from the west.

The cruiser steamed a little nearer and lowered a boat. The sealers watched in heartbroken silence. They could see the white bulk of the boat as it was slacked away to the water, and its crew sliding aboard. They could hear the creaking of the davits and the commands of the officers. Then the boat sprang away under the impulse of the oars, and came toward them. The wind had been rising, and already the sea was too rough to permit the frail craft to lie alongside the tossing schooner; but watching their chance, and taking advantage of the boarding ropes thrown to them, an officer and a couple of men clambered aboard. The boat then sheered off into safety and lay to its oars, a young midshipman, sitting in the stern and holding the yoke-lines, in charge.

The officer, whose uniform disclosed his rank as that of second lieutenant in the Russian navy, went below with the captain of the *Mary Thomas* to look at the ship's papers. A few minutes later he emerged, and upon his sailors removing the hatch-covers, passed down into the hold with a lantern to inspect the salt piles. It was a goodly heap which confronted him — fifteen hundred fresh skins, the season's catch; and under the circumstances he could have had but one conclusion.

"I am very sorry," he said, in broken English to the sealing captain when he again came on deck, "but it is my duty, in the name of the tsar, to seize your vessel as a poacher caught with fresh skins in the closed sea. The penalty, as you may know, is confiscation and imprisonment."

The captain of the *Mary Thomas* shrugged his shoulders in seeming indifference, and turned away. Although they may restrain all outward show, strong men, under unmerited misfortune, are sometimes very close to tears. Just then the vision of his little California home, and of the wife and two yellow-haired boys, was strong upon him, and there was a strange choking sensation in his throat, which made him afraid that if he attempted to speak he would sob instead.

And also there was upon him the duty he owed his men. No weakness before them, for he must be a tower of strength to sustain them in misfortune. He had already explained to the second lieutenant, and knew the hopelessness of the situation. As the sea-lawyer had said, the evidence was all against him. So he turned aft, and fell to pacing up and down the poop of the vessel over which he was no longer commander.

The Russian officer now took temporary charge. He ordered more of his men aboard, and had all the canvas clewed up and furled snugly away. While this was being done, the boat plied back and forth between the two vessels, passing a heavy hawser, which was made fast to the great towing-bitts on the schooner's forecastle-head. During all this work the sealers stood about in sullen groups. It was madness to think of resisting, with the guns of a man-of-war not a biscuit-toss away; but they refused to lend a hand, preferring instead to maintain a gloomy silence.

Having accomplished his task, the lieutenant ordered all but four of his men back into the boat. Then the midshipman, a lad of sixteen, looking strangely mature

and dignified in his uniform and sword, came aboard to take command of the captured sealer. Just as the lieutenant prepared to depart, his eyes chanced to alight upon Bub. Without a word of warning, he seized him by the arm and dropped him over the rail into the waiting boat; and then, with a parting wave of his hand, he followed him.

It was only natural that Bub should be frightened at this unexpected happening. All the terrible stories he had heard of the Russians served to make him fear them, and now returned to his mind with double force. To be captured by them was bad enough, but to be carried off by them, away from his comrades, was a fate of which he had not dreamed.

"Be a good boy, Bub," the captain called to him, as the boat drew away from the *Mary Thomas's* side, "and tell the truth!"

"Aye, aye, sir!" he answered, bravely enough by all outward appearance. He felt a certain pride of race, and was ashamed to be a coward before these strange enemies, these wild Russian bears.

"Und be politeful!" the German boat-steerer added, his rough voice lifting across the water like a fog-horn.

Bub waved his hand in farewell, and his mates clustered along the rail as they answered with a cheering shout. He found room in the sternsheets, where he fell to regarding the lieutenant. He didn't look so wild or bearish, after all — very much like other men, Bub concluded, and the sailors were much the same as all other man-of-war's men he had ever known. Nevertheless, as his feet struck the steel deck of the cruiser, he felt as if he had entered the portals of a prison.

For a few minutes he was left unheeded. The sailors hoisted the boat up, and swung it in on the davits. Then great clouds of black smoke poured out of the funnels, and they were under way — to Siberia, Bub could not help but think. He saw the *Mary Thomas* swing abruptly into line as she took the pressure from the hawser, and her side-lights, red and green, rose and fell as she was towed through the sea.

Bub's eyes dimmed at the melancholy sight, but — but just then the lieutenant came to take him down to the commander, and he straightened up and set his lips firmly, as if this were a very commonplace affair and he were used to being sent to

Into the dangerous waters where the Russian Bear kept guard

Siberia every day in the week. The cabin in which the commander sat was like a palace compared to the humble fittings of the *Mary Thomas,* and the commander himself, in gold lace and dignity, was a most august personage, quite unlike the simple man who navigated his schooner on the trail of the seal pack.

Bub now quickly learned why he had been brought aboard, and in the prolonged questioning which followed, told nothing but the plain truth. The truth was harmless; only a lie could have injured his cause. He did not know much, except that they had been sealing far to the south in open water, and that when the calm and fog came down upon them, being close to the line, they had drifted across. Again and again he insisted that they had not lowered a boat or shot a seal in the week they had been drifting about in the forbidden sea; but the commander chose to consider all that he said to be a tissue of falsehoods, and adopted a bullying tone in an effort to frighten the boy. He threatened and cajoled by turns, but failed in the slightest to shake Bub's statements, and at last ordered him out of his presence.

By some oversight, Bub was not put in anybody's charge, and wandered up on deck unobserved. Sometimes the sailors, in passing, bent curious glances upon him, but otherwise he was left strictly alone. Nor could he have attracted much attention, for he was small, the night dark, and the watch on deck intent on its own business. Stumbling over the strange decks, he made his way aft where he could look upon the side-lights of the *Mary Thomas,* following steadily in the rear.

For a long while he watched, and then lay down in the darkness close to where the hawser passed over the stern to the captured schooner. Once an officer came up and examined the straining rope to see if it were chafing, but Bub cowered away in the shadow undiscovered. This, however, gave him an idea which concerned the lives and liberties of twenty-two men, and which was to avert crushing sorrow from more than one happy home many thousand miles away.

In the first place, he reasoned, the crew were all guiltless of any crime, and yet were being carried relentlessly away to imprisonment in Siberia — a living death, he had heard, and he believed it implicitly. In the second place, he was a prisoner, hard and fast, with no chance of escape. In the third, it was possible for the twenty-two men on the *Mary Thomas* to escape. The only thing which bound them was a four-inch hawser. They dared not cut it at their end, for a watch was sure to be maintained upon it by their Russian captors; but at his end, ah! at his end —

Bub did not stop to reason further. Wriggling close to the hawser, he opened his jack-knife and went to work. The blade was not very sharp, and he sawed away, rope-yarn by rope-yarn, the awful picture of the solitary Siberian exile he must endure growing clearer and more terrible at every stroke. Such a fate was bad enough to undergo with one's comrades, but to face it alone seemed frightful. And besides, the very act he was performing was sure to bring greater punishment upon him.

In the midst of such somber thoughts, he heard footsteps approaching. He wriggled away into the shadow. An officer stopped where he had been working, half-stooped to examine the hawser, then changed his mind and straightened up. For a few minutes he stood there, gazing at the lights of the captured schooner, and then went forward again.

Now was the time! Bub crept back and went on sawing. Now two parts were severed. Now three. But one remained. The tension upon this was so great that it readily yielded. Splash! The freed end went overboard. He lay quietly, his heart in his mouth, listening. No one on the cruiser but himself had heard.

He saw the red and green lights of the *Mary Thomas* grow dimmer and dimmer. Then a faint hallo came over the water from the Russian prize crew. Still nobody heard. The smoke continued to pour out of the cruiser's funnels, and her propellers throbbed as mightily as ever.

What was happening on the *Mary Thomas?* Bub could only surmise; but of one thing he was certain: his comrades would assert themselves and overpower the four sailors and the midshipman. A few minutes later he saw a small flash, and straining his ears heard the very faint report of a pistol. Then, oh joy! both the red and green lights suddenly disappeared. The *Mary Thomas* was retaken!

Just as an officer came aft, Bub crept forward, and hid away in one of the boats.

Not an instant too soon. The alarm was given. Loud voices rose in command. The cruiser altered her course. An electric search-light began to throw its white rays across the sea, here, there, everywhere; but in its flashing path no tossing schooner was revealed.

Bub went to sleep soon after that, nor did he wake till the gray of dawn. The engines were pulsing monotonously, and the water, splashing noisily, told him the decks were being washed down. One sweeping glance, and he saw that they were alone on the expanse of ocean. The *Mary Thomas* had escaped. As he lifted his head, a roar of laughter went up from the sailors. Even the officer, who ordered him taken below and locked up, could not quite conceal the laughter in his eyes. Bub thought often in the days of confinement which followed, that they were not very angry with him for what he had done.

He was not far from right. There is a certain innate nobility deep down in the hearts of all men, which forces them to admire a brave act, even if it is performed by an enemy. The Russians were in nowise different from other men. True, a boy had outwitted them; but they could not blame him, and they were sore puzzled as to what to do with him. It would never do to take a little mite like him to represent all that remained of the lost poacher.

So, two weeks later, a United States man-of-war, steaming out of the Russian port of Vladivostok, was signaled by a Russian cruiser. A boat passed between the two ships, and a small boy dropped over the rail upon the deck of the American vessel. A week later he was put ashore at Hakodate, and after some telegraphing, his fare was paid on the railroad to Yokohama.

From the depot he hurried through the quaint Japanese streets to the harbor, and hired a *sampan* boatman to put him aboard a certain vessel whose familiar rigging had quickly caught his eye. Her gaskets were off, her sails unfurled; she was just starting back to the United States. As he came closer, a crowd of sailors sprang upon the forecastle-head, and the windlass-bars rose and fell as the anchor was torn from its muddy bottom.

"'Yankee ship come down the ribber!'" the sea-lawyer's voice rolled out as he led the anchor song.

"'Pull, my bully boys, pull!'" roared back the old familiar chorus, the men's bodies lifting and bending to the rhythm.

Bub Russell paid the boatman and stepped on deck. The anchor was forgotten. A mighty cheer went up from the men, and almost before he could catch his breath he was on the shoulders of the captain, surrounded by his mates, and endeavoring to answer twenty questions to the second.

The next day a schooner hove to off a Japanese fishing village, sent ashore four sailors and a little midshipman, and sailed away. These men did not talk English, but they had money and quickly made their way to Yokohama. From that day the Japanese village folk never heard anything more about them, and they are still a much-talked-of mystery. As the Russian government never said anything about the incident, the United States is still ignorant of the whereabouts of the lost poacher, nor has she ever heard, officially, of the way in which some of her citizens "shanghaied" five subjects of the tsar. Even nations have secrets sometimes.

43
CHRIS FARRINGTON, ABLE SEAMAN

CHRIS FARRINGTON, ABLE SEAMAN

"If you vas in der old country ships, a liddle shaver like you vood pe only der boy, und you vood wait on der able seamen. Und ven der able seaman sing out, 'Boy, der water-jug!' you vood jump quick, like a shot, und bring der water-jug. Und ven der able seaman sing out, 'Boy, my boots!' you vood get der boots. Und you vood pe politeful, und say 'Yessir' und 'No sir.' But you pe in der American ship, und you t'ink you are so good as der able seamen. Chris, mine boy, I haf ben a sailorman for twenty-two years, und do you t'ink you are so good as me? I vas a sailorman pefore you vas borned, und I knot und reef und splice ven you play mit top-strings und fly kites."

"But you are unfair, Emil!" cried Chris Farrington, his sensitive face flushed and hurt. He was a slender though strongly built young fellow of seventeen, with Yankee ancestry writ large all over him.

"Dere you go vonce again!" the Swedish sailor exploded. "My name is Mister Johansen, und a kid of a boy like you call me 'Emil!' It vas insulting, und comes pecause of der American ship!"

"But you call me 'Chris!'" the boy expostulated, reproachfully.

"But you vas a boy."

"Who does a man's work," Chris retorted. "And because I do a man's work I have as much right to call you by your first name as you me. We are all equals in this fo'c'sle, and you know it. When we signed for the voyage in San Francisco, we signed as sailors on the *Sophie Sutherland,* and there was no difference made with any of us. Haven't I always done my work? Did I every shirk? Did you or any other man ever have to take a wheel for me? Or a lookout? Or go aloft?"

"Chris is right," interrupted a young English sailor. "No man has had to do a tap of his work yet. He signed as good as any of us, and he's shown himself as good —"

"Better!" broke in a Nova Scotia man. "Better than some of us! When we struck

the sealing-grounds he turned out to be next to the best boat-steerer aboard. Only French Louis, who'd been at it for years, could beat him. I'm only a boat-puller, and you're only a boat-puller, too, Emil Johansen, for all your twenty-two years at sea. Why don't you become a boat-steerer?"

"Too clumsy," laughed the Englishman, "and too slow."

"Little that counts, one way or the other," joined in Dane Jurgensen, coming to the aid of his Scandinavian brother. "Emil is a man grown and an able seaman; the boy is neither."

And so the argument raged back and forth, the Swedes, Norwegians and Danes, because of race kinship, taking the part of Johansen, and the English, Canadians and Americans taking the part of Chris. From an unprejudiced point of view, the right was on the side of Chris. As he had truly said, he did a man's work, and the same work that any of them did. But they were prejudiced, and badly so, and out of the words which passed rose a standing quarrel which divided the forecastle into two parties.

The *Sophie Sutherland* was a sealhunter, registered out of San Francisco, and engaged in hunting the furry seaanimals along the Japanese coast north to Bering Sea. The other vessels were twomasted schooners, but she was a threemaster and the largest in the fleet. In fact, she was a full-rigged, three-topmast schooner, newly built.

Although Chris Farrington knew that justice was with him, and that he performed all his work faithfully and well, many a time, in secret thought, he longed for some pressing emergency to arise whereby he could demonstrate to the Scandinavian seamen that he also was an able seaman.

But one stormy night, by an accident for which he was in nowise accountable, in overhauling a spare anchor-chain he had

Fed him all of a pound of cake — chocolate

all the fingers of his left hand badly crushed. And his hopes were likewise crushed, for it was impossible for him to continue hunting with the boats, and he was forced to stay idly aboard until his fingers should heal. Yet, although he little dreamed it, this very accident was to give him the long looked-for opportunity.

One afternoon in the latter part of May the *Sophie Sutherland* rolled sluggishly in a breathless calm. The seas were abundant, the hunting good, and the boats were all away and out of sight. And with them was almost every man of the crew. Besides Chris, there remained only the captain, the sailing-master and the Chinese cook.

The captain was captain only by courtesy. He was an old man, past eighty, and blissfully ignorant of the sea and its ways; but he was the owner of the vessel, and hence the honorable title. Of course the sailing-master, who was really captain, was a thoroughgoing seaman. The mate, whose post was aboard, was out with the boats, having temporarily taken Chris's place as boat-steerer.

When good weather and good sport came together, the boats were accustomed to range far and wide, and often did not return to the schooner until long after dark. But for all that it was a perfect hunting day, Chris noted a growing anxiety on the part of the sailing-master. He paced the deck nervously, and was constantly sweeping the horizon with his marine glasses. Not a boat was in sight. As sunset arrived, he even sent Chris aloft to the mizzen-topmast-head, but with no better luck. The boats could not possibly be back before midnight.

Since noon the barometer had been falling with startling rapidity, and all the signs were ripe for a great storm — how great, not even the sailing-master anticipated. He and Chris set to work to prepare for it. They put storm gaskets on the furled topsails, lowered and stowed the foresail and spanker and took in the two inner jibs. In the one remaining jib they put a single reef, and a single reef in the mainsail.

Night had fallen before they finished, and with the darkness came the storm. A low moan swept over the sea, and the wind struck the *Sophie Sutherland* flat. But she righted quickly, and with the sailing-master at the wheel, sheered her bow into within five points of the wind. Working as

well as he could with his bandaged hand, and with the feeble aid of the Chinese cook, Chris went forward and backed the jib over to the weather side. This, with the flat mainsail, left the schooner hove to.

"God help the boats! It's no gale! It's a typhoon!" the sailing-master shouted to Chris at eleven o'clock. "Too much canvas! Got to get two more reefs into that mainsail, and got to do it right away!" He glanced at the old captain, shivering in oilskins at the binnacle and holding on for dear life. "There's only you and I, Chris — and the cook, but he's next to worthless!"

In order to make the reef, it was necessary to lower the mainsail, and the removal of this after pressure was bound to make the schooner fall off before the wind and sea because of the forward pressure of the jib.

"Take the wheel!" the sailing-master directed. "And when I give the word, hard up with it! And when she's square before it, steady her! And keep her there! We'll heave to again as soon as I get the reefs in!"

Gripping the kicking spokes, Chris watched him and the reluctant cook go forward into the howling darkness. The *Sophie Sutherland* was plunging into the huge head-seas and wallowing tremendously, the tense steel stays and taut rigging humming like harp-strings to the wind. A buffeted cry came to his ears, and he felt the schooner's bow paying off of its own accord. The mainsail was down!

He ran the wheel hard-over and kept anxious track of the changing direction of the wind on his face and of the heave of the vessel. This was the crucial moment. In performing the evolution she would have to pass broadside to the surge before she could get before it. The wind was blowing directly on his right cheek, when he felt the *Sophie Sutherland* lean over and begin to rise toward the sky — up — up — an infinite distance! Would she clear the crest of the gigantic wave?

Again by the feel of it, for he could see nothing, he knew that a wall of water was rearing and curving far above him along the whole weather side. There was an instant's calm as the liquid wall intervened and shut off the wind. The schooner righted, and for that instant seemed at perfect rest. Then she rolled to meet the descending rush.

Chris shouted to the captain to hold

tight, and prepared himself for the shock. But the man did not live who could face it. An ocean of water smote Chris's back, and his clutch on the spokes was loosened as if it were a baby's. Stunned, powerless, like a straw on the face of a torrent, he was swept onward he knew not whither. Missing the corner of the cabin, he was dashed forward along the poop runway a hundred feet or more, striking violently against the foot of the foremast. A second wave, crushing inboard, hurled him back the way he had come, and left him half-drowned where the poop steps should have been.

Bruised and bleeding, dimly conscious, he felt for the rail and dragged himself to his feet. Unless something could be done, he knew the last moment had come. As he faced the poop the wind drove into his mouth with suffocating force. This fact brought him back to his senses with a start. The wind was blowing from dead aft! The schooner was out of the trough and before it! But the send of the sea was bound to broach her to again. Crawling up the runway, he managed to get to the wheel just in time to prevent this. The binnacle light was still burning. They were safe!

That is, he and the schooner were safe. As to the welfare of his three companions he could not say. Nor did he dare leave the wheel in order to find out, for it took every second of his undivided attention to keep the vessel to her course. The least fraction of carelessness and the heave of the sea under the quarter was liable to thrust her into the trough. So, a boy of one hundred and forty pounds, he clung to his herculean task of guiding the two hundred straining tons of fabric amid the chaos of the great storm forces.

Half an hour later, groaning and sobbing, the captain crawled to Chris's feet. All was lost, he whimpered. He was smitten unto death. The galley had gone by the board, the mainsail and running-gear, the cook, everything!

"Where's the sailing-master?" Chris demanded, when he had caught breath after steadying a wild lurch of the schooner. It was no child's play to steer a vessel under single-reefed jib before a typhoon.

"Clean up for'ard," the old man replied. "Jammed under the fo'c'sle-head, but still breathing. Both his arms are broken, he says, and he doesn't know how many ribs.

He's hurt bad."

"Well, he'll drown there the way she's shipping water through the hawse-pipes. Go for'ard!" Chris commanded, taking charge of things as a matter of course. "Tell him not to worry; that I'm at the wheel. Help him as much as you can, and make him help —" He stopped and ran the spokes to starboard as a tremendous billow rose under the stern and yawed the schooner to port — "and make him help himself for the rest. Unship the fo'c'sle-hatch and get him down into a bunk. Then ship the hatch again."

The captain turned his aged face forward and wavered pitifully. The waist of the ship was full of water to the bulwarks. He had just come through it, and knew death lurked every inch of the way.

"Go!" Chris shouted, fiercely. And as the fear-stricken man started, "And take another look for the cook!"

Two hours later, almost dead from suffering the captain returned. He had obeyed orders. The sailing-master was helpless although safe in a bunk; the cook was gone. Chris sent the captain below to the cabin to change his clothes.

After interminable hours of toil, day broke cold and gray. Chris looked about him. The *Sophie Sutherland* was racing before the typhoon like a thing possessed. There was no rain, but the wind whipped the spray of the sea mast-high, obscuring everything except in the immediate neighborhood.

Two waves only could Chris see at a time — the one before and the one behind. So small and insignificant the schooner seemed on the long Pacific roll! Rushing up a maddening mountain, she would poise like a cockle-shell on the giddy summit, breathless and rolling, leap outward and down into the yawning chasm beneath, and bury herself in the smother of foam at the bottom. Then the recovery, another mountain, another sickening upward rush, another poise, and the downward crash! Abreast of him, to starboard, like a ghost of the storm, Chris saw the cook dashing apace with the schooner. Evidently, when washed overboard, he had grasped and become entangled in a trailing halyard.

For three hours more, alone with this gruesome companion, Chris held the *Sophie Sutherland* before the wind and sea. He had long since forgotten his mangled fingers. The bandages had been torn away, and the cold, salt spray had eaten into the half-healed wounds until they were numb and no longer pained. But he was not cold. The terrific labor of steering forced the prespiration from every pore. Yet he was faint and weak with hunger and exhaustion, and hailed with delight the advent on deck of the captain, who fed him all of a pound of cake-chocolate. It strengthened him at once.

He ordered the captain to cut the halyard by which the cook's body was towing, and also to go forward and cut loose the jib-halyard and sheet. When he had done so, the jib fluttered a couple of moments like a handkerchief, then tore out of the bolt-ropes and vanished. The *Sophie Sutherland* was running under bare poles.

By noon the storm had spent itself, and by six in the evening the waves had died down sufficiently to let Chris leave the helm. It was almost hopeless to dream of the small boats weathering the typhoon, but there is always the chance in saving human life, and Chris at once applied himself to going back over the course along which he had fled. He managed to get a reef in one of the inner jibs and two reefs in the spanker, and then, with the aid of the watch-tackle, to hoist them to the stiff breeze that yet blew. And all through the night, tacking back and forth on the back track, he shook out canvas as fast as the wind would permit.

The injured sailing-master had turned delirious, and between tending him and lending a hand with the ship, Chris kept the captain busy. "Taught me more seamanship," as he afterward said, "than I'd learned on the whole voyage." But by

daybreak the old man's feeble frame succumbed, and he fell off into exhausted sleep on the weather poop.

Chris, who could now lash the wheel, covered the tired man with blankets from below, and went fishing in the lazaretto for something to eat. But by the day following he found himself forced to give in, drowsing fitfully by the wheel and waking ever and anon to take a look at things.

On the afternoon of the third day he picked up a schooner, dismasted and battered. As he approached, close-hauled on the wind, he saw her decks crowded by an unusually large crew, and on sailing in closer, made out among others the faces of his missing comrades. And he was just in the nick of time, for they were fighting a losing fight at the pumps. An hour later they, with the crew of the sinking craft, were aboard the *Sophie Sutherland*.

Having wandered so far from their own vessel, they had taken refuge on the strange schooner just before the storm broke. She was a Canadian sealer on her first voyage, and as was now apparent, her last.

The captain of the *Sophie Sutherland* had a story to tell, also, and he told it well — so well, in fact, that when all hands were gathered together on deck during the dog-watch, Emil Johansen strode over to Chris and gripped him by the hand.

"Chris," he said, so loudly that all could hear, "Chris, I gif in. You vas yoost so good a sailorman as I. You vas a bully boy und able seaman, und I pe proud for you!

"Und Chris!" He turned as if he had forgotten something, and called back, "From dis time always you call me 'Emil' mitout der 'Mister!' "

44
THE SUNLANDERS

THE SUNLANDERS

Mandell is an obscure village on the rim of the polar sea. It is not large, and the people are peaceable, more peaceable even than those of the adjacent tribes. There are few men in Mandell, and many women; wherefore a wholesome and necessary polygamy is in practice; the women bear children with ardor, and the birth of a man-child is hailed with acclamation. Then there is Aab-Waak, whose head rests always on one shoulder, as though at some time the neck had become very tired and refused forevermore its wonted duty.

The cause of all these things, — the peaceableness, and the polygamy, and the tired neck of Aab-Waak, — goes back among the years to the time when the schooner *Search* dropped anchor in Mandell Bay, and when Tyee, chief man of the tribe, conceived a scheme of sudden wealth. To this day the story of things that happened is remembered and spoken of with bated breath by the people of Mandell, who are cousins to the Hungry Folk who live in the west. Children draw closer when the tale is told, and marvel sagely to themselves at the madness of those who might have been their forebears had they not provoked the Sunlanders and come to bitter ends.

It began to happen when six men came ashore from the *Search,* with heavy outfits, as though they had come to stay, and quartered themselves in Neegah's igloo. Not but that they paid well in flour and sugar for the lodging, but Neegah was aggrieved because Mesahchie, his daughter, elected to cast her fortunes and seek food and blanket with Bill-Man, who was leader of the party of white men.

"She is worth a price," Neegah complained to the gathering by the council-fire, when the six white men were asleep. "She is worth a price, for we have more men than women, and the men be bidding high. The hunter Ounenk offered me a kayak, new-made, and a gun which he got in trade from the Hungry Folk. This was I offered, and behold, now she is gone and I have nothing!"

"I, too, did bid for Mesahchie," grumbled a voice, in tones not altogether joyless, and Peelo shoved his broad-cheeked, jovial face for a moment into the light.

"Thou, too," Neegah affirmed. "And there were others. Why is there such a restlessness upon the Sunlanders?" he demanded petulantly. "Why do they not stay at home? The Snow People do not wander to the lands of the Sunlanders."

"Better were it to ask why they come," cried a voice from the darkness, and Aab-Waak pushed his way to the front.

"Ay! Why they come!" clamored many voices, and Aab-Waak waved his hand for silence.

"Men do not dig in the ground for nothing," he began. "And I have it in mind of the Whale People, who are likewise Sunlanders, and who lost their ship in the ice. You all remember the Whale People, who came to us in their broken boats, and who went away into the south with dogs and sleds when the frost arrived and snow covered the land. And you remember, while they waited for the frost, that one man of them dug in the ground, and then two men and three, and then all men of them, with great excitement and much disturbance. What they dug out of the ground we do not know, for they drove us away so we could not see. But afterward, when they were gone, we looked and found nothing. Yet there be much ground and they did not dig it all."

"Ay, Aab-Waak! Ay!" cried the people in admiration.

"Wherefore I have it in mind," he concluded, "that one Sunlander tells another, and that these Sunlanders have been so told and are come to dig in the ground."

"But how can it be that Bill-Man speaks our tongue?" demanded a little weazened old hunter, — "Bill-Man, upon whom never before our eyes have rested?"

"Bill-Man has been other times in the Snow Lands," Aab-Waak answered, "else would he not speak the speech of the Bear People, which is like the speech of the Hungry Folk, which is very like the speech of the Mandells. For there have been many Sunlanders among the Bear People, few among the Hungry Folk, and none at all among the Mandells, save the Whale People and those who sleep now in the igloo of Neegah."

"Their sugar is very good," Neegah commented, "and their flour."

"They have great wealth," Ounenk added. "Yesterday I was to their ship, and beheld most cunning tools of iron, and knives, and guns, and flour, and sugar, and strange foods without end."

"It is so, brothers!" Tyee stood up and exulted inwardly at the respect and silence his people accorded him. "They be very rich, these Sunlanders. Also, they be fools. For behold! They come among us boldly, blindly, and without thought for all of their great wealth. Even now they snore, and we are many and unafraid."

"Mayhap they, too, are unafraid, being great fighters," the weazened little old hunter objected.

But Tyee scowled upon him. "Nay, it would not seem so. They live to the south, under the path of the sun, and are soft as their dogs are soft. You remember the dog of the Whale People? Our dogs ate him the second day, for he was soft and could not fight. The sun is warm and life easy in the Sun Lands, and the men are as women, and the women as children."

Heads nodded in approval, and the women craned their necks to listen.

"It is said they are good to their women, who do little work," tittered Likeeta, a broad-hipped, healthy young woman, daughter to Tyee himself.

"Thou wouldst follow the feet of Mesahchie, eh?" he cried angrily. Then he turned swiftly to the tribesmen. "Look you, brothers, this is the way of the Sunlanders! They have eyes for our women, and take them one by one. As Mesahchie has gone, cheating Neegah of her price, so will Likeeta go, so will they all go, and we be cheated. I have talked with a hunter from the Bear People, and I know. There be Hungry Folk among us; let them speak if my words be true."

The six hunters of the Hungry Folk attested the truth and fell each to telling his neighbor of the Sunlanders and their ways. There were mutterings from the younger men, who had wives to seek, and from the older men, who had daughters to fetch prices, and a low hum of rage rose higher and clearer.

"They are very rich, and have cunning tools of iron, and knives, and guns without end," Tyee suggested craftily, his dream of sudden wealth beginning to take shape.

"I shall take the gun of Bill-Man for myself," Aab-Waak suddenly proclaimed.

"Nay, it shall be mine!" shouted Neegah; "for there is the price of Mesahchie to be reckoned."

"Peace! O brothers!" Tyee swept the assembly with his hands. "Let the women and children go to their igloos. This is the talk of men; let it be for the ears of men."

"There be guns in plenty for all," he said when the women had unwillingly withdrawn. "I doubt not there will be two guns for each man, without thought of the flour and sugar and other things. And it is easy. The six Sunlanders in Neegah's igloo will we kill to-night while they sleep. To-morrow will we go in peace to the ship to trade, and there, when the time favors, kill all their brothers. And to-morrow night there shall be feasting and merriment and division of wealth. And the least man shall possess more than did ever the greatest before. Is it wise, that which I have spoken, brothers?"

A low growl of approval answered him, and preparation for the attack was begun. The six Hungry Folk, as became members of a wealthier tribe, were armed with rifles and plenteously supplied with ammunition. But it was only here and there that a Mandell possessed a gun, many of which were broken, and there was a general slackness of powder and shells. This poverty of war weapons, however, was relieved by myriads of bone-headed arrows and casting-spears for work at a distance, and for close quarters steel knives of Russian and Yankee make.

"Let there be no noise," Tyee finally instructed; "but be there many on every side of the igloo, and close, so that the Sunlanders may not break through. Then do you, Neegah, with six of the young men behind, crawl in to where they sleep. Take no guns, which be prone to go off at unexpected times, but put the strength of your arms into the knives."

"And be it understood that no harm befall Mesahchie, who is worth a price," Neegah whispered hoarsely.

Flat upon the ground, the small army concentred on the igloo, and behind, deliciously expectant, crouched many women and children, come out to witness the murder. The brief August night was passing, and in the gray of dawn could be dimly discerned the creeping forms of Neegah and the young men. Without pause, on hands and knees, they entered the long passageway and disappeared. Tyee rose up and rubbed his hands. All was going well. Head after head in the big circle lifted and waited. Each man pictured the scene according to his nature — the sleeping men, the plunge of the knives, and the sudden death in the dark.

A loud hail, in the voice of a Sunlander, rent the silence, and a shot rang out. Then an uproar broke loose inside the igloo. Without premeditation, the circle swept forward into the passageway. On the inside, half a dozen repeating rifles began to chatter, and the Mandells, jammed in the confined space, were powerless. Those at the front strove madly to retreat from the fire-spitting guns in their very faces, and those in the rear pressed as madly forward to the attack. The bullets from the big 45:90's drove through half a dozen men at a shot, and the passageway, gorged with surging, helpless men, became a shambles. The rifles, pumped without aim into the mass, withered it away like a machine gun, and against that steady stream of death no man could advance.

"Never was there the like!" panted one of the Hungry Folk. "I did but look in, and the dead were piled like seals on the ice after a killing!"

"Did I not say, mayhap, they were fighters?" cackled the weazened old hunter.

"It was to be expected," Aab-Waak answered stoutly. "We fought in a trap of our making."

"O ye fools!" Tyee chided. "Ye sons of fools! It was not planned, this thing ye have done. To Neegah and the six young men only was it given to go inside. My cunning is superior to the cunning of the Sunlanders, but ye take away its edge, and rob me of its strength, and make it worse than

no cunning at all!"

No one made reply, and all eyes centred on the igloo, which loomed vague and monstrous against the clear northeast sky. Through a hole in the roof the smoke from the rifles curled slowly upward in the pulseless air, and now and again a wounded man crawled painfully through the gray.

"Let each ask of his neighbor for Neegah and the six young men," Tyee commanded.

And after a time the answer came back, "Neegah and the six young men are not."

"And many more are not!" wailed a woman to the rear.

"The more wealth for those who are left," Tyee grimly consoled. Then, turning to Aab-Waak, he said: "Go thou, and gather together many sealskins filled with oil. Let the hunters empty them on the outside wood of the igloo and of the passage. And let them put fire to it ere the Sunlanders make holes in the igloo for their guns."

Even as he spoke a hole appeared in the dirt plastered between the logs, a rifle muzzle protruded, and one of the Hungry Folk clapped hand to his side and leaped in the air. A second shot, through the lungs, brought him to the ground. Tyee and the rest scattered to either side, out of direct range, and Aab-Waak hastened the men forward with the skins of oil. Avoiding the loopholes, which were making on every side of the igloo, they emptied the skins on the dry drift-logs brought down by the Mandell River from the tree-lands to the south. Ounenk ran forward with a blazing brand, and the flames leaped upward. Many minutes passed, without sign, and they held their weapons ready as the fire gained headway.

Tyee rubbed his hands gleefully as the dry structure burned and crackled. "Now we have them, brothers! In the trap!"

"And no one may gainsay me the gun of Bill-Man," Aab-Waak announced.

"Save Bill-Man," squeaked the old hunter. "For behold, he cometh now!"

Covered with a singed and blackened blanket, the big white man leaped out of the blazing entrance, and on his heels, likewise shielded, came Mesahchie, and the five other Sunlanders. The Hungry Folk tried to check the rush with an ill-directed volley, while the Mandells hurled in a cloud of spears and arrows. But the Sunlanders cast their flaming blankets from them as they ran, and it was seen that each bore on his shoulders a small pack of ammunition. Of all their possessions, they had chosen to save that. Running swiftly and with purpose, they broke the circle and headed directly for the great cliff, which towered blackly in the brightening day a half-mile to the rear of the village.

But Tyee knelt on one knee and lined the sights of his rifle on the rearmost Sunlander. A great shout went up when he pulled the trigger and the man fell forward, struggled partly up, and fell again. Without regard for the rain of arrows, another Sunlander ran back, bent over him, and lifted him across his shoulders. But the Mandell spearmen were crowding up into closer range, and a strong cast transfixed the wounded man. He cried out and became swiftly limp as his comrade lowered him to the ground. In the meanwhile, Bill-Man and the three others had made a stand and were driving a leaden hail into the advancing spearmen. The fifth Sunlander bent over his stricken fellow, felt the heart, and then coolly cut the straps of the pack and stood up with the ammunition and extra gun.

"Now is he a fool!" cried Tyee, leaping high, as he ran forward, to clear the squirming body of one of the Hungry Folk.

His own rifle was clogged so that he could not use it, and he called out for some one to spear the Sunlander, who had turned and was running for safety under the protecting fire. The little old hunter poised his spear on the throwing-stick, swept his arm back as he ran, and delivered the cast.

"By the body of the Wolf, say I, it was a good throw!" Tyee praised, as the fleeing man pitched forward, the spear standing upright between his shoulders and swaying slowly forward and back.

The little weazened old man coughed and sat down. A streak of red showed on his lips and welled into a thick stream. He coughed again, and a strange whistling came and went with his breath.

"They, too, are unafraid, being great fighters," he wheezed, pawing aimlessly with his hands. "And behold! Bill-Man comes now!"

Tyee glanced up. Four Mandells and one of the Hungry Folk had rushed upon the fallen man and were spearing him from his knees back to the earth. In the twinkling of an eye, Tyee saw four of them cut down by the bullets of the Sunlanders. The fifth, as yet unhurt, seized the two rifles, but as he stood up to make off he was whirled almost completely around by the impact of a bullet in the arm, steadied by a second, and overthrown by the shock of a third. A moment later and Bill-Man was on the spot, cutting the pack-straps and picking up the guns.

This Tyee saw, and his own people falling as they straggled forward, and he was aware of a quick doubt, and resolved to lie where he was and see more. For some unaccountable reason, Mesahchie was running back to Bill-Man; but before she could reach him, Tyee saw Peelo run out and throw arms about her. He essayed to sling her across his shoulder, but she grappled with him, tearing and scratching at his face. Then she tripped him, and the pair fell heavily. When they regained their feet, Peelo had shifted his grip so that one arm was passed under her chin, the wrist pressing into her throat and strangling her. He buried his face in her breast, taking the blows of her hands on his thick mat of hair, and began slowly to force her off the field. Then it was, retreating with the weapons of his fallen comrades, that Bill-Man came upon them. As Mesahchie saw him, she twirled the victim around and held him steady. Bill-Man swung the rifle in his right hand, and hardly easing his stride, delivered the blow. Tyee saw Peelo drive to the earth as smote by a falling star, and the Sunlander and Neegah's daughter fleeing side by side.

A bunch of Mandells, led by one of the Hungry Folk, made a futile rush which melted away into the earth before the scorching fire.

Tyee caught his breath and murmured, "Like the young frost in the morning sun."

"As I say, they are great fighters," the old hunter whispered weakly, far gone in hemorrhage. "I know. I have heard. They be sea-robbers and hunters of seals; and they shoot quick and true, for it is their way of life and the work of their hands."

"Like the young frost in the morning sun," Tyee repeated, crouching for shelter behind the dying man and peering at intervals about him.

It was no longer a fight, for no Mandell man dared venture forward, and as it was, they were too close to the Sunlanders to go back. Three tried it, scattering and scurrying like rabbits; but one came down with a

Tyee saw Peelo drive to the earth as smote by a falling star, and the Sunlander and Neegah's daughter fleeing side by side

broken leg, another was shot through the body, and the third, twisting and dodging, fell on the edge of the village. So the tribesmen crouched in the hollow places and burrowed into the dirt in the open, while the Sunlanders' bullets searched the plain.

"Move not," Tyee pleaded, as Aab-Waak came worming over the ground to him. "Move not, good Aab-Waak, else you bring death upon us."

"Death sits upon many," Aab-Waak laughed; "wherefore, as you say, there will be much wealth in division. My father breathes fast and short behind the big rock yon, and beyond, twisted like in a knot, lieth my brother. But their share shall be my share, and it is well."

"As you say, good Aab-Waak, and as I have said; but before division must come that which we may divide, and the Sunlanders be not yet dead."

A bullet glanced from a rock before them, and singing shrilly, rose low over their heads on its second flight. Tyee ducked and shivered, but Aab-Waak grinned and sought vainly to follow it with his eyes.

"So swiftly they go, one may not see them," he observed.

"But many be dead of us," Tyee went on.

"And many be left," was the reply. "And they hug close to the earth, for they have become wise in the fashion of fighting. Further, they are angered. Moreover, when we have killed the Sunlanders on the ship, there will remain but four on the land. These may take long to kill, but in the end it will happen."

"How may we go down to the ship when we cannot go this way or that?" Tyee questioned.

"It is a bad place where lie Bill-Man and his brothers," Aab-Waak explained. "We may come upon them from every side, which is not good. So they aim to get their backs against the cliff and wait until their brothers of the ship come to give them aid."

"Never shall they come from the ship, their brothers! I have said it."

Tyee was gathering courage again, and when the Sunlanders verified the prediction by retreating to the cliff, he was light-hearted as ever.

"There be only three of us!" complained one of the Hungry Folk as they came together for council.

"Therefore, instead of two, shall you have four guns each," was Tyee's rejoinder.

"We did good fighting."

"Ay; and if it should happen that two of you be left, then will you have six guns each. Therefore, fight well."

"And if there be none of them left?" Aab-Waak whispered slyly.

"Then will *we* have the guns, you and I," Tyee whispered back.

However, to propitiate the Hungry Folk, he made one of them leader of the ship expedition. This party comprised fully two-thirds of the tribesmen, and departed for the coast, a dozen miles away, laden with skins and things to trade. The remaining men were disposed in a large half-circle about the breastwork which Bill-Man and his Sunlanders had begun to throw up. Tyee was quick to note the virtues of things, and at once set his men to digging shallow trenches.

"The time will go before they are aware," he explained to Aab-Waak; "and their minds being busy, they will not think overmuch of the dead that are, nor gather trouble to themselves. And in the dark of night they may creep closer, so that when the Sunlanders look forth in the morning light they will find us very near."

In the midday heat the men ceased from their work and made a meal of dried fish and seal oil which the women brought up. There was some clamor for the food of the Sunlanders in the igloo of Neegah, but Tyee refused to divide it until the return of the ship party. Speculations upon the outcome became rife, but in the midst of it a dull boom drifted up over the land from the sea. The keen-eyed ones made out a dense cloud of smoke, which quickly disappeared, and which they averred was directly over the ship of the Sunlanders. Tyee was of the opinion that it was a big gun. Aab-Waak did not know, but thought it might be a signal of some sort. Anyway, he said, it was time something happened.

Five or six hours afterward a solitary man was descried coming across the wide flat from the sea, and the women and children poured out upon him in a body. It was Ounenk, naked, winded, and wounded. The blood still trickled down his face from a gash on the forehead. His left arm, frightfully mangled, hung helpless at his side. But most significant of all, there was a wild gleam in his eyes which betokened the women knew not what.

"Where be Peshack?" an old squaw queried sharply.

"And Olitlie?" "And Polak?" "And Mah-Kook?" the voices took up the cry.

But he said nothing, brushing his way through the clamorous mass and directing his staggering steps toward Tyee. The old squaw raised the wail, and one by one the women joined her as they swung in behind. The men crawled out of their trenches and ran back to gather about Tyee, and it was noticed that the Sunlanders climbed upon their barricade to see.

Ounenk halted, swept the blood from his eyes, and looked about. He strove to speak, but his dry lips were glued together. Likeeta fetched him water, and he grunted and drank again.

"Was it a fight?" Tyee demanded finally,—"a good fight?"

"Ho! ho! ho!" So suddenly and so fiercely did Ounenk laugh that every voice hushed. "Never was there such a fight! So I say, I, Ounenk, fighter beforetime of beasts and men. And ere I forget, let me speak fat words and wise. By fighting will the Sunlanders teach us Mandell Folk how to fight. And if we fight long enough, we shall be great fighters, even as the Sunlanders, or else we shall be — dead. Ho! ho! ho! It was a fight!"

"Where be thy brothers?" Tyee shook him till he shrieked from the pain of his hurts.

Ounenk sobered. "My brothers? They are not."

"And Pome-Lee?" cried one of the two Hungry Folk; "Pome-Lee, the son of my mother?"

"Pome-Lee is not," Ounenk answered in a monotonous voice.

"And the Sunlanders?" from Aab-Waak.

"The Sunlanders are not."

"Then the ship of the Sunlanders, and the wealth and guns and things?" Tyee demanded.

"Neither the ship of the Sunlanders, nor the wealth and guns and things," was the unvarying response. "All are not. Nothing is. I only am."

"And thou art a fool."

"It may be so," Ounenk answered, unruffled. "I have seen that which would well make me a fool."

Tyee held his tongue, and all waited till it should please Ounenk to tell the story in his own way.

"We took no guns, O Tyee," he at last began; "no guns, my brothers — only knives and hunting bows and spears. And in twos and threes, in our kayaks, we came to the ship. They were glad to see us, the Sunlanders, and we spread our skins and they brought out their articles of trade, and everything was well. And Pome-Lee waited — waited till the sun was well overhead and they sat at meat, when he gave the cry and we fell upon them. Never was there such a fight, and never such fighters. Half did we kill in the quickness of surprise, but the half that was left became as devils, and they multiplied themselves, and everywhere they fought like devils. Three put their backs against the mast of the ship, and we ringed them with our dead before they died. And some got guns and shot with both eyes wide open, and very quick and sure. And one got a big gun, from which at one time he shot many small bullets. And so behold!"

Ounenk pointed to his ear, neatly pierced by a buckshot.

"But I, Ounenk, drove my spear through his back from behind. And in such fashion, one way and another, did we kill them all — all save the head man. And him we were about, many of us, and he was alone, when he made a great cry and broke through us, five or six dragging upon him, and ran down inside the ship. And then, when the wealth of the ship was ours, and only the head man down below whom we would kill presently, why then there was a sound as of all the guns in the world — a mighty sound! And like a bird I rose up in the air, and the living Mandell Folk, and the dead Sunlanders, the little kayaks, the big ship, the guns, the wealth — everything rose up in the air. So I say, I, Ounenk, who tell the tale, am the only one left."

A great silence fell upon the assemblage. Tyee looked at Aab-Waak with awe-struck eyes, but forbore to speak. Even the women were too stunned to wail the dead.

Ounenk looked about him with pride. "I, only, am left," he repeated.

But at that instant a rifle cracked from Bill-Man's barricade, and there was a sharp spat and thud on the chest of Ounenk. He swayed backward and came forward again, a look of startled surprise on his face. He gasped, and his lips writhed in a grim smile. There was a shrinking together of the shoulders and a bending of the knees. He shook himself, as might a drowsing man, and straightened up. But the shrinking and bending began again, and he sank down slowly, quite slowly, to the ground.

It was a clean mile from the pit of the Sunlanders, and death had spanned it. A great cry of rage went up, and in it there was much of blood-vengeance, much of the unreasoned ferocity of the brute. Tyee and Aab-Waak tried to hold the Mandell Folk back, were thrust aside, and could only turn and watch the mad charge. But no shots came from the Sunlanders, and ere half the distance was covered, many affrighted by the mysterious silence of the pit, halted and waited. The wilder spirits bore on and when they had cut the remaining distance in half, the pit still showed no sign of life. At two hundred yards they slowed down and bunched; at one hundred, they stopped, a score of them, suspicious, and conferred together.

Then a wreath of smoke crowned the barricade, and they scattered like a handful of pebbles thrown at random. Four went down, and four more, and they continued swiftly to fall, one and two at a time, till but one remained, and he in full flight with death singing about his ears. It was Nok, a young hunter, long-legged and tall, and he ran as never before. He skimmed across the naked open like a bird, and soared and sailed and curved from side to side. The rifles in the pit rang out in solid volley; they flut-flut-flut-flutted in ragged sequence; and still Nok rose and dipped and rose again unharmed. There was a lull in the firing, as though the Sunlanders had given over, and Nok curved less and less in his flight till he darted straight forward at every leap. And then, as he leaped cleanly and well, one lone rifle barked from the pit, and he doubled up in mid-air, struck the ground in a ball, and like a ball bounced from the impact, and came down in a broken heap.

"Who so swift as the swift-winged lead?" Aab-Waak pondered.

Tyee grunted and turned away. The incident was closed and there was more pressing matter at hand. One Hungry Man and forty fighters, some of them hurt, remained; and there were four Sunlanders yet to reckon with.

"We will keep them in their hole by the cliff," he said, "and when famine has gripped them hard we will slay them like children."

"But of what matter to fight?" queried Oloof, one of the younger men. "The wealth of the Sunlanders is not; only remains that in the igloo of Neegah, a paltry quantity—"

He broke off hastily as the air by his ear split sharply to the passage of a bullet.

Tyee laughed scornfully. "Let that be thy answer. What else may we do with this mad breed of Sunlanders which will not die?"

"What a thing is foolishness!" Oloof protested, his ears furtively alert for the coming of other bullets. "It is not right that they should fight so, these Sunlanders. Why will they not die easily? They are fools not to know that they are dead men, and they give us much trouble."

"We fought before for great wealth; we fight now that we may live," Aab-Waak summed up succinctly.

That night there was a clash in the trenches, and shots exchanged. And in the morning the igloo of Neegah was found empty of the Sunlanders' possessions. These they themselves had taken, for the signs of their trail were visible to the sun. Oloof climbed to the brow of the cliff to hurl great stones down into the pit, but the cliff overhung, and he hurled down abuse and insult instead, and promised bitter torture to them in the end. Bill-Man mocked him back in the tongue of the Bear Folk, and Tyee, lifting his head from a trench to see, had his shoulder scratched deeply by a bullet.

And in the dreary days that followed, and in the wild nights when they pushed the trenches closer, there was much discussion as to the wisdom of letting the Sunlanders go. But of this they were afraid, and the women raised a cry always at the thought. This much they had seen of the Sunlanders; they cared to see no more. All the time the whistle and blub-blub of bullets filled the air, and all the time the death-list grew. In the golden sunrise came the faint, far crack of a rifle, and a stricken woman would throw up her hands on the distant edge of the village; in the noonday heat, men in the trenches heard the shrill sing-song and knew their deaths; or in the gray afterglow of evening, the dirt kicked up in puffs by the winking fires. And through the nights the long "Wah-hoo-ha-a wah-hoo-ha-a!" of mourning women held dolorous sway.

As Tyee had promised, in the end famine gripped the Sunlanders. And once, when an early fall gale blew, one of them crawled through the darkness past the trenches and stole many dried fish. But he could not get back with them, and the sun found him vainly hiding in the village. So he fought the great fight by himself, and in a narrow ring of Mandell Folk shot four with his revolver, and ere they could lay hands on him for the torture, turned it on himself and died.

This threw a gloom upon the people. Oloof put the question, "If one man die so hard, how hard will die the three who yet are left?"

Then Mesahchie stood up on the barricade and called in by name three dogs which had wandered close, — meat and life, — which set back the day of reckoning and put despair in the hearts of the Mandell Folk. And on the head of Mesahchie were showered the curses of a generation.

The days dragged by. The sun hurried south, the nights grew long and longer, and there was a touch of frost in the air. And still the Sunlanders held the pit. Hearts were breaking under the unending strain, and Tyee thought hard and deep. Then he sent forth word that all the skins and hides of all the tribe be collected. These he had made into huge cylindrical bales, and behind each bale he placed a man.

When the word was given the brief day was almost spent, and it was slow work and tedious, rolling the big bales forward foot by foot. The bullets of the Sunlanders blub-blubbed and thudded against them, but could not go through, and the men howled their delight. But the dark was at hand, and Tyee, secure of success, called the bales back to the trenches.

In the morning, in the face of an unearthly silence from the pit, the real advance began. At first, with large intervals between, the bales slowly converged as the circle drew in. At a hundred yards they were quite close together, so that Tyee's order to halt was passed along in whispers. The pit showed no sign of life. They watched long and sharply, but nothing stirred. The advance was taken up and the manoeuvre repeated at fifty yards. Still no sign nor sound. Tyee shook his head, and

even Aab-Waak was dubious. But the order was given to go on, and go on they did, till bale touched bale and a solid rampart of skin and hide bowed out from the cliff about the pit and back to the cliff again.

Tyee looked back and saw the women and children clustering blackly in the deserted trenches. He looked ahead at the silent pit. The men were wriggling nervously, and he ordered every second bale forward. This double line advanced till bale touched bale as before. Then Aab-Waak, of his own will, pushed one bale forward alone. When it touched the barricade, he waited a long while. After that he tossed unresponsive rocks over into the pit, and finally, with great care, stood up and peered in. A carpet of empty cartridges, a few white-picked dog bones, and a soggy place where water dripped from a crevice, met his eyes. That was all. The Sunlanders were gone.

There were murmurings of witchcraft, vague complaints, dark looks which foreshadowed to Tyee dread things which yet might come to pass, and he breathed easier when Aab-Waak took up the trail along the base of the cliff.

"The cave!" Tyee cried. "They foresaw my wisdom of the skin-bales and fled away into the cave!"

The cliff was honey-combed with a labyrinth of subterranean passages which found vent in an opening midway between the pit and where the trench tapped the wall. Thither, and with many exclamations, the tribesmen followed Aab-Waak, and, arrived, they saw plainly where the Sunlanders had climbed to the mouth, twenty and odd feet above.

"Now the thing is done," Tyee said, rubbing his hands. "Let word go forth that rejoicing be made, for they are in the trap now, these Sunlanders, — in the trap. The young men shall climb up, and the mouth of the cave be filled with stones, so that Bill-Man and his brothers and Mesahchie shall by famine be pinched to shadows and die cursing in the silence and dark."

Cries of delight and relief greeted this, and Howgah, the last of the Hungry Folk, swarmed up the steep slant and drew himself, crouching, upon the lip of the opening. But as he crouched, a muffled report rushed forth, and as he clung desperately to the slippery edge, a second. His grip loosed with reluctant weakness, and he pitched down at the feet of Tyee, quivered for a moment like some monstrous jelly, and was still.

"How should I know they were great fighters and unafraid?" Tyee demanded, spurred to defence by recollection of the dark looks and vague complaints.

"We were many and happy," one of the men stated baldly. Another fingered his spear with a prurient hand.

But Oloof cried them cease. "Give ear, my brothers! There be another way! As a boy I chanced upon it playing along the steep. It is hidden by the rocks, and there is no reason that a man should go there; wherefore it is secret, and no man knows. It is very small, and you crawl on your belly a long way, and then you are in the cave. To-night we will so crawl, without noise, on our bellies, and come upon the Sunlanders from behind. And to-morrow we will be at peace, and never again will we quarrel with the Sunlanders in the years to come."

"Never again!" chorussed the weary men. "Never again!" And Tyee joined with them.

That night, with the memory of their dead in their hearts, and in their hands stones and spears and knives, the horde of women and children collected about the known mouth of the cave. Down the twenty and odd precarious feet to the ground no Sunlander could hope to pass and live. In the village remained only the wounded men, while every able man — and there were thirty of them — followed Oloof to the secret opening. A hundred feet of broken ledges and insecurely heaped rocks were between it and the earth, and because of the rocks, which might be displaced by the touch of hand or foot, but one man climbed at a time. Oloof went up first, called softly for the next to come on, and disappeared inside. A man followed, a second, and a third, and so on, till only Tyee remained. He received the call of the last man, but a quick doubt assailed him and he stayed to ponder. Half an hour later he swung up to the opening and peered in. He could feel the narrowness of the passage, and the darkness before him took on solidity. The fear of the walled-in earth chilled him and he could not venture. All the men who had died, from Neegah the first of the Mandells, to Howgah the last of the Hungry Folk, came and sat with him, but he chose the terror of their company rather than face the horror which he felt to lurk in the thick blackness. He had been sitting long when something soft and cold fluttered lightly on his cheek, and he knew the first winter's snow was falling. The dim dawn came, and after that the bright day, when he heard a low guttural sobbing, which came and went at intervals along the passage and which drew closer each time and more distinct. He slipped over the edge, dropped his feet to the first ledge, and waited.

That which sobbed made slow progress, but at last, after many halts, it reached him, and he was sure no Sunlander made the noise. So he reached a hand inside, and where there should have been a head felt the shoulders of a man uplifted on bent arms. The head he found later, not erect, but hanging straight down so that the crown rested on the floor of the passage.

"Is it you, Tyee?" the head said. "For it is I, Aab-Waak, who am helpless and broken as a rough-flung spear. My head is in the dirt, and I may not climb down unaided."

Tyee clambered in, dragged him up with his back against the wall, but the head hung down on the chest and sobbed and wailed.

"Ai-oo-o, ai-oo-o!" it went. "Oloof forgot, for Mesahchie likewise knew the secret and showed the Sunlanders, else they would not have waited at the end of the narrow way. Wherefore, I am a broken man, and helpless — ai-oo-o, ai-oo-o!"

"And did they die, the cursed Sunlanders, at the end of the narrow way?" Tyee demanded.

"How should I know they waited?" Aab-Waak gurgled. "For my brothers had gone before, many of them, and there was no sound of struggle. How should I know why there should be no sound of struggle? And ere I knew, two hands were about my neck so that I could not cry out and warn my brothers yet to come. And then there were two hands more on my head, and two more on my feet. In this fashion the three Sunlanders had me. And while the hands held my head in the one place, the hands on my feet swung my body around, and as we wring the neck of a duck in the marsh, so my neck was wrung.

"But it was not given that I should die," he went on, a remnant of pride yet glimmering. "I, only, am left. Oloof and the rest lie on their backs in a row, and their faces turn this way and that, and the faces of some be underneath where the backs of their heads should be. It is not good to look upon; for when life returned to me I saw them all by the light of a torch which the Sunlanders left, and I had been laid with them in the row."

"So? So?" Tyee mused, too stunned for speech.

He started suddenly, and shivered, for the voice of Bill-Man shot out at him from the passage.

"It is well," it said. "I look for the man who crawls with the broken neck, and lo, do I find Tyee. Throw down thy gun, Tyee, so that I may hear it strike among the rocks."

Tyee obeyed passively, and Bill-Man crawled forward into the light. Tyee looked at him curiously. He was gaunt and worn and dirty, and his eyes burned like twin coals in their cavernous sockets.

"I am hungry, Tyee," he said. "Very hungry."

"And I am dirt at thy feet," Tyee responded. "Thy word is my law. Further, I commanded my people not to withstand thee. I counselled—"

But Bill-Man had turned and was calling back into the passage. "Hey! Charley! Jim! Fetch the woman along and come on!"

"We go now to eat," he said, when his comrades and Mesahchie had joined him.

Tyee rubbed his hands deprecatingly. "We have little, but it is thine."

"After that we go south on the snow," Bill-Man continued.

"May you go without hardship and the trail be easy."

"It is a long way. We will need dogs and food — much!"

"Thine the pick of our dogs and the food they may carry."

Bill-Man slipped over the edge of the opening and prepared to descend. "But we come again, Tyee. We come again, and our days shall be long in the land."

And so they departed into the trackless south, Bill-Man, his brothers, and Mesahchie. And when the next year came, the *Search Number Two* rode at anchor in Mandell Bay. The few Mandell men, who survived because their wounds had prevented their crawling into the cave, went to work at the hest of the Sunlanders and dug in the ground. They hunt and fish no more, but receive a daily wage, with which they buy flour, sugar, calico, and such things which the *Search Number Two* brings on her yearly trip from the Sunlands.

And this mine is worked in secret, as many Northland mines have been worked; and no white man outside the Company, which is Bill-Man, Jim, and Charley, knows the whereabouts of Mandell on the rim of the polar sea. Aab-Waak still carries his head on one shoulder, is become an oracle, and preaches peace to the younger generation, for which he receives a pension from the Company. Tyee is foreman of the mine. But he has achieved a new theory concerning the Sunlanders.

"They that live under the path of the sun are not soft," he says, smoking his pipe and watching the day-shift take itself off and the night-shift go on. "For the sun enters into their blood and burns them with a great fire till they are filled with lusts and passions. They burn always, so that they may not know when they are beaten. Further, there is an unrest in them, which is a devil, and they are flung out over the earth to toil and suffer and fight without end. I know. I am Tyee."

45
WHERE THE TRAIL FORKS

WHERE THE TRAIL FORKS

The singer, clean-faced and cheery-eyed, bent over and added water to a pot of simmering beans, and then, rising, a stick of firewood in hand, drove back the circling dogs from the grub-box and cooking-gear. He was blue of eye, and his long hair was golden, and it was a pleasure to look upon his lusty freshness. A new moon was thrusting a dim horn above the white line of close-packed snow-capped pines which ringed the camp and segregated it from all the world. Overhead, so clear it was and cold, the stars danced with quick, pulsating movements. To the southeast an evanescent greenish glow heralded the opening revels of the aurora borealis. Two men, in the immediate foreground, lay upon the bearskin which was their bed. Between the skin and naked snow was a six-inch layer of pine boughs. The blankets were rolled back. For shelter, there was a fly at their backs, — a sheet of canvas stretched between two trees and angling at forty-five degrees. This caught the radiating heat from the fire and flung it down upon the skin. Another man sat on a sled, drawn close to the blaze, mending moccasins. To the right, a heap of frozen gravel and a rude windlass denoted where they toiled each day in dismal groping for the pay-streak. To the left, four pairs of snowshoes stood erect, showing the mode of travel which obtained when the stamped snow of the camp was left behind.

That Schwabian folk-song sounded strangely pathetic under the cold northern stars, and did not do the men good who lounged about the fire after the toil of the day. It put a dull ache into their hearts, and a yearning which was akin to belly-hunger, and sent their souls questing southward across the divides to the sun-lands.

"For the love of God, Sigmund, shut up!" expostulated one of the men. His hands were clenched painfully, but he hid them from sight in the folds of the bearskin upon which he lay.

"And what for, Dave Wertz?" Sigmund demanded. "Why shall I not sing when the heart is glad?"

"Because you've got no call to, that's why. Look about you, man, and think of the grub we've been defiling our bodies with for the last twelvemonth, and the way we've lived and worked like beasts!"

Thus abjured, Sigmund, the golden-haired, surveyed it all, and the frost-rimmed wolf-dogs and the vapor breaths of the men. "And why shall not the heart be glad?" he laughed. "It is good; it is all good. As for the grub —" He doubled up his arm and caressed the swelling biceps. "And if we have lived and worked like beasts, have we not been paid like kings? Twenty dollars to the pan the streak is running, and we know it to be eight feet thick. It is another Klondike — and we know it — Jim Hawes there, by your elbow, knows it and complains not. And there's Hitchcock! He sews moccasins like an old woman, and waits against the time. Only you can't wait and work until the wash-up in the spring. Then we shall all be rich, rich as kings, only you cannot wait. You want to go back to the States. So do I, and I was born there, but I can wait, when each day the gold in the pan shows up yellow as butter in the churning. But you want your good time, and, like a child, you cry for it now. Bah! Why shall I not sing:

> "In a year, in a year, when the grapes
> are ripe,
> I shall stay no more away.
> Then if you still are true, my love,
> It will be our wedding day.
> In a year, in a year, when my time is
> past,
> Then I'll live in your love for aye.
> Then if you still are true, my love,
> It will be our wedding day."

The dogs, bristling and growling, drew in closer to the firelight. There was a monotonous crunch-crunch of webbed shoes, and between each crunch the dragging forward of the heel of the shoe like the sound of sifting sugar. Sigmund broke off for his song to hurl oaths and firewood at the animals. Then the light was parted by a fur-clad figure, and an Indian girl slipped out of the webs, threw back the hood of her squirrel-skin *parka*, and stood in their midst. Sigmund and the men on the bearskin greeted her as "Sipsu," with the customary "Hello," but Hitchcock made room on the sled that she might sit beside him.

"And how goes it, Sipsu?" he asked, talking, after her fashion, in broken English and bastard Chinook. "Is the hunger still mighty in the camp? and has the witch doctor yet found the cause wherefore game is scarce and no moose in the land?"

"Yes; even so. There is little game, and we prepare to eat the dogs. Also has the witch doctor found the cause of all this evil, and to-morrow will he make sacrifice and cleanse the camp."

"And what does the sacrifice chance to be? — a new-born babe or some poor devil of a squaw, old and shaky, who is a care to the tribe and better out of the way?"

"It chanced not that wise; for the need was great, and he chose none other than the chief's daughter; none other than I, Sipsu."

"Hell!" The word rose slowly to Hitchcock's lips, and brimmed over full and deep, in a way which bespoke wonder and consideration.

"Wherefore we stand by a forking of the trail, you and I," she went on calmly, "and I have come that we may look once more upon each other, and once more only."

She was born of primitive stock, and primitive had been her traditions and her days; so she regarded life stoically, and human sacrifice as part of the natural order. The powers which ruled the daylight and the dark, the flood and the frost, the bursting of the bud and the withering of the leaf, were angry and in need of propitiation. This they exacted in many ways, — death in the bad water, through the treacherous ice-crust, by the grip of the grizzly, or a wasting sickness which fell upon a man in his own lodge till he coughed, and the life of his lungs went out through his mouth and nostrils. Likewise did the powers receive sacrifice. It was all

one. And the witch doctor was versed in the thoughts of the powers and chose unerringly. It was very natural. Death came by many ways, yet was it all one after all, — a manifestation of the all-powerful and inscrutable.

But Hitchcock came of a later world-breed. His traditions were less concrete and without reverence, and he said, "Not so, Sipsu. You are young, and yet in the full joy of life. The witch doctor is a fool, and his choice is evil. This thing shall not be."

She smiled and answered, "Life is not kind, and for many reasons. First, it made of us twain the one white and the other red, which is bad. Then it crossed our trails, and now it parts them again; and we can do nothing. Once before, when the gods were angry, did your brothers come to the camp. They were three, big men and white, and they said the thing shall not be. But they died quickly, and the thing was."

Hitchcock nodded that he heard, half-turned, and lifted his voice. "Look here, you fellows! There's a lot of foolery going on over to the camp, and they're getting ready to murder Sipsu. What d' ye say?"

Wertz looked at Hawes, and Hawes looked back, but neither spoke. Sigmund dropped his head, and petted the shepherd dog between his knees. He had brought Shep in with him from the outside, and thought a great deal of the animal. In fact, a certain girl, who was much in his thoughts, and whose picture in the little locket on his breast often inspired him to sing, had given him the dog and her blessing when they kissed good-by and he started on his Northland quest.

"What d' ye say?" Hitchcock repeated.

"Mebbe it's not so serious," Hawes answered with deliberation. "Most likely it's only a girl's story."

"That isn't the point!" Hitchcock felt a hot flush of anger sweep over him at their evident reluctance. "The question is, if it is so, are we going to stand it? What are we going to do?"

"I don't see any call to interfere," spoke up Wertz. "If it is so, it is so, and that's all there is about it. It's a way these people have of doing. It's their religion, and it's no concern of ours. Our concern is to get the dust and then get out of this God-forsaken land. 'T isn't fit for naught else but beasts? And what are these black devils but beasts? Besides, it'd be damn poor policy."

"That's what I say," chimed in Hawes.

"Here we are, four of us, three hundred miles from the Yukon or a white face. And what can we do against half-a-hundred Indians? If we quarrel with them, we have to vamose; if we fight, we are wiped out. Further, we've struck pay, and, by God! I, for one, am going to stick by it!"

"Ditto here," supplemented Wertz.

Hitchcock turned impatiently to Sigmund, who was softly singing, —

> "In a year, in a year, when the grapes
> are ripe,
> I shall stay no more away."

"Well, it's this way, Hitchcock," he finally said, "I'm in the same boat with the rest. If three-score bucks have made up their mind tò kill the girl, why, we can't help it. One rush, and we'd be wiped off the landscape. And what good'd that be? They'd still have the girl. There's no use in going against the customs of a people except you're in force."

"But we are in force!" Hitchcock broke in.

"Four whites are a match for a hundred times as many reds. And think of the girl!"

Sigmund stroked the dog meditatively. "But I do think of the girl. And her eyes are blue like summer skies, and laughing like summer seas, and her hair is yellow, like mine, and braided in ropes the size of a big man's arms. She's waiting for me, out there, in a better land. And she's waited long, and now my pile's in sight I'm not going to throw it away."

"And shamed I would be to look into the girl's blue eyes and remember the black ones of the girl whose blood was on my hands," Hitchcock sneered; for he was born to honor and championship, and to do the thing for the thing's sake, nor stop to weigh or measure.

Sigmund shook his head. "You can't make me mad, Hitchcock, nor do mad things because of your madness. It's a cold business proposition and a question of facts. I did n't come to this country for my health, and, further, it's impossible for us to raise a hand. If it is so, it is too bad for the girl, that's all. It's a way of her people, and it just happens we're on the spot this one time. They've done the same for a thousand-thousand years, and they're going to do it now, and they'll go on doing it

for all time to come. Besides, they're not our kind. Nor's the girl. No, I take my stand with Wertz and Hawes, and —"

But the dogs snarled and drew in, and he broke off, listening to the crunch-crunch of many snowshoes. Indian after Indian stalked into the firelight, tall and grim, fur-clad and silent, their shadows dancing grotesquely on the snow. One, the witch doctor, spoke gutturally to Sipsu. His face was daubed with savage paint blotches, and over his shoulders was drawn a wolfskin, the gleaming teeth and cruel snout surmounting his head. No other word was spoken. The prospectors held the peace. Sipsu arose and slipped into her snowshoes.

"Good-by, O my man," she said to Hitchcock. But the man who had sat beside her on the sled gave no sign, nor lifted his head as they filed away into the white forest.

Unlike many men, his faculty of adaptation, while large, had never suggested the expediency of an alliance with the women of the Northland. His broad cosmopolitanism had never impelled toward covenanting in marriage with the daughters of the soil. If it had, his philosophy of life would not have stood between. But it simply had not. Sipsu? He had pleasured in camp-fire chats with her, not as a man who knew himself to be man and she woman, but as a man might with a child, and as a man of his make certainly would if for no other reason than to vary the tedium of a bleak existence. That was all. But there was a certain chivalric thrill of warm blood in him, despite his Yankee ancestry and New England upbringing, and he was so made that the commercial aspect of life often seemed meaningless and bore contradiction to his deeper impulses.

So he sat silent, with head bowed forward, an organic force, greater than himself, as great as his race, at work within him. Wertz and Hawes looked askance at him from time to time, a faint but perceptible trepidation in their manner. Sigmund also felt this. Hitchcock was strong, and his strength had been impressed upon them in the course of many an event in their precarious life. So they stood in a certain definite awe and curiosity as to what his conduct would be when he moved to action.

But his silence was long, and the fire nigh out, when Wertz stretched his arms and yawned, and thought he'd go to bed. Then Hitchcock stood up his full height.

"May God damn your souls to the deepest hells, you chicken-hearted cowards! I'm done with you!" He said it calmly enough, but his strength spoke in every syllable, and every intonation was advertisement of intention. "Come on," he continued, "whack up, and in whatever way suits you best. I own a quarter-interest in the claims; our contracts show that. There're twenty-five or thirty ounces in the sack from the test pans. Fetch out the scales. We'll divide that now. And you, Sigmund, measure me my quarter-share of the grub and set it apart. Four of the dogs are mine, and I want four more. I'll trade you my share in the camp outfit and mining-gear for the dogs. And I'll throw in my six or seven ounces and the spare 45-90 with the ammunition. What d' ye say?"

The three men drew apart and conferred. When they returned, Sigmund acted as spokesman. "We'll whack up fair with you, Hitchcock. In everything you'll get your quarter-share, neither more nor less; and you can take it or leave it. But we want the dogs as bad as you do, so you get four, and that's all. If you don't want to take your share of the outfit and gear, why, that's your lookout. If you want it, you can have it; if you don't, leave it."

"The letter of the law," Hitchcock sneered. "But go ahead. I'm willing. And hurry up. I can't get out of this camp and away from its vermin any too quick."

The division was effected without further comment. He lashed his meagre belongings upon one of the sleds, rounded in his four dogs, and harnessed up. His portion of outfit and gear he did not touch, though he threw onto the sled half a dozen dog harnesses, and challenged them with his eyes to interfere. But they shrugged their shoulders and watched him disappear in the forest.

A man crawled upon his belly through the snow. On every hand loomed the moose-hide lodges of the camp. Here and there a miserable dog howled or snarled abuse upon his neighbor. Once, one of them approached the creeping man, but the man became motionless. The dog came closer and sniffed, and came yet closer, till its nose touched the strange object which had not been there when darkness fell. Then Hitchcock, for it was Hitchcock, upreared suddenly, shooting an unmittened hand out to the brute's shaggy throat. And the dog knew its death in that clutch, and when the man moved on, was left broken-necked under the stars. In this manner Hitchcock made the chief's lodge. For long he lay in the snow without, listening to the voices of the occupants and striving to locate Sipsu. Evidently there were many in the tent, and from the sounds they were in high excitement.

At last he heard the girl's voice, and crawled around so that only the moose-hide divided them. Then burrowing in the snow, he slowly wormed his head and shoulders underneath. When the warm inner air smote his face, he stopped and waited, his legs and the greater part of his body still on the outside. He could see nothing, nor did he dare lift his head. On one side of him was a skin bale. He could smell it, though he carefully felt to be certain. On the other side his face barely touched a furry garment which he knew clothed a body. This must be Sipsu. Though he wished she would speak again, he resolved to risk it.

He could hear the chief and the witch doctor talking high, and in a far corner some hungry child whimpering to sleep. Squirming over on his side, he carefully raised his head, still just touching the furry garment. He listened to the breathing. It was a woman's breathing; he would chance it.

He pressed against her side softly but firmly, and felt her start at the contact. Again he waited, till a questioning hand slipped down upon his head and paused among the curls. The next instant the hand turned his face gently upward, and he was gazing into Sipsu's eyes.

She was quite collected. Changing her position casually, she threw an elbow well over on the skin bale, rested her body upon it, and arranged her *parka*. In this way he was completely concealed. Then, and still most casually, she reclined across him, so that he could breathe between her arm and breast, and when she lowered her head her ear pressed lightly against his lips.

"When the time suits, go thou," he whispered, "out of the lodge and across the snow, down the wind to the bunch of jackpine in the curve of the creek. There wilt thou find my dogs and my sled, packed for the trail. This night we go down to the Yukon; and since we go fast, lay thou hands upon what dogs come nigh thee, by the scruff of the neck, and drag them to the sled in the curve of the creek."

Sipsu shook her head in dissent; but her eyes glistened with gladness, and she was proud that this man had shown toward her such favor. But she, like the women of all her race, was born to obey the will masculine, and when Hitchcock repeated "Go!" he did it with authority, and though she made no answer he knew that his will was law.

"And never mind harness for the dogs," he added, preparing to go. "I shall wait. But waste no time. The day chaseth the night alway, nor does it linger for man's pleasure."

Half an hour later, stamping his feet and swinging his arms by the sled, he saw her coming, a surly dog in either hand. At the approach of these his own animals waxed truculent, and he favored them with the butt of his whip till they quieted. He had approached the camp up the wind, and sound was the thing to be most feared in making his presence known.

"Put them into the sled," he ordered when she had got the harness on the two dogs. "I want my leaders to the fore."

But when she had done this, the displaced animals pitched upon the aliens. Though Hitchcock plunged among them with clubbed rifle, a riot of sound went up and across the sleeping camp.

"Now we shall have dogs, and in plenty," he remarked grimly, slipping an axe from the sled lashings. "Do thou harness whichever I fling thee, and betweenwhiles protect the team."

He stepped a space in advance and waited between two pines. The dogs of the camp were disturbing the night with their jangle, and he watched for their coming. A dark spot, growing rapidly, took form upon the dim white expanse of snow. It was a forerunner of the pack, leaping cleanly, and, after the wolf fashion, singing direction to its brothers. Hitchcock stood in the shadow. As it sprang past, he reached out, gripped its forelegs in mid-career, and sent it whirling earthward. Then he struck it a well-judged blow beneath the ear, and flung it to Sipsu. And while she clapped on the harness, he, with his axe, held the pas-sage between the trees, till a shaggy flood of white teeth and glistening eyes surged and crested just beyond reach. Sipsu worked rapidly. When she had finished, he leaped forward, seized and stunned a second, and flung it to her. This he repeated thrice again, and when the sled team stood snarling in a string of ten, he called, "Enough!"

But at this instant a young buck, the forerunner of the tribe, and swift of limb, wading through the dogs and cuffing right and left, attempted the passage. The butt of Hitchcock's rifle drove him to his knees, whence he toppled over sideways. The witch doctor, running lustily, saw the blow fall.

Hitchcock called to Sipsu to pull out. At her shrill "Chook!" the maddened brutes shot straight ahead, and the sled, bounding mightily, just missed unseating her. The powers were evidently angry with the witch doctor, for at this moment they plunged him upon the trail. The lead-dog fouled his snowshoes and tripped him up, and the nine succeeding dogs trod him under foot and the sled bumped over him. But he was quick to his feet, and the night might have turned out differently had not Sipsu struck backward with the long dog-whip and smitten him a blinding blow across the eyes. Hitchcock, hurrying to overtake her, collided against him as he swayed with pain in the middle of the trail. Thus it was, when this primitive theologian got back to the chief's lodge, that his wisdom had been increased in so far as concerns the efficacy of the white man's fist. So, when he orated then and there in the council, he was wroth against all white men.

"Tumble out, you loafers! Tumble out! Grub'll be ready before you get into your footgear!"

Dave Wertz threw off the bearskin, sat up, and yawned.

Hawes stretched, discovered a lame muscle in his arm, and rubbed it sleepily. "Wonder where Hitchcock bunked last night?" he queried, reaching for his moccasins. They were stiff, and he walked gingerly in his socks to the fire to thaw them out. "It's a blessing he's gone," he added, "though he was a mighty good worker."

"Yep. Too masterful. That was his trouble. Too bad for Sipsu. Think he cared for her much?"

"Don't think so. Just principle. That's all. He thought it wasn't right — and, of course, it wasn't, — but that was no reason for us to interfere and get hustled over the divide before our time."

"Principle is principle, and it's good in its place, but it's best left to home when you go to Alaska. Eh?" Wertz had joined his mate, and both were working pliability into their frozen moccasins. "Think we ought to have taken a hand?"

Sigmund shook his head. He was very busy. A scud of chocolate-colored foam was rising in the coffee-pot, and the bacon needed turning. Also, he was thinking about the girl with laughing eyes like summer seas, and he was humming softly.

His mates chuckled to each other and ceased talking. Though it was past seven, daybreak was still three hours distant. The aurora borealis had passed out of the sky, and the camp was an oasis of light in the midst of deep darkness. And in this light the forms of the three men were sharply defined. Emboldened by the silence, Sigmund raised his voice and opened the last stanza of the old song: —

> "In a year, in a year, when the
> grapes are ripe —"

Then the night was split with a rattling volley of rifle-shots. Hawes sighed, made an effort to straighten himself, and collapsed. Wertz went over on an elbow with drooping head. He choked a little, and a dark stream flowed from his mouth. And Sigmund, the Golden-Haired, his throat a-gurgle with the song, threw up his arms and pitched across the fire.

The witch doctor's eyes were well blackened, and his temper none of the best; for he quarrelled with the chief over the possession of Wertz's rifle, and took more than his share of the part-sack of beans. Also he appropriated the bearskin, and caused grumbling among the tribesmen. And finally, he tried to kill Sigmund's dog, which the girl had given him, but the dog ran away, while he fell into the shaft and dislocated his shoulder on the bucket. When the camp was well looted they went back to their own lodges, and there was a great rejoicing among the women. Further, a band of moose strayed over the south divide and fell before the hunters, so the witch doctor attained yet greater honor, and the people whispered among themselves that he spoke in council with the gods.

But later, when all were gone, the shepherd dog crept back to the deserted camp, and all the night long and a day it wailed the dead. After that it disappeared, though the years were not many before the Indian hunters noted a change in the breed of timber wolves, and there were dashes of bright color and variegated markings such as no wolf bore before.

46
DUTCH COURAGE

DUTCH COURAGE

"Just our luck!"

Gus Lafee finished wiping his hands and sullenly threw the towel upon the rocks. His attitude was one of deep dejection. The light seemed gone out of the day and the glory from the golden sun. Even the keen mountain air was devoid of relish, and the early morning no longer yielded its customary zest.

"Just our luck!" Gus repeated, this time avowedly for the edification of another young fellow who was busily engaged in sousing his head in the water of the lake.

"What are you grumbling about, anyway?" Hazard Van Dorn lifted a soap-rimed face questioningly. His eyes were shut. "What's our luck?"

"Look there!" Gus threw a moody glance skyward. "Some duffer's got ahead of us. We've been scooped, that's all!"

Hazard opened his eyes, and caught a fleeting glimpse of a white flag waving arrogantly on the edge of a wall of rock nearly a mile above his head. Then his eyes closed with a snap, and his face wrinkled spasmodically. Gus threw him the towel, and uncommiseratingly watched him wipe out the offending soap. He felt too blue himself to take stock in trivialities.

Hazard groaned.

"Does it hurt — much?" Gus queried, coldly, without interest, as if it were no more than his duty to ask after the welfare of his comrade.

"I guess it does," responded the suffering one.

"Soap's pretty strong, eh? Noticed it myself."

"'Tisn't the soap. It's — it's *that!*" He opened his reddened eyes and pointed toward the innocent little white flag. "That's what hurts."

Gus Lafee did not reply, but turned away to start the fire and begin cooking breakfast. His disappointment and grief were too deep for anything but silence, and Hazard, who felt likewise, never opened his mouth as he fed the horses, nor once laid his head against their arching necks or passed caressing fingers through their manes. The two boys were blind, also, to the manifold glories of Mirror Lake which reposed at their very feet. Nine times, had they chosen to move along its margin the short distance of a hundred yards, could they have seen the sunrise repeated; nine times, from behind as many successive peaks, could they have seen the great orb rear his blazing rim; and nine times, had they but looked into the waters of the lake, could they have seen the phenomena reflected faithfully and vividly. But all the Titanic grandeur of the scene was lost to them. They had been robbed of the chief pleasure of their trip to Yosemite Valley. They had been frustrated in their long-cherished design upon Half Dome, and hence were rendered disconsolate and blind to the beauties and the wonders of the place.

Half Dome rears its ice-scarred head fully five thousand feet above the level floor of Yosemite Valley. In the name itself of this great rock lies an accurate and complete description. Nothing more nor less is it than a cyclopean, rounded dome, split in half as cleanly as an apple that is divided by a knife. It is, perhaps, quite needless to state that but one-half remains, hence its name, the other half having been carried away by the great ice-river in the stormy time of the Glacial Period. In that dim day one of those frigid rivers gouged a mighty channel from out the solid rock. This channel to-day is Yosemite Valley. But to return to the Half Dome. On its northeastern side, by circuitous trails and stiff climbing, one may gain the Saddle. Against the slope of the Dome the Saddle leans like a gigantic slab, and from the top of this slab, one thousand feet in length, curves the great circle to the summit of the Dome. A few degrees too steep for unaided climbing, these one thousand feet defied for years the ad-

He made a last supreme effort
and gripped the coveted peg

venturous spirits who fixed yearning eyes upon the crest above.

One day, a couple of clear-headed mountaineers proceeded to insert iron eye-bolts into holes which they drilled into the rock every few feet apart. But when they found themselves three hundred feet above the Saddle, clinging like flies to the precarious wall with on either hand a yawning abyss, their nerves failed them and they abandoned the enterprise. So it remained for an indomitable Scotchman, one George Anderson, finally to achieve the feat. Beginning where they had left off, drilling and climbing for a week, he at last set foot upon that awful summit and gazed down into the depths where Mirror Lake reposed, nearly a mile beneath.

In the years which followed, many bold men took advantage of the huge rope ladder which he had put in place; but one winter ladder, cables and all were carried away by the snow and ice. True, most of the eyebolts, twisted and bent, remained. But few men essayed the hazardous undertaking, and of those few more than one gave up his life on the treacherous heights, and not one succeeded.

But Gus Lafee and Hazard Van Dorn had left the smiling valley-land of California and journeyed into the high Sierras, intent on the great adventure. And thus it was that their disappointment was deep and grievous when they awoke on this morning to receive the forestalling message of the little white flag.

"Camped at the foot of the Saddle last night and went up at the first peep of day," Hazard ventured, long after the silent breakfast had been tucked away and the dishes washed.

Gus nodded. It was not in the nature of things that a youth's spirits should long remain at low ebb, and his tongue was beginning to loosen.

"Guess he's down by now, lying in camp and feeling as big as Alexander," the other went on. "And I don't blame him, either, only I wish it were we."

"You can be sure he's down," Gus spoke up at last. "It's mighty warm on that naked rock with the sun beating down on it at this time of year. That was our plan, you know, to go up early and come down early. And any man, sensible enough to get to the top, is bound to have sense enough to do it before the rock gets hot and his hands

sweaty."

"And you can be sure he didn't take his shoes with him." Hazard rolled over on his back and lazily regarded the speck of flag fluttering briskly on the sheer edge of the precipice. "Say!" He sat up with a start. "What's that?"

A metallic ray of light flashed out from the summit of Half Dome, then a second and a third. The heads of both boys were craned backward on the instant, agog with excitement.

"What a duffer!" Gus cried. "Why didn't he come down when it was cool?"

Hazard shook his head slowly, as if the question were too deep for immediate answer and they had better defer judgment.

The flashes continued, and as the boys soon noted, at irregular intervals of duration and disappearance. Now they were long, now short; and again they came and went with great rapidity, or ceased altogether for several moments at a time.

"I have it!" Hazard's face lighted up with the coming of understanding. "I have it! That fellow up there is trying to talk to us. He's flashing the sunlight down to us on a pocket-mirror — dot, dash; dot, dash; don't you see?"

The light also began to break in Gus's face. "Ah, I know! It's what they do in wartime — signaling. They call it heliographing, don't they? Same thing as telegraphing, only it's done without wires. And they use the same dots and dashes, too."

"Yes, the Morse alphabet. Wish I knew it."

"Same here. He surely must have something to say to us, or he wouldn't be kicking up all that rumpus."

Still the flashes came and went persistently, till Gus exclaimed: "That chap's in trouble, that's what's the matter with him! Most likely he's hurt himself or something or other."

"Go on!" Hazard scouted.

Gus got out the shotgun and fired both barrels three times in rapid succession. A perfect flutter of flashes came back before the echoes had ceased their antics. So unmistakable was the message that even doubting Hazard was convinced that the man who had forestalled them stood in some grave danger.

"Quick, Gus," he cried, "and pack! I'll see to the horses. Our trip hasn't come to nothing, after all. We've got to go right up

Half Dome and rescue him. Where's the map? How do we get to the Saddle?"

"'Taking the horse-trail below the Vernal Falls,'" Gus read from the guide-book, "'one mile of brisk travelling brings the tourist to the world-famed Nevada Fall. Close by, rising up in all its pomp and glory, the Cap of Liberty stands guard —'"

"Skip all that!" Hazard impatiently interrupted. "The trail's what we want."

"Oh, here it is! 'Following the trail up the side of the fall will bring you to the forks. The left one leads to Little Yosemite Valley, Cloud's Rest and other points.'"

"Hold on; that'll do! I've got it on the map now," again interrupted Hazard. "From the Cloud's Rest trail a dotted line leads off to Half Dome. That shows the trail's abandoned. We'll have to look sharp to find it. It's a day's journey."

"And to think of all that travelling, when right here we're at the bottom of the Dome!" Gus complained, staring up wistfully at the goal.

"That's because this is Yosemite, and all the more reason for us to hurry. Come on! Be lively, now!"

Well used as they were to trail life, but few minutes sufficed to see the camp equipage on the backs of the packhorses and the boys in the saddle. In the late twilight of that evening they hobbled their animals in a tiny mountain meadow, and cooked coffee and bacon for themselves at the very base of the Saddle. Here, also, before they turned into their blankets, they found the camp of the unlucky stranger who was destined to spend the night on the naked roof of the Dome.

"What's that for?" Gus asked, pointing to a leather-shielded flask which Hazard was securely fastening in his shirt pocket.

"Dutch courage, of course," was the reply. "We'll need all our nerve in this undertaking, and a little bit more, and," he tapped the flask significantly, "here's the little bit more."

"Good idea," Gus commented.

How they had ever come possessed of this erroneous idea, it would be hard to discover; but they were young yet, and there remained for them many uncut pages of life. Believers, also, in the efficacy of whisky as a remedy for snakebite, they had brought with them a fair supply of medicine-chest liquor. As yet they had not touched it.

"Have some before we start?" Hazard asked.

Gus looked into the gulf and shook his head. "Better wait till we get up higher and the climbing is more ticklish."

Some seventy feet above them projected the first eye-bolt. The winter accumulations of ice had twisted and bent it down till it did not stand more than a bare inch and a half above the rock — a most difficult object to lasso at such a distance. Time and again Hazard coiled his lariat in true cowboy fashion and made the cast, and time and again was he baffled by the elusive peg. Nor could Gus do better. Taking advantage of inequalities in the surface, they scrambled twenty feet up the Dome and found they could rest in a shallow crevice. The cleft side of the Dome was so near that they could look over its edge from the crevice and gaze down the smooth, absolutely vertical wall for nearly two thousand feet. It was yet too dark down below for them to see farther.

The peg was now fifty feet away, but the path they must cover to get to it was quite smooth, and ran at an inclination of nearly fifty degrees. It seemed impossible, in that intervening space, to find a resting-place. Either the climber must keep going up, or he must slide down; he could not stop. But just here rose the danger. The Dome was sphere-shaped, and if he should begin to slide, his course would be, not to the point from which he had started and where the Saddle would catch him, but off to the south toward Little Yosemite. This meant a plunge of half a mile.

"I'll try it," Gus said, simply.

They knotted the two lariats together, so that they had over a hundred feet of rope between them; and then each boy tied an end to his waist.

"If I slide," Gus cautioned, "come in on the slack and brace yourself. If you don't, you'll follow me, that's all!"

"Ay, ay!" was the confident response. "Better take a nip before you start?"

Gus glanced at the proffered bottle. He knew himself and of what he was capable. "Wait till I make the peg and you join me. All ready?"

"Ay."

He struck out like a cat, on all fours, clawing energetically as he urged his upward progress, his comrade paying out the rope carefully. At first his speed was good, but gradually it dwindled. Now he was fifteen feet from the peg, now ten, now eight — but going, oh, so slowly! Hazard, looking up from his crevice, felt a contempt for him and disappointment in him. It did look easy. Now Gus was five feet away, and after a painful effort, four feet. But when only a yard intervened, he came to a standstill — not exactly a standstill, for, like a squirrel in a wheel, he maintained his position on the face of the Dome by the most desperate clawing.

He had failed, that was evident. The question now was, how to save himself. With a sudden, catlike movement he whirled over on his back, caught his heel in a tiny, saucer-shaped depression and sat up. Then his courage failed him. Day had at last penetrated to the floor of the valley, and he was appalled at the frightful distance.

"Go ahead and make it!" Hazard ordered; but Gus merely shook his head.

"Then come down!"

Again he shook his head. This was his ordeal, to sit, nerveless and insecure, on the brink of the precipice. But Hazard, lying safely in his crevice, now had to face his own ordeal, but one of a different nature. When Gus began to slide, — as he soon must, — would he, Hazard, be able to take in the slack and then meet the shock as the other tautened the rope and darted toward the plunge? It seemed doubtful. And there he lay, apparently safe, but in reality harnessed to death. Then rose the temptation. Why not cast off the rope about his waist? He would be safe at all events. It was a simple way out of the difficulty. There was no need that two should perish. But it was impossible for such temptation to overcome his pride of race, and his own pride in himself and in his honor. So the rope remained about him.

"Come down!" he ordered; but Gus seemed to have become petrified.

"Come down," he threatened, "or I'll drag you down!" He pulled on the rope to show he was in earnest.

"Don't you dare!" Gus articulated through his chattering teeth.

"Sure, I will, if you don't come!" Again he jerked the rope.

With a despairing gurgle Gus started, doing his best to work sideways from the plunge. Hazard, every sense on the alert, almost exulting in his perfect coolness, took in the slack with deft rapidity. Then, as the rope began to tighten, he braced himself. The shock drew him half out of the crevice; but he held firm and served as the center of the circle, while Gus, with the rope as a radius, described the circumference and ended up on the extreme southern edge of the Saddle. A few moments later Hazard was offering him the flask.

"Take some yourself," Gus said.

"No; you. I don't need it."

"And I'm past needing it." Evidently Gus was dubious of the bottle and its contents.

Hazard put it away in his pocket. "Are you game," he asked, "or are you going to give it up?"

"Never!" Gus protested. "I am game. No Lafee ever showed the white feather yet. And if I did lose my grit up there, it was only for the moment — sort of like seasickness. I'm all right now, and I'm going to the top."

"Good!" encouraged Hazard. "You lie in the crevice this time, and I'll show you how easy it is."

But Gus refused. He held that it was easier and safer for him to try again, arguing that it was less difficult for his one hundred and sixteen pounds to cling to the smooth rock than for Hazard's one hundred and sixty-five; also, that it was easier for one hundred and sixty-five pounds to bring a sliding one hundred and sixteen to a stop than vice versa. And further, that he had the benefit of his previous experience. Hazard saw the justice of this, although it was with great reluctance that he gave in.

Success vindicated Gus's contention. The second time, just as it seemed as if his slide would be repeated, he made a last supreme effort and gripped the coveted peg. By means of the rope, Hazard quickly joined him. The next peg was nearly sixty feet away; but for nearly half that distance the base of some glacier in the forgotten past had ground a shallow furrow. Taking advantage of this, it was easy for Gus to lasso the eye-bolt. And it seemed, as was really the case, that the hardest part of the task was over. True, the curve steepened to nearly sixty degrees above them, but a comparatively unbroken line of eye-bolts, six feet apart, awaited the lads. They no longer had even to use the lasso. Standing on one peg it was child's play to throw the bight of the rope over the next and to draw themselves up to it.

A bronzed and bearded man met them at the top and gripped their hands in hearty fellowship.

"Talk about your Mont Blancs!" he exclaimed, pausing in the midst of greeting them to survey the mighty panorama. "But there's nothing on all the earth, nor over it, nor under it, to compare with this!" Then he recollected himself and thanked them for coming to his aid. No, he was not hurt or injured in any way. Simply because of his own carelessness, just as he had arrived at the top the previous day, he had dropped his climbing rope. Of course it was impossible to descend without it. Did they understand heliographing? No? That was strange! How did they —

"Oh, we knew something was the matter," Gus interrupted, "from the way you flashed when we fired off the shotgun."

"Find it pretty cold last night without blankets?" Hazard queried.

"I should say so. I've hardly thawed out yet."

"Have some of this." Hazard shoved the flask over to him.

The stranger regarded him quite seriously for a moment, then said, "My dear fellow, do you see that row of pegs? Since it is my honest intention to climb down them very shortly, I am forced to decline. No, I don't think I'll have any, though I thank you just the same."

Hazard glanced at Gus and then put the flask back in his pocket. But when they pulled the doubled rope through the last eye-bolt and set foot on the Saddle, he again drew out the bottle.

"Now that we're down, we don't need it," he remarked, pithily. "And I've about come to the conclusion that there isn't very much in Dutch courage, after all." He gazed up the great curve of the Dome. "Look at what we've done without it!"

Several seconds thereafter a party of tourists, gathered at the margin of Mirror Lake, were astounded at the unwonted phenomenon of a whisky flask descending upon them like a comet out of a clear sky; and all the way back to the hotel they marveled greatly at the wonders of nature, especially meteorites.

47
JAN, THE UNREPENTANT

JAN, THE UNREPENTANT

Jan rolled over, clawing and kicking. He was fighting hand and foot now, and he fought grimly, silently. Two of the three men who hung upon him, shouted directions to each other, and strove to curb the short, hairy devil who would not curb. The third man howled. His finger was between Jan's teeth.

"Quit yer tantrums, Jan, an' ease up!" panted Red Bill, getting a strangle-hold on Jan's neck. "Why on earth can't yeh hang decent and peaceable?"

But Jan kept his grip on the third man's finger, and squirmed over the floor of the tent, into the pots and pans.

"Youah no gentleman, suh," reproved Mr. Taylor, his body following his finger, and endeavoring to accommodate itself to every jerk of Jan's head. "You hev killed Mistah Gordon, as brave and honorable a gentleman as ever hit the trail aftah the dogs. Youah a murderah, suh, and without honah."

"An' yer no comrade," broke in Red Bill. "If you was, you'd hang 'thout rampin' around an' roarin'. Come on, Jan, there's a good fellow. Don't give us no more trouble. Jes' quit, an' we'll hang yeh neat and handy, an' be done with it."

"Steady, all!" Lawson, the sailorman, bawled. "Jam his head into the bean pot and batten down."

"But my fingah, suh," Mr. Taylor protested.

"Leggo with y'r finger, then! Always in the way!"

"But I can't, Mistah Lawson. It's in the critter's gullet, and nigh chewed off as 't is."

"Stand by for stays!" As Lawson gave the warning, Jan half lifted himself, and the struggling quartet floundered across the tent into a muddle of furs and blankets. In its passage it cleared the body of a man, who lay motionless, bleeding from a bullet-wound in the neck.

All this was because of the madness which had come upon Jan — the madness which comes upon a man who has stripped off the raw skin of earth and grovelled long in primal nakedness, and before whose eyes rises the fat vales of the homeland, and into whose nostrils steals the whiff of hay, and grass, and flower, and new-turned soil. Through five frigid years Jan had sown the seed. Stuart River, Forty Mile, Circle City, Koyokuk, Kotzebue, had marked his bleak and strenuous agriculture, and now it was Nome that bore the harvest, — not the Nome of golden beaches and ruby sands, but the Nome of '97, before Anvil City was located, or Eldorado District organized. John Gordon was a Yankee, and should have known better. But he passed the sharp word at a time when Jan's blood-shot eyes blazed and his teeth gritted in torment. And because of this, there was a smell of saltpetre in the tent, and one lay quietly, while the other fought like a cornered rat, and refused to hang in the decent and peaceable manner suggested by his comrades.

"If you allow me, Mistah Lawson, befoah we go further in this rumpus, I would say it wah a good idea to pry this hyer varmint's teeth apart. Neither will he bite off, nor will he let go. He has the wisdom of the sarpint, suh, the wisdom of the sarpint."

"Lemme get the hatchet to him!" vociferated the sailor. "Lemme get the hatchet!" He shoved the steel edge close to Mr. Taylor's finger and used the man's teeth as a fulcrum. Jan held on and breathed through his nose, snorting like a grampus. "Steady, all! Now she takes it!"

"Thank you, suh; it is a powerful relief." And Mr. Taylor proceeded to gather into his arms the victim's wildly waving legs.

But Jan upreared in his Berserker rage; bleeding, frothing, cursing; five frozen years thawing into sudden hell. They swayed backward and forward, panted, sweated, like some cyclopean, many-legged monster rising from the lower deeps. The slush-lamp went over, drowned in its own fat, while the midday twilight scarce percolated through the dirty canvas of the tent.

"For the love of Gawd, Jan, get yer senses back!" pleaded Red Bill. "We ain't goin' to hurt yeh, 'r kill yeh, 'r anythin' of that sort. Jes' want to hang yeh, that's all, an' you a-messin' round an' rampagin' somethin' terrible. To think of travellin' trail together an' then bein' treated this-a way. Wouldn't 'bleeved it of yeh, Jan!"

"He's got too much steerage-way. Grab holt his legs, Taylor, and heave 'm over!"

"Yes, suh, Mistah Lawson. Do you press youah weight above, after I give the word." The Kentuckian groped about him in the murky darkness. "Now, suh, now is the accepted time!"

There was a great surge, and a quarter of a ton of human flesh tottered and crashed to its fall against the side-wall. Pegs drew and guy-ropes parted, and the tent, collapsing, wrapped the battle in its greasy folds.

"Yer only makin' it harder fer yerself," Red Bill continued, at the same time driving both his thumbs into a hairy throat, the possessor of which he had pinned down. "You've made nuisance enough a' ready, an' it'll take half the day to get things straightened when we've strung yeh up."

"I'll thank you to leave go, suh," spluttered Mr. Taylor.

Red Bill grunted and loosed his grip, and the twain crawled out into the open. At the same instant Jan kicked clear of the sailor, and took to his heels across the snow.

"Hi! you lazy devils! Buck! Bright! Sic 'm! Pull 'm down!" sang out Lawson, lunging through the snow after the fleeing man. Buck and Bright, followed by the rest of the dogs, outstripped him and rapidly overhauled the murderer.

There was no reason that these men should do this; no reason for Jan to run away; no reason for them to attempt to prevent him. On the one hand stretched the barren snow-land; on the other, the frozen sea. With neither food nor shelter, he could not run far. All they had to do was to wait till he wandered back to the tent, as he inevitably must, when the frost and hunger laid hold of him. But these men did not stop to think. There was a certain taint of madness running in the veins of all of them. Besides, blood had been spilled, and

upon them was the blood-lust, thick and hot. "Vengeance is mine," saith the Lord, and He saith it in temperate climes where the warm sun steals away the energies of men. But in the Northland they have discovered that prayer is only efficacious when backed by muscle, and they are accustomed to doing things for themselves. God is everywhere, they have heard, but he flings a shadow over the land for half the year that they may not find him; so they grope in darkness, and it is not to be wondered that they often doubt, and deem the Decalogue out of gear.

Jan ran blindly, reckoning not of the way of his feet, for he was mastered by the verb "to live." To live! To exist! Buck flashed gray through the air, but missed. The man struck madly at him, and stumbled. Then the white teeth of Bright closed on his mackinaw jacket, and he pitched into the snow. *To live! To exist!* He fought wildly as ever, the centre of a tossing heap of men and dogs. His left hand gripped a wolf-dog by the scruff of the back, while the arm was passed around the neck of Lawson. Every struggle of the dog helped to throttle the hapless sailor. Jan's right hand was buried deep in the curling tendrils of Red Bill's shaggy head, and beneath all, Mr. Taylor lay pinned and helpless. It was a deadlock, for the strength of his madness was prodigious; but suddenly, without apparent reason, Jan loosed his various grips and rolled over quietly on his back. His adversaries drew away a little, dubious and disconcerted. Jan grinned viciously.

"Mine friends," he said, still grinning, "you haf asked me to be politeful, und now I am politeful. Vot piziness vood you do mit me?"

"That's right, Jan. Be ca'm," soothed Red Bill. "I knowed you'd come to yer senses afore long. Jes' be ca'm now, an we'll do the trick with neatness and despatch."

"Vot piziness? Vot trick?"

"The hangin'. An' yeh oughter thank yer lucky stars for havin' a man what knows his business. I've did it afore now, more'n once, down in the States, an' I can do it to a T."

"Hang who? Me?"

"Yep."

"Ha! ha! Shust hear der man speak foolishness! Gif me a hand, Bill, und I vill get up und be hung." He crawled stiffly to his feet and looked about him. "Herr Gott! listen to der man! He vood hang me! Ho! ho! ho! I tank not! Yes, I tank not!"

"And I tank yes, you swab," Lawson spoke up mockingly, at the same time cutting a sled-lashing and coiling it up with ominous care. "Judge Lynch holds court this day."

"Von liddle while." Jan stepped back from the proffered noose. "I haf somedings to ask und to make der great proposition. Kentucky, you know about der Shudge Lynch?"

"Yes, suh. It is an institution of free men and of gentlemen, and it is an ole one and time-honored. Corruption may wear the robe of magistracy, suh, but Judge Lynch can always be relied upon to give justice without court fees. I repeat, suh, without court fees. Law may be bought and sold, but in this enlightened land justice is free as the air we breathe, strong as the licker we drink, prompt as —"

"Cut it short! Find out what the beggar wants," interrupted Lawson, spoiling the peroration.

"Vell, Kentucky, tell me dis: von man kill von odder man, Shudge Lynch hang dot man?"

"If the evidence is strong enough — yes, suh."

"An' the evidence in this here case is strong enough to hang a dozen men, Jan," broke in Red Bill.

"Nefer you mind, Bill. I talk mit you next. Now von anodder ding I ask Kentucky. If Shudge Lynch hang not der man, vot den?"

"If Judge Lynch does not hang the man, then the man goes free, and his hands are washed clean of blood. And further, suh, our great and glorious constitution has said, to wit: that no man may twice be placed in jeopardy of his life for one and the same crime, or words to that effect."

"Unt dey can't shoot him, or hit him mit a club over der head alongside, or do nodings more mit him?"

"No, suh."

"Goot! You hear vot Kentucky speaks, all you noddleheads? Now I talk mit Bill. You know der piziness, Bill, und you hang me up brown, eh? Vot you say?"

"'Betcher life, an', Jan, if yeh don't give no more trouble ye'll be almighty proud of the job. I'm a connesoor."

"You haf der great head, Bill, und know

somedings or two. Und you know two und one makes tree — ain't it?"

Bill nodded.

"Und when you haf two dings, you haf not tree dings — ain't it? Now you follow mit me close und I show you. It takes tree dings to hang. First ding, you haf to haf der man. Goot! I am der man. Second ding, you haf to haf der rope. Lawson haf der rope. Goot! Und tird ding, you haf to haf someding to tie der rope to. Sling your eyes over der landscape und find der tird ding to tie der rope to? Eh? Vot you say?"

Mechanically they swept the ice and snow with their eyes. It was a homogeneous scene, devoid of contrasts or bold contours, dreary, desolate, and monotonous, — the ice-packed sea, the slow slope of the beach, the background of low-lying hills, and over all thrown the endless mantle of snow.

"No trees, no bluffs, no cabins, no telegraph poles, nothin'," moaned Red Bill; "nothin' respectable enough nor big enough to swing the toes of a five-foot man clear o' the ground. I give it up." He looked yearningly at that portion of Jan's anatomy which joins the head and shoulders. "Give it up," he repeated sadly to Lawson. "Throw the rope down. Gawd never intended this here country for livin' purposes, an' that's a cold frozen fact."

Jan grinned triumphantly. "I tank I go mit der tent und haf a smoke."

"Ostensiblee y'r correct, Bill, me son," spoke up Lawson; "but y'r a dummy, and you can lay to that for another cold frozen fact. Takes a sea farmer to learn you landsmen things. Ever hear of a pair of shears? Then clap y'r eyes to this."

The sailor worked rapidly. From the pile of dunnage where they had pulled up the boat the preceding fall, he unearthed a pair of long oars. These he lashed together, at nearly right anles, close to the ends of the blades. Where the handles rested he kicked holes through the snow to the sand. At the point of intersection he attached two guyropes, making the end of one fast to a cake of beach-ice. The other guy he passed over to Red Bill. "Here, me son, lay holt o' that and run it out."

And to his horror, Jan saw his gallows rise in the air. "No! no!" he cried, recoiling and putting up his fists. "It is not goot! I vill not hang! Come, you noddleheads! I vill lick you, all together, von after der odder! I vill blay hell! I vill do eferydings! Und I vill die pefore I hang!"

The sailor permitted the two other men to clinch with the mad creature. They rolled and tossed about furiously, tearing up snow and tundra, their fierce struggle writing a tragedy of human passion on the white sheet spread by nature. And ever and anon a hand or foot of Jan emerged from the tangle, to be gripped by Lawson and lashed fast with rope-yarns. Pawing, clawing, blaspheming, he was conquered and bound, inch by inch, and drawn to where the inexorable shears lay like a pair of gigantic dividers on the snow. Red Bill adjusted the noose, placing the hangman's knot properly under the left ear. Mr. Taylor and Lawson tailed onto the running-guy, ready at the word to elevate the gallows. Bill lingered, contemplating his work with artistic appreciation.

"Herr Gott! Vood you look at it!"

The horror in Jan's voice caused the rest to desist. The fallen tent had uprisen, and in the gathering twilight it flapped ghostly arms about and titubated toward them drunkenly. But the next instant John Gordon found the opening and crawled forth.

"What the flaming —!" For the moment his voice died away in his throat as his eyes took in the tableau. "Hold on! I'm not dead!" he cried out, coming up to the group with stormy countenance.

"Allow me, Mistah Gordon, to congratulate you upon youah escape," Mr. Taylor ventured. "A close shave, suh, a powahful close shave."

"Congratulate hell! I might have been dead and rotten and no thanks to you, you — !" And thereat John Gordon delivered himself of a vigorous flood of English, terse, intensive, denunciative, and composed solely of expletives and adjectives.

"Simply creased me," he went on when he had eased himself sufficiently. "Ever crease cattle, Taylor?"

"Yes, suh, many a time down in God's country."

"Just so. That's what happened to me. Bullet just grazed the base of my skull at the top of the neck. Stunned me but no harm done." He turned to the bound man. "Get up, Jan. I'm going to lick you to a standstill or you're going to apologize. The rest of you lads stand clear."

"I tank not. Shust tie me loose und you see," replied Jan, the Unrepentant, the devil within him still unconquered. "Und after as I lick you, I take der rest of der noddleheads, von after der odder, altogedder!"